EL Gancho

A Saga
of an
Immigrant
Family's
Journey out
of Mexico

MICHAEL TRAVIS

FOREWORD BY JOE MINJARES

PUBLICATION
CONSULTANTS
We Believe In The Power Of Authors

PO Box 221974 Anchorage, Alaska 99522-1974
www.publicationconsultants.com

ISBN 978-1-59433-048-3

Library of Congress Catalog Card Number: 2006935284

Art Design by Natalie Travis
Graphic Enhancing by Clifford Sonnentag and Devin Stiller

Manufactured in the United States of America.

Dedication

To my family—Past, Present, and Future.

And, in loving memory to my son, Brant M. M. Travis: 1984-2003.

Acknowledgements

There are many people I wish to thank because, without their support and information, I would not have been able to complete this book. My uncle Joe Minjares provided narratives and letters written in the 1940s and 50s that described life in Mexico, Doña Ana, New Mexico, and Sidney, Montana. Uncle Joe also spent hours on the telephone with me retelling his father's stories and providing key information about the family's past.

My grandmother Anita Fine, my uncle Ben Minjares, my aunt Lupe Rodriguez, and my cousin Mary Lou Brese provided invaluable details to the family saga. I enjoyed listening to their accounts and found their stories consistent with other sources.

I deeply appreciated my brother Steven Travis taking time from his busy schedule to travel the mountains of Zacatecas, Mexico with me in search for Monte Escobedo—the village where our great-grandparents came from. Together, we found the village and discovered baptismal records that documented our family's existence.

Ms. Ruth Hammond of the Lincoln County News spent hours searching though dusty newspapers to find the accounts of my great-grandfather stopping the train south of Carrizozo, New Mexico. Her search found vital details that supported one of my grandfather's greatest tales.

Ms. Martha Proctor, City of Carrizozo Historian, dug up names and places associated with the train holdup. I could never have told the story in such detail without her efforts.

Ms. Claire Kluskens, Archivist with the National Archives and Records Administration, reviewed tens of old microfiche films before finding copies of my family's immigration registration cards. I greatly appreciated her time and diligence.

I thank my wife Barbara, my daughter Natalie, and my uncle Joe for giving me encouragement to continue writing when tragedies struck our family. While writing this book, we lost dearly-loved family members. My grandmother Anita and her husband died in a house fire. My uncle Ben succumbed to a liver aliment from complications of contacting malaria during World War II. My father, Lloyd Travis, died quickly from brain cancer, and most heart-breaking, my son died. To say that I developed a writer's block was an understatement. However, the very act of researching and writing was therapeutic for my soul.

Dr. Louis R. Sadler, emeritus history professor at the New Mexico State University, provided comments to clarify and strengthen the historical portions of the book. I am grateful for his time and efforts.

This book would not have been possible without the professional editing by Ms. Marthy Johnson. I am very appreciative of her patience and thoroughness.

Contents

Foreword
by Joe Minjares

Set in Mexico, during the final years of the iron fisted reign of Porfirio Diaz, Michael Travis takes us on an epic journey in time with powerful images that give startling clarity to the tumultuous events of the early 1900s. In a discontent Mexico, wrought with wild rumors and the lust for power, it was impossible to distinguish good from bad, righteous from evil, compassion from greed. A time of revolution and a social transition from nineteenth century Victorian ideals to the industrial and geopolitical visions of the twentieth century. A time when the government was in constant chaos, verging on disaster and threatening the very fabric of the Mexican people.

It is also a part of American history that is often overlooked. A time, just moments outside of our collective memory, that is as relevant today as it was then. It is if history is tapping us on the shoulder and asking us to take a good second look.

El Gancho is the story of a defeated people, joining a vast sea of brown faced refugees, heading north toward the promise of America. Moving away from a world that was spinning out of control, understanding only the hunger in their bellies and the cries of their children,

This stunning narrative centers around one of those brown faces. Prudenciano Nava. A towering, muscular man with a commanding presence. A leader by choice or by force, he was a person who never took kindly to not being listened to. Nothing in his life went quite the way he had planned, and to say that he had a life filled with bad luck wouldn't be quite true. He was a man who lived a long life of making bad choices.

Born into middle class Mexico, he grew up on the family ranch in Monte Escobedo in the state of Zacatecas. Unwilling to work on the ranch which he found uninteresting and a job that no one took notice of, he left it and spent much of his early life pursuing his first love and eventual source of fame, the Jaripeo (the rodeo).

His event was La Colleada, throwing the bull. La Colleada was a two man event in which upon releasing of the bull, one rider became the prey by waving red flags as he rode away from the charging animal. The second rider, the colleador, rode up from behind the bull, grabbing it by the tail and attempted to flip it onto it's back. It was a dangerous way to make a living but for Prudenciano and his partner Tereso Rodriguez, it was not only the ultimate rush, but at times very lucrative.

For Nava, just as important as the money was the fame and admiration it brought. He thrived on it. All over the region of Chihuahua and Zacatecas he was considered the finest colleador in the circuit. He was a star. An honor that he never hesitated to remind people of. It would take the death of his partner, Rodriguez, in another Jaripeo, to send him home to the family Ranch in Monte Escobedo, begging for a second chance.

As predictable as the coming of tomorrow, it didn't take long for the 49 year old Prudenciano to grow discontent and remember why he left the ranch in the first place. Restless feet, and his disdain for taking orders, led to a physical confrontation with his brother, and to his relief he was soon asked to leave.

As always, his exit would be in dramatic fashion. Love was not a concept he understood but before he left, he met a young woman who he fell infatuated with. Her name was Maria Paz. It wasn't difficult for women to fall under the spell of this magnificent looking man and Maria Paz was no different, but she was only fourteen.

When Prudenciano rode away from the ranch and into the night he took the soon to be child bride with him. Predictably they found themselves pursued by a very angry father and a posse more than eager to string up the kidnapper. Thus became their life of being pursued, moving from job to job, town to town; victims of his bad choices and events.

The years that followed brought physical hardship and uncertainty to the Navas. For Prudenciano, it was a daily struggle to stay alive while preserving both his dignity and sanity while working deep under ground in the silver mines of Torreon. When an outbreak of typhoid fever drove the Nava's from Torreon, Prudenciano took a job as a mounted policeman working for the wealthy haciandero Don Luis Terrazas.

Terrazas, was the owner of vast tracts of land in the state of Chihuahua, and was the symbol of private wealth and power. He controlled every aspect of life in this region from the arts to commerce and education. Thus he represented all that was wrong in Mexico in the eyes of revolutionaries such as Francisco Madero, Abraham Gonzalez and Francisco "Pancho" Villa.

Nava was not blind to the injustices of the status quo and found himself caught in the middle, working for Terrazas, yet sympathizing with the revolutionaries' doctrine. This led to him becoming a marked man. A man looking for a way out. He looked north to America.

Taking only what they could carry, the family, now numbering four, joined the growing exodus of refugees on the 235 mile trek to the United States. On the way, the family averted disaster when a party of Villistas looking for men to fill their ranks, stops the Nava family and several others. After Prudenciano is picked out of line and threatened to be shot, an old friend riding with the soldiers intercedes and Nava's life is spared.

After weeks of grueling travel by foot the family arrives at their statue of liberty. An old rope bridge that spanned the Rio Grande and into the town of El Paso. El Paso was the port of entry into the United States.

America, where dreams came true and nothing was impossible. Where a poor man could become rich, where a peon could be a king. It was 1913 and the Nava's were one family of many thousands of Mexicans that paid their two cents to enter that year. One hundred thousand to be exact.

This was a booming time for the American economy and the demand for cheap labor was high. All up and down the streets of El Paso, shops advertising work and a piece of the American dream recruited the Mexican worker. With promises of money and a decent place to live these recruiters fed the appetites of American industry for laborers. This was El Gancho. The hook.

It was this hook that snared the Nava family and brought them to a desolate spot in the New Mexican desert called Corrizozo. Sharing an old boxcar, they set up house. Every morning Prudenciano set out before first light riding with a crew of men up and down the El Paso and Northeastern railroad line repairing track for two dollars and fifty cents a day. It was a start and it was more money than he had ever earned before.

There is an old American saying that goes "Wherever you go, there you are." The one thing Nava could not escape was himself and his own bad choices. With a reason to celebrate and few bottles of tequila, he would soon find himself involved in a controversy that was to effect the rest of his life, driving him and his family out of Corrizozo, forcing him to change his name and eventually costing the life of one child.

A few years later, the final hook took the family north to eastern Montana and a little town named Sidney. Sidney was the home of the Holly Sugar refinery and it was here that the now Minjares family would take root. It was in Sidney that Prudenciano would live out his final days but not before he would commit one final act that defined his life and the time from which he came.

Michael Travis has written an important story. A true story. A story about his great grandfather, my grandfather. He has taken the bits and pieces of family history that have been handed down and put the puzzle together into a colorful mural of our family history. A history that at times has made us blush.

But in a larger sense, this book is a testament to the struggle of the immigrant family and their tenacity against extreme adversities that would make common men surrender to these uncommon circumstances. They are the exploited, expendable souls whose backs empires are built upon.

And it was this exploitation and expendability that didn't go unnoticed by idealistic heroes in the likes of people like Francisco Madero, Emiliano Zapata, and Francisco Villa. And it didn't go unnoticed by our grandfather, for I think it was the basis for many of his choices—good or bad. The choice to stand and fight. The choice to protect at any cost. The choice to, as Zapata preached, to die on ones feet rather than live on one's knees.

Yes, Prudenciano Nava was a flawed man, with an insatiable thirst for tequila and hand rolled cigarettes. A self centered braggart who chose a "blood in, blood out" allegiance to his friends before anything or anyone, including family. A code of honor that cost him dearly. Including his own name.

But there is something about the man that is alluring to us. Seduces us. He was a handsome, hard drinking, hard fighting man with a free, wreckless soul. A complex man of contradictions who could be a deep well of compassion one moment and a cold, ruthless killer the next. Walking that fine line between hero and villain, idealistic patriot and the sap. He was the man we wish we could be and the man that we thank God we're not. He is the macho man that has been handed down and sleeps quietly inside all of us.

Introduction

There comes a time in every person's life when they wonder who stares back at them in the mirror. They ask themselves what events led to their creation and who are the people responsible for their blood flowing through their veins. Some say that we are the result of random meetings and fate, but I believe that we are more than a series of chance events. We are the product of our ancestors' hopes, dreams, fears, recklessness, and boldness. Every one of us exist because our ancestors chose a path to follow, sometimes with enormous risk.

My search for the people responsible for my existence began one December night when I asked my Grandmother Anita about her parents. She smiled and said, "Well, I suppose you are old enough to know about your great-grandfather. You see, our last name was not Minjares. It was Nava. My father had to change it because . . ." Two hours later, my jaw was still on the floor. The story that she told sounded so unbelievable that I had to investigate it.

This book is the result of balancing facts, family stories, and historical accounts. My great-grandfather, Tereso Minjares (a.k.a Prudenciano Nava) was known for telling fantastic adventures and my relatives gave them little credence. However, when I arranged the stories in chronological order and compared them to actual historical events, I was amazed how well the stories correlated to documented history. Therefore, I decided to weave the stories and history together to develop this fictional novel.

While most the book is based on my great-grandfather's stories, some adventures were real events. The most noteworthy were the border crossing at El Paso, Texas and the train holdup at Carrizozo, New Mexico. With the help of the National Archives and Records Administration, Lincoln County News, and the Carrizozo city historian, I was able to accurately reconstruct these events.

To keep the story flowing, I greatly simplified the description of the Mexican Revolution. In reality, the revolution was very complex and tumultuous. If the reader desires an accurate account of the revolution and Pancho Villa's role in it, I highly recommend reading Centaur of the North by Manuel A. Machado.

I am not a historian and some of the historical events may not be completely accurate. However, I believe that I captured my family's beliefs and convictions of regional events as they struggled to escape the revolution and survive in America.

I wrote this book out of love for my family. I hope it inspires you to seek your past and embrace it—the good and the honorable along with the bad and the deplorable.

Michael D. Travis
2006

The home where my Grandmother Anita, Aunt Angelita, and Uncles Ben and Joe were born. My Uncle Joe took this picture in the 1950s. The house had been standing for at least 30 years. It still displays the metal roof put on after the sod roof collapsed on Paz.

My great-grandparents, Tereso and Paz Minjares, taken in December, 1923 in Sidney, Montana. Paz's left hand was atrophied from a roof collapse in Doña Ana. She was self-conscious of it for the rest of her life.

Chapter 1
Reflection

Midsummer heat hung in the afternoon air over the sugar beet field like a heavy blanket. The low droning of locusts barely penetrated the silence that prevailed over the workers. Tereso Minjares took a rest from his backbreaking work to straighten his massive aging body and stretch his aching muscles. He wore a wide-brimmed hat that covered his long, flowing gray hair that parted in the middle and hung almost to his shoulders. It perfectly matched his full gray beard. He stood six feet, four inches, with a powerfully built torso—an imposing figure for seventy-four years old.

As he wiped his brow with his handkerchief, Tereso scanned the field for his family. He found his two daughters and his son spaced evenly throughout the rows. They steadily thinned and weeded the beets in a squatting position that required strength and endurance. His son used the most hideous tool devised by man, the short-handled hoe. With this two-foot long device in one hand, he either scooted on his knees or waddled like a bent duck as he chopped the weeds and excess beets and removed them with his free hand. The girls followed behind and further thinned the row, leaving a single beet plant spaced every ten to twelve inches.

The Holly Sugar Company owned these fields, which consisted of several hundred acres and surrounded the newly built sugar refinery. The large facility consisted of enormous silos and a sugar reduction plant. The factory was located two miles east of Sidney, Montana along the railroad. The plant had its own rail spur and track sidings to bring sugar beets in from distant fields and to export the refined sugar to market.

The Minjares family contracted with Holly Sugar to weed and thin the sugar beets for five dollars per acre. Like the other Mexican families working their contracted sections of distant fields, the Minjareses toiled alone. If they failed to thin the crops according to their contract, Holly Sugar would not pay them and the family would starve.

Tereso signaled to his oldest son, Augustine, that he needed a water break and chance to sit in the shade of one of the massive cottonwoods that bordered the field. The family had appointed Augustine as their leader. He nodded his head but added in Spanish with a stern voice that carried across the field, "But only for ten minutes, *comprende?*"

Tereso grunted his response and strolled directly to the nearest tree. Augustine was always lenient to him because of his age. Tereso often exploited his privileges to the maximum and used his breaks to brag to other workers about his past exploits or counsel others, usually his children, on how to work better. Augustine kept an eye on his father, ready to rescue some unfortunate recipient of Tereso's wisdom by dragging Tereso back to work.

Tereso stopped under a broad cottonwood and found the canvas water bag that he had left to cool in the shade. After taking a couple of deep swallows, he screwed the cap tight and returned the bag next to the tree. Slowly he took out his Prince Albert tobacco can and rolled a cigarette. He lit the end and flicked the burning match into the irrigation ditch that flowed behind the tree.

He took a long drag and released the smoke through his beard. His thoughts of the hard labor that faced him dissipated in the smoky wisps. As he surveyed the field, he realized that this was not the life that he had searched for these past thirty years. He did not own a house or a car, which were Mexican symbols of wealth. He still worked hard six days a week, and, despite being respected, no one outside Sidney knew him if one discounted that altercation in Carrizozo, New Mexico. But that suited Tereso fine. He subconsciously ran his fingers over the old dents in his skull and chuckled to himself about that memory. Life was different then, with many new challenges and opportunities to exploit.

For Tereso, a better life had always beckoned from the north and he had always answered its call. As a result, life relentlessly dragged him north like a fish hooked on a line. He had tenaciously moved north for so many years in search of the easy life that he found it hard to believe that he had nowhere else to go. Now he was in the most northern state of America and life was still hard.

To make matters worse, the year was 1930 and America was amidst a great economic depression. Tereso knew that he was luckier than most. Unfathomable hordes of Mexicans were jobless and living in abysmal poverty. Ironically, many were returning to Mexico, where the job opportunities were much better. Tereso had chased the American dream to Sidney and now he was stuck. "Hooked" others would say. Yes, he had swallowed *el gancho* offered by a labor agent in Las

Cruces, New Mexico and now he was caught. For better or worse, Tereso's search had come to an end.

Tereso took another puff and drifted back to a time past, a time before he had begun his epic journey north. A time when many knew him by another name. A time when life was grand.

Chapter 2
Jaripeo

His back hurt and his mind reeled with confusion as he dragged himself from the depths of sleep. Prudenciano Nava had no idea of what had aroused him. The dust from the nearby corral hung thick in the late afternoon air. It coated his face and hair like talcum powder and made him choke. As he lay on the ground on top of his jacket, Prudenciano heard the disturbing noise again.

"Wake up, Nava! It's time. The crowd is waiting."

Prudenciano shook the cobwebs from his mind and slowly opened one eye. It was Tereso Rodriguez. It was always Tereso. The two of them had been nearly inseparable over the past twenty years while competing in Mexican-style rodeos called *jaripeos*. They moved from town to town following the *jaripeo* circuit and performing in local corrals or any roughly assembled field. At first, the traveling and drunken brawls called *parrandas* had been exciting, but now it felt like hard labor.

Tereso was a small, wiry man with the stout bowlegs and long torso of the Mexican Indian. In contrast, Prudenciano had the tall, lean physique of a Spaniard. These ethnic differences were confirmed by Tereso's smooth face and Prudenciano's full, thick beard. Both men were forty-eight-years old—much too old to be sleeping on the ground, throwing bulls, and living day to day.

Prudenciano felt the effects of the tequila that he had drunk a few hours ago. It made his mood foul. He readied himself to curse Tereso, but the chanting of the crowd within the ring carried to him and drowned out any attempts to retaliate. "¡*Colleada! ¡Colleada!*" It was time for tailing the bull.

"See? I told you. Your time has come," said Tereso. He studied Prudenciano for a moment and realized he was in poor condition. In fact, during these last few months, he had seldom looked better. This life was consuming them. "You must try to get ahold of your senses. The bull will have his and I bet our last peso on us."

El Gancho

At this, Tereso had Prudenciano's full attention. Prudenciano spoke roughly. "You are right." With a great effort from sheer will, he lifted his aching body and began dusting himself off. He had chosen a place by their horses to sleep. Tereso had already saddled and prepared them for today's performance. All that remained was for Prudenciano to get dressed.

He slowly pushed his feet into his worn boots. Then he put his riding shirt on. His shirt was his only possession that still had some fashion left. It was black with sequins and silver buttons. Some of the sequins were missing, but all the buttons were present. He strapped his thick leather belt around his trim waist and centered his silver belt buckle. Prudenciano put on his leather chaps and then tied his spurs to his heels. Finally, he finished off his apparel with a frayed, wide-brimmed hat with a string that hung under his neck. He was ready.

Tereso led the horses over to Prudenciano. Tereso wore simple pants and a plain white shirt with a black vest. His outfit was frayed, but still had a distinguished look. However, the most important part of his equipment was not worn by him. These were the two bright red flags attached to the pommel of his saddle. Without them, their task would have a very low probability of success.

Their horses were strong and healthy. Anyone who saw them knew they were from good breeding stock. Onlookers also wondered how two ruffians could possess such magnificent creatures. The horses and saddles were reluctant gifts from Prudenciano's father.

As they mounted their horses, Prudenciano looked over to Tereso and asked, "What were the odds?"

Tereso answered, "Good. They say that we are getting old." Neither Prudenciano nor Tereso could read, and they had only a very rudimentary understanding of money and betting odds. To them, odds were either good or bad. Good odds made lots of money. Bad odds barely paid more than what was put in.

The two of them rode side by side to the large crowd of men surrounding the corral. There would be no women in this unruly mob except for a few *señoritas* trying to make many *pesos* in one evening. Already the men were driven to a roaring drunken frenzy. Warm *cerveza* and tequila loosened every inhibition. The prior events of bronco riding, calf roping, and impromptu attempts at bullfighting had warmed the crowd to the final event of *la Colleada*—grasping the tail of the bull.

Only a handful of men in Mexico could throw a full-grown bull by its tail. These men were called *colleadores*. The bulls that charged the *colleadores* appeared to be the same animals that faced *matadores* in

22

a bullfight. They possessed the same immense, powerful shoulders and neck that supported broad sharp horns. Each animal exceeded a ton. However, they were actually quite different. These bulls had faced men and horses in past competitions. They were used in training *matadores*, *picadores*, *rejoneadores*, and other *colleadores*. Unlike reputable bulls of the ring, these canny beasts had been taught the lessons of combat. They no longer charged blindly at any motion. If a horse and its rider faked one direction and quickly veered to the other, the bull anticipated the dodge and swung his horns to meet the horse's rib cage with deadly accuracy.

This is what made *la Colleada* dangerous and the crowd knew it. Bets quickly changed hands. Most of the men were placing odds on the bulls. A self-picked extrovert was the center of the confusion. He stood in the middle of the crowd with wads of pesos and shouting confirmations of wagers. The cacophony of yelling men, disturbed animals, and breaking bottles filled the air around the *jaripeo*.

As Prudenciano and Tereso approached the corral, the same manager of betting also became the self-appointed master of ceremonies. He looked up from the gambling and saw them ride toward the starting gate. He quickly closed all bets and vaulted over the fence. He strutted to the middle of the corral with his trouser pockets bulging with betted pesos. Of course, none of the bets had been recorded. Every man depended on his memory of the exact wager and odds placed. Inevitably, disagreements flared at the conclusion of the events and this only added to the uproar of the *parranda* that always followed the *jaripeos*. Prudenciano knew that invariably this man would pocket some of the money he was carrying, but without the benefit of math or literacy, cheating would be hard to prove.

The ringmaster spread his arms to attain some air of authority and quiet the crowd. "Welcome to Jerez, Zacatecas on a fine August day of the nineteen hundred and fourth year of our Lord."

"Oh, get on with it, Octavio!" shouted someone from the crowd.

Unruffled, Octavio continued, "All three teams of *colleadores* are here! By the order chosen by the crowd, the first team will be Anastacio Currandas and Luis Cato." The crowd's subdued response was mixed with voices of support and hisses. Ignoring the lukewarm response, the orator continued, "Next will be José Para and Antonio Castillo." Now the crowd's reaction was more boisterous.

The crowd must have bet more money on their success, Prudenciano thought dryly.

"Finally, the third team will be the famous Prudenciano Nava and Tereso Rodriguez!" shouted Octavio. At this, the crowd started banging the fence and screaming derogatory remarks at the two of them.

This confirmed what Tereso had said earlier. The crowd had bet against them.

Just three years before, this very town had showered Prudenciano and Tereso with admiration. Now the hero's welcome had died. This awareness awoke a deep anger within Prudenciano, and his big hands and square jaw clenched in rage. Tereso was acutely tuned to his partner's emotions. He spoke evenly to Prudenciano. "Think of the money we'll make today. Think only of that and we will leave rich!" Prudenciano nodded his acknowledgment, but he continued to stare at the crowd with eyes of hatred. Slowly he began to compose himself and review the steps of tailing a bull in his mind.

La Colleada required exquisite teamwork and timing. First, a rider got the attention of the bull with fluttering flags and initiated a charge. As the bull committed to the moving target, a second rider came in from behind. This rider must exhibit superb horsemanship and strength as he leaned very far and low and gripped the tail. At this critical moment, three components must occur simultaneously to ensure a successful throw. The bull must be taken by complete surprise. The horse must accelerate at top speed. The rider must maintain his grip. Failure of any one of these would result in the bull impaling a horse and maybe its rider. If the throw was successful, the bull would tumble forward as the rider used his leverage and speed to virtually overrun his victim. When the bull landed fully on his back, the *jaripeo* judge declared that the team successfully threw the bull. If other teams successfully threw the bull, the winner was chosen by the speed, style, and skill of the throw.

Luis Cato of the first team entered the corral while Anastacio Currandas sat on his horse at the entrance. Luis wore clothing similar to that of the men in the audience, simple off-white cotton pants and a long, square-cut pullover shirt with a rope cinching his shirt around his waist. Unlike the spectators, he wore boots with spurs. The only color that punctuated his apparel was a large set of multicolored flags connected to the pommel of his saddle. His horse was short and rangy like a rugged pony, but it moved well and seemed comfortable within the noisy corral.

Currandas was a large man. His girth seemed to shorten his six-foot frame. His arms and hands were massive, a sure sign of a veteran *colleador*. Differing from Luis, Currandas wore a colorful sombrero that was secured with a strap under his chin, and leather gloves to improve his grip. His mustache drooped down both sides of his mouth, which fitted his bloated, unshaven face.

The bull was released into the chute as Luis positioned himself directly across the corral. To reach Luis, the bull would have to run in front of the corral entrance where Currandas sat. Thus, Luis must immediately catch the attention of the bull and hold it for Currandas to surprise the bull from behind.

The bull shot out of the chute like an iron ball fired from a cannon. It was a magnificent creature with a shiny black hide and massive, sharp horns. The horns glinted in the late afternoon sunlight as if they were polished. His shoulder and neck muscles looked like living granite. In one fluid motion, the bull sighted the horse and rider with his waving flags and charged.

Luis checked his horse and held it broadside while waving his flags back and forth. The bull rumbled toward him like a freight train. As the bull passed the corral entrance, Currandas spurred his horse and they leaped behind it at a full run. Currandas immediately leaned forward and low. The fence and Luis were coming up very fast. Currandas strained outward and concentrated on the bobbing tail. Then suddenly he grabbed it. At the same time, Luis's horse bolted. The bull was about to slam them through the fence and into eternal oblivion.

As Luis's horse skimmed past the horns, Currandas pulled the tail up. The bull tried to brake by stiffening his front legs and sliding to a stop, but it was too late. The fence was only a few feet in front of them. As his horse continued to race forward, Currandas grunted from the exertion of lifting the bull. The bull began to flip over. Then they met the fence. The bull struck the thick timbers with his back. The wood cracked like a rifle shot from the impact. At the same time, Currandas's horse vaulted the rail. Currandas instinctively held onto the tail and was savagely ripped backward from his mount. One of his boots caught in the stirrup and yanked off, wrenching his leg in the process. Bull and man fell hard onto the earth.

The crowd momentarily went silent with shock. Life and death for Currandas were separated by a razor's edge. As he lay unconscious next to the dazed animal, Luis galloped toward him. Abruptly, the beast came to life with a monstrous fury. Luis brushed by the bull and it gave chase.

As Luis lured the bull away, Prudenciano bolted his horse toward Currandas. Galloping at full speed, he leaned out, snagged the hefty man, and dragged him back through the corral gate with Currandas's heels scarcely touching the ground. The crowd erupted with cheers and Luis dodged the bull again and led it to the chute. The bull, still furious but obviously hurting, charged up the chute and into a small wooden pen, where he could sulk and rest.

Tereso slapped Prudenciano's back. "You are a hero, Nava! Just listen to the crowd."

But Prudenciano looked back at the crowd with disgust and said, "It pays nothing. Now I probably wrecked our odds too." Prudenciano was right. Several people were engaged in a heated debate with Octavio, but it wasn't over their odds. Everyone wanted to know Octavio's ruling if Currandas had thrown the bull. A lot of money rode on his decision and some men were going to be mad either way the ruling fell.

Octavio sensed this and immediately began formulating a plan. He slowly strolled to the middle of the corral as he put the final touches to his plan. Octavio again raised his hands to silence the crowd and put on a grave face. "My friends." Octavio began. "I have a very difficult decision to make." The crowd, stone quiet, leaned forward to catch every word. "First, we all know the rules of a successful throw. The bull's back must fully touch the ground." At this, part of the crowd groaned while others shouted triumphantly "*Sí ! Sí !*" Octavio threw out his hands again and the crowd quickly quieted. "However, we all witnessed Currandas's excellent horsemanship and had this town built its corral to the correct dimensions in the first place …" Octavio paused to let this thought sink in. Several men in the crowd coughed and shuffled nervously. "Currandas would have completed the throw. Therefore, I declare this match a draw and all bets will be transferred to the next competition." Shouts of disbelief and relief echoed through the men, but Octavio wasn't finished. "Just to make it up to you," Octavio shouted, "I will reopen the bets for Nava and Rodriguez. I am sure you were impressed by Nava's display of bravery and strength. He obviously is not the old man you thought he was."

"Damn that man!" shouted Tereso. "We will lose our odds!" Prudenciano could only smile at Octavio's craftiness. By calling a draw, there was no loss of money or cause for violence. Octavio was still able to protect his commissions. Tereso walked over to where the betting was resuming. In a few minutes, Tereso returned with a resigned posture. He shook his head as he said, "The odds are only half as good as before. We'll make money but not as much."

Before Prudenciano could reply, the second team readied itself for the next bull. José Parra and Antonio Castillo looked scarcely older than boys. José was the *colleador*. He lacked the typical massive build required to hold the bull, but his arms and shoulders were lean and hard from years of ranching. Neither of them had hats or special garb. Everything they had, including their horses, was bottom-dollar quality. Most of their equipment was borrowed, but if they were successful today, they could easily afford their own saddles and clothes for the next *jaripeo*.

The trauma of the last match must have unnerved José. With great anxiety, he scanned the broken timbers where bull and man had collided with such force. Then he returned his gaze to the chute. "We can call this off and come back another day," José told Antonio softly.

Antonio bristled at the comment. "You know that there is no turning back!" he said sharply. "We borrowed too much from too many to stop now. I would never be able to look our foreman in the eyes again if we quit. He's probably betting on us right now."

I bet he's not, thought José. He gulped his fear back and nodded to Antonio. "Better get ready."

Antonio held his head up high and trotted his horse to the far end of the corral. The men began jeering at him as soon as he positioned himself. "Hey, little man! That bull is going to get you! Ha, ha …" Antonio pretended not to hear. He clenched his right hand on his flags and abruptly raised them to signal that he was ready.

In response, the second bull rumbled down the chute and burst into the corral. José blinked in disbelief at the size of him. The bull was actually larger than the first one. A skilled eye would have noticed that he was about one year older and thus a veteran of tailings, but all José could recognize was his sheer mass.

Instead of immediately charging Antonio, the bull swayed his head side to side and scanned the entire corral. When he satisfied himself that Antonio and his flags were the only targets within sight, he charged, but only at three-quarters speed. As he ran past the entrance gate, José quickly fell in behind him for a few seconds and prepared to grab the tail. Suddenly, the bull spun around and faced him. He knew this game well.

José's shock and disbelief at this turning of the tables paralyzed him, but thankfully, his horse instinctively countered and broke diagonally to dodge the horns. Now, the hunter became the hunted as the bull pursued him. José's mind could not keep up with the quickly unfolding events. His horse behaved like a chicken caged with a fox. Its eyes bulged from sheer terror and it breathed heavily through its mouth. José could barely keep his mount as the horse twisted and turned to shake the bull.

Antonio rode closely behind the bull screaming obscenities and even slapping his rump with his flags. He tried everything he could think of to attract the bull's attention. The bull was totally focused on destroying the man who tried to grab his tail. The spectacle would have been comical had it not been for the deadly intent of the bull.

Then, as abruptly as the bull had chased José, he whirled around and stabbed Antonio's horse through the rib cage. The horn jammed up to the hilt. Antonio dove forward over the horse's head, barely escaping injury. He landed on his shoulder and rolled onto running feet in a swift fluid motion that carried him to safety. The bull now had the advantage of leverage and easily lifted the entire horse off the ground and began to shake it viciously. The horse let out an agonizing scream that struck terror in every living creature within earshot.

José directed his bucking, panic-stricken horse through the entrance gate. A man who was paid to lure bulls jumped into the corral and ran past the enraged beast. The dead horse hung limply from the horn. The bull spotted the man and charged him. The dragging horse hardly slowed the bull as he chased the man to the chute. The man agilely ran up the ramp and the bull followed. The horse caught on a side rail and peeled off the horn. As the man entered the holding pen, he quickly scampered up one of the sides and escaped to safety. The bull crashed in and the door closed behind to secure him in his pen.

The crowd went wild with relief and the aftermath of an adrenaline rush. It was a great show with no one hurt and only the loss of a range horse. Those who had bet on the bull were satisfactorily rewarded. Everyone except José and Antonio was in a festive mood until yelling was heard from the bullpens.

"He has broken his leg! How could you have let this happen?" shouted a ranch foreman at one of his men. The young man exhibited a submissive posture with his head bowed and shoulders slumped. He stood next to the holding pen that held the third bull. The bull held his front leg slightly up. The bone below the joint was dangling at an unnatural angle. When the previous bull ripped into Antonio's horse, the piercing screams had startled the penned bull and his leg struck one of the fence timbers. Obviously, it was an unfortunate accident that the young man could not have prevented, but the foreman showed no mercy. His boisterous rebuke attracted the crowd's attention and Octavio came over to investigate.

"What's the ruckus about?" he inquired.

"This poor excuse of a man let the bull break his leg!" answered the foreman. One look at the large animal and the wiry young man and Octavio doubted that the kid could have done anything to avert it.

"Never mind how it happened," snapped Octavio. "What are we going to do about it? We have one more match and there are too many bets on it to stop." The foreman knew that the almighty peso would dictate the solution. He put his hand to his chin and rubbed his coarse stubble for a moment before reaching a solution.

"Here's the situation," the foreman began. "The third bull is done. We'll butcher him tonight for the *parranda*. The first bull may very well have cracked some ribs when he hit the fence. He appears too sore to put on a good show. Thus, I suggest that we reuse the second bull for the final match." Octavio's eyes popped open with disbelief. The bull was newly experienced and therefore deadly to anyone trying to tail him. There was no way he could talk the last team into tangling with this bull. He raised his hand to protest, but the foreman quickly cut him short by saying, "You could offer a financial incentive to Rodriguez and Nava. Say four-to-one odds?"

Now Octavio had something that he could control and manipulate to his advantage. "*Sí.* I see now that you are a shrewd businessman. All right, ready the second bull, I'll make Nava an offer." Octavio walked quickly to the entrance gate with a renewed spring to his step.

When Prudenciano saw Octavio coming, he became immediately suspicious. The man looked too confident and jovial after just quieting an argument in the bullpens. Prudenciano leaned over to Tereso and said, "Here comes the jackal. I'm sure he has an interesting proposition for us."

"My good men," exclaimed Octavio, "I have some terrible news, but an interesting solution."

That clinches it, thought Prudenciano. *Here comes the pitch.*

"It appears that your bull broke his leg during the unfortunate last match," explained Octavio. "Now, the only alternative is to use the previous bull again."

"You are completely *loco!*" snarled Tereso. "That bull would have us as soon as he was out of the chute!" Prudenciano said nothing. He only stared straight at Octavio.

"Now, now, *Señores*. I realize that you may have some doubts so I'm going to make it worth your while. Say four-to-one odds?"

"What does that mean?" asked Prudenciano. Octavio instantly realized that he had the distinct advantage of knowledge.

"Well, let's see." Octavio pretended that he was engaging in deep computation. "Tereso bet twelve pesos on today's match. So, if you win, you will get thirty-eight pesos." Octavio's voice was as smooth as satin as he glossed over his lie. However, Prudenciano knew men and he could sense when one was lying. The way Octavio's eyes flickered away from them as he explained the profit betrayed his dishonesty. They were obviously entitled to more, but Prudenciano did not know exactly how much more.

"We want two hundred pesos for the match. No odds," said Prudenciano.

Octavio quickly sucked in his breath. He was not expecting this reply. "Too much. I'll give you seventy-five pesos. Take it or leave it."

"We are out of here!" said Tereso quickly. "Let's get our gear and leave this godforsaken place." Octavio suddenly panicked. If they refused to tail the bull, he would have to refund the match bets and lose a significant portion of his profit. Besides, there was only a very slim chance that they would win. Thus, the gamble was tilted in his favor.

"How about one hundred pesos?" Octavio blurted out. The men stared at him. "Okay. This is my final offer: one hundred twenty-five pesos." This was a lot of money. More than they had seen in a while.

Tereso pulled Prudenciano to the side. "Can we do it?" he whispered.

Prudenciano flashed a reassuring smile at him and said, "For a hundred and twenty-five pesos, I would pull the dress up of the queen of Spain!" Prudenciano then turned to Octavio and said, "We'll do it."

"Excellent!" exclaimed Octavio as he smacked his lips and rubbed his hands together with delight.

As he quickly turned to leave, Prudenciano grabbed him by the upper arm and yanked him back. He stuck his face into Octavio's and said sternly, "If you try to cheat us, I will kill you." Prudenciano said this as a matter of fact, not as a threat, and Octavio knew it.

When Prudenciano released him, Octavio walked more slowly and not so cocksure as he went back to address the crowd. When Octavio approached the corral center, he composed himself and produced a wide, friendly smile. He raised his hands to hush the expectant crowd. "My *amigos*. I have some exciting news." The audience had already a memorable day, so they smiled back with anticipation for more entertainment. "The third bull has broken his leg and therefore will be the main course tonight. So, the third match will proceed as planned with the second bull."

The crowd was stunned and took a little time to comprehend the implications of the match. Slowly murmurs turned into voices and voices expanded into shouts and cheers. Immediately, massive side betting began. Most doubted that Prudenciano Nava could tail this bull, especially after the bull had just successfully evaded tailing in the last match.

Prudenciano took this time to plan his attack. As they saddled their horses, he quietly explained his strategy to Tereso. Tereso solemnly nodded his approval and understanding. When they finished discussing their scheme, they swung up into their saddles and adjusted their equipment.

Sitting high in their saddles, they signaled to Octavio that they were ready to begin. Tereso began trotting his horse into the corral. Octavio turned and motioned to the foreman to let the bull out. At that moment, he heard the audience gasp. He spun around to see Tereso backing his horse up the chute with his flags draped over the horse's rump. The horse's tail naturally flipped the bright red flags back and forth. It made an irresistible lure.

Prudenciano had also entered the corral and tucked his horse and himself in the crook where the chute protruded into the arena. From this perspective, the bull would not be able to see Prudenciano waiting in ambush when he came down the chute. The position also gave Prudenciano precious seconds and distance to tail the bull than if he had started from the traditional entrance gate.

Octavio began babbling in a high-pitched voice, "Stop! Stop! You can't do this! Don't let the bull out! Stop!" But it was too late. The foreman had already opened the pen and the bull started his run. Suddenly, he stopped, bewildered by the unaccustomed intrusion in the chute. The bull was transfixed by watching the flags twitching back and forth. Then the movement began to enrage him. He lowered his head and saw the legs of the horse under the flags. The sight was too much. The bull exploded forward. Tereso, anticipating this response, spurred his horse to a gallop. The bull was inches behind with the flags flapping tauntingly in his eyes.

Prudenciano shot forward from his concealed lair, leaned out, grabbed the tail, and straightened his muscular torso. His horse instantly accelerated. The bull was taken by complete surprise. His front legs began braking as his haunches lifted from the ground. The bull was going over.

Then suddenly, Prudenciano experienced something that he had only heard about from old *colleadores*. As the bull began to flip, his tail snapped off just above his hand. Astonished, Prudenciano was left holding the limp, broken appendage. The bull momentarily balanced on his forelegs, then came back down on all fours. By now, Prudenciano and Tereso had blown by the bull and scattered in separate directions. The crowd went wild with excitement.

The bull's entire body shook in anger and pain. He began to paw the earth and snort in rage. Looking up, he sensed one of the riders circling behind. The bull spun around and charged Prudenciano, who quickly aborted his attempt and evaded the bull. As Prudenciano pulled away, he slowed the horse slightly to allow the bull to come close. The bull quickly became transfixed on destroying the horse, and lost his wariness. Tereso stealthily slipped in and grabbed the stub of the tail. The bull bellowed in surprise and whirled on

Tereso. Tereso never intended to throw the bull, but just to keep him off balance. He let go and dodged the swinging horns. The crowd shouted with glee. This was a fine sport.

Now the bull forgot Prudenciano and roared after Tereso. This time Tereso held his flags behind him, letting them flutter. When the bull was within a few feet, Tereso let go of the flags and they wrapped around the bull's face. The bull slid to a stop and began shaking the flags off. This was the precise moment when Prudenciano struck. At a full gallop, he grabbed the tail stump and pulled up with all his strength.

The whole process worked like a second-class lever. The bull's haunches rose as the horse ran forward. The bull's front hooves acted as a fulcrum and the torso and the front legs provided the leverage for Prudenciano to flip the entire bulk over. The beast fell with a resounding thud as he crashed onto the earth.

The crowd produced a deafening roar. Octavio stood with his mouth agape as both *colleadores* lifted their hats to the crowd and rode triumphantly out of the arena.

———

The *parranda* was in full earnest by the time the moon rose. The entire male population of Jeréz and the surrounding countryside was present. This included citizens of the nearby towns of Huejucar, Mal Paso, Lobato, and Valparaiso. The moonlight cast a soft light over the adobe buildings with tile tops and wooden timbers protruding from the roof-line. A large bonfire lit the town square and a huge roasting pit was positioned only a few feet away. The unfortunate third bull had been split and skewered, and was turning slowly over the cooking coals.

Liquor of all makes flowed from any type of container that a man could get in his hands. Although *cerveza* and tequila were the usual drinks, some whiskeys and bourbons were also selectively available at a higher price. The day's *jaripeo* had been exceptionally good, which elevated the men's spirits. They sang, joked, and fought. As the night matured, the men did not. Frequently, a skirmish broke out and someone flew through an open doorway or window. Large groups locked arms and swaggered through the town square knocking over unsuspecting bystanders and even shoved the cooks and their utensils into the fire. Occasionally, a shot rang out. It was a grand time.

Offset from the plaza and under a store awning, Prudenciano and Tereso sat with their backs against the wall. A rough-cut table was between them and it held a bottle of the coveted whiskey with two clay mugs. They had bought the bottle with a portion of their winnings. The aroma of the meat cooking over the nearby fire wafted over and made their mouths water. Their moods were relaxed with the elated feeling that comes after flirting with danger and emerging victorious.

As they watched the drama unfolding in the plaza, Tereso took a long draft from his mug. He reached over and grabbed the half-drunk bottle, uncorked it, and poured another cupful of the precious whiskey. "Any problems collecting the hundred twenty-five pesos from Octavio?" Tereso asked.

"Not really," sighed Prudenciano. A jar thrown from the crowd smashed against the wall beside them. Oblivious to the near miss, Prudenciano continued, "He was easy to find. There were many men surrounding him demanding their winnings. In fact, two of them had him pinned against the fence. The others were trying to rip the pesos from his pants pockets."

Tereso chuckled and asked, "What did you do?"

"I went back to our gear and got my pistol. Then I persuaded everyone to let him go. Naturally, it is only fitting that the *colleadores* get paid first. So after Octavio gave me our money, I let the wolves have him."

Tereso smiled and thought to himself, *Sometimes, this is such a good life.* Suddenly, a large man lumbered out of the crowd and limped toward them. Momentarily, they thought him drunk, but as he drew near, they recognized him immediately.

"Anastacio Currandas! Please have a drink with us!" exclaimed Prudenciano.

"Ah, *gracias, amigos,*" replied Currandas. He grabbed a chair from the wall and laboriously sat down. He was obviously in much pain from his backward somersault with the bull. Prudenciano poured a mug full of whiskey and handed it to him. Currandas gulped it down like he was taking a large dose of medicine. As he finished his mug, he screwed up his face and exhaled forcibly through his mouth. "Prudenciano," Currandas began, "I first want to thank you for saving my life." Then Currandas looked deep into Prudenciano's eyes, "I will never forget it."

"*De nada,*" Prudenciano said as he waved off Currandas's gratitude. However, even a blind man could see that Prudenciano was deeply touched.

"Now, I have a favor to ask of you." Currandas continued. "You are a highly skilled *sobador* and I need your services. My leg is killing me." A *sobador* was a combination country doctor and masseuse with no formal training. Like many intelligent but illiterate men, Prudenciano had developed a phenomenal memory to compensate for the lack of written instructions. In many aspects, it was photographic. As a young man, he had watched with fascination as the *sobador* in his hometown of Monte Escobedo treated sprains, dislocated joints, and pulled muscles with a combination of massaging, herbal medicines, and bandages. He had memorized every treatment the *sobador* utilized to relieve suffering. Much to his family's surprise, Prudenciano displayed an instinctive talent to effectively administer the healing remedies. Now, people sought him out during his travels to alleviate their aches and pains. Often his services supplemented his and Tereso's meager income.

Prudenciano looked over to the roasting meat. The cooks were battling knife-wielding men who surrounded the pit. It would be a little longer before the meat was ready. "I suppose that I could have a look at you before dinner," capitulated Prudenciano. "Let's find a place to stretch you out." He slowly stood up and drained his mug at the same time. Currandas struggled up by bracing himself with the table.

Prudenciano turned and opened the door to the store that they sat against. The front room had a long table with several inebriated, unconscious men draped over the top. He reached down, picked up two of the men by the collar, one in each hand, and threw them out the door as one pitches out garbage. Prudenciano repeated the process until the table was clear and a heap formed outside.

"Now, let's have a look at your leg," Prudenciano said as he laid Currandas on his back on top of the table. The table groaned under the weight. Carefully, Prudenciano removed Currandas's boot and rolled up his pants. He skillfully examined the leg and made his assessment. The knee and ankle were swollen and bruised, but did not appear broken. Prudenciano determined that a precise hip realignment and a knee support would allay much of the pain. To do this properly, he would need his medical supplies from his saddlebags.

"Tereso!" shouted Prudenciano. Tereso stuck his head into the store. "Go to our gear and get my medical bag." Tereso disappeared into the noisy night. "Now then, I need to realign your hip while we wait for Tereso. Roll over on your stomach." Currandas complied and Prudenciano put his knee into the small of Currandas's back. At the same time, he grabbed Currandas's leg around his calf and twisted the leg to the inside. Viciously, Prudenciano yanked the leg outward while pushing Currandas's torso in the opposite direction. Currandas yelled out once and breathed deeply. Prudenciano rolled off Currandas and said, "You'll feel better tomorrow."

Tereso came back within a few minutes carrying the medical kit. Prudenciano took out a small glazed pottery jar with a wire latch that secured the lid and long strips of cloth for bandages. He opened the jar and took out the thick, rubbery leaves of an aloe vera plant. He broke two of the leaves and squeezed out the milky pulp into his left hand. Then, using both hands, he massaged the pulp into the injured knee and ankle. When Prudenciano was satisfied with his work, he bandaged the joints in such a fashion that Currandas could still flex them.

"*Gracias, amigo*," grunted Currandas. "It feels better already." Currandas sat up and slid off the table to test his leg.

"Buy me a drink and we'll call it even," Prudenciano replied. The three of them walked out of the store, stepped over the pile of men that still lay in front of the door, and strolled into the plaza. The crowd had finally overwhelmed the cooks and was hacking chucks of meat from the carcass. Large vats of beans were bubbling on the coals. Men would use their drinking mugs to scoop out a serving. As a result, the average dining man staggered in a drunken stupor with a dripping mug of beans in one hand and in the other a hunk of beef skewered by a knife.

Tereso found a plate and a set of bowls in the store. He handed the bowls to Prudenciano and heaped meat onto the plate. Prudenciano filled the bowls with beans and brought them back to the table. Currandas came limping back with a fresh bottle of tequila.

The three of them sat down and began eating from the bowls and the platter with their hands. They would wash it down with a mug full of alcohol. Despite the lack of utensils, they looked like highly civilized men when compared to the rest of the plaza population. They ate in silence. When they were finished, Prudenciano wiped his hands on his pants and poured himself another drink. "Well," he said as he lifted his mug, "Where is the next big *jaripeo*?"

"Oh, I guess I forgot to tell you," said Currandas nonchalantly. "It's time for one of the biggest *jaripeos* in Zacatecas."

"Um?" mumbled Prudenciano through his mug.

"*Sí*. In fact, we will perform in a real bull arena. Lots of people and women. Within two weeks, we meet in Fresnillo."

"Fresnillo! Are you sure? Is it really time for Fresnillo?" asked Prudenciano. He almost split his drink in his excitement. Fresnillo represented a chance to perform in front of hundreds of people who dressed for the occasion and cheered with colored ribbons and hats thrown high into the air. The *colleador* who won this event also earned respect, some fame, and many pesos. This was in stark contrast to today's event in Jeréz .

It was Tereso who pulled him back to reality. "You know, Prudenciano," Tereso said carefully, "that your family always makes the trip from Monte Escobedo to Fresnillo for the *feria* and *jaripeo*. Do you think that this time you can meet them without fighting?"

Prudenciano flared at Tereso. The night's drinking was finally taking effect. In his anger, he clenched his fist to hit him, but when he pulled his arm back, a strange vision manifested itself in front of him. Momentarily, Tereso's body appeared mangled and lifeless next to a gruesomely pulverized horse. Then, as swiftly as it came, the vision left and a wide-eyed Tereso was staring back at him. The whole episode lasted only a split second, but it was enough to unnerve Prudenciano. It defused his rage and he slowly lowered his fist.

Tereso quickly apologized, "I'm sorry. I shouldn't have said anything about you and your family." Prudenciano said nothing. He slid back into his chair and nursed his drink. Prudenciano gave great credence to his visions. He had experienced fleeting prescience in the past. They always bore out some truth within a short period of time. Suddenly, he had a deep foreboding about Fresnillo.

Chapter 3
Fresnillo

Prudenciano and Tereso rode slowly through the stark, rugged valleys of the Sierra Madre Occidental. The valleys contained small, scattered farms with irregularly-shaped fields that conformed to the mountainous contours and ravines. Each plowed field revealed the red soil characteristic of the land. As they rode northeast along the only road to Fresnillo, the elevation imperceptibly decreased as the countryside began to open into rolling hills. There were no towns along the eighty miles from Jeréz to Fresnillo.

The *ranchos* they passed housed poor people. Most of these destitute residents were sharecroppers working for rich landowners called *hacendados*. Once a man started down the narrow road of sharecropping, he never returned. All his hard-earned money was quickly consumed by the barbarous share due to the *hacendado*. Any money left barely covered daily necessities and operating expenses. Commonly, the sharecropper had to borrow money from the *hacendado* to continue ranching, thus burying himself deeper in unrelenting debt.

Long ago, the land had flourished in newfound treasures. In the mid-1500s, the Spanish discovered silver here. Henceforth, Zacatecas became the source of Spain's wealth as silver ingots and bars flowed outside at the expense of the Mexican Indian. Spain required slave labor to mine the precious ore. When the wealth dried up, Spain discarded Zacatecas and its people like one would crush and throw away an empty tobacco pouch.

Zacatecas was now in a severe economic depression as the result of the polices of Mexico's dictator, Profirio Díaz. Díaz had taken control of Mexico's government in 1876. Since then, Zacatecas's economy had begun sliding downward to ruin. Only the *hacendados* prospered because they ruled large landholdings with an almost feudal style.

As Prudenciano and Tereso quietly rode east through the high chaparral, the country was cool and arid and possessed the vegetation of the high-altitude plains. Any fold in the terrain that could provide shelter and trap water contained hardy trees and grasses.

The Trujillo river was the only watercourse they crossed during the trip and its dry bed testified that it was only an intermittent flowing stream. The rest of the land depended on the year's rainfall to determine the type of flora it would support. In good years, the land was green with lush grasses that could nourish thousands of cattle. In drought years, the country resembled a desert with only a few tufts of grass. Therefore, the people's fortunes ebbed back and forth with the unpredictability of the seasons.

The men's slow pace matched the quiet and enduring rhythms of Zacatecas. Everything here happened slowly and in its own time. The country road they followed was deeply worn by millions of footpads over eons of years. The land was not despairing, but it was relaxed, old, and poor.

Within this environment, Prudenciano and Tereso were in constant pursuit of opportunity. They moved from town to little town following the *jaripeo* schedule. They were always hoping for that big score that would make them rich, but never quite attaining the goal. They would make a lot of pesos and lose them in a single night. Sometimes, they lost their money from gambling after a hearty *parranda*. Other times, it was just bad luck. Whatever the reason, they had always looked forward to the next *jaripeo*, until now.

Prudenciano felt great anxiety over what lay ahead in Fresnillo. The vision he had in Jerez was still etched vividly in his mind. He tried to rationalize his dark premonition as a drunken hallucination, but a feeling of dread followed him. He had a gut feeling that Fresnillo was going to be a disastrous venture.

Tereso noticed his dark mood, but waved it off as Prudenciano's brooding about fighting with his family. Some would be attending the *feria* and Prudenciano always fought with them. Tereso turned in his saddle and addressed Prudenciano. "Hey! Let's cheer up. Fresnillo is going to be lots of fun. It always is. Many friends and women. Great food. Tequila flows in the streets! So, forget about your father and brothers. Just concentrate on throwing bulls and having a good time."

"Easier said than done," Prudenciano replied dryly. He couldn't bring himself to tell Tereso of the vision. He flexed his right hand, the one he used to tail the bulls. The hand felt stiff. Prudenciano continued, "Maybe I am getting too old for this stuff."

"Oh, and what would you do instead?" asked Tereso.

"My father wants me to come back to the ranch. He would like to retire and have his sons look after things. Being the oldest, I could be the boss."

Tereso snorted in full disagreement. "Your father would never let you be the boss. Remember? You must first learn to read and write. That is your father's rule and that is why we are here today." Prudenciano's eyes darkened with anger. Tereso sighed and let the argument go. The way Tereso saw it, the dilemma was a no-win situation. Prudenciano would never stay in one place long enough to be schooled. Looking up, Tereso spotted the rising dust and buildings along the distant horizon. "Look, Prudenciano! Fresnillo! Our destiny lies ahead."

"Fresnillo." Prudenciano spoke quietly. "I hope we live through our destiny."

"Come on, man. Get yourself together. It's time for the second bull," urged Tereso. "What's the matter? Did you hurt yourself?"

"It's my hand," growled Prudenciano. "It feels weak. Kind of stiff." He flexed it several times.

"I warned you," answered Tereso, "that you should wear a glove like everyone else."

"A bare hand gives me a better grip."

"Or a sore one," finished Tereso. "Look. We got a good time on that last bull. We are in the running to take the top prize of five hundred pesos. All we have to do is equal our last time and we got it. Just think, Prudenciano. Five hundred pesos plus our bets! We could take a rest on that much."

"*Sí*. A rest would do us good," replied Prudenciano. "A long rest to heal these sore muscles. Let's do it!" They got up and dusted off their saddle blankets which they were sitting on to rest for the upcoming match. Prudenciano stretched and looked around him. Fresnillo always threw a grand *jaripeo*. The town proudly supported a large stadium with high bleachers that formed a semicircle around the enclosed field. The stadium provided spacious corrals for the horses and men in the back of the arena.

Prudenciano smiled as he reminisced about the last three days in Fresnillo. He and Tereso had mingled freely between the narrow streets and tightly packed buildings that characterized the town. They enjoyed themselves more than they had in many years. They met old acquaintances and drank copious amounts of *cerveza* while they relived past times. The nights were filled with festivities.

Fresnillo's *feria* differed dramatically from the drunken melee in Jeréz. Primarily, men and women equally enjoyed the activities. Instead of the hard drinking and fighting that was the main attraction at the Jeréz *jaripeo*, Fresnillo offered exhibits, assorted vendors selling crafts and foods, and dancing. The streets were plugged with people. Wagons laden with wares regularly tried to negotiate the crowded pathways. Shouts and cursing rose between the drivers and unfortunate bystanders. Every building had colorful flags and banners flapping gaily in front.

Prudenciano's spirits were so high that he completely forgot about the horrible vision he had in Jeréz. In fact, he felt as if he didn't have a care in the world. Tereso and he were in the running to win the competition and the top prize. Life would be truly grand if they could grab first place.

Prudenciano eagerly began saddling his horse when he heard a young voice pipe behind him. "Uncle Prudenciano, *Tío*, it's me, José." Prudenciano spun around and found his eleven-year-old nephew José Nava standing behind him. José wore simple woven pants with a matching pullover shirt that hung loosely over his slim frame. He used a rope to cinch up his clothes around his waist. He wore sandals, and no hat covered his thick bushy black hair. His eyes beamed with excitement and awe. "I saw you, *Tío*. You threw that bull faster than anybody in the whole world!"

Prudenciano smiled back at the boy. He liked the kid despite his aggravating adoration. José was his brother Abundio's son which, according to Prudenciano, was Abundio's only positive attribute. *Abundio may know how to read and write*, thought Prudenciano, *but he has no horse sense.*

"*¡Hola!* José. You are growing like a weed." The boy beamed back. He was obviously happy that Prudenciano remembered him.

"*Tío*, can I watch you and Tereso tail the bull from the gate?" asked José.

"*Sí*, but stay out of the way." Then Prudenciano asked carefully, "Are your father and grandfather here?"

"Oh, yes! I'll go and get them!" exclaimed José. Before Prudenciano could protest, the boy bolted into the crowd and disappeared. Tereso watched the two from the horses. He chuckled. *Well, the fuse is lit. Now for the family reunion fireworks.*

Prudenciano sensed Tereso's amusement and turned back to the horses. "Let's saddle up and move to the starting gate."

"Too late, Prudenciano," laughed Tereso. "Here they come!" Tereso pointed to the figures emerging from the multitude. Prudenciano was abruptly filled with trepidation. Slowly, he dropped his reins and turned to face his family. José was skipping forward leading two men toward him.

Abundio was a year younger than Prudenciano. He was a couple of inches shorter and stockier than his older sibling, but he still bore a strong family resemblance to him. Abundio wore black pants with a white shirt and a matching black vest and hat. *Always playing the rooster*, thought Prudenciano.

Emilio, his father, was in his late sixties. He was still tall, but his back slightly bowed from years of eking out a living on a small ranch. He wore solemn clothing to match his formal face. His shirt had red and blue embroidered designs, which was the only color found on his black and white clothing. A bolo tie secured his collar.

"Here they are, *Tío*. I brought them here just like you told me," exclaimed José proudly.

"*Sí*. You did a great job," Prudenciano said dryly. "Father. Abundio. How are you?" His father and brother stood stone-faced in front of him. Neither of them extended a hand of greeting.

Finally, his father spoke first, "Did you not think to stop by the *hacienda* before traveling to Fresnillo? Your poor mother died last year and we could not find you for the funeral. Do we displease you so much that you had to stay away?" It was an evasive statement because everyone knew the real reason why he did not want to go home. Prudenciano had left his wife, Julia Villaviceneio Nava, and their son, Brigido, to fend for themselves many years ago. Family life had never suited him.

"Father," replied Prudenciano with a voice thick with emotion. "This is my work. After we are finished here, I will come back ... "

"Work!" spat Emilio. "You call this work? Prudenciano, you play hard, but you don't know the meaning of work. If it wasn't for me, you wouldn't even have a decent horse!"

"*Sí*. No horse," chimed Abundio.

"*¡Silencio!*" Prudenciano roared straight back at his brother. Abundio cowered and stepped behind Emilio. Prudenciano directed his reply to his father. "This is my work. I earn a living doing this and I am famous."

"Right," scoffed Emilio. "Well, come along, Abundio and José. Let us leave our famous relative alone so he can work." Emilio put special emphasis on *famous* and *work* to sound especially sarcastic. "I just hope that after the drinking, gambling, and whoring, you can possibly find it within yourself to go home and assume your responsibilities." With that retort, the Navas turned to leave. However, José remained behind to speak one last time to Prudenciano.

"*Tío*, I bet five pesos on you," exclaimed José with absolute glee.

Prudenciano chided, "José, you are too young to gamble."

"But I love to gamble. It's great fun!" laughed José. "I'll be back before your match." The boy whirled toward his father and grandfather as they made their way to the grandstands.

Tereso began clapping. "Congratulations, Prudenciano. You chased your family off in three minutes flat. That must be a new record." The jibe made Prudenciano very mad. In his anger, he grabbed the saddle horn with his right hand and started to swing himself into the saddle. As he pushed off the stirrup with his left foot, his hand unexpectedly slipped off the horn which caused him to flop awkwardly across his horse.

"What kind of mount was that?" asked Tereso.

Stunned, Prudenciano looked down at his right hand. "I don't know," he replied. "My hand just slipped."

———————

The late afternoon sun lay heavy on the horizon. Its blood red rays painted the entire town in its hue. The lateness of the day did not dampen the excitement in the stadium as the competition narrowed to the two final teams, Anastacio Currandas and Luis Cato versus Prudenciano Nava and Tereso Rodriguez. The two teams were virtually tied in points as they began their final matches.

As Prudenciano predicted in Jeréz, Currandas had healed completely. *He recovered too well*, thought Tereso as he watched Currandas tail the bull in record time. Currandas and Cato had performed flawlessly in the previous match and therefore, everyone anticipated a grand finale. The competition was closely matched and the competitors were highly skilled and motivated. This was the perfect combination to end the *jaripeo*.

It was within this atmosphere that Prudenciano and Tereso readied themselves to throw their final bull. Prudenciano especially liked to perform in front of large crowds and women. If it hadn't been for his family feuds, Prudenciano's spirit would have been at its zenith. Nonetheless, he enjoyed the excitement and the attention. Nothing would please him more than hearing the screams and shrieks of women as he threw the bull within a first-place time. Then, as he rode to the judge's stand to receive his prize, the crowd would pelt him with roses, hats, and admiration. *Ah!* dreamed Prudenciano, *That would be grand. All that stands in the way of glory is throwing this last bull.*

"Prudenciano!" snapped Tereso. "If you could be so kind as to give this last match your full attention, we will be on our way shortly with real money. How about it?" Prudenciano startled from his fantasy. He snorted in agreement and made an effort to regain his composure. Then he refocused his attention to the activity in the stadium.

The master of ceremonies was walking to the middle of the arena. His rotund body was housed in an expensive tuxedo and he carried a megaphone in one hand. When he reached the center, he raised the amplifier to his mouth and shouted his announcements with a booming voice. As he spoke, he swivelled his torso side to side to ensure that his message carried throughout the grandstands.

"For the final round, we have saved our finest bulls. Each one is precious." Precious was the term reserved for magnificent bulls that were brave and aggressive. Since nobody really knew how a bull would react in the ring, every owner and event organizer said that their bulls were precious. The crowd knew this but always accepted the term with excitement.

The orator continued, "By the drawing of lots, I will determine the order of the two teams." As he finished with this declaration, a young woman in a beautiful long dress flowed onto the field. She carried a large black jar with a screwed-on lid. Her dress was adorned with bright colors that perfectly matched the colored ribbons in her hair. Catcalls and hoots of male appreciation rang throughout the stadium. The woman pretended not to notice and strode regally to the announcer. As she reached him, she smiled and lifted the jar to him. Before the man accepted the jar, he lifted up his megaphone and asked the spectators, "This is my niece. Is she not a beautiful sight today?" The crowd roared their agreement back for several minutes. The man beamed with pride and accepted the jar. He opened it and removed a set of dice. One die was black and the other red. He placed the dice in one hand. With his free hand, he lifted the amplifier and said, "The black die is Anastacio Currandas's team and the red one is for Prudenciano Nava's."

Prudenciano shuddered involuntarily at the mention of the red die. The symbolic color of violent death momentarily brought back his vision of several weeks ago. Then, as swiftly as the emotion came, it was gone. Prudenciano shook the remnants of the icy feeling out of his head and let the exhilaration of the afternoon consume him.

The master of ceremonies placed the dice into the jar and handed it back to his niece. She gracefully accepted the jar and gently but thoroughly jiggled it. After it was thoroughly mixed, she presented the jar to her uncle. Instead of taking the jar, he only removed the lid and turned his head away from her. Then without looking, he reached in and removed a die. His big hand completely engulfed it and hid it from view. After much fanfare, he raised his hand in full view of the crowd and flicked his fingers up to display the die. It was red.

"By the luck of the draw, Prudenciano Nava and Tereso Rodriguez will start first," announced the ringmaster. The crowd erupted with roaring cheers. Prudenciano's magnificent style was always a crowd pleaser.

"*¡Tío!* Tereso! I'm back!" The two men turned and saw José leaping onto the entrance gate. He clung to the wooden slats like a tick on a dog's back. His eyes danced with excitement. A couple of stadium hands made motions to remove him, but Prudenciano halted them with a sharp rebuke.

"The boy stays!" The men threw up their hands and turned away. Prudenciano then addressed José, "I want you to stay out of the way. If you don't, you will have me to answer to, *comprende?*"

"*Sí,*" answered the boy as he squirmed on the gate. Prudenciano's stern warning did not diminish his spirit. José was absolutely bubbling with exhilaration.

Prudenciano smiled and returned his gaze to the ring. The announcer had finished his oration and was escorting his niece back to his booth. The chute was being readied for the bull. Deafening shouts of "*¡Colleada!*" echoed through the stadium. Men waved their hats and women wagged colorful scarves in their hands. The entire scene heightened the thrilling anticipation within Prudenciano and Tereso. This moment was the highlight of their haphazard lives. They felt strong, alive, and invincible.

Prudenciano looked over to Tereso and smiled widely. In the deafening roar, he mouthed, "Let's do it!" Tereso smiled back and spurred his horse forward. He rode to the middle of the grounds, took out his red flags, and readied himself. The crowd quieted and an eerie hush fell over the stadium. Everyone leaned forward in expectation.

The master of ceremonies signaled to release the bull. The door opened and the bull blew down the chute and into the arena. He was truly a tremendous animal. His shiny black hide rippled from well-developed muscles. His long sharp horns possessed a glossy amber color that glinted in the low-angle sunlight. He shook his magnificent head to survey his surroundings. He took in deep breaths through his wide black nostrils and analyzed the smells. Even the most inexperienced spectator could see that the bull was intelligent, fearless, and in his prime.

A woman's piercing scream shattered the magical spell that held the bull in check. He bolted toward Tereso and the crowd emitted a thunderous roar. The bull's head lowered as he committed to the charge. Tereso began riding away from the animal with his flags trailing. He did not ride too fast, but with just enough speed to lure the bull away from the starting gate. Suddenly, Prudenciano came swooping across the field. He seemed to float above the ground as he leaned far and low to grab the tail with his right hand.

Now, time began to slow down as adrenaline surged into Tereso's brain. Microseconds seemed to turn to hours and seconds lasted for an eternity. The sounds of the crowd muffled to a low drone. He could now distinguish the sound of each horse hoof below him, and each deep breath it took. He could feel the ominous presence of the bull only a few feet behind him. Tereso's mind raced ahead in crystal clarity as he took in each complicated detail of his surroundings and calculated minute, three-dimensional changes to his situation. He saw the exact angle of Prudenciano's assault. At the same time, he observed the bull's subtle increase in speed toward him.

Only in situations of extreme danger did a man experience the total awareness of life within a heartbeat. These pinpoints of time attracted men like Tereso Rodriguez and Prudenciano Nava to sports and battle. It felt like standing on the edge of a giant abyss and screaming at the face of death. Once a man lived it, he was either addicted or repelled by it. For Tereso and Prudenciano, it was the elixir of life.

The stadium field was oval shape. Tereso was now approaching the far end of the arena. His maneuvering room was quickly disappearing. He glanced back and saw Prudenciano forming a grip on the tail. *He's got him!* thought Tereso. Instinctively, Tereso slowed his horse and prepared to veer, but the converging sides of the stadium restricted his movements. Desperate, Tereso flattened his horse against the wall to give Prudenciano maximum space to throw the bull.

Prudenciano secured the tail with his right hand and wrenched upward with all his strength. The bull faltered slightly, then fired forward with startling speed. Prudenciano shot a look to his hand. It was empty. His hand had slipped off the tail!

Prudenciano glanced up and saw the terror in Tereso's eyes. Again, time seemed to stand still. Prudenciano tried to shout a warning. It sounded in his ears like a distorted moan. He could see every agonizing detail in slow motion. He saw the flying dirt clods spinning off the bull's hooves as the bull slowly drove into Tereso's horse. Prudenciano saw the horns momentarily dimple the horse hide before beginning their long plunge into the ribcage. Last, he saw the finality of Tereso's life being driven out of him when the bull crushed man and horse against the wall. The final scene was exactly as Prudenciano had foreseen.

Chapter 4
Monte Escobedo

After that fateful match in Fresnillo, Prudenciano practically begged his father to take him back home. The tragedy unnerved Prudenciano and forced him to assume a humble demeanor as he pleaded with his father. Emilio was also overwhelmed by the turn of events. The bull had struck Tereso directly in front of their stadium seats. José had witnessed the whole event from the starting gate. The episode reduced the boy to an emotional wreck and he hung on his grandfather. Emilio eventually accepted Prudenciano back to the *rancho* against his better judgement. They left Fresnillo abruptly, not even staying for Tereso's funeral.

The five-day ride back to Monte Escobedo was a long, silent affair. They covered the 135-mile trek with each brooding over special problems. Prudenciano blamed himself for the death of his best friend. José struggled with the haunting memory of Tereso's death too, but he was also upset about losing his bets over the ill-fated match. Abundio worried about how he and his family would get along with Prudenciano. Finally, Emilio fretted about how he was going to control Prudenciano so he didn't lapse into his old ways.

The road slowly gained altitude and the mountains gradually enclosed them. They first traveled southwest for thirty-five miles before coming to a fork in the road. At this junction, they had to choose a route to return home. They could continue southwest for another sixteen miles to Lobato and then turn south on a rough, deserted trail for forty miles more to Monte Escobedo. The other choice was to take the fork south for forty miles to Jeréz, then thirty miles southwest to Huejucar, and eventually thirty more miles west to home. The latter route was longer, but the road was easier with more amenities along the way. Thus, Emilio chose it without much thought.

The gravel road to Huejucar was wide and adequately maintained. It provided one of the main pathways to the bustling city of

Guadalajara in the southern state of Jalisco. Residents of Zacatecas regularly made the long trek to the city to trade and barter their goods for products that were not readily available from the rural merchants. The road ran directly into Huejucar and narrowed between houses and stores that rose abruptly from the road's edge. This formed a bottleneck for traffic as carts, horses, and pedestrians mingled and pressed forward.

As the road wound through the town, the Navas could have easily missed the small sign that pointed up a side street to Monte Escobedo if they had not known the way. The cobblestone street led up a densely packed neighborhood and climbed a hill overlooking the town. As the road crested the hill, it suddenly left the town's boundaries and became a narrow dirt road that steadily climbed up the mountains behind Huejucar.

The road rose about one-thousand feet above Huejucar by following a series of switchbacks that twisted up the steep terrain. As the Navas progressed up the winding road, the vegetation changed from thick hardwoods and lush underbrush on the valley floor to sparse shrubs that hugged the dry mountain sides. They would often pass small *ranchos* that clung to tiny, level tracts of land within small draws and niches along the road. When the Navas reached the summit, they stopped to rest and gaze across the eastern and southern vistas. The air was so clear that they could see for a hundred miles. The travelers took a last look at Huejucar nestled in lush vegetation below and then continued riding west.

The next twenty miles were relatively flat. The road headed due west across wide open grass plains that typified the vegetation of the semiarid high chaparral. The land sloped slightly to the south with few trees to break the monotonous scenery; however, hand-built rock fences seemed to stretch to infinity along both sides of the road. The fences contained no mortar but maintained their structure through carefully placed stones wedged tightly together. Walls consisted of mostly weathered igneous rock that was light brown in color. Every so often, sections tumbled, which left gaps in the line. These four-foot high structures represented uncountable hours of labor, some forced and some driven by necessity. They formed crude property boundaries and helped contain wide-ranging livestock.

As the Navas pressed westward, a large plateau rose from the plains in front of them. The road led directly to the mountain and crossed several large dry riverbeds that flowed along the base. The small village of Gomez lay nestled along the last riverbank about one mile south of the road. Then the road rose steeply up the mountain. As they met the summit, they entered a thick hardwood forest and caught their first glimpses of Monte Escobedo in the distance.

Night fell as they entered the town. The streets were deserted, but each felt the secretive glances of residents peeking through parted curtains. They were too tired to care and rode on, shoulders hunched with fatigue, to the southern edge of town. In the blackness, Emilio's horse found the narrow trail that led them the final six miles home.

———— ◆••••◆ ————

Monte Escobedo was at the end of the Zacatecas road system. The town resided in a shallow bowl on top of a high plateau, which exceeded seven thousand feet in elevation. The surrounding landscape tilted slightly to the south and created the headwaters for the Río Cotolán and the Río Balaños, which flowed into larger rivers that finally made their way into the Pacific Ocean. The rugged mountains on the west prevented the continuation of roads.

The rugged topography also generated an anomaly in the normally dry climate that pervaded the high plains of Zacatecas. Warm, moisture-laden air rose out of the Pacific Ocean about 150 miles to the west. As the air moved east across Mexico, it pushed up against the Sierra Madre Occidental mountain range. The rising air began to cool and release its water as rain. The rain usually fell on the west side of the mountains and there was little left for the high, thirsty plains to the east. However, Monte Escobedo was located within a rain trap because the mountains continued to push the air over the village. The increased rainfall with the high elevation produced thick green forests of pines and hardwoods within the bowl that was unique to Zacatecas.

The soil on top of the plateau was very rocky and not suitable for tilling. Therefore, residents were primarily ranchers and utilized the higher rainfall to sustain their livestock throughout the year. The increased rainfall helped stabilize Monte Escobedo's economy during troubled times. The valley bowl was small, though, and once a person left the forest perimeter, the dry plains quickly depleted any excess water. The lack of suitable agricultural land and water restricted Monte Escobedo's population to a few thousand permanent residents.

It took Prudenciano eight months to remember why he had left his father's *rancho* in Monte Escobedo. He hated the endless tasks that required little skill and impressed few people. But most of all, he loathed his father telling him what to do every day.

Emilio Nava owned a small ranch about six miles south of town along the fringes of the life-giving forest. The *rancho* had a modest home that housed the Nava clan. Prudenciano, however, preferred to live in the small bunkhouse behind the home and next to the corrals. Both structures were well built from the native wood and rock of the area. The main house was a standard frame construction that Emilio had designed to enlarge by telescoping additions. Emilio and his sons had done this several times to accommodate their growing needs. The bunkhouse was a single-story rock-and-mortar home. It was built rugged to withstand the rough treatment the hired hands inflicted upon it.

Besides his four sons, Emilio employed five ranch hands. Abundio, the second-oldest son, lived on the ranch with his wife, Antonia, and their four children. Antonia taught at a one-room schoolhouse in town. Abundio's son José and his stepdaughter, Maria Paz Esparsa, also helped with the daily labors. José followed the men and assisted in any way he could. Maria Paz was now fourteen years old, fully schooled, and was fast becoming the chief cook. Abundio also had two young daughters under the age of five, who stayed with their mother when she was teaching.

Emilio was aware of the value of his property. A large demand and a small supply always generated high prices. He had many attractive offers from *hacendados*, but he steadfastly refused. He justified his stubbornness partly by principle—he hated the way the *hacendados* treated their sharecroppers—but mostly because he truly wanted his sons and their families to inherit and thrive on the land. This would ensure his immortality and the welfare of his future generations. Thus, he worked his sons hard and demanded not only that they learn the lessons of operating the ranch profitably, but that they learn to read and write. Emilio had succeeded with all his sons except one, Prudenciano.

Prudenciano had a lazy streak that manifested itself whenever he was not strictly supervised. Because of his superior strength and equestrian skills, he could outperform the best of men when working on the ranch. This was especially true when his father or some important town official was watching. He was absolutely unbearable when women stopped to observe his labor. His men suffered miserably from his exaggerated antics. However, when left on his own, he would begin to bully the hired men or his brothers into doing his share of the work. He justified this by claiming that he was supervising their efforts as he walked or rode casually through the fields.

Emilio was not oblivious to Prudenciano's slack habits. Not only had he witnessed him threatening his help, but he listened daily to his sons' and his workers' complaints. Emilio now confirmed his earlier doubts about taking back his oldest son. Prudenciano was quickly reverting to his old ways. In desperation, Emilio began to rebuke Prudenciano daily about his sloth and supervised him closely. The tension and emotional stress on the ranch were starting to rise.

Prudenciano began to reflect why he had decided to come back to Monte Escobedo. Every day, life began and ended the same way. Breakfast was served at dawn. Work started shortly afterward. Lunch and a short siesta were taken during the noon heat. Then work continued until darkness provided a respite from labor. After they made their way back to the *hacienda* and washed, dinner was served. Sleep was the only recreation available.

This routine burned the days, weeks, and months away. Prudenciano felt his mind stagnate and become oblivious to the world around him. As Prudenciano viewed it, each day brought endless tasks with little reward. Over the past eight months, he had slowly come to grips with Tereso's fatal accident. Thus, Prudenciano was now looking to go on with his life and pick up where he had left off. He felt the days beginning to drag.

The inevitable confrontation took place one afternoon. Thinking that he was alone with a small crew of ranch hands, Prudenciano decided not to partake in rebuilding the rock fences that bordered the distant pastures. Instead, he began to shout orders and direct the men with exaggerated bravado. The men bowed their necks at his unwanted supervision. Quickly, tempers flared and voices escalated. Prudenciano continued to bully the men until he had successfully provoked them to the verge of rioting.

Emilio and Abundio were riding along the fence line not far from Prudenciano and the crew. They heard the commotion and goaded their mounts into a gallop to investigate. Soon they came upon Prudenciano as he was about to brawl. "Prudenciano," shouted Emilio. His voice stopped Prudenciano in his tracks. "Why are you causing so much trouble? Are you so bored that you must antagonize my help?"

"What do you mean by that?" snapped Prudenciano. "They need strong leadership and I intend to give it to them!"

"No!" roared his father. "You should be setting an example by working hard instead of terrorizing them. I am warning you. Stop bossing these men around or leave!"

"*Sí*, leave," repeated Abundio. Prudenciano wanted to hit him badly. It took an extreme effort to refrain and turn to face his father.

"I know that if these *campesinos* are not dealt with harshly, they will eventually steal you blind."

"You know nothing!" blurted Emilio. By now, Emilio had reached the end of his rope. "This is it. You know my rule. If you live here, you must know how to read and write. Starting tomorrow, you will go to school every day until you are satisfactorily educated. Do I make myself clear?"

"You mean I have to listen to Abundio's wife every day and sit with children? That's a fate worse than death!" lamented Prudenciano.

"I mean it! Tomorrow!" With that, Emilio and Abundio spun their horses around and rode off to the corrals.

I should leave, thought Prudenciano. *But where would I go? Maybe school will not be so bad.* Subdued, he left the jeering men and sauntered toward the road. He wanted to walk through his problems. As he strolled along the wooden fence that lined the road, he faintly heard beautiful harmonica music ahead in the distance. When Prudenciano neared the gate that led to the ranch, he saw Abundio's stepdaughter playing the instrument. Maria Paz seemed not to notice him; however, her eyes betrayed her as she stole a quick glance at his face. Then she started to play with alacrity.

Intrigued, Prudenciano walked over to her. He leaned on the top rail next to her and listened to her music, an old folk tune of the area. Prudenciano enjoyed the familiar melody and watched her with more interest. She certainly had grown into a beautiful young lady. She was just entering the ripeness of womanhood.

Maria Paz was born on January 22, 1891 when her mother has thirty-five years old. Antonia was unmarried at the time and was ashamed of her predicament. She waited a full month before officially reporting Maria's birth to the Municipality of Monte Escobedo. For some reason, people preferred to call Maria by her middle name, Paz, which meant "peace" in Spanish. The name stuck and almost no one ever called her Maria.

Paz Esparsa and José Nava had the same mother, but they bore little resemblance to each other. Paz had inherited the Indian features of the Aztecs from both her father and mother, with the exception that she had fair skin. She was barely five feet tall with long, thick brown hair that flowed down past her shoulders. She possessed the rugged beauty of the native people who had thrived in these mountains for hundreds of years. José expressed the Spanish slim build and bone structure he inherited from the Nava side.

Prudenciano spoke softly, "You play very well. Why is it that I never heard you before?"

Paz looked up at him with those very dark brown eyes that contained infinite depth. At first she held his gaze, then quickly dropped her head. Paz felt her pulse race. How could she tell him that it had taken all her courage to sit here and play for him? "I always play here in the afternoon. You must be too busy to notice," she said meekly.

"*Sí.* It looks like I have missed a very nice concert every day." Then an awkward silence fell upon them. Neither one wanted to say goodbye, but the lack of spontaneous conversation made them uncomfortable. Finally, Paz broke the stalemate.

"I think I need to start dinner. I better go." She slid off the fence and slipped her harmonica into the fold of her dress. Prudenciano was suddenly struck by her smallness. He seemed to tower over her and that made him feel like he was her big, strong protector. It was a good feeling.

Paz felt his strength and virility engulf her. Her heart began to pound like never before. All of this was a strange and exciting feeling. "I really must go," Paz stammered. She quickly turned and ran to the ranch house.

Prudenciano watched her go and shouted, "I'll meet you here tomorrow." Paz flashed him a smile of acknowledgment before she ducked into the kitchen door. *Why did I say that?* thought Prudenciano. *I must be getting soft.* He laughed it off and shook his head. He turned and continued down the dusty road.

After breakfast on the following day, Prudenciano set out for the short walk into town to begin his schooling. The fall air was moist and fresh. The night rain had thoroughly soaked the land and the warmth of the morning sun brought out the vegetation's vibrant health. The country exuded a feeling of abundance and well-being. However, Prudenciano could not share the upbeat mood. He was dreading the small one-room schoolhouse that was located in the village.

Monte Escobedo was built within a small bowl. From the outskirts, all roads led downhill toward the village's square. The homes and shops were mostly flat-roofed, blocked-shaped buildings. Although white was the predominant color, some buildings were painted a warm gold or a dull red. The stores and homes were packed tightly together along narrow streets with sidewalks scarcely wide enough for one person. A pedestrian who met someone walking in the opposite direction would have to step into the street or duck into a shop to let the traffic pass.

In the center of the village was a beautiful town square. Each square side was a full block long. The north and south sides had a low cement wall with a tall, black iron fence. The fence consisted of iron pickets that terminated in sharp spears at the top. The west and east sides had tall block walls. Each side had a gate denoted by fancy stone arches that guarded the entrance. The outside walls had cement benches along the entire length of each side. Like spokes of a wheel, cobblestone paths led straight to the park's hub. In the middle of the hub stood a large gazebo made from white stone and capped with a red tile roof. Between the spokes were immaculate gardens with exotic flowers and trees.

The town kept the square locked to keep children from trampling the gardens, and vagrants from sleeping in the gazebo at night. On special occasions, the town opened the gates and the residents strolled inside to admire the gardens closely and enjoy a *mariachi* band playing in the gazebo. The shops that bordered the streets next to the square profited by people who stopped daily to gaze through the iron fence at the lovely scene and loitered on the park benches.

Monte Escobedo had built a new Catholic church in 1893. It replaced the older one that was only one block north of the town square. The town renovated the older church to house the municipal offices. They placed a large clock in the bell tower that rang softly every hour to proclaim the time.

The new church was much larger and was located on a hill about four blocks west of the town square. The combination of height and elevation gave the church a dominating presence that could be seen anywhere in the village. It was the norm for all towns in Zacatecas to have the church be the most predominant structure in the community.

The new church was also where Prudenciano's cousin José de Jesús Nava was the presiding priest. Father José had baptized Prudenciano's son, Brigido, in this church on October 8, 1895. He vehemently opposed Prudenciano's way of life and had chastised him severely for leaving his wife and son. After ten years of Prudenciano's absence, Father José finally annulled the marriage and granted Julia her freedom. For these reasons, Prudenciano stayed far away from the church steps.

The schoolhouse was located a few blocks from the town square. Much to Prudenciano's dismay, many people had seen him walk up the stairs and enter the school. He was sure they were all laughing at him. Prudenciano paused at the steps of the school before entering. In his youth, he had teased and harassed village children and his own brothers as they climbed these very steps. Now, life was playing a cruel joke on him. Four decades later, Prudenciano was finally going to school while his peers and brothers laughed at his predicament.

"Now, Prudenciano. You may sit there," said his sister-in-law, Antonia Nava, as she directed him to a small chair in the back of the classroom. The twelve children who shared the class giggled with delight to have such a big and old student with them. Prudenciano was totally humiliated. First, his sister-in-law was teaching him. Second, these kids were making fun of him. Last, none of them knew how smart he was.

He tried to sit in the chair assigned to him, but his knees came almost to his chest. Suddenly, the chair's legs gave out and Prudenciano crashed to the floor. The children shrieked with laughter. Antonia ran over to him. "Are you hurt?" she asked.

"No!" said Prudenciano gruffly as he tried to pick himself off the floor. This promised to be a long day. "I'll just sit here on the floor." He gathered what was left of his dignity and leaned against the back wall as he sat upon the hardwood floor.

Antonia walked back to the front of the class. "All right, children. Let's review our letters." She began writing on the blackboard. Although Prudenciano had a photographic memory, he had no interest in learning the alphabet. His mind began to drift off.

"Prudenciano!" Prudenciano snapped his head up. The startled look in his eyes told Antonia all she wanted to know. "You haven't heard a word that I said to you."

Prudenciano shook his head clear and said, "I'm sorry. What did you say?"

"I thought as much," sighed Antonia. "Let's try again ..."

The morning dragged on until the noon church bell signaled the end of the school day. Prudenciano picked himself off the floor and stretched the kinks out of his legs. "We will see you tomorrow," smiled Antonia. Her voice almost carried a question with it. Prudenciano sighed heavily and nodded his head. Without saying a word, he put on his hat and walked out of the school. He kept his head bowed so that his hat would cover his face as he came down the steps. As he reached the bottom, he turned quickly to stride down the street. In his haste, he bumped into a woman who was also on the sidewalk.

"*Perdón*," muttered Prudenciano awkwardly as he tipped his hat back to see if the woman was all right. Suddenly he recognized her and shock swept across his face. When the woman saw his face, her eyes grew wide with surprise and then narrowed with disgust.

Julia Villaviceneio wore a simple, dull red dress with white lace around the throat and sleeves. It was old with some of the edges frayed, but it was clean and well mended. She wore sandals and a white scarf over her head. Her face was still handsome, but was beginning to show lines from hard work and personal hardship. "Prudenciano," she began in a calm voice, "I heard that you were back. How long are you going to stay this time?"

He was totally unprepared to meet his ex-wife. He fumbled with a few words and finally blurted, "For a little while. I am going to see what develops. How have you been?"

Julia's expression hardened and she responded through clenched teeth, "You do not care about my welfare. You only care for yourself. Do you even care that our son is an eighteen-year-old man now? Do you even know where he is or what he is doing?" Prudenciano remained speechless. Julia shook her head, "I am just wasting my time." She replaced her scarf on her head and, without another word, continued walking down the sidewalk and out of his life forever.

Prudenciano continued to stare after her and watched her turn the corner and disappear. She didn't look back once. The meeting had unnerved him. In some ways, he regretted leaving her and his son, but he found that life too restricting. Seeing her again only intensified his feeling that he had to leave this town. He turned and started walking toward home.

Prudenciano strolled along the country road deep in thought. Gradually he became aware of the faint harmonica music in the distance. As he drew nearer to the ranch, he saw Paz sitting on the fence where she had been the day before. He watched her quickly glance at him and begin to play louder and with more feeling. Paz's actions broke his melancholy and he chuckled at her response and stopped to listen.

"Ah, Paz. Imagine seeing you here today." She flushed and avoided his gaze. She was truly beautiful. Her long, dark brown hair was full of golden highlights. Although small, her body was strong and athletic. Prudenciano felt his interest pique. Watching her play stirred a deep wanting within him.

Paz sensed that his attention was more than appreciation of her music. She stopped playing and looked up at him with her lovely dark eyes and asked, "How was school with Mother today?" Prudenciano's mood instantly darkened. Paz saw the shadow pass before his eyes and quickly looked down. "I'm sorry for asking," she said quietly.

Mollified, Prudenciano replied, "Your mother is a good woman. I just don't belong there. Now, how about another tune?" Paz smiled back and nodded in agreement. She started to place the instrument back to her mouth when a loud, booming voice startled them.

"What are you doing here?" roared Abundio. He marched up to them with his fists clenched and his teeth clamped tight. "Paz, you should be in the kitchen and, Prudenciano, you should be in the fields!"

"You sound like a little rooster crowing his head off," answered Prudenciano calmly. "Leave us alone."

"You leave her alone!" shouted Abundio with a finger pointed at him. "She's too young for you."

"I'm getting tired of people telling me what to do," growled Prudenciano. He felt his temper brewing. "Now get out of here before I crush your head!"

Abundio flushed with rage. He grabbed Paz by the arm and yanked her toward the house. Paz winced in pain, but she did not make a sound. The sight of Abundio hurting her evoked a protective response within Prudenciano. He took a step toward Abundio with his fist drawn back. Abundio saw his brother coming for him and released his grip from Paz's arm. "Hit me and Father will toss you off this land!" charged Abundio.

Prudenciano halted and quivered with anger. As much as he thought about it, he still was not ready to leave home. Hitting Abundio would feel exquisite, but he knew he would lose too much at this time. He spun away from Abundio and briskly strode back to town. "I need a drink," he said to himself. He ignored his father's fields and men along the way to the *cantina*. His mind focused only on escaping behind a bottle.

"I'm telling you," said the half-drunk man at the bar, "You can make a lot of money up north. *Sí.* I mean it." He leaned forward to Prudenciano to stress his point. "Lots of work up north. Torreón and Chihuahua are crying for good men. You can make good money."

Prudenciano looked skeptically at the inebriated fellow. He had heard these stories before and they always came from drunks like this one. Prudenciano scanned the room to see if anyone was listening to their conversation. The *cantina* was almost deserted at this time of day. Anyone with any fortitude was busy earning a living, not drinking and dreaming about get-rich-quick schemes. Only the bartender was paying any attention to them. Judging by the scowl on his face, Prudenciano knew that he was objecting to the drinks that he was charging to his father's account. *What the hell!* thought Prudenciano. He turned back to his drinking partner and asked, "How do you know about these jobs?"

"Because I was there!" exclaimed the man. "I hurt my back so I couldn't work anymore."

Right, thought Prudenciano sarcastically, but he didn't want to discourage the man. He enjoyed discussing buried treasures and ways of making fast money. "Why did you come south?"

"I made lots of money and I wanted to rest," the man replied. "Now the money is gone and I still can't work." Prudenciano grunted his understanding and refilled the man's tequila glass.

"*Gracias.* You are right, however," continued the man, "I should have gone north. There is so much opportunity up there."

"You mean in Chihuahua?" asked Prudenciano.

"No! I mean *los Estados Unidos de América!*" shouted the man. "I hear that if you work hard there that in three years you can own a house. There you can make five times the wage that you can earn in Torreón."

The thought of going to the United States of America hit Prudenciano like a thunderbolt. "*Estados Unidos,*" he repeated. He suddenly visualized himself rich and important there. *Of course*, dreamed Prudenciano. *That's where a man can make his fortune!*

"*Tío!* Are you going to *América?*"

Prudenciano snapped out of his daydream and turned on his stool. José was standing behind him and was eavesdropping on his conversation. The boy must have slipped in while he was fantasizing about becoming rich. "José, what are you doing here? You are too young to be in a *cantina* and you should be working."

The boy laughed at Prudenciano's questioning. "What am I doing here? I think we both should be working, huh?" José's eyes sparkled with mischief. "Don't worry, *Tío*. I'm not here to drink. I am placing a bet on tomorrow's cockfight. I'm going to win a lot of money!"

Prudenciano couldn't help admiring the boy. He reminded him so much of himself. Prudenciano knew that he would have done the same thing at José's age. He smiled back at the boy and nodded his head toward his drinking partner. "He thinks a man should go north to become rich. Perhaps, even go to *los Estados Unidos*."

José became intensely interested as he listened to the man sitting next to his uncle ramble on about the opportunity in America. According to this man, Prudenciano shouldn't even waste his time in Mexico. He should just make his way to the border and cross into America by way of El Paso. The trek was long, but the crossing was cheap and U. S. immigration officials asked few questions. As soon as a man entered El Paso, there were many labor agents who helped good men like Prudenciano get work.

When the man's recital finally trailed off into incoherent phrases, José momentarily fell into deep thought. Then he looked up to Prudenciano and declared, "Some day, I will live in *los Estados Unidos*." Prudenciano studied his face for a few moments and saw the firm conviction in his jaw. Suddenly, a vision flashed through Prudenciano's mind—José dressed in a woven suit with a derby hat in his hand waving from a train station platform. The train was pulling away and the surrounding country was strangely different from Zacatecas. There were huge trees with large golden leaves in the background and large railcars heaped with what looked like turnips.

"*Sí*. I believe you," answered Prudenciano. Then he wondered where they would meet each other in *los Estados Unidos*. *What destiny awaits us?*

School was an excruciating experience this day as it had been for the last three days. *How much longer can I suffer this treatment?* thought Prudenciano. His back hurt from trying to write on the low tables. His bottom smarted from sitting cross-legged on the floor. The children had lost their reserve and now openly laughed and teased him when he fumbled with his letters.

The ranch work in the afternoons was equally dissatisfying. His father monitored his every move. If he stopped and offered advice to one of the ranch hands, his father immediately rebuked him and ordered him to back to work. There was nothing that Prudenciano hated worse than being told what to do.

The event that finally pushed Prudenciano to his limit began when he slipped away to see Paz at their usual meeting place along the fence. As Prudenciano was enjoying her company, Abundio crept up behind them. He was seething at the fact that Prudenciano had defied his orders not to see his stepdaughter again.

"Enough!" raged Abundio as he surprised them. Abundio seized Paz by the collar and yanked her off the top of the rock fence. Her dress ripped from behind as Abundio dragged her to the ground. Prudenciano exploded into his brother. With one hand, he lifted Abundio off his feet by the front of his shirt. With his other hand, he pried Abundio's grip from Paz's torn clothing. When Abundio released Paz, Prudenciano drew back his fist to deliver a devastating blow.

Abundio quickly croaked, "Hit me and Father will throw you out!" Prudenciano hovered in indecision. Striking him would vent his anger and avenge Paz, but was it worth it? Prudenciano slowly lowered his fist, but kept Abundio suspended. Then with both hands, he drew Abundio close to his face and snarled, "If you ever touch her again, I'll kill you!" Prudenciano dropped him in a heap on the ground.

Paz picked herself up and tried to cover the torn dress the best she could. Her eyes filled with tears of hurt and embarrassment. She turned and started to run into the house. "Wait!" called Prudenciano. He stooped down and picked up the harmonica from the dirt. He patted it against his leg to clean it and handed it back to Paz. She held it to the torn fabric and fled. The sight of her distress squeezed his heart. He knew now that he had to leave the ranch soon. Prudenciano looked down in disgust at his brother, then left him where he lay.

The evening meal was a tense affair. The entire family knew what had happened that afternoon and they were split on who was right. Paz quickly served the meal on the table and kept her gaze lowered. Everyone ate in silence.

Abundio finally broke the quiet with a clumsy attempt at casual dialog. "Father, I was thinking…"

"You think?" retorted Prudenciano. "Now there's a new concept."

"¡Silencio!" commanded Emilio. The dam of verbal restraint was broken. "Ever since you arrived home, you have disrupted this ranch and it's going to stop now! I want you to do as you are told and stop trying to be the boss." Abundio smirked from across the table. The anger building within Prudenciano was almost unbearable.

"Perhaps I should leave, Father. I can make a lot of money up north," declared Prudenciano.

"And you'll be rich!" exclaimed Emilio sarcastically. "You are always chasing buried treasures. Grow up!"

"*Sí*. Grow up!" mocked Abundio. Prudenciano snapped. He grabbed the dining table and pushed off the floor with both legs. The table, food and all, vaulted up and overturned onto Abundio. With powerful athletic prowess, Prudenciano leaped over the table and swung with all his might. The blow caught Abundio totally unprepared across the skull. Abundio's head whipped to the side and he slumped to the floor unconscious. It gave Prudenciano an instant rush of satisfaction.

The surrounding family members were on their feet with their mouths agape in horror. "Enough!" cried Emilio. "Get off my land and never come back!" The look on his father's face was one of genuine outrage. Prudenciano had crossed the bridge of no return. Without an ounce of regret, he stepped over his brother's prostrated body and strode out of the room. He never looked back when he turned the handle and slammed the door behind him.

Paz had witnessed the entire explosive conflict from the kitchen doorway. She placed her hands over her face as she gasped at the savagery Prudenciano unleashed. Abundio lay on the floor totally incapacitated. Her step-grandfather had ordered Prudenciano to leave and he had just marched out of the house and out of her life forever. She could not stand here and watch her world crumble around her.

Paz ripped off her apron and quickly slipped out the back kitchen door. She grabbed her skirt with her left hand and ran as fast as she could to the front of the house. Prudenciano was not there. "*Where could he be?*" she quailed to herself. She felt her anxiety rise. Any minute now, the men would be coming out of the house to check on the whereabouts of Prudenciano.

Just then, she heard a horse nicker from the corral. Paz whirled toward the sound and ran. The night was very dark now. The moon had not risen and the stars blazed brightly in the heavens. She almost ran into Prudenciano as he saddled his horse. "Don't go!" pleaded Paz.

"I have no choice," he replied without turning around.

Paz felt time was quickly running out. She knew that she was at a major crossroad of her young life. She had always done what others commanded, but now she was going to make her first independent decision. She had very little here on the ranch. Her mother was her only true family. The others had tolerated her adoption into the Nava clan, but there was no real love binding her to this place. Thus, she looked to the man in front of her as an escape from this mediocrity.

"Do you love me?" Paz asked in a clear, quiet voice. The question stopped Prudenciano in his tracks. He turned slowly away from his saddling to face her. He knew that she stirred some deep unexplained emotion within him, but he had no idea if it was love. At forty-nine years old, Prudenciano had yet to tell a woman that he loved her, even Julia.

He looked down at her. She bent her head back to see his face. Avoiding the question, he asked, "Do you want to come with me?"

Paz appeared hurt by his reluctance to answer her direct question, so she tried another tactic. "I will go with you if you promise to marry me at the first church we come to." Prudenciano's mind began to race. How could he go to *los Estados Unidos* with such a young woman? Although her company at times would be enjoyable, she would cramp his style.

Abruptly, they heard Abundio's unsteady voice yell out of the darkness. "Find him! I want him now!" The sound of rushing feet was everywhere. They would find Paz and him very soon. The sound of Abundio's irritating voice rekindled Prudenciano's anger. Suddenly, a thought flashed into his mind. If he ran off with Paz, Abundio would be twisted with rage and there would be little that he could do about it. It would gnaw at his guts for a long time. What's more, his father would be without a cook. Perfect!

Prudenciano smiled and looked down at Paz. She was still waiting for a response. "All right. I agree to marry you. I will be back tonight in front of the fence to take you." Paz sucked in her breath. She had done it. Now, she had to follow through with her plan. "Remember to pack light," Prudenciano added. Paz nodded her head, turned, and disappeared into the night.

Prudenciano quickly finished strapping his saddle to his horse. With the addition of Paz, he would need another horse. A young mare stood nearby. *She will do fine*, thought Prudenciano. As he reached up to grab a light bridle for the second horse, he heard a man running and breathing hard come up from behind. "He's here!" cried the man. In one fluid motion, Prudenciano flicked the bridle out by one rein. The free rein wrapped around the man's neck and Prudenciano yanked him forward. As the man stumbled to regain his balance, Prudenciano smacked him in the face with his fist. The man fell hard.

Prudenciano pulled the rein from the fallen man and put the bridle over the mare. Leading the mare, Prudenciano ran back to his horse and leaped upon the saddle. He could hear several men running to the corral entrance.

"*¡Vámanos!*" shouted Prudenciano to the horses. His horse bolted forward toward the entrance. He led the mare with his left hand. As they neared the passage, two men appeared out of the darkness. One man was running in front of the other. Prudenciano goaded his horse into a full gallop, leaned to the right, and stretched out his arm as if he was going to tail a bull. His right hand caught the front man by the collar. The forward momentum of the horse ripped the man off his feet and sent him flying backward into the man behind him. Both of them were knocked senseless by the impact. Prudenciano dropped the man and continued riding out of the corral.

He turned sharply and began galloping toward the road. It was only a few hundred feet away, but Prudenciano could tell that several men were angling to block his path and one of them had a gun. "I want him stopped! Shoot if you have to!" screamed Abundio.

Prudenciano goaded his horse for maximum speed to reach the gate, but the men were already beginning to cut him off. He quickly veered into their angle of attack and headed directly toward the fence. The maneuver caught the men in complete surprise. The man with the rifle came down on one knee, aimed, and fired at Prudenciano. The gun barked a sharp report as the muzzle flash lit up the night. Prudenciano flattened himself against his horse just as the bullet whizzed past his head. The fence loomed out of the darkness. With the smooth motion of an expert horseman, Prudenciano nudged his horse forward and jumped the rock fence. The mare followed easily behind and the three of them disappeared silently into the night.

Paz heard the fighting outside and narrowly escaped detection when she fled back to the house. She almost ran into two men who were racing toward the corral. Only by jinxing off the path did she slip past them. The gunshot terrified her. *Had Prudenciano been shot? Did they catch him?* These thoughts paralyzed her with fear.

The sounds of the approaching men and a very upset Abundio broke her anxiety. "How could you have let him go? Idiots!" Abundio spat venomously. Paz hid herself behind the kitchen door so she could hear the conversation.

"Abundio!" cried Emilio. "This is nothing to kill a man over. Let him go. He will never bother us again."

"But he stole your horse! I say we track him down and hang him for being a thief!" replied Abundio.

"No! Let him have it. It's a small price to pay," said Emilio. Abundio reluctantly capitulated and shuffled toward his room, mumbling all the way. He massaged his aching head as he walked.

He is alive! Paz almost said aloud. She breathed a great sigh of relief and quietly crept into her room. She started packing a few cherished items that she would need for her journey. Paz had very few possessions. When she was a little girl, she had followed her mother from a small *rancho* ten miles to the northeast of town to live with Abundio. They had carried few belongings with them and after years of toiling on the ranch, she still had little to show for it. Leaving this place would be easy. She would miss her mother and José, but she would live on with Prudenciano.

Suddenly, she stopped and thought about what life would be like with him. He was certainly tall and handsome, but lacked social graces. Perhaps she could help nourish that side of him, but did he love her? Paz contemplated this for a few moments. He did protect her from Abundio, but did he have another motive for doing so? Prudenciano was kind to her. Was he just being nice? The doubts eroded her newly found self-confidence.

"I have nothing here," whispered Paz. "So, I am going." With that declaration, she shoved the rest of her belongings into a small bag. Finally, she removed her harmonica, which was her most cherished possession, from under her pillow and placed it into the bag. Now, she must wait until the family slept before she could sneak away and join Prudenciano.

The hours dragged by slowly. Gradually, the sounds and stirs within the house died. Paz slowly lifted herself off her bed and crept toward her bedroom door. She carefully cracked it open and peered into the hallway. The way was clear. Moonlight shone through the windows and cast long dark shadows along the walls. Paz grabbed her bag and quietly tiptoed into the kitchen. There she hefted some corn tortillas from the counter and wrapped them in a cloth. She placed them carefully in her bag.

The back door was bolted. It required Paz to set the bag down and use both hands to move it. The bolt made a metallic "clink" when it slid out of the latch. She froze and waited for someone to come running to investigate the noise. After several seconds, she exhaled and pulled the door open, picked up her bag, and stepped outside. Then she carefully closed the door behind her.

The moon had risen high in the night sky and fully illuminated the entire countryside. Paz had little trouble negotiating the path to the road. When she reached the fence, she hunkered down in the weeds to wait for Prudenciano. As she made herself comfortable, Paz began to feel the weariness of the long day. *Why isn't he here yet?*

Paz came awake with a start. The moon had moved across the sky which indicated several hours had past. *How long have I slept?*

thought Paz. *Oh, where is Prudenciano?* Her anxiety grew by the minute. *He's not coming, is he?*

Suddenly, she heard a low whisper next to her say, "Good evening, Paz. Waiting for someone?" This scared her so badly that she jumped up and almost hit her head against the rock wall.

"Prudenciano! You scared me!" Paz said breathlessly. She was a bit angry, but very relieved. "What took you so long? I thought you would never come."

"I had to wait until the men in the bunkhouse were asleep," Prudenciano chuckled. He enjoyed giving her a start. "Being shot at once in one night is more than enough for me. Now, let's get going." He picked up her bag, took her hand, and led her to where he had stashed the horses. They were well hidden about a half mile down the road in a shallow ravine. He lifted Paz up onto the mare.

"I'm sorry," said Prudenciano. "I didn't have time to get a saddle for you. I'll carry your bag and you just hold on the best you can." Paz nodded that she understood, leaned forward, adjusted her large hat, and grabbed handfuls of the mare's mane.

Prudenciano mounted his horse and grabbed the reins of the mare. He pushed back his sombrero and looked up into the beautiful clear night sky. The stars shone brightly against the dark heavens. He searched until he found the Big Dipper constellation. At this time of year, fall of 1905, the star formation was high above the northern horizon. The front two stars of the Dipper pointed to the North Star. Satisfied with his bearings, Prudenciano began leading them north on the rugged road to Lobato.

"Where are we going?" asked Paz.

"North," answered Prudenciano. He looked back to the North Star. *North to rich jobs. North to los Estados Unidos de América. North away from Monte Escobedo forever.*

Chapter 5
North

"She's gone!" bellowed Abundio. He held his head as he staggered down the hall. On the side of his skull was a lump the size of an egg. There was no doubt that he suffered from the effects of a concussion.

Antonia cried on Paz's bed. She had discovered the abandoned bedroom earlier that morning. After she frantically searched the house and the surrounding yard, she instinctively knew what had happened and went back into the house to tell Abundio. "She is so young," sobbed Antonia. "She can't marry him. He is too old for her. This is terrible!" Her lamentations infuriated Abundio further. He began ranting and raving and calling out for his father.

Emilio and several ranch hands came running to Abundio. "What is it?" Emilio asked.

"Prudenciano took Paz. That's why he stole the mare last night. It looks like she packed some things before she left. He must have come back for her." Emilio first looked stunned, then began to get angry. He knew he should have anticipated this. He had seen the eyes that Prudenciano and Paz made at each other.

"When do his insults to this family stop?" said Emilio half to himself. "Now he has stolen your daughter. We must stop him before he tries to marry her." He turned to three of his men, "Saddle the horses. We must leave quickly."

The men raced out the door and began preparing the horses. In their haste, they forgot to fill the water bags. One of the men ran to the Navas and told them that all was ready. Abundio and his father jogged back fully dressed and carrying rifles. Within seconds, the five men rode out onto the road to Huejucar.

Emilio now faced the problem of determining where they went. The closest town with a church was Huejucar, which was thirty-five miles to the east. The road was easy and would be the perfect place to elope to. If they struck out last night, they would be there by now.

Emilio and his men would have to hurry if they were going to prevent a wedding. Emilio faced his men, "Everyone! I think they went to Huejucar. We must hurry. *¡Vámanos!*"

They were about to spur their horses into a gallop toward Huejucar when one of the men spotted trampled vegetation in a small ravine next to the road. "*Señor* Nava! Wait, *por favor!*" pleaded the man. He quickly dismounted and ran down the gully. The ground was stomped in a small circle. It was obvious that someone had tethered two horses here during the night. At closer inspection, he found two sets of human footprints clearly depressed into the soft earth. One set was large and had left a deep imprint from a big man. The other set was small and delicate, like that of a girl. "It is them!" declared the man. Emilio, Abundio, and the rest of the men brought the horses over.

The man quickly explained his observations and Emilio agreed with his assessment. "The wily fox!" mused Emilio. "Of course, he would have assumed that we'd think that he'd go to Huejucar. So he decided to take the rough trail to Lobato."

"Lobato!" muttered Abundio. "That's almost forty miles!"

"Do you want your daughter back?" replied Emilio in disgust. Sometimes Abundio's lack of drive grated on his nerves. He turned to his man who was still studying the tracks. "How much of a head start do they have?"

The man touched the edge of the track. The sharp dirt edge fell into the print. The sign was very fresh. "They left here about five hours ago," the man said with confidence.

"Then we must ride hard. Now!" said Emilio as he immediately took the lead and struck out at fast pace. The rest of the men galloped after him. Abundio grimaced and sucked in his breath. The rhythmic gait of his horse sent shivers of pain from his aching head to the rest of his body. This was going to be a long ride. He squinted to the east and saw the bright sun rising into the cloudless sky. Not only was the ride going to be long, but it was also going to be very hot.

———

Prudenciano set a steady and sustainable pace north. He resisted the urge to stop for a rest. When the sun rose to the noon position, Prudenciano estimated they had been traveling for nearly ten hours. Paz had fallen asleep on the mare's neck, but she still maintained a death grip on the mane. The sun beat them unmercifully. Sage and cactus dotted the surrounding landscape. There were no trees to provide shade. The heat produced shimmers of light on the horizon as the convection currents rose from the earth.

Prudenciano's plan was to strike the main road at the small town of Lobato. Lobato shared a priest with the larger town of Valparaiso and Prudenciano knew that chances were slim that he would be in Lobato today. He planned to stop only long enough to water the horses and then follow the road west for eight miles to Valparaiso.

Prudenciano figured they had been averaging a little better than four miles per hour. He had ridden this land for forty years and memorized every contour. He knew they were very close to Lobato and not a minute too soon. The horses were tiring fast from thirst. "Where is that town?" Prudenciano said to himself. "We should be seeing it soon." Then, as they crested a hill, Lobato abruptly loomed in front of them.

Satisfied, Prudenciano turned to wake Paz. As he reached over to her, something caught his eye. At first, he thought it was just a heat mirage on the southern horizon, but as he continued to stare at it, distinct figures began to emerge. He suddenly realized that the images were men on horseback riding hard toward them.

Emilio set a grueling pace north. Hour after hour, they sped forward. Abundio's head ached in the scorching sun until it made him sick. Finally, Abundio pleaded, "Let's stop for a short rest, Father."

Emilio looked back at him briefly and realized that he was in great pain. He reluctantly reined in his horse and ordered a ten-minute rest. "Everyone grab a drink of water and give some to the horses." The hired hands looked helplessly at each other and then back to their employer.

"I'm sorry," said one man timidly. "We forgot to bring water."

"Numbskulls!" cursed Emilio. He knew that they were in a predicament. They were more than halfway to Lobato. *Do we continue in hopes of finding water or turn back and let Prudenciano and Paz go?* He looked at the men and horses. They would not last long in this heat without water. He walked away from them and stared out across the wide, stark valley.

The trail that led to Lobato was rugged and intermittent. It led north out of the mountain bowl that surrounded Monte Escobedo. As one traveled this lonely path, the mountains opened into a wide valley that ran east to west. The country consisted of the high, arid plains with sparse vegetation and few creatures struggling to survive.

Amidst this environment, Emilio stood facing north and looking at the two sets of horse tracks that disappeared into the shimmering horizon. He shook his head at the daunting task in front of him and called his tracker. "How far ahead are they?"

Again, the man brushed his fingertips along a hoof print. The tracks possessed a sharper edge than earlier this morning. "I think they are about two hours in front of us," he replied.

Emilio took a deep breath. The air was dry, hot, and dusty. It seemed to suck the last bit of moisture out of his mouth. "We can make it to Lobato," Emilio said with conviction. "Let's try to catch them." With his mind made up, Emilio ordered everyone into their saddles and resumed pushing north.

They rode on in silence for an hour. Each man and animal was suffering from thirst and heat. As the sun punished them, the men began to see images and occasionally muttered incoherent phrases. No one paid anyone much heed as each described his visions. When finally one of the men exclaimed, "There they are!" The rest of them were dubious, but stopped their horses for a better look.

"I don't see anything," said Abundio as he squinted into the quivering heat waves. His head was filled with a dull aching. He would need to rest soon.

"I could have sworn that I saw two figures on top of that hill," said the man as he pointed toward a distant hill. No one else spoke to his defense and now after a thorough search there clearly was nothing on the ridge

"Let's continue," Emilio said softly. Under his breath he muttered, "The heat is getting to us."

"Paz! Wake up!" shouted Prudenciano. He bolted the horses off the hill and down into a gully. *Have they seen us?* wondered Prudenciano. He struggled hard to think of what to do next, but his mind was not sharp after riding all night and through the heat of the day. He was amazed that Abundio and his father had found them so quickly.

"What is the matter?" asked Paz groggily as she tried to shake the sleepy confusion from her head.

"Your father and grandfather are chasing us," replied Prudenciano evenly.

"How do you know this?" Paz now had fear in her voice. She obviously had not expect anyone to come after them. Up to this point, she had thought Prudenciano cruel for not stopping and resting during their long trek. Now, she saw the wisdom of his actions.

Prudenciano replied, "Who else would ride fast across the plains at this time of day?" Paz knew he was right. She became fully alert.

"What are we going to do?" asked Paz.

"I don't know!" he answered gruffly. He hated to be pestered with questions while he struggled with a problem. A thought flashed through his mind to abandon her. He could make a quick break and they would most likely give up chasing him once they had retrieved Paz. However, one long look at her and he dismissed the idea. He would not extract his revenge on his family if he gave up now.

"So, what's next?" Prudenciano thought out loud. "They probably found our tracks where we left the road in Monte Escobedo. If we could just trick them in following the horses ..." His voice trailed off as his mind began to race. He looked to the west and scanned the road that stretched between Lobato and Valparaiso. The road was entirely open with no cover. If they decided to make a run for it, their pursuers would immediately see them and run them down. However, the tiny town of Lobato was only a few hundred feet in front of them. They would have to try to lose them among the buildings.

"Come," ordered Prudenciano. He galloped into town with Paz following behind. As she caught up with him, she saw Prudenciano hailing two young men sitting in the shade under an awning. Prudenciano put on a broad smile and addressed them confidently.

"*Buenos días, Señores*," began Prudenciano. The men smiled back. No matter where you were in Zacatecas, people were poor but always friendly.

"*Buenos días, Señor y Señorita*," replied one man. "Where are you and your daughter traveling to today?"

Prudenciano bristled at his question, but quickly recovered. "This is not my daughter, but the woman I will marry." Although there was a large age difference, this was not unusual in Mexico. Sometimes when a man had finally sowed all his wild oats and desired to settle down, he chose a much younger woman to bear him many children and take care of him in his older age. Both young men looked appreciatively at Paz and were impressed with Prudenciano's choice. Prudenciano quickly continued, "However, her father does not have a favorable opinion of me. In fact, if you look to the south, you can see him and his men coming for us." The men squinted toward the direction that Prudenciano was pointing. Sure enough, five distant figures could be seen riding this way.

The men looked back to Prudenciano quizzically. "Do you want us to help you? We have no weapons or horses," said one man.

"Ah, but see. This is how we can benefit each other," Prudenciano responded reassuringly. Time was running out. He needed to convince them of his plan quickly. The men leaned forward in anticipation of the offer. Excitement for young men was so hard to come by these days. "I'll give you these two fine horses. In exchange, I want you two to wear our hats and ride east as fast as you can and hide, *comprende?*"

"You can't do this!" cried Paz. "What will we do without the horses?"

"Enough!" barked Prudenciano. He turned back to the men. "How about it? Horses for a wild ride and, oh yes, two bags of water."

The youths looked at each other, nodded their agreement, and then looked back to Prudenciano with wide smiles. "*Sí*. We will do it."

"*Bueno*. Get off your horse, Paz. We have no time to waste," ordered Prudenciano as he jumped off his horse and removed his saddle bag.

Paz jutted out her chin in solid defiance. "I'm not giving them my horse."

Prudenciano had no time to argue. He roughly snatched her from the horse. With one hand, he held her and with the other, he ripped her hat off her head. "Here!" he said as he thrust the hats to the men. "Wear these. Now, give us some water." One man quickly ran into the house and within a minute, came out with two leather bags with water still streaming down the sides. He had obviously dunked both bags into a bucket to fill them quickly. Each bag had a corked spout and a leather shoulder strap.

"*Bueno*. Quickly give your horses a short drink and ride!" The men led the horses to the well in the center of town and drew several buckets of fresh water into the adjacent watering trough. The horses plunged their snouts into the trough and eagerly slurped up the water while barely stopping to breathe. Prudenciano glanced to the south for his pursuers. They were only a mile away. *They have been riding too hard and long,* he thought. *Their horses are nearly spent, so they will have to rest here for a while. Paz and I will have to hide while they do.* Prudenciano turned to the men. "You'll have to ride now, but before you do, we will need a hiding place."

The young man pointed to a barn on the eastern edge of town. "That barn is my uncle's. Nobody will bother you there." The young men dragged the horses away from the trough. The horses strained to return to the water, but a full horse cannot run and it was time to flee. The men leaped on top of the horses, adjusted the large floppy hats, and began to gallop to the east.

Prudenciano still had ahold of Paz. "Now we must hide," he told her. He led her to the barn. It was an old frame building with the typical ten-foot-high double doors and a hayloft above. Prudenciano opened one of the doors and let them in. He quickly shut it and threw the bolt from inside. The barn was deserted and the ground floor was covered with the offal of cows, chickens, and sheep. Prudenciano found a ladder that provided access to the hayloft. He climbed up with the water bags in one hand and the saddle bags draped over his shoulder. When he reached the top, he opened the trap door and motioned for Paz to follow him. The hay loft was clean and had soft stacks of straw mounded along the walls. It had a small door on the front of the barn to load straw and hay by a pulley mounted on a beam. Prudenciano carefully cracked the door open and peered out. The height gave him an excellent vantage point. He could see over the tops of most of the buildings and scanned the southern plains. He saw the Nava clan entering Lobato.

"There they are!" cried Abundio. The men looked where he was pointing. In the distance were two figures riding fast along the road to the east. The familiar sombreros flopped in the wind as the riders hunched over to help their horses gallop at maximum speed. Emilio's men wanted to give chase, but he knew that their horses were nearly spent. They were already lathered up from the hard push across the trail. The horses would need a short rest and water before they could pursue Prudenciano and Paz.

At least we prevented a marriage in Lobato, thought Emilio. *They will have to go all the way to Fresnillo now and we will catch them before then.* Emilio ordered the men to rein in their horses and water them in Lobato. As they entered the town, they spied the last signs of the riders disappearing into the eastern shimmering haze.

Prudenciano observed the men discussing their options. They had definitely seen the two young men ride out of town. Most of the Nava party wanted to pursue them, but Prudenciano saw Emilio disagree and direct them to the water well. Prudenciano felt a trickle of respect for his father. He was a wise man and knew the limits of his resources. To follow the riders with spent horses in this blazing heat would be folly. Prudenciano had guessed right that they would first rest and water the horses, then continue the pursuit. Paz and he would have to lie low until they left. Then, under the cover of darkness, they would make their way west to Valparaiso.

Prudenciano sighed and slowly closed the door. He turned to Paz and said, "I guess we'll have to stay here until tonight. Your father and grandfather are in the town square watering their horses. They'll probably rest for a couple of hours before chasing our horses." Prudenciano got up and walked over to a straw pile, fluffed up a nest, and fell backward into it. He uncorked a water bag and took a long swig. As he wiped his mouth with his shirt sleeve, he handed the bag to Paz. She quietly accepted the bag and also took a drink. The water tasted cool and sweet. Until now, she had not realized how thirsty she was because of the excitement of the last hours. She drank deeply.

As she corked the bag, she assessed her feelings. Prudenciano's rough handling of her during this last hour and the loss of her horse grated deeply within her soul. However, in retrospect, he'd really had little choice. There was no time to explain his plan and he had acted decisively. Paz admired that trait in a man, but there was something in the way he had wrenched her off the horse that disturbed her. Could she really trust him? She shook her head and put the thought away. She decided she would have to watch him closely.

Paz picked up her bag and took out the corn tortillas. They were a little crumbled, but edible. She offered one to Prudenciano. He took it from her and smiled his thanks back. After they had eaten, Prudenciano lay back and folded his hands behind his head. He spoke softly to her, "We will leave for Valparaiso when it gets dark. So, in the meantime, might as well enjoy ourselves, eh?"

Paz shot him a venomous stare and hissed, "Don't you dare touch me, Prudenciano Nava! You will not lay a hand on me until we are married!" She had expected this, but his comment still startled her.

"All right," Prudenciano chuckled as he threw his hands into the air in a show of resignation. "Just testing the waters." He dropped his hands on his chest and closed his eyes. Prudenciano was still smiling as he said, "I suggest you calm down and get some sleep. It's going to be a long walk tonight." Within minutes, Prudenciano was sleeping hard and snoring lightly.

——————

Paz woke with a start. Prudenciano's hand was placed over her mouth and his body was pinning her to the floor. In the first wild instant, Paz thought he was going to test the waters he had spoken of earlier, but when she looked up he had his finger to his lips signaling to stay quiet. Then slowly he removed his hand from her mouth and quietly moved off her. Paz froze and looked around her. The sun was just setting and burnt orange rays pierced through the knotholes and gaps in the wall. She could faintly hear men's voices outside.

Prudenciano crawled over to the cargo door and peeked through a crack around the hinges. His father and brother were with the rest of the men in front of the barn. Prudenciano fought down his irrational thoughts generated from his panic. Had they found them? How could they have known? No, it must be something else. Then it dawned on him. They required feed for their horses. He had not foreseen that need and had unknowingly hidden Paz and himself in a location where they were in peril.

Paz moved up along the side of him and squinted through the crack. She gasped when she saw her relatives. Prudenciano shook his head to prevent her from asking a question. The two of them waited to see what would happen.

"¡Hola! Anyone home?" yelled Emilio. "We wish to buy grain."

"Sí." answered an old man as he came out of the house next door.

He walked with a stoop that required him to crane his head up to see the men as he approached. "I don't have much, but I may have a pinch to see you through."

"*Gracias, Señor.* We only need enough for a couple of days," replied Emilio. Emilio had a deep respect for hard-working elders such as this man. He made a mental note to pay this man well for his fodder.

The old man lumbered up to the barn doors. All five riders of the Nava clan were still mounted and positioned directly in front of the doors. The man grabbed a door handle with both hands and yanked backward. The door barely budged. The owner was definitely surprised. He grabbed the other door handle. This door responded exactly the same way as the first. "The doors must be bolted from the inside. Now, how could that be?" the man said scratching his head. "Maybe my good-for-nothing nephew has something to do with this. You know him and his brainless friend just disappeared this afternoon and I can't find them anywhere."

Emilio stared at the man for a moment. Something was not right here. But what? Suddenly, he had a real need to explore the barn. "*Señor*, please let us help you." Emilio pointed at two of his hired hands. They quickly dismounted and walked over to the doors. After a quick examination, they discovered that the bolt was a simple board pushed through a catch. One man pulled out his knife and worked the board off the mounts. The doors easily swung open.

Prudenciano whispered to Paz, "They're in. Come on. Let's move over to the trap door." They both crept across the floor and peered through the crack along the edge of the door. They could see the men coming into the barn. Prudenciano noticed that Emilio was exceptionally alert. *He looks like he is searching for something more than grain.*

"Now where did I leave that bag of grain?" said the old man as he scanned the animal pens. He pressed his hand on his lower back to alleviate a nagging pain. "You know. I bet I had my nephew stored it in the loft. Why don't you send one of your boys up there to find out?" The old man pointed toward the ladder that led up to the hayloft. Emilio noticed that the dust had recently been knocked off the ladder rungs.

"*Señor*, has anyone been in here lately?" asked Emilio. His breathing was becoming rapid. Could it be that Prudenciano and Paz were hiding in here? If they were, then who had they seen riding out of town? Was there any connection to the disappearance of the two young men? No, that would be too convenient.

"Well, my nephew and his friend are always knocking around here," answered the man. Emilio felt his excitement dampen a little. He motioned for Abundio to climb up the ladder.

Prudenciano frantically searched the loft for a place to hide. Except for the hay, there was nothing to conceal them. He knew he could leap out of the loft cargo door and steal one of the horses. He would be long gone before the others could react, but he had Paz. She would hinder his escape. *She is going to tie me down*, thought Prudenciano bitterly. Acting quickly, he dug the straw away from the wall behind the trap door. Thus, when the door swung up, they would be shielded from Abundio's view. Then he and Paz lied down in the nest and Prudenciano threw the straw back over them.

From below, they heard Abundio grumbling as he negotiated each rung of the ladder. Then, the hinges of the trap door began squeaking as he pushed the door up. Prudenciano tensed as Abundio rose from the opening. Prudenciano placed a foot against the wall to aid him in bolting forward if they were discovered. If he hit the trap door with sufficient force, Abundio would be knocked senseless from the blow and would most likely fall back into the barn. This would give him enough time to jump out the cargo door and steal a horse. He would leave Paz behind because her life was not at stake.

Paz felt Prudenciano's body wind up like a tight spring. She knew something explosive was about to happen. Suddenly, Paz felt a trickle of fear rise up her spine as she spotted her bag in front of the straw pile. She had dropped it in her haste and forgotten to cover it. Paz reached behind her and tapped Prudenciano on the shoulder. He followed her stare and riveted his eyes onto the bag. He was helpless to retrieve it. Their only hope was that Abundio would not see it.

From their concealed lair, Prudenciano could barely see the top of Abundio's head. His brother slowly looked around the loft, but he did not make the effort to glance behind the door. Satisfied, Abundio grunted down to his father, "There is no grain here." With that declaration, he began to lower the trap door. Prudenciano shot forward and retrieved the bag. He quickly replaced the straw and froze.

Just then Emilio hollered back to Abundio, "Are you sure? I didn't see you look behind you."

Abundio sighed in deep resignation and pushed the door open again. This time he climbed all the way into the loft and took an extended look around. He seemed to stare a long time at the straw pile directly behind the door. Paz thought for sure he had seen them, but after a few seconds, Abundio continued to scan the other walls.

"*¡Dios mío!*" exclaimed the old man from below. "Now I remember where I stashed that bag of grain." The man strode over to some old blankets stacked against an animal pen and pushed them aside, exposing a grain bag. "Here it is. Sorry for the trouble."

"He says he's sorry," Abundio muttered sarcastically under his breath.

He immediately walked over to the door opening, lowered himself down the ladder, and closed the trap door behind him. Prudenciano let out a sigh of relief, but stayed immobilized. Paz felt his muscles relax.

Within a few minutes, Emilio had purchased the grain and thanked the old man. Then, without delay, the five men saddled up and rode off to the east. Prudenciano knew his father was going to take advantage of the cool night to ride hard and try to catch the impostors by dawn. "I would love to see the look on my father's face when he catches up with the boys," Prudenciano chuckled to himself. "Well, hopefully the ruse will give us a two-day reprieve."

Prudenciano and Paz shook the straw off them and removed their belongings from the pile. Both of them wore their relief on their faces. "We will wait a couple of hours after dark before moving onto Valparaiso," Prudenciano said softly to Paz. Now that he had almost lost her, he felt emotions bordering on love for her. *Could I have actually had left her?* he asked himself as he studied her face again. She looked so small and helpless that it squeezed his heart. For the first time, he was actually looking forward to their marriage.

"Paz," he said quietly. "Tomorrow, we will find the priest and get married. Then we can stop running and start our life together."

Paz reached up and touched his face. It sent shivers of emotion through him. "I will enjoy that very much, my brave man." Her words slew him harder than the worst melee that he had ever encountered during a *parranda*. Without thinking, he put his arms around her and held her gently to him. They stood embraced without moving for what seemed like an eternity while night fell and the five riders disappeared far to the east.

The midnight sky was illuminated by the bright moon and brilliant stars. The night sky over the high chaparral always possessed exceptional clarity and definition. During the autumn season, the region exhibited pronounced diurnal fluctuations in temperature. The sizzling hot days gave way to chilly nights. As Prudenciano and Paz walked in silence along the road to Valparaiso, they buttoned their clothing tightly and Paz wrapped a shawl around her neck and head. Since Prudenciano had given his hat away, he resigned himself to pulling his collar up as high as it would go and hunkering his head down to his chest. Despite their discomfort, they could not help but appreciate the natural wonder and beauty of the surrounding country. The moon backlit the dark outlines of the surrounding mountains, sage, and tall cactuses. Every once in a while, a yapping coyote or hooting owl punctured the silence.

They encountered no other travelers on the road. About one hour before dawn, they reached the outskirts of Valparaiso. The town was still sleepy and no one stirred in the streets. Because he had participated in many past *jaripeos* here, Prudenciano was familiar with the town and knew where they could find shelter. He led Paz to the rectory next to a magnificent church. Like most established towns in Zacatecas, the church was the predominant structure in the community.

He knocked on the massive, polished wooden door. They waited a few minutes and were about to knock again when the door creaked open and a fully clothed nun stood in the doorway holding a candle in a glass lamp. She glanced at the two of them with a little suspicion—they could tell that the glare from the lamp was impeding her night vision. Sensing her hesitation, Paz spoke first, "We traveled all night and we were wondering if you had a place for us to rest."

The nun immediately smiled with sincere warmth and relief at hearing a young woman's voice. "Of course we do," answered the nun. "We were just preparing to begin our morning prayers when I heard you knock. We occasionally get married couples from out of town to visit us for prayers and counseling."

"Oh, we are not married yet," Paz interjected. "That's why we have come. We want to see the padre as soon as possible to wed."

"Not married?" repeated the nun. She thought there was something familiar about the outline of the tall man in front of her. She lifted up the lamp so it shone directly onto Prudenciano's face. The sister's eyes flicked open wide in recognition and she almost dropped the lamp in her alarm. "You!" lashed out the nun. "How can you even show your face around here? Do you even realize the grief you caused this town from the last time you and your swine friends met here? Now you are dragging a poor innocent girl around! Come with me, honey." She reached out and grabbed Paz by the hand and began pulling her into the house.

Paz was taken totally off guard by the sister's response. She glanced at Prudenciano and saw him standing motionless in front of the door. "No, you don't understand," pleaded Paz as she resisted the nun's efforts to get her inside. "I came with him on my own free will. Please understand. We want to be married!"

The sister stopped in disbelief and stared at Paz. Could it be this Nava had a strange hold over women? Didn't she know that he would break her heart like he had done to so many girls in this town?

"All right," declare the nun. "We'll let Padre Miguel sort this out later today. Until that time, I want you to stay in here with us. But you," she said, pointing at Prudenciano and looking at him like he was a filthy pig, "I want you to stay in the barn in back. Now scat!" With that, she slammed the door shut in his face.

Prudenciano woke to the sounds of children playing in the street. Judging by the hot air drifting inside, it must be early afternoon. He stretched upon the fluffed straw and sat up. He felt surprisingly good for walking half the night. *You know,"* he thought, *I could get used to sleeping on straw.* He looked up and saw several horses standing in their stalls. The horse smell brought back a twang of bittersweet memories of when Tereso and he had caroused these very streets and slept where they fell, usually by their mounts. He was ripped away from his pleasant daydreams when a middle-aged woman dressed in a severe black and white habit marched into the barn. She placed both hands on her hips and looked him up and down in disgust. Prudenciano recognized her as the nun who had thrown him out early that morning.

"You and the girl will see the padre in about two hours," she said with a snarl on her lips. "We can't have you meeting him like this. He'd die from your stench!" The sister wrinkled her nose as she spoke. It was obvious that duty compelled her to help him, not human love. "We will set up a tub next to the first stall. When you are bathing, we will try to do something about your clothes."

"May I have something to eat also?"

"*Sí*, but after you take a bath," the sister answered. She turned to disappear, but halted and pivoted back to him. "I don't know what you promised that young girl, but none of us can make her see any reason. So help me, Nava, if you destroy her, I will chase you to hell!" She quickly made the sign of the cross for her curse and glanced upward for forgiveness. Then she abruptly left. Almost immediately, two younger sisters dragged a tub into the stall and, in rapid procession, carried in buckets of hot and cold water. Within minutes, they filled the tub and placed a bar of soap and a towel next to it.

Prudenciano noted that the women never looked directly at him or made any attempt at conversation. After their tasks were complete, they left without delay. *The old battle ax must have told them to stay away from me*, he thought.

He sighed, stood up, and walked over to the tub. The water looked inviting. He quickly stripped and lowered himself into the tub. After the initial shock of the heat, the warm water spread a relaxing glow throughout his body. He was just about to relax when the first nun reappeared. She said nothing, but gathered up his clothing with great abhorrence and abruptly left.

Prudenciano stayed in the tub until his skin wrinkled. He had scrubbed himself thoroughly several times, partly to pass the time until his clothes were returned to him and partly because he felt certain that if he didn't, the nun would return and finish the job properly. Still, no one brought his clothing. Grumbling, he stepped out of the tub and wrapped the towel around his waist. He walked over to a pile of straw that was immersed in sunshine. He sat down and closed his eyes. The sun felt good as it dried his skin.

He dozed briefly and when he opened his eyes, his favorite nun was glaring coldly at him. "Here," she said, handing him a stack of neatly folded clothes. "We tried our best but there is only so much we could do with these." Prudenciano did not recognize his own clothes. Contrary to the sister's evaluation, they were spotless and mended. He thanked her and took the clothing. "I'll be back to cut that hairy mane and beard of yours," she said and promptly left.

Prudenciano put on the clean clothes. They felt and looked good. True to her word, she came back with a stool, comb, and scissors, tools of the barber trade. Without waiting for a command, he sat down on the stool and allowed her to start combing his damp, thick hair into place. His lustrous mane was dignified with strands of gray, especially around his temples. In spite of herself, she reluctantly admitted that he was a very good-looking man.

Within half an hour, the hair cutting and beard trimming were done and the sister stepped back to study her work. She had done her job too well. He sat there with a devilish smile on that handsome face. *How could a woman resist him?* she thought.

Prudenciano guessed what was on her mind and smiled as he asked, "*Gracias*. Now, may I have some food?"

The nun shook the spell he wove in her mind. "*Sí*. I will get some now. Then you will see Padre Miguel." She was plainly flustered and flattened her gown with her palms to fully recover and left. Within a few minutes, she came back with a large plate heaped with beans, rice, squash, and tortillas. Prudenciano wolfed the food down hungrily and drank mightily from his water flask. For the first time, the nun seemed to look appreciatively at him for his healthy regard to her cooking. When he was finished, she took his plate and motioned for him to follow her.

She led him to the front of the rectory and signaled for him to stay put. The nun went inside and within a few minutes emerged with Paz. Prudenciano sucked in his breath, for he had never seen her more beautiful. She was freshly scrubbed and her clothes were clean and pressed. Her thick brown hair was tied with a piece of colored yarn into a tail that bounced along her back. Her golden highlights shone in the sunlight. Paz smiled and walked up to him. She took his hand and together they followed the sister to the church.

As they reached the church door, the nun turned and said, "Padre Miguel is waiting for you inside. He may be praying so please do not disturb him." They walked past the sister and entered the building. Valparaiso was approximately four times the size of Monte Escobedo and thus could support a luxurious cathedral. The vaulted ceilings were adorned with murals of the angels attending to the needs of Jesus and the Holy Father. A golden crucifix above the altar reflected the sunlight with brilliant rays. A beautiful statue of the Virgin Mary was placed on the left side of the cross. Padre Miguel was kneeling in front of the altar with his head bowed in deep prayer. He wore the white robe of priesthood and a wooden cross hung from his neck by a leather thong.

Prudenciano and Paz shifted uneasily in the back. The movement caught his attention and Padre Miguel quickly concluded his prayer and made the sign of the cross. He stood up and turned to address them. He was in his early fifties, not much older than Prudenciano. His hair was beginning to recede and gray. However, his eyes and the way he held his stout body indicated that he still had plenty of fire and determination. He smiled, opened his arms in welcome, and walked toward them. *They certainly are a striking couple*, thought Padre Miguel, *but he is so much older than she*. This was not so unusual here, though. He had seen and married several couples of similar age differences. Actually, many of the marriages had survived happily. However, the real problem was not age, but Prudenciano Nava. Padre Miguel had heard many confessions from distraught *señoritas* and raging fathers concerning this man. He also knew Padre José Nava, the priest from Monte Escobedo, and his disdain for his cousin Prudenciano. It was only after extreme reluctance that Padre José had dissolved Prudenciano's previous marriage. Padre Miguel's brow wrinkled as he wondered if Prudenciano had matured so that he could actually remarry.

"*¡Hola!*" said Padre Miguel. "Please sit down." He motioned to a pew next to them. They seated themselves and got comfortable. Paz instantly liked him. He seemed to possess a deep understanding that comes with years of serving as a Catholic priest. However, Prudenciano felt exposed like an open book in front of the padre's gaze. He fidgeted uneasily. Padre Miguel began the conversation. "Now then, I understand you two wish to get married. So, before I grant your wish, I want to know why you are not getting married in your hometown, Monte Escobedo?" By the look on their faces, Padre Miguel knew that he had struck at the very heart of the situation.

"I take it that you know my father?" asked Prudenciano. He felt certain that this man knew a lot more about him than he was letting on.

"*Sí*. He is a good man," answered the padre. "So, are you running from him?"

"Well, we wanted to get married and my father objected. So, we decided to come here to get married." The response was not the full truth, but it sounded good.

"I see, but just because your father objected doesn't mean that you have to come all the way to Valparaiso," replied Padre Miguel. He turned to Paz. "What did your family have to say about all this? Do they approve of your marriage plans?"

Paz always made it a point to tell the truth, especially to a priest. She knew that Prudenciano would be angry, but it had to be known. She started slowly and soon recounted the entire last three days. Paz left nothing out and when she concluded she bowed her head and folded her hands on her lap. Padre Miguel sat back in the pew and whistled softly. He was impressed with the two of them. To risk life and limb for the sake of being together was the ultimate expression of love, but he still needed to confirm Prudenciano's sincerity.

Padre Miguel stood up and faced Prudenciano. "Stand up," he commanded. Prudenciano slowly rose to his feet. Although he towered over the priest, he felt vulnerable in front of the man. "Now take my hands and look at me." It seemed strange to hold another man's hands, but when Prudenciano looked at him he felt Padre Miguel's eyes reach deep into his soul. He knew any deception that he might concoct would be instantly detected. "Prudenciano, answer me truthfully. Do you love this girl?"

Prudenciano squirmed in front of those searching eyes. "*Sí*" was all he could say.

"*Sí? Sí* what?" pressed the padre. He tightened his grip on Prudenciano.

"*Sí*, I love her," admitted Prudenciano. Then, like a dam bursting, words spilled from his mouth and came cascading down before he could curtail them. "At first, I meant only to hurt my brother and father by taking her." Prudenciano flashed a glance over to Paz. She was looking up at him and listening intensely. "But I now realize that I also took her because I didn't want to be without her. She possesses a goodness within her that makes me feel right and happy when I am around her. When we were being chased, I knew that all I had to do is give them Paz and they would let me go, but I just couldn't do that. I love her very much." The truth was out and Prudenciano felt drained.

Padre Miguel realized too that Prudenciano had finally looked within himself and found the truth. Confident of what to do next, he released Prudenciano's hands and turned back to Paz. "My dear child, after what you just heard, do you still want to marry this man?"

"Oh, yes!" exclaimed Paz. "More than ever." She looked approvingly toward Prudenciano.

"All right then, I'll get two of the sisters to act as witnesses and we will hold the ceremony now," said Padre Miguel with a broad smile. He stood up and walked out the main door. As he left the church, he thought with a little trepidation, *How am I ever going to explain this to Emilio Nava?*

The wedding was a simple affair. The only difficulty encountered was the signing of the marriage record. Paz had to help Prudenciano spell his name and shape his letters, but after the laborious operation was over, they were free to leave as husband and wife. Arm in arm, they strode down the church aisle, opened the door, and came face to face with the dusty, tired Nava search party.

The couple's eyes widened in shock and disbelief. The five men stared down at them from their horses. Prudenciano's horse and the young mare were tethered to one of the hired men. This told Prudenciano all that he needed to know. No one uttered a word. A horse nickered and another swished its tail to brush off flies. Prudenciano finally broke the silence. "*Hola*, Father, Abundio. What a pleasant surprise to see you again."

"You bastard!" hissed Abundio. He pulled his pistol from his holster.

"No!" shouted Emilio. "You are not going to kill your brother and especially not on the steps of the church. Put that thing away now!" With a tremendous effort, Abundio obeyed his father and holstered the weapon. Emilio dismounted and walked up Prudenciano and Paz. It was obvious that they were too late to prevent a marriage. He was torn between the mixed emotions of admiration for his son for so brilliantly outmaneuvering his pursuers, and rage at his reckless disregard for Paz's welfare.

"Ah, Emilio Nava," greeted Padre Miguel. "I prayed that I might be given a chance to explain this marriage to you. Please, *Señor*. Come inside with me alone so we can discuss this." The priest took Emilio by the arm and led him inside. Emilio was too tired to argue and complied without utterance.

The minutes dragged by slowly as Prudenciano and Paz stood on the church steps. The four men never dismounted, but sat watching them wearily. The afternoon sun baked them unmercifully. Finally, Emilio and Padre Miguel emerged with the padre's arm around Emilio's shoulder. Emilio had the certain look of resignation on his fatigued face. He left the priest, walked up to the newlyweds, and addressed them. "Padre Miguel has convinced me that you two actually love each other and should be married. I have the greatest respect for the padre, so I will accept his decision."

"However," continued Emilio pointing at Prudenciano, "I am still not totally convinced that you are right for her. Prudenciano, you are just too unpredictable. I pray that you will not someday abandon her because this marriage has lost its novelty. Son, you have a wife now. You can't be chasing rainbows anymore. You are going to have to work to support her and your children. *Comprende?*"

The lecture rankled Prudenciano's pride. He could feel his anger rising. He was certain that his father was heading for something, so he remained quiet.

"So," resumed Emilio, "after you two travel a bit, come back to Monte Escobedo and live with us."

Prudenciano and Abundio simultaneously yelled a resounding "No!"

Emilio sighed and shook his head at the two of them. "You both are forgetting what's best for Paz. All right, so be it. Prudenciano, I am taking my horses back with me. You are on your own now, but before I go, I must talk to Paz alone." He motioned for her to follow him away from the crowd. When they walked behind the corner of the building, he stopped and faced her. Paz felt a little embarrassed to talk privately with her step-grandfather. In many ways, he was like a father to her. She kept her eyes lowered in front of him.

"Well," he started, "if you must run off with Prudenciano, then you will need all the help you can get. I know that he has no money, so I want you to have this." Emilio pulled out a pouch and handed her some coins. "It's not much, but it will help give you a start. Please, take it. Think of it as a wedding gift. Just don't let Prudenciano know you have it."

Paz was deeply touched. Tears began to well up in her dark brown eyes. "*Gracias.* I will use it wisely." She stood up on her toes and kissed Emilio on the cheek, then quickly hid the pouch in her dress.

Emilio smiled broadly for the first time that day. He thought, *She is a smart one. Because of her, they just might make it.* "Let's go back now," Emilio said to Paz. "Remember, do not tell your husband about the money. You must watch over these matters now." Paz nodded her understanding and they walked back to the men.

Emilio walked up to Padre Miguel and thanked him for his services. Emilio deftly slipped some money into his hand. "Just a little something for the church, Padre," he said.

"You are so generous, *Señor* Nava," answered Padre Miguel with a bow.

Emilio took his reins and mounted his horse. But before he could signal them to leave, Abundio leaned out and asked Paz, "Where can I tell your mother that you went?"

Paz gazed uncertainly up to Prudenciano. Prudenciano responded directly to Abundio, "Torreón. Tell her Torreón." The men started laughing and Emilio shook his head as he led them away toward home.

Prudenciano clenched his hands into fists and stiffened his arms straight down along his sides as he glared after them. "They'll see," he muttered. "We will see who is laughing when I am rich." Suddenly, his mind's eye activated and he saw a vision of Abundio hunched over like an old man, leading a horse with two young girls on it. The grief and torture that Abundio wore across his face instantly deflated Prudenciano's anger. Then, as quickly as the vision came, it was gone. All Prudenciano could see were the five men disappearing down the street.

Paz could feel the tension leave him. "What's the matter?" she asked.

"Oh, nothing that I can put my finger on," answered Prudenciano as he stared after his father and brother. "But I have the feeling that I will never see my father again and the next time we see Abundio there will be much sadness." Paz looked up at him with a puzzled look upon her face and then followed Prudenciano's gaze back to the men. A cold shiver went through Prudenciano even though it was very hot outside. As his family went out of sight, he thought, *Why do these damn visions follow me? Why must I know?*

Chapter 6
Torreón

Paz stopped to adjust the strap on her bag and blow a nagging wisp of hair off her face. The heat was beginning to rise to an uncomfortable level and the dust made her skin feel gritty. They were climbing a small hill near the outskirts of Torreón. She wished that they would stop and rest at a *rancho* or under a quiet tree, but it was hard to pause so close to their final destination. During the first five weeks of her married life, she had grown to anticipate and cherish the quiet times they shared during the noon siesta and the late evening. Prudenciano liked to stretch out and think out loud about the great things he was going to do once they got to Torreón. She loved to lie next to him and listen to his dreams. He made them sound so powerful and attainable that she quivered with excitement. But most of all, during these precious times, he was totally hers. She did not have to worry about him showing off to others or treating her gruffly in front of strangers.

She shuddered involuntarily when she thought about what had happened two weeks ago in Fresnillo. It was the first time Paz had ever visited that city. She was so excited. It was all so new to her. However, Prudenciano acted like he knew the town like the back of his hand and proceeded to round up old *jaripeo* cronies. One thing led to another and before she knew it, Prudenciano had disappeared into one of the many *cantinas*. By the time she found him, he was totally inebriated and incapable of walking. She nursed him in a back alley for two days until he was able to function again. She spent a few of the coins that Emilio had given her for food and medicine. Paz knew they had to leave the town quickly before Prudenciano went rogue and abandoned her completely. It was the closest they had come to arguing, but in the end, Prudenciano shouldered his pack and they marched out of Fresnillo and headed north.

When they were alone, Prudenciano proved to be a loving and

capable partner. He was knowledgeable about the land and told her fascinating stories about the country while they walked. At night, he was a very gentle lover and when they were done, she would snuggle deep into his arms and chest and fall asleep.

They were poor, but she felt so alive. Every day brought new country to see. The people they met along the way were also impoverished, but always extended a helping hand. A cup of cool water, a small meal, and sometimes a place to sleep were offered regularly. Prudenciano often exercised his skills as a *sobador* and relieved the aches and pains of the residents. Many times, a family would be so thankful for his services that they sent a runner ahead advertising Prudenciano's skills. As a result, people would be waiting for them with a meal or shelter in return for the *sobador's* talents.

They averaged about twenty miles per day. At that pace, they covered the 235 miles to Torreón in about two weeks. As they left the state of Zacatecas and entered Durango, the country began to fall away from the Sierra Madre mountains and open into the rolling hills of the great plains. Vegetation was confined to the gullies and protected lowlands. The exposed land yielded sparse grasses, which withered away in the heat.

The road they walked was well engineered and maintained. The main traffic between the United States and Mexico City traveled up and down this corridor. In essence, it was the backbone of Mexico's transportation system. No other road offered such direct access to Mexico's main cities such as Juarez, Chihuahua, Torreón, Zacatecas, and San Luis Potosí. The traffic was mostly horse-drawn carts, but once in a while, a motorcar would rattle and bang noisily down the road. When traffic was heavy, the dust rose high into the hot blue sky and coated the weary travelers below.

It was during one such dusty episode that Prudenciano and Paz reached the suburbs of Torreón. Three communities, Torreón, Gómez Palacio, and Lerdo composed the sprawling metropolis before them. The Ora Nazas river separated Torreón from the other two. The Ora Nazas also served as the boundary between the states of Durango and Coahuila. Torreón was in Coahuila and the others were in Durango.

In the late 1600s, the Spanish had conquered this land and enslaved its residents to mine the silver from the surrounding hills. Unlike Zacatecas, the mines continued to produce silver to the present day. This allowed the Spanish to invest their wealth into large architectural projects such as cathedrals, sports arenas, and a university.

From the hilltop, they stopped to take in the view of the enormous city before dropping down and vanishing into its urban sprawl. Neither of them had ever seen such a mass of humanity. It seemed to spread out forever before them. Paz was filled with excitement and fear at the prospect of this being their new home. Random thoughts filled her mind. *What will we do? Where will we live? How can I keep Prudenciano out of trouble?* The last thought troubled her the most. Her experience in Fresnillo was still fresh in her mind.

"Well, we made it," declared Prudenciano. "Let's go down and see what opportunities are available." He squared his shoulders and set off down the hill with a renewed energy and a determined pace. Paz hesitated for a second and readjusted her pack. Then with the same determination, she strode off to follow him.

The residents of Torreón lived in areas determined by their wealth and social status. Subtle pressures of society discreetly drew lines so that compatible levels of humanity could coexist. The few extremely wealthy residents lived in the northwestern outlying areas. Their large homes and ranches spread neatly along the bordering countryside. The affluent government bureaucrats and business owners lived closer to the city and provided a buffer between the extremely rich and the working poor majority. As one moved south through the heart of the city, the residents became poorer and the living conditions degenerated. The progression continued until society had effectively corralled the uneducated working class in the southern portion of Torreón. Thus, the majority of citizens lived in the densely populated and impoverished southern half of town while the wealthy families occupied spacious neighborhoods of the northern quarter.

Prudenciano and Paz entered the city from the south. They were among thousands of economic refugees that immigrated from the dismal prospects of rural communities in hopes of building a new life in Torreón. The reality of life within the city sobered them. They did not see the thriving and bountiful images that others had painted for them. Here, people lived from day to day, competed for whatever work was available, and tried to maintain some sort of privacy within the tightly packed multitudes. The poor people of this area cooperated and helped each other through the poverty. Crime was low and the laughter of children playing in the streets could be heard throughout the neighborhoods.

Prudenciano stopped in front of a small adobe building that had an office in front and living quarters in back. Paz told him that the crudely made wooden sign said "People's Labor Agent." Prudenciano thought this would be a good place to start. He entered the office and was mildly surprised and irritated that Paz followed him closely behind. This was a man's affair and she had no business inside.

Before he could complain, a heavyset man in his fifties came through a doorway screened by a hanging woolen blanket. He walked up to a rough-cut wood counter and eyed the two of them like a man judging livestock. He had a knack for analyzing the worth of people. With the enormous influx of labor into Torreón these last few years, he'd had countless times to practice. His appraising eye told him that these two migrants might make him a profit. The man before him was tall, broad shouldered, healthy, and looked intelligent. The mines would pay a substantial finder's fee for a man like this. The young woman with him was beautiful and appeared not to have any children, but her penetrating stare let him know that she was nobody's fool. The man sighed and thought, *Too bad.* If she had been gullible, he could have convinced her to provide certain entertainments to wealthy clients for a considerable fee, but he would have to settle for finding her a position as a cook or maid.

"My name is Don Luis Manos," the man said without a smile. His demeanor was all business. "How may I help you?"

"My name is Prudenciano Nava and this is my wife," Prudenciano jerked his head toward Paz. "We just arrived in town and I was wondering what jobs are available."

Don Luis nodded his understanding and asked, "What skills do you have? I get a lot of men looking for work nowadays."

"I handle horses and cattle," replied Prudenciano.

"I have no jobs for farmers," Don Luis replied curtly. "Can you work in a mine?"

Before Prudenciano could answer, Paz cut in, "What does it pay and how dangerous is the work?"

Don Luis looked straight at Prudenciano as he pointed at Paz and said, "Does she speak for you, Nava?" The comment embarrassed Prudenciano immensely, which was exactly Don Luis's intention. Don Luis had seen wives try to drive hard bargains for their husbands before. He had to put an end to it now.

"I speak for myself!" declared Prudenciano as he glared back at Don Luis. "I can outwork any man, anywhere. What do you need me to do?" Paz shot a venomous look at Don Luis. She did not trust him at all.

Don Luis was totally unscathed by the scrutiny. He casually replied, "I want you to come back here early tomorrow morning. We'll talk over the details then. *Adios.*" He turned to leave.

"Wait a minute," Paz commanded. "Where can we stay?"

Don Luis turned around and shrugged his shoulders. "That's not my problem. I only find people work." Just then, the curtain parted and out marched a confident middle-aged woman. She placed her hands on her hips and snarled at Don Luis. The way she addressed him showed that they were married.

"You can be such a dog at times, Don Luis," she rebuked him. "You can't just throw a woman out into the streets like you do with your men." She turned to Paz and Prudenciano. "Come back here with me. I'll get you something to eat and then we will find you some place to stay." Paz smiled her thanks to the woman and followed her to the back room. Prudenciano looked at Don Luis questioningly. Don Luis just threw up his hands and motioned for Prudenciano to follow the women into the home.

Mrs. Manos found a family that was willing to share their humble home with the Navas. The Martinez family had a two-room adobe house in one of the crowded subdivisions of south Torreón. Tomas and Rita were in their twenties and had four children whose ages ranged from two to six years. After the normal awkward introductions, the adults happily found each other's company agreeable. The children retreated to a corner and watched their new housemates with curious eyes.

The sun had completely set and the home was illuminated by an oil lamp and a few candles. The streets were quiet and people strolled comfortably down the sidewalks, enjoying the cooler air. Prudenciano felt his eyelids grow heavy and struggled to participate in the evening conversation. "I tell you," confided Rita leaning forward, "that you cannot trust Don Luis Manos. He will sell your soul if he could get away with it. His wife is good, I think. What she sees in him I will never know."

"*Sí*," replied Paz. "I fear that he may have some dangerous job for Prudenciano."

"Most likely," interjected Tomas dryly. "The men at the mine always start out a the bottom of the ladder." Tomas unconsciously rubbed his calloused and worn hands on the table. His hands were aged way beyond his years. "I work at the mine. The work is very hard, but the money is all right."

"*¡Dios mío!*" exclaimed Rita. "They work you like an animal and pay you very little. I still have to work to help support the family. I am a cook at a restaurant downtown."

"What kind of job will I get at the mine?" asked Prudenciano groggily. He could barely keep his eyes open.

"Well, I do not know for sure," answered Tomas as he noticed Prudenciano's weariness, "but one thing is certain. You will have to get a good night's sleep if you want to be fresh for it. Rita, let's put the little ones to bed so they can have the front room to themselves." Tomas got up and proceeded to scoop up the kids with one big hug. The children squealed with delight as their father carried them into the back room.

"I am sorry for keeping you up for so long," said Rita. "Tomas and I really enjoyed talking with you both. Please make yourself comfortable and we will see you tomorrow." Rita smiled, picked up the oil lamp, and moved to the other room.

"Oh, man," yawned Prudenciano as he stood up and stretched. The long day's walk and the excitement of Torreón had totally exhausted him. Paz motioned for him to follow her to the bedding that she and Rita had arranged along the back wall. He slowly undressed and lay down on the blankets. Paz blew out the remaining candle, lay down next to him, and snuggled up close to his warm, muscular body.

Paz softly called out in the darkness, "Prudenciano. Prudenciano? Are you awake?" She heard him grunt an incoherent affirmation, so she continued, "Do you think that everything is going to be all right? I mean, is Torreón going to be our home?" Again, she heard him mumble something unintelligible. Paz sighed, "I guess we will find out, my adventurous husband." This time there was no response from Prudenciano and she let sleep envelop her.

The morning began in a rush of confusion and noise. The small house was quickly filled with the cacophony of kids fighting and crying, scoldings from Rita, and sharp barks from Tomas and Prudenciano. One small sound of salvation rang through the turmoil. "Don't worry, Rita. I'll be happy to stay and watch the children," said Paz. Rita beamed her appreciation back and the house settled back into a manageable, hurried pace.

The men were worried about getting to Don Luis early enough in the morning to catch the wagons to the mine. Tomas insisted on escorting Prudenciano and showing him the ropes. The men left the house shortly after dawn and strode quickly to the office of the People's Labor Agent. When they got there, several wagons were already parked in front and men were lining up in front of the door to seek labor contracts from Don Luis Manos.

Don Luis represented a large silver mining company, several factories, and manual labor needs of the wealthy. Labor requests came to him and he found capable people to perform the work. Each request would pay him a fee depending on the type of labor needed. Maids, yard workers, and farmers generated the lowest fees. The mine paid the highest tariffs for capable and strong workers and the mine relied heavily on representatives like Don Luis to find them. If a worker proved to be a good investment, Don Luis received an additional bonus for his referral.

Prudenciano got into the line and Tomas waited next to him.

Within a few minutes, Don Luis opened the door and the People's Labor Agent began his business. The men shuffled in and Don Luis sized up each man and determined if he had a job for him. Some contracts were temporary, lasting only a day or two. Others received contracts for several months of work. If the employee was productive, the job could lengthen indefinitely. Tomas was one of these lucky few and he wanted Prudenciano to have chance at one of these coveted positions, too.

Each man took up only a few minutes of Don Luis's time. The line moved quickly and Prudenciano soon found himself facing Don Luis again. Tomas spoke first. "Ah, Don Luis. I trust you met Prudenciano yesterday? No doubt you noticed how capable he looks. Surely you have a good long-term position for him at the mine?"

Don Luis silently evaluated Prudenciano again. He certainly was tall and strong looking, but there was something about this man that made him wary. Was it that his back was too straight? Or was it the defiance in his eyes? This one could be trouble. After a few more moments of contemplation, Don Luis finally spoke, "Okay. I have a conditional position at the mine. You are on probation for one month. If you prove to be lazy or rebellious, you will never work through my office again, *comprende?*"

Prudenciano could feel his hackles rising. *Who does he think that he is talking to? I am not a child.* With a forced calmness, Prudenciano answered clearly, "I accept your terms." Don Luis nodded his acceptance and quickly produced a labor contract.

"You may want to read the contractual terms. If you accept, please sign at the bottom." Don Luis knew that most of his placements were illiterate, so he added, "Of course, I can just sign for you and save you some time."

"*Sí,*" Prudenciano answered a little too quickly. He gruffly pushed the paper back to Don Luis who casually printed Prudenciano's name on the bottom. As Don Luis was completing the paperwork, Prudenciano asked, "So, what will I do and how much does it pay?"

Prudenciano's comment confirmed Don Luis's suspicions that he could not read or write, because the contract provided this information. Don Luis replied, "You will do whatever the mine requires of you. The starting pay is three pesos per day. Now, get into one of the wagons. They will be leaving soon, but remember, Prudenciano Nava, one screwup and you will never work here again." With that declaration, Don Luis dismissed him.

"All right, Nava!" Tomas exclaimed as soon as they were out of the office. "You got a chance to get a permanent job!" They climbed into the wagon and made themselves as comfortable as they could. The wagon rapidly filled with men going to the mine. Only a few made any attempt at conversation. Most of them wore the hopeless look of sentenced criminals being taken to a penitentiary for hard labor.

After a few minutes of silence, Prudenciano turned to Tomas and said, "Three pesos per day is not much. I thought I would get more than that."

Tomas's demeanor turned serious and he leaned forward to answer in a quiet and confidential voice, "Prudenciano. You just got a peso more per day than most of these men. Until you prove your worth, you won't find a better job in all of Torreón! Be thankful for what you got." Suddenly, the wagon lurched forward as the driver snapped the reins to start the horses. Prudenciano's first day at the mine had begun.

Paz had no trouble controlling the children. She read them stories and played games. The kids thoroughly enjoyed having such a fun sitter. It was only when the neighborhood children began joining the Martinez kids that the situation became unmanageable. Soon there were twelve children competing for Paz's attention. Exasperated, Paz took out her harmonica and began playing. Like the Pied Piper, she captured their attention and led them outside. They sang songs and played "Guess that tune." The sounds of her music and the children's laughter filled the street. Women who stayed home to raise their children came out to see the ruckus. They smiled in their doorways and watched the children dancing and singing to the beautiful music.

Everyone in neighborhood seemed to be in a festive mood. Paz's music provided a respite from the monotonous daily chores that filled everyone's life. Some of the neighboring women gave her and the children hot tortillas with butter to eat. By late afternoon, Paz was entertaining at least thirty children. Most of these kids had been left unsupervised because both parents had to work. They were lonely and desperate for attention. Paz gave them a safe refuge to pass the day. *"Won't Rita be surprised when she comes home,"* thought Paz. Little did she know that her competent child-supervising skills were becoming the main topic of conversation in the surrounding households.

The wagon jostled and lurched as the horses strained to pull it up the hill on the outskirts of town. Prudenciano looked to the east and could see the entire city unfold before him. The crowded streets of the south side were in stark contrast to the neatly laid out parcels of the north. He saw Torreón's city center with its cathedral and large office buildings. As the dirt road continued to rise, he looked out across the great vastness of Mexico's central plains with a reddish-hued sky floating high overhead. When he turned toward the hillside, he spotted a dark plume rising just beyond the ridge.

As the wagon crested the hill, Prudenciano heard the mill houses and retorts rumbling in the distance. "We are not far now," said Tomas. "You will see the mine buildings soon." The wagon continued for several minutes with the mechanical noises building strength with each passing moment. Abruptly, the buildings emerged from behind the crest. They were mammoth and made of sheet metal. Some housed machinery that ground the ore into a powder. Others sorted and manipulated the rock to maximize recovery of the precious silver. Buildings containing the furnaces that melted the ore into an amalgam and eventually into silver ingots belched black smoke from their coal-fired combustion chambers.

Prudenciano was awestruck at the immensity of the plant. He asked Tomas, "Which building will I work in?"

"I am sorry, Prudenciano," Tomas replied, "but you will have to start in the mine. It's over there." He pointed to a wooden tower with cables running vertically through the structure. "That timber frame is actually an elevator. It takes you down to where you will work. I will be in one of the upper levels. Most likely, you will be deeper."

Prudenciano felt trepidation about working underground. He had never been in a mine before and was completely unsure of what experience lay ahead. His silence and deep brooding were similar to the demeanor of the rest of the men the wagons. These men provided the muscle that allowed the upper class to get rich and widen the chasm between the minority rich and the majority poor. Men like these would never work themselves out of this pit. Many would die here trying. Eventually, they would all give up when their spirits and bodies were broken. Then they would return home penniless and Don Luis would get another fee for a fresh set of recruits. The cycle of exploitation would continue until the silver ran out. Then the mine would become yet another derelict that testified to the abuse of mankind for the benefit of a few.

The wagons stopped in front of a one-story wooden building. Judging by the behavior of the men, Prudenciano surmised that it must be the main office. Everyone jumped out and formed a single line. A rough-looking man came out and began calling out names from a roster. Tomas leaned over to Prudenciano and said, "His name is Felix Pontes and he is the mine boss. Watch out for him. He cares nothing for your safety." Prudenciano nodded and paid attention to what was happening around him. As each man was called, Pontes checked off his name and pointed toward the mine elevator. Men were grouped according to their skills and physical ability. The company stationed the newer recruits in the lower sections of the mine. A seasoned miner could volunteer to join these men too. The mine paid these miners more to compensate them for the atrocious working conditions. Only the more developed sections of the upper levels had adequate ventilation and lighting. As Tomas predicted, Prudenciano was assigned to the lowest level along the new ore seam.

Each group of men rode the elevator together to their respective work levels. The company would load the men closest to the surface first and then move the groups destined for the deeper levels sequentially. Since Prudenciano's team was working in the deepest level, they were the last to be transported.

As he stepped carefully onto the elevator with his crew, Prudenciano wondered how he could trust his life to this rickety contraption. The platform consisted of a ten-by-fourteen-foot plank floor with a wooden rail that enclosed all four sides. The rail was haphazardly built with rough lumber. Some of the boards were not fully secured and the whole railing bulged outward if anyone leaned against it. The entire platform was secured to a single, four-inch metal cable that hung from a pulley high above. The elevator swayed as each man entered. With each movement, dark voids could be seen around the perimeter of the floor which revealed the bottomless pit below. As the last man stepped onto the platform, the whole structure groaned from the combined weight. It finally dawned on Prudenciano that their safety was totally dependent upon the elevator cable. The thought made him feel vulnerable. The crew stood shoulder to shoulder, packed like sardines.

Abruptly, the elevator plunged downward. The new recruits such as Prudenciano were always caught off guard. He felt his fear shoot up his spine and his sphincter tighten. *We're going to die*! he thought almost out loud. He flailed and grabbed the flimsy railing. It bowed and added to his anxiety. Quickly, the acceleration zeroed and the feeling of free-falling passed. The wooden structure descended quietly into the darkness. Periodically, Prudenciano looked up and saw the small circle of light overhead shrink away. After passing a depth of several hundred feet, they dropped by many lighted work levels. Prudenciano caught glimpses of men pushing ore carts or digging with picks and shovels. The temperature was pleasantly cool and he could sometimes feel a gust of ventilated air.

Now the cage began to slow and again Prudenciano tried to steady himself with the useless railing. The platform came to a stop with a jerk. He noticed in the feeble light that he now could see the bottom of the shaft, which was only a few feet below. He knew that they were far below the surface, but the actual depth of 900 feet was incomprehensible to him. Prudenciano followed the men off the elevator into a large cavern. As he left the platform, he noticed that one man stayed behind. The man opened a small box mounted on a railing post. The box had a slender black cable that ran up the main support line. The man reached into the box and tapped on a telegraph striker. After a few moments, the elevator shot silently upward. Prudenciano and his team were left alone in the near total darkness. He felt abandoned and cut off from the rest of the world. *Are they going to leave us here forever?* pondered Prudenciano forlornly.

The team leader spoke for the first time. "Okay. Light all the lamps. You two, move the water buckets to that wall. And you," said the leader pointing at Prudenciano, "move the food baskets next to the water." Prudenciano snapped out of his despair and responded to the command. As he gathered the baskets, the work area came alive with the flickering lamplights. He placed the food by the wooden barrels and stood up to face the crowd forming around the leader.

The team leader name was Victoriano Vallejo. He was a short, wiry man in his thirties. His hard arms and shoulders testified to his years of toiling in the mines. Victoriano also exuded an air of confidence as he gave commands. He efficiently directed his men to follow the exposed ore seam and, most importantly, to do it safely.

Normally, Prudenciano would have bristled under such close supervision, but he was totally out of his element. He followed the instruction exactly and without question. The pick given to him felt good in his hands. He partnered with two other strong men and chipped away at the broken face of the ore seam. Several others worked behind them gathering the rock and loading it into sturdy metal carts. The carts rolled on small solid wheels. When the men filled the carts to capacity, the weight caused the wheels to lock if they rolled onto the tiniest obstruction. Thus, the men were forced to jockey their loads back and forth to the elevator landing.

The seam that contained the silver ore was characterized by a gray-brown hue that followed a horizontal, four-foot-thick fold. Although the men concentrated their efforts on removing the crumbled rock, they inevitably had to remove some lower-grade material from above and below the seam. The entire working face was never more than six feet high, so tall men like Prudenciano had to stoop as they worked.

As the hours dragged on, the air began to degenerate. Without enhanced ventilation, the men began to breathe each other's respiration. The smell of a sweating humanity mixed with dust produced a stifling atmosphere. The foreman had a pocket watch on a chain attached to his belt. He punctually checked the time and called a fifteen-minute break every two hours. During this time, the men sat down and rested and drank from one of the water barrels. A communal tin ladle was passed among the men to dip water and drink. Victoriano never allowed a man to leave his group and seek water alone. There were too many dangers within their dark domain to permit a loner to wander around at will.

Around noon, Victoriano signaled the men to stop for a one-hour lunch and rest. The men collapsed exhausted along the rough-cut walls next to the elevator shaft. The mining company provided the food baskets and Victoriano distributed them among the men. Today, the meal consisted of corn tortillas with a bean and chili paste.

Prudenciano munched on his lunch and studied the faces of the men around him. He was surprised to find that he was the oldest one there. They were mostly in their late teens and early twenties. All of them wore solemn, dusty faces with perspiration streaking dirt down their foreheads. Every so often, a worker coughed up phlegm and spit on the floor. They ate in silence with only minimal talk.

Prudenciano turned to Victoriano and asked, "I noticed that we have been removing broken rock along the face. How does it get that way?"

Victoriano looked hard at Prudenciano for a moment to see if he was joking. When he failed to detect any sarcasm, Victoriano thought, *This man truly doesn't have a clue how to mine.* He replied in a low and authoritative voice that carried clearly through the cavern, "After our work is done today, drillers will place explosive charges along the seams at every level. During the night, they will detonate the explosives and allow the dust and loose rock to settle by the next morning. Our powder men are very good. They usually generate deep cracks in the rock that take us all day to remove. But sometimes ..." Victoriano's voice trailed off as if he was contemplating a perplexing problem. Prudenciano made a special note of Victoriano's muted thought. He would investigate it later.

After lunch, the elevators began descending again. Each trip was coordinated for maximum efficiency. The elevator shuttled timbers for cribbing and empty ore carts to the lowest levels. Every upward trip took filled ore carts to the surface. Within two hours, the full carts had been replaced with empties and the timbers were stacked along one wall.

Victoriano then directed everyone to start building braces under areas that he had previously marked with rough lines of red paint. Victoriano had developed a keen eye for the strike and dip of rock. He could sense sheer zones and unstable ceilings just by reading the surface stratigraphy. The company had long ago learned to trust his judgement and allowed him complete control in the placing of the supports. The men knew that their safety depended on him. In the event of a cave-in, a man could scream forever down here without anyone above hearing his desperate cries for help.

The shoring took the rest of the day. Victoriano told them that to-morrow they would open a new section opposite the elevator shaft. For the first time, Prudenciano comprehended their mission. They were to open and prepare new levels for others to mine. His group was the first on site, encountered untested rock, and worked in un-ventilated spaces.

Victoriano Vallejo looked at his watch and found that the workday had come to an end. He signaled for the men to gather at the eleva-tor landing. They carried the oil lamps and the empty water barrels with them. Soon, Prudenciano felt a rushing of air push down upon them. He looked up and saw the black bottom of the platform falling toward them like an enormous bat with its wings outstretched. After working underground for nine hours, Prudenciano was going back to live among the surface dwellers.

The setting sun greeted Prudenciano like a long-lost friend. He had to squint until his eyes became accustomed to the piercing light. Tomas met Prudenciano by the elevator house. Like Prudenciano, he looked tired and dusty. "How did it go today, *amigo?*" Prudenciano tried to talk, but a thick coat of dust caught his voice in his throat. All he could do was shrug and signal that the day went well. "Fol-low me," continued Tomas. "I know just how to make you feel bet-ter." He led him to several long water troughs. Rows of men were kneeling before the troughs and dunking their entire heads into the water. Then they abruptly rose and let the water stream down their chests and backs. Many repeated the ritual several times. Lye soap was available, but few bothered to use it. The water in the troughs turned a muddy brown.

Tomas steered Prudenciano to a gap in one of the rows. They knelt side by side. Prudenciano did not even hesitate. He plunged his head and part of his chest into the trough, wiggled back and forth, and then quickly raised his head up. "That's the way to do it, Pruden-ciano!" laughed Tomas. Then he took his turn to wash his head.

Tomas was right The water felt marvelous. It cleared his vision and nasal passages and magically revitalized him. He felt that he could go on. They stood up and grinned at each other with water dripping off their hair and clothes.

Tomas pointed at the wagons and they started walking toward them. They stopped to get one last drink of water from a water barrel. As they walked the last few feet, Prudenciano noticed that Tomas was favoring his right leg. "Tomas, did you hurt yourself today?" he asked.

"*Sí*," replied Tomas. "I twisted my leg and back when I was carrying a timber. It's just a sprain." As Tomas reached up to grab the wagon railing and jump in, he felt his muscles in his back bunch up. He let out a low groan and sucked air through his clenched teeth. Prudenciano knew what was happening and quickly helped him into the wagon.

"Everyone, let him lie down!" barked Prudenciano. The men quickly scattered and made room along the middle board. Tomas collapsed on the floor. "Roll onto your stomach." Tomas slowly complied. Prudenciano straddled him and pressed the heel of his palms into the small of Tomas's back. He expertly massaged the tight muscles and gradually adjusted his spine. Tomas first resisted and cried out in pain. Then as the treatment progressed, he began to relax. To his amazement, his back began to feel better. By the time the wagons started, Tomas could sit up and comfortably ride home.

It was dark by the time they walked into the house. The children ran to Tomas and he gingerly stooped down to hug them. Paz skipped up to Prudenciano and wrapped her arms around his waist. He smiled and kissed the top of her head. It always amazed him how much he enjoyed having her around. *Perhaps this married thing isn't so bad after all*, thought Prudenciano.

"Yuck!" blurted Paz as she recoiled from him. "You are dirty and you stink!" Prudenciano sneered and reached out to drag her back to him, but she dodged and began backpedaling.

"Don't worry, Paz," said Rita. "They always come back smelling like this. You will get used to it. Tomas, please show Prudenciano where to wash and change before he gets into trouble."

Tomas laughed and slapped Prudenciano on the back. "Come on, man. You can chase her later." Prudenciano faked as if he was going to bolt toward Paz, but turned and followed Tomas out the back door.

In the alley, a large wooden crib that was capable of holding several hundred gallons of water hung along the wall with stout ropes. The crib caught rain water from the roof. A hose connected to the bottom of the reservoir allowed water to gravity-feed with considerable pressure. A partition built with rough-cut lumber provided the user with some privacy as he opened a valve at the end of the hose to wash.

Tomas motioned to Prudenciano to follow him. He walked behind the screen and stripped off his clothes. Then he reached up and turned the valve open. Lukewarm water gushed out and drenched Tomas. When he was thoroughly soaked, he turned the water off and soaped himself up. Prudenciano copied him and soon the two of them were scrubbing themselves clean. As they were rinsing the soap off, the women came out with towels and clothes.

"We are looking for two clean, naked men," announced Rita. "Any takers?" Even in the darkness, Prudenciano could see Paz blush.

"*Sí*. We both could use a woman right now," taunted Tomas. Rita threw a towel at him in mock anger. Tomas laughed as he caught it.

Paz handed a towel to Prudenciano. He grabbed her hand instead and pretended to pull her into the stall. "Prudenciano!" squealed Paz. Prudenciano chuckled as he released her and took the towel.

"We'll see you two inside. Hurry up. Dinner is ready," said Rita. The men quickly dried and dressed. The darkness was almost complete when they walked toward the door. Prudenciano noticed that Tomas still limped slightly. He made a mental note to bandage the leg after dinner. As they opened the door, the smell of beans and fresh tortillas wafted toward them and made their mouths water. In the front room, the dinner table was set and the food laid out, but everyone was waiting for the men to sit and serve themselves first before beginning their meal. Tomas and Prudenciano took their assigned chairs and began heaping their plates. It was only after the men were fully engrossed in their food that the women and children sat down and started their dinner.

After the first five minutes of rapid consumption had dulled the hunger pains, casual conversation arose around the table. Prudenciano described his first day at work with Tomas clarifying some details. The description of the underground conditions disturbed Paz. Paz talked about how nice the children and women were in the surrounding neighborhood. The children chattered about Paz's music and games. Rita smiled at Paz in gratitude for her services.

When the dinner was done, the men relaxed around the table while the women cleared and washed the dishes. The lamplight cast a friendly glow over the room. Prudenciano leaned forward and said, "Tomas, let me wrap that leg for you. Your knee needs support if you expect to work tomorrow." Then he turned to Rita and asked, "Do you have anything that I could make a bandage out of?" Rita nodded and went into the back room. Prudenciano found his bag and brought out his aloe vera jar. Rita returned with an old towel. "That will do nicely," Prudenciano said as he took it from her. He then cut it into long, narrow strips.

A knock on the door interrupted Prudenciano. Rita hurried across the room and opened it. Two women from the neighborhood greeted Rita and came in. Both of them said hello to Paz and were about to launch into a friendly discussion when one saw Prudenciano kneeling in front of Tomas examining the knee. "Rita, what's wrong with Tomas? Is this man a doctor?" asked one of the women.

"He is a *sobador*," answered Rita. "Tomas strained his back and knee today at work. Prudenciano relaxed his back so he could ride the wagon home. Tomas says that he is very good." The women watched Prudenciano with deep interest and fascination. Prudenciano did not look up as he continued his treatment. He broke the rubbery leaves and squeezed the pulp into his left hand. Then he rubbed the ointment into the joint as he massaged the knee. When he was satisfied with his work, he skillfully wrapped the knee securely with the towel strips, but in such a fashion as to allow the joint to flex.

"Damn, Prudenciano!" exclaimed Tomas as he stood up and tested his bandaged knee. "It feels great. *Gracias!*"

"My Diego could use your services," said one of the women. "His shoulder has never been the same after he fell from a horse. Maybe I can get him to come over here soon."

"*Sí.* I can think of several people in the neighborhood that could benefit by your skill," added the other woman. "But the main reason that we came over was to ask Paz if she could watch over our children, too. Our children enjoyed you so much today. We both work and have to leave them alone. It just kills me to do so, but we really have no choice. We can't pay you much, but we can give you some food for your troubles. Please, we would be so very grateful."

Paz turned to Prudenciano for his support. He responded by merely shrugging his shoulders. The decision would be hers alone. The idea of earning a little money and bringing food into this household appealed to her. Thus, she smiled back and nodded, "*Sí,* I would be happy to do it." Her simple agreement started her day care and Prudenciano's *sobador* business because these women were not known for their discreetness.

When Prudenciano reflected on it, he could not believe how fast the past three months had gone. It seemed like yesterday when Paz and he crested that last hill outside Torreón. Now he had a good-paying job since he had passed his probation, albeit it was mind-numbing and back-breaking work. He also made more money in the evenings when people sought his services to remedy wrenched backs and other aches and pains.

Prudenciano's thoughts shifted to Paz and he shook his head in disbelief. Families kept coming with their children for Paz to watch. She enlisted two older girls to help her watch the growing numbers of kids. The money and food that her services brought astounded him.

Who would have thought that Paz and her music would produce such a bounty. Their combined efforts allowed them enough money to move into a house of their own not far from the Martinez household.

The jostling of the wagon jarred him back to the present. He shook his head to clear his thoughts and looked around him. Tomas dozed by his side. The other men wore the same forlorn faces that Prudenciano had seen during his first ride up to the mine. He looked back over the city below. The trees were beginning to leaf and the smells of spring rose into the air. Of the wagon full of men, only he seemed to notice the rebirth of life occurring around them.

The wagons soon topped the hill and rolled to the mining office. As his cart stopped, Prudenciano nudged Tomas awake and jumped out to begin lining up. This time the mine boss came out of the office with Victoriano beside him. The two men were engaged in a heated discussion. Victoriano's fists were clenched in rage as he confronted Pontes. "The blast was wrong! Your powder monkeys shot too deep last night. We need to explore the cracks first before working on that level."

Pontes was a bull of a man. His thick neck bowed at Victoriano's comments. The veins in his massive head bulged out from his building anger. Through clenched teeth, he towered over Victoriano as he squared his shoulders and growled back, "That would take too much time and cut back production. I know you, Victoriano. You would peck at each crack for hours and accomplish nothing! We would lose an entire day's work from your scratching."

Victoriano was not fazed by Pontes's superior size. He tilted his head back and pointed his finger straight at the man. "You know it's not safe," responded Victoriano. "If you force me to take these men down, then you stand to have a mutiny on your hands if something goes wrong."

"Are you threatening me?" asked Pontes as he took a step forward. Victoriano just glared back at him without budging an inch. Pontes gave Victoriano a long, hard look and then turned to the gawking men standing around him. "Line up!" he barked. The men hesitated at first, but then slowly formed a line. They obviously sided with Victoriano. The boss read each name off the roster and every man responded grudgingly. Pontes formed the groups and sent them to their respective levels. Prudenciano's team assembled last.

Tomas walked by Prudenciano and spoke in a hushed voice, "Be very careful, *amigo*." Prudenciano grunted an acknowledgment and watched Tomas and his group enter the elevator platform. As the elevator began its plunge, Tomas never took his eyes off Prudenciano. His expression seemed to say, *Beware. Danger!*

Prudenciano turned to Victoriano and asked, "What was all that about?"

"One of the shaped charges misfired and exploded incorrectly," answered Victoriano. "It may have weakened the rock above the seam. That donkey's ass over there is more concerned with meeting his daily quota than the safety of the men." Victoriano's shoulders suddenly slumped forward. He looked tired and old. "They always think about the silver first," he mumbled half out loud. With a great effort, he picked up his tools and shuffled toward the elevator. The men grabbed their gear and followed him.

As they descended into the abyss, Victoriano seemed to recover and became his normally alert self. He constantly scanned the walls of the shaft as they drew closer to the bottom level. The men began to share his apprehensiveness and wearily studied the rocks around them. Finally, the platform reached their work level. The men automatically began to step off the elevator and move into the work area. "Stop where you are!" commanded Victoriano with a hiss like a rattlesnake that grabbed their attention. "No one moves until I have had a chance to check the rock." He turned to the elevator operator. "Better signal to them to hold until I clear the level." The man nodded, opened the protective metal box that contained the telegraph on the railing post, and tapped the order to hold.

Victoriano cautiously moved off the elevator with a pick in one hand and a lantern in the other. The lamp cast a flickering yellow light along the rock walls. He deliberately placed each foot carefully in front of the other as he slowly made his way around the empty ore carts and proceeded down the new corridor. Every so often he would stop and chip away at a fissure or some anomaly he detected along the ceiling. As he ventured down the tunnel, the glow of his lamplight began to wane. Soon, all the men could detect of his investigating was the sound of his pick testing the rock.

Prudenciano's sixth sense began to tingle up his spine. He knew danger lurked for his foreman. A warning surged within Prudenciano. "Quick. Give me that lamp!" He snatched it from a man and struck a match along the lamp base. He lit the wick and turned the flame up. The uneven light shimmered along the rock leading to the tunnel. Prudenciano swiftly trimmed the flame to steady the light, but the rock continued to vibrate.

"The rock is moving!" whispered a man next to Prudenciano.

"Everyone, get back!" shouted Prudenciano. 'Victoriano! Get out of there, now!' The sound of breaking glass shattered the silence within the tunnel as Victoriano threw his lantern aside and began to run. The entire ceiling started buckling and large cracks opened above. *He'll never make it*, thought Prudenciano. Hunks of rock began crashing down along the entire corridor. Within the rising dust and moving earth, he could just make out Victoriano fighting to make the entrance. Prudenciano looked down at the ore cart. Without thinking he bolted forward and grabbed it with both hands. With adrenaline-stimulated strength, he shot the cart down the collapsing tunnel. His legs churned beneath him as he drove ahead. The cart bounced back and forth among the fallen rock. He could barely see where he was going. Rocks struck glancing blows along his back and shoulders.

The cart struck the wall, tipped over onto its side, and continued sliding down the corridor before coming to a stop. Prudenciano stumbled and pitched forward. He took the fall on his shoulder and rolled into the bin. Miraculously, Victoriano blundered in beside him. Prudenciano's head bled profusely from multiple scalp cuts, but fear kept his mind clear. The earth fell thunderously around them. The stout metal of the ore cart bowed from unceasing pounding, but steadfastly protected the men inside. Prudenciano thought the deafening cave-in would never end.

As quickly as it started, the falling rock stopped and an eerie silence prevailed. They were now in total darkness and could not even see their hands in front of their faces. They inhaled dust with every breath, which caused them to cough.

"Are you all right?" rasped Prudenciano.

"*Sí,*" answered Victoriano. "Feel how much space we have around us." Prudenciano groped the top and sides of the cart. He could just make out a six-inch gap along the top edge. He shoved his arm through it and found a free space above, but his hand felt loose rock encapsulating the cart.

"I think there is a void above us. There is rock blocking the tunnel on both sides." Prudenciano's voice had a thin tremor of panic underlying it. Victoriano recognized it immediately and knew he had to contain it now. To be trapped underground was stressful enough without being confined with a madman.

Victoriano spoke in the darkness with a calm and logical sound. "Prudenciano, listen to me. We must preserve our air if we expect to be rescued. The men know that we are here. They will come. Now we must help each other through these next hours." He could hear Prudenciano mutter something unintelligible and shift around in the cramped quarters. Victoriano could sense that his breathing had slowed and he was gaining control of his fear. If they sat up against the opposite ends of the cart, they could just barely stretch out their legs. This was the best they could do under the circumstances. All they could do was wait. As he closed his eyes to rest, Victoriano allowed himself one last wild thought, *I wonder if my men survived?*

The elevator operator watched in horror as Prudenciano disappeared into the collapsing tunnel. "Damn fool! Hold on everyone! We're getting out of here!" He ripped the cover to the telegraph open with such force that it tore off from the box. A rumbling cloud of shot rock bellowed out toward them. He began tapping the striker in a rapid-fire motion without stop. The company's emergency retrieval code was an unceasing entry of dots. The operator had no problem adhering to this protocol. "Come on! Come on! Oh God!" Some of the men screamed as the flowing rock seem to engulf them and roll onto the platform. Suddenly, the platform shot upwards with such a wrenching force that everyone was flung to the floor. Earth filled the shaft below and the displaced air blew dust hundreds of feet upward.

Every man within the mine knew something had happened. The ground shook as if a blast detonated from below. Then the elevator looked like it was shot out of a cannon as it roared by with an expanding cloud of dust underneath it. Quickly, the dust infiltrated the upper levels and caused the workers to abandon their tasks. They all knew what had happened without discussing the situation. The lower level had collapsed.

When the elevator reached the surface, Pontes was there to meet it. The platform was covered with broken rock and dirt. The men were crazed with terror. He knew that only a cave-in would generate such hysteria. He searched for Victoriano to give him a status check. Then he realized that Victoriano and that other large man were missing. He thought, *Damn! There are men trapped below.* The implications extended much further than a couple of men dying. He would have to act quickly to minimize the potential of a worker rebellion. Pontes barked, "Everyone, get off the platform, now!"

The men spilled off the platform. Pontes grabbed the operator by the collar and threw him back. "Not you. Get back down there and start evacuating the levels!" The man shuffled toward the control box. His posture and demeanor exuded fear. He looked back to the boss in hopes that he would reconsider, but saw nothing that indicated that he had changed his mind. The operator sighed in despair and tapped a signal on the striker. The elevator quickly fell back into the dusty depths.

Pontes sent messengers to town to summon medical staff and, of course, notify the mine's management of the situation. When he was satisfied with these preparations, he began assembling the rescue teams. By now most of the men were removed from underground. Each foreman was taking roll call and accounting for his men. The mine went through the motions that they cared for every worker and were willing to expend a great deal of effort to recover the missing men, although management really viewed their men as expendable slaves. However, mutiny was disruptive and bad for business. Therefore, the mine had to at least make a good-faith effort to save their employees.

A call rang out for volunteers. Tomas Martinez stepped forward and was the first to be counted. A few others followed and, after much coaxing, Pontes recruited a full rescue team. He sent the rest of the men home in the wagons. There was no sense in having idle, troublesome men hanging around the mine.

The rescue team consisted of forty men. Each one was focused on re-covering the trapped miners in the shortest possible time. Pontes made a special note that none of rescue members were part of the lower-level team. *Whatever they saw must have scared the hell out of them.*

The first task was to open the elevator shaft to the original lower-floor level. This required implementing a dangerous process of lowering men and equipment on half a platform. Reducing the platform size allowed the men to move their equipment off the elevator once they reached the depth were the cave-in filled the shaft. The men would work off the half platform until they reached the lower level.

They removed part of the wooden flooring and stacked ore carts, tools, and a dozen men onto the remaining small perch. The dark void beneath the floor seemed to open its deadly mouth to swallow them. The platform tilted awkwardly to the loaded side. The men wore bandannas across their faces to filter dust from the air. Fear registered in every set of eyes that peered over their scarves, but no man balked at the job at hand. It was their love for their fellow man that strove them to continue. For Tomas, it was also the additional love for a friend that gave him the courage to dangle hundreds of feet above an abyss on a slanted, overloaded ledge.

"Okay. Send them down," ordered Pontes. After a little more than one hour after the cave-in, the rescue team began their first descent to the lower level. The elevator fell more slowly than usual because the load was unbalanced. The dust had settled somewhat, but it grew thicker with depth and obscured everyone's vision. The shaft was much darker than normal. One of the men lit a lamp and held it over the void. Even with this additional illumination, they could see only a few feet below.

The elevator fell at a constant speed for several minutes and then began slowing. The crane operator knew the depth of each level by the markings on the cable. Since he did not know the exact depth of the lower level, he had to be cautious. He also depended on the plat-form operator to signal when they sighted the floor. Men peered over the platform edge in anticipation of the bottom. Suddenly, they hit with a bone-jarring force. Nobody saw it coming. The men, already off balance, pitched forward and sprawled onto the rock. The crane operator saw the cable go slack and knew they hit hard. He quickly noted the depth. It was twenty feet shallower than before.

Tomas picked himself up and felt his guts convulse in terror. Total darkness completely enveloped them. The lamp had snuffed out on impact and absolutely no light filtered down to them. He could hear men moaning and swearing as they tripped over their equipment. He yelled, "Quickly, someone! Light anything. Just a match!" More fumbling, then he heard the unmistakable sound of a wooden match striking a rock. The feeble light looked like a beacon of hope as the floating dust made halos around its glow. Another man found a lamp and lit it with the same match. Order was beginning to return.

Within a few minutes, the men pushed the carts and tools off the elevator. The operator signaled that all was clear and the platform rose away. A second group of men established operations on the level above the rescue team. These men took the full carts of dirt from the excavation below and dumped them into a mined-out corridor. This process took careful and tedious coordination between the platform and crane operators, but proved to be effective, and the men moved large quantities of rock in a relatively short time.

After two and a half hours of nonstop back-breaking work, the men had removed enough rock to allow thirty men to work without hampering each other. The support team hung large ventilation tubes down the shaft to supply fresh air and remove the dusty remnants of the cave-in. To increase their efficiency, the men decided to dig in a slant to the collapsed tunnel. They started excavating directly above the tunnel entrance and move the rock away from their work. Tomas asked the platform operator what time it was. He was surprised to learn that it was 1 P.M.. Four hours had passed since the accident. *How much longer could they live?* he asked himself.

News about the cave-in spread like wildfire through southern Torreón. Rita left work as soon as she heard about the accident in the restaurant. She ran all the way to Paz's home, where she was tending to her day care business. Paz looked up from a circle of children to see a wild-eyed Rita gasping for breath with her hands to her breast. "Rita! What's wrong? Please tell me!"

Rita caught her breath, "Paz, have you not heard?" She gulped another lung full of air. "There has been a cave-in at the mine. The company is sending most of the men back home. Come! We must find out if our men are safe!"

"I can't just leave these children alone," quailed Paz. She felt her own anxiety rising. Rita was absolutely beside herself and the children could sense her terror. They started to wail and whimper.

One of the older girls that Paz had hired to help with the day care came forward and said, "Go, Paz. Rosemary and I will watch the kids. They will be safe." Paz produced a worried smile of thanks and followed Rita. They alternated between running and walking to the house of Don Luis Manos, People's Labor Agent for Torreón. Here, the wagons came and went daily to the mine. As Paz and Rita approached the house, they saw over a hundred people milling in front. Some were angry and demanded answers from Don Luis. Others were silent with fear.

Don Luis stood calmly on his porch with his arms folded across his chest. He listened to the crowd's demands, then shook his head and said, "Look. I know nothing more than you. The wagons will be here soon. Then we will be able to find out what has happened." Don Luis finally tired of the questioning and walked back into his front office leaving the angry crowd to wait in frustration. Once inside, Don Luis smiled and rubbed his hands together. *I hope there were a lot of men killed,* he thought. *Then I will collect much more recruitment fees.*

Rita and Paz started asking everyone there if they knew anything. The answer was always the same—nothing. They would have to wait with the others. Rita slumped down next to the house wall. She pulled up her knees and buried her head in her arms. Suddenly, her body racked with sobs. Paz bent down and put her arm around her. She spoke softly. "Rita. Don't worry. They will be fine. You'll see."

Rita wrenched herself away from Paz and lashed out, "You don't get it, do you? I have four young children. If Tomas is dead, what am I going to do? What man would have me with so many kids? You're different. You are young and pretty with no children. You can just pick up where you left off, so don't tell me everything is going to be fine!" Her words stung Paz like a slap to her face. Rita collapsed again and continued to sob. Paz got up and left her alone.

As Paz walked into the crowd, she began peering up the street toward the hills. Somebody shouted. The people began stir. Just then, the wagons rounded the corner and began coming down the street. "Give them room. Everyone. Get back." Few people heeded the warning. The horses had to weave through the multitudes before stopping in front of the house. Most of the men looked no worse for wear. However, the last wagon contained Victoriano's men. They stood out by their grimy faces and dust-covered clothing.

Relatives embraced each other. Wives cried as they held their husbands. Brothers and uncles slapped each other's backs. Over the crowd,

Rita's voice rose above with a chilling resonance, "Tomas! Tomas! Oh, God! Tomas! Where are you?" Everyone froze in their tracks.

One of Victoriano's men grabbed her by the shoulders to quiet her. "Tomas was not one of the men trapped in the cave-in. But he volunteered to go back down and try to rescue them," he said.

"But why would he put himself in such danger?" Rita asked, totally bewildered. By now Paz had walked up next to her. The man knew that this young woman next to Rita was Prudenciano's wife. He cursed himself silently for being the one who had to tell her.

The man replied, "Tomas went back down because his friend is one of the men trapped." Rita's eyes flew wide open with comprehension. She turned and looked at Paz. "That's right," continued the man, "Prudenciano was in the cave-in." Rita let out a moan. Paz felt like she was in a play, somehow unreal and unimportant. Prudenciano could not be trapped in the mine.

Paz faced the man with her brave chin lifted up. "How do you know this? Are you sure he just isn't with Tomas helping with the rescue?"

The man shook his head sadly. "No, *Señora*. I saw it with my own eyes. It was the bravest thing I have ever seen. As the tunnel started collapsing, he pushed a cart inside to save our foreman. That was the last we saw of him before we had to evacuate. We barely escaped with our lives."

Paz look down to the ground. Tears began to well up in her eyes. She had been brave too long. Rita put her arm around her. "I'm so sorry for my harsh words, Paz. I really didn't mean them. Come on, let's go home. They will send word to us when they know something." Rita led Paz down the street.

Don Luis heard the news from his porch. *Possibly only two men dead. Oh well,* he thought as he watched Rita and Paz walk back home. An evil smile formed on his lips. *Maybe I can still make a profit on Paz if everything works out.*

Prudenciano's own choking awoke him from a troubled sleep. His throat felt like the dust had crept down it while he slept. He desperately needed a drink. As he hacked, he involuntarily jerked his head up and smacked the top of the cart.

"Ouch!" came Victoriano's voice in the darkness. "That must've hurt."

Prudenciano recovered his breath. He rasped, "How long have we been here?"

Victoriano took out his pocket watch. It had luminous watch hands. "Um, let's see," he said, "Looks like its about five o'clock, so we have been here about eight hours. How are you holding up?"

Prudenciano replied, "I have to pee. Other than that, all right I guess."

Victoriano managed a quick laugh. "Well, if that's all then you are doing pretty good. Hold on for a little while longer. Then we'll deal with it the best we can." They waited in silence for a few minutes, then Victoriano continued. "Prudenciano, regardless what happens, I want to thank you for saving my life. If you hadn't pushed this cart in here, I would have been squashed like a bug." Victoriano let that sink in for a minute and then added, "Do you realize that if you had stayed with the others you would probably be safe? Why did you do it?"

Prudenciano could not answer him. He brooded over why he had acted so impulsively. He loved the attention of others and often tried to act the hero in front them, but this was much more than he had ever bargained for. Prudenciano hated what he was feeling now because, if the truth be known, he wished that he had just let Victoriano die.

Tomas refused to be replaced and worked alongside the second team. As he stretched a weary arm out to retrieve another boulder, the rock rolled a few inches away from him. Tomas blinked and thought his eyes were playing tricks on him. Just to be sure, he reached down and pushed on the rock. It gave under his pressure and slid back several feet, revealing a gaping hole. Tomas quickly slid down the small chute on his stomach and peered inside. "Quickly, somebody, give me a lamp!" A lamp was handed to him and he wiggled it into the crevice. The light revealed a tight void running along the top of the collapsed tunnel.

Tomas yelled out, "Prudenciano! Victoriano! Can you hear me?" Prudenciano and Victoriano lifted their heads and opened their eyes. They could see a feeble light peeking along the top of the cart. Prudenciano shoved his arm through the gap and waved it.

Prudenciano shouted back, "*Sí!* We're over here!"

Tomas heard Prudenciano and saw his arm at the same time. He wiggled back up and yelled to the workers, "They're alive! They live! *¡Dios mío!* Come on men! We got to get them out of there!" With renewed energy and purpose, the men redoubled their efforts. By seven o'clock that evening, Prudenciano and Victoriano stepped off the elevator platform on the surface and breathed the sweet night air.

The mining company had a doctor and first-aid equipment available. Oil lamps threw soft orange glows on the monstrous buildings and lit the night. The feeling was joyous and the entire rescue team smiled and laughed with each other. No one had died and everything ended well. The only grim-faced man in the crowd was Pontes.

He stepped forward as the doctor finished his examination of the men and addressed Victoriano. "Well, Vallejo. You just cost the mine a full day's production!"

Victoriano lowered his head in a submissive manner, but Prudenciano could see that there was fire in his eyes. Calmly, Victoriano said, "You know, a man can do a lot of thinking when he is trapped underground. And I think I know how to repay the company."

"Now how is that?" sneered Pontes with his hands folded in front of him in a show of defiance.

"Like this." Victoriano uncoiled and struck like a snake. His fist hit the man directly on the point of the chin. With his arms folded, Pontes could not block the blow. His head ripped backward and then snapped forward. For a second, the blow did not seem to faze him. Then slowly he teetered backward and fell with a resounding thud. Everyone stared in utter disbelief.

Prudenciano stood up and walked over to the fallen boss. He nonchalantly unbuttoned his fly and urinated on the man. He sighed with relief and said, "Finally got that chance to relieve myself. It never has felt so good!" Tomas bursted out laughing. Then everyone followed suit. Some laughed so hard they cried. Everyone enjoyed themselves so much that no one saw the two well-dressed men in the back slip away from the crowd and disappear into the night.

Tomas wiped the tears away from his eyes and said, "Come on, Prudenciano. Let's go home. We'll deal with him tomorrow." The wagons were waiting and the joyous men jumped aboard. As the wagons rumbled to town, the men sang songs. Victoriano retold the story of how Prudenciano saved him. Everyone cheered and made Victoriano retell it several times. The time flew quickly and before they knew it, they were entering the city limits. The wagons stopped in front of Don Luis's home.

The men unloaded noisily. Victoriano embraced Prudenciano and thanked him heartily. His laughing was cut off suddenly as he looked up and saw Don Luis standing on the front porch of his house eyeing him with brooding malice. Don Luis's eyes moved slowly from him to Prudenciano and he spoke with a voice as cold as ice. "So, Nava, you live."

"Sí. Much to your disappointment, I'm sure," replied Prudenciano.

Don Luis sneered down at him. "Remember what I said about causing trouble? If you start any upheaval at the mine, I can assure you that you will not be as lucky next time. Comprende?" Prudenciano just stared back him with hatred in his eyes. He did not like the undertones of this conversation. Was Don Luis threatening him?

Don Luis continued, "Vallejo, I think you have just come to the end of your rope, so to speak." Victoriano clenched his teeth, spun on his heels, and strode away.

"Forget him, Prudenciano," said Tomas as he led him away. "I bet our wives will give us a special welcome tonight, *¿qué no?* Let's go home." They turned and walked briskly down the street. Within a few minutes, they had forgotten Don Luis.

There were no lights on at Prudenciano's house so they continued a block further to Tomas's. There they found the home fully lit. "Hey everyone," said Tomas as he bounded through the door, "Look what I dug up." Prudenciano entered behind him. Rita let out a shriek and ran to Tomas. He grabbed her and hugged her hard.

Paz practically jumped into Prudenciano's arms. She couldn't quite get her arms around his torso, but she embraced him fiercely. Her face was buried into his chest. Suddenly, her whole body shook with sobbing convulsions. Prudenciano pushed her head back to reveal a terror-stricken little girl with tears streaming down her face. He was deeply touched by her concern. He wanted to tell her that he loved her, but found it hard to speak the words. So, he settled for a simple, "Did you miss me?"

Paz nodded and continued to hug him. "I thought I lost you," she whispered.

Prudenciano stroked her hair and said, "It would take a lot more to get rid of me. You know that." He continued to hold her and looked up to see Rita and Tomas. They looked like they were about to embark on a second honeymoon. Prudenciano nuzzled Paz and said, "Let's go home." He gently led her to the door. When he opened it, he noticed that neither Tomas nor Rita had looked up from their long passionate kissing. He chuckled and softly closed the door behind him.

The pounding on the door woke Prudenciano and Paz from their bed. Judging by the full daylight, they both knew that they had slept well into the morning. The knocks came again. This time Prudenciano got up, put his pants on, and shuffled to the door. His body was stiff and his joints ached. For an instant, he felt like he had just slept on the ground next to his horse at some distant *jaripeo*. He cracked the door open and peered outside. A man stood on the step with his sombrero held in his hand. Prudenciano recognized him immediately. He was one of the wagon drivers for the mine.

The old man addressed him. "*Señor* Nava, I have been told to come and bring you to the mine as quick as possible." The man was very uncertain about telling Prudenciano to do anything. His demeanor showed that he held Prudenciano in great respect.

Prudenciano opened the door all the way and faced the driver. He noticed that the wagon was parked next to the house. "Why me?" he asked.

The man shifted to his other foot and said, "There is trouble brewing with the men at the mine. The bosses think that you might be able to help."

Although this gesture bolstered his ego, Prudenciano could not help but wonder why he was chosen. He asked, "Where is Victoriano? He can handle any problem there."

The driver suddenly became very nervous. He leaned toward Prudenciano and said in a quiet voice, "Victoriano has disappeared. Nobody knows what happened to him. Please *Señor*, come with me. It will be better for all."

Victoriano is gone? thought Prudenciano, *Something is very wrong.* He looked carefully at the driver. He appeared sincere enough. Prudenciano thought about it some more and then came to his decision. "Did Tomas Martinez show up for work today?" The man shook his head. "Then we will first pick him up and the both of us will go to the mine with you. Wait here."

He shut the door and turned back to Paz. She wore one of his shirts and walked bare-legged to him. Relaxed with sleep, she leaned against him and asked, "What does he want?"

"I really don't know," he answered, "but I'm going to get Tomas to come with me and we are going back to the mine. The driver says that there is some trouble up there." Prudenciano gave her a reassuring hug and started to get dressed.

Paz watched him for a moment and then said, "You don't have to go. Stay here with me."

Prudenciano stopped dressing and shot her a look of annoyance. "The bosses asked for me to come. It must be important." Paz knew then that the real reason that he was returning to the mine was for self-satisfaction. He would never pass up a chance to look important. Within minutes, he was dressed and ready to leave. "I'll be back by dinner," he said as he opened the door and left without looking back.

The driver waited anxiously for him in the wagon. As soon as Prudenciano climbed onto the front bench, the driver snapped the reins and the horses moved forward. They continued down the street and halted in front of the Martinez home. Prudenciano jumped down and pounded on the front door. After a few minutes and more knocking, Tomas creaked the door open. "Prudenciano," he spoke with a heavy dry tongue. "What are you doing out of bed? I thought you would sleep the entire day."

"The mine bosses sent this wagon to fetch me," replied Prudenciano as he pointed with his thumb over his shoulder to the driver and the wagon team. "I want you to come also."

"But why? You don't need me."

Prudenciano then leaned toward Tomas and whispered in his ear, "Victoriano is missing. If you come, there is less chance that something will happen to me." The information jolted Tomas awake.

Tomas nodded his comprehension and said, "Just one minute. I got to tell Rita where I'm going." He closed the door. Within a short time, Tomas came out tucking his shirt into his pants. "Man, she is mad! I'll probably hear more about it tonight. ¡Vámanos!"

It was close to noon when the wagon started up the hill. They followed the well-worn road for a short distance. Then, without warning, the driver turned quickly onto an abandoned trail. Prudenciano became alarmed. He shot out his hand and grabbed the driver by the throat. He snarled, "What are you doing? Tell me now or I will break your scrawny neck!"

The man croaked, "Please, Señor!" He started choking as he tried to quickly explain, "They wanted me to take you here so you can meet with them in secret."

"You mean kill us in secret, you bastard!" hissed Prudenciano as he applied more pressure.

Suddenly, a voice boomed out, "Release him, Nava! He speaks the truth." Prudenciano looked up to see four men walking toward him. They strolled in pairs. The two older men were in front with two younger ones in back. They were well dressed. Each wore a fine black felt hat that matched his black leather vest. Their shirts were different colors, clean, well pressed, and accented by a bolo tie. Their boots were made from finely tooled leather and buffed to an exceedingly bright shine.

Prudenciano dropped his grip on the man. The driver responded by immediately gasping for breath and massaging his throat. Tomas leaned over to Prudenciano and spoke quietly through the side of his mouth, "Be careful, Prudenciano. A scorpion looks beautiful too." The men came up to the wagon and stopped. One of the older men waved for Prudenciano and Tomas to come down. They slowly dismounted while never taking their eyes off the four men. The working class frequently circulated stories of how the rich would dispose of a man at a mere whim and neither Prudenciano nor Tomas wanted to validate those rumors.

The dignified looking man spoke with the strength and confidence that reminded Prudenciano of his father. "Let me introduce ourselves. This is Francisco Bollas and I am Juan Trujillo. We own the silver mine. These young men are our sons. They…"

"They were at the mine when Victoriano Vallejo and I were rescued," said Prudenciano as he finished Juan's sentence.

Juan cracked a smile and said, "You are very observant. *Bueno.* Then you know about the unrest and bad feelings that the men harbor. That is why we want to talk with you and, I believe your name is Tomas Martinez. Correct?" Tomas nodded his head but kept silent.

Prudenciano squared his shoulders and looked Juan straight in his eyes. "Before we talk, I want to know what happened to Vallejo. Did you kill him?"

Both Francisco and Juan whipped their heads back like someone hit them. Obviously, the comment caught them unprepared. Francisco asked, "How do you know that Vallejo is gone?"

Prudenciano replied evenly, "I never said that he was gone."

Juan could tell that the conversation was not going the way he had planned. He immediately confronted Prudenciano. "Last night, we reassigned Vallejo to a mining operation close to Chihuahua. He and his family are on their way there as we speak. We did this because our sons tell us that he was becoming increasingly dissatisfied with our management. We felt that if we left him here he would incite a riot. Vallejo is an experienced miner and we thought it better to utilize him elsewhere."

Prudenciano thought that this explanation was plausible, but he was still wary. "Why do you want to talk with me?"

Juan answered without taking his eyes off him, "The men think of you as a hero. They are all talking about the way you pushed that ore cart into the collapsing tunnel and saved Vallejo. In addition, I hear you are a very good *sobador*. These men idolize you."

Prudenciano's ego was thoroughly pumped up by Juan's words. Tomas could actually see Prudenciano swagger under the compliments. Tomas thought, *I'll have to be his conscience.*

Juan continued, "I have come here to ask your advice on how to prevent a strike at the mine and bring contentment back to the men." This last comment completely collapsed Prudenciano's defenses. To have a rich man and important man ask him for advice boosted his pride and conceit higher than the mine's elevator building. Tomas shifted his weight to the balls of his feet and prepared to launch a barrage of reason into Prudenciano. Juan anticipated this and derailed Tomas's plans by adding, "Of course, we expect you, Martinez, to be Prudenciano's assistant to help him maintain peace, and we will pay you extra for this." Tomas rolled back to his heels. His words lodged in his throat.

Prudenciano's head tilted back as he straightened his back. He felt very important and wise. "I think you should have the mining boss take over Vallejo's job. This way the men will immediately see justice being done."

Juan nodded in agreement. "There is wisdom in what you say. Who would we get to fill the boss's old position?"

Prudenciano answered immediately, "Your son. He needs to learn the ropes anyway. *¿Qué no?*"

"*Sí*," replied Juan. "It seems that we were correct to seek your advice. We will do as you suggested. Now, I need you to go up to the mine before us and tell the men that these things will be done. We will follow you shortly and initiate the changes."

"One more thing," countered Prudenciano. "I want out of the bottom crew with no reduction in pay."

"Done!" proclaimed Juan. "You must go now. We will talk with you later today." Juan held out his hand and Prudenciano shook it. He was surprised at the firm grip the older man possessed. Juan released it and led his group back up the road where they had staked their horses.

When they were out of earshot, Francisco asked, "Do you trust him?"

Juan considered this for a moment and then replied, "No, not really, but I think he will serve us well for a while. Did you see the way he puffed up his chest when I paid him a few compliments? The man seeks recognition. Don Luis thinks Nava is a troublemaker. He even asked me if I wanted him killed. Well, Don Luis is a good judge of character, but I'm going to try and use him for a time. However, if Nava cannot be controlled, Don Luis can have him."

Prudenciano's wagon took another thirty minutes to reach the mine. As they drew closer, they heard men shouting. It took Prudenciano a minute to realize that something besides the men was amiss. Then he realized that no mechanical noise emanated from the milling plant and retorts. This meant that the entire mine was shut down. When the wagon swung around the first building, they saw most of the work force standing outside the elevator. Several guards on horseback were trying to restrain the crowd. The mood seemed ugly.

Someone in the mob recognized Prudenciano and Tomas coming up the road. Several yells rang out and the crowd's attention shifted to them. Someone shouted, "Prudenciano has come to join the strike!" Another said, "Let him speak!" Prudenciano could not believe that he was the center of attention. He awkwardly moved to the center of the wagon bed and stood up. From this vantage point, he could see over the top of all the mens' heads. In the back next to the elevator, he found the focus of the horde's anger. There stood Pontes with a black and blue lump on his chin and looking exasperated among the confusion. Prudenciano made a point of catching his eye before he spoke to the men.

"My *amigos*," he began. "I share your outrage for this mine's lack of concern for our safety. Tomas and I have just met with the owners of this mine. They assured us that there will be some changes. For starters, Juan Trujillo's son will be the new mine boss and you," Prudenciano pointed over the crowd toward Pontes, "will lead the bottom team." The men cheered.

Prudenciano spread his hands to silence the men and continued, "Trujillo assured me that Victoriano is alive and well. They have sent him to Chihuahua to oversee a mining operation there. Now, I want everyone to load into the wagons and go home. Tomorrow is a big day. After all, we have a new bottom team foreman to break in." The men guffawed. This was the ultimate joke. Many things could happen to man in the lowest reaches of the mine. Pontes had his work cut out for him if he wanted to survive. Prudenciano smiled as he saw Pontes pale at his future prospects.

The men jumped into the wagons. Everyone had a sense of accomplishment. They had forced the management to amend their ways. Sending Pontes to the bottom of the mine was icing on the cake.

The four men watched from a nearby hilltop as the wagons pulled away. "Nava did it," proclaimed Francisco. "The men are leaving without destroying the mine."

"*Sí*," replied Trujillo, "he can be useful. Well, we will see." As the wagons made their way down the road, the four men looked down upon the wagon train as they sat on their fine horses. They were hidden behind some brush at a distance of at least a half mile. However, no one had trouble picking Prudenciano out of the crowd with his large frame perched on the front bench of the lead wagon. They all felt a deep chill when for some unexplained reason Prudenciano turned in his seat and looked at them. They all thought at once, *How did he know?*

———

Life gradually returned to normal at the silver mine. Production was up. The men's bravado slowly dissipated into the day-to-day realization that they would never leave the mine. The junior Trujillo quickly learned the ropes and proved to be a fair and just manager. Prudenciano enjoyed his improved working conditions in the upper mining levels.

Don Luis still sent up new recruits. One of the new conscripts was a middle-aged man from Zacatecas. Like many new employees, management assigned him to work on the bottom level. He kept to himself and did whatever task Pontes ordered. He was puzzled why so many of the men ignored Pontes or made fun of him. Finally, after being bombarded with insults, Pontes lashed out, "I am the boss down here. Nava can't protect you when you are with me!" The ribbing stopped, but the men still did not follow his orders.

During the following lunch, the new man broke his silence. He leaned toward one of the men and asked quietly, "Who is this Nava?"

The other man answered, "Prudenciano Nava. He saved our last foreman from a cave-in that Pontes said would never happen. Nava speaks to the management from time to time when we need attention to a matter."

The new man contemplated this for a moment and then asked, "Is this Nava from Zacatecas?"

"Why yes, I think he is. Do you know him?"

"If it's the same Prudenciano Nava that I know," replied the man, "then you have one of the best *colleadores* in the country working in your mine! If you see him, tell him that Luis Cato is here."

Within a few days, word swept through the mine that Prudenciano was a famous *jaripeo* star. Prudenciano finally received word that Cato was at the mine and tried to find him after work, but the bottom-level team had a different shift than he. Prudenciano resorted to sending an invitation back through the grapevine for Luis to come to his house in the evening.

That night, Luis came to visit after dinner. He brought a bottle of tequila to help with the evening's discussion. Paz gave Luis an annoyed glance. She had so far dissuaded Prudenciano from drinking since they arrived in Torreón. Now she felt that Luis had let the genie out of the bottle. Once Prudenciano tasted the liquor, he was apt to seek out more.

Paz stayed in the background darning clothing, but she could clearly hear the conversation. The lantern that hung from the ceiling painted the men with a flickering yellow glow. They both sat around the wooden table with the bottle in the middle. Prudenciano was both intrigued and happy that Luis had searched for him. Paz listen to the friendly banter when the mood suddenly changed as Prudenciano asked, "So, why did you leave Zacatecas and part from Anastacio Currandas?"

Luis looked into his mug for a long time before answering. "There are two reasons," he finally said. "First, I was there when that bull crushed Tereso Rodriguez to death. Tereso was one of the best in the business and he still got killed. It started me thinking that no matter how careful I was, I could die very easily in the ring." Prudenciano responded with intense silence. Getting no reply, Luis continued, "Then came the typhus epidemic that swept through the mountain lands." Paz looked up from her sewing in horror. Prudenciano increased the grip on his cup. "It hit first in Jeréz, then spread to the surrounding communities. I thought it was time to leave while I was still alive. Anastacio understood. He said that if I ever found you to tell you that he will always remember you."

Silence descended upon the room and allowed each to brood about a particular concern. Paz wondered if her mother and half-brother and sisters were alive. Prudenciano questioned if his elderly father could survive such an outbreak. Luis cursed himself for having to deliver such morbid news to this household.

The conversation slowly dried up and Luis graciously excused himself to leave for the night. When they were alone, Paz sat down in Prudenciano's lap and held him tightly. She whispered to him, "Do you think our family is all right?"

Prudenciano had seen typhus sweep through a village before. It was nonselective and its fierce fever left its survivors marked for life. He took a deep breath and said, "To be honest with you, there is no way to tell. I suppose we will hear sooner or later if they made it." As he held Paz and stroked her hair, his inner eye activated and flashed the same vision he had on the church steps in Valparaiso. Abundio and the two young girls looked like refugees from some distant war. Then the vision was gone. Paz could feel his body tighten and breathing quicken.

"What is it?" she asked. Prudenciano just shook his head as he suddenly understood the meaning of his vision. How could he tell her that most of her family was dead?

Although the *Cinco de Mayo* holiday was two weeks away, the men were busy planning for a grand celebration. The highlight of the celebration was a *jaripeo* to be held in nearby Gómez Palacio. The men pleaded with Prudenciano to represent the mine in the *Colleada*. He steadfastly refused. When the young Trujillo asked him to come to his office and talk with him, he had a hunch that the management wanted to persuade him, too.

Trujillo sat in a leather chair with a high back behind a solid oak desk. His office was neat and clean. There was no trace of the dust that permeated the mine. Prudenciano felt that his mere presence defiled the wooden floor he stood on. Trujillo tried to offer him a chair, but Prudenciano refused and preferred to stand. The young man stared at him for a moment while he twirled a pencil in his hand. "Did you know that my father posts a rather large wager on the *jaripeo* held at Gómez Palacio every year?" Prudenciano did not reply, but stared back at the man. Trujillo sighed and continued, "He lost last year to the team from Lerdo. My father not only lost a fair sum of money, but he felt his reputation had been tarnished. He always boasts of having the best *jaripeo* team in Durango." Trujillo leaned across the desk toward Prudenciano to accent his desire, "Nava, my father wants you to compete in this year's *Cinco de Mayo jaripeo*. He would consider it a special favor. One that he is most willing to compensate you handsomely for."

Prudenciano was deeply stirred by the offer from such an important man. The chance to impress many people was just too irresistible to refuse. "Why not?" shrugged Prudenciano. Trujillo smiled and leaned back in his chair. "However," continued Prudenciano, "I need a few things first."

Trujillo thought, *I knew it*. He got out a paper pad and a pencil. "All right, what do you need?"

Prudenciano straightened his back and pursed his lips for a second and then replied, "I need two good horses with well-fitted saddles. I must have the rest of the time off with pay to practice. Next, I require Tomas Martinez and Luis Cato to assist me during this time period, with pay, of course."

"Is that all?" asked Trujillo. He knew Prudenciano was keeping the best for last.

"Just one more thing. If I win, I get two hundred pesos for my time."

Trujillo shook his head as he finished writing the last demand and said, "You drive a hard bargain, Nava. But I think my father will approve. In fact, consider it done. You can practice at our ranch north of town. You and your friends can come over tomorrow morning and we'll assign two horses to you. Martinez knows the way." Prudenciano nodded, turned, and started to leave, but Trujillo's voice halted him. "Nava, my father wants you to win. *Comprende?*"

Prudenciano thought, *Is he warning me?* He answered, "I usually do." Then he opened the door and strode out.

That night, Prudenciano excitedly told Paz about the deal he had made with Trujillo. Paz had mixed emotions about Prudenciano returning to the ring. She was happy that he was not working underground, but competing in the *jaripeo* presented other dangers. The bulls were deadly, but the perils of the *parrandas* were just as frightening to Paz. She disliked the types of men and women that were attracted to such events. Therefore, she made it known to Prudenciano that she was going to attend the *jaripeo* in Gómez Palacio. Prudenciano grimaced when Paz told him of her intent, but one look at her eyes told him that the manner was settled.

Prudenciano then reached up and got his hat. Paz asked with a puzzled look on her face, "Are you going somewhere?"

"*Sí*," answered Prudenciano with one hand on the door handle. "I've got to convince Luis Cato to be my partner. He is almost as good as. . ." Prudenciano caught himself before he could say his long-lost friend's name. He thought, *It still hurts.* Without another word, he put on his hat and went out into the night.

The next morning Tomas, Luis, and Prudenciano headed for the Trujillo ranch. They walked north at a brisk pace. They quickly strode through the heart of the city and gradually entered the more wealthy sections. Soon they encountered the manicured lawns and cultivated pastures of the ruling class. Tomas pointed to a large home on a hill and said, "There is the Trujillo ranch."

The ranch had a paved road leading up to a large mansion. A white rail fence surrounded the land and bordered both sides of the driveway. As they started up the road, they passed through a black iron archway with the Trujillo crest of arms sculptured on top. It struck Prudenciano how different his life was compared to that of the Trujillo family. He doubted that they ever had to worry about shelter, food, or poor working conditions. He brooded on these thoughts until he saw a man riding a horse down the road to meet them.

"*¡Hola!*" the man greeted them. "You must be the men from the mine. I have been expecting you. Come. I will show where you will be training." He dismounted and walked with them up the road. Just before they got to the house, he led them to a trail that went around the home and to a stable in back. Inside were two well-bred geldings, all brushed and well cared for. Prudenciano admired the animals as he walked around them, stroked their glossy coats, and inspected their hooves. *They would do nicely.*

Then he noticed the two saddles that straddled the stall partitions. They were made of finely tooled leather. The pummel was graciously spaced in front of the seat to allow for plenty of room to maneuver. *Sí. First class all the way.*

Prudenciano straightened up and asked the servant, "Where do we train?" The man pointed to the back of the stable. The men stepped outside and saw the training corral. It was a circular field enclosed with a rail fence. A chute and holding pens were available on the far side. "*Bueno*," said Prudenciano. "For the next three days, we will train by ourselves. However, by the fourth day we will need some animals to practice on. Nothing fancy. A couple of steers will be fine." The servant nodded, wished them luck, and left.

The training started in earnest. Prudenciano immediately barked orders to Tomas and Luis. Within a short time, they saddled the horses and brought them out to the corral. Tomas did any task required to help with the training. Luis practiced pacing himself in front of

Prudenciano in mock matches. Prudenciano rehearsed riding fast and stretching out low to the ground.

On the fourth day, the servant brought two steers to the holding pen. Tomas readied the chute and released one for Luis to attract and lead. Prudenciano's first attempt was perfect. He threw the steer in one quick, fluid motion. His old instincts were coming back. By May 4, Prudenciano had thrown real bulls with consistent efficiency. They were ready.

—•••—

The *Cinco de Mayo* celebrated the defeat of French forces at the Battle of Puebla on May 5, 1862. Although the French eventually defeated the Mexican army, the *Batalla de Puebla* became a symbol of Mexican unity and patriotism. Mexicans, rich or poor, enthusiastically observed this holiday with at least three days of parties, *mariachi* dancing, parades, and *jaripeos*.

Sadly, even though *Cinco de Mayo* brought the economic classes together for celebration, it actually exacerbated the rift between the rich and the working class. On September 16, 1821, about three hundred years after the arrival of Cortes, Mexico finally shed the yoke of Spanish rule. However, foreign interests and internal strife tore the economic fabric of the country. The Mexican-American War of 1846-48 left the country financially devastated and conceding nearly half of its territory to the United States. On July 17, 1861, President Benito Juarez temporarily suspended all foreign debt payments for two years. Juarez promised to resume payments after this period. His decree angered England, Spain, and France. They simultaneously launched independent invasions of Mexico with the intent of procuring payment by conquering land. After a tumultuous period, England and Spain eventually withdrew, but the quest to establish another French empire consumed Napoleon and he persisted in his advance.

Commanded by General Ignacio Zaragoza, about five thousand poorly equipped Mestizo and Zapotec Indians defeated the French army at the *Batalla de Puebla* on the fifth of May. The defeat incensed Napoleon and he committed more forces to his captured stronghold at Vera Cruz.

Meanwhile, the conservative political movement within the major cities of Mexico were secretly assisting Napoleon. The conservatives consisted of prominent members of the Roman Catholic church, military, and large landowners. Numerous among them were the Creoles who were Mexican citizens of Spanish descent. The conservatives wanted large land holdings returned to the Church that President Juarez had nationalized. They believed that their only hope to reestablish their once unchallenged economic status was in European intervention. After all, the Spanish had recognized the necessity of a noble few ruling the impoverished and down-trodden majority. It maintained stability.

With this help, Napoleon captured Mexico City in 1864. Napoleon chose Maximilian of Hapsburg, younger brother of Emperor Franz Josef of Austria, to rule the new French territory. Maximilian proved to be an inept monarch with no aptitude to be a ruler. Within a very short time, he managed to alienate every political alliance. He angered his conservative backers by refusing to rescind Juarez's liberal reforms. Then to completely cut himself off from the Mexican people, he treated the working class ruthlessly. Mexicans responded by unrelentingly harassing the French troops. Ex-president Juarez and General Porfirio Díaz led a successful campaign of guerrilla warfare. Napoleon eventually tired of trying to maintain his newly acquired province and began withdrawing his support.

Maximilian sent his wife, Carlota, to Europe to plead for continued backing. She met in vain with the Pope and Napoleon. When word came that Mexico City was soon to fall back into Mexican hands, she launched a frantic, desperate plea for help to anyone who would listen. Alas, no one would lift a finger to help. In 1867, France received information that Juarez had executed Maximilian by firing squad at Queretaro. By this time, Carlota had driven herself into a neurotic frenzy and the news of her husband's death pushed her into the hazy realm of insanity.

Benito Juarez reestablished himself as the president of Mexico. However, in 1872, Juarez died of a heart attack. Juarez's vice pesident, Sebastian Lerdo de Tejada, assumed the presidency. Shortly after, Lerdo de Tejada faced civil unrest. Pofirio Díaz overthrew the government and appointed himself president on November 29, 1876. Díaz quickly became addicted to power and eventually replaced his predecessor's democratic ideas with dictatorial policies. He ensured his tenure by empowering the rich, placing faithful military followers into governor seats, and assigning high-level government positions to family members. With the army and police at his disposal, he ruled over the working class with an iron fist. Thus, the gulf between rich and poor grew even wider.

Rita and Paz sewed the finishing touches to their dresses for the upcoming folk dancing. Paz had never owned a party dress before and she was absolutely beside herself with joy as she stopped to admire her work. Rita had tailored the top of the dress to fit snugly along her slim body. A ruffled collar enhanced the yellow fabric, but the flowing skirt made the dress magnificent. It contained hoops of color that surrounded the entire skirt. When a dancer twirled it, it produced rapid shimmers of blue, red, and green that resembled the spinning spokes of a wheel. Paz and Rita planned to dance barefooted because they could not afford matching shoes. This did not detract from their enjoyment because most of the women at the dance would be dressed similarly.

Rita looked up from her sewing and said excitedly to Paz, "Let's try them on and practice our dance!" Paz giggled delightedly as she slipped out of her clothes and into her dress. Rita joined her. They had to help each other with the buttons along the back of the new dresses. When they were done, they stepped back and appraised their work. The dresses transformed them into stunning creatures. The design hugged their slender bodies and flared at the hips to produce a curtain of color. "We look beautiful! Don't you think?" Paz nodded in agreement. She was too awed to speak.

"Now," continued Rita, "do as I do." Rita lifted her right hand over her head, arched her back, and held her skirt with her left. She then proceeded to twirl and dance. Her dress responded by floating and flashing colors in step with her movements. Paz watched with earnest for a few moments and began to mimic Rita's steps. Within a short time, the two women were gracefully dancing in unison. Like their husbands, they too were ready for tomorrow's celebration.

—◆—

The *Cinco de Mayo* celebration started with a parade down the city streets of Torreón. Musicians, clowns, horse drawn displays, and firecrackers filled the plazas with noise and fun. Everyone came to enjoy the holiday, young and old, rich and poor. It was time to forget your troubles and loosen your inhibitions.

Most of the activities were centered around the town square. Prudenciano and Paz walked to the square together. She carried her new dress and would change with Rita when the dancing began. Her intent was to first enjoy the festivities with her husband. She left him for a few minutes to store her dress. When she returned she saw that he had found friends and liquor. He was so engrossed in his story telling that he had forgotten that Paz existed. Dejected, she mingled among the crowd in hopes of finding someone she knew. Within a few minutes, she heard someone calling her. She turned and saw a couple of mothers of the children that frequented her day care. Paz waved back and quickly joined them. When she told them what happened to Prudenciano, both women just laughed. "Men can act like little boys sometimes," said one woman with a voice of authority.

"It usually amounts to nothing, but you have to make sure that they don't get into trouble."

Paz glanced back to where Prudenciano was standing. He was surrounded by men who seemed to hang on his every word. "*Sí*. I guess there is nothing wrong with telling stories, but when he drinks, bad things happen. I think I will hang around here until the dance starts."

The two women nodded their understanding. "That's probably a good idea. Well, we will be watching you at the dance. *Adios*." As they left, one said secretly to the other, "What does she see in him anyway?"

Paz spent the time visiting the vendors that surrounded the square. From time to time, she glanced over to Prudenciano. She frowned with concern as she saw how much he was drinking. Workers put the final touches to the performing stage in the middle of the square. The frame consisted of rough-cut timbers, but the floor was smooth and polished. The platform elevated the performers four feet above the crowd. The edges of the deck were adorned with bright colored ribbons.

The dance must be starting soon, thought Paz. *I should start getting ready*. She looked back to Prudenciano and saw that he was going nowhere. Satisfied, she retrieved her dress and went to the back of the stage. There were already several women there in various stages of preparation. Rita was among them and had just slipped into her dress.

"Paz. You are just in time. Please help," asked Rita. Paz helped her button the back. Then Rita assisted Paz with hers. They brushed their hair back and used a brooch to pin their hair into a bun. Rita smiled at Paz and reached into a nearby box. She produced two beautiful orchids. "Compliments of the City. They will look gorgeous in our hair, *¿que no?*" They carefully pinned the flowers behind their ear. When they were finished, they stood back and admired each other. They looked truly stunning.

The program announcer was a distinguished older man. He wore a tight-fitting suit and polished pointed boots. He stood on the stage and shouted last-minute commands to the *mariachi* players who lined up along the bottom of the platform. The musicians wore matching costumes that consisted of a black vest and pants, white shirts with red ties, and black sombreros with bright sequins. The announcer held his megaphone to his mouth and cried out in a loud voice, "Everyone. May I have your attention, please. We have some of the most beautiful women in all of Torreón to dance for you. Please welcome them!"

He motioned for the music to start. They began playing a familiar folk tune of the area. The music gave a lively mood to the crowd. All heads turned toward the stage as the women twirled onto the floor. Their dresses flashed colors as they spun on their toes. They swayed to the music and bowed their backs.

Prudenciano abruptly stopped in the middle of one of his stories and looked up to the stage. "*¡Dios mío!*" exclaimed a man next to him as he pointed toward the stage, "Look at the small one next to the end. Damn! What a beauty she is." It took a full second for Prudenciano to recognize the figure on the platform. It was Paz. He sucked in his breath. His mind filled with strong, conflicting emotions—pride for how beautiful she was, anger for the hungry thoughts flowing through the men around him, love for his wife, and jealousy for her sudden limelight. The liquor he had consumed energized his unrest. He felt like he was about to snap. All he needed was for someone to pull his trigger.

By the second dance, the audience was cheering and clapping to the music. The women were performing with fluid, synchronous movements. They effectively entranced every man in the square. Then, unknowingly, the man next to Prudenciano pulled the trigger. "Man, what I wouldn't give to have that small one!" he said. The liquor had oiled Prudenciano's well-muscled machinery. He unleashed a very satisfying blow into the man's face. He crumpled to the ground.

A man yelled, "Hey! Why did you do that?"

What the hell? thought Prudenciano and he decked that man, too. Two men jumped on Prudenciano and tried to wrestle him. He stripped both off and threw them to the ground. Another man leaped at Prudenciano. Prudenciano caught him by the neck and punched him with his free fist. Several men loyal to Prudenciano stepped forward and met the next charge. Within seconds, a melee erupted within the crowd.

As Prudenciano battled, he noticed another fight occurring close to the stage. One of the men looked familiar. Then he recognized him. It was Tomas. Apparently, Prudenciano was not the only man having problems with his wife dancing on the stage.

Screams from women came from the stage and the crowd. The clamor of the fight rang in Prudenciano's ears. He lashed out as fast and hard as he could. Faces seemed to blur. Suddenly, several loud gun blasts fired from the stage. Momentarily, all fighting stopped. The announcer had returned with a shotgun and shot harmlessly into the air. He stood boldly in front of the crowd as he worked the action to pump another shell into the chamber. "Enough!" he roared. "Break it up now, or I'll blow your heads off!" He looked like he meant it. Everyone released their hold on each other. The man continued, "I don't care who started it, but it ends now. The dance is over. I want everyone to go home. Tomorrow is another day."

The crowd moaned and began to break up. Prudenciano dusted

himself off and strode over to where he had last seen Tomas. He found him massaging his chin by the stage. Blood trickled from his nose. Tomas asked, "Well, Prudenciano. Did you hear the same comments about your wife that I did?"

Prudenciano replied, "*Sí*. There is only so much a man can take." Their backs were turned to the stairs leading from the stage. Rita abruptly appeared from behind and savagely tore into Tomas. She looked like a wildcat filled with rage.

"Tomas!" she shrieked, "How could you wreck my show?" Her wrath silenced them. Paz came quickly behind Rita. Although she was more restrained, the men could tell that she was seething, too.

Paz spoke evenly, but with very angry undertones, "Do you know how long it took Rita and me to sew our dresses? Why is it, Prudenciano, that you have to drink and fight at gatherings?" She did not wait for a response. She and Rita stormed off together, leaving the men standing speechless in the thinning town square.

———•••———

The *jaripeo* at Gómez Palacio was a grand affair. The arena was spacious, which allowed easy maneuverability for the horses and their riders to perform their event. Spectators were seated in wooden grandstands that surrounded the fenced field. The chutes were designed to simultaneously release animals and riders side by side.

The *jaripeo* lasted most of the day. Calf roping and horse riding competition occurred in the morning. As the day wore on, the events became progressively more dangerous. This was purposely done to maintain the crowd's interest. Bronco riding and steer wrestling were scheduled in the afternoon. The grand finale in the late afternoon was the *Colleada*.

The team from the Torreón mine had done well through the *jaripeo* so far. They unexpectedly won the bronco riding, but to no one's surprise lost the horse-riding competition. When all points were tallied, the mine closely trailed a team from one of the largest ranches in northern Torreón. The ranch owner was an archrival of Juan Trujillo. The *Colleada* would decide the winner.

Prudenciano scanned the bleachers for Paz and Rita. He found them sitting rigidly on the benches and sighed. Both had given their husbands a cold shoulder and silent companionship during the previous night and all today. The mine had sent a wagon to carry the Navas, Martinezes, and Luis Cato to the *jaripeo*. The women frosted the air around the men during the entire trip. Now they showed total indifference to the upcoming event.

Prudenciano shifted his gaze toward the judges' box. Inside he recognized Juan Trujillo and Francisco Bollas watching him preparing for the upcoming match. Trujillo gave him a slight nod of acknowledgment. Prudenciano grunted and reciprocated the gesture. Prudenciano had no doubt that Trujillo expected him to win and there might be dire consequences if he did not, but this did not trouble him. He reveled in being the center of attention and made a show out of adjusting his equipment and bossing Luis and Tomas around.

The heat of the day began to dissipate as the late afternoon sun threw low-angle shafts of yellow light through the stadium. The bulls were ready in their holding pens. The men and their horses found their positions. The *Colleada* was ready to begin. Each team would compete twice and the judges would select the winner with the most points from their combined performances. By rules of the festival, the teams with the lowest scores went first and progressively continued until the first-place team competed last. Prudenciano and Luis would be the fourth team to compete. The leaders would perform fifth.

The crowd warmed to the occasion and as their excitement rose, their inhibitions waned from the enormous consumption of tequila. Entire sections of the stands stomped their feet in anticipation. A thundering noise resulted and cascaded onto the field. The bulls stirred nervously in their pens.

A judge signaled for the first bull to enter the chute. The crowd momentarily paused and watched as the holding pen's gate slid up. The bull immediately bolted forward and began to follow the twisting maze into the chute. He quickly found the entrance, jumped into the box, and fired down the ramp. As the bull shot out of the chute, the crowd roared in exhilaration.

A hapless young man was waiting to attract the bull. Between the roar of the crowd and the ferocity of the bull, he froze in his tracks. The bull ran unchecked straight into the horse. The poor animal and its rider were instantaneously pulverized. The boy lived, but with many broken bones.

The next two teams had varying degrees of success. Each finally threw their bull, but not after endless cat-and-mouse chases where the wary bull whirled and chased each team member around and around the arena.

Of course, all of this was good news to Prudenciano. If he could throw two good bulls, his team would win. He readied his horse and sat poised at the starting gate. Luis brought his gelding into the middle of the field directly in front of the chute. His left hand held the colored flags. Luis raised them high to signal to the judge that he was ready. Everyone leaned forward in anticipation. Word had gotten around that these two men were the very best in the sport.

Paz and Rita were caught up in the moment, too. They momentarily put aside their resentment and watched in fascination as the bull was readied. Although Paz had heard plenty of stories from Prudenciano about his *jaripeo* days, this was the first time that she had actually seen the event. The first match had unnerved her. The next two showed her that a bull could be thrown by his tail, but it was a very dangerous venture. She crossed herself and said a silent prayer for Prudenciano's protection.

The judge gave the handlers a nod. The bull launched into the chute and came crashing down the ramp. Luis held his horse until the very last second. Then he bolted forward with his flags waving in back. The bull totally committed to the charge. Luis began riding toward the far rail. He rode at just the right speed to infuriate the bull and keep his interest.

Suddenly, the crowd emitted an enormous roar as Prudenciano burst out of his gate. He rode with his weight up on the horse's front shoulders and flattened his body along the neck. This allowed the horse to accelerate up to top speed without its lower back and leg muscles being hampered by the rider. Prudenciano rode like he was just shot out of the gates of hell. His hat blew off his head and his thick black hair streamed behind him. His eyes focused on the bull's tail like a hawk diving for a mouse. He wore a thin smile, which proclaimed that he loved every millisecond of this event.

Prudenciano hung low to the right side and reached out for the tail. Luis began turning and riding dangerously close to the fence. As he kicked his horse in the ribs to urge it faster, his right knee struck a fence post. He heard the distinct sound of crunching bone. Luis clenched his teeth to keep from yelling out and rode on. Prudenciano snatched the bull's tail and yanked it up. Simultaneously, he spurred his horse forward. The bull immediately responded by bunching up onto his front legs. As the horse blew by, the bull somersaulted forward and fell resoundingly onto his back.

The crowd clamored its approval. Men threw their hats into the air and jumped up and down on the stands so hard that its foundations threatened to break. For most of them, this was the most perfect toss they had ever seen. Paz and Rita were leaping with joy. All past transgressions were forgiven. Even Trujillo and Bollas congratulated each other.

Prudenciano soaked up all the praise as he rode out of the arena. His exhilaration ceased as soon as he saw the pain on Luis's face. "Cato. What's wrong?" he asked.

"I screwed up," wheezed Luis through his teeth. "I struck the fence with my knee. Damn, it hurts bad. Very bad." Prudenciano could tell by the way Luis dismounted that he had broken something. Luis hopped on his left leg to the fence and sat down. Prudenciano immediately rolled up Luis's pant leg and examined his knee. It was swelling before his eyes and already turning black and blue. Prudenciano knew that he would not be competing any more tonight. He would need a new partner.

The first-place team readied themselves. Despite the last spectacular throw, they showed complete confidence. Both men sat tall and straight in their saddles, totally committed to their task. The flagger signaled to the judge that he was set. The bull came out of the chute with a half-hearted trot. Every now and then, a bull entered the ring with no interest in playing games with men. Some were cowards. Others were simply passive and did not care who or what shared their domain. This bull was the latter and he presented an easy target.

The *colleador* galloped out of his gate and promptly threw the bull. It was all over in a few seconds. Prudenciano was stunned. It was a legal throw, no matter how unfair. He knew that the overall time was far superior to his own. Shouts and boos of displeasure rang out from the crowd. The judge shook his head, but awarded the full points. The team was still in first place. The only bright spot was that the other teams forfeited and would not be competing in the last match. The last two teams would compete for the championship.

Prudenciano searched quickly for a substitute and spotted Tomas adjusting the saddles on the horses. Prudenciano took one look at him and knew that he was the best that he could find under the circumstances. Prudenciano pointed at him and ordered, "Tomas, saddle up. You will replace Cato."

Tomas whipped his head back in surprise, pointed his finger at himself, and mouthed, "*Me?*"

Prudenciano replied, "*Sí*. You! Now get ready. We are next." Tomas was scared. He had watched Prudenciano and Luis practice over the last weeks, but he had never participated. He cursed himself and began to get ready. Tomas knew that it would be futile to argue with Prudenciano now. Besides, he was the next logical choice.

Tomas walked over to Luis and took his flags. Then he leaned down to him and asked, "Luis, any advice?"

Luis just shook his head as he held his bent knee, "Just stay in front of the bull. Whatever you do, don't freeze and pray that Prudenciano tails him quickly."

Tomas shook his head and stood back up. As he walked over to his horse, he muttered, "How does Prudenciano get me into these things?" He swung on to his horse, wrapped the reins around his left hand, and held the flags in his right. A couple of men opened the gate, and a very frightened Tomas rode into the arena.

Paz and Rita were chattering like birds to each other when they heard that the next match was beginning. As they turned to watch, they both realized that something was different. Rita was the first to recognize Tomas. She put her hands to her mouth to muffle her cry of horror. "That's Tomas! There must be some mistake!" Paz was flabbergasted, too. She could tell by the way Tomas slouched over his saddle that he was very unsure of himself. Previous matches had showed her that men who lacked confidence usually suffered dearly in this sport.

Paz tried to comfort Rita. "Rita, Luis must of have been hurt. Don't worry, Prudenciano will protect him."

But Rita would not listen. She stood up and screamed, "Somebody stop him! He doesn't know what he is doing! Oh, no! Somebody please stop him!" However, the cacophony of the crowd overwhelmed her pleas. A man grabbed her from behind and forced her to sit down. She resorted to clinging to Paz and crying hysterically. When the judge signaled to release the bull, Rita buried her head into Paz's shoulder and refused to watch.

The bull rumbled out of the chute. He was magnificent! Shiny black with a mature, muscular build; he definitely was the largest animal yet to be encountered during the competition. Within a fraction of second, the bull spotted Tomas weakly waving the flags in front of him. It fired forward with unbelievable speed.

Tomas had never before seen such an incredible and terrifying animal. The sheer size of it made him quake. It looked a speeding locomotive rumbling toward him. His first inclination was to freeze, which he did until he heard Luis's voice in his head, *Whatever you do, don't freeze* ... "Freeze, hell! I am out of here!" shouted Tomas. He threw the flags into the air and spurred his mount into action. Tomas rode like a man possessed with the bull chasing him close behind.

Suddenly, he heard the cheers of the crowd. Tomas turned in his saddle to see Prudenciano riding up beside him with a tremendous smile across his face. The bull was just rolling off his back and trying to regain his senses. "Now, that wasn't so bad, was it?" laughed Prudenciano as he slapped Tomas on the back. "You did great waiting there until the very last second for the bull to chase you. That gave me time to catch it. Good job, my brave *amigo!*"

"*Sí*, brave. Right," muttered Tomas weakly. He could not believe that it was over. He would have to check his pants for soiling once he dismounted.

The crowd went wild with hysteria. The throw was even better than the last one. Paz pried Rita off her shoulder and said, "They did it! They did it! Oh, Rita. Tomas was so brave. You should have seen him!" Rita shook from nervous energy. Her swollen eyes showed waves of relief.

The judge smiled broadly in the box as he checked the time on his stopwatch. Then he leaned over and whispered something into Trujillo's ear. Juan returned the smile and began sharing the news with Francisco. Prudenciano watched this interplay in the box and knew he had a winning time. Now, if the next team just faltered once during their next try, he would have the victory.

The competing team readied their riders. The flagger rode proudly out into the arena carrying his flags high. He stopped in the center and made a show out of signaling that all was prepared. The judge nodded and the bull was released into the chute. This animal was younger than the last. His shoulders and neck were not as developed, but he appeared more agile and lithe. Where the other bulls of the day had rumbled as they ran, this one bounded like a gazelle. He quickly sized up the arena and swiftly charged the flagger with energetic leaps. The bull gracefully swung his head back and forth as he bore down on the rider.

The *colleador* bolted from the gate and quickly intercepted the bull, but the man found it impossible to latch on to the tail. The fluid bounding motion caused the tail to bob in a corkscrew motion, which made grasping the tail extremely difficult. The man was forced to concentrate totally on snagging the tail and was oblivious of the fact that he was riding parallel to the bull. The bull finally spotted him in his peripheral vision and deftly twisted his head under the horse. The horse's momentum carried it over the bull's head and up onto his neck. Then with a powerful surge, the bull flipped the horse and its rider over its back. The man hit the ground first and the horse landed of top of him.

The crowd went momentarily silent. Then the silence was pierced when someone yelled, "Damn, man! You are supposed to throw the bull! Not the other way around!" People started cautiously laughing. The hapless *colleador* slowly stood and began to shake himself off. Miraculously, he only had the wind knocked out of him. At seeing that he was not seriously hurt, the whole crowd began guffawing. The judge did not even bother totaling the scores. He reached over and clasped Trujillo's forearm. Then he stood up and brought Trujillo to his feet. They raised their arms together over their heads to proclaim the winning team. The crowd thundered their approval throughout the stands.

———•◦•◦•———

The wagon ride home was much more pleasant than the ride in.

Paz and Rita clung to their men. Luis was relaxed but gingerly braced his knee on a pile of straw. Prudenciano had expertly wrapped the leg before they left. There was a festive mood in the air. Groups held parties wherever people could meet. All in all, the evening proved to a pleasant cap to an eventful *Cinco de Mayo*.

The wagon stopped in front of the Navas' house first. Prudenciano leaped to the ground and then reached up to catch Paz. She jumped down into his waiting arms. He caught her and kissed her fully on the mouth, then placed her on the ground. Paz blushed at this public display, but enjoyed it nonetheless. Prudenciano waved goodbye to everyone as the wagon pulled away and turned to open their door. He abruptly stopped and shifted his weight to the balls of his feet.

Paz noticed his sudden change in mood and asked, "What's wrong?"

"Somebody was in our house," replied Prudenciano. He pointed toward the door. It was slightly ajar as if someone was in a hurry. He carefully moved Paz behind him and opened the door. As he stepped in, he tripped over something placed haphazardly by the entrance. This confirmed that someone had been there. He carefully crept in and scanned the dark interior. He could tell something had changed, but it was difficult to tell exactly what. He needed a light. He felt for a lamp, found one, and quickly lit the wick. As he adjusted the flame and the light illuminated the front room. Paz gasped from the doorway. The room was filled with bags of beans, rice, corn, flour, and sugar.

Paz put her hands up to her face and exclaimed, "Where did all this food come from?" Prudenciano reached over to one of the sacks and plucked an envelope from on top. He handed it to Paz. She opened it and removed wads of pesos and a note. Then with trembling hands, she read it silently at first. She looked up to Prudenciano and said, "It's from Juan Trujillo. He says, 'Congratulations on a fine performance. As agreed, here is two hundred pesos. Please accept the food as a small token of my appreciation.'"

Prudenciano smiled smugly as he listened to the words. To get praise from such an important man was almost indescribable. Paz sensed what was going through his mind. She snuggled up to him and said, "I too want to show you how appreciative I am." Prudenciano chuckled and then swooped her off her feet and carried her into the back room.

Chapter 7
Transition

Life at the mine improved dramatically for Prudenciano Nava and his friends Tomas Martinez and Luis Cato. The mine boss appointed Prudenciano as his special assistant. This meant that he did little work and lots of directing, which suited him fine. Management promoted Tomas to foreman of one of the upper levels. Luis performed menial tasks around the mine on crutches while his knee mended.

The men treated Prudenciano with great awe. They overlooked his daily show of bravado. He could do no wrong. Not only did he keep the peace at the mine, but he soothed their aches and pains from their hard labors. On top of all this, he was a famous rodeo star. All of Torreón knew of his performance at Gómez Palacio. Prudenciano reveled at being an overnight celebrity.

Through all of this, the Trujillos and Bollases tolerated Prudenciano's excesses. He was unknowingly keeping the men in line and thus maintaining the mine's production. They constantly watched and occasionally cautioned him. The management kept him on a long leash, but did not give him enough slack to hang himself. The arrangement was beneficial for both sides.

The home lives of Prudenciano and Tomas also greatly improved. Before the winning of the *jaripeo*, they would return home dead tired and dirty. After dinner, each did little more than go to bed. Now because of their easier workloads, they came home every night with energy and vigor. The women greatly appreciated this benefit. Their husbands had more time to socialize with them. Tomas could now play with the children before they had to go to bed. Prudenciano told stories and massaged the aching muscles of men who visited them.

During the last week of July 1906, Prudenciano and Paz were just finishing their dinner and preparing to enjoy a relaxing evening when Prudenciano heard a knock at the door. He stood up to answer it when a cold feeling of dread crept through his body. He hesitated before going forward. Paz saw his delay and thought it strange. "It's probably just someone wanting your services," said Paz as she picked up the dishes. Prudenciano grunted and turned back to the door. He felt a deep ominous feeling well up from within his bones. Whatever was behind the door was not an ordinary customer.

He moved slowly and halted in front of the door. He took a deep breath and swung it open. Abundio stood on the porch holding the reins of a bony old horse with two little girls clinging on the back. Abundio looked like a hunched, sickly skeleton. His clothing was in tatters. The girls were cold and dirty. Prudenciano felt a queasy lump slide deep into his stomach. He was seeing a replay of his vision from the church steps in Valparaiso over a year ago. Paz gasped and dropped a plate. It shattered on the floor.

Abundio tried to mumble something, but instead he pitched forward and fell into Prudenciano's arms. Prudenciano had to turn his head to the side to keep from retching from the stench. Paz ran outside to the girls. "*¡Dios mío!* My little sisters! We must get them inside!" Prudenciano dragged Abundio into the house and laid him on a blanket. Then he went back out to help Paz with the girls. When he took them down from the horse, he was shocked to feel their bones protruding from under their skin. Their bodies possessed the emaciation of starvation. In addition, lice crawled throughout their hair. Prudenciano shuddered as he brought them inside.

Paz was horrified at the condition of her half sisters. She wailed, "Oh, my poor little ones. What has happened to you?" The girls were beyond conversation. They sat like zombies on the floor with blank stares.

Paz quickly fetched a tub and began to fill it with water. She stripped the girls and tossed their clothing into the alley. Then she promptly began to scrub each one thoroughly. In desperation, she cropped their knotted hair close to their scalps to ensure that she had removed all the lice and nits.

Prudenciano concentrated on tending to Abundio. He gave him a drink of water and some food. As he ate, Prudenciano reflected how strange life could be. Just one year ago, his brother had tried to kill him and now he sought him for help. Prudenciano shook his head as he contemplated this twist of fate. After Abundio had eaten and appeared slightly rested, Prudenciano sat a little closer to him and asked in a low voice, "Tell me, Abundio. What has happen to you and the family?"

Abundio stared down at the floor forlornly for several minutes. Twice he tried to speak, but deep sobs racked his body. Finally, he regained his composure and began to talk in a halting voice. "Typhus. It came without warning. Spread through the land. Dead. They are all dead. Government troops took the land. I had to get out with the girls ..." Abundio's body began to shake again. He had to stop.

The region around Monte Escobedo was notorious for hosting a particularly virulent strain of typhus. The disease was louse-borne and spread like wildfire among poor people living in rural conditions. When the economy suffered, so did the normal hygiene habits of the people. Deteriorated living conditions caused typhus to rush through poverty-stricken people like a lion.

Prudenciano slumped against the wall. Although he had fought with his family, he still loved them, especially his father. Now they were gone. His heart began to fill with remorse. Suddenly, Prudenciano sat up with a nagging feeling that something was missing. While his brother cried beside him, he concentrated on the problem. *Of course!* he thought. *I had a vision of José in the cantina in Monte Escobedo. I saw him much older. He must be still alive!* Prudenciano turned to Abundio and asked, "What happened to José?" Abundio looked like he did not understand, so Prudenciano repeated slowly, "Where is José?"

"José?" answered Abundio, "Oh, I remember now. He got sick with typhus. He developed a rash all over his body. The boy's fever went rampant and he gradually became delirious. I thought he was going to die. When the troops came, I asked them to take him to a hospital. They said that they would under one condition. That he joins the army when he is cured. I agreed and signed his enlistment papers. There was nothing else that I could do."

Prudenciano replied with anger in his voice, "But he is only thirteen. The army is no place for a boy of his age." He was going to further chastise Abundio when a moan came from Paz. Prudenciano sprang to his feet and quickly ran to her. She was holding a bed pan that her sisters had just used. The pan contained a dark fluid like molasses.

"Oh, heaven help them!" cried Paz, "What would cause such urine?"

Prudenciano winced when he saw the excretions. He turned to Abundio and asked him sternly, "What have you been feeding these children?"

Abundio spread out his hands as a show of helplessness and replied weakly, "I never took care of such small children before. I did the best that I could. I fed them sugar and water."

"What else?"

"Nothing more. Just sugar," answered Abundio. Paz's face displayed her disbelief and shock. She wondered if Prudenciano's assessment of Abundio's low intelligence was accurate. How could a man be so dumb? Prudenciano had all he could take. He marched out of the house and slammed the door behind him. At least he could take care of the horse.

For the following week, Paz let others run the day care business while she tended to her family's needs. The girls needed frequent baths and scrubbing to fully rid themselves of the lice. By the end of the week, they began to put on weight and show signs of youthful health. Abundio looked like a new man with clean clothes he borrowed from his brother, and regular meals.

Prudenciano still had a hard time socializing with Abundio. Although he sympathized with his brother's plight, he bristled every time he thought of how Abundio treated his children. Prudenciano frequently thought about poor José conscripted into the army. With the growing civil unrest around Mexico, Díaz frequently called the army to use force to put dissenters in line. No young boy should be expected to kill a man. It usually scarred him for life.

The sleeping arrangements had the greatest impact on Paz and Prudenciano's simple life. Paz insisted that the girls sleep with her until they were stronger. This decision forced the two men to sleep together in the front room and only reinforced Prudenciano's disdain for his brother. By the end of the second week, Paz noticed a distinct change in Prudenciano's behavior. He seemed constantly irritable and quickly snapped at the smallest provocation. She intuitively knew that their nightly separations were probably the cause of his intense emotions. Thus she decided that the girls could now sleep on their own, and moved them into the front room with their father.

After their lovemaking that night, Paz snuggled comfortably alongside Prudenciano. She whispered softly to him, "Prudenciano, are you awake?" She heard him grunt something unintelligible in reply. She continued, "Promise me, Prudenciano, that when we have a baby girl we will name her Alcaria."

The discussion of future baby names grabbed his full attention, because Pax had never mentioned the topic before. Prudenciano came fully awake and rolled over to Paz. He asked, "Are you pregnant?"

Paz smiled at him. "No, silly. But I am sure it will happen soon. Now promise me. Alcaria if it's a girl and you may name it if it is a boy."

"*Sí*. I promise," said Prudenciano, "I think that is a very good idea." He kissed her and rolled onto his back. He stared at the ceiling until he started to drift off to sleep. His last thought was, *Why doesn't the thought of having children scare me?* He smiled and concluded, *I must be getting soft.*

The Mexican celebration that generated the most national patriotism was not the *Cinco de Mayo*, but Mexican Independence Day, held on September 16. It recognizes the fact that in 1821 Mexico finally won its independence from Spain. The working class especially embraced this day because the revolt had started with a priest named Miguel Hidalgo y Costilla leading a band of poor Indians and *Mestizos* against a far superior Spanish army. The date of this revolt was September 16, 1810.

For three hundred years, Spain tightly controlled the economy, culture, and sociology of Mexico. At birth, a Mexican citizen was predestined to follow ingrained standards. An Indian peasant could expect to live a life farming the very soil that his ancestors had tilled. A *Creole*, a native-born Mexican of pure Spanish descent, could expect a better life, which consisted of higher education and a dependable government job. However, toward the end of the eighteenth century, the Spanish unknowingly implanted new ideas into Mexicans that threatened to tear the very fabric of Spanish dominion over Mexico. The Spanish King, Charles III, instituted more local rule and independent management of the Mexican and South American empires. Under these changes, the Spanish gave *Creoles* increased access to government offices. This stimulated the Mexican government to become more self-reliant and confident. The *Creoles* quickly developed a definite taste for independence much like the American revolutionaries did with England.

At the turn of the century, Spain became concerned about Mexico's growing confidence and deliberately began replacing the *Creoles* with native Spaniards to temper any possible secession. The *Creoles* saw their power being eclipsed and started to voice their concerns. Their chance for independence came quickly in 1808 when Napoleon Bonaparte's troops overwhelmed Spain and Portugal. Napoleon kidnapped the Spanish king, Ferdinand VII, and placed his brother Joseph on the throne. Spanish juntas sprang up across the country to fight the French invaders.

Between 1808 and 1810, the *Creoles* responded by revolting against the new Spanish regime. They notified King Joseph that Mexico was determined to govern itself in Ferdinand VII's name, and awaited his restoration. Racial and social revolutions erupted throughout the country. Hordes of Indians waged war against all whites, both Spaniards and *Creoles*. Spain was helpless to stop it because they were engulfed in their own civil strife.

In September 1810, a *Creole* plot to overthrow the Spanish viceroy was revealed and the conspirators were warned to flee for their lives. Father Miguel Hidalgo decided to lead volunteers into battle anyway. He firmly believed that the poor Mexicans would never have justice until the Spanish rule was broken. In the dawn hours of September 16, 1810, he held a meeting in Dolores and passionately called for all able men to stand forth and fight for freedom. His moving speech was remembered in history as the *Grito de Dolores*. Hidalgo succeeded in persuading Indians and the working-class Mexicans to join the battle. However, the *Creoles* did not trust the Indians because of the past racial fights and refused to unite with them. The revolutionaries adopted a Mexican saint, the Virgin of Guadalupe, as the patron of the movement. Within days, Hidalgo had formed an army of sixty thousand men armed with only spears, slings, and machetes.

The army marched directly to Gunanjuato and promptly razed the city. They butchered every white resident they encountered, *Creole* and Spaniard. The Hidalgo's soldiers lashed out in racial fury and destroyed everything they could get their hands on.

The Gunanjuato massacre demonstrated to the *Creoles* that the independence movement had taken a monstrous turn. It also threatened the *Creoles'* social and economic status. Thus, *Creoles* and the Spanish formed a temporary alliance and battled Hidalgo's army.

As the revolution proceeded, Hidalgo's decrees became increasingly radical. He preached the abolition of taxing Indians for simply being Indians. He favored restoring property taken from Indian communities. Although the *Creoles* favored independence from Spain, they were unwilling to agree to Hidalgo's demands. Had Hidalgo won their support, history might have been different. However, his tactics were not organized and he had only limited resources to fight a war.

In 1811, the Spanish army with the *Creole* militia confronted Hidalgo's soldiers near Mexico City. Hidalgo now commanded nearly eighty thousand men, but they were poorly trained and armed. After a fierce battle, Hidalgo retreated and destroyed Valladolid and Guadalajara in the process. His army gradually disintegrated from the constant attacks from the Spanish-*Creole* troops. Finally, the Spanish captured Hidalgo and executed him by firing squad.

In 1812, another priest, José Maria Morelos, rose to take Hidalgo's place. Morelos proved to be a gifted military tactician. He continued to push Mexico to independence. A profound Mexican nationalist, Morelos rallied Mexicans of all colors to join the revolution. He preached far-reaching visions that were truly ahead of his time. For example, he declared all inhabitants except Europeans would no longer be designated as Indians, mulattos, or other castes, but they would be known as Mexicans. He abolished the mandatory church tithe and slavery. Morelos also perpetuated the idea of transferring lands to Indians. Naturally, the *Creoles* saw these principles as threats to their way of life and refused to join Morelos's cause.

Morelos failed to capture Mexico City or Acapulco. Like his predecessor, Morelos was captured and executed on December 22, 1815. With his death, the Mexican revolution stalled until five years later.

In 1820, the *Creoles* ironically revived the independence movement. A general named Agustin de Iturbide became sympathetic to the Mexican cause and met secretly with the rebels. Iturbide joined the rebels, taking most of his loyal army with him. With the combined forces of the aristocrats and the laborers, they quickly overwhelmed the beleaguered Spanish. By September 28, 1821, Mexico formally declared its independence.

As in most wars throughout the world, the working class took the brunt of the fighting. *Creoles* commanded the infantry and laborers carried out the orders. The majority of the Mexican casualties were the working class. Thus, the common folk of Mexico felt that they had sacrificed the most for their sovereignty. These feelings carried forward to the present time.

Although Mexicans of all levels of society possessed deep feelings of pride for fighting for their independence, the working class felt that they had given the most for the cause. Therefore, they rationalized that it was their national right to celebrate Independence Day with gusto. Prudenciano was an ardent believer in this principle. Throughout his adolescent and adult years, he had never missed a celebration. The festivities had always centered around a *parranda*. However, this year was different. This time he was married.

As September 16 approached, he began to contemplate his situation. Paz despised his social drinking, but what woman did otherwise? She would probably give him a cold shoulder for several days afterward. He weighed the consequences and quickly came to a decision. He would enjoy Independence Day to the fullest. It was worth it.

Prudenciano smiled at his choice and began to make preparations. He spread the word among the men that there was going to be a big party along the hillside below the mine. Everyone was expected to show and bring a bottle. Drinking would start in the morning and last until either the booze or men were depleted. Like all hastily organized *parrandas*, no thought was given to food or other logistics.

Young Trujillo caught wind of the upcoming event and promptly summoned Prudenciano. When he bounded into his office with a cocky grin on his face, Trujillo knew that he had to deal with him swiftly. Trujillo intentionally studied Prudenciano silently for a few minutes from behind his meticulously clean desk. He methodically thumped his pencil in front of him as he stared. Finally, he spoke with an even and authoritative voice. "I understand that you are planning quite a party for Independence Day, no?"

"*Sí*," answered Prudenciano. He could tell where this conversation was going.

Trujillo continued, "A party is one thing. The mine will be closed during the holiday. However, incapacitating the men for the following day's work is another matter. I will not have you destroying this mine's production. *Comprende?*"

Prudenciano nodded his understanding. Instead of feeling chastised, he felt his irritation rising. He thought, *This kid is wrecking my plans.*

"I mean it, Nava," said Trujillo sternly as he pointed his finger at him. "If you lead these men to a drunken brawl and none show up to work the next day, I will fire you."

Instinctively, Prudenciano lifted his chin in defiance. "I understand. May I go now?" Trujillo stared at him for a few seconds then shook his head sadly. Without saying a word, he dismissed him with a wave of a hand. Prudenciano turned and strode briskly out the door.

Trujillo slowly got up and walked over to the window with his hands clasped behind his back. From this second-story vantage point, he could survey the entire work yard. Looking down, he saw Prudenciano strut into the yard and continue to recruit potential participants for the *parranda*. Trujillo sighed and spoke out loud, "I guess I should inform Father about this."

Paz could tell that Prudenciano had something up his sleeve. Independence Day was tomorrow and he acted like he was not aware of this fact. He was on his best behavior and sought every opportunity to please her. From hearing stories of his past carousing, she knew he was probably planning a wild drinking party. She started to ask him about the next day, but caught herself. She thought, *No. I'll wait for him to tell me in his own way.*

By late that evening, Prudenciano had not spoken of his plans. So, Paz decided to goad him in revealing his intentions. While she was sewing a quilt with her sisters, she smiled sweetly at him and asked, "I was thinking that it would be nice to have a picnic tomorrow. *Sí?*"

Prudenciano jolted upright at the suggestion. He shook his head and said lamely, "I don't think that will work out."

"Oh? And why not?" replied Paz with feigned innocence.

Prudenciano shuffled his feet. He appeared to be at a loss to explain why. Paz reveled in his discomfort and waited patiently for his response. When he finally answered, Prudenciano could not look at Paz. "Actually, I was planning on getting together with a few of the men from work. We were going to trade a few stories and have a few laughs."

Paz put down her sewing and fired a direct question. "Are you going to drink?" The little girls cringed at this exchange. They felt that something explosive was about to happen.

"Well, yes. Some of the men will have a bottle or two."

Paz stood up and walked over to him. She looked him right in the eye. "You are lying!" Prudenciano abruptly stood up with his stool flying against the wall. His eyes bored his anger into her. Paz bent her head back to maintain her stare and did not even flinch at his aggression.

Prudenciano gritted his teeth together and pointed his finger at her. "I am going to celebrate Independence Day like any other man in Mexico. I always have and always will. You will not tell me what I can do! Do you hear me?"

Paz met his glare head on. She sternly replied, "One of these days, you will drink yourself into so much trouble that you will never recover." With that she promptly turned and marched into the back room, slamming the door behind her. In unison, the girls looked at the bedroom door and then back to Prudenciano. The cold lonely night had started.

The site Prudenciano had chosen for the *parranda* was the very gully he and Tomas had met the Trujillos and Bollases months ago. It was perfect for their needs because it was just out of the city and secluded. Yet, the men could easily find it. They only had to follow the road to the mine up the hill a short distance to the first right-hand turn they encountered.

Prudenciano, Tomas, and Abundio were the first at the gully. Prudenciano had taken Abundio and left a quiet and uncomfortable home early in the morning. He went straight to the Martinez house and dragged Tomas out of his warm bed. Rita raised such a ruckus at them that they could still hear her blocks away. The three of them rode awkwardly on Abundio's old horse. The weight of the men burdened the worn-out animal, but they had only a short way to go.

The first order of business was to gather enough firewood for a bonfire. They cleared the land of any dry brush available. As they were stacking the wood, the men began to arrive. Some walked and others rode horses. By noon, over a hundred men had arrived and began drinking in earnest. By mid-afternoon, hunger started to set in. The men began complaining and threatened to go home early. The alcohol dulled any discriminating tastes that a man might have, so no one except Abundio complained when Prudenciano pulled out his pistol and shot Abundio's horse in the head. Volunteers started the fire and butchered the carcass. Within an hour, the horse was quartered and skewered over a large cooking fire.

By early evening, they had finished eating and were polishing off the last of the booze. The blazing sun began to mellow and take on deep blood-red hues as it melted into the western horizon. The party had been a great success. Some of the men felt that it was a shame to stop the *parranda* so early. Prudenciano shared this view, but he was wrestling with the choices facing him now. He could declare the party over and send everyone home at a decent hour as Trujillo had requested or find some more drink and continue. Management dictated that he do the responsible thing. However, the party had invoked strong patriotic emotions among the men and Prudenciano was caught up in the moment, too. Therefore, he prevailed on fate to decide what he should do.

Prudenciano asked the men if they knew where they could procure some more alcohol. "*Sí*," replied one man, "I bet there are a few bottles at the mining office!" There were mumbles of agreement in the crowd.

Prudenciano asked, "How do you know this?"

The man answered, "Management always has a few bottles to do business with. All *Creoles* do this." It must have been the copious amounts of tequila that Prudenciano had consumed or the horse meat that clouded his judgement, but the man's reasoning sounded logical. In fact, Prudenciano looked around him and could not find a single man doubting this proclaimed truth.

Prudenciano shouted, "Okay, let's go up there and find out!" Everyone cheered. Several men shouted "*¡Viva Mexico!*" and the mob began to climb the rest of the way up the hill to the mine. The evening sky gradually darkened and the stars sprang out across the dark background. By the time the crowd reached the mine, the night was fully upon them. No one had thought of bringing a torch. They stumbled around the mining yard and finally found the office building.

Prudenciano tried the door. "It's locked!" he said in dismay.

Someone shouted from the darkness, "Break it down!" Two men responded by ramming the door with their shoulders. The door cracked on the first try. By the third rush, the door broke up and the crowd pressed forward.

Suddenly, the mining yard was flooded with light. Several lamps were lit simultaneously around the perimeter of the yard. About twenty men on horseback rode out from behind equipment and buildings. Each man was armed with a rifle. Prudenciano had the sinking feeling that he was trapped. His men were speechless and frozen like deer in a spotlight.

A familiar figure rode out in front of the armed men. It was not until he took off his hat and spoke that Prudenciano recognized him. "*Buenas noches, Señores*. For those who do not know me, my name is Don Luis Manos. Señor Trujillo asked me to pay you a visit on this fine night. He wants me to escort you boys home before you get into trouble. If you refuse, well, my partners will shoot you. Any questions? *Bueno. ¡Vámanos!*"

Don Luis waved his hand forward and the guards responded by riding menacingly toward the men. At first no one moved. Then panic swept thorough the crowd and the men broke into frantic attempts to flee. The net result was people slamming into one another, tripping and being trampled. During the melee, the guards continued to press forward. The men had to make a serious effort to keep from being crushed by the horses. Don Luis constantly scanned the moving mass of men as if he was searching for someone. Finally, he shouted, "There he is! Get him. I want him!" Prudenciano realized that Don Luis was pointing at him.

Prudenciano ducked into the office. The guards were forced to dismount and secure their horses before entering the building. This gave Prudenciano time to jump out the back window and flee into the night. When he crested the hill, he almost fell down the steep incline. He had to fumble his way down the rocky terrain. He dared not make his way back to the road in fear of encountering more of Don Luis's lynch mob.

After an hour of hard travel, he stumbled into the city. There he slunk among the street shadows and alleys until he made it to his house. He jumped inside and swiftly shut the door behind him. His body fell backward against the door and slowly slid downward. Exhausted, he collapsed in a heap on the floor. His clothes were in tatters and his arms had cuts and abrasions from careening down the mountainside.

As he sat on the floor trying to catch his breath, he had the feeling that someone was watching him. He looked up and saw Don Luis sitting comfortably by the kitchen table. Paz and her sisters were cowering together in the corner. Prudenciano made a halfhearted move toward Don Luis, but Don Luis quickly produced a pistol from under the table and pointed it directly at him. He motioned for Prudenciano to sit back down. "What are you doing here?" demanded Prudenciano in a ragged voice.

Don Luis replied, "You know quite well what I am doing here, Nava." He wore a wide evil grin on his face. "I knew that you would screw up some day. I can read troublemakers like you a mile away." Don Luis laughed and waved his gun toward Paz, "Oh, don't worry about your beautiful young wife. I haven't laid a hand on her ... yet!" He seemed to get a chuckle out of this. Then he abruptly became very serious. He leaned toward Prudenciano to drive his final point home. "I want to kill you, Nava, but Juan Trujillo says that because of your past good service, he is going to give you one last chance.

So, here's the deal. You live right while you are here in Torreón and I will give you no more trouble. You cause problems again and you will disappear like Vallejo. Then I will have to take care of Paz, *comprende?*" Don Luis stared intensely at Prudenciano to let his threats sink in. After a few moments he rose, holstered his gun, and strode out the door without saying another word.

Prudenciano picked himself off the floor and walked over to Paz and the girls. The girls were deeply traumatized and Paz kept trying to soothe their fears by stroking their trembling heads. Prudenciano groped for the right words and finally asked, "Are you all right?"

Paz looked up at him with contempt. "Your drinking almost got us killed! You care more about your parties than about us." She nearly spit her words at him.

Prudenciano was filled with deep remorse. He knew that he had needlessly endangered himself and his family. He wrung his hands and said solemnly, "I promise never to drink like that again."

Paz shot back, "Don't make promises that you can't keep!" She quickly prodded the girls to stand up and led them to the back room. Prudenciano was left alone in the front. He slumped into one of the kitchen chairs, placed his elbows on the table, and propped up his head. He felt miserable. He searched his soul for some respite from his trouble, and for resolve to live up to his promise. Suddenly, his mind's eye opened and flashed a vision. Paz was standing in front of him with a baby in her arms and two little girls holding on to her skirt. She seemed both scared and disgusted as she looked directly at him. The room was long and narrow, similar to a large, rectangular box. Then the vision gone. It left him with a feeling of despair.

Prudenciano shook his head to rid himself of the remnants of his vision. He had the sneaking hunch that history would eventually repeat itself. Just then, Abundio stumbled through the door. He looked exhausted. He said, "Man, I'm beat. I never want to repeat this Independence Day again." Then he noticed Prudenciano's expression. He asked, "What's the matter with you? You look like you saw a ghost."

Prudenciano shook his head and answered, "I wish that it was a ghost."

———

The months flew by as the Nava family settled down into a daily routine. Prudenciano continued to organize the men at the mine. After Independence Day, his demeanor seemed subdued. He no longer was the braggart he once was. Every once in a while, he would become a little cocky, but all it took was one hard look from young Trujillo to sober him.

Paz continued to run her day care. She watched about twenty children. Her harmonica music was still a big crowd pleaser.

Life at home improved with time. Paz eventually forgave Prudenciano and reestablished the sleeping arrangements. Abundio decided to move to the state of Durango and investigate the opportunities there. He finally demonstrated to Paz that he now knew how to care for the girls. She reluctantly released them into his custody. After they left, the house seemed strangely empty.

Paz contemplated why she had felt so lonely since her little sisters were gone. She ultimately decided that it was time to start raising her own family. By April 1907, she instinctively knew that she had gotten her wish. Paz was absolutely ecstatic over being pregnant. She shared her secret with Rita, who squealed with delight. Now the final hurdle was to break the news to Prudenciano without frightening him.

Paz chose the place and time with infinite care. After serving an excellent meal, she soothed him with a few tunes from her harmonica. He was in a relaxed and excellent mood. Then she sat in his lap and held him for a while. As her head snuggled into his chest, she asked, "Do you remember when we discussed names for our children?"

Prudenciano's eyes were closed. "*Sí*," he murmured, "Why do you ask?"

Paz said, "Well, it's time to get ready to use one of them." She held her breath as she waited for his reaction. Whether it was his full stomach or being so relaxed, Prudenciano was very slow in grasping what she meant. As the minutes ticked by, comprehension began to sink in and Prudenciano's eyes came open with a start. He slowly pushed Paz away from him and lifted her chin up so he could look into her eyes.

He asked, "Are you going to have a baby?"

Suddenly, she felt very shy and replied softly, "*Sí*. Rita and I think that the baby will probably be born in the last of November or early December." Prudenciano smiled broadly at her. He leaned over and kissed her forehead. Again, he wanted to tell her that he loved her, but he could not crack his masculine shell to do this. He was now fifty-one years old and, except for his confession in Valparaiso, he still had never told anyone that he loved them. In the end, Paz had to settle for, "I am glad."

The following months flew by. Paz's abdomen gradually began to swell. Rita and she spent many enjoyable evenings sewing maternity dresses and skirts to fit around her expanding girth, and baby clothes. As the due date approached, Paz developed an acute case of nesting syndrome. She industriously cleaned the home from top to bottom. She directed Prudenciano to make a wooden crib which she meticulously lined with soft blankets.

At the mine, Prudenciano carried on with his normal duties, but without the normal fanfare that was his trademark. He and Luis Cato competed in the next *Cinco de Mayo jaripeo* and won. Tomas graciously assisted them from behind the wooden rails. Prudenciano did not repeat last year's performance of Independence Day. The only noteworthy change at the mine that occurred was the inflow of refugees from Zacatecas. These people were fleeing either the hopeless economy or the typhus epidemic that still ravaged the country. Don Luis conscripted many of these hapless souls to work the mine for rock-bottom wages. The experienced miners resented these new workers because they were driving down everyone's base pay.

On the cold winter night of December 6, 1907, Paz felt the first distinctive contractions of labor. Although Prudenciano was an accomplished *sobador*, he felt absolutely helpless to assist Paz with the birth. He ran down the street and fetched Rita.

Because Prudenciano was a big man, Rita was deeply concerned that Paz was carrying a large baby. Paz was petite and giving birth to a large baby would be very difficult. However, Paz was seventeen and strong and thus stood a good chance of surviving it. Prudenciano stayed in the front room. He could do nothing but pace and wait as Paz moaned and screamed in pain. The night wore on slowly.

As the dawn broke across the dark sky, the agonizing sounds from the back room ceased and were replaced by soft baby cries. Within a few minutes, Rita came out holding a bundle in her arms. Rita looked exhausted, with strands of sweat-soaked hair hanging down over her face. She smiled wearily at Prudenciano and lifted the blankets up to him. She spoke in a husky, tired voice, "Your firstborn is a beautiful daughter. Here, you can hold her."

Prudenciano did not know how to hold the baby. He tried positioning his arms in several different configurations, but none felt right. Finally, Rita kept the baby and pulled the covers away from its face. Prudenciano immediately felt his heart jump up his throat. The little girl was perfectly formed. She was the most beautiful child he had ever seen. He knew instinctively that he loved her more deeply than he had ever thought possible. Prudenciano smiled widely and asked, "How is Paz?"

"She is very tired," answered Rita. "She had a rough time with it. Why don't you check in on her? I think she would like that." Prudenciano nodded and quietly walked to the back room and opened the door. The smell of sweat was thick in the cluttered room. He could see soiled sheets crumpled against the wall from a hasty attempt to clean up from the birth. Paz lay quietly on the bed with a wool blanket over her. Her breathing was deep and even, but her face still contained lines of pain and exertion from the night. Her hair was plastered against the sides of her head.

He moved slowly toward her and knelt beside her bed. He bent down and kissed her forehead. She opened her eyes and stared at him. At first, no recognition registered in her dark brown orbs. Then her lips formed a weak smile. Paz mouthed, "Did you see her?"

Prudenciano whispered, "*Sí*. She is beautiful. Just like her mother."

Paz closed her eyes, but maintained her smile. "Alcaria," she breathed, "Remember, you promised. Alcaria."

The years 1908 and 1909 were very good to the Navas. Work went well for Prudenciano at the mine. He continued to maintain worker stability, but his task was increasingly difficult because of the desperate and sometimes sickly recruits Don Luis sent them. Paz turned her day care business over to others and devoted her time to raising Alcaria. At first, Paz did not think that she could fill a day with only her daughter, but as the child neared her "terrible twos," she became quite a handful. Prudenciano once remarked that she could crawl faster than a man could run.

Alcaria had a calming effect on Prudenciano. He curtailed his habit of joining his friends after dinner for a bottle and story swapping. Many evenings he was content to stay home and bounce her on his knee. Often Paz caught him staring at Alcaria while she slept. He marveled at her creation and the joy she brought him.

In December 1909, Paz announced that she was pregnant again. This time Prudenciano welcomed the news with open arms. He wondered, though, how he could ever squeeze another child into his heart. He loved Alcaria so much. Prudenciano contemplated this as he rode in the wagon up the hill to work. Tomas could tell that something was on his mind.

"So, Prudenciano," remarked Tomas, "What seems to have captured your thoughts this morning? You haven't told me a single story yet." The men were packed tight together. A new employee was pressed against Tomas. He looked like death warmed over. The veteran miners called men of this one's condition a "Don Luis special." These "specials" worked more cheaply than donkeys.

Prudenciano lifted his head with a start. "Uh, did you say something?"

"*Sí*," replied Tomas. "What's troubling you?"

Prudenciano shook his head and replied, ""Oh, nothing I guess. Well, actually I was just thinking what it will be like to have another baby. You know. You kind of get used to having one, then bang! Here comes another one. How do you handle four?"

Tomas laughed so hard that the man next to him jolted. "Man, I can't believe that you are the same guy that can throw a full-grown bull on its back! Don't worry, Prudenciano. The kids won't get the better of you. Just let it happen."

The wagon crested the hill and soon entered the mining compound. When the wagon stopped, the men leaped from the bed and began to form lines. The sickly man who sat next to Tomas could barely make it off the wagon. He stood hunched over in line.

Young Trujillo stood tall in front of the office building with his hands on his hips. He scanned the men and noticed that some of the new recruits were weak and in poor health. He shook his head and thought, *How can my father put up with Don Luis's poor selections? The man must be pocketing a small fortune at our expense. I must have a word with Father.*

Trujillo turned to Prudenciano, "Get these men down to work."

"*Sí*," answered Prudenciano. He quickly organized the men in groups and sent them to their respective levels, including the sick man to work in the bottom level. *After all*, Prudenciano rationalized, *we all started at the bottom.* The group foreman was furious with the decision, but let it go. Chances were that the man would not last the day.

The bottom floor group was the last to take the elevator. The men shuffled onto the platform with their equipment and water barrels. Then they plunged into the inky depths of the mine. Work began as usual with everyone taking their positions and removing rock. The sick man could barely pick up his shovel and coughed excessively. He also had severe diarrhea and thus he constantly crawled to the makeshift latrine along one of the corridors. The foreman finally gave up trying to motivate the man and placed him out of harm's way for the time being.

The man slumped up against the water barrel for support. Soon, the gagging dust and his thirst overwhelmed him, so he opened the lid and scooped out the cool clean water with the ladle cradled in his soiled hands and drank copious amounts. Several men close by thought the water looked good and broke the rule of never taking an unsupervised water break. The sick man offered the ladle to the other men who eagerly accepted it and began drinking and passing the utensil around.

When the one o'clock elevator arrived, the infirm man was loaded with the ore carts and sent home. "He was useless," declared the foreman to the elevator operator. The operator just nodded and signaled to raise the platform. He had seen this scene all too often. As the elevator rose, the foreman lifted his lantern to light the way back. He noticed that the water barrel lid was ajar. Grumbling, he walked over to adjust it. As he held the lamp in one hand and grabbed the lid with the other, the lamplight illuminated the water surface. The foreman could see a frothy foam on the surface. He winced and made a point of telling everyone to stay away from this water.

At the end of the day, the men lined up to dunk their upper bodies into the water troughs. It was the only way to strip the dust that had caked on them during the day. Several men from the bottom level felt unusually warm today and the water felt extra soothing this time. They wanted to dwell, but several lines of men were waiting their turn behind them. Thus, the men slowly got up with water dripping from their clothes and hair and strode to the waiting wagons.

Within a few days, over a quarter of the mine workforce complained about weariness, headaches, and fevers. Prudenciano never examined the men until Tomas complained about pains in his lower right abdomen. Prudenciano laid Tomas down on one of the wagon beds and took his shirt off. Prudenciano spotted the dark red "rose spots" on his upper stomach and lower chest and knew the culprit—a water-borne disease called typhoid. He gasped, "Typhoid! *¡Dios mío!* Where have you been, man?"

His friend's revelation shook Tomas. He asked in a scared voice, "Are you sure? Can it not be something else?"

"No," answered Prudenciano with fear in his voice. "You and a good portion of the mine has typhoid. I want you to stay here, *comprende?*"

As Prudenciano jumped off the wagon and starting running toward the office, he heard Tomas yell back, "What about Rita and the children? Prudenciano! What about my family?" Prudenciano felt a lump of dread shift within his stomach. He knew that once typhoid had a hold in a densely populated area like Torreón, it would race through its inhabitants like wildfire.

Prudenciano bounded through the door and flew up the stairs. He smashed Trujillo's door open and faced the young manager who was scanning yesterday's production figures. The serious look on Prudenciano's face silenced any protest that Trujillo may have voiced. Prudenciano was concise and to the point, "The men have typhoid!"

Trujillo's head whipped back like he had been hit in the jaw. He quickly whirled away from his desk and confronted Prudenciano. "How do you know?"

"I saw the signs on a man and the others have the same symptoms."

Trujillo took a deep breath. *Could it be?* he thought, *Could Nava be mistaken? No. He is a sobador. He would know.* Trujillo walked over to the window with his hands clasped behind him. He needed to think. What should he do? Prudenciano remained motionless, but followed him with his eyes. After a moment, Trujillo began talking as he stared out the window. He could plainly see men lying on the ground around the buildings. "We must try to contain the sickness here at the mine."

"I agree," replied Prudenciano, "but many of the men stayed home today because they were too sick to work."

Trujillo asked, "Then what do you suggest?"

Prudenciano replied, "Try to keep the sick men here. Better to keep the sickness in one location. Next, drain every water container that you have at the mine. Then lime the containers and latrines. Make sure everyone washes thoroughly with lye soap. Finally, let me get a warning out to the people in Torreón so that they may prepare."

Trujillo thought that his logic was sound. At least, it was a plan. He replied, "Go. I will see that your instructions are carried out."

Prudenciano turned to leave, but suddenly halted. He took one last look at Trujillo and said, "By the way, if I was you, I would tell Don Luis to stop sending men to the mine."

Trujillo's eyes flashed in fury. "Do not worry, Nava. My father and I will see that Don Luis is properly notified!"

Despite his fear, Prudenciano smiled and quickly left the office. He thought, *Perhaps some justice will be done after all.*

Prudenciano ran back to Tomas. He found him with his shirt on and sitting in the wagon. "Tomas, listen to me. Trujillo will try to treat all the men here. I am going back to town to warn the others. I want you to stay here."

Tomas grabbed Prudenciano by the shirt and said, *"Por favor,* check on Rita. I beg you!"

Prudenciano could barely pry his fingers from his clothing. He replied gruffly, *"Sí.* I will try." He stepped back and took one last look at this friend. The image of Tomas Martinez desperately stretching his hands out for help riveted in Prudenciano's mind. He turned and ran as fast as he could down the road to town. He ran fast to give the alert, but he also ran hard to erase Tomas's grieving face.

Prudenciano told every person he met on the way into town. He also quickly spread the word through key individuals that loosely regulated the civil business in southern Torreón. All the time, he kept working his way toward home. He finally arrived at his house just when Paz and Alcaria were leaving. His breath was ragged from the many miles he had traveled. It took him a minute to regain his speech.

Pa asked, "Prudenciano, why are you home so early? We were just going to see Rita. She says her children have stomachaches and fevers …"

Prudenciano cut her off in mid-sentence. "No! You must never go there again! *Comprende?"*

"But why? What do you mean that I should never see her again?" Her husband's command deeply troubled her.

Prudenciano answered sharply, "Tomas has typhoid. Most likely he infected his family, too." Paz put her hands to her anguished face. Prudenciano continued, "I don't think I am infected yet, but typhoid is highly contagious. You and I may survive it, but Alcaria and the baby won't. Paz, we must leave Torreón now!"

All of this was too sudden for Paz to comprehend. She was paralyzed by the news and their need for quick action. She quickly ran to him and buried herself into his big, strong arms and chest. She whispered into his body, "Please help us, Prudenciano. Please." Little Alcaria walked over to her parents and reached up to be held. If Mama got a hug, then so did she.

By late that afternoon, the Navas had fashioned two backpacks and stuffed their necessities into them. They were leaving a lot behind, but that did not matter. Only the well-being of the family counted. Paz secretly slipped the coin pouch that Emilio Nava had given her into her dress. She had managed to save a few pesos for emergencies. They left their safe, warm home without looking back. Prudenciano led wearing a backpack and carrying Alcaria. Paz wore a smaller pack. Besides the clothes they wore, this was all they possessed.

Prudenciano decided to take the southwestern road out of the city where it joined with the main north-south highway. It was the same road by which they had entered Torreón three years before. The streets were strangely quiet as if some evil lurked within the neighborhoods. They were almost to the outskirts of town when they heard a woman scream from the next block. Prudenciano quickened his stride, then abruptly halted. The scream had come from the office of the People's Labor Agent.

Several horses were tied to the front porch. Their fine condition and breed told Prudenciano that they belonged to the Trujillo family. Suddenly a man was thrown through the front window and landed on the front porch. Shards of glass flew in every direction. Now that the window was gone, voices from inside carried clearly out into the street.

A woman wailed, "But he didn't mean to spread the disease!" Paz and Prudenciano knew it was *Señora* Manos.

A man yelled, "Keep her away from me! Get out there and finish the job!" The voice belonged to Juan Trujillo. Several young men bolted out the door and lifted the body up. It was then that Prudenciano realized it was Don Luis. He face was bloodied and one of his arms appeared broken. He was barely conscious. The men pitched him over the porch railing and into the street. He landed only a few feet away from the Navas.

Juan bounded out the door with his son holding *Señora* Manos behind him. Juan jumped off the porch and commanded his men,

"Burn this house down, now!" The young man released *Señora* Manos and she ran and fell to her knees next to her husband. She cried as she rolled him over and saw his beaten face.

"We must get out of here," said Prudenciano quietly to Paz. He carried Alcaria and led Paz by the hand.

Juan Trujillo's voice rang out, "Ah, Nava. How fortunate for me to see you." Prudenciano stiffened. He wanted nothing to do with this matter although he had instigated it. He turned slowly to face Juan. He could already smell and hear the crackling flames from the house. Juan continued, "Are you going somewhere?"

"*Sí*," answered Prudenciano. "I am taking my family away until the sickness has passed."

Juan nodded his understanding. "Any idea where you are going?"

Prudenciano replied, "We are going north." Frankly, it never occurred to him to go in any other direction.

"All in all, Nava, you have served me well. So, I will tell you what I'm going to do," said Juan as he walked closer to Prudenciano. The flames from the house were beginning to shoot through the roof and backlit Trujillo as he came nearer. "I want you to go to Chihuahua. I have a close friend and business associate there by the name of Luis Terrazas. He owns most of the property and cattle in that area. He tells me that ruthless bandits are rustling his cattle and vandalizing his construction projects. I want you to help him fight these hooligans."

Prudenciano was taken back by this order. He sputtered, "What do I know about policing? I probably…"

Juan cut him short with a wave of his hand. "Nonsense! You are a man accustomed to danger and thrive on it. You ride better than most men walk. No, Nava. You will serve him well and he will pay you generously. I will telegraph him tomorrow. Now go! I have to finish destroying this filthy place." Juan turned and walked back to the horses. The house was completely engulfed in flames. The heat was becoming unbearable. The crackling of the fire drowned the sobbing of *Señora* Manos as she held her husband's head to her breast and rocked him softly.

Prudenciano felt neither pity nor righteousness at the fate that had befallen Don Luis. Luis had chosen to misuse his power and now he was suffering the consequences. The Mexican people handed down their own justice. There was nothing else for Prudenciano and Paz to do, but to continue walking out of the city and into the dark countryside. As they crested a hill, they turned to catch one last glimpse of the city. Except for the glow of the house fire, Torreón appeared tranquil. Prudenciano broke the stillness and said quietly, "I wonder if Chihuahua will be a safer place to live."

Paz looked up to him and replied, "How could it be any worse?"

Chapter 8
Chihuahua
September 22, 1894

The day's heat was finally waning as the sun sank below the Sierra Madre mountains. Doroteo Arango felt dead tired from toiling in the fields all day without a single break. He stored his hoe and shovel in the shack bordering the field. Doroteo took off his hat and wiped his sweat-streaked brow with the back of his dirty sleeve. He thought grimly, *Another day behind me, and another day to tackle tomorrow.* Such forlorn thoughts for a sixteen-year-old boy. Actually, he had put away adolescent views when his father died last year. Since then, circumstances had forced him to become the head of the household. His mother and four younger siblings depended on him to keep the family together.

Sometimes he felt that his burden was too hard to bear. Frequently, he stopped his ceaseless chores and stared out into the distant mountains. They seemed to beckon to him to leave everything behind and ride into them. There was unlimited freedom there. "Well, some day," Doroteo would say out loud, "Some day." Then the reality of his situation would hit him. He had to work every day as sharecropper for a bastard of a man named Don Agustín López Negrete. No matter how hard he worked, Negrete seemed always to get richer and Doroteo's family got poorer. Negrete also despised his sharecroppers and treated them with open disdain. The whole situation grated on Doroteo's sense of justice.

Doroteo began to stroll home. There was no need to hurry. Dinner would be a simple affair of the usual staples of beans and tortillas. The adobe *hacienda* was very small for six people, but his mother kept it clean. Afterward, sleep was his only recreation. There was no excitement for a young man around this small farming community of San Juan del Río in the state of Durango. Since he was also illiterate, he knew his future choices were limited.

Suddenly, he heard his mother screaming from the direction of his home. Doroteo sprinted the remaining distance. As he reached the low hill in front of him, he spotted the horse carriage of López Negrete parked in front of the *hacienda*. A couple of Negrete's henchmen waited next to the carriage and seemed to laugh and rib each other as his mother screamed again. "My baby! You cannot have her! She is only twelve years old. I beg you, Señor Negrete, leave her alone!"

Doroteo knew exactly what was happening. Two days ago, he had seen Negrete casting lecherous eyes at his sister Martinita. Now the swine was claiming her as he would his huge share of the field's profits. If he was going to save his sister, he was going to have to act fast.

Doroteo jumped off the road and moved quickly through the bushes to avoid detection. He went directly to his cousin's nearby house. No one answered when he beat on the door, so he let himself inside. Nobody was home, but that did not deter Doroteo. He knew exactly what he was looking for. He went straight to the bedroom and found the cap and ball pistol in its holster still strapped around the bed post. His cousin always liked to be prepared. Doroteo removed the pistol, checked it, and found it ready. He stuffed it in his rope belt and ran out the house.

The evening was maturing by the time he crept back to the *hacienda*. Doroteo pressed his body against the wall and peered in through the window. He could see Negrete dragging his sister toward the door. His mother was holding on to Martinita's right arm and trying fruitlessly to pull her back. Doroteo slipped around the front and charged through the door. Negrete's back was turned toward Doroteo as he gave his young prize his full attention. Doroteo raised the pistol and fired three quick shots into his back. The lead balls smacked Negrete forward like he had been hit with a bat. Martinita and her mother fell backward when Negrete let go of Martinita's hand.

Doroteo twisted around to look out the front door. The two guards were running toward the house with their guns drawn. Doroteo fired a shot at one of them and the ball barely missed his head. They both dove for cover. "Stay back," yelled Doroteo, "or I'll kill you, too!" He had only two loaded chambers left. He would have to be very careful if he was going to live through this one.

His mother wailed, "*¡Dios mío!* Doroteo! What have you done?" She pressed her hands against her face as she gazed down upon Negrete's body. The back of his stylish black suit coat was frothing with fresh blood.

Doroteo urged, "*Madre*, get down!" His anger was changing to fear as he realized that the odds were mounting against him

His mother quickly recovered her wits. She grabbed him and looked him straight in the eyes. "You must escape and never come back. Go, my son. Remember always that I love you. Now, go!" She practically threw him toward the back door. Doroteo stumbled against the wall to regain his balance. He took one last look at his mother and sister before jumping out the door and disappearing into the night.

The guards finally worked up enough courage to storm the front door. They bolted in unison with their pistols drawn and bodies held low. The men dove into the front room and braced themselves for a fusillade. Instead, all they saw was Negrete lying face down on the floor in a pool of blood and a woman and girl cowering in the corner. One of the men demanded, "Where is the boy?"

"Forget him," a voice said weakly. "You must first help me." The men looked wildly around the room for the source of the voice.

Then Señora Arango gasped, "He is alive!", made the sign of the cross across her chest, and pointed to Negrete in amazement. The men quickly put their pistols away and rolled Negrete onto his back. The bullets had not exited his chest. He was gravely wounded with three lead balls lodged deep in his body.

Negrete croaked, "Help me back to the carriage." The men complied and carried him outside. It took their full strength and concentration to keep Negrete level and off the ground. When they discovered Doroteo stealing one of the horses, they were powerless to prevent it. Doroteo rode off into the night unchallenged.

The guards brought Negrete home and laid him in his bed. The short trip had nearly killed him. When he regained some of his strength, Negrete ordered his men to fan out and capture the boy. He spoke with his eyes closed. "I want him brought back alive. *Comprende?* Now go!"

The following day, Negrete was still alive, but in agonizing pain. He knew death was near and thus the capture and punishment of Doroteo Arango must happen soon. He asked for a status report from his men. When they reluctantly admitted that they could find no trace of the boy, Negrete sent an urgent request to the law officials in nearby Canatlán to form a posse and hunt him down. It took two days for them to respond and arrive in San Juan del Río. By this time, the trail was cold and Negrete was dead.

Doroteo rode deep into the mountains that had reached out for him for so long. Within them, he found the freedom he hungered for. He slept as long as he wanted, rode where he fancied, and played games with the men who pursued him. He learned to live off the land and thrive in the remote environment. Unfortunately, like most unsupervised adolescents, he met and joined with several unsavory characters. These lawless men taught Doroteo the finer points of life such as thievery, cattle rustling, and eventually murder. Within a few years, Doroteo Arango became a man badly wanted by the law in the states of Durango and Chihuahua.

In 1909, Doroteo became tired of his nomadic life and decided it was time to settle down. To prevent detection, he changed his name to Francisco Villa. Villa was the name of his paternal grandfather, Don Jesus Villa. The fact that Villa was also the name of a notorious nineteenth-century bandit only added icing to the cake. His friends, though, made fun of his first name and called him Pancho. Thus, the name stuck—Pancho Villa.

Villa's brief venture as a respectable citizen started ambitiously when he tried to operate a butcher shop in Hidalgo del Parral about one hundred miles south of the city of Chihuahua. Within eight months, the wealthy and powerful land owner Luis Terrazas drove Villa out of business by channeling the flow of cattle to his own slaughter houses. Destitute and bitter, Villa felt that another *hacendado* had unfairly robbed him of a living. Thus, he started a grass-roots campaign against Terrazas. Villa led cattle rustlers to steal large herds from the surrounding country and sell the bounty to unquestioning buyers from El Paso who never bothered to check brands. By 1910, Villa boldly moved his operations to Terrazas's front door, Chihuahua. In addition to rustling, Villa began to disrupt Terrazas's construction projects within the city. Vandalism and violence commonly erupted at each project site.

Luis Terrazas was part of the Porfirio Díaz "machine." As ex-governor of Chihuahua, Terrazas received lucrative railroad subsidies to expand the rail system throughout the state. The Mexican government paid for the track and Terrazas eventually owned it. The railroads were usually built to substandard specifications, possessed narrow-gauge tracks, and the rail consisted of cheap-grade steel. Terrazas received an average of $12,880 per mile of track in Mexican silver. This huge sum was taken out of the national treasury.

Terrazas's true wealth was in his enormous land holdings. Díaz's method of procuring land and distributing it to his loyal machine was through land registration. Díaz enacted a law that permitted anyone to claim land to which there was no recorded title. Until this time, few Mexicans recorded land titles. If a man resided in a home that his father and grandfather had lived in, the common law decreed that he owned the property.

If Díaz felt that his new law was in the best interest of the country, he would have sent agents to educate the populace and help them register their lands. However, he informed only members of his machine of the strict registration requirement. Díaz, his father-in-law, and cronies like Terrazas formed land companies that systematically registered the choice lands throughout the country. The scheme robbed thousands of small farmers of their property.

To acquire even more land, Terrazas manipulated property assessments throughout Chihuahua. He eventually paid few or no taxes on his holdings while the poor farmers were levied heavy assessments. The farmers who survived the land registration law succumbed one by one under the strangling tax burden. Then Terrazas absorbed the repossessed land at bargain prices. When the plunder was finally over, Terrazas had embezzled over fifteen million acres of prime land in the state of Chihuahua.

Terrazas epitomized the corruption of wealth and power that Villa despised. Villa venomously struck at Terrazas at every opportunity. He organized bands of men who had lost their lands and shared Villa's feelings. More men were joining his ranks every day. Soon, Villa would have a small army to command. The city of Chihuahua was electrified with the ominous feeling that something explosive was about to happen. The brown kettle of discontent was about to boil over.

Prudenciano felt his patience wearing thin. He was not used to waiting and moving slowly during extended travels. Frequently when he carried Alcaria, she demanded to be let down to run and play along the road as most two-year-olds do. She often soiled her diaper, which required more stops to change her. Other times she would become so cranky from hunger that her parents had to halt and fix her something to eat.

In addition to Alcaria's needs, Paz was beginning her third trimester of her pregnancy. Her protruding abdomen coupled with her heavy pack caused excruciating pains in her lower back. During especially painful times, Prudenciano would lay her across their packs and massage her back to loosen her muscles. Her condition also caused her to tire easily.

Thus, Prudenciano was learning a universal truth that men have discovered and rediscovered since prehistoric times. No one with kids and a pregnant wife migrates very fast. This fact grated on his nerves. They were making only eight to ten miles per day and Chihuahua was about three hundred miles north of Torreón. The slow pace stretched the trip to almost two months. Prudenciano constantly fretted about Señor Terrazas forgetting that he was coming to join his police force. *Perhaps he won't need me anymore*, Prudenciano contemplated.

The people they met along the way generously opened their doors to them. Like the poor people who helped them while they traveled between Fresnillo and Torreón, everyone enthusiastically invited them to stay for dinner and the night. Again, Prudenciano's skills as a *sobador* were welcomed and eventually sought out by people further up the road. The women took pity when they noticed Paz and her condition and often ran out of their homes with a jug of water or some baby food for Alcaria.

One day, the Navas topped a high hill that provided a vantage point. They could see the road stretching north until it disappeared over the horizon with people moving north along its entire length. To them, the road seemed like a giant river draining the country of its residents. The road was the main transportation corridor through the heart of Mexico. It literally bisected the entire length of the country. Like a river, it collected traffic from peripheral roads and funneled them to its mouth—El Paso, Texas.

The Navas encountered travelers even when they crossed long stretches devoid of settlements. When Prudenciano questioned a few, their reply was always the same. They were heading north where better jobs awaited, less sickness prevailed, and a better economy existed.

The highway bordered the eastern foothills of the Sierra Madre Occidental and the fringes of the barren plains and mountains of the Bolsón de Mapimí. The eastern view was always uninterrupted as one could look forever across the desolate landscape. The western view was quite different in that wooded mountains and hills paralleled the road. Sometimes the road went directly across the desert to skirt a mountain or another geologic formation. When this happened, the heat became almost unbearable and slowed them further.

The Navas were now only a day's hike away from Chihuahua. The population density was increasing as they drew closer to the city. It was here that Prudenciano's patience wore out and he could stand their slow pace no longer. He shouted, "Damn it, Paz! Why can't you walk any faster?" Alcaria had fallen into an uncomfortable sleep in his arms. For hours previously, she had fussed and cried in the afternoon heat and finally succumbed to exhaustion.

Paz was so tired that she almost staggered. She hurt from carrying a backpack and a baby in her womb. The heat was insufferable and only added to her discomfort. Dust from the road caked her face and hair. However, Prudenciano's rebuke ignited her anger and renewed her energy as she prepared to battle. "I am doing the best I can," she replied with an edge to her voice. "You have been on my case for the last two weeks and I have had it! If you can't wait for your family, then why don't you just go ahead and we will catch up with you. Your choice!"

Prudenciano stopped and faced her. She straightened her back and marched up to him. He could tell that she was definitely not bluffing and she was waiting for an answer. Actually, the thought had crossed his mind, but this was no place to leave a two-year-old child and a pregnant wife. Instead, he chose to avoid her question and said, "We will find a place to stay soon." He resumed his march north, albeit at a slower pace. Paz let out a deep, irritated sigh and followed.

A woman met them on the road just a few minutes later. She heard that a skilled *sobador* was coming and she was determined to meet him. She hailed Prudenciano, "*Buenos días, Señor*. I understand that you are a *sobador* and am in need of your services. If you and your wife would follow me to my home, you may stay with us for the night. *Sí?*"

"*Sí*," replied Prudenciano as he smiled and turned to look at Paz. He gave her one of his "I told you so" looks. Paz was simply too tired to care. She gratefully nodded and followed the woman. Mercifully, the home was close and their host had cool water and a place to wash. Paz had never thought water had tasted so good. After her and Alcaria's thirst were satiated, she set about washing the two of them. The water rejuvenated them and, afterward, Paz sought out their benefactor to socialize.

The woman's name was Antonia. Paz judged that she was in her fifties. Her hair was peppered with gray and put back in a tight bun. She had a solid build from years of hard labor, but her face was kind. Antonia took a sincere interest in Alcaria and Paz found her easy to converse with.

Paz asked her, "Do you have a health problem that my husband can help you with?"

"Oh, no. Not me," answered Antonia. "My brother has been having painful back spasms for several months. He can not work or sleep. I fear for his life."

Prudenciano overheard the conversation and came into the house. "Should I go and see him now?"

Antonia shook her head. "No. My husband, Manuel, will bring him here after his work is finished. You can see him here after dinner."

Prudenciano nodded and scanned the house. He would need a flat, comfortable place to work. The adobe home had only one room. Each of the four walls supported a particular function. The south wall contained the shelves and wash basin for the kitchen area. The west wall was the sleeping portion. The north wall and center of the house served as the living room. The east wall had many wall pegs to hold clothing. The floor was stone, which Antonia kept swept and clean. The walls were adorned with weathered pictures of the Virgin Mary, Jesus, and several patron saints.

After a quick look, Prudenciano chose to examine the man in the living room. "When the time comes, I will work on your brother there," said Prudenciano as he pointed toward the center of the living room. "I will need to lay him on those cushions too."

Antonia answered, "*Sí*. That will be fine." She was pleased that he was thinking ahead. She thought Prudenciano must be a professional.

Paz helped Antonia prepare the evening meal. Antonia had just harvested the first growth in her backyard garden. The beans and tortillas were augmented by fresh carrots, lettuce, radishes, and onions. Paz had craved vegetables for the last several days. Her advanced pregnancy sucked nutrients from her body. The sight of the vegetables made her mouth water and she had to exercise great restraint to wait until dinner to eat them.

Antonia's husband, Manuel, arrived home after sunset. He was a stoutly built man of average height. Paz thought he was the perfect match for Antonia. Their similar builds and age made them look like each other. Manuel gingerly helped his brother-in-law into the home. The older man's face was twisted in pain. Prudenciano eyed him warily as Manuel placed him gently in a chair.

According to custom, the men were served first. The women and child ate only after the men had taken their fill. Alcaria wailed with hunger as she waited her turn. When the time came for everyone else to eat, Paz filled Alcaria's plate first. She tore a tortilla into small finger food pieces and gave her some beans and carrot sticks. Alcaria quickly stuffed her mouth with food and quieted down with satisfied smacks.

Paz eagerly gobbled the vegetables and beans. They tasted so good tonight. Her body was telling her that she needed the vitamin-rich food.

At the end of the meal, the men adjourned to the living room while the women cleaned up. The men talked about various affairs as Prudenciano casually opened his medical bag and took out a leather pouch. The pouch was old, and had a draw string. He nonchalantly untied the knot and opened the bag. First, he pulled out some tobacco papers and selected one. He placed the rest back into the pouch. Next, he deftly knocked some dried leafy material into the paper. The leaves looked different from tobacco. Manuel recognized it as marijuana. Prudenciano finished rolling his cigarette, struck a match, and lit an end. After drawing on it for a couple of puffs, Prudenciano handed it to the crippled man and told him to smoke it. "It will relax your muscles so I can work on you."

As the man began puffing on the drug, the men continued their light conversation for some time until Manuel focused the discussion by asking, "So, what brings you to Chihuahua?"

Prudenciano sat up a little straighter and said, "I have a job with

Señor Luis Terrazas." He noticed the announcement startled the men. Manuel's lifted his head sharply and his brother-in-law began choking and coughing from inhaling too sharply. This was not the reaction that he sought.

Manuel asked sharply, "What business do you have with him?"

Prudenciano replied calmly, "He has need for guards and he is supposed to hire me." He could tell that he touched on a tender subject.

"You mean one of his lynch men!" shouted the brother-in-law a little too loudly. Prudenciano noted that the drug was starting to work.

Prudenciano answered, "I don't understand. I heard that there has been some trouble in these parts and he might need some help."

"Terrazas, Terrazas," muttered the brother-in-law. He shook his head in an exaggerated motion as he took several long drags on the cigarette. Prudenciano knew that it was almost time to examine him.

Manuel explained, "Many people around here feel Terrazas stole their land. He is incredibly rich and powerful. I think he is ruthless. He sneers at us working people and treats us like ants. Little wonder that people are stealing his cattle and vandalizing his construction projects." Manuel leaned forward on his chair toward Prudenciano to emphasize his next point. "You must be careful that you do not help Terrazas in his tyranny. If you do, the people of Chihuahua will remember and they will eventually kill you in retribution. And if they don't kill you, then Pancho Villa will!"

His threat bothered Prudenciano, but he had a sneaking feeling that he did not have all the facts about Terrazas either. *Who was Pancho Villa? Another mystery to solve.*

Prudenciano nodded to Manuel that he understood and stood up to check on the older man. He took a quick look and announced, "I think you are ready." He pried the hot stub out of the man's hand and threw it out the open door. The red hot ash glowed as it bounced on the ground and rolled into the darkness. Prudenciano laid several pillows on the floor and gently arranged the man on top. Manuel, Antonia, and Paz came over to watch. For the time being, Manuel put aside his hatred for Prudenciano's future position.

Prudenciano took off the man's shirt and began to examine his back. By running his fingertips along the spine, he quickly found what he was looking for—a misaligned vertebra. He started his treatment by massaging the man's back muscles. The brother-in-law at first winced in pain, but gradually relaxed and began to enjoy the therapy. After a half a hour of expert rubbing, Prudenciano casually slid one hand to the side of the disorder and another hand between the shoulder blades. With one violent motion, Prudenciano stretched the man's spine by pushing forward and driving the man into the pillows while striking the vertebra with his free hand. The man bellowed in surprise, then relaxed. Prudenciano rolled off and knelt beside him.

Prudenciano commanded, "I want you to get up now." The man blinked at him in disbelief. Then, gingerly, he slowly lifted himself off the pillows and sat up.

"¡Dios mío!" exclaimed the man as he looked at the faces staring at him. "I feel no pain!" The man jumped up and stretched his arms upwards. "I feel no pain!" he repeated with almost a childlike expression. He laughed and danced around the room. Suddenly he embraced Prudenciano and almost lifted him off the ground. "Gracias, Señor. ¡Gracias!"

Prudenciano quickly rebuked him, "Whoa there! Be careful. Your back is not strong yet. You must take it easy for a while or you will be right back where you started."

Antonia's eyes were filled with tears as she hugged her brother. She looked up to Prudenciano and said, "I don't know what you and my husband were arguing about, but you must be a good man. Only a good man can heal like you do. Gracias." Prudenciano smiled down at Antonia. His happy expression masked the growing uneasiness he felt deep down inside. He was having some serious doubts about his big, important job in Chihuahua. When he looked up, he saw Paz staring at him from across the room. She had heard what Manuel had said earlier and she shared Prudenciano's misgivings.

The Navas reached the outskirts of Chihuahua in the early afternoon. As the road entered the southern section of the city, it passed the train depot. Its large sheltered porches held hundreds of travelers while they waited for their respective trains. However, today's traffic was particularly heavy. Over a thousand people were seeking passage to somewhere. The majority had to wait in the merciless sun. A gallant few called out to the crowd to offer space for children and women under the awning, but the request went unheeded.

Looking north, the tracks bent slightly to the right and crossed the north fork of the Conches River by a new metal suspension bridge. The girders were still highly reflective and glinted the sunlight uncomfortably back. Terrazas's construction crews had built the bridge as a showpiece for arriving visitors.

Across the street from the depot stood a finely built brick building with a tall brick wall surrounding it. An ornamental iron gate secured the entrance. The one-story, flat-roofed building was unremarkable except that it was kept immaculate. The brick had been painted a dull white. The gate was a flat black. Obviously, someone of wealth had built this place and took the time and money to maintain it.

Probably a place to store valuable freight, thought Prudenciano as they walked along its wall. He had to stop briefly to readjust Alcaria. She had just fallen into her afternoon nap. Paz caught up with him, pushed a strand of hair out of her face, and tucked it behind her ear. She looked across the road and tracks at the horde of people at the station.

She asked her husband, "I wonder what's going on? Why is everyone leaving?"

Prudenciano did not answer. He stood watching and listening to the crowd. He noticed a large horse-drawn carriage parked at the far end. The carriage had a large awning that kept the blazing sun off the driver and two rows of passenger seats behind him. Prudenciano noticed that the driver and the doorman were heavily armed and positioned themselves strategically around the wagon. The horses, one black and the other white, were alert. Whoever owned this team could leave at a second's notice. The owner must be expecting trouble.

Thirty-foot tall poles led the telegraph wire to the depot. The railway station seemed to be the focus of both transportation and information. The wire reminded Prudenciano that Juan Trujillo had supposedly sent a message to Terrazas. Prudenciano thought, *I wonder if it happened?*

No one paid particular attention to the poor couple and their baby as they stood across the tracks and along the barren white wall. The Navas looked like another *peon* family drifting in from the south. Their clothing was dirty and, despite Paz's best efforts, torn and frayed. What they owned, they carried on their backs. In contrast, most of the people leaving were well dressed. They were all higher-class citizens.

Suddenly, a shout rang out. The crowd turned to see the cause of the uproar. Brusquely, an armed man shoved the office door open and barked orders for people to step back. Whoever failed to respond quickly enough was thrown aside by the guard. A tall man dressed in a black suit walked briskly through the cleared path and went directly to the waiting wagon. The doorman saluted as he opened the door. The man never acknowledged his existence. The doorman vaulted up to the driver's bench and the horses bolted forward. As the wagon pulled away, someone in the crowd yelled, "Hey, Terrazas! You own the land, but you can't control the people!" There were many shouts of agreement.

"*So,*" thought Prudenciano, "*That's Luis Terrazas. I will try to meet him tomorrow.*"

"Prudenciano," said Paz as she tugged on his shirt for his attention, "these people are fleeing town! Why, Prudenciano, why?" He felt uneasy not knowing the answer, but he had a feeling that tomorrow he would find out.

———•••———

Prudenciano was up early the next morning. He left Paz and Alcaria in a makeshift camp on the banks of the Conches river. Paz barely stirred when Prudenciano rose from their bedding and dressed. The two months of hiking had drained her.

As the sun rose, Prudenciano made his way back to the train depot. That was where Trujillo had sent his telegram and the place where he had seen Terrazas. Thus, he thought it was a good place to start. By the time he got to the station, the air had warmed to a comfortable temperature. Judging by the cloudless horizon, the day was going to be a scorcher.

Prudenciano found the station open and let himself into the main lobby. Across the vast hardwood floors, the ticket agent was busy preparing for the upcoming day. The clerk was a middle-aged man of medium height. He wore a leather visor, wire-rimmed glasses, and a dress shirt with a black bow tie, which was typical of ticket clerks at train stations. He was bent over reading in deep concentration and did not hear Prudenciano walk up until he said, *"Buenos días."* Startled, the man jumped. He quickly ran his eyes over Prudenciano and his expression showed that his evaluation was not favorable.

The man quickly regained his composure. He smiled and asked, *"Buenos dias, Señor.* How may I help you?" Prudenciano noticed his right hand sliding along the lower shelf that was hidden from his view. The man flicked his eyes to his hand as it stopped against something. Then he resumed looking at Prudenciano.

Prudenciano thought, *Probably has a gun. Must be a rough town.* He smiled reassuringly at the clerk and stated his business. "I am Prudenciano Nava. *Señor* Juan Trujillo sent *Señor* Luis Terrazas a telegram two months ago from Torreón. He asked Terrazas to hire me as a guard. So, I thought you could tell me if Terrazas got the message and where could I find him?"

The clerk looked at him incredulously. The man asked, "You are a guard?" A sarcastic smile formed on his face. "You have got to be kidding!"

Prudenciano's eyes flashed in fury. He subconsciously balled his hands and tensed his muscles. *Who did this imp think he was?* The clerk must have read his body language because his smile disappeared and his eyes twitched to the shelf again to reconfirm that his gun was ready. Prudenciano let out some breath and composed himself. The clerk had the clear advantage this time. He was armed and possessed the information that Prudenciano sought. "Look," capitulated Prudenciano, "please check the messages. I know that it's there."

The clerk looked over to a pile of telegram copies that were sitting on a corner shelf. He sighed, grabbed them, and set the papers in front of him. "All right, you said two months ago that a *Señor* Trujillo sent a message to *Señor* Terrazas. I'll look once, but I really don't remember such a telegram." He fumbled through the copies, then abruptly stopped. He scanned it quickly then looked up to Prudenciano and exclaimed, "Well, what do you know? Is this what you are looking for?" He pulled the paper from the pile and handed it him.

Prudenciano made a show out of reading it and gave it back to the clerk. "I'm having trouble reading this copy," he said, "Could you help me?"

The clerk stared at Prudenciano and blinked once. He should have anticipated that this big clod did not know how to read. *Campesinos* were usually not literate. What would Terrazas want with a man like this? The clerk took back the paper, adjusted his glasses, and read the telegram out loud. "To: Luis Terrazas - stop- From: Juan Trujillo -stop- Closed mine temporarily from typhoid outbreak -stop- One of my men traveling to Chihuahua -stop- Name is Prudenciano Nava -stop- Use him -stop- Good with horse and controlling men." The clerk looked up and said, "That's it."

Prudenciano smiled to himself and repeated the sentence in his mind, "*One of my men ...*" The statement pumped up his ego. He asked, "Now, where can I find *Señor* Terrazas?"

The clerk now felt that he was entering dangerous waters. He could not very well send this vagrant to the Terrazas estate, but he could not ignore the telegram either. Thinking quickly, he came up with a compromise. The clerk pointed across the tracks and said, "Nava, if I were you, I would go across the street to the armory. It's that large white brick building over there. A freight train is due in about a half an hour. Terrazas's militia will be there to receive the shipment. Take this copy of the telegram and show it to the captain." The clerk smiled and handed the copy to Prudenciano.

It sounded like a logical plan. So, Prudenciano tipped his hat to the man, stuffed the telegram in his shirt pocket, and walked out of the lobby. The day's heat enveloped him like a furnace. He stood under the porch as he looked across the tracks at the large white building. Paz and he had stood by that white wall only yesterday. The building looked unoccupied for the moment. He waited a few minutes longer till five soldiers arrived on horseback. They were dressed in blue jackets and pants. They wore flat black caps and shiny black boots.

One man jumped off his mount and unlocked the large iron gate. He held the gate open and let the others through.

Prudenciano jumped off the deck and ran across the tracks. The soldier was just closing the gate when Prudenciano shoved out his arm and blocked it open. The man instantly pivoted on the balls of his feet and barked at Prudenciano through the bars with a little too much emotion, "What do you want?" This was a big rough-looking character staring at him and the metal gate suddenly seemed very flimsy.

Prudenciano thought, *He's scared of me.* He put on his most charming smile and said, "I am reporting for a position as a guard." The soldier's face displayed total disbelief. Prudenciano chose this moment to push the gate open and step in.

A man on horseback rode up to them and thundered, 'What is going on here?" He wore stripes on his sleeves that signified a captain's rank. He drew his pistol and eyed Prudenciano. This rough character meant trouble. "State your business," he commanded.

Prudenciano fished the telegram out of his pocket and said, "My name is Prudenciano Nava. My last employer in Torreón sent this telegram to Terrazas. It says that I should be hired as a guard." He handed the telegram to the captain. The man ripped it out of his hand and quickly read it. When he finished, he carefully returned it to Prudenciano. Prudenciano could tell that the captain's demeanor had changed slightly. Perhaps he would believe him.

The captain studied Prudenciano for a moment. God knew that he desperately needed good men. Villa and his mob were killing them at a fast rate, but could he trust this one? The captain sighed, "Bring him to the office. Terrazas will be here shortly. He will decide if *Señor* Nava will join us." The gate closed behind Prudenciano and the soldier pointed toward the central building. Prudenciano obliged and allowed the men to escort him to the office. The interior of the building was cool because the thick walls protected it from the summer heat. Prudenciano was shown a chair, where he seated himself to wait.

The captain went to his desk and began to plan the day's work. A supply train was due in town within the next thirty minutes. It was carrying a shipment of guns and ammunition for Terrazas's forces. The transfer of goods to the armory would take priority over all other responsibilities. His dwindling troops desperately needed the supplies to protect the various construction sites in town. With this thought, the captain involuntarily sighed. Terrazas's most ambitious project, *El Palacio de Bellas Arté* (the Palace of Fine Arts), had just started its ground breaking. The last thing the captain needed was a large controversial project to protect. His forces were already spread dangerously thin.

He looked up from his work and scrutinized the large man in front of him. He was certainly well over six feet tall with an impressive upper body build, but his hair was very long, almost to his shoulders and his beard was unruly. Judging by the wisps of silver in both, he was probably older than what he normally recruited. However, the captain knew that a man's eyes were windows to his soul. This man's eyes were intelligent, brave, and perhaps hard. Maybe he did possess the backbone he so desperately needed now. The captain made a special note to spruce him up if the decision was made to keep him.

A train whistle snapped the captain awake. He took out his pocket watch and shook his head. "Everyone to their posts, now!" shouted the captain, "Damn train is twenty minutes early!" The guards ran to their horses while another sprinted to the gate with his key in hand. Prudenciano lagged behind. He was both curious and excited to watch the event. As he approached the gate, he noticed two men walking along the porch of the train station. Because of the distance and the shade, he could not distinguish their faces, but one of them looked familiar. Prudenciano dwelled on that for a moment. It was how the man walked and carried himself that struck a chord of recognition. Regardless, both of them looked uneasy. They constantly searched for something up and down the track. In addition, each carried a pistol and a belt of bullets. To Prudenciano, all of this added up to one conclusion—these men were going to rob the train.

Prudenciano thought, *But they can't do it themselves. They need help. That must be what they are searching for.* He looked down the tracks. The train was just now crossing the river and would be arriving within the next three minutes. He would have to act fast. Prudenciano ran back to the captain and yelled, "Captain! Those men over there," Prudenciano pointed to the porch, "are going rob the train. I think they are waiting for reinforcements."

The captain looked up and saw the two men on the porch. He could question this man's allegations, but there was no time. The train was already braking. He shouted to a young guard, "Check those two out!" The guard saluted and ran across the tracks toward to the porch. The men had heard the captain's order and appeared agitated when the guard approached. The young man started up the steps when one of the men pulled his pistol and shot him. The captain screamed, "It's a holdup! Take them!"

The robbers flattened themselves behind the wooden posts that supported the roof and began firing in full earnest. The guards scattered behind the wall and entrance to shoot from prearranged vantage points. Prudenciano yelled to the captain, "Give me a gun!" The captain never gave it a second thought. He pulled his rifle from its scabbard and tossed it to him. "*Gracias!*" said Prudenciano as he ran to the far end of the compound. He climbed a ladder to the top of the north wall and started waving the train on.

The engineer realized something was amiss by the scurry of activity at the station. He could barely distinguish the shooting in front of the depot. Now the sight of someone flagging him to steam forward from Terrazas's armory confirmed his suspicions. "Stoke up the boilers!" the engineer ordered his fireman, "We are going through!" He let off the brake and began to open the steam valve. The train responded in its usual slow and consistent manner. It gradually began to build speed. "Remember to keep your head down," shouted the engineer as they neared the depot.

Prudenciano heard the brakes release and the train's boilers fire up. He knew that the train was moving through. He stopped waving and prepared himself to jump. He waited until the engine passed the station before he leaped to the ground. Prudenciano landed on his toes and rolled on the dirt. He sprang to his feet like a cat and started running toward the back of the train. When the last car passed, he jumped across the tracks and ran as fast as he could for the station. If the train hid him from the bandits' view, he calculated that he had a few seconds before they would start looking for someone pursuing them. He figured correctly. The men were still in their prone positions waiting for a clear shot at the armory when he rounded the caboose and sprinted their way.

Prudenciano's speed catapulted him onto the porch and he fired his rifle at the farthest man. The bullet smacked him in the ribs just under the shoulder and pulverized the heart. Prudenciano never broke stride as he bore down on the closest man. He was already turning to fire. Prudenciano knew he would never cock his lever action rifle in time. He hurled his rifle at the man, but it passed harmlessly overhead. The man drew his pistol and aimed. Prudenciano steeled himself. How could this man miss? He waited for the shot that he knew certainly must come, but incredibly the man held his fire.

Prudenciano flung himself at the man and they collided with a brutal force. His pistol knocked loose and skittered across the porch. They wrestled for position. Prudenciano found the man's throat with his free hand and began to squeeze with all his strength. The man's head lifted up into the sunlight as his hat fell away. Suddenly, all of Prudenciano's power drained from his grip and he gasped, "Victoriano Vallejo!"

Victoriano collapsed alongside, him wheezing for air. *No wonder you didn't shoot*, thought Prudenciano. The last of the train was passing though the station. He looked back to the north and saw a group of men riding hard to the depot. They were led by a barrel-chested man with a long full mustache. Prudenciano asked, "Are these your people?"

Victoriano looked up. "*Sí*. The early train threw us off."

"Well, it's over for today," said Prudenciano, "Hurry, before the train passes, run behind the station and join your men. I'll cover for you." Victoriano acted like he wanted to say something, but held it. This was not the time to catch up on the past. He jumped up and bolted for the back of the building.

Prudenciano glanced back to the group of men. The leader held up his hand and halted their advance. Prudenciano now had a chance to get a good look at the man. He was a couple inches shy of six feet tall. His curly short-cropped hair was tucked under a military style hat that had a moderately wide brim. The man would have been rather unassuming if it hadn't been for his eyes. Those eyes seemed to burn with a seething wrath, like glowing embers smoldering within his skull. They raked over Prudenciano as he stood to face him.

With a wave of the hand, the leader executed a retreat. With the train gone and the troops alerted, there was no point in fighting today. In a cloud of dust, the attackers turned toward the mountains and fled. Victoriano leaped upon the back of one of the horses and clutched the rider. As suddenly as they had arrived, they were gone.

The guards came running over as soon as the mob was out of sight. Prudenciano was still staring at the fleeing men when the guards came up from behind. "Man, that was fantastic!" exclaimed one of the young guards as he kicked over the dead bandit. "Where did you learn to fight like that?" Prudenciano did not reply. Instead he turned around and bent down to the guard that was shot. He felt for a pulse along the carotid artery and found none.

Prudenciano shook his head and thought as he stood up, *What a useless death*. He addressed the rest of the group, "Who was the man that led the riders? Have you ever seen him before?"

The captain answered, "*Sí*. His name is Pancho Villa and the men who follow him are called *Villistas*. They live only to rob and kill. I had a feeling that they would try for the arms shipment." There was that name again. Prudenciano needed time to think about all of this. He knew Victoriano would never lower himself to be a common thief. He was a man of principle. So what was the *Villistas'* mission?

"Captain!" shouted one of the guards. "Here comes Terrazas's wagon!" From the south, the same wagon with its black and white horses that Prudenciano had seen yesterday approached at a breakneck speed. It wheeled up to the landing as the driver pulled back on the reins. The passenger door blew open before the doorman could jump off the driver's bench. Out stepped a distinguished-looking man in his early sixties. He wore a finely tailored, three-pieced dark suit with a matching felt hat. His angry face was clean shaven.

He marched up to the captain and snarled, "What happened to the shipment? We need those supplies!"

The captain was still recovering from the adrenaline rush of the battle. Terrazas had flustered him and the combination caused him to clip his speech, "We saved it. Train passed through." Then the captain took a deep breath and continued more smoothly, "It was Villa and his gang again. They tried to rob the train. Nava here tipped us off in time to react." Terrazas seemed to relax a bit when he learned that the robbery was foiled. He turned his attention to the ruffian among them.

Terrazas asked, "Do I know you?"

Prudenciano realized that the most important man in Chihuahua was asking him for his name. He loved the attention and savored it for a moment before replying, "My name is Prudenciano Nava and Juan Trujillo asked me to see you. He said that you could use me as a guard."

For an instant, Terrazas's eyes flickered with recognition. "So, you are the one that Juan sent me a telegram about. Juan is an excellent judge of men." Terrazas ran an appraising eye up and down Prudenciano as he would a prize bull. The assessment made Prudenciano feel cheap. Terrazas turned his attention back to the captain. "I suppose he will do. After you get the arms secured, clean him up and get him to work." Terrazas almost tripped over the dead bandit as he walked over him without a second thought and returned to this coach.

As the coach pulled away, Prudenciano stared after it with mixed emotions. He had elated feelings about being hired, but he could not help noticing that Terrazas never commented once about the dead man on the porch. *To him*, thought Prudenciano, *we are all expendable*.

———•———

As he rode in front of his men, Pancho Villa could tell that they were too late. The train had come early and was passing through the station. It looked like one rebel was down and a huge man was getting the upper hand on Vallejo. The whole situation had gone bad.

Villa swore under his breath as he raised his hand to halt the advance. Victoriano seemed to escape. *Actually, he was let go,* thought Villa. *Strange.* Then the big man stood and faced him. Villa stared straight at him, but the man did not avoid his eyes. Villa mused, *This one is just a common man. Why does he fight for Terrazas?* He allowed himself a few more seconds to study the man and then ordered the retreat. They were low on weapons and men. No sense risking both by hanging around any longer.

They rode west out of town and into the Sierra Madre mountains.

They trotted their horses up the foothills and across the increasingly rugged terrain. The brush and trees became thicker as they rose in elevation. The vegetation screened their movements. As they rode deeper into the canyons, they split into four groups to confuse anyone tracking them. By the time night fell, they had regrouped and met at their hidden ranch.

The ranch was old, but in good condition. The men had done the repair work themselves. It consisted of a main house, barn, a corral, and tents to shelter additional men. A box canyon enclosed the entire facility. Many *federales* had searched fruitlessly for this hidden lair.

Inside, Villa counted his men and was surprised that Victoriano was with them. Villa had twenty good men in his group. They were men he could trust. He personally felt the loss of any of them. Men like these were precious, but it was getting tougher to keep them alive without guns and supplies. Villa gestured for Victoriano to come over and give his report. Victoriano walked to his leader and Villa put his arm around his shoulders and asked, "What happened?"

Victoriano began, "A series of events went wrong. First an old friend of mine from Torreón thought we were suspicious. He must have alerted the guards. Second, the train came twenty minutes early. You did not have time to get into position. Lastly, I underestimated my friend. He slipped behind the train and killed Diego before we knew that he was on us."

Villa pressed, "Why didn't you kill him?" Victoriano was known for his quick and accurate shots. Friend or enemy, Villa felt Victoriano had an allegiance to the cause. He should have avenged Diego's death.

Victoriano avoided Villa's gaze for a second. The entire room was silent. All eyes were studying him. Victoriano suddenly looked up at Villa and said, "He saved my life a few years ago. We were trapped in a cave-in. He risked his life to save mine. I couldn't shoot him. I owed him."

Villa studied Victoriano's face for a few seconds and then nodded. "I understand the responsibility of owing a life," he said gravely, "but the debt is now paid. Next time, I expect you to do your duty. *Comprende?*"

Victoriano responded, "*Sí.*"

"*Bueno,*" stated Villa. He clasped Victoriano on the shoulder and turned to the rest of the men. "Now, what do we have to eat?"

———

Paz was growing worried. It was late in the afternoon and Prudenciano still had not come back to their camp. She awoke in the morning and found him gone. She cared for Alcaria the best she could in the sweltering heat. Her swollen abdomen strained her back as she climbed the steep riverbanks after the toddler. She had little food and water to give Alcaria and her unborn baby pulled nutrients from her own body, which made her ravenous. All of this added to her growing anxiety. Paz dared to think, *Did he finally leave us?* She had certainly told him to leave them several times during their trek north. Had he really done it this time?

She pushed the thought away and busied herself by mending Alcaria's shirt. The youngster always seemed to be tearing her clothes. Within a short time, the feeling of dread began to creep back. Paz wailed, "Oh, where are you?" Alcaria stopped what she was doing and waddled back to her.

"Mama?" asked Alcaria as she reached up and held her mother's face. "Are you looking for Papa?" Paz was amazed how perceptive the child was.

"*Sí*, little one. I was just curious when Papa was coming home from work."

"Don't worry, Mama. He come soon," stated Alcaria with certainty. Then she returned to her play without any trepidation.

Paz said to herself, "I hope so, my little one. I hope so." As she was returning to her sewing, she heard a wagon approaching along the road that followed the river. The sound of horses pulling a cart grew louder, then stopped alongside them. She quickly put down her mending and scooped up Alcaria. Paz did not know what to expect in this town and she was not going to take any chances. She bolted into the brush and crouched down in the weeds with Alcaria held tightly to her breast.

Suddenly, Prudenciano stepped into the camp followed by two other men in uniform. He looked around and spotted Paz in the bushes nearby. He laughed and motioned for her to come out. She carefully rose from her hiding place and set Alcaria down. The little girl squealed and ran to her Papa. He laughed again, picked her up, and gave her a hug and kiss. Alcaria turned around and said, "See Mama. It's all right."

Paz came over to Prudenciano and stood by him. She was greatly relieved to see him, but tried not to show it. Prudenciano announced to the guards, "This is my family and this is all that we own. Let's load it up and go to our new home." The guards grinned at Paz and began to help her fill her packs. Within a short time, they were making their way back up to bank to the wagon.

Along the way back, Paz asked Prudenciano quietly, "What took you so long? I nearly died in the heat." Prudenciano began to say something, but choked it back. How could he tell her that he was in a gunfight during his first day in Chihuahua? She would never understand.

Prudenciano said simply, "I was delayed." Paz looked up at him and started say something, but thought better of it. He was back and taking them somewhere better than their camp. That was all that mattered.

———————

Terrazas's guards enjoyed housing provided by the estate. The homes were spacious and well built with brick. The foundations and flooring were poured concrete. Paz had never lived in such luxury before. Clean water was available nearby and used water could be disposed down drains in each home. Paz immediately began arranging the furniture and preparing the bedroom for their new baby. This work gave her great satisfaction and fulfilled her nesting instincts.

The guards gave Prudenciano a bath, haircut, and trimmed his beard neatly along his jaw. Then they issued him a new uniform complete with shiny black boots and a smart-looking cap. Paz had to alter the coat to fit across his wide shoulders. When he donned his outfit, he looked truly magnificent. His muscular torso tapered down to his trim waist, which accented his long, muscular legs. The boots gave him an additional one and half inches to his already impressive height. The cap fit nicely on his head and made him only more handsome, with streaks of gray along his temples. He was in tremendous shape for a fifty-four-year-old man.

Paz made him stand in the middle of the living room as she walked around him and inspected her work. Prudenciano asked, "Well, what do you think?" She had to hold her breath. She thought he looked incredibly handsome, but she could tell by the twinkle in his eye that he was fishing for such a compliment. Paz did not want to feed his inflated ego because she knew that once it grew unchecked he would strut around the house like a peacock.

Paz pretended to contemplate his appearance for a few moments and then said, "I think it will do." Prudenciano's smile faded for a second. Then he reached out for her and kissed her hard on the mouth. After several seconds, he released her and put his hand on her stomach. The baby seemed to move with emotion.

He whispered huskily, "You know that I look better than that." Paz felt weak in the knees. How could he have read her thoughts so accurately? All she could do was nod meekly and brush the rough kiss from her lips. Yes, he was going to be impossible to live with.

———————

Chihuahua was a relatively new city by Mexican standards. Before the early 1800s, Chihuahua was nothing more than a meeting place for traders and ranchers. The northern Indian tribes frequently attacked the Spaniards who tried to settle in the area. The fiercely independent Spaniards and *Creoles* refused to be intimidated and slowly enslaved the Indians. With an influx of money from the Díaz machine, the prominent families of Chihuahua such as the Terrazases, the Cuiltys, the Lujanes, and the Creels modernized the city. The upsurge in construction created many jobs for the working class. However, it also generated consternation among those who sought to regain property that was unfairly taken from them.

Prudenciano began his first day on the job with all the excitement of a child going to school for the first time. *It's incredible how a uniform commands respect*, thought Prudenciano as he rode his beautiful horse to work. People he'd never met tipped their hats to him as he passed. Women waved and children pointed and shouted greetings. He felt like he was ten feet tall. This was truly Prudenciano's kind of job. The captain assigned him to guard *El Palacio de Bellas Artes* construction site. His duties consisted of making his presence known around the project. In other words, his job entailed little work and lots of show. He shared the limelight with a young man named Felipe. Together, they spent their time riding slowly around the enormous compound.

El Palacio de Bellas Arté was in the early stages of construction. The crews concentrated on the foundations. Men hauled bags of cement in wheelbarrows to the wooden forms that acted as molds for the basement walls. The sheer size of the building required hundreds of men to transport thousands of bags to the work area. Wagons constantly arrived and left building materials at the premises. The whole area was a frenzy of activity. Thus, if Prudenciano really wanted to take his job seriously, he would have found it impossible to scrutinize every detail. His choice of simply being visible was unintentionally the best decision.

At the end of the day, they rode to the armory and regrouped with the rest of the guards . They traded stories and information. After all the banter, it was time for everyone to go home. For Prudenciano, the socializing was the perfect end to a perfect day.

———

Paz gave birth to their second daughter on July 13, 1910. The labor was easier this time and she had the assistance of several midwives from the guard housing to help her. Paz named her Joaquina because she thought the musical-sounding name suited her. The beautiful baby was perfectly formed and healthy. Alcaria was thrilled to have a living doll to love and she hovered around the bed hoping that her mother might need her assistance.

Prudenciano had hoped for a boy, but when he held her for the first time, his heart squeezed and he fell hopelessly in love with her. "Joaquina," he whispered, "you are the most beautiful baby I have ever seen." Paz watched him through partially opened eyes. She smiled as she observed him studying the baby's face while he fumbled to hold her just right. His big hands trembled with uncertainty as he tried to hold her level. Finally, he gave up and laid her down on the bed next to Paz.

She thought, *How can a man who can flip a bull over by its tail be so awkward with a baby?* She opened her eyes and asked Prudenciano, "Well, what do you think?"

He smiled, stooped down, and kissed her on the forehead. He smoothed back her hair and said, "I think we make beautiful babies."

Porfirio Díaz believed in the same myopic philosophy as most of the world's dictators—if they crush the working class, then the rest of the population will automatically obey them. As he strangled the working class into submission, he was blind to the smoldering discontent among the well-educated middle class that had been excluded from politics, land ownership, and financial credit from Mexican banks. As the presidential election drew near, a leader rose from this agitated group to oppose Díaz. His name was Francisco Madero of Coahuila.

Madero was a wealthy man. He kept his hair and long mustache impeccably trimmed. He often wore a stylish three-piece suit and fine leather boots, always crowned with a banded top hat. He looked like a *hacendado*, but his views were revolutionary. He believed that every man had a right to vote, possess land, and be assessed fair taxes. His words excited the masses in Mexico to back him as a candidate for the presidency of Mexico.

The Díaz machine reacted by blatantly rigging the voting booths and compromising the vote counting across the country. When the votes were counted during July 1910, Díaz miraculously won a landslide victory. Outraged, Madero lashed out at the Díaz machine and called for a national uprising to oust the president. Díaz responded by throwing Madero in prison. To prevent a jailbreak, Díaz kept Madero's whereabouts secret by constantly moving him from one prison to another.

During October of 1910, Díaz relocated Madero to the San Luis Potosí federal penitentiary. Madero's spirit was not broken and, during this dark time of his life, he prayed for strength to see his cause to its end. Fortified by prayer, he picked up a pen and eloquently wrote what was later known as the Plan of San Luis Potosí. His essay declared the presidential election illegal and argued that he was actually the lawful president of Mexico. He passionately asked citizens of Mexico to rise up in arms on November 20, 1910 and overthrow the Díaz regime.

Madero allowed some of the guards to read his writing. The letters moved them and they plotted to help Madero escape. A few nights later, two guards abruptly woke Madero and whisked him down the silent corridors and into a waiting coach. Within a few days, Madero safely crossed the United States border and went into exile in San Antonio, Texas.

Madero wasted no time in assembling sympathizers to his cause. Together they plotted the overthrow of Díaz. Their plan required two elements—a large force of fighting men and, perhaps even more difficult, leaders who would guide these men in the revolution. To solve these problems, Madero's followers infiltrated Mexico and began to recruit the men he needed.

Madero's first break occurred when a disgruntled banker from Chihuahua stepped forward to undertake the task of forming an army within the state. His name was Abraham Gonzalez. He was educated, possessed moderate wealth, and was extremely intelligent. He was smart enough to know that Díaz's economic policies would eventually ruin the country. Gonzalez had seen his own career dissolve when the Terrazases and Creels consolidated the banks in Chihuahua. The rich now became wealthier and offered credit only to a privileged few.

His unemployment forced Gonzalez to become a representative of an El Paso company that dealt with Mexican cattle. Through buying cattle from many suppliers throughout Chihuahua, he eventually met Francisco Villa. Gonzalez smiled when he spotted the Terrazas brand on several of the animals. It seemed fitting that he should make a living from the stolen property of the man who was corrupting the business practices of Mexico.

But Gonzalez could not forget Villa's burning eyes. Villa was filled with contempt for the current regime and he would not rest until it was demolished. Terrazas had tried every trick in the book to capture this man and failed. Thus, Gonzalez knew that Villa could lead men into battle and win. He was therefore Gonzalez's choice to command the Chihuahua forces. Gonzalez sent out messengers to find him and arrange a meeting.

———•••••———

"All right, gentlemen," said the captain as he motioned for everyone to gather around him. "I want everyone to pay attention." The men had just arrived at the armory after their day's work. Prudenciano was in a jovial mood today. Several women had batted their eyes at him when he was patrolling the construction site. This greatly boosted his self-esteem and made him feel cocky. The captain had to give him a stern look to bring him in line. "Take a good look at this poster. It's a drawing of Pancho Villa. Our sources tell us that he is in Chihuahua now. If you see him, you must report it immediately. *Comprende?*" Everyone nodded.

The captain continued, "Now, here are some composites of some of his main men. They too are in town." He handed out four more posters. Prudenciano scanned them. He did not recognize the first three. However, the fourth one almost took his breath away. It was Victoriano Vallejo. Prudenciano deadpanned and abruptly handed the posters to the next man.

Felipe raised his hand in the back. "Captain, how do you know this?"

The captain considered this question for a moment and then said in a quieter tone, "I can't go into specifics, but we have a man inside the Villa camp. Let it go at that." The men were intrigued, but it was clear that the captain was not going to reveal any more details. "Remember, if any of you see any suspicious characters, report them to me *pronto*. Now, go home. *Buenas noches.*" The captain dismissed them and each began to saunter home.

For Prudenciano, the elation of the day dwindled as he thought about Victoriano. *How could he be a wanted man? What am I going to do if I see him again?*

Faithful followers of Pancho Villa were called *Villistas* and only a select few knew of Villa's personal home in the city of Chihuahua. Villa had purchased it last year under a false name. He would wait until night to slip in the back door and he left the same way before dawn. The home was comfortable and provided a convenient safe haven.

Tonight began as a typical evening of sharing a meal with friends and planning future escapades. Villa always listened to his men for their ideas and plans. Sometimes he adopted them into his schemes. Other times he kept the main concept, but radically changed the method of implementation. All six of them were gathered around the kitchen table when a knock was heard at the back door. Immediately, the lantern was doused and guns were drawn. "Who is it?" demanded Villa through the unopened door.

A voice answered from the darkness, "Claro Reza. I come with a message." The *Villistas* had witnessed Reza's capture by Terrazas's men only a few months ago. Villa was concerned that the small man would crack under the interrogation and give away many facts about their operations. However, after a few weeks, no posse arrived at the ranch or at this house. Thus, Villa thought that either Terrazas had killed the man or he managed to convince his captors that he possessed no important information. Regardless, he was quite surprised to have Reza knocking at his door.

Villa slowly opened the door while keeping his gun at the ready. Reza was standing by himself on the porch. A quick check to each side of him verified that there was no one else hiding in ambush. Villa motioned for Reza to step inside. He responded by jumping into the kitchen and quickly closing the door behind him. Someone lit the lamp and Reza found himself surrounded by *Villistas*.

Pancho confronted him. "All right, Reza. How did you get out of jail?"

Reza was cursed with a weasel-like face, which bred mistrust among men. It always produced a bad first impression that Reza had learned to anticipate and diffuse. He needed his best performance tonight or he would not live to give another. "The guards finally let me go," said Reza confidently. "They said I was useless to them."

Victoriano interjected, "But, they caught you red-handed stealing cattle. We were with you, remember?"

For a split second, Victoriano's comment caught Reza off guard, but he quickly recovered and smoothly answered. "It turns out that no one actually saw me rustle cattle. So, after a few weeks, they decided to let me go." No one in the room bought this story, but on the other hand, no one could refute it either. Reza sensed that everyone was at the precipice of indecision, so he decided to press forward with his mission. "I come to you with a request from Abraham Gonzalez. He wants to meet with you."

Villa asked, "Who is Gonzalez and why would I want to meet with him?" He vaguely remembered him as a cattle buyer he had dealt with about a year ago.

"Gonzalez is organizing an army to overthrow Díaz. He wants you to lead the forces in Chihuahua." Someone whistled softly as others mumbled among themselves. Villa remained silent and studied Reza's face for signs of betrayal. Villa had to admit that the concept intrigued him, but he was having a tough time trusting Reza, let alone Gonzalez.

Villa finally responded, "I see. I want you to tell Gonzalez to meet me here tomorrow night. I want you to bring him here alone. *Comprende?*"

"*Sí,*" answered Reza. He could tell by the look on everyone's faces that he was no longer welcome. He put his hat on and exited the back door like a thief into the night.

"You know, Pancho," said Victoriano as he looked out the back window after Reza, "The guards never just let cattle rustlers go. We must keep an eye out for him." Villa nodded and unconsciously patted his pistol in its holster. The unspoken message was clearly received by all in the room.

The following night Reza led Abraham Gonzalez to Villa's home. Reza knocked on the kitchen door and waited for someone to answer. They had to linger for a few minutes until the door slowly opened. A man verified Reza's identity and motioned for the two to enter. Gonzalez was not used to these cloak-and-dagger precautions, but he understood their concerns. They were all wanted men. They all had a price on their heads, especially Villa—except his bounty was good whether he was dead or alive.

When the door closed and the curtains were drawn tight, the men lit the lamps. As the light filled the room, Gonzalez realized that he was surrounded by rough men. A stout man with the fiery eyes stood in front of him. His unforgettable appearance rekindled his memory. He looked more fierce than the last time they had met. Gonzalez stretched out his hand and said, "*Señor* Villa, I presume."

Villa reluctantly and slowly took the gentleman's hand. Gonzalez gave him back a sincere and firm handshake. Villa noticed that Gonzalez had the hand of a wealthy man. It was smooth and not accustomed to manual work. Villa always mistrusted upper-class people. He was suspicious of Gonzalez's intent. Gonzalez seemed to sense Villa's apprehension and made an overture to him. "May I sit down? We have a lot to discuss." Villa nodded his head and pointed to a chair by the table. "*Gracias*," said Gonzalez as he settled himself.

Villa took the chair directly across the table from Gonzalez and started the conversation. "I hear that you want to talk with me. Why?"

Gonzalez replied with a question, "Have you ever heard of Francisco Madero of Coahuila?"

Villa answered, "*Sí*. He ran against Díaz. I heard he is in San Antonio."

"Correct. He is building an army to overthrow Díaz and he wants you to lead it."

Villa asked, "Why should I?" He could not possibly see himself fighting for two *hacendados* such as Madero and Gonzalez. They represented everything that he opposed. They were rich, had never worked in the fields, and probably employed many people such as himself.

Gonzalez replied, "Madero seeks to provide equal opportunities for all men, regardless of social and financial status." Gonzalez spoke to Villa as a peer. He explained Madero's views to him as one intellectual to another. At no time did Gonzalez talk down to him. He passionately discussed Madero's plans for a new government. As the evening wore on, Villa's animosities gradually dissipated.

Villa thought, *Could it be that these men seek the same goal as I?* He stroked his long mustache as he contemplated Gonzalez's words.

Gonzalez, seeing that Villa was wavering, pressed forward. "*Señor* Villa, please come to Madero's reelection meeting tomorrow night.

You can meet others who are prepared to go to battle. When you see the type of men who are prepared to fight, you will agree that we stand for the same principles that you do."

Villa thought this was a very good idea. He asked, "How can I come undetected?"

"Here," said Gonzalez as he opened his suit coat and reached his right hand deep into his vest. "I have something for you."

Villa thought wildly, *"He's got a gun!"* He reacted out of the same instinct that had served him well for the past twenty years. Like a striking rattlesnake, he flicked his pistol out of its holster, cocked it, and pointed it between Gonzalez's eyes. Villa had adjusted the trigger pull to a mere four ounces. He only had to breathe and the gun would fire.

If Gonzalez was shaken by this affair, he did not show it. Without taking his eyes off Villa, he slowly withdrew his hand with a key. Gonzalez said evenly, "You may use this key to enter the back door." Villa grunted his acknowledgment, pulled the barrel up, and let the hammer down softly with his thumb. Gonzalez's cool impressed him. However, Villa could just make out the faint beads of perspiration forming along his brow. This man was human after all.

The day promised to be another scorcher. Not a cloud in the sky and it was already hot for so early in the morning. Prudenciano was tired from a night of broken sleep. Joaquina had demanded to be fed and changed every few hours. Although Paz did most of the care, her activities and Joaquina's crying disrupted his normally blissful rest. Today's heat was only going to aggravate his foul mood.

Prudenciano and Felipe began their daily circuit around the compound. The walls were going up quickly. Already the first floor was almost enclosed. As they started down the street, Felipe leaned over from his horse and tapped Prudenciano on the shoulder. "Nava," he said, "isn't that the captain?" Prudenciano squinted against the morning sun to see a uniformed man walking quickly to an alley close to the construction site.

"*Sí*," said Prudenciano. He hated it when a younger man noticed something so important and he did not. "I'm going over to find out what's happening. You stay here." Prudenciano threw the reins to Felipe and dismounted. Felipe was curious too, but reluctantly obeyed. He watched Prudenciano lope across the street and sneak around the building.

Reza was nervous as he waited in the alley. He hated these clandestine meetings, especially in broad daylight. There were too many prying eyes around. If anyone even breathed a word to Villa, he was a dead man. The sound of a foot kicking a rock startled Reza. He spun around to see the captain striding toward him. Reza exclaimed, "Damn, man! Anyone could have seen you come back here."

The captain asked mockingly, "What's the matter, Reza? Are you afraid that somebody will see us talking?"

"*Sí*," answered Reza. "Don't you care?"

"You should have thought of that before you tried to rustle Terrazas's cattle. If you hadn't agreed to our terms, you would be swinging from the end of a rope by now. At least this way you have a chance to live. Now, what did you find out?"

Reza stared at him for a moment as he considered his limited options. He sighed and recounted the meeting between Villa and Gonzalez. While the two were conversing, Prudenciano crept along a hedge nearby. He knelt on the grass and strained to hear the discussion.

"So, Madero plans to carry out his revolution?" repeated the captain. "Who is involved?"

Reza replied, "An ex-banker named Abraham Gonzalez is organizing Madero's reelection in Chihuahua. He wants Villa to lead the revolt."

The captain hissed through clenched teeth, "Villa! I should have known. Now, listen closely. This is what I want you to do. You must go to the next reelection meeting and note all who attend. Then report back to me, *comprende?*"

"*Sí*," answered Reza, "but what about my pardon? You promised that in a few weeks I would have it. I can't keep doing this."

The captain said sternly, "You will get a pardon. Just get me those names and tell me their plans. Then we will talk about your pardon." Reza did not like this response, but decided not to push the issue. He bent his neck in a submissive manner and kicked at the ground. The captain had him in a tight spot. For now, he had to play along.

"Don't think about leaving town, Reza," said the captain with a smile. "I'll just track you down and kill you. Save us both some trouble and get that information." The captain turned and left him shuffling silently in place. When the captain was gone, Reza violently kicked a rock through the hedge. It missed Prudenciano's head by an inch. Then he abruptly marched off in the opposite direction.

Prudenciano remained motionless for a few moments and then gradually made his way back. "So, what happened?" asked Felipe as he handed the reins back to Prudenciano. He mounted his horse and gathered the reins in his hands.

"The captain has a spy within the reelection movement."

Felipe whistled and asked, "Who was it? Did you recognize him?"

"No, but he had a face like a rat or a weasel. I could never forget it." Something Prudenciano said struck a chord in Felipe's mind. He just could not remember what and it bothered him.

They continued to ride their circuit in silence. After a few minutes, Felipe spoke again as he stared straight ahead, "I suppose we will be breaking up the reelectionists soon." Prudenciano grunted in response. He was deeply troubled. If he helped round up these revolutionaries, he would invariably have to confront Victoriano again. He knew he could not harm him.

Prudenciano thought, *Where does a man's loyalty to his employer stop and his service to his friends begin?* He felt that the lines of right and wrong were blurred. As he thought about it some more, he came to the conclusion there was only one thing to do. He had to warn Victoriano Vallejo.

Victoriano Huerta scowled as he led his pathetic troops into Chihuahua. Their mood was jovial, but Huerta could not share their elation. He followed orders to take land from poor farmers who rightfully owned it. The farmers had put up a futile resistance and his men trounced them. Only a coward would rejoice over such a victory. It disgusted him.

Huerta was a bull of a man. His six-foot height and muscular body gave him a commanding appearance. His square head and thick neck supported a stern-looking face. No one ever argued with Huerta because he always appeared ready to kill you at the slightest provocation. Through sheer intimidation, he bullied men to follow his orders. He was known throughout the federal army as a ruthless man, one who would use any means to get what he wanted.

What Huerta wanted now was power. The power to fight worthwhile causes instead of property squabbles. The power to build a government the way he saw appropriate instead of plodding along with the fruits of the Díaz machine. The power to be an important man.

The troops followed him to the garrison just south of town. He remained on his horse as he watched them dismount and unload their animals. He shook his head again. *All of them are oblivious to whom they serve. They would all die in a fair fight.* He now thought about the offer he had received a few weeks ago from Señor Gonzalez. A chance to build a new government. An opportunity to lead a determined army to overthrow the country's dictators.

That evening, Huerta came to his decision. Like any good military leader, he made decisions and acted upon them with absolute determination. He never lamented about bad choices. If a decision turned bad, he accepted the implications and moved forward. Huerta chose to follow Madero's revolution. *"Besides,"* smiled Huerta to himself, *"if everything went right, I could even become the governor of this state. I'd be a good ruler of Mexico, too."*

Paz knew that something was bothering Prudenciano. He had scarcely said two words during dinner. He usually was full of stories and bragging. Alcaria and he would trade teases, which made the meal an enjoyable family time, but tonight he appeared deeply troubled. When she commented about it, he brusquely denied that there was a problem. His behavior bothered her. Prudenciano was capable of getting himself into great trouble. If he was this agitated, she needed to know what it was.

Prudenciano stood up from the table and walked to the window. He noticed that a deep, restful night had fallen upon the city. It gave the illusion of tranquility and shrouded the simmering discontent among the residents. The streets were quiet and empty. He took a deep breath and let it out slowly. He knew what he had to do and it would be dangerous.

Prudenciano wore his civilian clothes. With his hat in hand, he started for the door. Paz stopped him short. "Prudenciano," she said in her most sincere voice as she walked up behind him. "I know that you are facing something that requires courage. Remember that I am here for you if you need me."

Her words slew him. Prudenciano hesitated at the door and turned to say something. He looked down into her eyes. She was truly a beautiful woman. Paz was no longer a girl. These last few years had forced her to mature ahead of her time—both physically and mentally. However, he just could not tell her that he had to warn a friend of impending disaster, especially if that warning meant betraying his employer. "I'll be back as soon as I can," he promised her. He put his hat on and disappeared into the night.

He knew just where to go. Terrazas's men had identified Villa's house several days ago. Since then, they kept it under surveillance. Prudenciano figured that it would be the most logical place to search for Victoriano. He chose to walk and blend into the shadows of the night. He set a quick pace that ate the miles away. Within an hour, he stood in the dark recesses directly across the street of the deserted-looking home.

Prudenciano patiently studied the situation. The entire street looked abandoned. He could not see any signs of men watching the premises, but he had the distinct feeling of someone watching him. There seemed to be something in the dark shadows of the trees, but he could not tell for sure. After several minutes, Prudenciano still could not see anyone and decided to take a chance. He walked slowly to the back of the house. Here, the darkness was complete and this worried him, for a man with a knife could easily hide and strike from behind. He felt his belly tighten and wished that he'd brought a gun.

As he approached the back door, he noticed a lamp burning dimly through the partially curtained window. Somebody was home. He made a move to knock at the door, but thought better of it. Instead, he threw a pebble and bounced it off the door. The rock made a surprisingly loud bang. Immediately, the light went out. Prudenciano heard the scurrying of feet and moving chairs. He definitely had their attention.

A couple of minutes went by without any response. Prudenciano threw another pebble. This time the door cracked open and a quiet low voice called, "Who's there?"

"A friend of Victoriano Vallejo," answered Prudenciano in the same hushed manner. The door closed for a while, then slowly opened a little wider.

Someone asked cautiously, "Who are you?" This time Prudenciano recognized Vallejo's voice. He was here!

"Prudenciano Nava. I must talk with you." The door opened even wider. An arm stuck out and waved him in. Prudenciano took a deep breath and came inside. As he entered the doorway, hands grabbed him and threw him forward. He stumbled to regain his balance, but someone knocked him to the floor. His temper flared and he rolled over to confront his assailant. The lamp flamed up and Prudenciano saw that he was surrounded by men pointing cocked pistols at his head.

They had him. All he could do now was play along. Prudenciano smiled at his hosts and held out his hands in surrender. A man knelt down and padded the sides of his body. "He's clean," the man announced. A few of the men holstered their guns; however, Prudenciano noticed that a young nervous recruit still held a bead on him. Prudenciano slowly rose to his feet. Victoriano appeared out of the darkness from an adjacent room. He motioned for a man to check the window. He peered through the curtain and then signaled to Victoriano that all was clear.

"Nava," said Victoriano shaking his head, "you know better than to come here. Why all the trouble?"

Prudenciano played it cool although his nerves were drawn tight. "I thought that I could get a drink with an old friend. That's all."

Victoriano looked dubious. "Right. You came all the way across town to drink with me. I'm honored. Now, what's the real reason?"

'Wait a minute," said the young man covering Prudenciano with his gun. "I remember you! You are one of Terrazas's guards at *El Pala-*

cio de Bellas Artes. Aren't you?" The rest of the men leaned forward awaiting his answer. Prudenciano knew this was a critical moment. If he answered wrong, these men would shoot him. He looked into each man's eyes to buy time to think about his response.

Victoriano intervened. "*Sí*, he works for Terrazas, but he is not one of them. See how he comes here unarmed and alone? Let's hear what he has to say." The man at the window did another a check and then nodded his approval back to the others. The men began to relax again.

Prudenciano thought, *Now we're even, Vallejo.* He composed himself and addressed Victoriano. "I saw my captain talking in secret with one of your men." This statement captured everyone's absolute attention. Betrayal was the worst possible offense. "Apparently this man was caught rustling. In exchange for his life, he agreed to spy for the captain and report the plans of the Reelectionists' revolt."

Victoriano gritted his teeth and asked, "What did this man look like?"

Prudenciano replied, "He had a very distinctive face. He looked like a weasel or a rat."

The men roared, "Reza!"

One man, Eleuterio Soto, drew his knife, slashed the air, and said, "I will personally kill him!" There were numerous rumblings of agreement amongst the men.

Suddenly, someone spoke out. "Wait a minute. Why are you warning us? You have nothing to gain by this."

Prudenciano stared straight at Victoriano and said, "I take care of my friends. No matter what the problem."

All could see that Victoriano was deeply touched. He smiled, embraced Prudenciano, and said, "I think you earned that drink, Prudenciano." The men agreed.

Later that evening, Prudenciano left the house considerably happier than when he came. A large man who was hiding in an adjacent room stepped into the kitchen and joined the men. He surveyed the group. Soto asked him, "Well, Villa, shall we kill Reza?"

"*Sí*, soon," answered Villa, "But I will need a third volunteer to see that justice is done. Who will help me?"

A determined young man named José Sánchez stepped forward. "I would be honored to help."

Villa smiled and said, "All right, you are in. Now, did that Nava fellow leave any tequila? Damn, that man can drink!"

————

During the next few days, Prudenciano kept a low profile. He had no idea if anyone had seen him enter or leave Villa's house. If so, no one was showing it. The evening meetings at the armory were routine. The same trading of stories and comradely banter were exchanged without exception. He began to believe that he had got away with it. He knew that he was lucky this time.

Several days later, the captain called the men together as usual for their nightly meeting. However, the stern look on his face signaled to everyone that he had something important to discuss. The captain addressed the men in a serious tone. "Tomorrow, we will provide protection for an undercover agent." The men watched him with fascination and excitement. Life as a guard can be very boring, but sometimes unusual assignments like this added spice to their jobs. "I want everyone to meet here at two o'clock. We will then ride over to the reelection meetinghouse and surround it from a distance. We are not to be seen, but if the agent needs help, we must move quickly to his aid. *Comprende?* I will brief you more tomorrow. *Buenas noches.*"

Well, it's started, thought Prudenciano as he headed for the door. After meeting and drinking with the infamous *Villistas*, he could no longer visualize them as a gang of thieves. They were determined men who were sick of living on the crumbs tossed to them by *hacendados*. Prudenciano felt for them.

"Nava," said Felipe as he punched Prudenciano in the arm. "Looks like we get to save that spy you saw the other day." Prudenciano just grunted and kept walking. Felipe persisted, "Hey, I finally remembered something about that description you gave of the man you saw talking with the captain. A few months ago, we arrested a man stealing Terrazas's cattle. He looked like a ferret. I think his name was Reza." Prudenciano pretended that he did not care. Felipe continued, "You know, he just disappeared. No hanging or shooting. Just one day he was gone. People say Reza lives in the shadows. He always sees who comes and goes. I bet that he is the spy. Kind of fits, huh?"

Suddenly, Prudenciano's stomach flopped as he remembered that feeling of being watched outside Villa's house. He thought, *Was he there? Did he tell anyone?*

The meeting started normally enough. Villa and his two trusted guards, Soto and Sánchez, arrived quietly at Abraham Gonzalez's house. Other determined men slipped silently through the back door. Much to Gonzalez's dislike, everyone was armed. Only half the men knew each other; however, they all recognized Villa. Reza floated in the background. He saw everything and said little. Only Soto and Sánchez paid him any attention.

Around a large oak table, Gonzalez led the discussions in his respectful and persuasive manner. They discussed tactics and logistical matters. Everyone became so engrossed in the conversations that the afternoon hours seemed to melt away. By five thirty, someone finally looked at the time and expressed his disbelief. Gonzalez sighed and quickly summarized the day's meeting. "Gentlemen, we have discussed and solved many important issues today. The hour of the revolution draws near. We must meet again soon to work out the last of the details, but we have stayed here too long. When you leave here, scatter as soon as possible and try to be inconspicuous. Go now."

The men all said their hasty goodbyes and slowly exited the house in pairs and threes. Villa caught Soto's eyes and nodded. Soto understood and grabbed Sánchez by the arm and pulled him to the back of the room. Villa casually waited until Reza moved for the door and then nonchalantly left beside him. The streets were filled with people walking home. Within a few feet of the house, a person could completely disappear within the crowd.

Villa turned to his right and spotted his men pushing up through the crowd from behind. He quickly looked forward and tried to resume a relaxed demeanor. Reza appeared nervous as his eyes darted from Villa to the crowd around him. *He suspects something,* Villa thought to himself. Villa could not risk losing this chance to kill him. He had to act now. The crowd would slow any response and provide the perfect screen to escape.

With a fast and fluid motion, Villa pulled his pistol from his holster and fired into Reza's head. Reza spun completely around from the force of the bullet. His eyes froze wide open in complete surprise. As his body turned, more bullets pummeled his chest and back from Soto and Sánchez. Miraculously, no innocent pedestrians were hit. The crowd erupted in panic, running in diverging directions like stampeding cattle. Villa and his men melted into the chaos and disappeared.

Prudenciano was hot and miserable in his dark uniform. He and Felipe had been standing for hours across the street of Gonzalez's home. Every once in a while, he saw another guard or the captain move around the house. Now the traffic was peaking and he could barely make out the front door. The meeting must be over because a few men had left, but it was impossible to tell how many.

When the shots rang out, all hell broke loose. Men and women were screaming and running in every direction. People fought with adrenaline-induced strength to flee the area. In the process, they pushed, punched, and tromped anyone in their way. Prudenciano bolted toward the gunshots, but the crowd pushed him back. He felt like he was swimming through a sea of people. He knew that if he stumbled he was dead. It took all his strength to keep his ground.

Slowly, the crowd thinned, he kept pushing forward, and suddenly he was through. What he saw sickened him. Tens of people were lying on the ground, all victims of the stampeding mob. Some were dead. Others still lived, but were grotesquely mangled and moaned for help. In the center of this destruction lay Reza, his body riddled with bullets. Prudenciano stood over him for a second. He did not bother to take his pulse. Relief should have came to Prudenciano, but he still had that nagging doubt. *Did he see me?*

The killing of Reza in broad daylight gave Villa and his men instant notoriety. The people of Chihuahua were torn between supporting the revolution and being appalled at such a vicious act. The event also gave Terrazas the justification he needed to impose martial law upon the city. He ordered his men to erect checkpoints at all the major roads. He increased surveillance of homes that were suspected of housing rebels. In the end, Terrazas tightened his grip on the economy of Chihuahua and ruled with an iron fist.

Paz kept dinner waiting for Prudenciano. Since the murder, he had been working very late every night. She worried about him. The *Villistas* were ruthless and Prudenciano had a knack for getting involved with the wrong people. She had to steer him in the right direction. After all, he had two little children to think about.

Paz had just put Alcaria to bed and rocked the baby to sleep when Prudenciano trudged through the door. His head and shoulders were slumped forward from exhaustion. She got up with Joaquina still in her arms and came to him. Prudenciano smiled, took his cap off, and gently put his arm around her. She asked, "How did it go today?"

"We ran around chasing our tails all day," answered Prudenciano bitterly. "Terrazas wants Villa captured and sent us on some wild-goose chases in the hills. We think that we know where he is right here in Chihuahua, but the captain wants us to just watch his house and report who comes and goes. Now, I'm beat from riding all day."

Paz said, "I have dinner waiting," and led him to the table. Prudenciano sat wearily in the chair while Paz served the meal with one free hand and cradled the baby with the other. He ate halfheartedly and his eyelids drooped heavily as he finished. He thanked her and stumbled to their bed. Paz came to him and softly broke the silence, "Prudenciano, I have something important to discuss with you."

Prudenciano replied, "Hum?" The hot food and warm, comfortable home cast their spell over his tired body. He was barely able to stay awake.

Paz pressed forward. "I want you to try to stay away from Villa and his gang." There was no response from her husband. "Prudenciano? Did you hear me?" The only sound was a deep snore.

———◆———

On November 17, 1910, three days before the official start of the revolution, Abraham Gonzalez brought a visitor to Villa's house under the cover of darkness. Terrazas's men who still watched the house from across the street could only make out silhouettes and not the faces of the men. Pancho Villa's curiosity was piqued at why Gonzalez would risk being seen here just to bring this man, who was definitely a warrior. His powerful build, square jaw, and glaring eyes declared that he was not to be trifled with. This should be an interesting visit.

"*Señor* Villa," began Gonzalez, "thank you for receiving us tonight." Villa preened over Gonzalez's comments.

"The pleasure is mine, *Señor* Gonzalez," answered Villa as he shook his hand. Then Villa looked questioningly at the stranger.

Gonzalez said, "Ah, let me introduce you two. *Señor* Francisco Villa, this is *Señor* Victoriano Huerta. *Señor* Huerta, this is *Señor* Villa." The two stared into each other's eyes for a moment—trying to see any weakness that might emerge under such close scrutiny. Neither saw any, and they slowly offered their hands for a formal shake. Each found the clasp solid and unwavering. They were equals in spirit and determination.

Gonzalez watched them size each other up for a few moments longer and proceeded with his business. "I came to announce a difficult decision," he said as he held Villa's gaze. Villa could tell by the tone of his voice that he was very uncomfortable with what he had come to discuss. "I have decided to have *Señor* Huerta lead the revolutionary troops. I know I promised that position to you, but he is a trained military leader and I cannot ignore his experience. I hope that you can accept this and continue to serve as Huerta's assistant."

Neither Huerta nor Villa spoke. Each was deep in separate thought. Villa was stunned and hurt. He felt that he alone could lead the revolutionaries to victory. So what if this Huerta had military experience? Villa had seen formal training fall apart when surprised by guerrilla warfare tactics.

Huerta could tell that Villa would be a hard man to win over. He knew he would never be able to trust him. He was too independent and cocky, but he needed him. Villa was too well known among the revolutionaries to dismiss him. Huerta required Villa's charisma to lead these men to battle. After the men had learned to follow him, Huerta could dispose of Villa, but not now.

Huerta finally spoke. "I want you to fight by my side. We will split the forces and you will have your own men to lead. Please stay with us."

Villa studied the man's face for a moment. Some sixth sense told him that he could not trust Huerta, but he could not put his finger on why. On the other hand, he trusted Gonzalez's judgement and he believed in the cause. Villa finally shrugged and said, "What the hell! We will fight together!" He clasped Huerta on the shoulder and gave him a leering smile and thought, *Yes, you better be a good leader or I'll kill you*! Huerta smiled back. He read Villa's facial language and knew exactly what it meant.

Chapter 9
The Revolution

Prudenciano knew something was different about the town on November 20, 1910. It took him a minute to realize that there was very little movement throughout the city. Usually around nine o'clock, the streets were filled to capacity with wagons and people traveling to their work, but not today. Only a few scattered souls moved quickly down the streets with nervous glances around them.

Strange, thought Prudenciano. He continued to the work site and Felipe was waiting for him. Felipe said nothing as he approached and nodded his head in the direction of the building. Prudenciano quickly saw that only a fraction of the workforce was present. "What's happening?"

Felipe answered, "Is not today the start of Madero's revolution? Something is brewing, Nava. Mark my words. We are in for an interesting time."

Prudenciano nodded as he considered these words. "Let's try to carry on the best we can. Keep alert. We may get some trouble." Felipe tipped his hat back and sat a little straighter in his saddle. Prudenciano knew that if the revolutionaries ever tried to overrun their position, there would be little the two of them could do to counter the offensive.

By two o'clock in the afternoon, the construction foreman announced that he was sending his men home. He explained to Prudenciano, "I got to. There are no more cement deliveries today. Something or someone has disrupted the train and supply wagons. We'll try again tomorrow." Prudenciano nodded and sat back in his saddle. He had the sinking feeling that Chihuahua's troubles had just started.

The revolutionaries struck from their mountain hideouts. Commanding a small force of 375 men, Huerta and Villa attacked federal wagons and trains. In one bold move, Villa ambushed federal troops as they stepped off the train at the small town of San Andrés, a small suburb of Chihuahua. He killed nearly a hundred before they could entrench themselves among the buildings.

Supplies and men were always in short supply for the revolutionaries. To help supply their needs, Villa demanded that all new recruits provide a horse and a gun. This requirement assured that the first revolutionaries were middle-class citizens, because the common peasants could not afford these items.

By the end of November, Villa and a few of his followers stopped at a small store in San Andrés to buy some supplies. Villa wore his normal scowl as he examined the goods and their prices. He stomped up to the counter to demand service and was stopped dead in his tracks by what he saw. There, sitting quietly behind the counter, was the most beautiful woman he had ever seen. The young lady was busily crocheting and pretended not to notice him. Villa thought there was more than just a physical beauty to her. She seemed to possess a lovely spirit and intellect that promised to blossom into a meaningful relationship if the right man came along.

For the first time in his life, Villa was tongue-tied. He made a feeble attempt at conversation, but she never looked up from her work. Just then, a serious-looking woman appeared and stood between Villa and the girl. She growled, "May I help you?" The woman was obviously the girl's mother and by her disapproving expression Villa knew that any further attempts to meet this girl would be difficult at best.

"Sí," said Villa in his most charming voice. "My men and I need some supplies."

The woman replied with disdain, "I know who you are. As long as you and your men don't try to steal anything here, I will help you. Give me your list and we will fill it." Villa handed over his list and the two women began to assemble the goods. Villa could not take his eyes off the girl. He stared at her while she worked. The girl was aware of the attention and it frightened her. She became so scared that she began to tremble when she wrote out the bill of sale.

Villa tried to alleviate her fears by saying, "Please, do not be afraid. I mean you no harm." But before she could respond, her mother intervened and told her to go into the back room. When she had left, the mother turned her wrath upon Villa.

"I will not stand to have a murderer and a thief making eyes at my daughter! Do you understand me?" Villa was not accustomed to being talked to like this. He nodded and ordered his men to help him with the materials. They all left without incident.

After a few minutes, the girl came out and asked, "Are they gone yet, Mamma? I was so scared!"

"*Sí*, the swine have left," answered her mother as she screwed up her face in disgust.

"You know, Mamma, he was kind of nice. Do you think that he is really as bad as they say?"

The mother looked at her daughter in disbelief and thought, *She could not be attracted to him, could she?* When her mother recovered, she responded, "You know what I think? I think that you should restack those canned goods that one of those hoodlums knocked over. Now scat."

The girl walked over to the can display next to the door. As she was stacking the cans, she again felt someone watching her. She turned around and put her hand to her face to stifle a scream. Pancho Villa was standing in the doorway with his hat in his hand. "Please," he said in a soft voice, "don't be afraid. My name is Francisco Villa and I should like to know your name."

The girl looked back to the counter. Her mother was gone. She probably was in the back room getting more goods. "My name is Maria. Maria Luz Corral. Now please go before my mother sees us."

Villa smiled and put his hat back on. "I will see you again, Maria." He turned and walked quickly out of the store.

———

By December, the revolution had severely impacted the economy of Chihuahua, but the attacks were still uncoordinated. A young man by the name of Pascual Orozco Jr. changed this situation. He racked up a series of successes in the northern state of Chihuahua, which elevated his stature within the revolutionaries. Now he reached out to Villa to join forces and capture larger prey, the main federal forces led by General Juan J. Navarro.

The revolutionaries acquired their intelligence of federal movements from the local farmers of the area. An intricate network of underground communications allowed the swift movement of information to move across the vast plains of Chihuahua. Inevitably, this information tended to become distorted with time and distance. Each carrier relied on his own ability to listen, remember, and convey the facts accurately. Unfortunately, human abilities to perform this task varied widely and the revolutionaries were about to discover this fact firsthand.

Reports trickled in about a major movement of troops traveling north along the major highway and train to Ciudad Juarez. Agents swore that the regiment traveling on the road was lightly armed and stretched thinly. Only a few supply wagons intermingled with the troops, but the greatest news was that Navarro himself led the men.

Villa and Orozco could not believe their good fortune. Here was their chance to deal a decisive blow to the Díaz government. Thus, on the evening of December 10, 1910, they decided to ambush the soldiers at a point of their choosing.

Orozco asked, "Shouldn't we notify Huerta?" He always believed in following protocol.

Villa would have laughed if Orozco had not been so sincere. He was still young enough not to harbor any suspicious about men. Villa answered, "Not enough time. We'll send word when we ride north." Under his breath he muttered, "By then it will be too late."

———•••———

General Navarro rode in silence with a deep worry in his soul. His men were lightly trained and untested in battle. They were as green as they came. Some of them were scarcely more than boys. Díaz had ordered him to bring reinforcements to Ciudad Juarez and he was executing that order, but he did not like being exposed. His troops followed the central highway north that wound along the foothills to the west. The landscape provided countless places for the perfect ambush. Navarro had read the reports of Villa, Orozco, and that traitorous Huerta terrorizing this very area. He knew that his men were a tempting target.

Juan Navarro had risen to the rank of general by his own determination and demonstrated skill—a feat that was very uncommon within the Díaz regime. He learned from his mistakes and vowed never to repeat them. One of the lessons learned was never to be caught off guard. Navarro's common sense finally erupted and he blurted out loud, "I'll be damned if I am going to let those bandits surprise us!" The general's outburst startled his captain awake from dozing in his saddle. "Captain, I want these men to ride four abreast, and each man to carry extra ammunition and a pistol."

"But, General," the man countered, "that will force all travelers that we will meet off the road."

Navarro turned in his saddle and squarely addressed the officer. "Captain, do you see those cliffs and hills along the road up there?" The captain looked to where Navarro was pointing and nodded. "That, sir, is your concern. Not some poor *campesinos. Comprende?* Now move!" The captain saluted with alacrity and immediately spread the order throughout the regiment.

When he was satisfied that his orders were implemented, Navarro relaxed a little and began to scan the horizon for movement. He thought, *Well, if they decide to come, at least we will have a fighting chance.*

José Nava responded to his lieutenant's command to fall back into groups of four. He was dead tired and followed the order without thought. The quartermaster came forward with an extra belt of bullets for his rifle and a pistol. These he stuffed into his saddle bags.

José was now seventeen years old. After recovering from typhus in an army hospital, he had served in the federal infantry for three years and there was still no release in sight. The army had become his family and his only hope for existence. At first, he had thought that he would eventually go home and pick up where he had left off, but when his regiment finally toured Monte Escobedo, he found that there was nothing left of the family *hacienda*. It had been burned and the land confiscated by Díaz. Villagers told him that his mother and grandfather had died, but his father and sisters had escaped. No one really knew where they had gone. So, he continued to serve his government although his debt for hospitalization had long been repaid. He just felt that he had nowhere else to go.

The entire regiment was now compressed to one third of its original length. The formation was easier to defend, but it slowed their progress. Some of the men grumbled about eating their companion's dust, but not José. From his position in the middle of the column, he saw the wisdom in the action and he tried to reason with them. "Look, you guys, this is a safer way to go. You know Villa and his men have been seen in this area."

"Right, Nava," snorted a cohort nearby. "I heard that the boogie man is here, too." Several men around him started laughing. José didn't answer. He eyed the high cliffs ahead and felt a dread pass through him.

———————

Villa passed his binoculars to Orozco. They lay on the ground on top of a mound that gave them a commanding view of the entire road for twenty miles in each direction. Hidden from view, their men and horses waited in the canyon behind them. Villa was upset. The federal troops had reformed and were proceeding forward as a defensive unit. This would not be as easy as they had first thought.

"He's a sly fox," stated Orozco as he analyzed the situation. The troops were still about five miles south of their position. "He knows that this is the perfect place for an ambush and he has prepared his troops." Orozco lowered the binoculars and turned his head to Villa. "So, what do you think? Do we still have a chance?"

After a string of recent successes, both Villa and Orozco were riding high on confidence. In addition, Villa always hated to admit when he was in over his head. Villa reached for the glasses and took a final look. He could not explain it, but it still felt good. "*Sí*, we'll do it. Original plan. No change." Orozco smiled back. He had known what Villa's answer would be all along.

Orozco rolled behind their perch to clear the skyline before standing and ran down the hill to his men. Villa did the same a few moments later. The men were eager and anxious to see their leaders mounting their horses. It was time. The butterflies they all had felt during the long hours while they waited were gone. Now the adrenaline began surging through their veins. Their nostrils began to burn with the increased blood flow and full breaths, typical symptoms for men as they prepared for battle.

Orozco and Villa clasped hands and gave each other a hearty shake. No words transpired, only looks of complete trust and confidence. The men saw and felt it, too. It fortified them.

Orozco gathered half of the troops and led them down a mountain path that would lead them to the north of a steep hill next to the highway. Here they would wait hidden until the troops crossed their path. Then Orozco would attack the front of the regiment from the side. If done quickly enough, he should cut through the column and reform on the opposite side. The intent was to draw their attention to him. When this was done, Villa would attack from behind. Both men were aware that the *federales* outnumbered them four to one. Thus, the plan required exquisite timing and complete surprise.

Villa moved his men in position behind a small hill just south of Orozco. When he saw Orozco bust through the federal line, he would charge over the hill.

Villa and his men were so absorbed into the moment that they failed to notice a group of seven men ride quietly up alongside them. "*Buenos días, Señor* Villa. Pleasant day, no?" Villa's head snapped around and he saw Huerta walking up to him. He shook his head in disbelief. How could he have found him?

Being a military man, Huerta quickly and correctly interpreted the operation. *Not bad*, he thought to himself. *I probably would have done the same.* He drew up alongside Villa and burned him with his glare. "I never authorized this attack. You will learn to obey my command."

Villa was not intimidated. "You are too late to assert command. See! The attack begins." Orozco silently initiated the charge and the men were galloping forward to meet the front of the advancing troops.

Huerta only smiled back at Villa and said, "No. I am here at just the right time." As fast as lightning, he flicked his pistol out of his holster, cocked and aimed it at Villa's head. "You and your troops are going nowhere." He reached out and took Villa's pistol from him and then instructed his men to watch the other men. "No one helps Orozco. If anyone moves, you will be shot."

Villa knew that he was not joking. The man never joked. He felt his anger building and his own helplessness fuel it. "Damn it, man! This is more than just my insubordination. Those are our own people down there. If we don't help them now, they will all die!"

Huerta was unmoved. "Better to lose a few now, than losing everyone later. There can be only one commander and that man is me."

Orozco's men smacked into the front group. Both the surprise and the soldiers' inexperience allowed Orozco to cut quickly through the column like a knife going through butter. The initial assault killed thirty *federales* without a single casualty. *This is going better than I thought*, said Orozco to himself as they rode about three hundred yards onto the plain, just out of rifle range, and reassembled. They drew the *federales'* full attention to their position. Soldiers began firing wildly at their attackers. Their entire column was in disarray. Some tried charging, others held back, unsure of what they should do.

Orozco looked to the hills and said, "Come on Villa! Now's the time. Let's go!" From his vantage point, Villa could tell that the time to strike was now. Huerta never lowered the gun from his head. Villa was furious. This was just so useless.

Navarro was about to charge when he noticed some of his attackers gazing up at the ridge behind him. He thundered, "Hold your position!" He scanned the ridge again. A *clever plan*, he thought, *but why didn't they strike when our backs were turned?* Navarro waited a minute and realized that his assailants' scheme had for some reason turned sour. He smiled and turned back to the rebels. Their own people had left them to die. Navarro drew his sword and roared, "So be it! Gentlemen, charge!"

Orozco saw the entire column advancing toward them, billowing large clouds of dust into the air. Something had gone wrong. Villa was not coming. He had to take evasive action fast, but he could not flee because the *federales* would eventually run them down. Their only hope was to smack through the *federales* and escape to the safety of the hills. Orozco rallied his troops and yelled at the top of his lungs, "Everyone, group together. We have to concentrate our strength at one point and try and break through again. When we do, ride for the hills. We will reassemble there. *¡Vámanos!*" Orozco led the countercharge. His men packed closely together with weapons drawn.

Villa could see the whole battle unfold before him. Orozco correctly regrouped his men and charged the advancing *federale* line. Both sides were firing as they rode full tilt at each other. As the distance closed, the shooting became more accurate. Soldiers and revolutionaries began falling from their mounts. Some got their feet stuck in the stirrups and their horses dragged them across the abrasive ground. This quickly reduced the men to a bloody pulp.

Still Orozco pushed forward firing his pistol until it was empty. He threw the gun away and drew his knife just as his men slammed into the soldiers. Horses hit horses with a sickening thud. The force jarred many men from their saddles and they were trampled below. Guns were practically useless at this close range. Men fought hand to hand as the revolutionaries pushed forward to break free. Orozco's knife slashed through the air and became so slippery from blood that he could barely hold it.

The *federale* line quickly enfolded the revolutionaries and attacked from all sides. Orozco screamed at his men to continue forward, then suddenly he emerged from the other side. He rode like a wild man for the safety of the hills. Only a handful of his men followed. The rest died trying.

It was over. Villa felt drained. He turned to Huerta and saw him slowly lower his gun. The only lesson he had learned today was that he had to kill Huerta. What he just did was an outrage. He felt hatred for the man seething through his body. Huerta realized that Villa was now in a murderous state. He ordered Villa arrested and taken back to their hideout and incarcerated until he cooled off. But Villa carried a long, lasting grudge.

———✦———

José first realized that something was wrong when the front soldiers shouted with surprise. He shook himself from the half-dazed sleep that men lapse into during long marches and tried to comprehend the sounds and commotion around him. Several horses reared in terror. Their riders spilled over backward. Others milled around in tight circles. Suddenly, José saw a pack of riders emerge from behind a steep hill and slam into the forward column. They sounded like Indian warriors by their blood-curling screams, which only added to the horror of the attack. The soldiers barely got off a shot before they were literally mowed down.

The terror grabbed José by the stomach and wrenched him. He was paralyzed. He wanted to run, but there was nowhere to go. Chaos totally enveloped him. Men were shouting and crying while others tried to control their horses and help their fallen comrades. José found it impossible to do anything. He had never felt such crippling fear.

Then the attackers broke through the column and rode into the eastern plain. As they rode away, José thought, *Thank God! They are leaving.* The men seem to share José's relief and became bolder. Some made halfhearted charges at the rebels, stopped, and rode back as they shouted insults and fired haphazardly at them. José could barely hear Navarro yelling to hold their position. Navarro kept looking back up at the hills behind them. He looked like he was searching for something.

None of this made sense to José. Why were they just standing here? Why weren't they getting out of this place? There were probably more rebels just waiting to attack them again. Then the unthinkable happened. The revolutionaries on the plain regrouped and charged again! José gasped, "They must be madmen!" The bravado that the soldiers had just displayed evaporated when they saw the charge. The rebels were coming at them at a full gallop in a tight V formation. Even at this distance, José could see their teeth clenched tight with determination and their eyes wide open with desperation. The entire regiment went silent.

Suddenly, Navarro thundered the command to charge. The men moved slowly at first. The junior officers began prodding them into action. José sluggishly rode toward the advancing enemy. His fear erupted up through his gut and wrapped its icy fingers around his mind. It almost incapacitated him. Still he moved forward with his speed increasing.

The rebels were closing fast and started firing first. Bullets whizzed by José's head. A man next to him clutched his chest, winced once, and fell off his horse. José's fear now began to suffocate him. His vision began to tunnel with blackness rushing in around him. He laid his head down on his horse's neck and continued forward. He began to pray to the Virgin Mary for God's protection, which was quite unusual because he had never been a religious person. His prayers were half spoken in a weak and crying voice.

The gunfire was deafening. Men screamed. Terrified horses bucked wildly. The dust rolled thick in the air. Abruptly, a new sound thudded into the battle. At first, it reminded José of a butcher shop. He had heard the same smacking sounds when the butcher threw quarters of beef onto the cutting table. He looked up and saw the rebels plowing into the soldiers' horses. Horse hitting horse. Meat slapping meat.

Then the hand-to-hand combat began. Never in his life had José witnessed such unleashed violence. Even the most wicked bulls he had seen in the ring did not wreak such havoc. The rebels were using knives and pistol butts to fight their way through. The soldiers had their sabers drawn. Men grabbed each other by the neck and slaughtered each other with their weapons. All the time, they were eyeball to eyeball, staring at each other with fanatical hysteria.

José could not bear it any longer. He fell back on his horse and retreated into a dark, insane world within his mind.

Paz stopped in the middle of her chores to rest. She stretched and pressed her hands against her lower back. She closed her eyes, let out a long slow breath, and reflected on the times. Their lives had certainly changed over the last six months. The sporadic fighting within the city had forced her to keep Alcaria inside. The four-year-old was fit to be tied with bundles of unspent energy. Joaquina was actively crawling and added to the household unrest.

Their life in Chihuahua had started out so peaceful and full of promise, but after late November, things had changed rapidly. Because of shipment delays, construction on Terrazas's buildings had almost come to a standstill. Sporadic fighting in the streets erupted randomly throughout the town. Prudenciano spent much of his time responding to these skirmishes. Paz stopped her reminiscing for a second to shake the dread that she felt for her husband's safety. "He is always so darn visible," she spoke out loud to no one particular. The girls never even looked up from their play.

Then came the work cutbacks. Terrazas ordered all his guards to work only half days. They still could use the guard housing, but the family barely got by on the meager income. The revolution had caused shortages of food and goods. Thus, inflation soared in Chihuahua. Paz had to stretch every peso and sometimes even dip into the money pouch that her father-in-law had given her. She could tell that Prudenciano was worried about their future.

Paz had never seen Terrazas, but Prudenciano spoke about him often. To her, his actions appeared increasingly desperate. He would order the guards to immediately assemble around one of his properties and then direct them to race to another location and secure that area. Prudenciano thought that the man was paranoid. Paz felt that Terrazas was fighting a losing battle. Slowly, everyone was turning against him and his regime.

Paz noticed that some days Prudenciano came home all agitated and restless. When she asked him what was wrong, he denied that anything was bothering him. He would gruffly walk past her and take off his uniform. Sometimes his clothing showed signs of a scuffle, a torn sleeve or blood stains on the chest. However, the most troubling sight to her was when he removed his pistol from his holster to clean it. She saw the empty cartridges slide from the chambers. The smell of burnt gunpowder wafted across the room. She thought, *Why don't we just leave this place before it was too late?*

The door swung open hard and startled Paz from her contemplation. Prudenciano bounded in and closed the door behind him. His face was stamped with shock and disbelief. Paz asked, "What is it?" She was almost too scared to hear his answer.

Prudenciano sat down at the table, shook his head, and replied, "The telegraph operator ran to the armory with a message." Prudenciano stopped, looked up at Paz, and continued, "The message was from General Navarro. It said Ciudad Juarez has fallen to the revolutionaries!"

Pancho Villa sat on his horse at the southwestern outskirts of Ciudad Juarez with his men awaiting Huerta's orders to attack. Orozco had positioned a similar army on the other side of the city. Navarro had sealed his men in the garrison and was preparing for the final battle. It was going to take a lot of fierce fighting to pry him out. Villa shifted in his saddle as he recalled the events that had led him to this point.

Huerta had kept him in confinement for nearly a month. During this time, Villa finally came to recognize his insubordination and cooled his hatred for Huerta. It still simmered, but he could control it. After that, his thoughts turned to Maria. He was determined to have her and mapped out his plan to court her.

When Villa finally had his freedom, he traveled to San Andrés every chance he got. His frequent visits not only won Maria's heart, but also soothed her mother's disgust for him. Villa's charm captured them and they developed sympathy for his revolutionary cause. Slowly, *Señora* Corral allowed Villa to escort her daughter around town without supervision and, within a short time, Francisco and Maria fell in love.

Huerta, Villa, and Orozco lobbied Madero for his support to attack Juarez. Their efforts were stymied for two reasons. Madero was a very cautious man and his military advisors, both foreigners, recommended against it. Only after Madero had exhausted every possible diplomatic avenue to get Díaz to step down from the presidency was the approval given.

Villa coordinated the flow of arms across the United States border to the rebels. Abraham Gonzalez and Huerta recruited the men needed for the assault. Huerta, Villa, and Orozco planned the battle. Now, everything was set. Villa wanted to surprise Navarro, but assembling this many men always attracted attention. So, the rebels had to settle for fighting a well-prepared and alerted enemy.

"Captain!"

Villa snapped out of his thoughts and turned his attention to a messenger riding up alongside him. "General Huerta orders you to attack when the cannon fire begins."

"*Sí*," answered Villa. "Tell the general that we will be ready." The messenger snapped a sharp salute and nudged his horse forward. Villa watched him ride off to repeat the command to Orozco's group. Villa turned and addressed his men, "*Señores*, mount your horses and prepare yourselves. When the cannons start, we will charge!" Immediately, everyone climbed onto their saddles and assembled their gear. Butterflies rose in every stomach. The easy banter that usually rolled between the men was squelched. Each man was now steeling himself for battle and this required a quiet meditation. Soon, the last of the individual adjustments were made and the men sat silently on their horses. Now came the long, agonizing wait for the battle to begin.

After inspecting his men, Villa turned his attention to Juarez. The city was nearly as large as Chihuahua, but not as modern. Some of its structures looked like they were haphazardly thrown up and the streets were poorly laid out. The entire city was unusually quiet as if the populace was waiting for some calamitous event.

Villa knew that Navarro would be fortified within the federal armory. The garrison was located in the center of town. Villa muttered under his breath, "Cowards. He knows that we will have to fight through citizens just to get at him." Villa uttered a small prayer that Huerta's cannons would fire accurately.

Although they were anticipating the sound, the first cannon volley startled the men. The cannons produced successive booms followed by the hissing of the iron balls flying through the air and finally the explosive crashing of impacts. Villa raised his pistol in the air and gave the command to charge. The battle of Juarez had begun.

——◦•••◦——

The railroad boxcars finally came to a stop along a lonely, deserted stretch of track south of Ciudad Juarez. Crammed inside each boxcar were at least seventy men, all survivors of Navarro's troops. The interior air was stifling hot and reeked with fear. They all had heard stories of how the revolutionaries dragged federal soldiers into the remote areas for execution. Now they were going to find out firsthand if those stories were true.

José Nava lay in a fetal position among the men in one of the middle cars. Since the battle had began yesterday afternoon, he had felt like he was trapped in a non-ending nightmare. The rebel cannon fire had been unceasing. The balls pelted the garrison walls with devastating effect. Shrapnel buzzed through the air as thick as flies over rotten meat. One moment a man would be standing next to José. The next instant he would be decapitated by flying iron and his lifeless body would slowly collapse to the ground.

After the bombardment, the frontal assault began. The rebels howled and screamed as they charged the walls. The constant roar of gunfire was deafening. The federal troops repelled them over and over only to have them regroup and charge again. As the night wore on, the rebels slowly beat down the federal troops. By the next morning, the *federales* had half their strength and limited ammunition. With their spirits broken and no interest in repeating the Alamo, Navarro exercised the only option available to him. He surrendered and opened the gates to the rebels.

The revolutionaries wasted no time in corralling their *federale* prisoners and herding them into railroad boxcars. José could still hear their taunting and jeers through the plank walls before the train begin moving to the southern desert. "We are going to kill all you *federale* pigs soon! Ha, ha, ha …" There was no doubt in each federal soldier's mind that the rebels were going to butcher them like livestock.

Fear had crippled José throughout the battle. He shook so badly that he could barely hold his rifle and fire. Now he could not even sit up. He curled up in a ball on the boxcar floor and whimpered for help.

Abruptly, there were new sounds coming from the first car. Men shouted orders at their captives to get out and line up. Through narrow slits between planks, men next to José could see the rebels dragging and kicking federal soldiers into a single line. The *federales* could barely stand. Many swayed and struggled to remain upright. A big, broad man rode forward on a horse, and directed the rebels to prepare their rifles.

"*¡Dios mío!*" exclaimed the man next to José. "They are going to shoot them all!" The large man raised his hand and glanced along both sides of the firing line. Satisfied, he dropped his hand and the soldiers were cut down in a bellowing fusillade.

José cried, "Oh, no, no, no!" He clasped his hands behind his head and pinned his ears down with his forearms. He rocked back and forth trying to escape this hell.

The man next to José turned from the wall and slouched to the floor. He said with a resignation, "The rebels are working their way down the cars." Already they could hear them opening the next boxcar. This time the rebels grabbed each *federale* and threw him to the ground in front of them. A rebel held a gun to the head of each man and asked, "Will you join us?" If the man hesitated or looked like a troublemaker, the rebel shot him. They spared only the truly repentant except, every so often, the rebels pulled out three men and shot them just to keep the *federales* guessing their fate.

The sounds of pleading men and random gunfire kept growing

louder as the rebels neared José's boxcar. "Oh, please, Blessed Mother," prayed José, "make them stop!" Then the anticipated and dreaded sound of the door unlocking rattled the men inside. The door slid open and the blinding afternoon sun blasted into their confines. At least twenty men stood smiling at them with rifles readied.

A rebel greeted them with an evil grin and said, "*Buenos días, Señores.* Who is first?" Terror paralyzed the *federales* and no one dared to breathe. Each agonizing second dilated into what seemed liked hours. Then a laugh from one of the rebels broke the spell. They reached in and began dragging out whoever they could grab. Some of these men struggled and were promptly shot. Others resigned themselves to the situation and let fate cast its dice. Surprisingly, the rebels spared most of these.

José was neither rebellious nor ambivalent. He simply was incapable of any action. He maintained his fetal position, closed his eyes, and tried to block out the sounds. For a long time, the rebels did not even know he was there. Gradually as they pulled the men from the car, they found José. A rebel snorted in disgust and yanked him out and onto the ground. José let out a whimper and tried to curl up again. A man roared, "Kill the dog!" The man standing over José casually raised his rifle to shoot him in the head.

Suddenly, a thunderous voice bellowed, "Halt!" José's executioner froze as an enormous man rode into the crowd. José slowly looked up as the horse stopped in front of him. The sun shone directly behind the large man, so José had to squint to make out his features. The glare made it impossible to see his face, and yet he looked vaguely familiar. The man dismounted with surprising agility. He stood over José for a moment and then said quietly, "Get up, Nava. Your uncle would be ashamed of you."

José blinked in amazement and slowly pushed himself up. He asked, "How is it that you know me?"

The man towered over him. He answered without emotion, "I last saw you when you were a boy in Fresnillo."

With his curiosity piqued, José managed to stand wobbly. He peered up at the man for a moment while his eyes adjusted to the light. Suddenly José recognized him and gasped, "*¡Dios mío!* Anastacio Currandas!"

"*Sí,*" replied Currandas. "And now you are going to fight for the revolution, *comprende?*" José slowly nodded. "*Bueno,*" said Currandas. He turned to his soldiers and announced, "I owe his uncle my life. Therefore, I say he lives. Any problems with that?" No one stepped forward to challenge him. Seeing no opposition, Currandas uttered only one word to his troops, "Continue!"

Pancho Villa and Pascual Orozco were furious! They could not believe what Huerta had told them. Victoriano Huerta repeated the order, "You are to release General Navarro unharmed. Immediately. *Comprende?*" By the expression on his face, both Villa and Orozco knew that Huerta bitterly disagreed with the command. "Madero personally delivered the order. He thinks that the release will demonstrate to Mexico that he is a fair and just man."

Orozco snarled, "It will prove that he is stupid! Navarro will just regroup and fight us again. How many of our men died taking this garrison?" When nobody answered he continued, "Over three hundred! And for what?" Orozco let his question hang in the air as he stared defiantly at Villa and Huerta. Neither of them could disagree or meet his gaze.

Finally, Huerta walked over to the window and looked out across the garrison yard. The rebels had removed all the bodies of the fallen men. Only yesterday the ground was littered with the blue coats of the *federales* and tattered clothing of the rebels. Both sides had suffered staggering losses. There were still blotches of deep red stains throughout the grounds. Huerta let out a long sigh of resignation and modified his order as he continued to study the battlefield, "You can keep Navarro in his cell until tomorrow, but then you must release him unharmed in the morning. Villa, I want you to carry out my order."

Orozco swore and bolted out the door slamming it shut behind him. Huerta appeared unaffected by his junior officer's behavior. He continued to watch Orozco stride quickly across the yard. When the rebel guards hailed him at the gate, Orozco brusquely shoved them aside and kicked the gate open. "He carries a deep anger within him," said Huerta watching him stomp out of the compound. "But he is a young man and may reflect upon this differently when he is older." Villa said nothing. He was still trying to control his own seething wrath. Navarro had killed too many of his men to be freed unpunished. Huerta seemed to sense Villa's thoughts. He turned from the window and faced him. "However, there comes a time when a soldier must contemplate if his commanding officer is fully competent to lead."

Villa's head snapped back from the implication of Huerta's words. Despite his anger, he despised treason even more. Villa asked, "What do you mean?"

Huerta looked at Villa with a slight smile across his lips. "What I mean is, that there comes a time when a man should evaluate the actions of his commander." Seeing that this was the time to press a point, Huerta leaned toward Villa and continued in a clear low voice, "Do you really think that a man who could release a criminal like Navarro is worthy to lead Mexico? Mark my words, Villa. It's blind trust like this that will be the death of Madero."

Villa had to take a step back from Huerta. For a moment, he saw the lust for power simmer within Huerta's eyes. He now knew Huerta's true alliance and it was all for himself. Huerta's voice "It will be the death of Madero" echoed through his mind. Villa's eyes met Huerta's again and stared hatred back. *I have not forgotten the massacre you caused at the highway ambush in Chihuahua. And I will not forget your traitorous words today."*

The sun rose above the dawn and changed its orange rays to yellow against the blue and dusty sky, which signaled another hot day. Villa had been walking the garrison yard before sunrise. From time to time, his fingers traced the pockmarks in the walls from the recent fierce gun battle. The fresh bullet marks were white blemishes against the gray rock wall. He could not sleep thinking about what Huerta had said and his duty to release Navarro today. He reluctantly had to admit that much of what Huerta had voiced had some truth in it. He did not understand Madero's aversion to killing enemies, but Villa still had a deep unwavering faith in Francisco Madero and Abraham Gonzalez. These men had always been truthful and open with him. Villa believed that they could rid Mexico of the corruption that infested the current government like a malignant cancer.

Villa was lost in thought and did not hear Orozco slip beside him. "Villa, may I speak with you?"

"Uh?" Villa felt a flash of anger at being startled. He always boasted how he knew that a stalker was nearby. At seeing that it was his trusted friend, his agitation quickly evaporated. He smiled and said, "Sí. I am happy to see you back."

Orozco did not return the smile. Instead, he drew closer and spoke in a quiet and low voice, "Pancho, I have the most important information. It appears that Navarro is up to his old tricks again."

Villa's interest was piqued. "What do you mean?"

Orozco put his hand on his arm and drew him closer. "Last night I wandered through town. I was very upset and could not sleep. It was very dark when I passed by a *cantina*. When I looked inside I saw a couple of the federal officers that we released a few days ago." He stopped talking for a moment and held on to Villa's arm. The momentary silence seemed to accent the importance of what he was about to say. "I slipped inside and began to mingle with the crowd.

Soon I got close enough to hear what they were saying. The men said that Navarro knows that Madero wants to release him. Within his cell, Navarro apparently has orchestrated a counterstrike before our men return from the south." Villa appeared incredulous so Orozco pressed his point further, "Villa, if they launch a surprise attack, we will be overwhelmed!"

Villa was shaken. *Of course! It would be the perfect trick.* He felt his anger rise and yelled, "We will see about that!" He pulled his pistol from his holster and marched straight to the jail. Orozco held back with a sly smile on his face.

General Juan Navarro lay on top of his hard bunk trying to capture a little more rest. He had slept fitfully through the night. The airy, concrete jail gave scant protection against the cold, breezy nights and sweltering hot days. His body shivered violently during the night and sweated profusely during the day. The only respite came during the brief transition of night and day. As dawn broke, Navarro felt his aching body relax and slip into an exhausted stupor.

The door to the front room kicked open and crashed into the wall. The abrupt noise startled Navarro out of his sleep. With his vision still blurry, he raised his head till he could see the cause of the commotion. He squinted through the bars and could barely distinguish the outline of a stocky man with a long-barreled pistol. Navarro thought bitterly, *So this is how it's going to end? I thought it would be at the end of a rope.*

The man inserted a key into the cell lock and jerked the door open. Only when he stepped inside did Navarro recognize him. "*Buenos días, Señor* Villa," Navarro greeted him with a calm but croaking voice. "Are you going to invite me to breakfast?"

Villa flared at Navarro's insolence. He snarled, "Get up, you swine, or I swear I will kill you where you lie!" When Navarro slowly stirred, Villa impatiently yanked him to his feet and placed the pistol against his temple. Navarro swayed unsteadily and looked at him without emotion. Villa asked with an acid edge to his voice, "So, you thought that you could kill us all with a surprise attack?" Navarro recognized the tone of an angry and betrayed man and knew that Villa was now capable of anything, even cold-blooded murder. Villa continued, "Madero was foolish enough to let you go, but I found out about your little plan and I am going to put an end to it!"

Navarro knew that his only chance was to try to reason with Villa. Exuding a calm that he did not feel, Navarro quietly addressed him. "Villa." The use of an angered person's name was always the best way to start. "How could I have planned such a strike? You kept me under twenty-four-hour guard, isolated, and locked in this cell. Look at me, Villa. Do I look like I have been having a good time?" Navarro felt the pressure of the gun against his head lessen. He felt a surge of relief knowing that Villa was reconsidering the situation. It bolstered him and he pushed his argument further. "Villa, I swear to you. I did not know of Madero's decision until now. It comes as a surprise to me. I thought for sure I was destined for the gallows."

Villa uncocked the gun and removed it from his head. Then he suddenly returned it and asked with renewed menace in his voice, "What about the federal soldiers talking about you leading a counterattack?"

This time Navarro slowly turned and faced Villa. The pistol was now pointed at his forehead and he could see Villa's finger twitching at the trigger. Navarro chose his words carefully, "Villa, I can imagine that many men are upset that Madero wants to free me. Some men probably want to kill me, but they do not want to violate an order. So, they invented a story that others will believe that I am too dangerous to release. What do you think?"

Navarro's logic temporarily stunned Villa. He felt his anger subside and lowered the gun. He thought, *Could it be that I was tricked?*

At that moment, Villa heard a thunderous voice, "Villa! What are you doing? I told you to release him now! That's an order!" Villa turned and saw Huerta standing in he doorway. His hand was on his pistol and Villa could see a trace of smile on his face. It was the kind of expression that said "Just give me an excuse to kill you."

Villa reluctantly released Navarro and shoved him back into the cell. He holstered his weapon and walked past Huerta into the courtyard. He saw Orozco fidgeting nervously against the far wall. Orozco's guilt prevented him from looking at Villa. He slunk out the gate and disappeared.

Villa felt a flood of emotions pour through his body. He was just betrayed by his best friend. He had almost let Huerta manipulate him into a situation where he could have been shot and no one would have questioned it. But the most heart-wrenching thought was his attempted insubordination. Villa would be the last one to violate an order from Madero. He had too much respect for the man.

"I am so tired," Villa spoke softly to himself. "I am tired of the killing. I am tired of watching my back and trusting no one. I am tired of it all." He closed his eyes and let his thoughts wander. Quickly a picture of Maria formed in his mind. It brought comfort and a long-lost feeling of well-being. Villa sighed and said, "*Sí*, I must go to her and make her mine. My time here is done."

Chapter 10
The Calm

The *jaripeo* of June, 1911 in Chihuahua was beneficial for three reasons. First, it aided the healing of emotional scars left by the revolution. This event would be the first celebration since the *Cinco de Mayo* of last year. Second, the sponsor was no other than Francisco Villa and his lovely new wife Maria, whom he had married the previous May. Lastly, the Villas would donate the proceeds to the orphans and widows of the revolution, regardless of what side their men had fought on.

Although Madero had captured the presidency, Mexico was still at war with some of its citizens. Emiliano Zapata stirred up revolts within the southern provinces, but this did not concern Villa. Last March, Villa had resigned from Madero's army and reopened a butcher shop in San Andrés. He wanted only to tend to his business matters, love Maria, and perform some public relations functions such as the *jaripeo*.

The new Chihuahua governor was Abraham Gonzalez. He governed with a fair and just hand. He broke up the Terrazas-Creel banking monopoly, but still allowed Luis Terrazas to possess about half of his property and continue constructing his projects. With the supply trains now running unmolested, building activities resumed at pre-revolution levels. Terrazas reinstated Prudenciano's full-time job protecting *El Palacio de Bellas Artes*. The new influx of supplies drove down the prices of food. Thus, the Navas' standard of living rose with the improved economy.

Prudenciano sat alone at the dining table with his mixed brew of thoughts. He felt excited about the upcoming *jaripeo*. With the encouragement of his fellow guards, he decided to compete in the *Colleada*. However, he was filled with doubts about the event. Unlike in Torreón, Prudenciano had no chance to practice and he reluctantly agreed to accept Felipe as his flagger. Felipe's eyes danced with jubilation when Prudenciano finally capitulated to his unceasing begging. Prudenciano thought, *The boy has no idea what he is getting himself into.* Above all, Prudenciano admitted to himself that he just was not young anymore. His fifty-five-year-old body was still hard and in peak condition, but he ached in places that betrayed his age. In addition, he knew that his reflexes and night vision were slowly waning. The combination of no practice, an inexperienced partner, and an aging *colleador* did not paint a picture of success.

Prudenciano subconsciously stroked his graying beard. The front door opened and two little tornados of energy blew in. Alcaria was in front and Joaquina wailed with frustration as she waddled close behind. They raced straight for their father's lap. The commotion jolted Prudenciano from his thoughts and he turned in his chair to receive the girls. "Come here, both of you. Now, what did you do with your mother?"

Alcaria easily clambered up, but Joaquina needed a little help getting her diapered bottom on top of Papa's leg. Within seconds, they sat on opposite sides of his lap. They stretched their arms around his neck and hugged him fiercely. Prudenciano felt his heart tighten when he wrapped his arms around them and pressed their little bodies against his. Alcaria spoke first, "Mama is right behind us."

Joaquina blurted out, "We go store!" Prudenciano was always amazed how fast his little girls learned to talk. At only one year old, Joaquina could chatter like a bird. She was a strikingly beautiful child with shiny black hair and long, dark eyelashes. Prudenciano thought with a sudden protectiveness, *What am I going to do when you get older?* He abruptly remembered his own behavior and thoughts when he chased beautiful *señoritas* and made a silent vow to thwart any future advances made by similar males.

He looked up when he heard a heavy sigh at the door. Paz stood in the doorway with a heavy shopping bag in each arm. She looked bedraggled and at the limit of her patience. "I almost sold your children today!" stated Paz in a serious tone as she moved to the table and deposited her bags with a thump. "They do not mind. I constantly had to chase them and pull them out of trouble. Buying food was a horrible experience."

Prudenciano replied, "*Sí*, I bet it was." He gave the girls a quick wink and hug. They wiggled with delight.

Paz massaged her lower back, walked over to the counter, and poured herself a drink of water. The cool liquid revived her. She came back to the table, shook her head, and said with a smile, "Well, perhaps I will keep them. They are kind of cute." The girls beamed their smiles back to their mother. They were obviously pleased that their transgressions had been forgiven.

Paz turned her attention to her husband. "Prudenciano, do you still plan on competing in the *jaripeo* next week?"

"*Sí*, I was just sitting here thinking about that. I want to try it one more time."

Paz studied his face for a second and started to say something, but she caught herself. She had learned long ago that any criticism would only galvanize his decision. She thought, *When will he realize that he is not a young man anymore?* She let out a sigh of resignation and said as she walked back to one of her bags, "Well, in that case, I bought you a present." She reached into the bag and pulled out a folded ream of cloth. Paz brought it over to him and unfolded it. It was a rugged cotton material that had been bleached bright white. It represented an unusual and extravagant gift.

Prudenciano fingered the cloth and asked, "What is it for?"

Paz lowered the material and kissed him on the forehead. "Well, if my husband is going to perform in front of hundreds of people, he should look like a star instead of the ruffian that he is. I am going to sew you a shirt. Your other clothes are not suitable for wearing in public."

Prudenciano tilted his head back and Paz responded by kissing him on the lips. He felt his pride and love for her soar. *She makes me feel so young*, he thought. *Maybe I'm not getting old. I probably have lots of jaripeos within me yet.* Paz seemed to read his mind and shook her head at him as if he were a little child. Then she kissed him again full on the mouth. The girls giggled with glee.

The *jaripeo* began with a beautiful midmorning. The sky was unusually blue without a hint of clouds on the horizon. The event took place in Terrazas's newly built arena. The magnificent facility could accommodate several thousand spectators around the center field. The circular stadium walls were solid concrete and rose two stories. People entered the center gate that was marked with an enormous arch and many ticket booths along its base. The seating arrangements depended on social status and the ticket price. If you were a major property owner or politician, you could look forward to being seated close to the judges' booth, which was positioned in the middle of the field, just above the wooden fence that enclosed the arena. From this point, the expensive seats were located closer to the field of competition with the top of the stadium providing shade from the afternoon sun. The cheaper and more plentiful seating was situated toward the top of the stadium within the glaring daylight.

The stadium walls were adorned with colorful banners and ribbons. Surrounding the arena, red, blue, and green streamers fluttered gallantly on tall flag poles against the blue sky. People packed into the seating aisles. They were all wearing their Sunday best. Their moods were gay and an infectious feeling of excitement wafted through the crowd. It had been so long since the city of Chihuahua had had anything to celebrate. With the return of prosperity and a semblance of peace, the citizens could at last sit back and enjoy a day of sporting events.

The judges' booth contained the attending dignitaries. Among them was Abraham Gonzalez, the new governor for the state of Chihuahua. In his finely tailored suit he looked distinguished as he sat next to Francisco Villa. The audience realized the significance of him being seen with Villa.

Directly across the field from the booth, Don Luis Terrazas sat with his family. Terrazas wore his traditional black Spanish-cut suit with a black leather vest and a large black sombrero. His wife and sons sat next to him. They all had somber expressions. It was as if none of them wanted to be at the *jaripeo*, but tradition and social protocol dictated that they attend.

Villa's stocky frame arose and he held his arms out to quiet the crowd. The excited droning slowly diminished as all heads strained to see this man. For better or worse, all of Mexico had heard of him, but only a few had actually seen him. Within the last five years, he had made a legend of himself. He was dressed in a smartly cut, brown three-piece suit with a white flat-rimmed hat. His mustache was neatly trimmed and his face was cleanly shaven. His beautiful wife sat proudly next to him. This man hardly looked like the barbarian his reputation painted him.

Villa lifted a megaphone to his mouth and boomed, "*Buenos días*, my countrymen and ladies. My name is Francisco Villa and this is my wife, Maria. We are both very happy to share this day with you." The crowd clapped and hooted wildly in response. When the crowd settled down, Villa continued, "Today we have some exciting events planned for you. We have some of the finest *vaqueros* in the country to entertain us with their riding, roping, and wrestling skills. Also, we have three matadors who will bravely slay ferocious bulls. I can assure you that each bull is precious." This comment was always made at these competitions regardless how true, but somehow it seemed real coming from Pancho Villa.

Villa went on, "The final event will be *la Colleada*! We have two fine colleadores who will give us an exciting show this afternoon." Murmurs of anticipation buzzed through the stadium. The *Coleada* would be an excellent conclusion to such a grandiose *jaripeo*. "Now my friends, I want you to know that these fine events are sponsored by Villa Meats. My business provides Chihuahua with the finest meat products in Mexico ..." His advertisement droned on for several minutes as people began to roll their eyes at its length. Others snickered at Villa's gall for boasting about his business when much of his cattle wore the brand of Terrazas, the very man who had built the stadium in which he was making his long-winded promotion and who sat directly in front of him. Villa seemed oblivious to the crowd's reaction. When he was finished, he looked extremely pleased with himself and smiled broadly at the people seated around him.

Villa reached down to a shelf and produced a small revolver that he loaded with blanks. He lifted his arm high into the air and fired a single shot that rang sharply throughout the stadium. In a loud and booming voice, Villa shouted, "Let the parade begin!" Cheers erupted from the stands as two large wooden doors swung open at the far end of the arena. Two *rejoneadores* on white horses led the procession with brightly colored ribbons dancing on top of their long spears. Behind them the *vaqueros*, or cowboys, walked proudly behind with their broad hats pushed back on their heads. Most of these young men had never competed in such a facility. They soaked in the cheers and admiration of the crowd as they walked around the field. Some actually swaggered with bravado.

Next came the three *matadors*. They were young men dressed in sequined black uniforms that fit tightly against their lean, muscular bodies. When they gallantly entered the arena with their capes folded neatly over one arm, feminine shrieks and sighs could be heard throughout the stadium. Many women threw long-stemmed roses down upon them as they strutted by. Each *matador* would deftly swoop down, pick up as many flowers as possible, and gather them in his free hand. One man brazenly put a stem in his mouth and broke from the parade. He waltzed up to the wall where he had noticed a beautiful *señorita* waving emphatically to him. He plucked the rose from his lips and handed it to her. She reached down and coyly took it from him, brushing his fingers in the process. Then she held the rose to her lips. The crowd loved this symbolic display and boomed their approval as the *matador* bowed low to the woman and bounded back to his position in the parade.

Lastly, in walked the two *colleador* teams. Prudenciano and Felipe walked in front. Prudenciano looked magnificent in his simple white shirt. Paz had tailored it to fit snugly around his waist but with ample room for his broad shoulders and chest. He wore his pants and black boots from his guard uniform, which accented his long, lean legs. His beard and long, flowing thick hair contained streaks of gray and added an air of dignity. His gait was strong and confident.

Felipe wore a fancy blue shirt with red designs embroidered along the collar. Over this, he slipped a tight leather vest that was polished a deep brown. Prudenciano had scowled with disapproval when he first saw his outfit. He wondered how the young man could maneuver with such restrictive clothing. As he looked at him now, Felipe appeared to be enjoying himself immensely. He walked beside Prudenciano and drank in the cheers from the crowd like a fine beer. He smiled and waved gaily back.

Prudenciano also enjoyed the banter and shouts of encouragement. He held his back straighter and lifted his head higher. As he scanned the audience, he felt a twinge of disappointment that Paz was not able to come. They could not afford a ticket for her. "Besides," Paz explained to him softly, "there is no one to take care of the kids." It was true. Since moving to Chihuahua, they had never found a family they trusted like the Martinezes in Torreón. Thoughts of Tomas stretching his hand out to him and pleading for help caused a quick shiver of remorse to flow through his body. It was not until Felipe spoke to him that he broke from his spell.

"Hey, Nava," said Felipe with his hands waving up to the crowd. "Why do you look so glum? Man, this is living! Just look at those women over there. I think they love me!"

Prudenciano looked to where he was pointing and saw a group of *señoritas* swooning and casting their eyes toward them. Judging by their expensive dresses and prime seating, Prudenciano surmised that they were probably daughters of rich *hacendados*. Prudenciano smiled and thought, *I haven't the heart to tell him that these girls perform the same way for all the competitors.*

Felipe tilted his head toward the judges' stand and asked, "Nava, isn't that Pancho Villa?" Prudenciano looked up as they passed the booth and spotted the familiar stocky figure. He stopped and faced him fully with his legs securely planted and his arms held slightly away from his body as if he was issuing a challenge. In response, Villa rose and looked down upon him. His eyes seemed to burn with a deep fury. They resembled two rutting bulls preparing for battle. The crowd sensed it too and began to quiet.

Villa became transfixed on Prudenciano's stare. He felt his heart quicken and his blood roar through his veins. *So, our paths cross again, Nava. Why do I always feel like fighting you? You are just a man.*

Prudenciano studied Villa with the detached interest of a man appraising a horse. Random thoughts filled his mind, *Who is this man? What is it that he wants?* Suddenly, his clairvoyant eye opened and flashed a dramatic vision. Villa rode laughing on his horse as he led his hordes across the barren landscape. His rampaging horsemen butchered hundreds of men, women, and children. From horizon to horizon, destruction and death surrounded him. Then Prudenciano saw a man and a woman with two small children and a baby cowering on a road. The barbarians surrounded them like a pack of wolves and prepared to devour them. Then he recognized the family. It was Paz and himself trapped with their children.

Felipe startled Prudenciano back to reality by placing a hand on his shoulder. "Nava, what are you doing? You are holding up the line." Prudenciano turned around and saw the other *colleador* team waiting for him to continue. The parade column was several hundred feet ahead. Felipe looked concerned as he asked, "What's going on, Nava? Are you all right? You look like you've just seen a ghost."

Prudenciano did not answer, but wiped the sweat from his brow and turned back to look at Villa with a new understanding. He had never before felt such utter fear in a vision. He spoke softly to himself, "This is just a lull before the storm. I must leave Chihuahua soon before that bastard kills us." Felipe turned Prudenciano around and led him back to the parade.

Villa felt his fury boil through his body. Why did Nava stop and stare at him? It was as if he saw something that shocked and infuriated him. Then he felt the soft and gentle caress of Maria's hand along his arm. "Come, Francisco," she said soothingly. "Please sit down. Do you know him?"

"*Sí*," said Villa gruffly, as he abruptly seated himself. "He fought for Terrazas, but helped our cause, too. There is something about him that I can't put my finger on. He always seems to know too much. I have a feeling that we will meet again." They watched Prudenciano finish the parade. As he walked past Terrazas, they gave each other a nod of acknowledgment. Then Prudenciano disappeared into the corrals.

———◆◆◆◆———

The mid-afternoon heat was stifling, but a light breeze from the west gave some relief and kept the air fresh. The lack of haze caused the sky to maintain its brilliant blue throughout the day. A thunderous roar from the crowd compelled Prudenciano to glance toward the wooden gate that led to the arena. He could not see above its ten-foot height, but judging by the loudness of the cheers and occasional hats thrown high into the air, he surmised that the *matador* had struck a fatal blow to the bull. It also meant that he and Felipe had to wait another two hours before their event began. Another *matador* still needed to fight.

Compliments of Villa Meats, some tequila and food was brought to the *colleador* teams. At first, Prudenciano was wary of accepting the refreshments from the very man his vision told him was dangerous. He still felt that helpless feeling of dread slide down his spine from his prophecy. However, after a few swigs of the bottle, his misgivings magically left and he began to wolf down a sandwich.

Felipe's excitement seemed to wane as time dragged on. The liquor and food relaxed him, but soon he became bored. This was not the action that he had dreamed of earlier. He was impatient to start the competition. Finally out of desperation he blurted, "Damn, Nava! How can you sit there so calmly? Doesn't this wait bother you?"

Prudenciano smiled at his agitation. He knew what it was like to be young and feel like a caged wild animal when waiting to compete. He wondered if soldiers felt like this when they reach the battlefield and then waited for the time to fight. The wait was always the hardest part. Prudenciano held up his bottle as sort of a toast and said, "Here's to our luck. Enjoy this time together. The bull may have other plans for us. You must be patient and wait for our turn. It will come soon enough."

A voice answered from behind, "And did you learn about patience when we decided to sit together in the mine, *amigo*?" Prudenciano jumped up and spun around to face the familiar voice.

"Victoriano, it is good to see you!"

Victoriano Vallejo vaulted lightly over a rail and heartily clasped Prudenciano's shoulder. Felipe could tell that a strong bond existed between the two. He thought Victoriano looked vaguely familiar, but dismissed it as a whim. Victoriano spoke first, "Nava, I heard that you were going to perform today. Can't get enough, eh?"

Prudenciano smiled back, "*Sí*. I thought that I would try to show Chihuahua how it's done. How have you been?"

Victoriano replied, "*Muy bien*. I'm supervising a mining crew at a small operation west of town. The work is good and stable." He stopped and looked in back of him. Prudenciano followed his gaze and saw a large man making his way toward them through the men and animals like a child walking through a wheat field. "Actually, Nava, besides coming to see you, this big hulk wanted to meet you, too." The man pushed a steer to the side to clear the final distance. As he did, Prudenciano and Felipe had their first good look at him. Felipe shuddered at the immense and powerful man standing before them. However, Prudenciano grinned broader than before and stepped forward to greet him.

"Anastacio Currandas! It is good to see you again!" Felipe and Victoriano looked at each other in disbelief as Prudenciano and Currandas warmly embraced.

Victoriano asked, "You know each other? How can this be? Anastacio was never in Chihuahua during ..." Victoriano let his voice trail off.

Prudenciano replied, "We go back a long ways. We competed as *colleadores* in Zacatecas for many years." Turning to Currandas, he asked, "Why are you not competing today?"

Currandas replied, "I am afraid that my days as a *colleador* are over, *amigo*. These last few years have been hard on me." Currandas was ten years younger than Prudenciano, but his body showed evidence of the rampages of war. Prudenciano nodded with understanding.

A voice rose out of the cacophony of the corrals. "*Perdón*, but I must speak with Prudenciano Nava."

"I am here," shouted Prudenciano and waved his hand over his head so the man could see. A young man dressed in a white shirt with a black bow tie and dress pants waved a pad of paper back at Prudenciano. He wore an expression of relief on his face as if he finally found the object of his search. He slid under the rail and came up to Prudenciano.

"Ah, *Señor* Nava," the man addressed Prudenciano as he pulled out his pencil. "Within the hour your team will start *la Colleada*. So, what shall we call you? Do you have any special name? You know, like *El Zorro* or *El Hombre*?"

Prudenciano shrugged his shoulders and replied, "You can just call us…"

Victoriano interrupted, "Wait a minute, Nava. Come on. Let's have a little fun here. The way you hook those bulls, you deserve a special name."

Felipe interjected, "*Sí*. Since I must dance my horse across the arena in front of a bull, I want a name that indicates that I can't be touched. I know! *La Mosca*, the Fly! *Sí*. That's it! *La Mosca*."

Prudenciano laughed and shook his head. "That's just great. Nava and *La Mosca*. That sounds frightening, doesn't it?"

Grinning, Currandas put his arm on Prudenciano's shoulder and said, "You know, Nava, it does have a certain ring to it. Perhaps though, you should have a performing name, too. How about building on what Victoriano said, *El Gancho*, the Hook?"

Prudenciano looked incredulously at Currandas and found that he was serious. Prudenciano rolled the names on his tongue, "*El Gancho y La Mosca*. *Sí*, it does have a good sound to it." Prudenciano turned to the young man who was now smiling from ear to ear. Prudenciano smiled back and said, "You may name us *El Gancho y La Mosca*!"

"*Sí*," answered the man as he scribbled down the name. "That's a grand name! The crowd will love it! Good luck, *Señores*." He closed his notebook and walked quickly out of the corral.

As Prudenciano watched him go, Currandas stepped closer and said seriously, "Prudenciano, there is another matter that I must discuss with you." Prudenciano suddenly became very interested in what Currandas had to say and nodded for him to continue. "Your nephew, José, is in good health. He...", Currandas was going to say "fought," but struggled to find a more accurate verb. "...*stayed* with me during the revolution."

Prudenciano's face brightened. "José is alive? Where is he?"

"I don't know," replied Currandas. "We discharged him two months ago. He said that he was going to the *Estados Unidos.*" Prudenciano looked down for a second and concentrated on a distant memory in Monte Escobedo. In the *cantina,* José had announced that he was going to America. The boy was fulfilling his dream. It made Prudenciano both proud and jealous.

———

Prudenciano and Felipe sat on their horses behind the tall wooden gate and waited for their announcement. The last bullfight had ended only minutes ago. Judging by the crowd's horrified shrieks and groans, the *matador* must have been on the losing side. They would have to wait a few minutes longer while the field hands cleared the arena.

Prudenciano studied Felipe for a moment. He wore the grin of a man who faces uncertain danger and excitement. *This is good*, thought Prudenciano. *He is not overconfident.* He cleared his throat and addressed the young man. "Felipe, there are some words of advice that I would like to give you." Felipe looked at him expectantly. As Prudenciano opened his mouth to speak, Tereso Rodriguez's mangled body flashed through his mind. The vision scared him.

Prudenciano shook the fear from his body and leaned closer to Felipe. "Look, Felipe, I don't want you to play the hero. When that bull comes out, you try to lead him straight to the far end of the field, *comprende?*"

"*Sí,*" answered Felipe. Butterflies fluttered in his stomach.

Prudenciano continued, "Now, do not wait for the bull to come at you. Just trail the flags and start moving away from him. I will be right behind to grab the tail."

"*Sí,*" answered Felipe again. Then his face became grave as he added, "I only have one regret."

Prudenciano thought, *I knew it. He probably wishes that he had not come.*

Felipe saw his scowl and continued with a straight face, "I wish that I could have found someone to cover a few bets for me like you did." A large smile broke across Felipe's face. Prudenciano returned the smile. Currandas had loaned him a few pesos to cover the betting. The informal gambling circuit was offering 2-to-1 odds today. Prudenciano interpreted that to mean average odds that paid more than what he put in. If he failed, he would be in debt to Currandas.

He also could not reveal any of this betting to Paz. She would be furious at his frivolous spending of their meager income.

Suddenly, the large wood doors began to creak open. They quickly sat up straight in their saddles and pumped up their chests. Slowly the opening gate revealed the arena and the waiting crowd to them. A booming voice introduced them to the cheering spectators. "*Señores* and *Señoras, la Colleada* is about to begin! The first *colleador* team is *El Gancho y La Mosca!*" The crowd went wild as Prudenciano and Felipe galloped onto the field. Each held a hand high as they rode around the arena.

Prudenciano's horse's gait faltered for a split second and then regained its footing, momentarily throwing Prudenciano off balance. He looked back to see what had caused his horse to slip. The hoofprints showed a skid mark directly behind him. He turned his horse back to investigate. When he arrived at the spot, he swore at what he found. The field hands had simply covered the blood from the past bullfighting with some dirt. The congealed blood created a hidden trap that could easily stumble a horse. The dark red mass oozed ominously into the tracks.

Prudenciano galloped back to Felipe. "Watch out for hidden pools of blood. The idiots didn't shovel it out. They just covered it up." Felipe gave Prudenciano a quick nod.

"*Señores,*" the announcer addressed them. "Please take your positions." Felipe winked at Prudenciano. Despite his discovery, Prudenciano felt the old excitement trickle through his body. He nodded back and smiled.

"Let's do it! Now remember, Felipe, just take the bull for a walk across the field. I'll do the rest."

"You worry too much, Nava," answered Felipe with a laugh. With that, he whipped out his flags and trotted to his position directly in front of the chute. Prudenciano nudged his horse forward and set up behind the starting gate.

The crowd began to quiet as they leaned forward in anticipation. Some of the spectators in the higher rows had to shield their eyes with their hands because the late-afternoon sunlight slanted toward them. The announcer checked the positioning of Felipe and Prudenciano. Satisfied that they were ready, he looked over to the man by the chute. He nodded that all was well. Then with much fanfare, the announcer lifted his hand, held it in the air for a breathless second, and dropped it like an executioner's blade. The gate fell open and the bull rumbled down the chute.

The bull bounded proudly into the arena. He tossed his head back and forth while he snorted great volumes of air through his widened nostrils. Within a heartbeat, he spotted Felipe sitting motionless on his horse holding a drooping flag in his hand. The bull lowered his head and charged forward.

Felipe momentarily quailed at its ferocity. He had never been the focus of such a powerful creature so bent on his total destruction. A wild thought crossed his mind to pitch the flags and ride away, but he checked it and began a mild gallop to the end of the field. The eyes of his horse rolled with terror as Felipe reined it in to keep it from bolting. The bull was now inches from his rear. His horns practically straddled the horse's width. Fear rippled through his body as Felipe screamed, "Nava, where are you?"

The crowd's sudden roar caused him to twist in his seat and behold the laws of physics in action. The bull was pitching forward with Prudenciano seemingly lifting the bull's hind end up by his tail. The bull's front legs locked forward as he flipped completely onto his back. Dust flew high as the bull hit the ground.

Prudenciano rode up to him with a triumphant look on his face. Little did Felipe know that Prudenciano was as surprised as anyone how easily the bull was tailed. It was a textbook throw. They might not be as lucky next time. Prudenciano winked at Felipe and yelled over the deafening roar of the crowd, "Did I hear you say something, Felipe?" All Felipe could do was shake his head and trot back to the gate. He was so scared that he could not even acknowledge the admiration of his fans.

When the noise subsided, the announcer stood up and boomed through his megaphone, "That, *Señoras* and *Señores*, is why he is called *El Gancho!*" People shouted back their approval. Even Villa had to admit that he had just witnessed the finest throw he had ever seen. He sat stroking his mustache as he watched Prudenciano wave to the crowd and disappear into the corrals. Villa sensed too that they seemed to be hooked together in some predestined fate. It took Maria's beautiful smile to break his thoughts.

———◦••◦———

Felipe looked astonished at Prudenciano. "What do you mean we're tied? That was a weak throw!" The competing *colleador* team just finished their match. Although it lacked the finesse and grace of Prudenciano's throw, the team still had a good time.

"It was their time," answered Prudenciano evenly. "Our next match must be much faster. *Comprende?* Now, this is what I want you to do. I want you to sweep across the chute as the bull is released. Try to drag him across the middle of the field." Prudenciano stopped for a moment and waited for Felipe's reply. He slowly nodded, but his eyes betrayed his fear. This maneuver would place him very close to the bull. Prudenciano continued, "When you start to arc back to the middle, I will strike then. If all goes well, it will be over in a few seconds." Felipe blinked. As far as he was concerned, "over" meant either for the bull or for him.

Prudenciano had Felipe repeat his plan and corrected him where he varied slightly. Then they prepared themselves for the second and final match. As they sat in their saddles and waited for the announcer to signal them to enter the arena, Prudenciano suddenly had a sad and melancholy feeling descend upon him. *This will be my last match*, he thought. *I know in my bones that I will not throw anymore bulls. My age is catching up with me.* As to accent this premonition, his throwing arm ached back in response. *Sí, this is it. Well, I will make it my best!* Prudenciano wrapped the reins tighter around his left hand and clenched his jaw in determination.

They received the signal and rode back into the arena. The crowd shouted cheers of *"¡El Gancho!"* Prudenciano and Felipe barely responded. The two men looked at each other for the last time and assumed their positions. Felipe brought his horse to an oblique angle to the chute. Prudenciano threw himself forward on his horse to prepare for maximum acceleration. The audience quieted as the announcer looked at the *colleadores* and then glanced at the gate operator. All was ready. As he lifted up his hand, Felipe nudged his horse forward and began his sweeping run. It was a calculated risk, but the gamble paid off. As Felipe approached the chute, the announcer signaled to release the bull. Felipe brushed past the ramp as the bull exited. It immediately gave chase.

Felipe kicked his horse to sprint and leaned to the left to start his swing back to the center of the field. The bull tracked directly behind with the horse's tail swishing in front of his eyes. Amidst thunderous cheers, Prudenciano exploded from his gate. His hair and beard flowed along his head as he shot his horse along an intercepting tangent. He planned to catch the bull at the peak of Felipe's arc.

The adrenalin rush caused Prudenciano's mind to race. Time seemed to slow almost to a standstill. The stadium noises now sounded like a low drone. He could hear his own heart beating like a steady drum. His breath seared his nostrils as his blood pressure soared. His horse seemed to move in a slow fluid motion. Spittle flew in tiny globules from its mouth and hung momentarily in the air. Prudenciano registered every movement, every minute detail of this unfolding drama, and every thought in crystal clarity. His whole being absorbed each thrilling microsecond as if it were a narcotic.

The bull behaved exactly as planned. As Felipe and the bull crossed the apex of their curve, Prudenciano reached out and snatched the tail. The bull's trajectory was slightly skewed to Prudenciano, so he tried to compensate by leaning farther that usual. At that critical point, the bull's legs slipped out from under him. Prudenciano' horse slid at the same time. His mind was operating at light speed and screamed the warning, *The blood! You've hit the blood!*

A double dose of adrenalin coursed through his body. It electrified him. Now his entire universe focused on the bull and his horse. There was no sound. His vision tunneled as his mind omitted frivolous details. Each movement played out before him like a stop-frame movie. The bull's horns slowly grazed the flank of Felipe's horse. Blood spurted along the neat cut. The bull locked its forelegs outward, but its momentum was carrying him sideways. His weight was not fully transferred forward. Prudenciano held on to the tail, but the shift in weight nearly wrenched him from his saddle.

The bull hit solid ground first. His front right hoof dug in and acted as the fulcrum to pitch his entire body over. The horse recovered its balance and Prudenciano yanked the tail upwards with all his might. The bull corkscrewed into the air and fell on his back.

The crowd exploded with exhilaration. The noise rumbled into Prudenciano's awareness and broke into his racing mind. The whole event had lasted only a few seconds, but it seemed like an eternity to Prudenciano. He was wasted in both mind and body. His body reeked from fear, exertion, and excitement. He felt waves of exhaustion move through him as the adrenalin left his system. He would remember this pinpoint of time for the rest of his life.

Felipe rode up to him. He looked deeply shaken. "You couldn't have cut it much closer, Nava!" He pointed to the blood trickling down his horse's leg.

Prudenciano gulped to catch his breath. He was quickly losing that delicious "fight or flight" feeling. After a few seconds, he managed to reply, "I bet we got a good time." He lifted his hand as a salute to the crowd and rode out of the corral.

The judge looked in disbelief at his stopwatch. His practiced hand had started the timer when the bull exited the chute and instinctively clicked the stop button when the bull hit the dirt. The watch read 4.5 seconds. Although the throw was unorthodox, the time was phenomenal. It would be very hard to beat.

He showed the time to the announcer who would not have believed it if he had not seen it. He raised the megaphone and shouted, "Four point five seconds! *¡Magnífico!* Let's hear it for *El Gancho y El Mosca!*" The crowd went wild for a few minutes. When some semblance of calm prevailed, the announcer continued, "The final team is ready to answer *El Gancho's* challenge!"

The second team began to settle into their positions. They had witnessed Prudenciano's tactics and concluded that they would like to repeat them. The *colleador* was in his thirties and a veteran of many tailings. His flagger was only a few years younger. Unlike Felipe, he also had many years of experience.

To beat Prudenciano's and Felipe's time, they knew that they had to cut the margin of safety closer. When the announcer lifted his hand to start, the flagger began to move slowly toward the chute. He waited until the bull was charging down the ramp before he spurred his horse into action and barely brushed by the animal as it entered the arena. With the bull literally pushing the horse from behind, he led the beast along Felipe's same arc. The *colleador* fired from his gate to quickly intercept the bull.

Their plan to perfect Prudenciano's method was good except for one fatal flaw. They forgot about the blood. The flagger looked ahead as he turned his horse into the center of the field. Suddenly he saw the thick, dark red soil directly in front of him. It looked like a deadly ambush waiting for its victim. Instinctively, he yanked the reins to veer to the right. His horse had to shift its weight to the opposing side of travel to initiate the command and faltered slightly. The bull slammed into them from behind and pushed the horse forward into the jaws of the trap. At that precise moment, the *colleador* grabbed the bull's tail.

The three of them were locked together as they hit the blood. The front horse fell first and the bull's horn struck the rider below his right shoulder blade. It slid under the bone and buried itself deep into the back. The bull lost its footing and fell sideways, twisting the flagger grotesquely into the air. The *colleador* flipped forward onto the bull as he kept his grasp of its tail. The trailing horse skidded into the heap. The spectators gasped at the melee.

Field hands from both sides of the stadium jumped into the arena to help. The bull found his footing, stood up, and shook the body from its horn. A man attracted its attention and led it back to the chute. The others found that there was nothing they could do to save the young man's life. The impalement had traumatized his entire chest cavity.

The death threw a black shroud over the day's events. The subdued crowd began to rise and shuffle out of the stadium. The judge simply noted that the final team failed to complete a throw and officially named Prudenciano as the winner.

Prudenciano and Felipe watched the field crews lift the ragged body onto a stretcher and carry it away. The scene dampened their jubilation. "That could have been us," commented Prudenciano. Felipe kept silent as he continued to watch the death procession.

"Nava!" shouted a familiar voice from behind. Prudenciano turned and saw Currandas grinning broadly. He was holding a fistful of pesos. "We did quite well, *amigo*. I brought you your share."

Prudenciano returned the smile and thought, *Perhaps something good came from today.* He took the money from Currandas and counted it. He did not know exactly how much he had made, but it felt like a lot. Prudenciano peeled off a few pesos and handed it to Felipe. "You did a good job out there, my *amigo*. Here is a little something for your time."

"*Gracias, amigo*," replied Felipe. The site of the mangled flagger still bothered him, but the money helped some. "I think I just might see if one of those adoring *señoritas* would like dinner." Felipe's spirits were rising.

Currandas laughed. "You just do that. Good luck!" Felipe adjusted his hat, waved goodbye, and rode out of the corral. Prudenciano and Currandas watched him go. When he disappeared, Currandas asked quietly, "Why is it that the inexperienced seem to make it and the experienced die?"

"Huh? What do you mean?" The question bothered Prudenciano. He had a feeling where Currandas was leading him.

"I mean, here Felipe has never competed before and comes out without a scratch, but experienced players like Tereso and that last flagger are killed. It doesn't make sense." Currandas's comment completely squelched the last bit of festive mood inside Prudenciano. He winced at the memory of the bull smashing the life out of Tereso—a bull that had slipped out of his hand.

"Come on, Currandas," said Prudenciano with a weary voice. "Let's put this money to good use and buy a bottle of tequila. I suddenly have a need for a drink."

Paz was beside herself with worry. Rumors sailed through the neighborhood that a *colleador* was killed at the *jaripeo*. No one knew who it was nor had she received word about his safety. All she could do was wait until he either came home or an officer delivered the official ominous news.

It was now one o'clock the following morning. To pass the time, she checked on the girls. Alcaria and Joaquina were snuggled together in their bed, both in a deep sleep. Paz felt a stab of envy as she looked upon their innocent little faces. They appeared oblivious to all of the world's problems. Paz thought wistfully, *I wish that my life was so simple.*

She carefully closed the door and resumed her slow pace around

the room. Within a few minutes, she heard the voices of men singing a rowdy Mexican folksong drunkenly off key. Paz looked out
the window to see a wagon coming slowly down the street. When it
drew closer, she could see a man driving the wagon with two large
men swaying in the back. All three were singing the bawdy tune.

As the wagon pulled up alongside the house, it stopped. Paz recognized Prudenciano with his arm draped over a very large man.
They each had a bottle in their free hand. In a final salute, they
toasted each other and flung a huge gulp of drink down their throats.
Prudenciano tried to get up once, but fell back down. The other two
men laughed until they both succumbed to choking and hacking fits.
Prudenciano gathered up his wits and this time cleared the wagon
and landed unsteadily on his feet. His left hand held tightly to his
bottle while his right grasped onto the wagon.

The driver waved to Prudenciano and said, "*Adios, amigo.* Pleasant dreams." Without waiting for a reply, he snapped the reins and
the horse started forward. Prudenciano still held on to the rail and
pitched forward with the wagon. He dropped the bottle as he frantically tried to regain his balance. The bottle smashed like a gun shot
and sprayed alcohol over his pants. He continued to hold on to the
wagon, which was the only stable force in his world for the moment.
He lost his footing and started to drag down the street.

The man in the back thundered, "Victoriano! Stop! You *federale*
idiot!" The driver pulled back on the reins and turned around. By the
look on his face, he was very surprised to see that Prudenciano was
still attached to them.

Victoriano exclaimed, "*¡Dios mío!* Are you all right?"

"*Sí,*" answered Prudenciano as he staggered to stand up. "Thanks
to Currandas. *Buenas noches.*" He waved them on and wiped his
grubby hands on his new cotton shirt. His hands left long grimy
streaks along down the front. He turned and slowly made his way
back to his house.

Paz had witnessed the whole undignified scene. By the time Prudenciano had made it to the door, her anxiety changed to total disgust.
With her arms crossed tightly in front, she lifted her little chin in solid
defiance as she steeled herself for her husband's entrance. The door
creaked open as Prudenciano tried to creep in silently. He had already
convinced himself that Paz had not heard them pull up. He tripped
over a chair trying to close the door and almost tumbled to the floor.
He caught himself on the table as the chair noisily tipped over. He
took a deep breath and looked up to see Paz standing across the room
glaring at him through the feeble light of a single candle.

A sequence of thoughts coursed through Prudenciano's mind. His first thought was his wife looked beautiful and he wanted to express his love for her. However, after his drunken stupor allowed Prudenciano to realize that she was very angry, his feelings changed to remorse and some guilt. Then when the look of contempt crept across her face, irrational anger rose within him.

Paz snarled, "Prudenciano! Do you have any sense of what time it is?"

"It's nighttime," he quipped. "What time do you think it is?"

His flippant response inflamed her. "You are so drunk that you can hardly stand! What would your children think if they saw you?"

Paz's verbal attack struck him low in the gut. He could think of no fitting retort to parry her thrust. He suddenly felt a wave of nausea pass over him like a breaking surf. He grabbed the table to steady himself. It drenched his anger and left him weak and exhausted. Subdued, he spoke to her in a tired and dejected voice, "Paz, I had two visions today."

His words stopped her cold. She knew that he seldom talked about his deep insights. When he did, the visions eventually foretold future events with uncanny accuracy. She felt a disturbing foreboding shift silently through her stomach. He sensed her uneasiness and continued, "One of the visions told me that I would never compete as a *colleador* again." He slowly shook his drunken head. His matted hair and beard only emphasized the filth on his clothes. "But my body has been telling me that for some time. I did not need a vision to point that out." He took a deep breath to clear his mind and smiled. "I won today! They called me *El Gancho!*" He pretended to snatch an imaginary tail with his hand and hook it upward.

Paz had not known that he had won. She allowed a little trickle of pride to enter her being, but her hardened features did not show it. It also explained why he had drunk so much tonight. However, any soft feelings for him were tempered when she gazed upon the shirt that she had taken so long to sew. It looked like he had wallowed in a pig pen with it. Her voice was even and angry, "You said you had two visions."

Prudenciano nodded his head and seemed to stare at the dark recesses behind her. In the soft glow of the candle, she saw his pupils dilate as he began to recall the vision. His silence scared her. He pursed his lips before answering. His voice was husky with emotion. "I saw Villa leading an army of ruthless bandits. They swarmed over the land like locusts, devouring everything in their path." His breathing became ragged and he stopped for a moment.

Paz felt herself being drawn into his vision. "Go on," she whispered.

Prudenciano gulped and continued, "I saw us on a lonely road and the smell of death was in the air. Then Villa's jackals swarmed down and encircled us." He again stopped and became silent.

Paz felt a sickening dread in the pit of her stomach. She asked breathlessly, "What happened then?"

Prudenciano shook his head. "I don't know. The vision was broken. I don't know what became of us." Paz lowered her chin and began to unfold her arms. Prudenciano's vision unnerved her and she needed the comfort of his arms, but before she could move to him, the stench reached her. The smell of stale tequila, beer, and tobacco wafted across the room. It rejuvenated her repulsion to his carousing.

"Well, that is a fine story," she said as she moved to the bedroom door. "Make yourself comfortable out here because you are not sleeping with me tonight." Before Prudenciano could reply, the door slammed shut.

Prudenciano felt sick, lonely, and a little mad. His body began to stiffen and ache from the afternoon's lopsided throw. He was going to hurt tomorrow. Prudenciano staggered to a corner and collapsed on the floor. His last thought before the spinning darkness enfolded him was, *Some way for El Gancho to finish his night!*

———

Life was good for the Nava family during the year 1911. Construction projects continued to increase, which kept Prudenciano steadily employed. His work was easy and allowed him to strut around the work site on the pretense that he was protecting the workers. Don Luis Terrazas finally left Chihuahua for a safer and more respectable place. Governor Gonzalez covered the construction costs and kept the economy moving.

Many Chihuahua residents continued to migrate north to the United States. Reports, some exaggerated, trickled in daily that described unlimited opportunities in America for agricultural jobs. It appeared that the economy was booming up there and Americans were begging for laborers. Some described wages three times higher than what Prudenciano was making.

The opportunities tempted Prudenciano, but he thought, *Where else could I ride all day wearing a uniform, boss people around, and get paid for it? Besides, it was hard enough to travel here from Torreón with one child. Now I have two. No, I think I will stay around here for a while.*

With his self-esteem inflated at work, Prudenciano found himself spending more time at home with his family. He would actively seek out Paz and tease her with seductive advances, some of which were playful, and some urgent. She enjoyed his attention, although she thought some of his antics were rather crude in front of the children. The girls loved to be held by him and would beg unceasingly to be picked up. Since last June, he had shown good behavior for three months without going on another drunken debauchery. Paz appreciated this above anything else. Her spirits rose so much that she began to play her harmonica regularly during the evenings.

On an October evening, Paz surprised Prudenciano by proclaiming that she was pregnant. She was now twenty-one years old and entering the prime of her life. If you looked closely at her face you could see traces of the past six years of child bearing, walking vast distances, times of scant food, and other hardships. She was still very strong and determined, but she had lost her young-girl beauty and replaced it with the attractiveness of a seasoned woman. Her pregnancy seemed to add a freshness in her cheeks. She radiated a healthy glow that seemed to enhance her allure.

Prudenciano's behavior toward her changed dramatically after the announcement. Every day after returning from work, he held her gently and place his hand on her abdomen in a loving way. At night after the girls were asleep, he used his *sobador* talents to rub her aching shoulders and lower back. Paz loved every minute of it.

For most, life in Chihuahua was finally peaceful. However, there was one young man who was not content with the new government and the changes that had occurred. Peace had no place in his heart. He sought the glory of the big fight and reveled in war's violence. But most of all, Pascual Orozco Jr. sought recognition and power and to achieve this, he was about to spark the bloodiest revolution of all time.

Chapter 11
Discontent

The January winds blew in the new year of 1912. Among the cold air, it brought the chill of unrest. Many of the conservative *hacenda-dos* longed for the old ways so that they could rule over the masses once again. They had lost too much money and land under President Madero. They needed a spokesman and a warrior to represent their selfish plans and they believed Pascual Orozco was that man. Bought off, he was skillfully groomed by the *hacendados* to lead a rebellion that would reestablish the old rule of the rich.

Sitting in a fashionable restaurant in Chihuahua, Orozco was accompanied by Alberto Terrazas, son of Don Luis Terrazas, and the notorious banker and land baron, Juan Creel. Alberto was a middle-aged man who was always impeccably dressed. He held an expensive cigar with a dignified grace and blew smoke through his finely trimmed mustache. Juan was older and incredibly rich. He had attained his wealth through the corruption of the Díaz machine. He also had personally pushed Abraham Gonzalez out of the banking business, an act that he later regretted.

They sat at a corner table in full view of all the dining patrons. Orozco bitterly cursed not requesting a private room. There were too many eyes that could report his unsavory company to Madero. Many would find it strange that the presidentially-appointed head of the military department of Chihuahua would dine with such arrogantly proclaimed enemies of the government. He had already caught several men looking at him from the corners of their eyes. He sighed and tried to concentrate on what Juan was saying.

"… as you can see," said Juan Creel as he swirled a goblet of port, "the major landowners of the region are becoming extremely concerned about your president's intentions." Orozco winced at the mention of "your president," but said nothing. Juan took a sip and continued. "You see, we can't possibly pay the back property taxes that your president says we owe. We were assessed and taxed according to the previous government's policies. Our money is currently tied up in investments that will keep our state moving forward. If your president demands that money, then I fear it may wreck our prosperous economy."

"We also want our original landholdings given back to us," injected Alberto as he exhaled his cigar smoke. "My father lost half of his land and over half his cattle."

Orozco sighed again and took a sip of his bourbon. It slid nicely down his throat without burning and left a delightful aftertaste. It had been a long time since he tasted such a high quality liquor. This was just one of the advantages of associating with men of wealth. He reached to the center of the table and pulled a fine Cuban cigar from the humidor. As he fumbled with the tip, he spoke for the first time. "I agree with your analysis, Juan, but I fail to see how I could help you."

"Ah, but contrary to what you think, my young man, you are in a very enviable position," answered Juan, leaning forward to make his point. "You have the ear of Madero himself and can glean from him how he intends to implement his policies. At the same time, you control a large militia in Chihuahua. That's a very powerful combination, my *amigo*."

Orozco countered, "But the men need a reason to revolt."

Juan replied evenly over his glass, "We will give them that reason and help you achieve the overthrow of the government. Alberto, tell him what we are offering."

Alberto tapped his cigar ash into a tray and seemed to collect his thoughts for a moment. Then he looked straight into Orozco's eyes and held his gaze as he spoke. "We are prepared to increase your compensation most handsomely and supply you with any weapons and support that you need to secure the state of Chihuahua. The landowners will assist you in convincing the state militia to follow you."

The grandeur of their plan stunned Orozco for a second. He had known all along that this was their ultimate goal, but the suddenness of their actions still surprised him. "*I knew the assessment of back taxes would smoke them out,*" thought Orozco bitterly as he recalled trying to convince Gonzalez and Madero not to embark on the ridiculous plan. Orozco narrowed his eyes at the men and said, "What about Villa? The men still think of him as a god and he continues to believe that Madero and Gonzalez walk on water. How do we handle him?"

"He is just a man, Orozco," answered Alberto. "Just an ordinary man that can be manipulated, bought, or killed. Nothing more."

You mean like me, thought Orozco angrily. He started to realize now how far he had sold his soul. In addition, he still liked Pancho Villa. They had been through too much together and they both hated Huerta. He calmed his anger and asked, "What do you have planned?"

Alberto slowly pulled his cigar from his mouth and pretended to examine it as he rolled the fat tube in his fingers. The silence amplified the suspense. Through the cigar smoke, he finally spoke, "Sometimes a man gets caught up in situations that cause him to lose control of his destiny. Then he becomes a pawn of circumstances. I believe that Mr. Villa's passions will cause him to do our bidding." Then without much fanfare, Alberto Terrazas explained the *hacendados'* plan to rebuild the Mexican government to their liking while Pascual Orozco Jr. felt his future slip from his control.

Governor Abraham Gonzalez was not a dumb man. From the governor's palace, he stood at his third-story office window with his hands clasped behind his back. It provided an excellent view of Chihuahua. The city appeared peaceful this evening, but Gonzalez knew better. Misguided men were stirring up trouble. He had heard the reports of Orozco spreading discontent throughout the land. Now he had been seen collaborating with political enemies. *In full view of the public,* thought Gonzalez as he shook his head in disbelief at Orozco's brashness.

To make matters worse, Madero refused to believe that anyone would harm him. He could not convince Madero to remove Orozco from his post. Gonzalez sighed with dismay at the discovery of his president's most glaring fault. He trusted people too much. Gonzalez knew if he did not do something soon, the pot would boil over into another civil war. He felt a chill trickle down his back at the thought. He reflected sadly, *So many have died already.*

Gonzalez possessed the supreme ability to concentrate and analyze problems. As he continued to stare out across the city, he concisely reviewed his options. He knew that his very life depended on his next decisions. His face scowled in deep thought for a few moments and then he looked up with a renewed purpose in his eyes. The scowl left but his jaw set in a determined line. He knew what he had to do.

Walking quickly to his chair, Gonzalez grabbed a notepad and wrote out a detailed order. Then he shouted for his aide, "Cástulo!"

A young man came briskly through the door. *"Sí, Señor?"* Gonzalez smiled with admiration for the man. No matter how late, Cástulo was always there for him. He had so few people that he could totally depend on nowadays.

"Cástulo, I know that it is late, but I need this message telegraphed immediately to President Madero in Mexico City."

"*Sí*," said Cástulo, "I understand. I will do it immediately." He turned to leave, but Gonzalez stopped him with a hand.

"Cástulo," said Gonzalez in a serious voice, "Thank you for your hard work and dedication. You are a tremendous asset to our government." Cástulo was slightly taken aback by the unsolicited praise. He grinned back, embarrassed, and managed to mutter an uncomfortable "*Gracias*" before leaving the room. Gonzalez watched him leave before reviewing his plans one more time.

Gonzalez planned to officially recall Francisco Villa and have him organize new military units under his command. He knew Villa would remain loyal to the Madero government. Villa was a natural leader of men. He could swing the alliances of the citizens to Madero and oppose the *hacendados*' influences. Behind his desk, Gonzalez placed his tired head on his hands and massaged his aching temples. He whispered to himself, "I just pray that Villa can organize the men in time."

———•••———

The guards began to gather at the armory for the evening debriefing. Prudenciano enjoyed the return of the old familiar camaraderie and rituals that the revolution had disrupted. He joked with the men and swapped stories about the day's events. To Prudenciano, it was the perfect way to end the day.

The captain, also a survivor of the revolution, asked for their attention before dismissing them. "*Señores*, if I could have a minute of your time, we will be on our way home." The laughing and murmurs died down, and the captain continued, "The construction is going well at all sites. The latest reports estimate that *El Palacio de Bellas Artes* will be completed by early next year." The captain nodded to Prudenciano in recognition of his territory. Prudenciano preened under this attention.

Now the captain's demeanor changed to a serious tone as he continued to address them. "I'm sure you all have heard the rumors of another revolution brewing." He stopped and stared across the room at every face. Everyone fell silent and knew something important was about to be announced. Satisfied that he had their undivided attention, the captain carefully told them the latest news release from the governor's office. "President Madero has recalled Francisco Villa into active service. He is organizing separate fighting units in this state to operate under his command. This is just a precaution. You are to carry out your duties as before, but I want you to be aware of the possibility of civil unrest."

The announcement froze every heart in the room. The jovial banter was gone. In its place seeped the dread of total social chaos. They all had suffered from the last upheaval. The lack of work brought hunger and the constant danger in the streets kept them prisoners in their own homes. Prudenciano had an additional worry. Paz was due to deliver their baby in four months. He closed his eyes and hoped that this would all just blow over.

Pascual Orozco burst into Juan Creel's office unannounced. An exasperated clerk followed behind yelling, "You can't do this! *Señor* Creel, I am sorry, but he just broke in here!" Juan appeared unruffled by the disturbance. In fact, he seemed to have anticipated it. His two visitors, however, were deeply upset. They both choked and hacked on their cigar smoke from the surprise.

Juan dismissed the clerk by saying, "It's all right, please close the door." When everyone settled down, Juan smiled at Orozco and asked, "Is something wrong?"

"Something wrong?" repeated Orozco sarcastically as he stood up and stormed around the office. "*Sí*, I would say that there is something wrong! Did you know that Villa is organizing a militia? I'm going to have to fight him!"

Juan was interestingly unimpressed by Orozco's news. He calmly addressed him like he had not heard, "Pascual Orozco, I want you to meet two associates of mine. This is *Señor* Cuilty and *Señor* Lujane."

Orozco had seen them before. Their families were major land owners in the state. He gave them a cursory acknowledgment and turned his attention back to Juan. "You act like this is a trivial matter."

"On the contrary," replied Juan, "this is a monumental turn of events and one that I am very thankful for."

Orozco was stunned. He asked, "How can you be grateful for the mounting opposition?"

Juan smiled and motioned to a chair. "Please, Pascual, sit down and calm yourself. We were just discussing how to turn this to our advantage." Subdued and bewildered, Orozco slumped into the offered chair. "That's better," continued Juan, "Now let's rationally discuss our options, shall we?"

Lujane adjusted the suspenders of his elegant suit, tapped his cigar into a brass ashtray, and finally spoke, "As I was saying before the interruption, we need to start an insurrection among the citizens. This way, the opposition will divide itself and fail to unite against us."

"True," injected Cuilty, "but how do we maintain control?"

Juan replied while smiling like a Cheshire cat, "Ah, but that is how

Señor Villa and our friend *Señor* Orozco can help us, *¿qué no?*" Orozco felt that the *hacendados* had something big in store for him. He brooded silently and watched his destiny unfold.

"*Sí*," continued Juan, "if we can convince Villa that a rebellion has occurred, he just might kill many innocent law-abiding citizens trying to stamp it out. That's when our young man who controls the government-recognized militia comes to the rescue and saves our fair city from the clutches of such an evil man. Think of how grateful Chihuahua will be! Visualize also how appalled the entire nation will be when it is known that Madero himself orchestrated the whole event!"

The room went silent as each man contemplated the scheme. It was simple enough that it stood a good chance of succeeding. All that remained was determining how to stage a small, convincing riot. Again, Juan laughed and provided the perfect solution, "A prison is the ideal place to fake a rebellion. The residents are always eager. You can usually contain it within the facility and any casualties are quickly forgotten. We just want you, Pascual, to be ready to respond with all the muscle that you can flex. We will call for you when the time is right."

Orozco closed his eyes and felt the iron jaws of the trap being set. They were going for a big prize, which included killing an innocent man and defaming a righteous president. It was an ominous start for the new government he was trying to promote.

————•◦•————

On February 2, Prudenciano rode his horse to the construction site in the early dawn. The cold wind forced him to button his coat tightly around his neck and pull his cap farther down on his head. He looked up and saw the gray, boiling sky spit flecks of snow through the air. This was promising to be a cold, hard day.

The workers had finished the walls and roof of *El Palacio de Bellas Artes*. Now they could complete the construction within the comfort of shelter, but Prudenciano and Felipe had to suffer the elements while they patrolled the perimeter. On days like this, they hated this job.

Prudenciano trotted up to the front of the building, quickly dismounted, and tied his horse to the front rail. Then he ducked through the large, solid oak doors and headed for a small makeshift kitchen where the men brewed coffee and gathered to talk. He walked into the main chamber and eyed the workmanship. The cavernous room always held him in awe. The ceiling soared three stories above and stained-glass windows lined the upper walls. Scaffolding hung from ropes and Prudenciano could see the beginnings of Michelangelo-style murals being painted across the entire ceiling. The huge space echoed the sounds of the workers. Even the distinctive clicking of boots walking across the tile floor was magnified tenfold and resonated through this enormous chamber. However, this morning he heard only faint noises of a few workers setting up for the day's activities.

This is wrong, thought Prudenciano as he continued to look around him. *There should be four times this many workers by this hour.*

Prudenciano made his way to the kitchen and spotted the elderly man who always kept the coffee brewing. The man was a dependable as a Swiss clock. Neither rain or snow would keep him from arriving early in the morning and making the coffee, and the coffee was good, too. The man derived a deep satisfaction from both feats.

Prudenciano grabbed a mug and began pouring himself a steaming cupful. He nodded at the old man and said, "*Buenos dias, amigo.* How goes it today?"

The old man flashed a toothless grin and replied, "I am sure that you can tell that it does not go well today, *¿qué no?*"

Prudenciano nodded and took another sip. Even the coffee tasted different. Something other than this was brewing. He could just feel it, but what? Prudenciano smiled nonchalantly back and asked, "*Por favor, amigo.* Tell me what you know."

The old man chuckled and shook his head as if he had heard a good joke. "You young men always think that I am hard of hearing. You talk of secret things in front of me as if I don't exist. Now you want me to tell you what I have heard. That is very funny." Prudenciano scowled back, but did not argue. Seeing that he had made his point and being very eager to share his knowledge, the old man continued, "Take heed, Nava. There are big changes in the wind today."

Prudenciano asked, "What are these changes, *amigo?*" He could feel a deep dread rising and thought, *Why must things change when I have finally found happiness?*

The man lost his smile and shifted in his chair. He leaned closer to Prudenciano and lowered his raspy voice to a whisper. "I heard that several men paid by Orozco and his *hacendados* slipped into the federal prison last night and are posing as troops. They are up to no good and our workers fear that a riot will erupt today. That is why everyone has stayed home."

Prudenciano sucked in his breath and thought, *What would a riot in the prison accomplish? Does it call attention to something?*

The old man watched Prudenciano contemplate this news for a few moments and then hastily interjected his opinion. "You know what I think?" He waited a split second to see if Prudenciano cared and then continued, "I think somebody is trying to set someone up." The old man pointed his craggy finger at Prudenciano and finished his prediction, "And I think that anyone that tries to quell that riot will be killed!"

Of course! thought Prudenciano, *It's the perfect trap, but for who?* Prudenciano stood up, tilted his cup back, and drained it. He smacked his lips and wiped his mouth off with the back of his hand. "*Gracias, amigo.* Now excuse me. I have work to do."

The old man cackled back, "I bet you do, *Señor.* I bet you do."

———•····•———

Villa was buried in supply requisitions. He loathed the paperwork associated with militias. Since he was the general for Madero's special troops, he was ultimately responsible for all monetary decisions. Villa did not let the fact that he could barely read or write stand in his way. He recruited two young men who possessed these skills to plow into the mountains of paper and explain their meaning. Thus, Villa sat with his head in his hands massaging his temples and radiating an extremely agitated disposition. His assistants sat across the table as they each took turns reading a work request. A sea of ledgers and forms floated between them. Villa hated this work!

A breathless messenger broke into the room. The swinging door blew the neatly stacked and well-organized papers across the room. The young men groaned in dismay. However, Villa greeted the distraction with relief.

Villa asked, "What is it?"

The young man heaved for breath from the long ride to deliver his message. He spurted his reply between gasping for air, "The troops are rebelling at the federal prison! They are demanding the overthrow of the Madero government."

Villa's eyes narrowed as he contemplated the news and said, "So, Orozco's revolt has begun. It is time to squash it!"

"No, General Villa", the man interrupted, "It cannot be General Orozco for it was he that sent me to get you." This greatly surprised Villa. He had always thought that Orozco would have launched a sneak attack. After several seconds of silence, the messenger continued, "General Orozco requests your immediate attendance at his office to discuss this situation."

Villa blinked bewilderedly for a second. Then he told the man to go back to Orozco and tell him that he would be coming shortly. When the messenger ran out the door, Villa turned to gaze out the window. This whole thing did not feel right. He was under explicit instructions to take orders only from Madero or Gonzalez. Now Orozco wanted his assistance. Was this a trick?

Villa quickly decided what needed to be done. He chose ten of his best men, armed them, and rode fast to Orozco's headquarters. "Keep your eyes open," Villa warned his men as he dismounted from his horse. "Make sure your chambers are loaded." The men obediently checked their rifles then rested the barrels in the crook of their arms. They were ready.

Villa strode into his archenemy's lair. He felt like a fly deliberately walking into a spider's web. When a soldier opened the office door, Villa saw Pascual Orozco sitting behind his desk talking to two captains standing before him. Orozco did not seem to notice him. As Villa watched him, he felt that old feeling of camaraderie flow through his veins. They had been through so much together. Could it be that everyone was mistaken about Orozco's intentions?

As if he heard Villa's thoughts, Orozco looked up from his discussion and spotted Villa standing by the door. He broke into a wide smile, stood up, and walked around his desk. He extended his hand as he approached him. "Pancho, it has been a long time! *Gracias, amigo*, for coming at such short notice." His handshake was warm and sincere.

Again, Villa was taken off guard by such a friendly greeting. He gathered his wits and replied, "I came as soon as I heard about the prison revolt."

"*Sí*," Orozco replied. His tone became quickly serious. "It appears that I have a revolt within my own troops. There is nobody I can trust. I need you to quell the uprising while I figure out the extent the mutiny planned by my soldiers."

Villa thought, *It all seems so plausible.* All he could do was simply nod and say, "I will try."

"*Bueno!*" exclaimed Orozco. "Will you need any assistance?"

Villa shook his head. "No. I have men I can trust. I am sure we can handle this situation. I will notify you when order has been restored."

Orozco appeared relieved and appreciative. He clasped Villa's shoulders with both hands. For a moment, Villa thought that he was going to kiss him, but Orozco smiled broadly and said, "We knew we could depend on you."

Villa awkwardly pried himself out of Orozco's grip and walked quickly out of the room. As he strode down the long halls to leave, he reviewed his brief meeting with Orozco. He had been just a little too gushy and this made Villa uneasy. A thought flicked across his mind, *Wasn't Jesús betrayed by a kiss?* Something in Orozco's words also disturbed Villa. He thought, *Who was this "we" that Orozco spoke of? He didn't say "I." He said "We knew that we could depend on you."* By the time Villa had reached his men, he felt even more confused about everyone's intentions.

When Prudenciano reached the armory, he found the compound bustling with activity. Men were quickly saddling horses and issuing rifles. He made his way to the captain's office and found him in deep discussions with a few junior officers. The captain looked up as Prudenciano entered the room. His face was tired, but serious, as he greeted him.

"Ah, Nava. Thank you for coming so quickly. I just sent Felipe for you only a few minutes ago." Prudenciano remained quiet and the captain continued, "It appears that Pancho Villa is leading a revolt at the federal prison. We will be assisting General Orozco's troops in rounding the rebels up."

Prudenciano felt a trickle of fear move through his guts. It must be Villa who Orozco is trying to kill! Everything was happening just like the old man had predicted. The captain read the concern in his face. Had it been any other man, he would have deciphered it as cowardice, but this was Prudenciano Nava, who had proven himself to be a very capable soldier. Thus, the captain realized that he probably had some important information. He asked, "What is wrong?"

Prudenciano answered, "I heard that this is a setup. Orozco and the *hacendados* want Villa dead, so they staged this riot."

The captain demanded, "What is your source?" If this was true, he had some serious decisions to make very quickly.

Prudenciano hesitated and shuffled his feet. How could he tell the captain that the coffee maker at the *Palacio de Bellas Artes* had told him? Finally he answered, "It is the talk on the streets."

The captain stared at him for a full three seconds before barking, "You expect me to hold back our garrison because of gossip? Get out of here and help the men to prepare to leave!"

Prudenciano shouted, "Wait! Let me ride to Governor Gonzalez's office and verify that we are ordered to mount an offensive against Villa."

The captain considered this request. It was true that his orders came from General Orozco and not Gonzalez. This new government was just so mixed up. It was hard to tell who to follow. This whole event just might be a trick. Then he and the rest of the guards could be implicated in some sort of scandal. With deep resignation, the captain nodded and said simply, "Do it."

Prudenciano tipped his hat and ran out the door. He leaped upon his horse and galloped as fast as he could for the governor's palace. The palace was on the other side of town and the clutter of the downtown streets would slow him down. Thus, he detoured to a road that skirted around the edge of the community. It was a longer route, but he could travel much faster.

As he rode, he suddenly realized that he would pass by Villa's garrison. In a snap decision, he diverted into the compound and galloped into the yard. About a hundred men were preparing for battle and no one paid him any heed as he dismounted. Prudenciano grabbed a nearby soldier and asked gruffly, "Where is your general?" The man shook off Prudenciano's grasp and pointed toward a small office building. Prudenciano turned and marched through the front door.

Before Prudenciano saw him, he could hear Villa yelling orders to his subordinates. "I want your men ready in ten minutes, *comprende*? Make sure that they take extra ammunition, water, and food. We may have to stage a siege. Now go!" Harried men scurried past Prudenciano. When the room cleared, Villa looked up and spotted him. Their eyes locked for a full two seconds before Villa recovered and resumed his tirade. He thundered, "What do you want?"

Prudenciano did not waste any words. They were both men of action and demanded that the bare facts be laid out on the table immediately. He spoke frankly, "You are riding into a trap."

Villa replied curtly, "Is that so? And how do you know this?"

Prudenciano neatly dodged that question by answering with another, "Who gave you the order to quell the riot?"

Villa's back stiffened as he responded, "General Orozco."

"And didn't Madero commission you to organize an independent militia to stand up to Orozco?"

Villa could see where this conversation was going. His body relaxed some as he slowly nodded. He thought, *Could it be that all of this was just some massive evil trick to kill me? After all, Orozco has deceived me before.* He felt his anger rising as he remembered how he almost betrayed Madero in Juarez. "*Sí.* You are right. I will wait until I have specific instructions from Governor Gonzalez. *Gracias.*"

Prudenciano smiled and turned to leave, but Villa halted him with another question. "Why did you come here and warn me?"

Prudenciano stopped abruptly and faced this square block of a man. Although he still harbored a deep foreboding about Villa, he knew that Villa fought for the common man. In Mexico, the working class always got the short end of the stick. For once, someone was wrestling that stick away from the *hacendados* and fighting back. Prudenciano summarized his response in a short sentence, "You fight for the common man." Villa appeared to accept this and said nothing as Prudenciano left and rode out of the garrison.

———

Pascual Orozco kicked Juan Creel's door open and stormed into his office. Again, Creel's secretary followed helplessly behind babbling a series of short apologies to his employer. Juan stood by the window with his hands clasped behind his back. Without turning around, he sighed and dismissed his servant with the wave of his hand. He had anticipated Orozco's rude entry, but it still annoyed him. The young man lacked maturity.

Orozco screamed, "He didn't take the bait! Somehow Villa knew that it was a trap. I think that one of your men tipped him off."

"Sit down," said Juan calmly as he continued to stare out the window. Orozco tried to burn holes into the back of Juan's skull with his fury. When Juan failed to respond, he flung himself into a soft leather chair and sulked. Juan waited a few minutes for Orozco to cool before he turned around to address him. "It appears that our man Villa is a bit more sophisticated than we anticipated."

Orozco hissed, "I told you that he is not to be trifled with."

Juan countered with an edge to his voice, "And I told you that he is just a man! And because he is just a man, we will still manipulate him to do our work. All right, so we failed to trick him. We will try to buy him."

Orozco snorted in disbelief. "He will never be bought."

"Every man has his price," replied Juan. "We just need to find out what it is."

Orozco jumped to his feet and said, "Good luck! I am going home."

Juan commanded, "Sit down! You and I have much to discuss, but you were right to wish the venture luck. For you will deliver the bribe to Villa yourself. Now, let's discuss how we are going to seize Chihuahua and promote you as our next leader." Orozco sank back into the chair. He felt his whole life slip away from him.

———

Maria watched her husband from the corner of her eye as she cleared the dinner dishes. Francisco sat brooding quietly by himself at the end of the table. His entire face appeared distraught with his frown bending his mustache downward. Her heart squeezed for him because she knew he felt deeply about the nation's state of affairs and by being betrayed again by his old friend. She also knew better than to question him about his thoughts. "He will discuss his problems with me when he is ready," she spoke quietly to herself.

The knock at the door startled both of them. Villa instinctively went for his gun. He made a physical effort not to draw it as he stood up. He pushed the pistol back into his holster and gave Maria a quick look. She gestured her head to door and managed a worried smile to mask her apprehension. Villa walked up to the door and shouted, "Who is it?"

A voice of an old man answered, "*Señor* Villa, this is Pascual Orozco. I am your friend's father." Villa's eyes sprang open with surprise. He wondered what the young Orozco could be up to now. Cautiously, he opened the door and found an old man with his hat in his hands standing by himself in the doorway. Villa darted a glance outside. Satisfied that Orozco Sr. was by himself, Villa stood aside and let him in.

The senior Orozco stood humbly in their front room. He looked around and saw the modest accommodations. His face seemed to reflect a confirmation of some secret mission. When his eyes fell upon Maria, he bowed respectfully. She smiled back and offered a chair and a refreshment. Orozco accepted the chair, but refused any other gratuity.

Villa cut straight to the point. "So, *Señor* Orozco, what brings you to our home tonight?"

The old man remained quiet for a minute to collect his thoughts. Then he addressed Villa in an even tone. "*Señor* Villa, my son's government wants to make you their ambassador to the United States. They are willing to pay you three hundred pesos for you and your wife to move temporarily there and lobby for their support."

At first, Villa sat silently staring at the older man. Orozco thought Villa had not heard him and was about to repeat the offer when he noticed Villa beginning to turn red. Within seconds, Villa began shaking and then exploded in a fit of rage. "Your son is a traitorous liar and a coward, too! He sends his own father to spread his treachery. He just wants me out of the way so he can capture this land and rule it like a dictator. You can tell him that he can shove his money up his ass so far that he will be crapping paper for months! Now get out of here before I kill you where you sit!"

Orozco did not even waste time trying to argue with Villa. He could tell that he was in a murderous fury and capable of anything. With amazing agility for such an elderly man, he bolted from his chair and ran out the door. As the senior Orozco rode off into the night, Villa felt a deep certainty fill his heart. His old friend was now his most deadly and hated enemy.

Abraham Gonzalez was a frightened man. He crouched behind a wooden crate with his trusted aide, Cástulo. They were hiding in a dilapidated shed on the outskirts of Chihuahua. The sunlight waned through a broken windowpane as the evening progressed. Villa would be here soon to take them to the safety of Mexico City. They just had to hold out a little longer until help arrived. Occasionally, they heard rebel troops galloping by searching for them. If Orozco found them, they were dead men.

Gonzalez closed his eyes and let his mind drift back to the start of this madness. During the entire month of February, Gonzalez had tried to stem the flow of dissension by implementing several economic programs designed to jumpstart the state. By funneling millions of *pesos* into irrigation and land distribution projects, Madero and Gonzalez had hoped to get the country back on its feet. However, the currents of deceit from Orozco and his *hacendados* undermined any hope of success.

Finally, on March 1, Pascual Orozco Jr. had stepped forward and officially denounced the Madero government. Immediately, thousands of misled citizens took to the streets. They systematically rooted out government officials associated with the president's regime and killed them. Their cries of "*¡Tierra y Justicia!*", (Land and Justice), still rang in Gonzalez's ears. He shook his head sadly as he recalled the irony of the situation. The very citizens who just a few years ago were brought to their knees by land swindles and injustices were now rebelling against the very government that was striving to restore their rightful property. He held no hate against them. Instead, he could almost cry at the thought of his countrymen again being shackled by an arrogant few.

Gonzalez and Cástulo had barely escaped from the governor's palace when a mob broke down the front door and razed the building. He had the forethought to send a messenger to Villa just before the fall of Chihuahua to arrange for a meeting. There was a good chance that the message got through, but would Villa honor its entire content? Gonzalez was so tired now. He subconsciously brushed the back of hand against the rough stubble on his cheek. These last two days had been hard on him.

His tired mind worried with a untested question. Would Villa follow his orders not to fight these people? He wanted so much to avert needless bloodshed. He had to convince Villa that there were alternatives to fighting his fellow countrymen.

The sound of horses startled Gonzalez out of his stupor. He motioned for Cástulo to stay down. They heard the riders stop in front of the door and dismount. Slowly the door creaked open and a stocky man stepped into the room. The last shafts of yellow sunlight lit his back and caused a dark shadow to mask his face beneath his sombrero. Gonzalez was uncertain who this man was, so he remained motionless with his fear rising. He could almost hear his heart pounding against his rib cage.

The man slowly turned and surveyed the room. The light slipped under his hat and showed his face. It was Villa! Gonzalez let out a sigh of relief and announced their presence. "*Señor* Villa. It is I, Abraham Gonzalez. I have my aide with me. We are coming out." At the sound of the voice, Villa drew his pistol, but lowered it when he saw the men stand up from behind the boxes.

Villa smiled and said, "Governor Gonzalez. You look like you have seen better days. Quickly, now. We must leave the city before we are seen." He led the two refugees out to a small band of waiting men who held two additional horses. Villa motioned to Gonzalez and Cástulo to each take one. They mounted and immediately rode out of the city as the full darkness fell.

Just out of the city, they dove into a small ravine where the rest of Villa's hundred-man army awaited. With very few words, Villa ordered the men to ride to the eastern plains. They silently filed up the gully and began riding in pairs into the country. Villa made sure that he was next to Gonzalez as they rode out. He turned to the fallen governor and said quietly, "With any luck, we will have you on a train to the capital by morning."

Abraham Gonzalez scarcely had time to express his relief when a shout rang out in the night. A man yelled, "The rebels have found us. Look! They are coming!" All heads turned west toward the city. Against the twilight sky, over two hundred men could be seen riding at full speed toward them. As all good leaders do, Gonzalez seized the moment. He reached out and grabbed Villa by the arm and shook his words into him. "Francisco Villa, remember my orders. Do not fight your countrymen! Let me first try to find a peaceful solution. Please! Order the retreat!"

Villa snatched his arm out of Gonzalez's desperate hold. He avoided Gonzalez's pleading eyes as he wrestled with deep conflicting emotions. His pounding blood and surging adrenaline screamed for him to confront the enemy. His felt his men too, begging for a chance to fight. But, Villa had a deep respect for Gonzalez and could not bring himself to disobey an order. His honor would not let him accept insubordination. With a deep breath, he made his decision. "Everyone, fall back. *Pronto*! That's an order." Villa could see their bewildered faces in the dark. Villa snarled at them and the men began to retreat, but not fast enough for Villa. He growled at them again, "Ride hard. *¡Vámanos!*" With more pushing and prodding, he shoved the whole regiment quickly into the plains.

As they retreated, they could hear the jeers and catcalls of the rebels in the distance. "Look at the cowards. They run like jackrab-bits! *¡Tierra y justicia!* We have won!" These insults ground deep into Villa's gut.

I will return and even the score, thought Villa. *And you will not be laughing then.*

Chapter 12
Refugees

On the hot morning of May 28, 1912, Paz gave birth to their first son. She named him Augustine after the Roman Catholic saint of the day. The neighboring women tended to her needs and helped her clean herself. Alcaria and Joaquina scampered quietly among the skirts with wide, worried eyes as they tried to assess their mother's condition and catch a peek at the crying baby. One of the women wrapped the baby in a cotton cloth and bent down to show them their new brother. The girls cooed and giggled at the tiny face. After a few moments, the woman cleaned herself and dutifully took the baby outside to present him to his father.

Prudenciano was nervously waiting on the front porch. He had slept little that night after Paz had gone into labor and demanded that he fetch help. He smoked a newly-rolled cigarette. Crimped butts of last night's smokes littered the porch. Throughout the night between Paz's anguished cries, Prudenciano had contemplated his family's future. Work was sporadic and the street fighting frequent. The city no longer held the promise of prosperity that it once did. Now, with one more mouth to feed, it was going to be even harder to make ends meet. He took another long drag and blew the blue smoke through his graying beard.

The swinging door interrupted his brooding. He looked up to see a woman carrying a bundle coming through the doorway. The midwife showed signs of fatigue that lined deep into her face. Sweat plastered her hair to her forehead. She solemnly walked forward like an altar boy approaching a crucifix. She stopped in front of Prudenciano and slowly raised the child to him. "His name is Augustine," she announced in an almost defiant tone.

Prudenciano bristled for a moment as he reached for the baby. The father always named the child, especially if it was a boy. His annoyance only lasted until he felt the weight of the boy in his arms and gazed upon his angelic face. "Augustine," he murmured gruffly.

"That is a good name." He and Paz had their first son! He felt a tremendous pride trickle through his body.

The midwife watched him with guarded approval for a few minutes, then firmly removed Augustine from his grip. "He must be brought back to his mother," she said flatly. "You must help out around here until Paz regains her strength." As soon as those words left her, she realized that Prudenciano would never lift a finger to help with the daily chores and child raising. She would have to help Paz herself. With a disgusted huff, she marched back into the house with the baby. Prudenciano watched as the screen door slammed shut behind her.

———

The city of Chihuahua was in a constant uproar. The economy was in shambles. Sporadic fighting slowed construction. The aid that Pascual Orozco promised never materialized. The working-class families suffered the greatest during this period. The lack of employment and low wages forced many families to live a destitute existence or flee for the American border.

The cool winds of December were beginning to blow. Mexico usually embraced this month with Christmas spirit and joy, but any visitor to Chihuahua would find a drab and desolate city. The hunger, poverty, and civil dishevel stamped out any holiday happiness the people could generate. No banners or gala colors garnished any building. A dismal feeling hung over the entire city.

Prudenciano sat on the front porch smoking a hand-rolled cigarette. He frequently spent his time here pondering his uncertain future. As he fretted, he could hear the cries of his children inside. They cried regularly nowadays. There was never enough food to fill their empty stomachs. The streets were too dangerous for children to play outside. Their mother was becoming insane from the despair and the constant wailing. Prudenciano just wanted to turn his back on the nightmarish reality.

His mind kept replaying that day so long ago in the Monte Escobedo *cantina* when José and he had listened to an old drunk tell them about the riches in America. The dream that he wove was so inviting then. Until now, he had forgotten the drive that had pushed him north. The good jobs he had in Torreón and Chihuahua had slowly defused his goal to travel to America. Prudenciano was now reevaluating his lost dream.

He took another deep draw from his cigarette and blew the smoke high into the air. His mind toyed with perplexing questions. How could he make the trip with a wife and three children? The trip from

Torreón had been hard enough with just Alcaria. It would be impossible with two more, but what other choice did he have?

Prudenciano then thought about the option of traveling to America by himself. The more he thought about the idea, the more he liked it. He would travel quickly, find work, and send money home. It would be the most expedient solution. Paz would fight it, though. He would have to keep this plan to himself until the last moment.

Now it was just a question of when to bolt north. Prudenciano thought about this for a few minutes. The longer he waited, the worse the situation would become for them all. "It will have to be soon," he said out loud. As on cue, little Augustine bellowed loudly. Prudenciano could hear Paz trying to comfort him and then suddenly lash out at the girls. "*Sí*, soon," he said with finality.

Smug with his decision, Prudenciano leaned back in his chair and looked down the deserted street. Only a year ago, the traffic had been so great that it was hard to cross during business hours. Now only a few desperate souls skittered down the wooden boardwalks. People always walked with their heads bowed low and their faces concealed by a broad hat or tight shawl. Some said that the December winds forced people to move this way, but Prudenciano knew that everyone wanted to keep a low profile. To be noticed was dangerous.

Thus, when Prudenciano spotted a man running down the street, he sat up and watched him carefully. The man appeared to be exhausted, but determined to deliver an urgent message. Despite the cool December breeze, sweat poured from his brow. He did not slacken his gait until he reached Prudenciano's porch. Only then did Prudenciano recognize him as one of the security guards with his attachment.

"*Señor* Nava," the man wheezed as he put one hand on the rail to steady himself. "The most incredible thing has just happened." Again his shortness of breath cut him short.

"What happened?" asked Prudenciano dryly. "Did our illustrious leaders poison themselves on a bad bottle of tequila?"

"No," gulped the man as he shook his head. "It is Terrazas. He is back! He wants the guards to meet at the armory this afternoon. Can you make it?"

"Terrazas is back?" repeated Prudenciano in an unbelieving voice. "How can this be? *Sí*, I will be there. *Gracias*." The man and reluctantly shuffled off to his next stop. Prudenciano watched him go. The news stunned him. He stroked his beard as he thought, *Why did he return? I guess I will find out soon enough. ¡Dios mío! What does all this mean?*

The armory was packed. There had not been a meeting like this for over a year, since the nightly debriefing sessions had dwindled after the rebellion. Not knowing what to expect, many men, including Prudenciano, did not wear their guard uniforms. The men crammed into the meeting room and mumbled excitedly to each other. This meeting was a welcome break from the idleness of the past year.

Being one of the tallest men, Prudenciano scanned the room above the heads of the crowd. The captain had not entered the room yet. He would probably do so from the side door at the front of the room. The only peculiarity Prudenciano could see was a podium erected in front. It presented an unspoken message of formality and importance of the speaker that was to address them.

Suddenly, the door swung open and the captain walked briskly into the room with Don Luis Terrazas close behind him. Although only a year had passed since Prudenciano had last seen him, Terrazas looked much older. He seemed to have withered and was his back bowed. His three-piece suit appeared baggy and hung on his slight frame. In an uncharacteristic show of patience, Terrazas allowed the captain to address the crowd first.

The captain grabbed the podium with both hands and stood stoically while the men ceased their murmurs. When he was satisfied that he had their attention, the captain began, "Men, thank you for gathering here at such short notice. *Señor* Terrazas has returned to Chihuahua under the protection of President Madero. Several major events have occurred in Mexico that makes this possible." The captain hesitated for a moment and scanned the faces in the room. He saw every face staring silently back. He could see the hardship and hopelessness in their eyes and it made his heart falter for an instant. He thought, *Our people can be such pawns. These men deserve a better life.*

The captain glanced back at Terrazas as he stood beside and slightly behind him. The man looked like a bent statue staring straight ahead. The captain could see no emotion displayed on his hard, aging face. He collected his thoughts and continued with a confident and authoritative voice. "First, Pascual Orozco has agreed to leave the city. He will no doubt lead an army of revolutionaries in the state. Second, the Madero government has imprisoned Pancho Villa in Santiago Tlatelolco on charges of robbery and insubordination." Murmurs and hushed comments rumbled through the crowd and the captain waited until order returned before finishing his speech. "Men, *Señor* Terrazas has returned to reclaim what was once his. We are to protect his property during these troubled times."

As by signal, Terrazas moved slowly forward and brushed the captain aside. He stopped and looked over the podium at the crowd. The platform seemed to magnify his presence. The men quickly quieted and stared back at this once powerful man. For a moment, a person could hear a pin drop. Then Terrazas started his address in a low and strong voice that seemed unnatural for his aged body. "My guards, life may have been tough for you when I was gone, but it will get worse if we do not make a stand now. The *Villistas* have stolen most of my cattle and ransacked my properties. My wealth is greatly diminished. President Madero has allowed me to return to Chihuahua to reclaim what is rightfully mine." As he said this, his body seemed to straighten and the old brash Terrazas began to manifest himself in front of them. His eyes burned with hate and the need for revenge. He clenched his fists and raised them above the podium. "I want to rebuild and make certain that this never happens again."

Terrazas abruptly stopped his ranting and pointed a bony finger at the crowd. "I know that there are some here that oppose my return and I know who you are." The men shot fleeting glances at each other. Prudenciano could feel his pulse rise. Could it be his imagination or was Terrazas pointing directly at him? Terrazas calmed himself before resuming, "Do you remember Claro Reza?" Fear stabbed through Prudenciano's body. Terrazas seemed to check a few faces for signs of recognition, then continued, "Sure you do. Villa and his gang gunned him down in broad daylight. You know why? Because he was my spy and someone in this room turned him in to Villa. But I know who you are and I kill traitors!"

Prudenciano almost bolted for the door. Only his instincts held him securely in place. Fleeing was the exact reaction Terrazas was hoping for, but no one moved. The room was deathly quiet. Suddenly, Terrazas tilted his head back and cracked the silence with a wicked laugh. "Well, I couldn't smoke you out, huh? But I know who you are and I will have my revenge. Captain, take over." Terrazas whirled away from the podium and exited by the side door.

When Prudenciano stumbled into the house in a state of panic, Paz knew something had gone terribly wrong at the armory. Except for that time when she had seen him run from the mine in Torreón, she had never seen him so scared. As she stood holding Augustine to her breast, she watched wide-eyed with worry as he searched for his pack. Finding it, he began to quickly stuff a few meager possessions into it.

Paz was dead tired from comforting baby Augustine and supervising the girls. Her own hunger gnawed at her guts and made her dizzy. However, her dulled senses could understand what her husband was planning. *He is going somewhere without us. And he will never come back. I can't let him leave me alone with the children.*

How would we survive? She gathered up her courage and stepped up to him. He had his back turned to her as he crammed more stuff in the pack. "Prudenciano!" she said in a loud, calm voice. He froze for a moment, but remained silent. Paz could see his shoulders slump forward slightly. "Prudenciano, I want you to turn around and talk to me." Prudenciano slowly turned and faced her. He still held on to the pack. She saw the haunted look in his eyes. "*Por favor*, tell me what happened. Why are you leaving?"

Prudenciano looked down at this woman whom he still loved holding his son. She had aged considerably this year. Lines of deep anguish and exhaustion were etched across her face. She met her hardships head-on and would never give up on her family. He felt his nerve dissolve slightly. Slowly, in a quiet voice, he answered her. "I must leave. Terrazas is going to kill me if I don't go now. I am going to *los Estados Unidos* and find work. I will send money back as soon as I can."

Paz walked up to him and tilted her head back to see his face more clearly. "No," she said with clenched teeth. "The family must stay together. If you go, we all go. *Comprende?*"

Prudenciano slowly shook his head, "No, Paz. That is not possible. By myself, I can reach the Texas border in a few weeks. With you and the children, it will take us months. Besides, there is a revolution going on out there. Bandits are killing everyone they find. It is too dangerous."

"You just don't want us along," said Paz defiantly. "If you go now, I will never see you again and these children need you." She saw his neck bow and quickly decided to try a different approach. "Prudenciano, I know things are bad now, but times will get better. We told Padre Miguel and God that we would love and care for each other forever. Remember? Why are you forgetting your promise now?"

Prudenciano clenched his bag with both hands and closed his eyes. He could almost feel the Padre squeezing his own hands and asking him if he loved Paz. That seemed almost a lifetime ago, and yet, in some ways it felt like only yesterday.

Paz continued, "Do you also remember your father saying that he hoped you would not abandon me when times got tough? Do you recall how angry that made you feel? Please do the right thing and stay with me."

Prudenciano let out a deep breath and opened his eyes. Paz thought his eyes looked moist. "You are right. I promise to take you and children with me. We will have to leave soon."

Paz nodded and readjusted Augustine in her arms. She felt waves of relief flow through her. "All right," she answered, "but we should wait until February when the weather is a little warmer. In the meantime, you need to stay in the house and out of sight."

Prudenciano nodded, but did not disagree with her. He did not know if Terrazas would let him live that long, but the dangers of a long, slow march to America were just as perilous. These were desperate times in Mexico and a poor Mexican had two terrible choices—stay and try to keep from getting killed or flee and face the ruthless trek to the border. This time Prudenciano's inner eye provided no vision. He would lead his family the best he could into an uncertain future.

———•••———

The cold night wind blew across Francisco Villa's face as he plodded across the desert. The lights of Tucson, Arizona glowed brightly ahead and dark, rugged mountains silhouetted the background. His fugitive trek from Mazatlán had exhausted him, but Tucson signified the end of hiding on trains and lying in back seats of dilapidated vehicles. A few revolutionary supporters had dropped him off before reaching the Mexican-American border at Nogales, Arizona. Although this meant that Villa was faced with a couple of days of hard marching, it was a necessity. There were too many eyes that would announce his crossing and he needed time to organize his counterstrike in secrecy.

Villa adjusted his hat over his long hair and pulled the collar of his coat against his bearded face. The date was January 2, 1913, over three months since he had been thrown into prison on charges trumped up by Victoriano Huerta. During most of his incarceration, he had been in solitary confinement, which had aged him significantly. He look scraggly and his skin had taken on that prison-pallor color. A haircut and a shave would have helped considerably, but that luxury was impossible because of his hasty escape.

He still had a few miles to walk, so he let his mind drift to pass the time and escape from his discomfort. Suddenly he was back in his damp, dark cell. He felt the familiar feeling of dread and hopelessness that came with isolation. But silence increased his senses and during the quiet of the night, Villa could hear faint murmurs from the cells above him. There was one theme he heard clearly from different men. Huerta was going to kill President Francisco Madero soon. The stories varied, but they agreed that time was short. He had to get word back to Madero, but how?

Villa stumbled in the darkness and interrupted his thoughts momentarily. When he regained his stride, he let his mind drift again. Huerta was the root of the Mexican unrest. Even Orozco aligned with him. Villa had to stop him. He felt his anger rise within and give him strength. Yes, he would get his revenge. After he rested for a few days in Tucson, he would make his way to El Paso, Texas and assemble a counterforce. He would chose loyal and ruthless men to rid Mexico of scoundrels like Huerta and Orozco.

Pancho took comfort in his plan and quickened his pace. As he entered the city, the wind abated and he felt more relaxed, but a deep lonesomeness ached within his weary body. He missed Maria terribly. It had been many months since he had last held her. Villa thought, "I must send for her immediately. Besides, I want her out of Mexico because it will soon be a very dangerous place to live."

On March 7, 1913, Abraham Gonzalez stood on a low ledge in Bachimba Canyon overlooking the north-south rail line that ran the length of the state of Chihuahua. He wore a three-piece suit that seemed to trap every ray of the blazing sun. The afternoon heat was building and caused the tracks to disappear into the shimmering horizon. Gonzalez took out his handkerchief and wiped his brow and the back of his neck. The silence was almost crushing.

Fate had trapped him like a boxed squirrel in this remote spot and he felt his fear creep up his spine. *If Madero had only listened to Villa's warnings*, he mused. *I would not be in this predicament*. He kicked a rock over the ledge and watched it fall to the tracks below. The rock seemed to take what was left of his spirit with it. Someone had assassinated President Madero only two weeks ago and now Gonzalez knew that his life was doomed too. Reports and hearsay speculated that Victoriano Huerta had something to do with the murder. Gonzalez laughed cynically to himself and shook his head, *Madero trusted people blindly. Could he not see that his own army commander despised him?* But, Gonzalez knew in his heart that he was also to blame. He had misread Huerta too and arranged for him to lead the army instead of Villa.

His laugh slowly changed to crying and tears streamed down his face as he looked across the canyon. *Madero and I could have done such great things for Mexico. We could have been a free nation, no longer ruled by a selfish few. If we'd just had the chance …* His thoughts wandered off. He got ahold of his emotions and straightened his back and squared his shoulders.

Now reality began to take hold of him. He started reviewing his actions that had led him to this spot. He had sent instructions and 1,500 pesos to Francisco Villa to return to Mexico and fight Huerta, but he doubted that Villa could organize an army quickly enough to help him. So that left him with only one more choice—negotiate a peace with Huerta. Huerta had chosen this spot to discuss the details in private. Gonzalez now had the feeling that he was acting as foolishly as Madero in trusting Huerta, but he just had no choice.

His horse nickered and raised his head to sniff the air. As Gonzalez turned to see what caught its interest, he spotted Huerta flanked by two men and riding slowly up the hill to the ledge. Then he saw Huerta's smirking face and felt his fear rise again.

"*Buenos dias, Señor* Gonzalez," Huerta greeted him as he reined in his horse. He put a hand casually on his hip and gave Gonzalez a toothy grin much like a cat about to pounce on a mouse. Gonzalez subconsciously step backward closer to the ledge. Huerta nonchalantly reached into his coat pocket and pulled out his pocket watch without ever taking his eyes away from Gonzalez. He deftly flicked the cover up and checked the time. "Hmm …," he said as he studied the watch. Then he quickly clicked it shut and appeared to look to the north at something distant on the tracks. His voice sounded detached as he said, "*Sí*, it appears that both you and fate are on time today."

The word "fate" shot stabs of foreboding though Gonzalez. He glanced at the other two men. Their faces were emotionless, but their piercing eyes never left him. They had the look of murderers, not the negotiators that he had hoped for. He fought for control of his voice and managed a reply. "General Huerta. Thank you for meeting me here today. We have lots to discuss."

Huerta dismounted and walked toward Gonzalez. Gonzalez could hear something mechanical faintly rumbling in the distance, but he forced himself not to take his eyes off Huerta. The noise barely registered in his mind.

Huerta smiled as he stopped in front of Gonzalez and said, "No, *Señor*. I can assure you the pleasure is mine. Now what is it that you want to discuss?"

Gonzalez spoke with a voice that was much calmer than his true feelings, "General, I propose that we temporarily share governmental control of Mexico. I could govern the northern states and you could direct the southern." Gonzalez stopped for a moment to see if Huerta was responsive to this suggestion, but he only stood there with an infuriating grin. The noise in the background was building. Gonzáles wondered, *What was that noise?* He quickly threw the thought out of his mind and pressed his proposal further, "I have a plan that we could implement until a new president can be elected." Gonzalez reached into his vest pocket and pulled out a handwritten document. He held it in front of Huerta.

Huerta quickly snatched the papers from his hand and threw them into the air. The breeze scattered them down the canyon. Then he reached out with both hands and grabbed Gonzalez by his lapels.

With his massive strength, he lifted the older man off his feet and dangled him above the ground. Gonzalez's eyes bulged as he strangled from the hold. The machine sounded very close and loud now.

Huerta's expression changed to a snarl as he spoke through clenched teeth, "Why would I want to govern with you? A mere weakling?" The noise was almost deafening with the distinct "click-clack" sound of metal wheels rolling on rails. He roared, "I am already president! Now its time for you to join Madero. It's time to die!"

Huerta took two quick steps forward and hurtled Gonzalez backward over the ledge. Screaming and windmilling his arms, he plunged in front of the speeding southbound freight train. The big black steam engine sucked him underneath and crushed his life.

As the train blew by, Victoriano Huerta turned to his men and gave them a victorious smile. "Now, nothing will stop me from becoming the rightful ruler of Mexico. Nothing!"

On the evening of March 13, Maria Villa stood on the banks of the Rio Grande near Isleta, Texas. Her husband was strapping his final supplies onto his saddle. They spoke little during this final hour. Each were deep in separate thoughts. Maria knew that her husband grieved for the two men whom he highly respected. When news had come to them three days ago that Abraham Gonzalez had been murdered, Pancho had lapsed into deep despair. Slowly over the days his demeanor changed to a seething anger that could only be quenched with the blood of Victoriano Huerta.

Maria had never seen him like this. Even his eyes seemed to burn for revenge. Then he spontaneously ordered his eight men to prepare to ride back to Mexico. Without saying a word, the men picked up their belongings and began to pack.

Maria shivered and wrapped her shawl tighter around her shoulders. She looked over to the other men. Some of them had already mounted their horses and were waiting. Each one of them was a determined and hardened man, but one stood out from the rest. His name was Rodolfo Fierro. Women who did not know him thought he was the most handsome man that they had ever seen. However, Maria knew that his heart must be black because she had heard rumors that he was exceptionally ruthless. Some said that he actually crucified prisoners to set an example to others. She had questioned her husband about the wisdom of keeping such company, but he had steadfastly believed that he needed him to complete the liberation of Mexico.

"The road to victory will be washed in blood," her husband would tell her. "I need men who will not hesitate to do what is necessary."

As if he had read her mind, Fierro slowly turned in his saddle and faced her. His black eyes seemed to burn with a consuming evil. With a cigar clenched in his teeth, he slowly produced a wide grin and chuckled quietly at her. Maria quickly diverted her gaze and looked at her husband's back. Fierro gave her the creeps.

Villa closed the final flap on his saddle bag and turned around to face his wife. For the first time in days, his eyes seemed to soften. He reached tenderly for her and drew her to him. "I must go now. I really don't know when I will return."

Maria tilted her head down. Tears began to well up in her eyes and slowly dripped off her cheeks. Villa softly put his hand under her chin and lifted her head up. She spoke in a quiet sobbing voice, "Will I ever see you again?"

Villa felt a lump form in his throat and had difficulty in responding. "I don't know, but whatever happens, you will always be in my thoughts." He bent down and kissed her gently on her salty lips. He lingered for a moment and then quickly mounted his horse and rode in front of his waiting men. Silently, he directed them into the river.

Maria stood on the bank still tightly clutching her shawl and watched the nine men wade their horses across the shallow Rio Grande and enter Mexico. She continued watching them until they disappeared into the evening darkness. "Goodbye, my love," she said softly. "Please come back to me."

Paz Nava had never been so exhausted in her life. The past three weeks had been a never-ending ordeal. She had successfully delayed Prudenciano until mid-May before starting their long, slow march to El Paso. However, instead of beginning with better weather and more favorable conditions, the civil fighting had escalated in Chihuahua and the spring season was hotter than normal. As a result, the road north was clogged with desperate people trying to flee the violence and famine in unbearable heat. Countless families dressed in rags and carrying their meager possessions on their backs walked past Paz, hardly giving her a glance. When they did, their eyes contained the haunted look common to all refugees of war. Their ghostly expressions were shaped by starvation, horrors, and despair. They were all walking north to an uncertain future in a foreign land.

Paz shifted baby Augustine in her tired arms. He still needed constant breast feedings, which drained her body of nutrients and energy. She felt her bones begin to bend and wither from the lack of food. Her guts gnawed at her for something to fill it. This made her very light-headed and weak.

The air was always choked with dust from so many travelers. It coated her hair and face and sucked the moisture from her skin. She felt dirty, old, and ugly and she wanted to cry, but her body had little water for tears. So she gulped down silent sobs and put one bare foot in front of the other and continued the best she could.

The girls walked next to their mother and held hands to comfort each other. They, too, were barefoot and their rough dresses were torn and dirty. Dirt caked on their faces and matted their hair. They whimpered quietly as their empty tummies growled inside them. With Joaquina sucking her thumb, they created a pathetic image that could break even the hardest heart of whoever saw them. Every so often, Alcaria would try to carry Augustine for a while to give her mother a rest. For a five-year-old, this quickly proved to be an overwhelming task and she would have to give him back to her mother after only a few minutes.

Prudenciano walked in front of his family with a heavy pack that contained their scant possessions. His back bent forward under the load. He wore boots from his security guard uniform, but his pants and shirt were the simple Mexican dress. He sheltered his head with a floppy broad sombrero.

They marched at a pace of eight to ten miles per day. With three small children, the Nava family could push no faster. Their pace, though, was equal to that of the thousands of other migrants that shared the highway. If a person could climb a nearby mountain to look over the country, the view would consist of a mass of humanity strung along the road from horizon to horizon, a never-ending string of people moving north.

This great migration of people stripped the land bare of anything edible. Gardens were raided and trampled. People broke into homes and food storage. They stole livestock hidden in barns. The starving hordes even consumed fodder meant for horses. As the famine continued, families resorted to picking through horse dung to find precious kernels of undigested corn.

In these turbulent times, a good horse was fed much better than a poor Mexican. The government and revolutionary armies needed horses to fight and horses were in short supply, but they had plenty of illiterate and beaten men for soldiers. Thus, a horse was worth vastly more than a common man and was treated as such.

Paz had managed to barter for some corn and beans from a small village several days earlier. She had only two items of any value, the small purse from her father-in-law and her harmonica. Her intuition told her that she would need the few coins in her purse for some unrevealed purpose. So, she reluctantly traded her musical instrument that she had cherished above all her possessions for a pitifully small pouch of food. Paz felt that she had lost a valuable part of her life as she handed the harmonica to the man. She winced as she watched him laugh and try to blow a tune. He dismissed her by throwing the food pouch at her feet and walking away without a single glance back. Paz gathered what was left of her pride, picked up the pouch, and trudged back to her family.

Starvation aside, the Nava family was luckier than most because they were still together. Countless families became separated during the march north. People were always looking for an easier mode of travel than walking. Thus, when a wagon rambled by or a freight train stopped for water and fuel, travelers would pile on the sides like ants. Fathers would frantically throw their children on board and turn to reach for their wives or older relatives. The result was usually chaos, especially when the wagon or train unexpectedly bolted forward, spilling some family members or leaving others behind. Sometimes a large family would not discover that they were missing a member until they reached the next stopping point, which could be a hundred miles away. Stories about families reunited with lost loved ones months later were common among the Mexican migrants.

The long, arduous walk from Chihuahua to El Paso, Texas was about 235 miles. At their rate, the Navas could expect to arrive at the American port of entry by the first week in June. It was during the final week of their travel that they entered the most torturous part of their journey. Just a few miles south of Juarez, the highway stretched through a desolate valley that was the hottest and driest region of the Chihuahuan desert. There were no water holes or shade trees along its thirty-mile length to sustain a weary traveler or livestock.

Mexican travelers of this time were also subjected to an additional hazard that was proving to be even deadlier. This desert valley was also the brutal fighting ground of revolutionary and governmental forces. Migrants were often caught in the crossfire of frequent skirmishes or "recruited" into one of the several armies that scoured the countryside.

It was on a hot, dusty afternoon in late May when Paz plodded through this valley in an exhausted daze. Her back and shoulders ached from carrying the baby. Suddenly, Prudenciano pulled up short and Paz blindly walked into him. "What is the matter?" she croaked with a dry throat.

Prudenciano stood silently with his back ramrod straight. Paz could not see around him and his behavior puzzled her. She quickly became aware that other people around her were stopping and staring straight ahead. Some gasped and children began crying. Paz grabbed her husband's shirt for support and moved to his side. She was not prepared for what she saw and put a hand to her mouth to stifle a scream.

Telegraph poles lined the road ahead and seemed to stretch to infinity. Hundreds of corpses hung on the cross-members of each pole. Some swung from their necks with their hands tied behind their backs. They hung in pairs which counterbalanced the weight along the top. Others were literally crucified with their arms stretched out wide along the cross-member and large nails driven into their hands and feet.

Judging by what was left of their uniforms, these men had once been government soldiers. The bodies were in a state of advanced decay and a faint odor of death still lingered in the air. The birds and wind had stripped any exposed flesh from the bones and the sun had bleached the skulls white.

An eerie silence prevailed and as the travelers started slowly moving forward, Paz could hear the wind blowing across the empty eye sockets. The hollow skulls produced a low moaning sound that sent shivers up and down her spine. It gave her a deep feeling of foreboding and she subconsciously held on to Prudenciano's arm. The girls pressed close to their parents and sometimes buried their heads into their mother's dress in an attempt to hide.

Prudenciano felt something else too. Like a past dream, he sensed that he had seen this place before. The mountains with low foothills, the killing field, and the desolate highway looked hauntingly familiar.

He squinted his eyes and gazed along the distant ridge line. An instant later, he saw them. Barely visible in front of the glaring late-afternoon sun, a line of armed men on horseback were descending upon them like a pack of wolves. Over a hundred men rode with reckless abandon screaming at the top of their lungs and brandishing their guns. Prudenciano felt his blood run cold. These men were not soldiers, but unpredictable revolutionaries.

The refugees in front of the Navas began throwing down their possessions and fleeing backward. Women screamed and ran with their children clutched to their breasts. The men's eyes were wild with fear. Their panic was infectious as the people scattered in all directions.

Prudenciano was not immune to the influences of the human stampede. He savagely shook Paz's grip from his arm and threw off his pack. He started to bolt when he heard Paz scream, "Don't you dare leave me, Prudenciano!" Her words held him in check. He looked at her and saw her face fill with contempt for him as she securely held a whimpering Augustine.

He glanced back up the road and saw the revolutionaries already beginning to corral up potential recruits. If a man escaped through the driving line of armed men, a handful of the bandits would chase him down and either shoot him or rope the man and drag him back.

Prudenciano thought that one bandit in particular who had fierce eyes seemed to greatly enjoy the sport.

Prudenciano felt his fear soar. He glanced back at his wife. She stood staring at him with the same expression of loathing. The girls had grabbed each side of her skirt and were burying their faces into the folds. Terrified people blindly knocked into them as they ran. Paz clutched her baby tighter and held her ground without taking her eyes off her husband. "Don't leave us," she repeated in a strong voice.

Prudenciano perceived that he was a trapped animal. He had nowhere to run. The revolutionaries were almost on top of them. He could hear their laughing and jeering voices as they formed a large circle around them and quickly closed it. They drove the people into a tight knot that impeded movement. At this point, many people just gave up and began making whimpering sounds of resignation. The Navas crunched together in the center of the crowd. Prudenciano glanced at the men surrounding them. Some of them looked oddly familiar, but he could not quite place where he had seen them before. They all wore sombreros and ragged shirts and pants. Most wore boots, but some were barefoot and balanced in their stirrups like a monkey on a branch. All of them strapped bandoliers of ammunition diagonally across their shoulders, backs, and chests. They looked tired, dirty, hungry, and desperate. Prudenciano knew that he was in grave danger.

The man with the evil eyes spoke first. "*Buenos días, Señores y Señoritas*. I demand your complete attention now. If you cooperate, this will take but a moment. If you fight or try to escape, we will kill you. However, we may have a little fun with the women first. *Comprende?*" Judging by his expression, no one doubted his threat. The man looked like he was enjoying himself immensely.

"*Bueno*," he continued. "Now let us begin. We need men to fight the *federales*. So, consider this an official recruitment to fight for freedom. Who wants to join us?" He paused and scanned the crowd. No man accepted the offer. "Just as I thought," he said shaking his head. "Seems like we caught a bunch of *federale* supporters." He lifted his hand and pointed his fingers along the telegraph poles, "Take a look at the poles and see what we do to *federales*."

He fell silent for a moment to let his words sink into their emotions. Only the light sounds of nickering horses and the gentle wind could be heard. Then he signaled to his men, "Pull the men out and line them up." The revolutionaries dismounted and began yanking the men from the crowd. The women protested and tried to hold their men back, but the bandits easily wrenched them away. Scared as he was, Prudenciano slowly began to move of his own accord toward the lineup. One of the rebels made a move to shove him forward, but reconsidered when he saw the size of Prudenciano. Within short order, the captured men stood uneasily in the line. They looked nervously at each other and at the rebels.

The leader rode his horse arrogantly down the line and surveyed his catch. His eyes lingered on Prudenciano as he passed him. Prudenciano stood head and shoulders above the rest of the men. Although he was now fifty-seven- years-old with graying hair, his body was still muscular and trim. The leader also noticed his posture and expression. Despite the man's obvious fear, it foretold strength and perhaps egotism. The combination of traits could spell trouble. The rebel made a mental note of this man and continued down the line.

"A bunch of sorry maggots," the man muttered with disgust. He turned in his saddle and motioned for his lieutenant to come forward. Then, in a loud voice so that all could hear, the leader pointed at Prudenciano and ordered, "Take that big man over there and string him up with the rest of the *federales*."

The younger man visibly blanched at the command. He looked down at the terror-stricken Prudenciano and suddenly realized that he knew him. He looked back up at his leader and said, "I cannot kill this man. I know him and he helped us in Chihuahua."

The leader was unmoved. "Are you disobeying a direct order, Eleuterio Soto?" The name jogged Prudenciano's memory. He had met him at Villa's hideaway. He felt a flicker of hope kindle within himself.

Soto seemed to steel himself and looked directly at his leader. "I am not going to kill an innocent man, Captain Fierro."

Fierro produced an infuriating grin and calmly pulled a cigar from his vest. He slowly bit the end off and spit it to the side. The uneasy silence was so solid that when Fierro struck a match, its flame seemed to roar as it jumped to life. He held it to his cigar for a second and drew a few puffs until it burned fully. Then he snuffed out the match with a deft snap of his hand. His entire procedure seemed to take a lifetime. Soto shifted uncomfortably in his saddle.

Fierro pulled the cigar from his mouth and appeared to examine it for a moment. Then he spoke with an even and deadly voice, "You know that I will not tolerate insubordination." Soto said nothing, but kept his eyes fixed on Fierro. Fierro slowly moved his vest to the side and revealed a revolver. Fierro continued, "I hope you reconsider." The tension began to build to an unbearable height. Fierro was rock solid with burning coals for eyes. Soto began to quiver from adrenaline surging through his veins. Their stares seemed to lock them together.

A huge bellow shattered the silence. "Enough!" Everyone except Fierro and Soto looked in the direction of the shout. A large man followed by a small and wiry rider galloped up to the dueling men. The huge man yelled, "Your butchery stops now, Fierro!"

Fierro never broke his stare with Soto. "I see you are pushing your fat gut where it does not belong, *Señor* Currandas. I am simply disciplining an officer here. Stay out of it."

Fierro's reply did not rebuff Anastacio Currandas. Currandas quickly pulled out his rifle from his saddle sheath and cocked the lever in one fluid motion. Fierro still projected the cold demeanor of granite and said, "Put that gun away, Currandas, or I will kill you too."

"Maybe," answered Currandas, "but either Soto or Vallejo will kill you before you get a second shot off. And that is fine with me because at least I will die knowing that your death will atone for all the needless violence that you have waged upon innocent citizens."

For the first time, Fierro broke his stare-down and looked at the two men next to him. Victoriano Vallejo was smiling with a pistol trained at his head. He knew that he did not have a chance to outgun them. Arrogantly, he smiled at them behind his smoldering cigar. "All right. Have it your way. I was getting bored anyhow. Do what you want with these pathetic varmints." Fierro spurred his horse forward and left for the hills. Only a few of his original troops followed him.

"*¡Dios mío!*" exclaimed Soto as he wiped his brow with the back of his hand. "That was close!"

"*Sí*," replied Currandas, "We will have to be careful from now on. Fierro carries a long grudge."

Vallejo looked into the crowd and exclaimed, "Well, what do we have here?" He half laughed as he bent down from his horse to shake the hand of a tall man.

Currandas turned to see whom Vallejo was greeting. At first he did not recognize the large, scruffy man until he saw the small woman holding a baby and two children crowd close to him. Currandas smiled widely and laboriously dismounted from his horse. He reached out with his bear-like arms and heartily embraced Prudenciano. "It is good to see you again, *amigo*. How goes it?"

Prudenciano answered, "Much better now that you and Victoriano stopped that madman. Who was he?"

Currandas lost some of his joy and replied with a solemn voice, "His name is Rodolfo Fierro. Although he fights for Pancho Villa, he is a ruthless butcher. Villa claims that he needs him, but I think otherwise. He is too mean." Then, Currandas quickly changed the subject, "So, you are taking your family to America, eh?"

"*Sí*," answered Prudenciano. "I hope to get work there soon. How much farther is El Paso?"

"Not much farther," replied Currandas as he looked at the rest of the Nava family. The wife and children looked half starved and exhausted. They probably were traveling slowly. "It should not take you more than two days to reach the Rio Grande." When Prudenciano nodded, Currandas continued, "Please take my advice, Nava. As soon as you reach Ciudad Juarez, move your family straight to the American border crossing. The streets are crawling with thieves and murderers. It is no place for a family."

"*Gracias, amigo*," said Prudenciano. "I will do that." Prudenciano then turned to Soto and extended his hand, "*Gracias.*"

Soto reached down from his horse and securely grasped Prudenciano's hand. "*De nada*," he replied with a smile. "It was my pleasure." He released his hand and tipped his hat to Paz. She smiled back and unconsciously preened her hair back behind her ear. It was the first time that she had smiled in many weeks. Currandas grunted as he heaved himself back onto his horse. He waved at the Navas and rode off with the rebels.

Victoriano quickly turned back and said, "Prudenciano, do not try to wade across the Rio Grande. It is too dangerous for little children. Take the swinging bridge, *por favor.*" Prudenciano nodded his understanding and waved him goodbye.

The people along the road watched the men quickly disappear back into the hills whence they had come from. Then the dazed migrants quietly retrieved their belongings and reassembled their families. Occasionally, a woman's temper flared at her husband for trying to flee during the conflict, but within an hour, traffic assumed its normal trudging pace north.

———

Prudenciano thought that Soto's and Vallejo's warnings were particularly wise. Juarez was chaotic and filled with unsavory characters. Paz had gathered her children close around her and scurried them through the bustling streets. Even Prudenciano, who normally sought the company of reckless men, felt that it was best that they skirt the city in a rapid manner. There were many young men with big guns and matching egos strutting down the boardwalks. Every so often, a bunch of uniformed federal soldiers galloped by, their faces tense and their hands next to their weapons. The entire situation reeked of trouble and Prudenciano wanted none of it. He led his family directly to the border crossing.

On June 9, 1913, after a month and a half of walking, the Nava family stood on the banks of the Rio Grande. Less than a hundred feet across, its muddy water flowed slowly to the southeast among low brown hills. The worn countryside had few trees and scattered brush. The heat of the day was rising, which seemed to evaporate the river before their eyes.

The swinging bridge to America loomed before them. It was a suspension bridge made from heavy timbers and thick ropes. At each bank, a twenty-foot-high tower stood solidly planted in the ground. The towers consisted of heavy, rough-cut timbers securely lashed together with rope. Ropes as thick as a man's wrist were tied to deadman anchors that were buried in each bank. These ropes held the towers upright. Two ropes of the same thickness spanned the entire width of the Rio Grande and produced gentle arcs across the water. Every ten feet, smaller ropes connected the main cables to a wooden boardwalk below. The boardwalk consisted of two-inch-thick, four-foot-wide planks that attached to thick ropes underneath. The resulting bridge had a somewhat level walkway, about six-feet above the river. In accordance with its name, the bridge tended to swing as people marched across its span. Thus, pedestrians used both hands to grab the cables to steady themselves as they walked in a weaving forward motion.

The bridge was a choke point for Mexicans migrating north. People carrying possessions often had a difficult time negotiating the swaying boardwalk and keeping their balance. In addition, the American authorities had guards that received immigrants and ushered them immediately into the ominous Port of Entry building. Many Mexicans opted to wade the river away from the bridge and its armed reception committee. This resulted in varying degrees of success. Some tripped or stepped into a hole and spilled their cargo into the brown water. When this happened, the unfortunate traveler recovered only a small portion of his belongings. American soldiers snagged many waders anyway and escorted them to the Port of Entry. Only the single and lightly loaded migrants successfully negotiated the river and evaded the guards.

Prudenciano and Paz waited in line for their turn to cross the swinging bridge. Because the bridge tended to sway wildly, the American guards allowed only small groups to cross at a time. Prudenciano did not trust the guards, but one look at Paz discouraged him from trying other options. After a few minutes, a border guard motioned for the Navas to cross. Paz took little Augustine in her arms and instructed the girls to hold on to her skirt with one hand and grab the rope rail with the other. As Prudenciano took an uncertain step onto the planks, Paz made the sign of the cross and sucked in her breath. The bridge seemed to wiggle under their feet. After a second's hesitation, Prudenciano bent forward to compensate for the weight of his pack and cautiously walked on the planks. Paz automatically followed close behind with Alcaria and Joaquina clinging to her dress, and her baby pressed close to her breast. As they approached the middle of the bridge, the swaying became more severe. Paz was terrified that she or one of her precious children would pitch over the rail and into the river, but she kept going with her eyes fixed on Prudenciano's back.

After a few long seconds, they crossed the bridge and stepped down onto American soil. The guard put his hand on Prudenciano's shoulder and directed him toward a flat-roofed, adobe building nearby. The American flag fluttered above the facility. As the Navas walked toward the building, Paz turned around for one final look at the country of her birth. She felt a deep sadness seep inside of her. Although she had known injustice and hardships within that country, it was still her homeland and Paz would always feel a strong connection with Mexico. Like thousands of other Mexicans who fled north, Paz only wanted to live someplace where hunger and danger were not her constant companions. If America could provide this basic need, then she would gladly live here, but regardless how good life would become in this country, Mexico would always be in her heart.

Paz shook off her melancholy and turned to face her future. She thought, *Perhaps, things would be better now.* She looked up at Prudenciano as he entered the doorway carrying the entire family's possessions on his back. She suddenly realized how much her and her children's welfare depended on him within this new land. *If he buckles down and works hard, we will be all right*, she thought as she entered the building behind him. Just to make sure, though, she decided that she was going to have to keep a sharp eye on him.

Chapter 13
America

During the year 1913, over 100,000 Mexicans migrated legally into the United States of America and at least the same number illegally. The social and economic chaos in Mexico forced Mexicans of all social classes to seek a better life in another country. The poor wanted employment and the rich immigrants sought safety and the preservation of their wealth.

Mexicans came to America to seek jobs within the booming economic growth of the southwestern states. Economic developments included completing the great southwestern railroads, planting cotton in new fields in Texas, Arizona, and California, and farming the newly irrigated lands in the Imperial and San Joaquin valleys. All these ambitious projects required plentiful and low-cost labor and Mexicans were ideally suited to fulfill these needs. Mexican unskilled laborers readily accepted employment for about thirty cents per hour because this was over five times greater than they had earned south of the border. It was far less than what the Greek, Italian, Chinese, and Japanese laborers accepted. In addition, Mexicans did not organize their labor force, and tolerated harsh working conditions. After the Mexicans completed their work, they moved on to the next job. This much relieved the conscience of American businessmen, and fortified their purses.

When the Navas entered America, Mexicans accounted for more than 60 percent of the total labor force on the southwestern railroad gangs, in the mines of Arizona and New Mexico, in the fruit orchards of Texas and California, and in the packing plants on the Pacific Coast. The cheap Mexican labor fueled the American economy. Since 1900, California orange output had risen over 400 percent. Southwestern lettuce and cotton production increased almost exponentially.

The year 1913 was a golden year for farming. Favorable weather, good prices, and a vast supply of cheap labor gave farmers a windfall of profits. Wheat was going for ninety cents a bushel. Corn, hay, and vegetable prices kept rising higher. Some farmers even experimented with a new crop they imported from Germany called sugar beets. United States senators and representatives from every southwestern state heard loudly and clearly from their constituents that nothing must prevent the Mexicans from coming into America. They were good for business and therefore good for the country.

The newly reorganized Bureau of Immigration and Naturalization had the gargantuan task of regulating immigration into the United States and registering qualified individuals as citizens. From the late 1800s to the early 1900s, immigrants flooded the American borders from all sides. Unable to cover all fronts, the Bureau opted to concentrate on two factions, the Chinese and the Europeans. To manage the Chinese, the Bureau implemented the Chinese Exclusion act of 1882 and simply refused all Orientals at all borders. The Bureau controlled European immigration by implementing a head tax of eight dollars for every man, woman, and child. Large European families found the tax financially daunting and stalled their immigration plans.

The Bureau put only limited resources into regulating the Mexican immigrants streaming across the American border. Bureau representatives along the southwestern border were often ill-trained and lacked central management. This resulted in numerous Ports of Entry implementing nonuniform procedures. For instance, the Port of Entry in Zapata, Texas did not charge any fee for Mexicans wishing to legally enter the United States, but El Paso charged two cents per head. Some Ports of Entry had detailed records of each entry whereas others had virtually none.

When Prudenciano and Paz entered the El Paso Port of Entry, Bureau employees hustled them to a large room with tables and government agents sitting behind them. Not knowing what to do, they moved quietly to the nearest vacant table and stood silently in front of a young Bureau agent who was busily completing a file card. The man wore tiny wire-rimmed glasses that pressed tightly against his meticulously oiled black hair. He had a shiny brass pin above his left breast pocket with the name Gattey inscribed across it. After a few moments, he looked up from his ledger and motioned for them to sit down. Prudenciano lowered his pack and took the chair that was directly across from the agent. Paz remained standing and positioned herself slightly behind her husband with Augustine balanced on her hip. Mr. Gattey counted the number of family members before him and then removed an equal number of index cards from a metal file holder. He laid them down in front of him and scribbled down the date on the bottom right of each card. Without looking up he asked, "Do you speak English?"

Prudenciano did not understand what the man said. He glanced behind at Paz for a clue. She shrugged her shoulders and shook her head slightly in response.

The Bureau agent looked up from his cards and was about to repeat his question, but stopped himself. Gattey had processed thousands of cases just like these and they were almost identical. The family did not speak or write English. The man was an unskilled laborer. They had no money. They had not the faintest idea where they were headed. The man sighed, took off his glasses, and massaged his eyes and the bridge of his nose. Shifting to Spanish he asked, "What is your name?"

"Prudenciano Nava."

The agent wrote it down, last name first, spelling it phonetically. This was an easy name to guess at the spelling. He knew that he had butchered others in the past by incorrectly using an "h" instead of a "j" or an "a" instead of an "e". But, who would even know? Gattey continued, "How old are you?"

Prudenciano balked for a moment on the question. He had never really know his birthday, but he thought he was close to fifty-seven. Prudenciano thought, *Fifty-seven! I can't be that old, especially with such a young wife. I will say something a little younger.* Prudenciano cleared his throat and said, "Fifty-four." Gattey never batted an eye as he wrote it down. Then he wrote "M" for male after the sex slot and "M" for marital status. Still without raising his head, he wrote "Mex" for race.

The agent asked with his pen on Prudenciano's card, "What do you do for a living, *Señor* Nava?" Prudenciano thought about this for a moment. A lot of occupations floated through his mind—rancher, miner, and guard. Finally, Prudenciano responded with a shrug. The man sighed again and wrote "laborer" for his occupation.

"Have you ever been in *los Estados Unidos*?"

"No."

"Can you read?"

Prudenciano was beginning to feel a little self-conscious. "No," he answered.

Gattey thought so. He also wrote "no" after "write". Then he wrote "family" after "Accompanied by."

"Your last residence was…?"

Prudenciano hesitated a moment before responding. He had been on the run for so long that he forgot what it was like to settle down somewhere. "Uh, Chihuahua." The agent wrote this down on his card.

When the agent was finally done, he looked up at Prudenciano and asked a routine question that he thought was totally useless, "What is your final destination?" The question stunned Prudenciano. This was partly due to the fact that he had not thought that far ahead and partly that he thought it was a trick question and, if he did not answer it correctly, he could not enter the country. Desperate, he looked back at Paz for help. She only raised an eyebrow in response.

The agent had seen this look of confusion before. "No matter," he said as he completed the entry cards. "I will just write 'El Paso.'"

He asked as he pulled another card out, "Is this your wife?"

"*Sí.*"

"And," continued the agent, a little irritated that he had to lead this man along, "what is her name?"

Prudenciano answered, "Maria Paz Esparsa Nava." Paz kept demurely quiet behind her husband. Although the baby squirmed in her arms, she closely watched the entire process.

"How old is she?"

Again, Prudenciano became sensitive to their age difference. "Ah, twenty-five," he answered as he put three more years to her real age.

"All right, and what are the children's names and ages?" The agent prepared to fill out a card for each of them.

"Well," replied Prudenciano, "the oldest is Alcaria. She is five now, but she will be six in December. Joaquina will be three on July thirteen. Augustine is one." Gattey hastily wrote the information down on separate cards. After "Accompanied by" he wrote "father." In the comment section, he wrote "Prudenciano Nava." On each child's card and Paz's, Gattey wrote the same last residence and destination.

Then he carefully laid down his pen and said with an air of finality, "Now there is the simple matter of the entry fee. I need two *centavos* per person for a total of ten *centavos*." Prudenciano was thunderstruck! He had no idea that registration required money and he had absolutely none. The agent could read Prudenciano's expressions like a painted billboard and began to smile. He had seen this reaction before. Paz walked up to the table and handed Augustine to her husband. "I have some money," she said. Both the agent and Prudenciano looked at her in surprise. Carefully, she untied a leather thong from around her neck and pulled a worn and dirty pouch from the front of her dress. She opened the pouch and emptied its contents onto the table. Several coins and pesos rolled out. It was all she had left from her father-in-law's gift from so long ago. Paz counted silently with her lips shaping each number until she had exactly ten *centavos*.

The agent was impressed and counted the rest of the money in the pouch. She had a total of three pesos and ninety *centavos*. Gattey wrote this amount down on Prudenciano's card after "money".

Prudenciano felt relieved that his had wife produced the required fee, but at the same time, he was angry with her for hoarding money. He thought, *What else has she kept from me?* He was oblivious to the fact that if she had not secretly stashed money, they could not have entered legally through El Paso. He would talk with her later on this matter. He reached for the remaining amount, but little Augustine hampered him. Paz deftly put her hands on it and pulled it to her. Then she carefully refilled the pouch and re-tied it around her neck.

The agent took the fee and signed the cards before filing them in the metal box. Then he stamped an entry document with Prudenciano's and Paz's names on it. He rolled this paper up, put a string around it, and handed it to Prudenciano. "You are free to travel within this country," he announced and then pointed toward another doorway. "Please exit that way."

Prudenciano and Paz looked at each other like there should be some sort of concluding ceremony. Then they picked their belongings and children and walked for the door. Paz turned around for one last look at the Bureau agent. She was surprised to see that another family had already taken their place and the agent was removing another card from the file. Paz faced back toward the door and escorted the girls out into the big new country called America.

In 1598, the Spanish adventurer Don Juan de Oñate named this area *El Paso del Rio del Norte* (the pass of the river of the north). For eons, the hills funneled people, horses, and wagons to this wide, braided ford of the Rio Grande. Travelers often took time to rest among the barren foothills that bordered the northern bank of the river. Afterward, the golden-hued mountains forced travelers to disperse into three directions, northwest, north, or east; toward the old Spanish settlements in Albuquerque and Santa Fe, the forbidding *Mal Pais* desert, or the Territory of Texas, respectively.

North of the crossing, plenty of level land existed within the mountain canyons and valleys. This area became a natural site for trading and defense. America built forts to monitor Mexican military and civilian movements. Businessmen established cattle lots and stores to replenish migrants. Mining companies based their exploration in the barren mountains. Gradually, people tired of the area's long Spanish name and shorten it to El Paso.

El Paso, Texas had had a tumultuous beginning. White settlers of the area originally named the town Franklin after a captain of the American cavalry. In 1859, residents voted to change the name back to El Paso and in 1873, El Paso officially became a U.S. city. Then in 1881, the Southern Pacific Railroad completed their east-west line that connected America's shores. El Paso became a critical hub for this traffic and the gateway to Mexico. In response, the town exploded and its population soared. Huge feedlots, mining ore stockpiles, and gigantic warehouses seemed to appear overnight. Americans and Mexicans flocked to El Paso to participate in the economic surge.

El Paso was not without its problems. Ruffians from all walks of life slipped into town. During April 1881, El Paso residents witnessed the famous "Four Dead in Five Seconds" gunfight. In 1895, John Selman gunned down John Wesley Hardin, the nation's most deadly gunfighter, in the Acme Saloon. Life in El Paso never seemed boring.

American business agents who set up labor contracts for Mexican immigrants descended on them like vultures on carrion. They often exploited the laborers' inability to understand or read English. In addition, Mexicans were usually totally unaware of their American rights. The concept of personal rights was foreign to them because they had lived their entire lives under the thumb of Porfirio Díaz. Mexicans who objected to conditions promulgated by an American labor agent were often met with a threat of deportation. Whether or not the Mexican had legally entered into the United States, he perceived this threat as real and quickly capitulated. Thus, the labor agents often cut deals with prospective employers to provide cheap labor for a fee and the Mexicans usually suffered the consequences.

When Mexicans first sought work when they entered America, they encountered conveniently located employment businesses close to all Ports of Entry. Sometimes these facilities were large single-story, adobe-brick buildings with a large meeting room and an office to conduct business. Others were simply a wooden stage where a labor agent announced with a megaphone voice that he had lots of high-paying jobs for willing Mexicans. The whole affair often reminded bystanders of the old medicine man shows where magical elixirs were hawked to innocent but ignorant citizens.

However, to people who had known only poverty, the labor agents sounded like angels from heaven. Typical promises from agents included high pay, unlimited job opportunities, housing and food included, and "Oh, of course you can take your family along. Do your wife and children want to work, too?" Usually, the Mexican became so enchanted with the incredible opportunity placed before him that he swallowed the whole sham line, hook, and sinker. He would quickly sign the contract that the labor agent slid in front of him with the blind faith of a cow led by a butcher to slaughter.

Within a few days on the job, the Mexican realized that he had been tricked. The working conditions were usually hard and dangerous. Employers offered substandard food, foul water, and drafty tents or boxcars for family housing. And, most irritatingly, the employer pulled a housing and food allowance from his hourly pay. Thus, a Mexican's net pay was much less than pledged.

The Mexicans had a name for the slick contract they signed. They called it *"El Gancho,"* (the hook). Once a man swallowed it, the labor agents would set the drag and reel him in. Then the only alternative was to work for what the real contract specified or face the threat of deportation. In reality, the Mexicans grumbled only between themselves. The work was plentiful and the pay was more than what they could earn in Mexico. It was just the thought of being promised so much, but getting much less in the end that rankled them.

John Dillon was a comfortably overweight man who had a fondness for good food, drink, and fine cigars. He always wore a wool three-piece suit, whether he was conducting business at his labor office or strolling down the street of El Paso. It was slightly frayed, which gave the owner the not-particularly-wealthy-but-still-professional look. It was the perfect costume for John Dillon because he was rich, but he dared not flaunt it yet. A wealthy labor agent always drew unwanted attention and mistrust, which was bad for business. Right now, business was very good. He just wanted to ride this Mexican wave of money for two more years and then he could retire comfortably for life.

Dillon was in a particularly good mood this early August morning. Another railroad company had just approached him for a large order of maintenance labor. They increased his normal fee plus dangled a bonus in front of him as an incentive. The company wanted him to round up a hundred men within the next week to replace and relevel railroad ties. The catch was that the laborers must be willing to work in the most godforsaken place known to man, the desert north of Orogrande, New Mexico, and of course, work for cheap.

Dillon stopped on the boardwalk in front of his office and tilted his head back as he faced the rising sun. He took a deep breath of early morning air and savored the mixture of smells. Among the odors of freshly cut lumber, burning wood and coal, cooking food, there were other smells of opportunity and progress. His trained nose detected whiffs of poverty and clustered humanity. He could almost taste the simple tortillas baking on hot rocks as the Mexicans stirred in their tent shanties to meet the day. Like a wolf smacking his lips as it detects the smell of helpless sheep, Dillon could barely contain his excitement and good fortune. *The smell of money is in the air*, he chuckled to himself. With that affirmation, he confidently put his key in his office door and readied himself for a productive day.

Upon receiving the railroad's enticing offer, Dillon hung a colored banner across the front of his office building. It loudly proclaimed, *TRABAJA ¡PRONTO!*, (Work now!). He hoped the sign would lure Mexicans to him, but Dillon was also a realist, and he knew that most of the men he needed were illiterate. To compensate for this flaw in his advertising, he brewed copious amounts of fresh coffee in the early morning and provided it, complete with sugar and cream, in the front receiving room. The aroma wafted through the dry air and infiltrated the minds and stomachs of men milling at street corners. The delicious smells often grabbed the men by their noses and dragged them unerringly back to Dillon's establishment. The crafty Dillon had discovered a fundamental truth that women throughout the world had known for centuries—the way to a man's heart was through his stomach.

Dillon's shop consisted of two rooms. As a potential client inquired for employment, the visitor entered a spacious reception area that was large enough for five men to wait in comfort. In a pinch, the room could accommodate ten standing men. Dillon conducted his business behind a closed door in the back room that functioned as his personal office. Scarcely large enough to contain a desk and two chairs, the room also contained a bookcase crammed full of intimidating and never-used law books and a worn typewriter that would create a work contract in rapid-fire motion before his awed client. To reinforce the effect, Dillon hung bogus diplomas and credentials upon the wall. If any of his clients could read and knew a little about America's university system, they would question such degrees as "Bachelor of Arts from the University of Four Corners, Arizona, in International Labor Relations" or "Honorary Degree from Havre, Montana in Western Law." However, this was generally not the case and each neatly framed sheepskin only added to the Mexicans' respect for and trust in Mr. John Dillon.

Dillon added one last feature to his office that completed the professional ambiance that he so meticulously tried to uphold. He installed a large window between the back and front rooms. This allowed waiting men to watch Mr. Dillon in action as he unfolded his drama before them. As they drank their steaming mugs of sweetened coffee, the men sat transfixed by Dillon's every move. They saw how he put his hand on their comrade's shoulder and explained the complicated details of the work contract. They noticed how Mr. Dillon considered looking up a reference in one of his important, looking books, but suddenly remembering the important detail and replacing the book upon the shelf. The men watched in amazement how he modified the work contract to help out their friend and type the correction on the paper in a lightning-fast manner. Lastly, and most importantly, they saw the smile appear across their companion's face and the hearty handshake after he had signed the contract. As the man opened the door and stepped back into the receiving room, Mr. Dillon always thumped him on the back and congratulated him on the incredible job opportunity he had just accepted. When Dillon asked who was next, he was nearly stampeded by willing participants.

Mr. Dillon felt especially jovial this beautiful, clear morning. He immediately busied himself by lighting the oil lamps underneath his large coffee brewer and filling the upper reservoir with water. He opened a fresh can of ground coffee and placed scoops of it into the coffee strainer. Dillon carefully placed the strainer and stand into the reservoir and pushed the metal lid onto the top until it locked securely in place. As the water heated, it rose through the strainer and produced the familiar perking sounds that people throughout the world found so reassuring in the morning. As a final touch, Dillon opened the windows to the street to provide adequate venting of the coffee aromas.

Prudenciano had grown accustomed to these early-morning gatherings along the street corners of El Paso. He bragged and traded stories with the clustered men. Every day brought either a newcomer to the crowd or someone saying *Adios* as he continued his migration into America. This suited Prudenciano just fine because this assured him that he always had fresh people to tell his exploits to.

Prudenciano had another enjoyable outcome of these morning gatherings. He had made a new friend and the man was proving to be an excellent *compadre*. His name was Rafael Silva and he was a scoundrel in his own right. He was a younger man in his midthirties and his eyes danced with the mischief of a twelve-year-old boy. The man was also blessed with a silver tongue and could talk a normal person into doing anything. He was boastful, lazy, articulate, and thoroughly enjoyed having a good time at someone else's expense. Prudenciano and Silva quickly discovered mutual interests and became fast friends.

While Prudenciano was enjoying himself, it never occurred to him that he and his family had been in El Paso for nearly a month and he had not secured a permanent job. Within the makeshift shelters that cluttered the outskirts of the city, the Navas eked out an existence among the thousands of other Mexicans arriving from Mexico. Although the family was safe, they barely stayed fed. Prudenciano earned some money and food by providing his *sobador* services.

Paz was growing increasingly terse with him. She prodded and pushed him to find the lucrative employment he had preached about for so long as they walked to America. Prudenciano appeared to comply with her wishes by rising before dawn and walking into the city. At first Paz thought he was looking for work, but after the third week she suspected that he had other motives. She made it very clear to Prudenciano that he should not expect his family to live like refugees much longer.

Thus, it was fate that the fresh-perked coffee aroma floated through the crowd of men and interrupted Prudenciano's storytelling and Silva's jibing. When Prudenciano asked where the smells were coming from, one man pointed to the office with a brightly colored banner over the door that was only a half block down the street. Prudenciano asked, "What is the place?"

A man replied, "That is *Señor* Dillon's shop. He is a local labor agent. Some say that he is a very smart man, but I think he is a bit of a snake. You can always tell when he has some work, though. He always brews coffee. It's *muy bueno.*"

"The coffee does smell good," muttered Prudenciano half out loud. It had been months since he'd had a cup. The smell made his stomach rumble. He thought about it some more and convinced himself that it was only proper for him to invite himself into the labor agent's office, have a free cup of coffee, and inquire about possibilities. "I think I will just go over there and see what is going on. What could it hurt, *¿qué no?*"

"*Sí,*" agreed Silva, "Let's have a cup or two on the house. What would it hurt?" He slapped Prudenciano on the back and started walking toward the smell.

A man warned, "Careful, *amigos!*" But Prudenciano and Silva laughed at him. They walked straight for the trap set by Mr. Dillon. John Dillon was like many animals who use odors and colors to create irresistible lures that draw unsuspecting prey within striking distance.

Prudenciano and Silva along with eight men stopped in front of the office with the colorful banner over the door. The coffee odors poured out of the open windows and smelled incredibly delicious. They all inhaled deeply before entering the building. Inside they found a large room with a huge container of hot brewed coffee and rows of clean mugs. Behind a window, they saw a professional-looking man hard at work among many thick books and a typewriter. The man looked up for a second, waved them to the coffee, and continued with his work.

"*Gracias!*" answered one man loud enough to carry through the glass. The owner nodded his head while he continued to busily scribble over a thick loose-leaf document. He appeared not to care who was outside, but in fact, he was very aware of what was going on and struggled to keep a nonchalant expression.

Got some bites, Dillon thought excitedly as he tried not to smile. *I will give them a few minutes to relax before I approach them*. Prudenciano poured himself a deep mug full of steaming coffee and mixed a generous amount of sugar and cream. He had not so richly indulged himself since working as a guard in Chihuahua. Then he spotted a comfortable-looking chair and slumped into it. He stretched his long legs out and took a long sip from his cup. It was as delicious as it looked and smelled. He closed his eyes for a second and savored the taste. When he opened his eyes, he was surprised to see the other men doing the same.

Silva settled into the chair next to him and smiled back, "This is *muy bueno, ¿qué no?*" Silva sighed and took another drink. He was thoroughly enjoying himself because the drink had all the necessary ingredients. It was hot, delicious, free, and he had someone's soft comfortable chair to drink it in.

When Prudenciano saw that the office owner had not come out yet, his curiosity piqued. He thought, *What kind of man would go through the trouble and expense to offer free coffee and not want something in return?* Prudenciano stood up and leisurely walked around the room and looked at the photographs on the wall. The pictures depicted men working happily on railroad crews or in large fields harvesting fruit. One picture that caught Prudenciano's eye showed a man dressed in a three-piece suit with his arm around the shoulders of a very happy Mexican worker. The Mexican had his wife standing next to him proudly looking up at his face. The two men were waving at the photographer. The picture appeared to have been taken in this very room. The professionally dressed man was obviously their benefactor in the back office. The picture affected Prudenciano deeply. It accurately portrayed what he craved. Prudenciano wanted to make lots of money, live a happy life, and have Paz think the world of him. He stopped and stared at the photograph for a few minutes longer.

John Dillon looked up from his play acting and saw a big man staring at what Dillon called his "success picture." *It never fails*, mused Dillon. *That photograph always holds them. Well, I guess it's time to recruit some men*. Dillon squeezed out from behind his cluttered desk and laboriously fought with the door because his one and only client chair impeded its opening. Finally out and dignified, Dillon casually walked up to Prudenciano and pretended to study the picture with him.

Mr. Dillon prepared to go fishing. "Ah, yes," said Dillon in his not-so-perfect Spanish with a gringo accent, "I remember that man well." Prudenciano flicked his eyes toward him in an attempt to goad him to tell the rest of the story. Dillon saw the man's reaction and calmly looked up to him to elaborate further. Prudenciano was a good six inches taller than he. Dillon also noticed the streaks of silver in the man's long, flowing hair and beard. He thought, *Damn, this man is big! If he was a little younger he would be perfect for railroad work, but he seems fit enough. It is so hard to tell the age of some of these Mexicans.* Dillon was crafty enough to realize that Prudenciano provided a huge benefit that could not be ignored. He was a natural leader and if Dillon could persuade him to sign up, tens of other men would blindly follow. He could fill his entire recruitment order within a day.

"That's right," continued Dillon. "His name is Miguel Lequina and he made a lot of money. See how happy he is?" Dillon paused as if he was reflecting on a pleasant lifelong memory and then added, "I think he is retired now. Lives in his own house somewhere in Colorado. Lucky man."

Prudenciano looked back at the picture. This Lequina certainly looked happy. He owned a house! His words blurted from his mouth before he could contain them, "How could I find the same work?"

Mr. Dillon baited the hook. "You are not going to believe this, but I just got a work order for a few capable men. The pay is very good."

Prudenciano replied, "*Sí?* What kind of work? How much would I get paid?"

Mr. Dillon threw the hook out and began fishing. Dillon answered in a loud conversational voice so all the men could hear, "Well, why don't you get another cup of coffee and step into my office? We can review the details in private."

Prudenciano smiled and said gruffly, "I think that I will do just that!"

Mr. Dillon had a bite. He set the hook and began to skillfully play the line. John Dillon slapped Prudenciano on the back and heartily laughed, "Great! I think that this is going to be your lucky day, *amigo!*"

"Nava," gasped Silva as Prudenciano passed him to refill his cup, "what are you doing? Are you completely *loco?* Let's just drink the man's coffee and leave, Okay?"

Prudenciano just laughed as he poured more steaming hot coffee into his mug and added a couple of sugar cubes. He stirred in a little cream and smacked his lips as he tasted his creation. He wiped his mouth off with the back of his hand and looked back at Silva with a new, serious look and said, "I want to make some good money. That is the reason that we came to America, *¿qué no?* This man says he has some good jobs and I am going to check them out."

Silva threw up a hand in disgust and slouched down in his chair. He pulled his hat down over his eyes and slowly sipped his coffee.

He pretended not to care what Prudenciano was going to do with his life, but in actuality, he was keenly aware of what was happening in the small back office. When he tilted his head back and squinted his eyes, he could just see under the brim of his hat and watched Prudenciano squeeze his big frame into a chair and close the door.

The other men in the front room also began watching Prudenciano through the back window. They noted every eloquent expression and movement that Dillon made as if they were watching a professional ballet. They noticed Prudenciano lean forward so he could study the details of the job and saw him begin to smile broadly.

"I am telling you, *Señor* Nava," Dillon waxed as smooth as silk. "There are no better jobs in all of America. The pay is excellent at $2.50 per day and the El Paso and Northeastern Railroad is one of the better companies to work for."

Prudenciano asked, "What is the work?"

"Line maintenance," replied Dillon. When he saw the look of bewilderment cross Prudenciano's face, he explained further. "The railroad line was built about twenty-five years ago. The rail needs some leveling and wooden ties must be replaced. It's good work. Outdoors. Plenty of fresh air. Good country." Prudenciano nodded as Dillon was explaining. Dillon sensed that he needed to throw out something that would seal the deal, so he asked, "Do you have a family?"

The remark caught Prudenciano off guard. "*Sí*," replied Prudenciano, "Why?"

"Well," smiled Dillon as he leaned across his desk as if he was sharing some sort of secret with Prudenciano, "The company is willing to bring your family along and provide housing and food for them. All of this at a nominal cost to you. So what do you say, *amigo*, eh? A fantastic job, great pay, and have your family with you. You can't find a better offer anywhere!"

Prudenciano rubbed his beard for a moment and appeared to contemplate the details of the job offer, but in reality he was already counting his money. A quick flash of Paz scolding him for not finding work was all it took for him to agree to the terms. He smiled and said simply, "Okay." He stuck out his hand and almost crushed Dillon's fleshy palm. Dillon grimaced, tried to smile weakly back, sucked in his breath to keep from screaming, and pushed a contract in front of Prudenciano for him to sign. Mr. Dillon had landed his fish.

As Dillon helped him put an "X" on the line and printed his name next to it, the men in the waiting room continued to watch in fascination. It appeared to them that Prudenciano had just won a lottery and was going to make some easy money. Even Silva almost spilled his coffee as he abruptly sat up and flipped his hat back so he could see better. Dillon had landed another recruit. When Prudenciano left the office with his contract in hand, Dillon was practically swarmed by eager men with Silva fighting to be first. All of them swallowed *El Gancho* and quickly spread the word through the Mexican community that Mr. Dillon had fantastic jobs for them. Their concerted efforts made Mr. John Dillon, labor agent, a lot of money as they filled his entire quota in one day.

The noontime sun was directly overhead when Prudenciano walked into the large encampment of shanties and mud huts on the western outskirts of El Paso. Laundry was strung between shacks. Dirty water flowed through the makeshift dirt roads that were really no more than alleys. The stench of garbage and untreated sewage hung in the hot air. Children ran unsupervised through the narrow roads in bare feet and played incredible games with newly found friends. An occasional dog would yap and bark at the children and strain at its leash to try to break free and participate in the fun.

This neighborhood was a cluster of very poor people just arriving in America. Most of the residents could not speak English and stayed less than six months. Within this time period, one of three things usually happened. They either moved on to find work, became so disillusioned that they returned to Mexico, or died from a disease spawned from unsanitary and crowded conditions. If an unfortunate mother gave birth within these hovels, chances were high that the baby would die within its first month. These people had no money for nutritious food or medicine and the American authorities cared little about their welfare.

Prudenciano made his way down several side streets and finally stopped at the front of a small adobe hut. The Navas had found the shelter empty when they arrived in El Paso and took it over as probably others had done over the years. The single-room hovel was about twelve feet square with a low roof and no windows. Prudenciano had to stoop to enter the doorway. He pushed the wooden door open and was immediately rushed by little Augustine. Like his sisters, Augustine never learned how to walk, but instead graduated from crawling to instant running. Moving quickly on his toes, the one-year-old boy would run forward with his weight shifted far forward and his arms outstretched to maintain his balance. He would continue in one direction until he ran into something that altered his course. Neighbors laughed and told Paz he reminded them of a billiard ball bouncing off bumpers.

Prudenciano scooped up his laughing son in his arms and held him to his face. "Hey, little *niño*, where are you going so fast, eh?" Augustine giggled and grabbed his father's beard with both hands. Prudenciano growled and shook his head like a bear. Augustine laughed again and thought this was great fun. Paz appeared in the doorway with an expression of concern. When she saw that it was Prudenciano, she relaxed and slumped down onto the dirt floor. She pushed a lock of dirty hair away from her face and looked dejectedly at the ground.

Paz said wearily, "I am so tired chasing these children around. I haven't the faintest idea where the girls are."

Prudenciano juggled Augustine lightly for a moment and set him softly on the ground. Augustine was clearly just warming up for a big romp with his father. He stretched his arms up and danced on his toes for more attention. Prudenciano settled down next to the doorway and placed his back against the mud wall. He tilted his head back and basked his face in the sun. He pretended not to notice Augustine scampering up onto his lap to resume his rough-housing. As the little boy jumped up and down on his father trying in vain to get a satisfactory reaction, Prudenciano and Paz sat silently in the dirt and listened to the noises of the neighborhood. Children played down the alley. A husband and wife roared in a heated argument. Laundry water was thrown out into the street. Dogs barked.

Finally, Paz broke their silence. "I don't know how much longer I can take living here." She said this as a sad statement and not as a threat. Prudenciano looked up at her and studied her face for a moment. The month living in this hovel had taken its toll on her. She looked beaten, tired, and dirty. Her youth had left her and now she looked much older than her twenty-three years. The time spent within these windowless mud walls with three small children had nearly driven her mad. For once, Prudenciano felt sorry for her and a little guilty about his selfish behavior.

Prudenciano grabbed his son and stuffed him under his arm like a rolled mat. Augustine squealed with delight. Then he turned to his wife and announced, "I found a job today."

Paz's eyes perked and the looked up to him in surprise. "What kind of job?"

Prudenciano suddenly remembered the photograph hanging in Mr. Dillon's office of the proud man and his adoring wife. He instantly had a rush of bravado and the feeling of importance. He puffed up his chest and held the squirming Augustine tighter. "A railroad company hired me to help maintain their line in New Mexico. They want all of us to come along. They will provide housing and food. It is a very good job with good pay. I will make lots of money."

Paz sat stunned. This news was too good to be true. "When do we leave?"

Prudenciano smiled and said, "Tomorrow morning we have to be at the train station to go to Orogrande."

Paz involuntarily put her hand up to her mouth to cover her astonishment. Then with a burst of emotion, she flung her arms around her husband's neck and buried her face into his chest. Her tears flooded down her cheeks and her body heaved with silent sobs. She was thoroughly relieved that her time here was almost over. Prudenciano stroked her head with his free hand and allowed Augustine to wiggle out of his hold. Like all little boys, Augustine became deeply disturbed when his mother cried. Sensing that something was wrong, he tried vainly to pry her head off his father's chest and comfort her. After a few moments, Paz relaxed and rose from Prudenciano. While managing a weak smile and wiping her tears away, she told her baby that she was all right and thanked him for his concern. Then she turned to her husband and asked, "Who else is going? Anyone else that we know?"

This was a logical question because everyone knew everybody's business within this shanty-town. Mexicans have a flair for keeping track of each other and if one family found work, chances were very good that the informal Mexican communications system notified other families of the same job opportunity. After all, Prudenciano was certainly not an introvert. Paz had a feeling that he had probably bragged about his good fortune and persuaded others to follow.

Prudenciano waved his hand in the air and nonchalantly said, "Oh, a few people perhaps."

Paz pressed, "Really? Like who?"

"Well, like Rafael Silva."

The euphoria that Paz felt over the job snapped away and was instantly replaced by suspicion. *I knew it*! she thought as she stepped back to study her husband. Silva represented everything that she despised in a man. He was reckless, undependable, and always loved to have a good time at the expense of others. He was also single, and without a good woman to temper and guide him, Paz thought he was absolutely worthless. To further grate on her nerves, Silva could talk Prudenciano into anything. Paz believed from the very bottom of her soul that this man meant trouble for her family.

The laughter from two girls broke Paz's icy stare. Alcaria and Joaquina came running down the street toward home. Judging by the dirt on their faces and clothes, Paz could tell they had been having a grand time. Alcaria yelled, "Mama! Papa!" She was almost breathless from running. "We have been making mud pies with a bunch of kids!"

Joaquina held out her upturned little hand and showed her parents her best mud pie. She said proudly, "See?" Her shiny black hair was matted with dried mud, but her bright smile lit up her face and made any dirt seem insignificant.

Paz sighed and managed a smile. It was no use rebuking them. Without good water, it was so hard to keep her children clean. She addressed them together, "Girls, your father has accepted a job in another place and we must get ready to travel. We are going to ride on a train! So, go tell your friends that we are leaving and come right back home. *Comprende?*"

The news surprised the girls and they responded differently. Alcaria let out a whoop and danced on her toes. The thought of riding on a train was just too good to be true. Then she took off down the alley to spread the news of her fantastic fortune. The younger Joaquina stood motionless as she tried to understand what was happening. The thought of leaving her friends was not particularly attractive because her last trip had shown her hunger, fear, and exhaustion. The prospect of traveling again terrified her. She slowly began to shake and get teary.

Paz instinctively knew what was bothering her and knelt down to hold her. Joaquina let her mother draw her into her arms and hold her. "Oh, do not worry, little one," cooed Paz as she stroked her hair. Big tears produced muddy streaks down Joaquina's face. "The train ride will be so much fun! We will be together and no one will hurt you." Joaquina seemed to take courage from this and slowly stopped crying. "There now," soothed Paz as she wiped her tears from her face with the hem of her dress. "Why don't you go tell the little girls down the street goodbye. It will make you feel better." Joaquina nodded her little head and cleaned up her last sniffles. Then with absolute faith that everything her mother said was true, she skipped down the street to tell her friends goodbye.

Paz stood up, turned back to her husband and said with a sarcastic voice, "I guess you do not have to say goodbye to anyone, do you? You are taking yours with you."

Prudenciano snorted in reply, "What do you mean by that?"

Paz looked him right in the eye and said sternly, "Silva is going to get you into a lot of trouble. He is going to talk you into doing something wrong and you will lose this good job. I know this will happen! The man is a coyote!"

Prudenciano prepared himself to rage back, but something in his wife's eyes stopped him. It was the look of certainty and he knew deep down that she was right.

Chapter 14
Tularosa Valley

The El Paso and Northeastern Railroad stretched northeast from El Paso through the desolate and beautiful Tularosa Valley in South-central New Mexico. The valley averaged about fifty miles in width and was about 130 miles long. A series of mountains ranges form its borders from north to south. The San Andres Mountains stretched along the valley's western border. With peaks rising over 2,000 feet above the valley floor, the San Andres mountains caught little of the moisture from the air masses moving predominantly from the west to the east. These mountains were starkly devoid of vegetation and form a jagged skyline of rocky needles.

The eastern border consisted of several mountain groups—the Sacramento, Capitan, and the Jicarilla mountains. Within these groups lay some of the tallest peaks in New Mexico. Approximately in the center of these formations stood Sierra Blanca at just shy of 12,000 feet. These formidable ranges wrung the last drops of moisture from the westerly winds. As a result, the mountains supported thick forests of spruce and fir and grassy meadows in the highlands. The mountains also accumulated deep snows in the winter that melted slowly during the spring and summer and provided precious water to the valley below.

Therefore, the borders of the Tularosa Valley contained very contrasting environments. The western side was dry with sparse vegetation. The eastern edge contained dense forests with pockets of lush vegetation around mountain springs and creeks fed by snowmelt.

The valley floor was rugged and devoid of human occupation. The southwestern section contained the White Sands Desert. As its name implied, this 270-square-mile desert contains sixty-foot-high dunes of shifting white crystallized gypsum that shimmered in the blazing sun. Scorching winds blew the sands across its thirty-mile width. Only sparse pockets of sagebrush and cactus survived between the high dunes. The high elevation caused the temperatures to plummet to freezing during the night and then rocketed to beastly highs during the day. The combination of fluctuating diurnal temperatures, lack of water, and unstable sand made this area almost impregnable.

Farther north in the White Sands Desert, the ground became more stable and less sandy. The country gradually turned into a rocky barren terrain with deep gullies carving through flat plains. Some hardy trees, shrubs, and grasses eked out an existence along the dry riverbeds. Mule deer lived as furtive shadows among these sparse habitats. Other than this, the land supported only scattered cacti. Locals called this area the *Mal Pais* (bad country). Travel through this area was extremely difficult due the rugged and unpredictable nature of the ground.

Two counties bisected the valley. Lincoln County covered the northern half the valley and Otero County contained the southern portion. Alamogordo was the county seat for Otero. Carrizozo, the seat for Lincoln County, was about fifty-eight miles north of Alamogordo and was much smaller. The railroad had been built along the east side of the valley to utilize the water and timber resources from the snow-rich mountains. Between Alamogordo and Carrizozo, the railroad had positioned tanks on wooden towers at dependable water sources to refill steam locomotives. These water stops, with names such as Polly Flats and Jake's Springs, had their own side track to allow the trains to take on water without blocking the main line.

Settlers had built several small communities along the section between Alamogordo and Carrizozo. These towns included Tularosa, Three Rivers, and Oscuro. All these towns were completely dependent on the railroad to generate their economic base.

In 1909, Lincoln County relocated their county seat from Lincoln to Carrizozo. Before this, the town of Lincoln had presided over one of the largest counties in the territory of New Mexico for more than thirty years. With the construction of the new railroad came the relocation of wealth and opportunities. Carrizozo blossomed because the new El Paso and Northeastern Railroad built a freight warehouse and stockyard in the town to service agricultural centers from Lincoln and Fort Stanton. Meanwhile, Lincoln, which was forty-two miles east of the rail line, had began to wither because of its isolation.

Carrizozo resided in the desolate and harsh country of the *Mal Pais*. People did not just go to Carrizozo for recreation or curiosity. There was usually a reason why they would end up in this small town, as pioneer Charles Mayer found out. He was on the first passenger train the El Paso and Northeastern Railroad offered. It stopped at Corona, New Mexico, and a tough, mangy cowboy boarded the train. He brusquely moved down the aisle and took a seat by himself. The ruffian pulled his hat over his eyes, checked the availability of his sidearm, crossed his arms, and slouched back in his seat. Mayer and the rest of travelers got the message that no one was to disturb him.

Within a few minutes, the conductor began collecting tickets. Everyone held their breath when he approached the cowboy. The conductor seemed undaunted. He had dealt with all types of men and this one was just another man. "Excuse me, sir," the conductor addressed the belligerent traveler. "May I have your ticket?" The cowboy sat unmoving and silent. The conductor moved closer and yelled, "I need your ticket!"

The cowboy slowly unfolded his arms and raised his hat. When Mayer saw that unshaven face with bloodshot eyes, he thought for sure that the conductor and half the train were going to die. The conductor did not waver. He continued to stare the man down. After a tense couple of seconds the cowboy straightened up and said, "Hell, I have no ticket, but if you will stop this train, I will go back to Corona and get one."

"I am afraid that is not possible," the conductor told him. "The next stop is Carrizozo and you could get a ticket there. So, supposing that you purchase one there, where do you want to go?"

The cowboy had expected to either buffalo the conductor or have him give up and let him ride for free. He was not planning on having to buy a ticket. He felt his anger rise and blurted out, "To hell!"

The conductor smiled and coolly replied, "Well, Carrizozo is as near as we can get you." When the train arrived in Carrizozo, the conductor threw the cowboy out and left him standing there bewildered. As the train quickly pulled away, Mayer watched him from the coach window as he gradually shrank in the distance. A mean, tough man marooned in a small, barren town far away from everywhere and close to nowhere.

Both counties had colorful histories. Otero adjoined the Mescalero Apache Indian Reservation. The federal government had designated the Mescalero reservation in 1880. The reservation was nestled between the Capitan and Sacramento mountains and included a portion of Sierra Blanca. Unlike other reservations, the Mescalero land was incredibly beautiful. Before the reservation, the Mescalero roamed freely and sometimes fiercely through southern New Mexico. They went on the warpath against the white settlers invading their lands and, for several decades, the Mescalero struck fear within every pioneer's heart. The U.S. cavalry fought a frustrating and elusive war against the Apache and finally settled for a truce. The Mescalero retreated to Sierra Blanca and its rich resources and the whites continued to eke out a life along its foothills.

In the late 1880s, a ruthless band of white and Mexican outlaws began stealing cattle from the Mescalero and neighboring ranchers and killing defenseless people indiscriminately. The white ranchers tried to fight back, but failed to stop them. The Mescalero appealed to their new "Great White Father" for help, but to no avail. Finally, Chief Augustine decided to take matters into his own hands and summoned a war council. Several years had passed since they had last fought and memories of that glorious past had faded. Even with the wild gyrations of his medicine man, Chief Augustine did not succeed in generating a killing frenzy among his young braves during the evening's war dance. He quickly decided that he needed something else to stimulate his braves into the appropriate frame of mind and that, of course, was whiskey.

The Territory of New Mexico strictly forbade the sale of liquor to Indians, but this did not deter Chief Augustine. With war paint smeared across his face, he rode a few miles northeast to a little settlement named Ruidoso next to the reservation, and stopped at a general store that had a hotel on the top floor. He knew the woman who ran the business, for he had traded with her for several years. She had always treated him and his people with respect. Augustine strictly commanded his braves to be kind to her and protect her family. While a brave watched the place one night, he noticed a white man carrying several bottles of firewater out of the store. The word spread like wildfire throughout the reservation that liquor was available, but the woman's husband would not sell it to them. Tonight was different because Augustine knew that her husband was managing a lumber mill several miles away. She had a soft heart that he thought he could exploit and, therefore, she was his best bet to acquire whiskey.

Augustine hid his horse in the brush outside the town and crept slowly to the back door. Only one room upstairs had a light burning. This was a great comfort to the chief because it meant that no boarders were staying the night. He waited a few moments to listen to the sounds of the night. All was quiet as it should be. Augustine reached up and rapped softly on the door. He waited and then rapped harder.

Mrs. Edith Lesnett was just putting her infant son, Tom, to bed when she heard the knocking on the back door. She put her hand to her breast as she felt fear surge through her body. Who could be knocking on the back door at this hour? Wild thoughts of the bandits that roamed the countryside entered her mind. Edith glanced at her baby and decided not to take any chances. She picked him up and placed him on a couple of pillows on the floor next to the bed. Then she scooted the pillowed baby under the bed where he would be hidden. She heard the beating on the back door again, only this time it was louder.

Edith's fear was almost crippling. She trembled as she picked up the lantern, tiptoed out of the bedroom, and closed the door behind her. She cried half out loud, "Why is Frank always gone when I need him?" When she approached the stairway, she grasped the railing tightly and steadied herself. "Get ahold of yourself, girl," she chided herself. "You knew what you were getting yourself into when you married him. Now, get tough and face this danger."

Edith had married Frank a few years before in the beautiful and exciting city of Chicago, Illinois. In her childhood, Edith had lived a comfortable life there and never dreamed of moving away until she met Frank. He was ruggedly handsome with strong shoulders and laughing eyes, but it was his confident manner that captivated her. None of the boys she had known in Chicago possessed such character. They usually followed the crowd, went to popular schools, sang popular songs, and sought comfortable employment from stable companies. They never struck out on their own.

Frank was different because he walked to the beat of his own drum. He had come to Chicago to secure financing for a lumber mill and ranch close to the Tularosa Valley. Financing proved to be difficult because the banks thought Frank was too young to manage a large, profitable business, and New Mexico was just too wild, but Frank persisted. The more rejection he met, the harder he tried. He had the character and strong determination usually found in someone much older.

Edith's father brought Frank home one night for dinner after Frank had tried valiantly to persuade him and his associates to back his plans. Edith's father succeeded in tabling the decision for the night instead of heeding his associates' wishes to issue an outright denial. When he introduced Frank to Edith, love thunderstruck the two. Edith scurried upstairs to return half an hour later dressed in a flowing gown and her hair nicely put up. Frank squirmed and preened in her presence. Of course, none of this was lost on her parents, who seemed to enjoy the spectacle of young courtship.

Over dinner, Frank explained his plan for a mill and ranch. He described the beauty and rich character of the land and expounded the tremendous opportunities available to people who were willing to work hard. Edith hung on every word. She could feel his passion and love of the land and belief that he could actually achieve his dreams. When dinner was over, she knew that she had one mission in life and that was to convince her father to finance Frank's proposition.

Frank's visit was over too soon and Edith almost cried in despair when he stood to get his hat and thanked her parents for dinner. Frank also looked disturbed to be leaving the presence of such a beautiful girl and walked slowly to the door. As he grabbed the doorknob, he quickly spun around, took her hand, and asked if he could see her tomorrow night. She smiled and said yes. The light that shone from his dazzling smile could have lit a Chicago city block and with that smile, Mr. Frank Lesnett captured Edith's heart.

The next two days were a living hell for Edith's father. Edith tenaciously pleaded Frank's case. Her pestering started in the early morning during breakfast and ceased only when he left to go to work. Edith then resumed her quest by midmorning when she paid the bank an uncustomary visit. She demanded a audience of each of her father's associates and had them uncomfortably explain to her why they did not favor financing Mr. Lesnett's proposition. Edith stayed long enough to accept a lunch offer by her father and argued unceasingly with him during the entire meal. She offered no respite during dinner. Finally, by the afternoon on the second day, her father and his associates called an emergency caucus and determined that if they wanted to recapture their peaceful lives, they would have to at least finance a smaller version of Mr. Lesnett's proposal.

When Frank learned of the bank's approval, he was ecstatic. He came over to her house every night to discuss arrangements with her father and then sit on the porch swing with Edith. Within the following weeks, they determined that they could not live without each other and announced their engagement. They were married in the early spring and after a joyous honeymoon, Frank struck out for New Mexico to build a house and construct the lumber mill.

One very long year later, Frank sent for her. She said goodbye to her frilly dresses and comfortable home and eagerly jumped on a train to Lajunta, Colorado. There she adventurously boarded a stagecoach and traveled to Fort Stranton, New Mexico where she and Frank were finally reunited.

She immediately embraced the Wild West and all its splendor. She fell in love with Ruidoso and the house Frank had built, but it sometimes took everything she had to be strong and not whine about the good life she had left behind. When Frank decided to build a store and hotel, Edith stepped forward and said she was going to manage them while he ran affairs at the mill. Thus, their division of labor started. Things went well and their business began to thrive. People from all over came and bought goods or stayed the night in one of the rooms upstairs.

The Apache scared her when they first came to trade for goods. The braves arrived with their children and wives following submissively behind them carrying buckskins and furs for barter. Although the men always wanted bullets and tobacco, Edith caught secret signals from the women that directed her to add a little food, medicine, or perhaps a piece of candy for the children. She slyly manipulated the men to accept an amended bargain. At the end of the trade, the Indian families would leave very satisfied. The men felt they got what they wanted and a little more. The women would wink and smile their thanks at Edith behind their men's backs as they walked away. Edith soon realized that they were people just like all the rest and made it a point to understand them and know their names. She could not prove it, but she suspected that they watched her place at night.

The pounding at the door snapped her back into reality. Frank had shown her how to use a shotgun, and stored it in a closet at the foot of the stairs. Edith crept down the stairs with the lantern eerily illuminating the wall in front of her. She opened the closet and retrieved the gun. She broke open the breach and found both barrels loaded with twelve-gauge buckshot. She snapped it shut and continued to the door. Edith carried the lantern in her left hand and held the shotgun under her right arm. "Who is it?" she asked with a loud and steady voice, but her knees almost rattled together.

A low, rough voice answered immediately back, "Augustine!"

She asked, "Chief Augustine?" Her anxiety dropped some, but she thought, *What does he want this time of night?*

A rough "Ugh!" grunted back. Edith placed the lantern on the kitchen table so she could use both hands to steady the gun. Its weight was already straining her arms and back. She glanced down at the breech and saw that she had forgotten to pull the hammers back to the cocked position. With all the strength that she could muster, Edith agonizingly pulled each hammer back with her thumbs until they clicked into place. Then she held the huge weapon straight out with the monster stock against her small right shoulder, and walked awkwardly to the door. With her left hand, she let go of the shotgun and groped desperately for the doorknob. Finding it, she freed the latch, pulled the door open, and took a step back with a renewed grip on the gun.

Edith's entire view of the world was through the open sights of the shotgun. The brass bead swayed and bobbed in front of her as the figure emerged from the dark. Lantern light had a way of enhancing features. Its yellow, wavering glow made normal images appear almost supernatural. When Chief Augustine stepped into the lantern light with his face and body painted a ghostly white with red and black stripes and circles, Edith almost blew his head off right then and there. The only reason Augustine survived was that he immediately threw himself to the floor and begged for mercy in his broken English.

"Please! No kill! Please! No shoot!" Edith took another step back and appraised the situation. The man appeared to be Augustine, but she was not certain. Her adrenaline pumped up her strength and ridded her of the ache in her back and shoulders. Right now, the shotgun was light as a feather.

Edith spoke with a renewed force, "For the love of God, Augustine, why are you pounding on my door at this hour dressed like a hellion?"

Augustine looked up from the floor at the two black tubes of the double-barreled shotgun weaving in front of his face. He knew in his heart that she would kill him at the slightest provocation. So, he assumed a submissive demeanor and pleaded his demand with one word, "Whiskey!"

Fear ripped through her mind as she thought, *Oh God! The word is out that Frank has brought a shipment of liquor into the store. I knew it would lead to trouble! Why didn't Frank listen to me? Now, I'm stuck with this!* Edith realized that her best card was to deny the existence of the liquor and decided to play it. "We don't have any whiskey here. Now scat before I pepper your hide!"

Augustine understood very little of what was being said. He caught the gist of her words that she was not going to give him any whiskey and she might kill him if he did not leave now. The chief started to slink back to the door, but stopped when he remembered his unmotivated braves. No, he must go back with some firewater. He smiled and opened his arms out wide in a gesture of friendship and said, "Please! Whiskey!"

Edith had about enough. She firmly leveled the shotgun at Augustine's face and restated her position. "We have no whiskey! Leave now or I will shoot!" An unsettling silence fell between the two of them. Augustine was not leaving empty-handed and Edith was not about let him have any whiskey. Events might have ended tragically at this point if the baby had not chosen this moment to wake up within the unfamiliar surroundings of the mattress springs and wail at the top of his lungs. Augustine's eyes flicked to the ceiling where the crying emanated and dropped his gaze back to the black barrels. Edith's maternal instincts fired up and instantly changed her perspective. She had to get this warrior out of her house immediately and if it took giving him some whiskey, then so be it.

"Augustine, listen to me. The whiskey is in the stable out back." Augustine sensed that she had changed her mind, but could not quite grasp what she was saying. He looked quizzically back. The baby's cries grew louder. Edith felt her anxiety rise. "The stable! You know, horses, stable? Whiskey? Stable?"

Augustine looked at her questioningly for a moment, then suddenly he understood. Stable. White man's house for his horses. Whiskey is there. He nodded enthusiastically while he backed out the door. "I tell no one. Many thanks! I tell no one. Many thanks! We kill bad men tonight. You see!" Edith could not care less. She prodded the Indian out, threw the door shut, and promptly locked it. As she slumped against the door and lowered the shotgun, she hoped Augustine would take the whole case of whiskey with him and never come around asking for it again. She would be damned if she was going to let Frank buy some more.

Little Tom's crying told her that she had more important things to worry about than what Augustine was going to do with the liquor. She felt a heavy weariness creep over her and her muscles began to ache deeply from lugging the shotgun. She gently released the hammers on the gun and place it across the table. Then she picked the lantern up and went upstairs to retrieve and comfort her son.

Augustine could barely contain himself when he found the large case of quart bottles of whiskey. This was not the rot-gut firewater he had sometimes consumed in his hut. He let out a whoop and performed an abbreviated dance of joy. Then he found a horse blanket and made a makeshift sling. He carefully placed each bottle into the cradle as though he was handling his own beloved babies. Augustine hefted the heavy bundle onto his shoulder and rode back home.

As Augustine predicted, the whiskey was a smashing success and produced such a frenzied furor that any observing military officer in the world would have been green with envy. Of course Augustine knew that the effect would be short-lived, so when the scouts pinpointed the bandits' camp and returned, Augustine assembled his braves to strike while the mood was hot.

The Apache attack caught the outlaws by surprise. Although the bandits were better armed, the Indians quickly overwhelmed them. Their blood-curdling screams, war paint, and absolute fearlessness struck terror into every man's heart. With tomahawks and knives, the braves ruthlessly hacked their way through the camp. Within a few minutes, the battle was over and the Apache collected many scalps.

Augustine signaled for his warriors to regroup and ride home. It was always a good policy to hit hard and then slip quickly away. However, most of his braves had never seen combat and were intoxicated by the savagery of it. Many continued to giggle and scream as they mindlessly stabbed at the bodies with their knives. They were experiencing a power that made them feel invincible and it felt delicious. Augustine had to drag several of the young men away from the mutilated bodies and clubbed a few to knock some reality back into them. With his men finally in line, Augustine let out a whoop and led them back to the reservation. As he rode through the ebbing night, he knew that life had changed for the once beaten Mescalero. Men would once again fear them.

A cavalry detachment from Fort Stranton happened to stumble upon the charred and grisly remains the following morning. When the cavalry Indian scouts dismounted and examined the battle, they found one Mexican barely alive. The Apache had purposely spared him as their messenger to proclaim what had happened. They had burned his eyes out, scalped him, and thrown him onto the mutilated corpses of his companions. The sergeant poured some water from his canteen over the Mexican's face to revive him. The man sputtered into consciousness and began screaming, "*¡Diablos! ¡Diablos!* Save me!"

The sergeant looked disgustedly at the man and kicked him hard to silence him. The Mexican curled into a fetal position and whimpered quietly. The sergeant barked, "What demons? Who finally gave you maggots what you deserve?"

The man seemed unable to understand or respond. He kept muttering, "*¡Diablos! ¡Muchos diablos!*"

"Bah!" spat the sergeant as he kicked the curled man and sent him flying into a heap of blood and twisted flesh.

"Sir!" The sergeant looked up to see one of his scouts pull a short spear from the back of a dead bandit. The scout examined the colorful markings along its shaft and the hawk feather attached at the base. "Apache, sir," the scout proclaimed. "Looks like Mescalero to me."

The sergeant exclaimed, "The Mescalero! They did this!" He studied the destruction around him and let out a long and low whistle. "Looks like we got ourselves a powerful ally in these parts." The sergeant made a mental note to fully report this to the proper authorities. He quickly realized that if the Mescalero could instill fear into the lawless, then the Tularosa Valley would become a peaceful place to live.

The sergeant's insight proved correct. Within weeks, outlaws got word of what the Mescalero had done and that they would not tolerate any harm or theft against the people of the valley. They gave the area a wide berth and whenever one decided to try his luck, the Apache dealt a swift blow. Even attempted escapes from the Lincoln or Alamogordo county prisons fell to an all-time low. Nothing could strike more fear into an escapee's heart than the knowledge of the Mescalero hot on his tail.

Lincoln County was also known for taking matters into its own hands. The Lincoln County War of 1878 was a classic example. In 1873, Lincoln was a small town of about four hundred Hispanic residents when a disgraced army officer named Lawrence Murphy rolled into town. Fort Stanton had kicked him out of the service for operating an unscrupulous business on the post. Undaunted, he brushed himself off, fixed his hat, put on a charming smile, and immediately resurrected a store and cattle-buying business in Lincoln. Within two years, he succeeded in convincing everyone that he was a scoundrel, and his business floundered. Murphy began burying his sorrow in liquor, which accelerated his business's demise.

Murphy's partner in crime was James J. Dolan. While Murphy was in a drunken stupor, Dolan seized the moment and bought out Murphy's interest for a pittance. He renamed the nearly bankrupt business the JJ Dolan & Company. Dolan quickly assembled a group of thugs to terrorize local ranchers and farmers into selling their goods to him at low prices. When they were not ostracizing people, Dolan's crew quietly bought stolen cattle from rustlers. For the next year, JJ Dolan had an iron grip on the Lincoln County economy.

In 1876, a wealthy young Englishman named John Tunstall and his Canadian partner, Alexander McSween, came into Lincoln and decided that the area was ripe for a competing mercantile. They founded the Tunstall & McSween Company in 1877 and area residents flocked to their store. The people found their prices fair and the service friendly, which was a welcome change. Conversely, Dolan's business cratered and this caused Dolan's anger to boil.

Dolan particularly disliked Tunstall. He hated his pompous fine suits or the way he elegantly tipped his hat to the ladies as he strolled down the street twirling his walking cane. But most of all, Dolan loathed the sound of his irritating English accent. He cringed each time Tunstall greeted him in the saloon while Dolan played poker with his gang. Tunstall would walk up behind him, slap him on the shoulder, and say, "Jolly good day, old chap! I say. I could use a drink. The pace at work has been frightful! Say what?" Damn, he hated that man!

Of course, the dashing Tunstall was not oblivious to Dolan's irritation. Like a boy tormenting his younger sister, Tunstall completely enjoyed prodding Dolan's ego. Tunstall savored each grimace he produced when he flaunted his success in front of Dolan. McSween cautioned his partner and told him he was playing with fire, but Tunstall was unabashed. To him, his friendly banter was nothing more than intellectual fencing. At least, this was what gentlemen in England would perceive his actions to be.

Dolan was not a gentleman. He had no code of honor and believed that disagreements were best settled with a bullet between his opponent's eyes. He also had a volatile temper he would release at the drop of a hat. Like an active volcano, Dolan's temperature was rising.

McSween was a lawyer and an asthmatic, which proved to be a

valuable combination. When in court and pressed for a defense, McSween could invoke strong sympathy from the jury by lapsing into an asthma attack while in the heat of an emotional delivery. The judge would immediately interrupt the court proceedings and order the bailiff to summon a doctor. McSween would make some feeble attempt to rise off the floor and finish his argument, but the jurors simultaneously stretched out their hands and waved him down. Women became teary and the men nodded their heads at McSween's valiant show of commitment. "The defendant must be innocent," they would say to each other. "Any man who would risk death defending his client must be telling the truth." By the time McSween had recovered enough to stand, the jury had made up their minds and the prosecutor could not provide any evidence, no matter how conclusive, that could make them see differently.

Unfortunately, McSween's tactics backfired in February 1878. A Hispanic woman lost her husband unexpectedly to a massive heart attack. Being a responsible man, her husband had secured a $10,000 life insurance policy to provide for her in the event of his untimely death. Unfortunately, Dolan had forced her husband to purchase a large sum of overpriced cattlefeed from JJ Dolan & Company. According to Dolan, the estate still owed him almost exactly $10,000 when one calculated the interest and the late payment fees. Dolan filed a lien against the insurance policy and began to pressure the woman to release the funds to him.

Desperate, the woman sought McSween's help. McSween quickly took charge and petitioned the court for a hearing. Judge John Wilson granted the request and rounded up eight upstanding citizens to serve as jurors. Since no one particularly cared for Dolan, the jury was heavily biased toward the plight of the widow. Nevertheless, McSween put on a performance that was worthy of a standing ovation. He pulled at the jury's heartstrings as he described the poor widow's plight. He eloquently recounted her husband's upstanding character and forthrightness. Then he ruthlessly tore into Dolan's business practices and exposed his outrageous interest rates and fees. At the crescendo of his delivery, McSween suddenly succumbed to a coughing fit which terminated in a gasping spasm on the floor. He weakly reached for the bannister to pull himself up, but the widow, weeping in sympathy for him, rushed to his side and told him to rest and forget her needs.

The whole scene greatly moved the entire court room—except for Mr. Dolan. Dolan thought that McSween was a farce and a clown, but one look at the jury faces told him that he had lost. His anger boiled over and he shot up from his chair. With teeth and fists clenched, Dolan hissed in a loud and evil voice, "You may have won this time, you Canadian charlatan. But I am going to run you and your English dung-head partner out of town!" Dolan threw a table over and stormed out of the courtroom. He did not even bother to await the jury's verdict.

On February 18, Tunstall was making his usual rounds through his company's holdings. He made a special point of greeting each of his employees by name. This small gesture fostered strong loyalty among the men and they enjoyed discussing the day's business with him. Many of the boys that were in his employ had never had a father figure in their lives and Tunstall fulfilled that need. He counseled them and insisted that they learn to read and write. Once the boys realized that Tunstall actually believed in them, they worked hard to be in his favor.

One boy in particular had taken a shine to Tunstall. His name was William "Billy" Bonney. Billy was a nineteen-year-old ranch hand who had bounced from one foster home to another since his mother died when he was ten. Until meeting Tunstall, he'd had no stable force in his life. He had frequent brushes with the law. He dabbled in petty theft, vandalism, and alcohol abuse. Tunstall recognized that Billy needed direction and positive reinforcement and made a point of seeing him at least once a day. Tunstall would greet him enthusiastically, "I say, kid! How does this world treat you today?"

Billy would flash a boyish smile back and push his stubborn lock of brown hair out of his face before walking over to Tunstall to talk with him. Tunstall's greeting of "kid" stuck with the rest of the crew and, hence, Bonney's nickname was born. The Kid worked for Tunstall for about a year and he developed a deep loyalty to the Englishman.

On this particular winter evening, Tunstall had just completed a visit to the company ranch close to Lincoln. He was bundled up in a tweed coat complete with a matching hat and scarf. Tunstall slapped the Kid on the back and said, "By jove, it is beastly tonight! I think I shall retire to my room with a strong bourbon."

Billy beamed a devilish grin and instinctively pushed his unruly hair back, "Yep. It smells like snow tonight, Mr. Tunstall. I reckon I will be shoveling tomorrow."

Tunstall laughed as he mounted his horse. "I have great faith in that nose of yours. Get a good night's sleep, Kid. Tomorrow will be full of challenges."

Billy suddenly felt a deep foreboding creep through his body that made his hair stand up on the back of his neck. His mind repeated Tunstall's words, *Tomorrow will be full of challenges.* He masked his trepidation and continued to smile as he said, "Ride careful-like, Mr.

Tunstall. See you tomorrow." Tunstall flashed him a thumbs-up sign and prodded his horse into the dark, cold night. The Kid watched the black veil of darkness cover his beloved boss and shivered as he saw its icy fingers grab him. He looked so vulnerable.

Billy continued to gaze down the dark road for several minutes. His instincts told him that something was not right. He shifted his weight uneasily as he stood watching and waiting. Finally, the Kid chided himself for his groundless worry and began turning around to go back to the ranch house when a rifle shot rang out. He froze and felt his blood run cold. The sound came from the road. Billy spun around and began running with all his might. His boots slipped and slid in the packed snow as he pressed on. Ahead, he could barely make out a riderless horse galloping away. As he watched the horse, he almost stumbled over a body in the middle of the road.

The Kid fell to his knees and grabbed the man. He was face down in the snowy road. Billy slowly rolled him over with the deep anxiety of knowing the terrible answer without asking the question. He recognized him immediately. "Oh, dear God! Mr. Tunstall! Mr. Tunstall! Can you hear me?" Tunstall groaned and rolled his eyes up to Billy. Then he let out a final sigh and died in his arms. Billy held Tunstall tight and rocked him as he cried, "No! Oh, God no!" Then the Kid gently laid him back down and removed his hand from his beloved mentor's back. It felt wet and sticky and when he examined it he saw that his hand was coated with blood. Suddenly, he heard another horse bolt from the brush along the roadside. Its rider pushed the horse into a fast gallop and sped toward town.

The sound of running men and the light of swaying lanterns distracted Billy. As they drew closer Billy cried out, "He's dead! He shot him! That damn Dolan killed him. I just know he did!" The lantern light caught the distraught face of William Bonney. It was smeared with blood, dirt, and tears.

The ranch foreman, Dick Brewer spoke first, "Billy! Kid! Are you all right? What happened?"

The Kid cried, "What the hell do you think happened? Either Dolan or one of his henchmen shot Mr. Tunstall in cold blood. I saw him hotfoot off to town. I say we ride right now and catch that son-of-a-bitch Dolan!" Billy's words fired up the men, but Brewer kept his head for the moment.

Brewer held up his hand and said, "Now just hold on a minute. We ride into town right now and the Dolan gang will ambush us just like Mr. Tunstall. No, what we are going to do is give Mr. Tunstall a decent burial and plot our strategy. Then we hit them real hard and final-like. You men understand?" Brewer looked hard at each one.

Everyone but Billy nodded their heads. The Kid's eyes roared like fire. "Look, Billy," continued Brewer, "I thought the world of Mr. Tunstall too, but we can't start running around like a bunch of chickens with our heads cut off, *comprende*? Now give me your word that you will fight with us, not on your own." Billy began to grit his teeth. "I mean it, Billy. Give me your word."

Billy bunched up his hands and quivered with anger. Then he abruptly nodded, turned, and stormed away into the darkness. One of the men tried to follow him, but Brewer caught him by the arm. "Let him go. He has got a lot grief to deal with. Now, someone ride into town and tell Mr. McSween what happened. The rest of you, help me with the body."

Dick Brewer was good to his word. He quickly formed a small army that he coined the "Regulators" whose sole purpose was to rid Lincoln County of the Dolan gang and avenge the death of John Tunstall. They began to systematically hunt down every man known to be loyal to Dolan. On April 1, the Regulators ambushed and gunned down the sheriff, his deputy, and another Dolan sympathizer. The act shocked the entire Territory of New Mexico. Although nobody knew exactly who was involved, everyone took for granted that Billy was there.

Many people felt that revenge was the Regulators' only motive, but Brewer knew that power and free enterprise for Lincoln County were in the balance. If Dolan succeeded in running all competition out of the County, the residents would forever be at the mercy of the unscrupulous JJ Dolan mercantile. As Brewer saw it, the Regulators were waging all-out war for the economic control of the whole County.

Unfortunately, Billy had a narrower view of his mission. According to Billy, Dolan had killed the only father he had ever known. Thus, Dolan was going to pay big time. Billy's vengeance burned like bitter acid in his stomach and changed him into a ruthless killer. Any man who rode with him saw his eyes squint wolflike and an evil grin creep across his face. When he finally cornered his victim, Billy would level his pistol at the man's forehead and say, "This is for Mr. John Tunstall from the Kid."

The bewildered man would reply, "The Kid?"

Billy answered, "Yep! Billy the Kid." With that explanation, Billy would put a bullet between his eyes while he laughed with glee. The whole affair put shivers down the backs of any man watching. It also bolstered the Kid's notoriety.

Both sides aggressively attacked each other. Skirmishes exploded in the surrounding hills and ranches. For the innocent bystander, it was difficult to remain neutral. Men were often forced into a kill-or-be-killed situation when violence erupted on their property. Within one month, Lincoln County was entirely sucked into the fray. Finally, on July 14, 1878, the Regulators and Dolan Company squared off in Lincoln and unleashed five days of fierce fighting. By the evening of July 19, the Regulators had beaten the Dolan gang and scattered the survivors throughout the hills. Regulators sustained heavy casualties during the battle, which included Alexander McSween.

With the breaking of the Dolan mercantile, Brewer called a halt to the killing, but Billy was too consumed by hate to listen. He assembled a splinter group and continued to pursue the remnants of the Dolan gang. Unfortunately, his passion for revenge drove him into a killing spree that was not limited to the Dolan stragglers. Within a very short time, Billy the Kid was a wanted man in the Territory of New Mexico.

On November 2, 1880, Lincoln County elected Pat Garrett as county sheriff. Garrett was an ex-buffalo hunter who had drifted into the area. He had married Apolinaria Gutierrez in January of that year and was finally ready to settle down. Thus, he needed a stable job with a good income and the sheriff position seemed to offer both. Garrett campaigned hard to gain the recognition needed to secure the majority vote. He recognized that the rampant violence sweeping the county was every resident's most pressing concern. He boasted that he was the man who could handle the situation and, in fact, Billy the Kid had once been his friend. This, of course, was a lie, but it sounded good to the voters. After all, who was more qualified to hunt down Billy the Kid than a past friend who knew how he thought?

On December 15, 1880, New Mexico territorial governor Lew Wallace decreed a $500 reward for the capture of Billy the Kid, "dead or alive." It proved to be a powerful incentive and many fortune and fame seekers like Garrett began their pursuit of the Kid. Over the next seven months, Garrett and Billy played cat-and-mouse with each other throughout the Tularosa Valley and surrounding mountains. Garrett even captured Billy once, only to have Billy escape from a jail in Mesilla, New Mexico, and kill both guards Garrett had assigned to watch him.

Finally, on July 13, 1881, Garrett got a tip that Billy's trusted friend Pete Maxwell was ill and near death. Garrett's informant said that Maxwell lay in his bedroom on the ground floor in the northeast corner of Maxwell's house in Fort Sumner. Garrett knew that his luck had finally turned because Billy was sure to visit Maxwell soon. Billy the Kid was a ruthless scoundrel, but he was steadfastly loyal to his friends. This was his major weakness and one Garrett intended to exploit.

During the darkening evening, Garrett slipped into Maxwell's house and hid in his bedroom. Pete Maxwell was too delirious and weak to notice Garrett hunkered in the corner with his pistol drawn. Shortly after midnight, Billy stealthily stepped through the bedroom door. As he walked to the bed, he carefully scanned the room. Months of being pursued like a wild animal had honed his senses to a fine edge. His sixth sense prickled. Something was not quite right.

Billy quietly removed his pistol from his holster. He heard his friend moan and continued to walk slowly toward him. His eye caught a slight movement from the dark corner. Billy cocked his gun and whispered hoarsely, "¿Quién es?" Garrett answered by firing two quick shots. One bullet struck the Kid squarely in the heart. Billy the Kid died with a pistol in his hand and Pat Garrett stepped firmly into stardom.

The next few years were good for Pat Garrett. With the help of others more skilled in literary matters, Garrett published several books on Billy the Kid's exploits and Garrett's heroic deeds. The American public was hungry for stories about the Wild West and ate up every word that Garrett printed.

Soon Garrett got bored with being a pseudo-author and decided to concentrate on ridding the New Mexico Territory of outlaws. He assembled a special group of Texas Rangers in the Fort Stanton area and began a campaign to crush cattle rustlers who operated along the New Mexico-Texas border. At first, the Rangers caught scores of men in the act of stealing cattle. The Rangers killed most of these outright and took only a token few to jail, promptly hanging them. After a few months of Ranger patrols, outlaws decided that cattle rustling in these parts was too dangerous and relocated to less protected areas. Rustler activity plummeted and, once again, Pat Garrett became bored.

What happened next was etched deeply into the minds of area Mexicans for decades to come. The Rangers reverted to rounding up "suspected rustlers" and punishing them on site. The majority of these unfortunate men were Mexican workers wandering across the border in search of their next job. Garrett and his men theorized that unemployed and poor Mexicans represented a huge risk to the New Mexican cattle industry and thus these people should be discouraged from roaming freely in the Territory. How Garrett could rationalize such discrimination and still be happily married to a Hispanic was an unexplained mystery. Nevertheless, the Rangers implemented their hazing across the southern portion of the Tularosa Valley with a vengeance. They hunted the migrants down like they were fleeing animals. The Rangers took bets with each other to see who could shoot the most Mexicans in a single day. They became so callous to the killing that the Rangers even once posed for a photographer and proudly displayed their typical daily catch, mounted on long poles as one would hang dressed deer.

As the years went by, though persecution slowly subsided, the Mexicans' hatred of law officials brewed, and mistrust grew deep within every soul. Over glowing campfires, they passed down terrifying stories of butchery at the hands of the law. Mothers held their babies close to their breast. Children hid behind their fathers and trembled. Men nodded and vowed never to cooperate with American lawmen.

This distrust resulted in Mexicans developing their own internal form of government and organization. Each informal band selected a leader called a *majordomo*. The *majordomo* was usually an elderly man who demonstrated maturity and experience, and possessed a large amount of common sense. People turned to this man for advice on settling squabbles within the group. The *majordomo* was the group's official spokesman to employers when they were seeking better working conditions or when they had a question of pay. Law officers also dealt with this leader when investigating alleged transgressions of a group member. Many times the *majordomo* was the only member of a Mexican group who would admit that he could speak and understand some English.

Garrett's methods of discouraging rustling rankled many residents of New Mexico. In 1890, Garrett ran for sheriff of Chaves County and was soundly defeated. People told Garrett that times had changed and his kind was not welcome in these parts. Garrett felt betrayed and bitterly left New Mexico to live in Texas.

Nine years later, Pat Garrett returned and bought a ranch in the San Andres Mountains on the southwestern side of the Tularosa Valley. Short of cash, Garrett crossed the Organ Mountains through San Agustin Pass to find work in Las Cruces, Doña Ana, and Mesilla. While in Las Cruces, Garrett managed to reestablish ties with old political cronies who had supported his reign of terror when he served with the Rangers.

On December 16, 1901, President Theodore Roosevelt appointed Pat Garrett as the United States Customs Collector at El Paso, Texas. Hispanics and whites of New Mexico and Texas were outraged. They claimed that Roosevelt's reasons for selecting Garrett were his love of Wild West stories and his romanticizing of Garrett's apprehension of Billy the Kid. Garrett's performance as customs collector proved his critics right. His deep-rooted prejudice against Mexicans surfaced frequently when he supervised the Ports of Entry. He bullied families that appeared weak from starvation and told them to go back home where they belonged. He arbitrarily jacked the admission fee up and down daily so that even his own employees were confused on what to charge the hapless immigrants. Even the Port's record keeping became abysmal and unsalvageable.

In December 1905, President Roosevelt had enough of Garrett and refused to reappoint him. Garrett returned to his ranch in the Tularosa Valley. He was restless and determined that it was time to move to Las Cruces, where there was more action and people willing to listen to his stories. He tried to sell his property, but interested parties were few. With his patience wearing thin, Garrett leased his cattle ranch for five years to Wayne Brazel. Brazel promptly imported goats and grazed them on the property.

In January 1908, Garrett found a buyer for his ranch. Ironically, the buyer was James Miller, a renowned cattle rustler and murderer, but Garrett could not care less. He was broke and needed the money badly, so he conveniently overlooked Miller's probable source of income and eagerly encouraged the sale. Miller traveled to the ranch to inspect the property before buying and immediately encountered two problems that threatened to sour the deal—the goats and Mr. Brazel. Miller, a cattleman, despised goats. He viewed them as completely incompatible with cattle. What he saw during his visit reconfirmed his beliefs. The goats had mowed the sparse grasses across the arid pastures to their very roots. The land could no longer support cattle and needed resting.

Mr. Brazel was furious that Garrett would try to sell the property while he still had a valid lease. Brazel told Miller in straightforward talk that he was not interested in canceling his lease and, as long as he was here, the goats stayed. Miller relayed this information to Garrett. Garrett was determined not to let this sale slip through his hands and arranged to drive his wagon back to the ranch to negotiate with Brazel. Unfortunately, Miller had other pressing matters to attend, but he sent his brother-in-law, Carl Adamson, with Garrett to bargain on his behalf.

On February 29, 1908, Garrett and Adamson met with Brazel at the ranch. Brazel seemed unnaturally quiet during their meeting and agreed too quickly to ride with the men back to Las Cruces to finalize the deal with Miller. As they rode back through the desert to San Agustin Pass, Garrett reined in his horses and leapt down from the buckboard. "Gotta take a leak," he announced as he walked off the trail. The sun was high in the blue sky and the day was pleasantly warm and still. Only the hint of a breeze moved among the desert silence. In the distance, the shimmering dunes of the White Sands Desert shone brightly on the horizon. Garrett loved this country and lazily scanned the scenery as he undid his fly. At that very moment,

Pat Garrett heard a faint metallic click from behind. His trained mind instantly told him what was happening and that he was going to die. He never heard the shot that blew his head off.

Adamson was stunned and wheeled on the buckboard to face Wayne Brazel. Brazel calmly chambered another shell in his rifle and said, "I have no beef with you, so take your paw off your pistol or else you will join Mr. Garrett there. I was just taking care of business. Now, I reckon that I ought to be going now." Brazel tipped his hat and rode back in the direction of the ranch and left Adamson to handle the sudden justice that was so common in these parts.

The residents of the Tularosa Valley were tough and sought to solve their problems themselves. When they saw a shady character come on to their property, they sent him packing or else he suffered the consequences. They dealt immediately with thieves, murderers, and other scoundrels. There was little tolerance, particularly if you were Mexican. The unwritten rule was, "Shoot first and ask questions later." This was especially true in Lincoln County and the areas next to the Mescalero Apache reservation. The Mexicans knew this and banded closely together. They all firmly believed that if their *major-domo* could not protect them, they were surely dead.

Chapter 15
Carrizozo

The early Tuesday morning of September 16, 1913, began like every other morning during the past sixty days since Prudenciano Nava had come to the El Paso and Northeastern Railroad as a laborer. Just before dawn, he began to stir under his woolen blankets on the straw bed he shared with his family. His breath steamed above his uncovered face in the cold early morning air of the high desert. Slowly Prudenciano stretched, retrieved an oil lantern from the wall, and lit the wick. As the lamp roared to life, the wavering light seemed to add warmth to the cold interior of the boxcar the Nava and Boca families shared for housing. Prudenciano hated the thought of leaving his warm, cozy nest, but he knew that others would look for him if he did not soon show signs of life. He sighed and gave his soundly sleeping wife an envious glance before flinging the blankets back and wrenching his aching body up. Paz moaned softly under the covers and the children snuggled closer together to compensate for the loss of their father's body heat.

The two families had divided the boxcar with blankets that hung from the roof. The curtain gave the illusion of privacy, but did little to block out sound. Over the past month, each family had learned more details of the other's private life than they cared to admit. The car provided a roof over their heads and a dry place to sleep. The unceasing wind infiltrated dust through the wooden plank walls and covered everything.

The Mexican families who worked for the railroad lived in company "housing" called *colonias*. *Colonias* consisted of a collection of old boxcars the railroad had pulled to sidings close to the work site. The Navas and Bocas were fortunate that their car had been used for hauling freight. Other families had to live in cars that had transported livestock. No matter how hard they scrubbed, they could not rid the planks of the animal stench.

Prudenciano scratched his ragged beard and staggered to his pants and shirt that Paz had hung from a nail on the wall. She had scrubbed them the previous night in a metal tub the company provided to the family. Unfortunately, the clothing was still damp and Prudenciano grimaced at the thought of putting them on in the chilly morning. He shot his wife another glare, but quickly realized that she was oblivious to his anger and he resumed dressing. He noisily sucked in his breath as he slipped each leg into his wet trousers and pulled them up to his waist. The cold seemed to penetrate to the very marrow of his bones. With teeth chattering, he grabbed his shirt, which was equally wet, and quickly put it on.

Now he was thoroughly chilled, which greatly increased his need to urinate. He fumbled for his shoes and shoved his feet in. Then Prudenciano bolted for the sliding cargo door and started to undo his fly. He suddenly stopped and emitted a muffled curse as he remembered the agreement he had made with the *mayordomo*.

The women of the camp, Paz included, bitterly complained to their husbands and then to the *mayordomo* about the men's urinating off the boxcar entrances. It seemed the whole *colonia* was in an uproar over it. The *mayordomo* convinced the men that life would be much easier if they all showed a little restraint and at least did their business behind the camp. Prudenciano felt that this was a challenge to his manhood, but reluctantly agreed to modify his behavior. However, times like these were a true test of his word.

With an almost superhuman effort, Prudenciano jumped down from the boxcar and ran behind it. As he quickly jostled his fly open, he could hear other men also in various phases of relieving themselves. Suddenly, a man swore loudly and Prudenciano looked to his side to see him wetting himself as he tried desperately to pull his member out. He looked incredibly funny and several men who witnessed it had a good morning laugh.

Prudenciano chuckled as he finished his business and rebuttoned his fly. His body heat had warmed his clothing and he felt a little better. His joints and muscles did not seem to ache as much as he made his way back to his boxcar. As he got to the door, he heard a familiar voice call out to him.

"Hey, Nava! What is the matter with you? Do not tell me that you obey the cackling of women! Next thing you know, they will be telling you to squat when you pee!" It was Rafael Silva standing in the entrance of a boxcar he shared with seven other bachelors. He was boldly urinating a steaming stream out the door in full view for everyone to see. "You are going to pee a lot today. I hope you can still stagger off the tracks by the end of the day or else you will wet yourself! Ha! Ha!" Prudenciano smiled and casually waved before he gripped the hand bar to lift himself up into his car. Silva did what he pleased and Prudenciano admired him for it. The *mayordomo* tried to reason with Silva, but it was like talking to a smiling scarecrow. Silva never listened.

Prudenciano parted the curtain to his family's compartment and found Paz wrapped in a wool blanket preparing a hot breakfast for him. He selected a comfortable spot to sit and watch her as she went about her business. She had her hair pulled back into a bun with unruly wisps hanging over her sleep-filled eyes. Paz had taken the glass from the lantern and placed an iron skillet across the flame. Three metal prongs supported the pan, but the makeshift stove was top-heavy. Twice in the past month, lantern stoves had tipped over and almost burnt the boxcars to their axles. The dry wooden floors and walls, straw mattress, and old blankets provided excellent kindling for errant fires. Once started, a fire would rage out of control so quickly that the occupants could barely escape with their lives.

Paz put flour tortillas on the pan, which puffed up with dark splotches when heated. Paz and the other women were grateful for the ground flour the railroad provided them. Although corn tortillas tasted better, she did not have to get on her aching knees to grind the corn meal in her *metate*. When she had a thick stack of hot tortillas wrapped in a cotton cloth, Paz threw two thick slices of bacon onto the skillet. The bacon sizzled loudly as it rendered its juicy fat and finally floated the shriveled remnants. Paz removed the cooked bacon and placed some on a tortilla with mashed beans. She folded it and slowly laid the sandwich in the grease. The grease sizzled again as it accepted the folded tortilla. She carefully fried both sides to a golden brown. Paz repeated the process until she had a stack of piping hot tortilla sandwiches. The smell made Prudenciano's mouth water.

Prudenciano's hunger distracted his thoughts from his aching body. His back and shoulders hurt from long days of swinging a sludge hammer or carrying railroad ties. His hands had developed thick calluses, which were a welcome relief from the normal oozing blisters and raw skin that he had when he had first started working. His fifty-seven-year-old body was feeling its age and there was no other *sobador* in the *colonia* who could massage his throbbing shoulders. He began to rub his right arm when Paz spoke without looking up or stopping her cooking, "I heard Silva calling you." When Prudenciano did not reply, she added, "He is such a filthy dog."

"Silva is all right," Prudenciano said calmly as he rested against the wall.

Paz finished stacking the tortillas and handed the plate to her husband. She asked, "What did he mean by relieving yourself a lot today?" Prudenciano shrugged as he started to wolf down the sandwiches. She watched him warily. Suddenly, her eyes flew open with comprehension. "Today is Mexican Independence Day, ¿qué no?" Prudenciano pretended not to hear and continued munching his food. Paz was not going to let this lie. She pressed the topic. "What happened to your pay last Friday? How come you did not give it to me?" Prudenciano looked up at her and smiled with his mouth full. Paz had learned from experience never to trust him with money. "Where is it?"

Prudenciano sighed and wagged his head toward his leather pouch. He usually carried his lunch, work gloves, and a water jug in it when he traveled to the work site. Paz went over to the wall and removed the pouch from a nail. She immediately began searching through its contents and found a few bills rolled up in an old tobacco pouch. She opened the roll and counted the money. "You are missing half of it. Where is the rest?"

Prudenciano waved vaguely in the air with a half-eaten tortilla and said, "Oh, I bought a few things." This line of questioning was starting to rankle him.

Paz pointed a finger at him and said, "You bought liquor, ¿qué no?" A week ago, the mayordomo had warned everyone to be on their best behavior during this Independence Day. Only a year ago, New Mexico had become the forty-seventh state in the Union and it still had some rough edges to smooth out. The mayordomo did not want any trouble and he was smart enough to recognize the ingredients of a major-class catastrophe among his people. They were working only one mile south of Carrizozo, where alcohol was available. A Mexican holiday was at hand that was noted for the consumption of copious amounts of hard liquor. And, finally, the men were paid in cash only a few days before the holiday. All of these elements together had the potential of creating havoc. Paz had listened to the mayordomo's lecture and followed the lesson with a sharp warning to Prudenciano. Now it appeared that all warnings had fallen on deaf ears. The men had spent at least half their earnings on liquor and now they were going to celebrate Independence Day their way.

Paz raised her voice and put fire behind her words, "You are going to get yourself in big trouble and your family will suffer from it!"

Prudenciano bristled under her charge. He had heard enough for one day. "I worked hard for two months straight. I deserve a little fun and I do not need you to tell me how to spend my money or when to drink!" He got up abruptly and ripped his pouch away from Paz's hands. He stuffed the rest of the tortilla sandwiches into it and cinched the pouch closed with the drawstring. He plucked his hat from the wall and turned to leave.

"Papa!" Prudenciano stopped and looked down at the bed. The loud argument had wakened Augustine. With sleep in his eyes, he got up and scampered to his father on his toes. The boy had proved to be an early walker. At one year old, he was literally running. He also was extremely fond of his father and would wait impatiently all day for him to return from work. Augustine latched on to Prudenciano's leg and begged to be held. Prudenciano's heart squeezed for a moment as he scooped him up and nuzzled him with his beard. Augustine threw his arms around his neck and squeezed him tight. It took all his reserve to pry his son's arms from his neck and set him down on the mattress. Prudenciano gathered his stuff and jumped out the sliding door without looking back.

The men assembled at the section house before loading onto the flatbed trailers that would take them north to the work site. The *colonia* was located at a railroad siding called Jake's Springs, which was about nine miles south of Carrizozo. A shallow well provided water to a tower that stored it for steam locomotives. The water was sweet and flowed year around. The railroad took advantage of this source to support a section foreman and his family and the needs of a mobile workforce.

The section foreman was Bill J. Ayers. He was a jovial and easygoing man. Never one to make waves, he was easy to please and often overlooked minor infractions his Mexican crew might have caused. He had raised his family at Jake's Springs and had just married his daughter to a local rancher only a year ago. He loved the land and the little prestige that his position gave him. He always walked with a bounce in his step that seemed out of character for his bulky carriage.

Ayers stood on his porch step with his hands on his hips, his hat pushed back, and a smile on his brown face. He was wearing freshly washed work clothes. He exuded the feeling that today was going to be great. As the men assembled in front of him, he acknowledged each one with a nod. When the elderly man who was their leader indicated that they were all there, Ayers addressed them in Spanish.

"*Buenos días, amigos,*" he began with a gringo accent. "Today should be a grand day indeed. We will continue working the soft section just north of Polly Flats." Polly Flats was another siding about three miles south of Carrizozo. "You men are making good progress on replenishing the gravel ballast and replacing the damaged ties. Remember that all rails must be secured by the time the five-thirty work train comes to pick you up. The Fox will be coming down at seven o'clock in the evening and it cannot be delayed."

The Fox was the southbound, nonstop freight train to El Paso. Some called it the "Limited." Others called it the Fox or "*El Zorro.*" It usually blew by the *colonia* in the early evening at a very high rate of speed. It carried freight bound for El Paso from paying customers. The freight haul generated needed revenue to feed the cash-hungry El Paso and Northeastern Railroad. Thus, the railroad would severely punish any work crew that caused it to be delayed.

Ayers asked, "Any questions?" He looked at all the Mexican faces staring blankly at him. As usual, no one spoke or even produced a comprehending expression. Ayers always half expected that someone sometime would at least say something, but no one ever did. He took a good look at his crew. One man stood out among them. He was at least a full six inches taller with a powerfully built chest and arms. His long, flowing hair and beard were streaked with gray, which bespoke his age. Standing next to him was a younger man with a cocky smile. Ayers could see that this younger one was a troublemaker. He made a mental note to keep an eye on him.

Ayers turned toward the elderly leader. His name was Antonio Ramos and Ayers depended on him to keep the Mexican crews in line. *The Mexicans called him something*, thought Ayers as he rubbed his chin. *What was it? Their mayordomo?* Ramos seemed to read his mind and nodded that everyone understood. Ayers sighed and realized that this was all the acknowledgment he would get. With a wave of his arm, he dismissed them and returned to the section house.

"All right, men," announced Ramos, "follow me to the train." The men turned and shuffled in single file to two flatbed cars pulled by a small tractor. The railroad had fitted the tractor with rail wheels so that it could travel the tracks unimpeded. The men climbed aboard the cars and sat or lay on the wood floor. When all had boarded, the engineer fired up the tractor and pulled the cars onto the main line and headed north to the work site.

The day was beginning to warm. The birds sang sweetly and small puffy clouds danced in the deep blue sky. Sierra Blanca soared majestically in the southeast. It seemed to fill the entire sky. The cars began to sing a rhythmic clacking as they picked up speed and warm air blew across the men. Some held their hats tight to their heads to keep them from sailing away.

Telegraph wires were strung over posts along the east side of the tracks. The railmen used a pole with two clips to connect onto the wires and send a telegraph message. This way they could report track conditions, their position, and receive lineup reports for other traffic. On the west side and offset by about half a mile was the newly built road from Carrizozo to Alamogordo. Every once in a while, the men would see a Ford Model T truck rattle down the road with a cloud of dust behind it.

Prudenciano was in a great mood today. The weather was nice and made the train ride enjoyable. The anticipation of drinking all day brewed within him. He smiled to himself as he looked out across the *Mal Pais* and toward the Organ Mountains in the west. He did not hear Silva come over to him until he spoke.

Silva laughed and said, "Nava, are you ready to have a good time?"

"*Sí*," answered Prudenciano. "Are you sure that you can buy enough liquor?"

"No problem," assured Silva. "I got it fixed. I will take one of the wheelbarrows from the site and wheel it into town. I have got enough money from you and the rest of the men to buy a full load. I will be back by noon and we can start celebrating."

Prudenciano smiled back at Silva. His beard and hair blew sideways in the wind. "We will have a grand time." They continued to chat about various topics until they passed another siding named Polly Flats. Polly was located about seven miles north of Jake's Springs. It provided a turnout for work trains and other equipment to get off the main line and allow passenger and freight trains to pass. The work train continued another two miles north to the work site. It was identified by abandoned wheelbarrows, tools, and stacks of new and old ties and rails. Only a mile north of the site was Carrizozo, which was easily seen in the distance. The train slowed and gradually came to a stop. The men jumped off the wagons and began to organize around the equipment.

Antonio Ramos divided the labors into units. One team pried the rail pins and metal saddles from the ties to release the rails. When this was done, others removed the rotten ties. Another team dumped fresh gravel over the old ballast and releveled the base. The men dragged new ties onto the ballast and pinned the rails in place.

The men assembled into teams and became absorbed into their tasks. Only a few noticed Silva casually grab a wheelbarrow and trot off toward town.

———•••••———

Ramos yelled sternly, "This is not right!" His rebuke fell on deaf ears. Ever since Silva had returned heavily loaded with whiskey and tequila, the men had been out of control. They threw down their tools and ripped into the bottles. Shouts of "*¡Viva México!*" blasted into the air and were often followed by a mighty swig. The Mexican

Independence Day celebration had started. The *mayordomo* threw his hands up in disgust and sat by himself in the sparse shade of a gravel berm.

By three in the afternoon, the men were roaring drunk. There were still several bottles left, but the men's rate of consumption fell and dribbled as the afternoon progressed. Many were already spinning into the ground and collapsing in a drunken stupor. Absolutely no work had been done during the afternoon. Ramos fretted silently that *Señor* Ayers would pay them a visit and fire them all, but the day wore on and the foreman did not arrive.

Finally, at five o'clock Ramos corralled two men who could barely stay on their feet and forced them to secure the few rails they had removed during the morning. By five thirty, the work train backed up from Polly Flats to pick up the crew. Ramos kicked and dragged the inebriated men onto the flatcars. Only Silva and Prudenciano defied him.

"Leave us," growled Prudenciano when Ramos ordered them to the cars. "We still have two bottles to finish."

Silva chimed in, "*Sí*, let us be. We will either walk back or stay here for the night. We are not done drinking." Ramos thought about it for a moment and then shrugged.

"So be it," he said. "I cannot make you come home. I hope you rot out here for all I care." Ramos jumped up on the last car and signaled to the engineer to drive on. Puzzled, the engineer looked back at the two men, each with a bottle in his hand, and leering at him. He shook his head in disgust, put the tractor in gear, and pulled forward.

"Have a nice trip," yelled Silva as the train picked up speed and moved away. Prudenciano laughed and threw a rock at the train. It corkscrewed and struck the tracks behind the cars. Ramos took one last look behind at the two belligerent men. He saw them laughing and making obscene gestures at him as they shrank into the distance.

Ramos shook his head in disgust and began sitting down when he noticed something brewing in the west. He saw massive thunder-heads building up over the dark Organ Mountains and moving eastward. The clouds were bruised deep blue with rain and boiled with thunder. *Bueno*, thought Ramos. *A cold dark night with a good rainstorm will beat some sense into those idiots.* With that thought, Ramos smiled smugly and hunkered down with the rest of the men.

Ben Cook wearily slowed the long freight train and blew the whistle before they entered Carrizozo. He drove the company's Limited and he was nervous about rolling through the upcoming town. Although the railroad gave him first priority on the line, this did not prevent residents from strolling in front of the train. Once he had even slammed into one of those newfangled motorized cars that stalled across the tracks. He hated blasting through towns with thousands of tons of freight pushing him forward.

He applied the brake lever with care and bled some steam from the cylinders. The train's velocity ebbed slightly, but its momentum continued to shove it forward. His fireman, Bill Leggett, stood next to him and watched the steam pressure gauge register the falling pressure. "Can't let it go too far under," Leggett said as he pushed his gray cap off his dirty forehead with a thick leather glove. "I'll be shoveling coal till Alamogordo to get it back up." As if to punctuate his statement, he stabbed his scoop shovel into the floor and leaned on its handle.

Cook replied, "I know, but I can't have us blowing through these towns either. Somebody is going to get hurt."

Leggett responded, "Nobody is going to be out this time of day. Just take a look at that storm brewing out there. Yes sir, it's going to be a doozy." Cook looked to the west where Leggett was pointing. He could see the dark, ominous clouds rumbling toward them. Already, big globs of rain pelted the windscreen.

Cook said, "I reckon you're right." He took out his pocket watch from behind his bib overalls and flipped open the cover. It read six fifty-eight. Right on time. They were approaching the edge of town and the place looked deserted. "No one in their right mind would be outside with a storm like that coming. The work party on the other side of town should be long gone by now, too. Why don't you stoke up the furnace a bit?"

Leggett took a deep breath as he made sure that his leather gloves were on tight. Then he bent over and slowly opened the firebox. The oxygen-starved fire seemed to leap alive as the heavy metal door swung wide. A solid wall of heat smacked Leggett in the face. He could feel his skin shrink in its presence. Leggett took a step back and readied himself to start throwing scoopfuls of coal from the holding bin into the fire. As he was about to pitch his first shovelful, he heard Cook yell out, "Do you see that up there? Looks like the track is out! Prepare to stop!"

Leggett barely had time to shut the firebox and brace himself as Cook applied the brakes and let the steam out of the pistons. His last wild thought was, *What the hell did Ben see?*

Prudenciano's and Silva's fun lasted about two seconds after the work train disappeared in the south. Then they heard the rumble of distant thunder from the west and spied the storm rolling across the *Mal Pais* toward them. They stood there with their mouths open and their half-drunk bottles at their sides watching the calamity unfold in front of them. It took a while for their drunken brains to comprehend that their private party was going to be rudely interrupted. Once the situation was fully realized, they immediately started running in the direction of the vanished train. After a fruitless, staggering run of only a few feet, they immediately realized several facts. First, the men were not coming back for them. Second, they were going to be very wet and very cold soon. Third, and most important, they were too drunk to walk back to Jake's Springs.

Like most inebriated men who suddenly realize that they are in way over their heads, they sat down in the middle of the tracks and sought solace in their drink. Prudenciano groused, "Why did you make me stay here with you?"

Silva snickered with bitter sarcasm and replied, "Right. I made you stay here and finish the bottle. Do not make me laugh." Prudenciano could be so dumb sometimes. Silva took another swig and grimaced as the brown liquid burned down his throat. The drink seemed to bring his world into focus. He thought, *Why is it that I have to think of what to do all the time? I guess we will sit here until someone comes.* He picked up a stone and threw it down the tracks. They made a pitiful scene of two dejected men sitting in the middle of the tracks with nowhere to go.

Suddenly Silva's face brightened and he yelled out, "*¡Dios mío!* That's it! *El Zorro* is coming! Get up, Prudenciano. We have work to do."

Prudenciano seemed dazed. "What do you mean we have work to do? How can *El Zorro* help us?"

"Yi! Yi! Yiiiii … !" exclaimed Silva. "Don't you get it? The train will come right through here in about an hour. It could take us right to the *colonia* in style. We all work for the same company, so it is all right that they give us a ride, *¿qué no?*" Prudenciano nodded as he tried to follow the logic. "So," continued Silva, "what we need to do is build a signal fire across the tracks so they know to stop and pick us up. Simple."

Prudenciano did not know if it was the liquor or Silva's persuasive words that convinced him that his plan would work, but it gave him some hope of getting home tonight. He growled, "Let's get this fire built," and forced himself to stand. He took one last gulp from his bottle and threw it in the direction of the oncoming storm as a show of defiance. It shattered against the rocks and the storm seemed to answer by releasing a bolt of lightning in the distance.

Silva and Prudenciano staggered back to the work area and stacked some old rail ties across the tracks. With an old axe, Prudenciano whacked chunks and splinters off for kindling. Silva made sure that he stayed far away from Prudenciano as he waved the axe over his head and took wide arcing swings. Soon they had a stack of kindling to work with. The wind gusted stronger and the smell of rain was thick in the air. Neither had a watch, but judging from the decreased daylight and the impeding storm, they knew that they had to light the fire now and try to keep it burning until the train arrived.

Starting a fire in the ripping wind would be a challenge. The wind tore at the tender, so they stacked a few more ties upwind to provide a shelter. Prudenciano fumbled in his pants pockets and found two old matches. This was all they had, so they had to be careful. Silva used his pocketknife to shave thin slices of wood into a small pile. Satisfied that he had enough, he stretched his hand up to Prudenciano for the matches. Prudenciano gave them to him without hesitation. Silva struck one against the rail and the match burst into flames. He quickly placed it under the shavings. A blast of wind poured around the rail ties and blew the infant fire out.

"Damn!" cursed Silva. He pointed to the pile of ties close by and shouted so his voice could be heard over the wind, "Drag two more ties over here and stack them alongside the others. Hurry!" Prudenciano opened his mouth to protest, but a brilliant flash of lightning caught his words in his throat. The thunder that quickly followed was deafening. The storm was very close now. Prudenciano muttered something unintelligible and ambled off to fetch the rail ties. Although it usually took two men to carry a tie, Prudenciano easily dragged both back by tucking one under each arm. He dropped them next to the wind screen and stood up to catch his breath. The rain was now softly pelting his face. It felt good.

Silva yelled, "Stack them now!" Prudenciano made a face of annoyance, but obeyed Silva's command. When he was done, the extra ties provided a wider shelter for the fire. Silva took the last match and struck it against the rail. It ignited and Silva cupped his hand around the little flame to protect it. He moved very slowly toward the woodpile and carefully fed it to the wood shavings. The flames licked the wood and gradually grew larger. With precision and patience, he added larger pieces of wood and nurtured the fire. Soon, the fire had enough strength to fend for itself and started devouring the large rail ties. The creosote-saturated wood burned hot and produced an oily smoke that could be seen for miles.

"Now we must wait, *amigo*," said Silva as he wiped the smoke and rain out of his eyes with his shirtsleeve. "*El Zorro* will be along soon."

Prudenciano responded, "I hope so or we are going to get very wet." As if on cue, they suddenly heard a train whistle blow from the far side of town. They turned in the direction of the sound and strained their eyes through the blowing dust and rain. Within a few moments, the train emerged from the town's edge. The enormous steam engine pierced the storm with its bright headlight. The train looked like a giant cyclops boring down on them. Thick black smoke streamed behind its black stack.

Silva let out a loud whoop. "It's here! It's here! It won't be long now. What did I tell you, Nava?" Prudenciano was deeply impressed with Silva's shrewdness. He smiled broadly and wished he had not thrown his last bottle away. This moment surely deserved a drink.

The train appeared to slow slightly. Suddenly, a whoosh of white steam belched from the stack and the engine emitted an ear-splitting screech as its metal wheels locked and skidded on the metal rails. The engineer applied the maximum amount of brakes allowable without causing a derailment. Thousands of tons of freight resisted the engine's attempts to stop and rammed it forward, but the engine fought valiantly and the train slowly bled off its speed. However, to Prudenciano and Silva, it seemed to rumble toward them like a charging bull. It filled the sky in front of them. Silva screamed, "Look out! It's going to hit us!" They jumped off the west side of the tracks as the screeching train slowly moved by and collided with their signal fire. The cattle-catcher deftly plowed the burning wood harmlessly to the side. The train continued another hundred feet before stopping.

With the braking sounds gone, the night became eerily quiet except for the raging storm. Chunks of burning wood were scattered along the tracks and crackled brightly in the wind. The engine chugged softly and deeply as if it was sulking from mistreatment. Silva grabbed Prudenciano's arm and tugged him forward, "Let's go." They bumbled toward the pilot house.

As they approached the engine, two men leaned over the side and peered down at them. Each wore blue bib overalls, a long-sleeved shirt, and a blue cap. The smaller man wore very thick leather gloves and held a scoop shovel in his right hand. His forehead was caked with soot. The larger man yelled out, "Is there something wrong with the tracks? Is there some sort of trouble?"

Prudenciano and Silva looked at them with uncomprehending stares. Prudenciano turned to Silva and asked, "What did he say? Can you speak any English?"

Silva smiled back and said, "A little. I will handle this. Watch." He grabbed the metal ladder and climbed up to the men. Prudenciano watched from below as the men stepped back and gave Silva room to enter. When Silva's feet hit the metal floor and he took one look at their wary faces, he knew he had his work cut out for him. He opened his arms wide and gave them one of his famous Rafael Silva smiles and said, "¡Hola! ¿Qué pasa, amigos?" His alcohol-scented breath wafted over the men and left no doubt about the Mexican's condition.

Severe doubts about the nature of the emergency began to creep into Ben Cook's mind. He turned to his fireman and asked, "What the hell did he just say?"

Bill Leggett shrugged his shoulders and replied, "I think he said 'Hello' and some sort of greeting afterward."

"Well, what the hell does he want?" asked Cook with anger rising in his voice. He had no time for a couple of drunk Mexicans. The company would kick his tail but good if they found out that he had stopped the Limited for these two.

Leggett pushed back his grimy hat and faced Silva. "Who are you? What do you want? *Comprende?*"

The only word that Silva fully understood was *Comprende.* Silva never relinquished his drunkenly sincere smile. He pointed to himself and said two of the few English words that he knew, "Good worker." This was Silva's attempt to tell them that he worked for the railroad.

"Damn," exclaimed Leggett, "I think he wants a job!" Silva knew that he had made some sort of impression, so he nodded in agreement and started pointing south. "You know," continued Leggett as he thoughtfully rubbed his chin, "they just might be from that work camp over at Jake's Springs. What do you think, Ben?"

Silva heard the camp's name and vigorously began nodding his head in affirmation and chanting, "*Sí! Sí! Sí!* Jake's Springs! Jake's Springs!"

Cook took off his cap and wiped his balding head as he studied Silva. "Well, I reckon that makes about as much sense as anything else," he said as he put his hat back on. "This is a work section. Bill, you stay here and watch these two while I go back and wire the Jake's Springs section house to check this out." Cook then looked over the side at Prudenciano. He thought, *Damn, he's a big one.* He pointed down to Prudenciano and said, "You stay right there, got it?" Prudenciano did not understand a single word he said, but got the general idea to stay put. He just stared back without comment. "Watch that guy down there, too," ordered Cook. "Don't let him up for anything." Satisfied that he had things under control, Cook climbed down on the other side of the engine and began walking back to the caboose where he stored the telegraph rod for communications.

Silva started to panic. He did not like the sound of the big man's voice and how he pointed at Prudenciano. Silva thought, *I bet he is going to get the sheriff.* This notion gave him a queasy feeling. Many stories were circulating around the *colonia* about the gringo law and how they always treated the Mexican with a ruthless hand in these parts. Silva felt that he had to convince these men that he meant no harm, but in his haste to explain the situation further, he managed to do the wrong thing. He stepped closer to the man and tried to pat him on the back.

Leggett responded by knocking Silva's hand away and brandishing his shovel threateningly in front of him. Silva took offense at the rebuff and his hot temper flared. The hard liquor clouded his mind and he exploded violently. Silva swung his fist wildly at Leggett. Leggett ducked under the punch and bunted Silva hard across the head with the shovel handle. The blow stunned Silva and caused him to see stars. The lightning cracked overhead and wind drove the rain unmercifully against the train. Blind with fury, Silva leaped at Leggett to bowl him over. Leggett had the enormous advantage of being sober. He anticipated Silva's charge even before he jumped. He stepped aside and let Silva's outstretched body fly by and slam into the wall. Then Leggett drove the handle of his shovel into Silva's lower back. Silva let out a screech and hung partly over the side before slowly sliding backward onto the floor in excruciating pain.

Silva's yell caught Ben Cook's attention. He turned just in time to see Silva draped over the pilothouse railing before falling back in. Cook thought, *Damn, they're fighting! I shouldn't have left them alone.* He ran back to the engine and climbed aboard. He saw Silva prostrated on the floor with Leggett standing over him with his shovel. "Bill," yelled Cook, "what the hell is going on here?"

Leggett looked up and said, "He started fightin' for no good reason. So I pasted him one." Silva looked up and saw Leggett distracted so he decided to take full advantage of the situation. He lashed out and kicked Leggett soundly in the groin. Leggett doubled over with a look of shock and agony on his face.

Cook was outraged and kicked Silva hard enough to skid him across the floor to the firebox. The blow almost knocked Silva unconscious. Leggett hissed, "I am going to kill that son-of-a-bitch!" He hobbled over to the firebox and opened the door. The heat and fumes engulfed Silva and ripped him back to reality. He looked up and saw the fire before him. Fear rippled through his body and enabled him to scream out at the top of lungs, "Prudenciano! Help me! They are trying to kill me!"

Prudenciano had been dancing impatiently alongside the engine. He could tell that something was wrong. The rain soaked him and he was tired of waiting. When he heard Silva cry out to him, Prudenciano leaped up the ladder and vaulted over the side. He saw the two men standing over Silva in front of the open firebox and bolted into action. He grabbed the bigger man with one hand and flung him hard against the wall. The impact drove the air out of Cook's lungs. He slid down to the floor gasping for breath.

Before Prudenciano could turn his attention to the smaller man, Leggett jumped back and swung his shovel at him like a battle axe. Prudenciano took the blow on his forearm and wrenched the shovel out of Leggett's hands. He twisted the big scoop shovel around and swung it with both hands at Leggett. The scoop caught Leggett across the side of his head and he went down hard.

Slumped on the floor, Cook looked up and saw the crazed expression on Prudenciano's face in the dying firelight. He stood towering over Leggett. He looked invincible with the powerful shovel in his hands and the wild wind blowing through his long hair. His body trembled from adrenaline coursing through his veins. It transformed him into a primitive creature. Prudenciano could not resist the fighting urge. He lifted the shovel above his head and swung with all his might and hit Bill Leggett at the base of the skull. The edge of the scoop tore his right ear off. Blood gushed from the wound and flooded the floor.

Cook gasped, "You murdering swine! You killed him!" The savage act galvanized him. He saw a ball-peen hammer hanging from a rack on the wall close to him. He grabbed it and swung it at Prudenciano. The blow hit Prudenciano in the hand and caused him to drop the shovel.

Silva yelled, "Run, Prudenciano!" Prudenciano looked to where Silva shouted and saw him going over the rail. He looked back just in time to avoid a deadly hammer swing. His hand throbbed and fear began to replace his aggression. He jumped over the rail and caught a ladder rung. Suddenly, his vision filled with a thousand bright stars. The pain seemed to rip his body apart. He squinted and saw Cook smack his head again with the hammer. The pain caused waves of nausea to ripple through him. Prudenciano felt his hands slip off the rail. The hammer struck home again and Prudenciano fell to the ground unconscious.

Silva cried, "*¡Dios mío!* We can't stay here. Wake up. We must run now." Silva lifted Prudenciano's head up and saw the blood racing down from the top of his scalp. The rain caused bright red rivulets to flow across his face. Prudenciano moaned and slowly opened eyes. Silva coaxed, "Come on, man. We have to go now." Silva slipped his shoulder under Prudenciano's arm and started dragging him away. Gradually, Prudenciano began to recover and started staggering forward. Together, they stumbled across the road and into the falling night.

Ben Cook shouted an obscenity at them and watched them disappear into the *Mal Pais* as the storm reached its climax. The raging rain seemed to swallow them up and gradually the sporadic lightning ceased to show any trace of them. He stood there for a moment until he heard a soft moan from behind. "Good Lord, Bill! You're alive! Stay right there and I will telegraph for help." Cook jumped off the engine and raced back for the caboose. Time was critical if he was going to save Bill and capture those scoundrels, and Cook wanted them bad.

––––—•••••—––––

Trainmaster Harold S. Fairbanks was a very unhappy man. He had been relaxing comfortably in his modest home until the Carrizozo section foreman banged on his door and reported an attempted holdup of the Limited just south of town, with a fireman injured. Through protests and ranting from his wife, he hurriedly threw on his coat and fired up his brand-new Model T Ford. He picked up Deputy Sheriff Albert T. Roberts and another fireman to replace the wounded one and drove quickly out of town. The hard rubber tires jarred the passengers violently as they plowed through water-filled potholes. The storm had passed, but a light drizzle continued to fall and blurred their vision through the windshield. The night air was damp and cold.

Fairbanks hunched his shoulders in an attempt to conserve his body heat as he drove. He grumbled, "Why did this have to happen on my watch? Just a few more months and I would have been out of this godforsaken country. Then all hell could break loose for all I care. Emma is never going to let me forget about this." It had been his choice to take a promotion and relocate to Carrizozo. He thought that the increased responsibilities and more pay would compensate for moving to a rough little town. However, Fairbanks had quickly learned the golden rule that most husbands learn in married life. That is, if your wife is not happy, you are not happy. Emma disliked Carrizozo from the first minute that she set foot in the town and never let her husband forget it. Now she would use this holdup as her latest weapon in her arsenal of insults. Fairbanks just shuddered at the thought of it.

Fairbanks directed the Limited to continue to the Polly Flats siding to clear the main line and wait for help. Thus, he had to drive a few miles south of the actual holdup site to where the train was parked to pick up the injured man and drop off the new fireman. Officer Roberts was anxious to start looking for the perpetrators, but he first had to get the suspects' description from the engineer and determine exactly what happened. He also knew that his chances of finding them in the pitch-black night were slim. He would probably gather a posse and mount a full search with Sheriff Hyde first thing in the morning.

The fireman broke into the thoughts of Fairbanks and Roberts by abruptly saying, "I'd slow down now if I was you, Mr. Fairbanks. I recollect that Polly Flats is real close and we just might mosey on by it if we are not careful-like." The men strained their eyes toward the railroad tracks that they knew were about a half mile to their left. All they could see was inky blackness. Suddenly the fireman yelled out, "Over there! Do you see it? A lantern flash." Fairbanks stopped the car and killed the headlights. After a few seconds, their eyes adjusted and a faint glow appeared in the distance. It seemed to float supernaturally ten feet off the ground. Then the lantern moved and briefly lit the entire pilothouse. It was the train.

"Well," said Officer Roberts, "let's walk over there and figure out what happened." They got out of the car and sloshed across the wet ground to the train. The mud caked the men's shoes and pants. The big black engine finally emerged from the darkness when they were only a few feet away from it.

Fairbanks called, "Hello, Mr. Cook, where are you?"

Cook cried, "Up here!" His voice sounded thick with relief that help had finally arrived. The men climbed the ladder and entered the pilothouse. They found the floor slippery with blood and Bill Leggett lying on his back with his head heavily bandaged. His face looked ghastly pale by the light of the dying embers in the firebox. They all stopped and stared for a second. Cook broke their silence. "You gotta catch the son-of-bitches that did this."

Officer Roberts nodded and said, "Yep, we will do just that. But first, we gotta get this man to a doctor and I need to get a statement from you on what happened, Okay?" Cook took a deep breath to relax and nodded. "Good," continued Roberts. "Now help us lift him up and carry him to the car. Then we will talk while they take him into town."

The men struggled to lift Leggett from the engine and gently lower him to the ground. Fairbanks had had the presence of mind to bring a stretcher and they used it to carry the wounded man to the truck. Officer Roberts turned to Fairbanks and said, "Take this man to the doctor. Then come back and get me. I should be done interviewing Mr. Cook by then." Fairbanks tipped his hat goodbye and drove back to Carrizozo.

"Well now," said Roberts in a very professional manner to Cook, "let's go back and discuss what happened." They walked back to the train in the thick darkness. Roberts, Cook, and the fireman climbed aboard the engine.

While the fireman busied himself with shoveling fresh coal into the firebox, Officer Roberts began his questioning. He had a pencil and a pad of paper ready to scribble notes. "So tell me, Mr. Cook, just what happened here?"

"Well," replied Cook as he took off his cap and wiped his forehead with the back of his hand, "as we left Carrizozo, I saw a fire across the tracks and two men waving their arms for us to stop. Since it was a work area, I thought something was wrong with the tracks, so I stopped the train."

Roberts looked up from his writing with a puzzled expression. "Okay. You stopped the Limited because you thought that someone was warning you that the tracks were out. Wasn't that kind of unusual? I mean, don't you usually get line reports about these sorts of things?"

Cook instinctively crossed his arms in defensive posture and replied, "Yes, damn it, it was unusual, but sometimes things slip through the cracks. I decided to play it safe and there is nothing wrong with that."

Roberts shrugged and returned to writing his notes. "You stopped the train. Now what happened?"

Cook continued, "Two Mexicans approached the train." He had the sinking feeling that Roberts was not going to file a very favorable report on his performance.

"What did they look like?"

"The one that did all the talking was a small guy in his thirties. A real cocky bastard. The other one was a great big son-of-a-bitch. He is the one that busted up Bill. They were both drunk as hell."

"Uh huh," mumbled Roberts as he jotted it all down. "What did they want? Did they take anything?"

Cook replied awkwardly, "Well, no, they didn't take anything. We kind of thought that they wanted a ride to Jake's Springs."

Roberts lifted an eyebrow in surprise and asked, "They just wanted a ride? That's it? What was the fight about?"

Cook shifted his weight uneasily as he sought to say the right words. "I don't rightly know what caused the fight. I left Bill alone with the smaller one to go back and telegraph Jake's Springs to see if they were missing two workers when all hell broke loose. I ran back to the engine to find Bill fighting with the Mexican. Then the big guy came aboard and beat the hell out of us. He hit Bill with the shovel when he was already down!" Cook paused for a second and added, "He had no reason to do that. The guy is a murderer. I got a few licks at him with a hammer, though."

"Really?" asked Roberts as he busily wrote. "Did you hurt him?"

Cook replied with a bit of pride, "I think I nailed him good once or twice in the head." This was the only good news that he had to offer this night. "I'm sure I rung his bell."

Silence filled the pilothouse as Roberts continued to write down Cook's statement. The fireman pretended not to pay attention to the interview and kept shoveling coal and adjusting the airflow into the firebox. He made an exaggerated show of reading the pressure gauge to mask his eavesdropping. Finally, Roberts signaled his completion by heavily planting the final period on the pad. He looked at the blood-stained floor and asked, "Well, I have one last question. Did you actually send that telegram to Jake's Springs?"

"No," replied Cook, "I never got the chance."

Roberts said, "Then do it. Maybe Mr. Ayers can identify the men responsible and hold them." Officer Roberts had a hunch that they might show up there later that night.

The torrential rain almost drowned them as they pitched over the embankment and tumbled down into the creek bed below. The usually dry bed was now a tumultuous stream that blasted them with cold water. Silva could feel its power rising as they let it flow over their beaten bodies. He wiped the mud from his eyes and squinted in the feeble light at his partner's prostrated body. Prudenciano could barely keep his head above the water. His head had large, swollen contusions that still bled. Silva could tell that he was suffering from a severe concussion.

Silva croaked, "Nava." When no reply came, Silva shook Prudenciano softly and said, "We got to get up. This creek is rising and it will swallow us up if we stay any longer."

He could barely see Prudenciano slowly nod his head. Finally he whispered, "Help me." Silva reached deep within himself for strength and pushed his stiff and aching body to stand against the current. When he secured a foothold on the creek bottom, he leaned over and grabbed Prudenciano by the shoulders. Then he leaned back and pulled Prudenciano to his feet. The big man swayed as he stood hunched over. He was barely conscious.

Silva was scared. They had been stumbling in the pouring rain and darkness for hours and he had no idea where they were. He tried to stay parallel to the road and head south, but the darkness gave few clues to his success. The country was rugged and the rain made the hills slick with mud. He felt the cold creep deep into his bones and his teeth chattered uncontrollably. To complicate his predicament, the man to whose strength he had become accustomed to see him through any hardship was gravely hurt. Silva had no one now but himself to get him out of this jam. It was a lonely feeling.

Silva slid his arm under Prudenciano's shoulder and helped steady him as they waded across the creek. "Hold on, Nava," wheezed Silva as they struggled up the other bank, "we are almost there. In a few minutes, you will be in your own bed with Paz in your arms. Sounds *muy bueno*, eh *amigo*?" Prudenciano gave no acknowledgment that he had heard him. His big head hung forward and swung with every step.

Silva thought, *We won't last much longer. Where in God's name are we?* His body convulsed with a massive fit of shivering. He fought to control himself, but it greatly weakened him. Through his blurred vision he saw a flash of light on his left. Not trusting his numbed mind, he stopped and blinked the rain out of his eyes. He stood still for a few moments and strained his eyes to see through the darkness. This time, several soft lights appeared and slowly ebbed away. He shouted with joy, "The *colonia*! Look, Nava. We made it!" Prudenciano's only response was to nod slowly. His breath was ragged.

Together they slogged their way to the camp. As they got closer, they could hear men's voices and an unusual amount of activity for this time of night. Although this was definitely strange, they were too tired and cold to care.

The telegraph from Ben Cook to Bill Ayers created a firestorm in the normally quiet Jake's Springs camp. The telegram struck like a thunderbolt. Ayers had never considered that any of his crew could have done such an outrageous act. Now, the accusation that possibly two of his men were involved hit him like a blow to his large gut.

Once he regained his composure, Ayers wheeled into action. He rustled the *mayordomo* from his dry boxcar and demanded that he assemble all the men in front of the section house on the double. Antonio Ramos was not accustomed to being treated so brusquely and asked irritably, "Why do you want the men so late while it's raining?"

Ayers snarled back, "Because two men held up the Limited this evening and the deputy thinks they came from here, that's why."

Ramos's jaw almost hit the ground. *Could it be Nava and Silva? Naw, they could not be so dumb, or could they?* The more Ramos thought about it, the more plausible the thought became. By the time Ramos had gathered his men, he was convinced that they were capable of doing anything.

Paz heard the commotion stirring in the *colonia*. Ever since Prudenciano had failed to return on the work train, she had feared that he would bring trouble back with him. She peered outside through the sliding door. The rain had subsided to a light drizzle and the wind and lightning had ceased. She saw the *mayordomo* gather the men in front of the section house. Some were grumbling and others looked scared as they glanced around them. Paz's intuition told her that her husband and his reckless friend were the cause of this meeting. She continued to watch as Mr. Ayers walked down the hastily assembled line and inspected each man. He held a lantern up to each face before continuing down the line.

Ayers did not know exactly what he was looking for. The men looked normal enough after being dragged out of their shelters on a late rainy night. Some appeared to have stomach problems and their faces showed signs of recent nausea and vomiting. *Must be spoiled food*, thought Ayers as he continued his inspection. *I will look into it tomorrow.* When he finished walking the line, he wondered what he was missing. Everyone was accounted for, but something bugged him. Ayers knew something was amiss. It resided in the recesses of his mind and hovered just out of his reach.

Ayers turned and lifted his lantern above his head and shone the light across the men. The light seemed to skip across the heads of the closest men before illuminating the men down the line. Ayers cried, "That's it!" He ran over to Ramos and yelled, "Where is the tall older man and his young sidekick? Answer me now!"

Antonio Ramos was now caught between telling the truth or remaining faithful to his people. He had no love for Nava or Silva. They were arrogant and lazy. The *colonia* would do well without them. However, the *mayordomo* shouldered the unspoken responsibility to protect every person in his group. If a *mayordomo* betrayed one man, then the rest would not respect his authority and command. Reluctantly, Ramos realized that he had no choice but to protect Nava and Silva. Ramos lifted his head in a dignified manner and said, "I do not know where they are. They refused to get on the work train with us and come home."

"Ah, ha!" proclaimed Ayers with a grin. He knew what they looked like. Now all he needed was their names. So he asked, "Who were they?"

Ramos looked Ayers right in the eyes and said without flinching, "Martinez and Vedris."

"That's it? What are their first names?"

Ramos repeated himself, "Martinez and Vedris."

Ayers quickly lost his grin. He tried to stare Ramos into divulging more, but the elderly man held his gaze and did not waver. Ayers finally said, "All right then, the deputy will be here in a little while. You can tell the story to him." Ayers whirled away and went back inside the section house.

Paz saw the whole exchange from the boxcar. She was just about ready to retreat to her children when two men stumbled in front of the car. At first, she did not recognize them. They were caked with mud and their clothes were completely waterlogged. It was only when the smaller man spoke that she realized who they were.

Silva rasped, "You must help me get Prudenciano inside. He is hurt bad." Paz put her hand to her mouth to stifle a gasp. She scarcely recognized the big man who stood swaying in front of her. His eyes were swollen shut. His drenched hair and beard were pulled down into stringy braids. He looked like death warmed over. Paz got down on her knees and stretched out an arm. Silva pushed Prudenciano forward and laboriously lifted him up into the car. Paz pulled him in and watched him collapse onto the floor.

Augustine waddled out of the family room at that moment and saw his beaten father lying on the floor. He wailed, "No!" He dropped to all fours and crawled over to his father. "Papa! Papa!" he cried to his father's puffy face. The boy was hysterical with fright.

Silva pried the boy away from his father and handed him to Paz. Then he grabbed Prudenciano by his shirt and dragged him into the Nava living quarters. The girls were shocked by the condition of their father. They quickly ran to their mother for comfort and protection. Paz walked up to her husband and gazed down upon his prostrated body. She asked Silva without taking her eyes off Prudenciano, "What happened?"

Silva plopped down on the floor next to Prudenciano and took off his filthy hat. He wiped his brow with the back of his hand and said, "We tried to catch a ride on *El Zorro* to bring us back here. Things got out of hand and Prudenciano got hit in the head with a hammer. See?" Silva bent over and moved Prudenciano's hair back to expose raw fleshy knots on his skull. Prudenciano moaned from Silva's touch. The girls wailed at the sight, which made Augustine cry even harder.

Paz stood solemn and clutched her baby tighter to her breast. After a moment's silence, she asked, "Were you drinking?" Silva stirred awkwardly under her stare and did not answer. She spat, "I thought as much." Her expression was filled with loathing as she looked down on her husband. "I told you that your drinking would bring trouble upon this family. *¿Qué no?* Now look what have you done."

At that moment, Antonio Ramos entered the room. He looked at both men on the floor as if to confirm his own suspicions before speaking, "Silva and Nava, you must get ready to leave soon. The deputy is coming tonight to search for you for stopping *El Zorro*. I will send a signal when I know he is near."

Paz asked, "Why flee? They cannot jail you for asking for a ride."

Prudenciano croaked, "Because I killed a man." It was the first time he had spoken all night. The room went deathly quiet. The only sound was the faint flickering of the oil lamp.

Ramos whistled softly and then asked, "Are you sure? This explains the railroad's interest in catching you guys."

"*Sí*," answered Prudenciano weakly. "I chopped part of his head off." Ramos looked over to Silva for confirmation. Silva dropped his eyes to the floor and nodded weakly. Paz stood in utter disbelief. She had always known Prudenciano would get himself in big trouble some day, but she had no idea that his drinking would lead to this.

Ramos muttered, "*¡Dios mío!* Then you must leave at my signal and never return. You will bring the lawman's wrath upon us all if you do. *Comprende?* Be ready." Ramos quickly turned and left the room to position sentinels on the road to Carrizozo.

It took Paz a few moments to compose herself. When she did, she spoke with confidence and authority. "Silva, leave us. You have done enough for one night." Silva did not argue. He got up, grabbed his hat, and shuffled out. Baby Augustine hid his face in his mother's dress and quivered with fright. The girls were speechless and stood behind their mother. Paz took another moment to study her husband before taking decisive action. She had to work with one arm because Augustine refused to be put down.

Paz directed the girls to use rags and water to clean their father's head wounds and face. Meanwhile, Paz gathered what food she had and stuffed it into a pouch. She worked quickly as if each second counted. Paz filled a canvas flask with water and corked it. She rolled a spare wool blanket and placed it on top of the pouch. Next, she pried the wet clothes off Prudenciano and helped him put on a dry shirt and his only spare pair of pants. When she was finished, Prudenciano looked and felt much better. With his face cleaned and hair and beard dry, he seemed to regain some of his strength. However, he could barely see through his swollen eyes.

Prudenciano sat on the straw mattress and looked around him as he tried to get his bearings. As meager as the room was, it contained his life possessions and his family. Everything that he had fought, struggled, and worked for was contained in this half of a boxcar that was parked in a lonely mountain desert. And now he was going to leave it all. He might never see his loyal wife and beautiful children again. Prudenciano began to feel sorry for himself. The thought that his drinking and rash thinking had brought him this fate never occurred to him. His family stood in front of him and watched him mired in his self-pity.

Silva suddenly appeared through the hanging curtain at the sliding door. "Nava," he whispered urgently, "they are here! We must go now!" Prudenciano got up, gathered the bundle that Paz prepared for him, and walked toward the door. His head throbbed fiercely. He stopped, turned, and took one last look at his family. His heart stopped cold at what he saw. There stood Paz holding a baby with a little girl on each side of her. Each grasped her skirt for emotional support. They stood in the center of the narrow box-shaped room. Paz had the expression of unforgiving contempt written across her face. The scene was exactly as he had foreseen so long ago back in Torreón. It left him with a feeling of despair.

"Come on, Nava," urged Silva. "They are coming!" Prudenciano turned and parted the curtain to leave.

Augustine let out a mournful wail that could be heard throughout the camp. "Papa! Papa!" Prudenciano hesitated for a moment, then continued forward. He let the curtain swing down behind him. "Papa … !" The little boy's plea was the last thing Prudenciano heard as he disappeared into the darkness.

Chapter 16
Escape

Dawn broke across the *Mal Pais*, shimmering with vivid reds and golds that reflected off the distant Organ Mountains. The previous night's storm had scrubbed the morning air clean. Most people rejoiced at waking to such a beautiful Wednesday morning, but not Sheriff C. Walker Hyde. He kicked the ground in frustration because the storm had washed away all traces of the fugitives' tracks. Behind him sat five men on their horses waiting for their instructions. They congregated just south of Carrizozo.

Sheriff Hyde ignored the men for the moment. He put his hands on his hips and stared across the rugged terrain as he contemplated the situation. Finally, he sighed when he realized that he had no choice. He had to scour the whole damn area to make sure that the suspects were not holed up in some canyon. Hyde knew that they would not be, but the town demanded a search anyway.

"No sense delaying it any longer," Hyde said as he turned to face the men. Sheriff Walker Hyde was known as a man of action. The citizens of Carrizozo thought that he was fair and they endorsed his strong-arm tactics when the situation required muscle. People considered Hyde and his able deputy Roberts as the main reason why crime was at its all-time low in the area. When criminal activity emerged, the residents expected Hyde and Roberts to find the suspects quickly and bring them to justice. Hyde was keenly aware that he occupied an elected position and his current standing was only as good as his last performance. To preserve his chances for reelection, he had to catch these Mexicans as soon as possible. The last thing the town wanted was a couple of drunk Mexicans trying to kill people along the countryside.

Sheriff Hyde pushed his cowboy hat off his face and appraised the hastily assembled posse. He was very lucky to have conscripted such able men. Each one was good in the saddle and could hold his own in a fight. "Steve," he said as he addressed the first man on his right, "I want you and Greg to search directly west of here. Jeff, and the rest of you, fan out and check out the country as far south as Jake's Springs. Rumor has it that the Mexicans are probably from the work camp down there, so I don't expect them to head north. Remember, you are looking for a big man with a younger, smaller guy. The big one is supposed to be meaner than hell. He almost killed a man last night, so be real careful-like. Any questions?" The men answered his question with a confident shake of their heads. They were ready.

Hyde was satisfied, too. "Okay. Let's get going. We will meet at Jake's Springs by this afternoon." The men wished each other luck and split up. As Hyde saddled his horse, he reviewed his decision to send Roberts back to Jake's Springs and try to find some leads. He concluded that it was the best course of action. He looked up into the blue sky and prayed silently that Roberts would find the suspects. If not and the search proved fruitless, he would enlist the Mescalero Apaches to sniff them out. Hyde muttered as he snapped his reins, "God help the Mexicans if we do."

———————

Deputy Sheriff Albert Roberts tried to interrogate the Mexican leader, but the old man claimed that they had a convenient language barrier between them. He wondered if Bill Ayers directed this *mayordomo* at all. He suspected that this man was purposely not cooperating.

"Okay," groaned Roberts as he readjusted his pencil and pad, "let's try this again. Your name is Antonio Ramos. Correct?" Ramos squirmed in front of him. He finally nodded, but did not reply. Roberts continued sarcastically, "All right. Now we are getting somewhere. Did Martinez and Vedris come by here last night?" He studied Ramos's face as he waited for a response. Ramos cocked his head and produced a puzzled expression on his face to signify that he did not have a clue as to what the deputy was talking about. Roberts came to the end of his patience. He gritted his teeth for a second and then shouted, "Ayers! Get your tail in here, now!"

Ayers came bounding through the door in a nervous sweat. He had not slept well last night. "Yes, Deputy Roberts," he said out of breath. "What's up?"

Roberts jabbed a finger at the scared little man and asked in a loud voice, "Does he speak English?"

Ayers would have thought Roberts was joking if he had not radiated hot anger. He replied, "He speaks English very well." Ayers turned and looked at Ramos. The *mayordomo* shifted in his seat again.

Roberts said with steel in his voice, "I thought as much. Well, let's see how our friend refreshes his memory after spending some time in our cozy jail. Let's go, *hombre*. We got some riding to do." Roberts stood up and grabbed Ramos by the collar. He jerked him up and threw him toward the door.

Ramos screamed, "Wait!" This was far more than he had bargained for. No one could expect him to go to prison for those two scoundrels. He had to give this deputy something. Ramos grabbed the door jam to steady himself and to keep from falling to his knees and begging for mercy. He blurted out, "They were here!"

"Well, well, well," snickered Roberts. "Looks like your English returned just in time. Good. Where did they go?"

Ramos looked up to Roberts and pointed toward Sierra Blanca. "They went that way."

Roberts thought that this was feasible. There was water and shelter in the forest. Still, he wanted to be sure. He took a step forward and asked, "They went into the mountains? Are you sure?"

"*Sí,*" answered Ramos enthusiastically. "They ran off into the mountains."

Roberts studied the man for a second and thought, *He's telling the truth.* He waved a hand at him and said, "You are dismissed." Ramos looked at him unbelievingly for second. "You heard me," barked Roberts, "Get out of here!" The old man jumped and ran out of the section house.

Ayers stood uncomfortably in the room. He watched the deputy think silently for a few moments. Finally, he asked, "What are you going to do now?"

Roberts replied in a calmer voice, "I reckon it's time to call upon our friendly neighbors for a little assistance."

Ayers asked, "Neighbors? What neighbors?"

"The Mescalero."

John Smoke Rider spotted the white man riding toward him when he was still two miles out. He sat on his stool and leaned back against the adobe wall of his hut and studied the man with his keen eyesight. He noted that the man rode strong and proud. He appeared one with the land and his horse ran fresh, which indicated that his owner knew how to care for it and pace it. Smoke Rider held all these attributes in high regard.

Smoke Rider's curiosity piqued when he noticed that the man rode directly toward him without distraction. The man wanted to see him. By the time the rider was a mile away, Smoke Rider recognized him and smiled. It had been a long time since he had seen Albert

Roberts. The man stood for justice and kept his word. Smoke Rider had fought beside him and found Roberts to be a mighty warrior. He looked forward to fighting next to him again. Maybe Roberts had another assignment for Smoke Rider and his Mescalero scouts. The thought gave Smoke Rider a rush of excitement.

John Smoke Rider was the grandson of Chief Augustine. He was twenty-eight-years old and exhibited the same natural-born leadership skills as his grandfather. The elders of the tribe recognized this and tapped him to become a chief in the future. They groomed him constantly for the responsibility. Smoke Rider did not shirk his destiny. He listened patiently to their instruction and became involved in tribal matters. However, his true love was to hunt criminals that were unfortunate enough to stray onto the reservation. Some even gave him a good hunt and fight, but most were as easy to track as a muddy dog walking across a clean floor. When he found them, they were usually too tired to fight. There was no sport in catching weaklings.

The Carrizozo and Alamogordo law officials often sought Smoke Rider's assistance in apprehending escapees and criminals at-large. He had a natural talent for tracking men and was as sly as a fox in trapping them. If Smoke Rider had one fault that the law officers would mention, it would be that he often shot too quickly. More than once Smoke Rider had returned with a dead man draped over his saddle.

Smoke Rider slowly came forward on his stool and stood to greet his friend. His dog shot out from a hole in the ground next to the house. It snarled and appeared ready to sink its teeth into the visitor's leg, but Smoke Rider stopped it with a sharp rebuke. The mongrel slunk into the bushes to watch the intruder in safety.

"I hope you are well, my friend," greeted John Smoke Rider as he stepped forward. Roberts swung off his saddle and grasped John's hand. They gave each other a solid handshake.

"And I hope you are well too, John Smoke Rider," replied Roberts with an honest grin upon his face. Roberts enjoyed John's company too, despite his rough edges. Roberts took a step back to appraise his friend. Smoke Rider stood five feet, seven inches. He had a muscular chest and strong arms and legs from years of running and riding hard. His dark eyes were set deep in his handsomely rugged brown face. He wore his thick black hair long and tied in a single braid that rested between his shoulder blades. His whole persona exuded wholesome health despite the poverty in which he lived. Roberts worried that John would someday get disillusioned and bury his self-pity in alcohol like so many of the young braves did on the reservation. To prevent this, Roberts and others slipped as many odd jobs as they could to John and his scouts to keep them employed.

Smoke Rider sensed what his friend was thinking and joked, "I would invite you in for a beer, but Indians aren't allowed to drink, no?"

Roberts seemed relieved to hear his humor. It verified that he was all right. He answered, "I'm afraid I will have to pass today, *amigo*. I do need your help, though."

Smoke Rider cracked a wicked grin across his face. "Well then," he said as he motioned Roberts to take a stool in the shade of his hut, "let us discuss the matter." He stuck his head into his house and yelled, "Maria! Bring us some water." As the men got comfortable, Smoke Rider's wife brought them each a clay jar filled with water. Roberts thanked her and peered suspiciously into the jar. He had seen the polluted water that some residents drank on the reservation, but this appeared sweet and clear. He sipped it first and could not detect any foul taste or smell, so he took a large gulp to quench his thirst.

After a few minutes of silence, Roberts began, "Appears that a couple of Mexicans stopped the Limited two nights ago. In the process, they nearly killed a man. We believe that they high-tailed it to these parts. We would like them captured. You interested?"

A hint of disappointment showed on Smoke Rider's face. He had hoped to chase a murderer or bank robber. These two prospects appeared to be minor players. "Doesn't appear to be a problem," he stated flatly. "What do they look like?"

Roberts replied, "One is a very big man, but he is older with a graying beard. The other is younger and smaller."

Smoke Rider asked, "Are they armed?"

"I don't believe so."

Great! thought Smoke Rider, *I am looking for an unarmed, old man with a young tag-a-long. That sounds like a great challenge.* He managed to ask Roberts without disappointment, "How bad do you want them?"

"Well," replied Roberts as he looked down into his jar, "it would be nice to apprehend them, but I wouldn't spend more than a week trying and I only want you to do it. I don't want your scouts on this one. Okay?"

Smoke Rider sighed. He had been without paying work for a while. His growing family could use the money. He looked out across the vast open territory to the west and slowly nodded.

"Good," exclaimed Roberts. He was relieved because he had half expected Smoke Rider to decline the offer. He stood up and fished a silver badge out of this breast pocket and said, "Stand and raise your right hand." Smoke Rider got up and lifted his right hand. He appeared bored, since he had done this countless times before. "By the power vested in me by the Lincoln County Sheriff's Department, I here by deputize you to carry out the apprehension of said suspects in the stopping of the El Paso and Northeastern Limited and the associated assault. Do you accept?"

Smoke Rider almost rolled his eyes when replying, "I do."

Roberts smiled and handed the badge to Smoke Rider. They spent the rest of the morning discussing the details and trading information. By the early afternoon, both men were satisfied that each was informed as much as possible. They shook hands and Roberts mounted his horse for the long ride back. Roberts waved and left with the grim satisfaction that he had done all that the situation demanded. Smoke Rider would begin his hunt at dawn.

———————

Prudenciano's stomach rumbled deeply with hunger. Yesterday, he and Rafael Silva had depleted the provisions Paz had packed for him. The cold nights, long marches, and his healing body all drained precious calories. Now his belly gnawed at him and magnified his unceasing headaches.

Silva suffered too from the lack of food. His muscles seemed to have no energy and he was becoming increasingly irritable. He tried to argue at the slightest provocation. Prudenciano avoided debating Silva and prodded him to continue moving. Silva was getting on Prudenciano's nerves.

They stumbled along for five days in a mostly southeastern direction. This was not fully by their choice, but by subtle influences of the land. The foothills along the eastern edge of the Tularosa Valley offered some concealment for the fugitives. They followed the folds and gullies as they walked along the majestic base of Sierra Blanca. The mountain's thick forests looked inviting, but the thought of scaling its steep slopes was daunting, especially since both men were very tired. Thus, they chose to distance themselves from Jake's Springs by taking the easier route through the hills. As they came to the southern base of the mountain, the terrain gradually turned to the east and gained elevation.

It had been six years since men had pursued Prudenciano with murderous intentions, when he took Paz from his father's *rancho*. He forgot the uneasy feeling that hangs on a man's back like a heavy blanket and makes him frequently glance over his shoulder. He was certain that the law was right on their heels, ready to pounce on them at a second's notice. His nerves were jumbled and he frequently jumped at the slightest sound.

Constantly being on alert sapped his energy even more. This caused him to sometimes fall asleep on his feet and abruptly startle awake. Silva often pulled him out of his daydream with a question.

"Nava. Nava! Can you hear me?" Prudenciano staggered ahead,

not acknowledging Silva's hailing. "Hey, *amigo*. I'm talking to you," continued Silva with irritation in his voice.

Prudenciano stopped abruptly in his tracks and looked quickly around. He saw Silva waiting impatiently for a quick answer with his hands on his hips and his chin jutted out. Prudenciano did not have a clue what he wanted. Prudenciano asked with a thick tongue, "*Sî?*"

Silva readied himself to launch into an irrational tirade, but checked himself when he saw his friend's face. Prudenciano's eyes were still swollen with dark blue swirls radiating from his sinuses and sockets. He also had large knots across his head, with black scabs. Silva thought, *They must hurt like hell*. He decided to give Prudenciano a break and calm down. With more control in his voice, Silva asked, "Where are we going? I need to get some *frijoles* in my gut before I fall over from hunger. What's the plan?"

Prudenciano seemed to sway on his feet as he looked blindly at Silva for a minute. Silva waited patiently for an answer. Finally, Prudenciano replied in a monotone, "We are going around this mountain."

Silva asked, "Why?"

Prudenciano stared back with dull eyes for a while longer. Then, with a pained expression, he explained, "Because if we go south, we will meet the Alamogordo law. If we go north, the Carrizozo sheriff will find us. If we go west, we will die in the *Mal Pais*. So, we must go east, around this mountain. *Comprende?*"

Silva thought that this was a satisfactory explanation about where they were going, but it did not completely answer everything. So he fired back, "What about eating, *hombre?* I'm hungry!"

Prudenciano's eyes seemed to flicker with anger. With steel in his voice, he barked, "We will eat when we are safe. Food will do you no good if you are hanging from the end of a rope!" Silva gulped at the thought of hanging. He knew that the *gringos* would kill him without a second thought. Prudenciano studied him for a moment to make sure that his point had sunk in. Mollified, he turned around and continued marching with renewed force. Silva buttoned his mouth and followed silently behind.

Soon, the terrain bent to the east around the base of Sierra Blanca. They found a narrow canyon to screen their escape into the mountains. They did not consider whose property they crossed. Their only concern was to conceal their movements and maximize their distance in the shortest possible time. The canyon provided both. Unknown to them, it was also the gateway to the Mescalero Apache reservation.

John Smoke Rider saw the movement in the corner of his eye. His honed hunting instincts told him that it was unnatural and could not be explained by a falling rock or a deer searching for water. He slowly turned his head in its direction. From his perch on a high ledge that jutted out from a rock wall, he looked like a stone statue. He had covered his face, hair, and body with the gray dirt of the canyon floor. Only his dark eyes shone through the disguise. He wrapped his rifle with an rumpled old wool blanket that broke the linear lines and masked it completely against the rock. He was invisible to the unwary eye, a ghost ready to appear out of nowhere and become a fugitive's worst nightmare.

Smoke Rider sat motionless for two days. He had chosen this spot because it provided a vantage point for surveying the most logical route for a fleeing man to pass. Smoke Rider recognized how the land would channel a man to this canyon. A fugitive needed to be hidden and travel fast. The canyon was a natural route that provided travelers with both. It funneled outlaws running from the north and directed them east across the reservation to Ruidoso and trails to Mexico. Thus, if Roberts was right about the criminals escaping south, they would most likely cross here.

Smoke Rider let his hawk eyes adjust to the distance. After a moment of concentrating, he saw two specks moving slowing up the canyon floor. They were still about three miles off, but Smoke Rider had already made some crucial observations. The specks were people. The one in front was larger than the one behind. They walked in a weary fashion as if they had been traveling for a long time. All these observations supported the possibility that these were the men he was seeking. In response, Smoke Rider slowly reached under the blanket with his right hand and cocked the lever. He would wait until they were closer before he made his move.

He was a patient hunter. His grandfather Augustine had taught him to "let his eyes do all the walking." That is, find a good perch that provide several angles for a good shot and wait and watch. The land provided many clues where animals and men chose to travel. By watching these areas over a period of time, the hunter was usually rewarded by his prey walking to him. Conversely, if the hunter elected to walk in search of an animal, they usually detected his presence and avoided him. Smoke Rider adhered strictly to his grandfather's principle. It had served him well for many years.

Smoke Rider watched the unsuspecting men come closer. Several days ago, he had paced out landmarks that denoted ranges of two hundred and one hundred yards from his ledge. He was an excellent judge of range, but knowing the distance took all the guesswork out of shooting. His rifle was a tried-and-true Winchester. He intimately knew its performance and windage for a variety of ranges and would instinctively compensate for the bullet's drop. If he missed, the rifle's quick lever action often allowed him another chance.

The men wandered single file up the narrow canyon. They walked in a zigzag motion as they negotiated the fallen rocks from the forty-foot-high walls. The sheer rock walls seemed to have been cut by God dragging an enormous knife across the barren landscape. The ragged rim serrated the blue sky above.

Two hours after Smoke Rider first spotted them, the men passed the two-hundred-yard marker. Smoke Rider could now pick out the men's features. They were both Mexican. The front man was big with a full beard. A smaller man walked closely behind him. Other than the big man's pouch, they carried nothing between them. They fit Roberts' description. Smoke Rider was satisfied that he had the right men.

Without taking his eyes off his prey, he slowly pulled his rifle from under the blanket. He let the blanket fall to his knees and assumed the kneeling position to aim. His buck-horn sights gave Smoke Rider an open view of the approaching men. He rested the front pin on the big man's shoulder. He had found through years of experience that it was best to first wound the meanest or biggest man of a group. Afterward, the other men usually surrendered immediately and John quickly subdued them. Then he led them away like docile sheep. Smoke Rider saw no reason to deviate from this proven method. He would shoot the front man in the shoulder. If that did not take the fight out of him, Smoke Rider would kill him with the next shot.

He held the gun motionless and controlled his breathing. The men continued their advance and steadily approached the one-hundred-yard marker. He steadied his aim. The distance was right. He gradually applied pressure to the trigger. It gave and smoothly slid back. As the hammer disengaged, the big man suddenly whirled with unbelievable speed and knocked down his companion. The rifle barked and released its bullet. It ricocheted harmlessly off a boulder behind where the man had been standing only milliseconds before. The shot reverberated down the canyon walls.

Damn! thought Smoke Rider as he recocked the rifle in one fluid motion without lifting his eyes from the sights. They disappeared behind a jumble of rocks along the north wall. He now had to wait until one of the men made a mistake and gave him a target. He knew that if he was patient enough, they would eventually expose a head, arm, or a leg. He was certain that they did not know where he was hiding. All he had to do was wait for them to move and he would nail them. John Smoke Rider assumed the posture of a statue aiming a rifle and waited. As he did, a troubling thought seeped into his mind, *How did that man know?* Smoke Rider had an eerie feeling that this job might not be as simple as he had once thought.

———•••••———

Prudenciano and Silva walked in silence up the narrow canyon. The air was so silent that it seemed to hang in front of them. The dry floor and the gray rock walls appeared completely devoid of life. The tight path they followed forced them to walk in single file as they curved around boulders and rocks that lay along the ground. Prudenciano led with Silva close behind. Each man was lost in his own thoughts and paid little attention to their environment

Silva's stomach wrenched in hunger. He was dog tired and day-dreamed of finding a comfortable *cantina* to drink and eat his worries away. His memories of working long days on the railroad were beginning to seem like a blissful vacation. At least there was food and shelter at the *colonia*. This forced march had neither and the prospects of finding any hospitality in the near future were bleak. Silva snapped out of his daydream for a minute and stared at the man's back that he had been following for so many hours. He suddenly put the entire blame for his misfortune on that back. His eyes shot daggers into Prudenciano as he thought, *If he did not hit that man, we would not be here. It is his fault*! Prudenciano appeared oblivious to Silva's wrath. Slowly, Silva simmered down and resumed his mindless march.

Although Prudenciano's head pounded like a small drum, the nagging feeling that someone was watching them tingled his senses. It seemed to creep along his spine like a slithering snake and it gave him the spooks. His eyes darted from rock to rock, but he saw nothing. The feeling intensified as they walked deeper into the canyon. Prudenciano had learned long ago to heed his feelings and intuitions. They had saved his life on more than one occasion. He began to walk on the balls of his feet and became more attentive.

As they rounded another large boulder, Prudenciano noticed a flat indentation on the ground next to the rock. It was faint and he would not have noticed it if he had not felt so uneasy. It seemed unnatural. Prudenciano noted it and continued. His sixth sense began to buzz like a rattlesnake. His pulse raced and his mind amplified all smells, sounds, and sights around him. Something was wrong, but he was lost for a reason why.

Within a few minutes they negotiated another large rock. Prudenciano spotted the same flat indentation along its side. He hesitated for a moment. It looked just like the last one about a hundred yards back. Suddenly, his mind flashed a brilliant intuition. He flicked his eyes up and focused them about a hundred yards forward. He knew what he was looking for and saw it. The rifle was pointed straight at him. With every ounce of strength he possessed, he flung himself backward, bowling over Silva in the process. He could feel the bullet whiz over his shoulder as he fell to the ground. The crack of gunfire quickly followed.

Silva shouted under Prudenciano, "What the hell is going on?"

Prudenciano hissed, "Keep quiet and stay down." He slowly slid off Silva and moved like a Gila monster behind some rocks. With a flick of his hand, he motioned to Silva to do the same and follow him.

Silva was almost hyperventilating by the time he slithered up to Prudenciano. His voice sounded scared and high-pitched as he asked, "Who is shooting at us?"

Prudenciano put his back against the rocks and shook his head. "I don't know, but this guy is very good. He has us pinned."

Silva looked at Prudenciano for a second and then said rashly, "I'm going to see who it is." He started slowly peering over the rocks. Prudenciano reached up and savagely pulled him down.

Prudenciano chastised him. "Are you completely *loco*? That *hombre* will shoot you the second you rise over these rocks." Silva looked back at him incredulously. Prudenciano shook his head and said, "Watch this if you don't believe me." He grabbed Silva's hat off his head and held it by the brim. Then he slowly lifted it above the rocks. A hole magically appeared in the top edge and another rifle shot rang out.

Silva was stunned! Prudenciano calmly handed his hat back to him. Silva sat speechless as he studied the hole. He finally whispered, "*Yi, yi, yi*. What are we going to do now? He will kill us if we move."

"*Sí*," answered Prudenciano, "he will do that for certain. We will have to wait until night, then slip away. It's our only chance. Might as well make yourself comfortable. We have a few hours before dark." Prudenciano got himself settled and closed his eyes. Within a few minutes, he was sleeping lightly. Silva marveled at how the man could sleep after narrowly escaping death. It was like he was resigned to the fact there was nothing else that he could do and accepted it. Silva fought a sudden urge to run and, instead, lay down next to him. He could not rest like Prudenciano, so he stared at the tall smooth walls of the canyon. They were trapped, and Silva knew that he would have to wait until nightfall to see how Prudenciano was going to get them out of this one.

Night fell suddenly in the deep narrow canyon. Smoke Rider had remained motionless since the first encounter with the fugitives. Other than firing at what he thought was a head, but what turned out to be a hat, he'd had nothing to do. The men had not moved. That surprised him. He had expected that they would have made a run for it by now. Slowly, Smoke Rider lowered his rifle and stretched out his legs. They felt stiff from hours of kneeling. He massaged them to bring back the blood flow and stop the aching. He would have to go down there and find them. They would probably wait until dark to make their escape. They were more disciplined than he had thought. He silently cursed at not having been able to bring a few of his scouts. He could really use them right now.

Smoke Rider slipped his rifle into a buckskin sheath he wore on his back. He checked that his knife with the elk bone handle was securely tied to his leg. Satisfied, he took a long drink from his flask and quietly climbed down the wall to the canyon floor. He dropped the last ten feet and landed like a cat on silent moccasins. He waited for a moment to make certain that all was right before stepping out in the customary toe-heel stride of an Indian hunter.

Like his name, John moved like smoke around the boulders and rocks, soundlessly gliding across the canyon floor. As he came to the rocks where the fugitives hid, he slowed, reached behind his back, and pulled his rifle from its sheath. He put his right hand into the lever and held the stock with his left. Smoke Rider stopped stone-still and listened. Within the deep recesses of the dark silence, he heard the faint sounds of movement from behind the rocks. *They are still there.* He was sure they would have left by now.

He took a deep breath and leaped over the rocks. He cocked his rifle in midair and brought the stock up to his face. John landed ready to shoot the first thing that moved—only there was no one there. He quickly scanned the area by looking through the sights of his rifle and jerking his body from side to side. He saw nothing. *Where are they?* He had heard something back here. What was it?

Just then, bits of fine dust rained down on his face. He looked up the sheer black canyon wall to see a big man reach down and pull a smaller man over the top. They were silhouetted against the twilight sky. For a moment, Smoke Rider stared in utter disbelief. When he recovered his senses, it was too late. The men were gone.

Smoke Rider walked up to the wall and ran his hand across its smooth face. He could find very few handholds in the dark. It was too treacherous to climb at night. He would have to go back to where he had hobbled his horse and backtrack along the rim until he crossed their tracks. This would mean that he would be half a day behind them. John cursed his bad luck. He had less than three days to find them again before his commission ended. That was not much time. He turned and started trotting up the canyon to his horse. It was going to be another sleepless night.

————•••••————

Prudenciano slept for only an hour. He woke quietly and lay motionless while he studied his surroundings. Silva finally settled into a fitful nap next to him. His punctured hat lay over his face to provide some shade from the afternoon sun. Every now and then, he twitched and shook as he fought and ran from demons in his dreams.

Prudenciano slowly slid his head against a rock pile and evaluated the path that led back down the canyon. Although there were plenty of boulders and rocks to take cover behind, the trail had many open spaces where a sniper could easily pick them off. Even under the cover of darkness, they would be open targets to a stealthy assailant. Prudenciano shuddered at that thought. He vividly remembered not seeing the man. He only saw the rifle that seemed to float in the air on its own power. Anyone who could hide like that could easily sneak up on them in the darkness and kill them. With these thoughts in mind, Prudenciano made a firm decision. They could not leave by the way they had come.

So, what other choice do we have? He looked around and saw the walls towering over him. *However,* mused Prudenciano as he studied the walls more closely, *the walls do present an alternative.* His eyes followed the smooth rock to the canyon rim. At closer inspection, he saw some hand- and footholds along a crack that stretched up the face. The crack bent and became discontinuous three quarters of the way up before reestablishing itself and continuing almost to the top. He tilted his head back to see if the wall and other rocks concealed the route from the sniper. It appeared sheltered from any line of fire. The more he looked at the ascent, the more feasible it seemed. He reasoned that they would climb it just as night fell. If they attempted it in daylight, they risked being discovered and shot. If they started to climb in the dark, they would not see all of the handholds and fall. Prudenciano knew that their window of opportunity would be very narrow.

Prudenciano spoke out loud for the first time, "We will do it just before nightfall. We have no choice." His voice woke Silva.

Silva muttered drowsily under his hat, "Huh? Did you say something?"

"*Sí,*" answered Prudenciano. "I see the way out of here."

Silva slowly pulled his hat away from his face and looked up to his partner and asked, "How?"

Prudenciano wagged his head in the direction of the wall and said boldly, "There. We will climb that wall just before dark."

Silva swore softly under his breath as he looked the wall up and down, "¡Dios mío! I fall asleep for a few hours and look what you dream up. Nava, there is no way we can do it."

Prudenciano chuckled. He knew that his friend would scoff at his idea. Then his demeanor turned serious. He needed to convince Silva that he had no choice and he would try with all his might or die. It was as simple as that. "Rafael," Prudenciano began, "that man out there is trying to kill us. He will come for us at nightfall. We can't run back the way we came. He would pick us off as easy as hunting rabbits. We have to climb this wall just as night comes to conceal our movements. If we fail, he will find us and kill us. Comprende, amigo?"

Silva reluctantly nodded. He could not think of a better plan. Climbing the wall was the only option. He slowly lay back down and placed his hat over his face. Silva whispered, "Wake me when it's time to act like a bat. And may God have mercy on our souls."

Prudenciano waited until the setting sun cast long shadows across the canyon floor before rousting Silva awake. He cautioned Silva with a finger to his lips to remain quiet. Then he motioned for them to crawl slowly to the north wall. The light was quickly falling. It made Prudenciano's anxiety rise. They had very little time to do this. When they reached the wall, he found the crack and thrust his fist into the fissure. It gave him a secure handhold to lift his body up and grab the next hold.

Silva watched him with deep trepidation. When Prudenciano was ten feet up the wall, he motioned with his head for Silva to follow. Silva took a deep breath and started up the crack. His hands were smaller than Prudenciano's and could not give him a decent grip. He almost slipped and fell back. His fear escalated to the point of paralyzing him. Only the thought of being killed by a bullet kept him prodding upward. After a few awkward tries, Silva managed to pull himself to within a few feet of his friend.

Satisfied, Prudenciano continued to work the fissure for holds and pull himself up. Night was falling quickly now. The light was failing and he could barely see the rock in front of him. He began operating on memory of how the crack played out along the wall. He remembered that it turned to the right for about twenty feet before angling upward again. He knew that he had to be close to that turn by now. With his nose touching the wall, he searched for his next hold. His entire weight rested on his left hand as he probed the rock for the fissure. He could not find it. His fear shot up his spine. He desperately swept his hand across the face. Far to his right, he latched onto a deep indentation. He grabbed it and swung his body across the wall. Hand over hand, he moved along the sheer rock until the crack turned upward again. Satisfied with his progress, he secured himself by forcing his fist into a fissure and digging his toes into a slight depression. He could now rest his tired muscles.

Silva saw Prudenciano stretch out and grab something, but in the feeble light, he could not see what it was. He also came to the dead end that had stopped Prudenciano. He weakly fanned the rock face with his right hand, desperately searching for another handhold. He felt nothing. He wheezed, "I can't go on, Nava. I can't find a handhold."

Prudenciano hissed, "It is there. You must try." Silva stretched further, but could not find any purchase.

"*Nada!*" he whined, "I can't go on!"

Prudenciano swore. He knew what he had to do. He released his left hand and moved back along the crack to Silva. When he got to the end of the crack, he secured his right hand and reached out with his left and said, "Take it. I will bring you across."

"No! I can't do it!"

Prudenciano fired back, "You must! Now take it or I swear I will pull you off this wall and watch you fall!"

Silva reeked with fear. The thought of being thrown off the wall and eventually shot was not appealing. He took one look at Prudenciano and knew that he meant it. So, like a trapped man who must choose between two evils, he slowly stretched his hand out to Prudenciano. He barely touched his hand when Prudenciano gruffly grabbed him and yanked his body across the wall. He swung him to the narrow ledge next to him and let Silva regain his handholds. "There now," stated Prudenciano in a hushed voice, "that wasn't so bad now, *¿qué no?*" Silva could not answer. He was too scared.

Prudenciano continued along the fissure and worked up the face. He could see that the rim was tantalizingly close. He reached up to pull himself forward and found that the crack was gone. Then he remembered that the fissure did not reach all the way. He would have to feel his way up for the final eight feet. He searched and found only fingertip holds. They would have to do. Inch by inch, he clawed his way up. Suddenly, the rim appeared and he pulled himself over the top.

Prudenciano was breathless and he lay on his stomach to rest and settle his nerves. After a few minutes, he saw no sign of Silva, so he peered over the edge. Silva was stuck at the top of the crack. Night had completely fallen and there was no moon to provide any light. It was almost completely black.

Silva cried, "I can't go on." Prudenciano recognized the sound of panic underlying his voice.

Prudenciano said soothingly, "You must try, *amigo.* Here, I will drop my belt to you and pull you up." He quickly took off his belt, lay down on the rock edge, and reached over the ledge. The belt dangled two feet above Silva's head. "Grab it," commanded Prudenciano.

Silva made a feeble attempt and wailed, "I can't."

"Climb just a little farther," coaxed Prudenciano. Silva appeared undecided. Prudenciano was about to say something more when a movement caught his eye. Something was moving along the canyon floor. "Hurry. The man is coming!"

The news seemed to galvanize Silva. He pulled himself up a little farther and grabbed the end of the belt. Prudenciano heaved him up the rest of the way and pulled him over the rim. "*¡Dios mío!*" exclaimed Silva, "I thought I was dead for sure!"

"Quiet!" snapped Prudenciano in a hushed voice. "He's below us!"

Despite his exhaustion, Silva's eyes snapped open in surprise. "*¿Verdad?* How do you know?" He started to lean over the edge to see for himself. Prudenciano savagely ripped him back.

"Get back here!" Prudenciano growled. "He'll shoot your head off! On your feet. *¡Vámanos!*" Prudenciano dragged Silva up and pushed him toward Sierra Blanca. The huge mountain formed a gigantic silhouette against the starlit night. "He will be tracking us by first light," continued Prudenciano as he struck a fast gait with his long legs, "and we had better be deep in the mountains by then or he will kill us by noon. The night will be a long one." Silva was already having trouble keeping up. He stumbled and sprinted to stay behind Prudenciano. He wondered if it would be more humane to die quickly from a bullet than to die slowly from exhaustion. One thing he knew was certain—tonight was going to be torturous.

Prudenciano led them northeast toward the south side of Sierra Blanca. Hour after hour they marched forward. They crossed the five miles to the mountain base and immediately started up the slope. The pines swallowed them as they moved into the dark forest. As the trees became thicker, their blistering pace slowed. By midnight, they were deep into the forest. Prudenciano called for a short break so that they could have a small drink and he could get his bearings.

Silva fell to the ground and gulped the thin air with ragged breaths. He was spent. He looked up to Prudenciano, who seemed none the worse for wear. *How could it be*, thought Silva, *he is so much older than me, but he is so much stronger? He must be made of steel.*

Prudenciano appeared oblivious to Silva's condition. He stood sloshing his rationed gulp of water in his mouth as he studied the constellations above them. Since the mountain covered the North Star and the Big Dipper, he had to navigate by other predominant star clusters. High above the horizon, he found Orion with his sword drawn against the charging bull Taurus. Prudenciano knew that these groups were in the southeastern sectors of the sky this time of year around midnight. He noted their position and oriented himself to his surroundings. Satisfied, he swallowed the last of his water and spoke to Silva. "Time to get moving again. You better get up now or you will stiffen up."

"Too late," replied Silva, "I feel like an old man. Don't you hurt too?"

Prudenciano looked down at Silva for moment. He seemed to study him as if he was looking for something. Finally, he simply said, "I want to live. Let's go." Prudenciano threw his pouch over his shoulder, reached down, and brought Silva gruffly to his feet. Without saying another word, he struck out in a northeast direction that continued their climb up the mountain, but would eventually bring them to the east side. Silva staggered behind him, stumbling over branches and hidden roots.

Dawn broke around six o'clock that morning and found them halfway up the mountain and on the eastern slopes. They looked like dead men on their feet. Their pace had slowed to a mere shuffle. They had run out of water hours ago and their tongues felt like leather in their mouths. Sleep tugged at them with each step they took. Silva had fallen asleep on his feet several times during the night. Prudenciano shook him awake each time. Now, Prudenciano was lapsing into a stupor and Silva was in no shape to revive him.

Deep in the recesses of his mind, an animal instinct nagged at Prudenciano's consciousness. He felt it tingle his nerves and tell him that a deadly force was tracking and closing fast. He startled awake and looked quickly around. All was quiet and serene with the steaming dew lifting off the grasses and leaves. Shafts of early, morning light beamed through narrow openings in the canopy above. Amidst the surrounding tranquility, Prudenciano knew all was not well. He trusted his inner sense with absolute certainty that their assailant was drawing nearer. They would have to quicken their pace to stay ahead.

Prudenciano turned to face Silva. He was swaying on his feet with his eyes shut. Prudenciano wearily reached out and shook him awake. "Rafael, wake up. We must keep moving. Rafael, do you hear me?"

"Huh? What's going on?" mumbled Silva as he struggled to open his eyes.

"The man is out there," continued Prudenciano, "I can feel it. We must try to stay ahead of him and lose him in the mountains. It is our only chance." Silva wanted to ask how he knew that they were being followed, but he did not have the energy. He nodded and tried to put a foot forward, but nearly fell in the process. Prudenciano watched him for a moment and decided that he would have to help him continue. He threw down his pouch and put his arm around Silva. With every ounce of strength he had left, Prudenciano dragged Silva forward.

They staggered along for hours while only managing to cover a few miles more. Prudenciano's arms and back were numb from carrying Silva. He knew he could not last much longer. His anxiety steadily rose with the feeling that someone deadly was coming. It steeled him to continue. Suddenly, they stumbled upon a dirt road. Prudenciano tripped while he tried to pull Silva up the shallow embankment and they sprawled upon the surface.

"Rafael," croaked Prudenciano as he tried to pick himself off the ground, "we must get up." Silva did not reply. He lay face down and motionless in the middle of the road. "Silva. I mean it. We ..." Prudenciano never finished his sentence. Fatigue, lack of food and water, and the subtle effects of his concussion finally took their toll. He saw his field of vision collapse around him until all he could see was a fuzzy ball of light. In the dark recesses of his mind, he could hear the faint clanging of bells as he pitched backward and blacked out.

———

Mrs. Edith Lesnett rode on the wagon buckboard next to her trusted and longtime hired hand, Canuto Reyes. Reyes expertly drove the team of four horses up the winding road to the Lesnett Lumber Mill where Edith's husband, Frank, and their son, Tom, ran the operations. The mill was located high on the eastern slopes of Sierra Blanca. The wagon was filled with supplies to keep the mill going until the heavy winter snow closed them down for the season.

Edith let the wind ruffle her thick salt and pepper hair. She loved this time of year. The trees were just showing signs of turning yellow. The air had a hint of autumn crispness and the high-bush cranberries emitted a mild, pungent smell. She sat with her eyes partly closed and her face tilted up to receive the lovely sunshine beaming down. She could hear the rhythmic clopping of the horses' hooves and the synchronized jangling of their harness bells. The sounds soothed her and made her feel glad that she had come. The hotel and store had been so hectic these past weeks that she had almost declined Reyes's offer to bring her up for a few days. But now she realized how much she had missed riding up into the mountains and the anticipation of seeing Frank and Tom again confirmed that this trip was the right thing to do.

Reyes smiled when he turned his head to watch her soak up the late morning sun. He thought she was a handsome woman and took pride in taking care of her. Canuto Reyes was a Mexican in his fifties. He stood just under five feet, nine inches. He sported a long, full gray mustache that filled his brown face. His brown eyes usually shone brightly under his cowboy hat, but on rare occasions when his anger flared, they boiled black. His hands were thickly calloused from years of hard labor. He almost self-consciously shielded them from Edith as he cradled the reins.

Reyes had migrated to New Mexico over twenty years ago. After trying his luck at various labors, he came across an advertisement for workers at the Lesnett Lumber Mill. The thought of working in a mountain forest appealed to him, so he signed up and traveled to Ruidoso. He enjoyed the work in the cooler weather and developed a deep respect for the Lesnetts. In return, the Lesnetts gave Reyes large responsibilities and a great deal of authority. He acted like a *mayordomo* with the crews and the Lesnetts treated him as a valuable employee.

During his frequent supply trips, he had witnessed the fierce pace Edith kept while managing the store and hotel. For her own good, he coaxed her into coming up to the camp. Seeing her in this relaxed state buoyed his spirits and made him happy. He turned his attention back to his driving and concentrated on the road ahead.

The Lesnetts had built a passable road to bring supplies to the lumber mill and haul the wood products out. It still had its rough spots from inadequate drainage and heavy wagons, but all in all they had constructed it well. In many portions, the road switched back and forth to flatten the grade as it climbed the mountain. They were now entering one of the switchback sections. Reyes held the reins tighter as the horses swung them around the first tight curve. Suddenly, Reyes spotted two bodies lying in the middle of the road. He yanked back on the reins and hollered, "Whoa!" Edith startled awake in her seat.

"What in the name of God. . ."she gasped as she lifted her hand to her face. She could tell that they were men. The smaller man lay face down in the dirt. The bigger man was sprawled out on his back with his arms stretched out wide. Neither moved and Edith feared that they had been shot. New Mexico still had its problems and a double murder on her road would not surprise her.

Reyes had the same thoughts and reached under the buckboard and pulled out his rifle. He passed the reins to Edith and said quietly, "Stay here. If anything happens, ride like hell out of here." Edith nodded and looked at him with nervous eyes as she took the reins. Reyes took a deep breath and stepped down from the wagon. He chambered a shell and pulled the hammer back to its firing position. He put the stock up to his shoulder and readied the rifle. Then he slowly walked toward them. Reyes was deeply concerned that the men were playing possum and would attack him when he drew nearer. He advanced with extreme caution and muttered, "If they so much as twitch, I'll blow their heads off."

Reyes carefully made his way to the smaller man. When he came close, he prodded him with the barrel of his gun. The man produced no movement or sound. He poked him harder and got no response. Reyes slid his boot under the man's ribs and rolled him over. The man flopped onto his back and his arms spread-eagled out. Reyes ran his eyes over his body and noted his ragged condition, but he could not see any wounds or blood. He looked closer and saw that the man was breathing slowly. His face looked totally exhausted.

Reyes turned his attention to the big man. He appeared much older than the other. Upon closer inspection, Reyes concluded that he was breathing too. Reyes bent down and pushed the man's head over to the other side. He saw raw wounds oozing from his scalp. Dirt caked the swollen knots and the gashes appeared infected.

Reyes took a step back to reassess the situation and was startled when he bumped into Edith. "*Señora* Lesnett, what are you doing here? You must get back to the wagon. It is not safe here."

"Nonsense, Canuto," stated Edith as she surveyed the scene. "These men are obviously hurt and we must help them." Before Reyes could protest, Edith bent down and began examining the men. Except for the larger man, she could find no wounds. "These poor men are exhausted, Canuto. They look like they have been chased by something."

"Or someone," added Reyes.

"Whatever the case may be, they need help or they will die. Help me get them into the wagon. We will take them to the camp."

"*¡Dios mío!*" exclaimed Reyes. "You can't just collect these men like stray animals you find along the road. They might be criminals for all we know. *Señora*, let's leave them here and notify the authorities, *por favor.*"

Edith flared back at him, "We will do nothing of the sort. Now, either help me or get out of my way!" Reyes knew that when Edith made up her mind, nothing, not even her husband, could dissuade her. He pushed his hat back and looked up into the sky as he swore under his breath. Then he reached down and grabbed the big man by the arm and dragged him to the wagon. After a few strenuous and awkward minutes, they managed to get both men loaded into the wagon. Against Reyes's wishes, Edith climbed in the back with the men and began tending to their needs. Reyes shook his head with frustration as he snapped the reins to start the horses. They slowly began to pick up speed and continued their climb to the camp.

They were gone only a few minutes when a man leaped out of the woods at the spot where they had found the men. His chest heaved from hard running and sweat soaked his buckskin shirt. He quickly scanned the ground for tracks and was confused by the signs he found. He could see where two men had lain on the road. Then, almost unbelievably, he saw two other sets of footprints. One set was made by a man. The other was smaller and lighter like that of a woman. As he followed the tracks, he found the unmistakable signs of dragging. The marks led to a wagon drawn by two—no, four horses.

John Smoke Rider memorized the information as he recreated the scene. He pulled his skin flask from his belt and took a small swig of water. Suddenly, the situation made perfect sense. He was on the Lesnett road. The woman was certainly Mrs. Lesnett and Smoke Rider knew that it would be just like her to help two total strangers. He kicked the dirt on the road in frustration. He thought when he had found the discarded flask several miles back that he finally had them. He had sent his horse home because of the thick forest and started running at a seven-minute-mile pace. Now this happened and snatched them from his clutches.

John shook his head in disbelief at his poor luck. He had no choice. He would have to run to the Lesnett camp. It was several miles up the road and he had only a few hours left before his commission ended. He pulled his rifle from the skin sheath that was strapped to his back. He checked its condition and put it back. Without delaying further, Smoke Rider put his head down and trotted off after the wagon. He knew in his heart that finding the fugitives was only a small part of the problem. Convincing Mrs. Lesnett to hand them over would be the real challenge.

———◦••◦———

The sun was setting when Prudenciano finally woke. As his eyes focused, he saw a woman place a damp cloth on his brow. Its coolness felt good against his hot, dry skin. When he mumbled, "*Gracias,*" she smiled back. Prudenciano thought that she had the face of an angel.

Prudenciano scanned his surroundings without moving his head. He was in a wall tent with a ridge pole made from an unpeeled spruce tree. He noticed something binding his forehead and lifted his hand to explore it. He found a bandage neatly wrapped around his skull to protect his hammer wounds. He let his hand fall to his side and it bounced slightly on a thin cotton sheet that draped over a tight canvas cot. When Prudenciano tried to lift his head, pain shot down and forced him to lie still.

Edith straightened up and smoothed her hair back with her free hand

and said, "You better take life easy for a while, Mister. You have a nasty set of bumps on your head." She looked at Prudenciano's bewildered face and realized that he did not understand a single word. Years of bartering at the store had taught her rudimentary Spanish, so she switched to the language and asked a simple question, "How are you?"

Prudenciano slowly nodded his head, "*Bien*, but I am very thirsty."

"I suppose you are," replied Edith. She went over to the table and poured a glass of water from a porcelain pitcher. She brought it back and gently put her hand under his head and lifted him to the glass so he could comfortably drink. He gulped the entire glass down. Edith chided, "I think that is enough for now. I will give you more in a little while. I want you to rest now." She softly lowered him to the pillow.

Prudenciano had never thought water tasted so good. Suddenly, he thought of Silva and tried to glance around the room for him. Edith guessed what he was looking for and calmed him by saying, "Your friend is sleeping over there." She pointed to the far wall. Prudenciano strained his aching head to peer in the pointed direction and saw a figure lying on a cot like his. Silva's mouth was open and he was snoring softly. The man was comatose in sleep. Edith continued, "He woke about an hour ago. After some water, he fell deep asleep again. You tired him out."

This struck Prudenciano as particularly funny, but when he tried to laugh, his aching body protested. His smile turned into a wince of pain. Edith watched him for a minute and decided to ask him about what had happened. As she began to speak, Canuto Reyes bolted into the wall tent. "*Señora*," he addressed her breathlessly, "I think we found who was chasing them! He is here now and wants them."

"Really?" Edith said in English as she stood up and prepared to meet her challenger. "We will see about that." She looked back at Prudenciano for moment as if to reconfirm her commitment. Then she threw back the tent flap and marched outside.

The sun was setting and signaled that it was time to shut down the lumber operations for the day. This was usually a peaceful time, when the men silenced the screaming band saws and ceased the banging of wood planks. Edith loved the easy banter among the men as the day slowed down. However, this was not the familiar scene she saw when she walked into the lumberyard. The men were crowding around someone and she could barely see Frank and Tom in the center. Tom seemed especially agitated.

In her usual brusque manner, Edith muscled her way through the men until she reached her husband. Frank stood with his hands on his hips with a concerned look on his face. His lanky six-foot frame bent forward as he cocked his full head of gray hair to the side and listened to a stranger converse with Tom. Edith stood next to Frank and gave the man a good looking over. He wore a combination of Apache and purchased apparel with a rifle tucked into a skin sheath that hung on his back. His face was streaked with dirt and sweat. He looked like a troublemaker. It was only when he turned his face toward her that she recognized him. Once she identified him, she wasted little time cutting to the heart of the matter.

Edith interrupted John in mid-sentence, "Johnny Smoke Rider! What is the meaning of this? Why do you trounce in here demanding we give up two men?" Edith had known John Smoke Rider since he was a baby and, much to his chagrin, she called him "Johnny" whenever they met. When he was a child, his grandfather Augustine would bring him by the store for a piece of hard candy. To Edith, it seemed like yesterday that John scampered across her floors in bare feet. She found it hard to believe that he now hunted men for a living.

Tom answered for John. "Maw, he says that those two Mexicans you brought up here are wanted felons. He says that he has warrants for their arrest."

Edith gave her big, muscular son a hard look before responding. "Johnny, show me the warrants." Smoke Rider suddenly seemed flustered and kicked his moccasin at the dust. "Johnny," repeated Edith, "I want to see your warrants."

Smoke Rider swallowed hard before responding, "I don't have them with me."

Edith remained expressionless. "Johnny, did these men steal anything?" Smoke Rider slowly shook his head "no." Edith continued, "Did they kill someone?" Again, Smoke Rider shook his head. He could have lied, but he had too much respect for Mrs. Lesnett. She was like a godmother to him. "Well then, I fail to see why I should turn these men over to you."

Frank had remained silent up to now. He turned and faced his wife. "Edith, it is not as simple as that. John says that they flagged down a freight train and hurt a man in the process. I think that we would be better off without them in camp. I say we give them over to John."

Edith snapped, "We will do nothing of the sort! If these men actually did something monstrous, wouldn't the law have sent a full posse instead of one man?" Frank had to admit that she had a point, but he still felt that they would be better off without them. Without waiting for an answer, Edith turned back to Smoke Rider and asked a very pointed question. "Johnny, doesn't your jurisdiction end at the reservation border?" Smoke Rider gave her a quick nod. "Well then.

That settles it. Since we are not on the reservation, we will keep the men here. You can return home and notify the authorities of their whereabouts and if they come, we will hand them over."

Frank sputtered his disagreement, "Now, Edith…"

Edith cut him off with a wave of her hand. Even Tom tried to protest, but he stopped at the futility of it. The rest of the men mumbled among themselves. Smoke Rider stood stunned in the middle. He knew that when Mrs. Lesnett had made up her mind that was the end of it. He had lost his prey again and would be returning empty-handed. He turned to leave.

"Wait," Edith said with sudden compassion in her voice. "Johnny, please stay and join us for supper. You can spend the night if you like and we will resupply you in the morning. You look like you could use a hearty meal and good night's rest." Smoke Rider's shoulders slumped forward with exhaustion. He could use something to eat. It had been five days since he'd had a decent meal. He lowered his head and nodded. "Excellent!" exclaimed Edith, "Canuto, please take Johnny over to the washtubs and then get him fixed up in one of the spare tents. Supper will be ready in one hour."

A low voice rumbled in the crowd, "That Injin ain't sleeping with me!" There were murmurs of agreement among the men.

Edith barked, "We will have no more of that! Johnny is an honored guest in this camp and I want each one of you to treat him with respect. Do I make myself clear, gentlemen?" The men shuffled their feet and avoided her piercing stare. Canuto came forward and led John away by the shoulder. Slowly, the men dispersed and the camp settled into its usual predinner activities.

———•◦•———

The brilliant moon rode high in the night sky when Prudenciano woke. Its soft white light lit the canvas roof like a large lantern suspended above the tent. He took a minute to gather his bearings and look around him. Silva still slept soundly on his cot. Only his imperceptible breathing indicated that he was still alive. Prudenciano envied how he could sleep totally oblivious to the world.

The pain in Prudenciano's head receded to a dull ache. He reached up and felt the bandage again. It felt dry and secure. It also reminded him that someone was taking good care of Silva and him. This caused him to pause and reflect on the day. He remembered dragging Silva onto a road. They fell and he could not get up. When he had opened his eyes again, they were here. The woman treated them kindly, but he saw a ferociousness beneath her eyes. It showed its fury when a man burst inside the tent and she left abruptly with him. Prudenciano barely heard the ruckus outside. It sounded like an argument. After a few minutes she returned with more water. The woman had a triumphant look on her face. He thought, *But why? Had their pursuer arrived and demanded their apprehension?*

He pondered these thoughts for a while. His eyes finally grew heavy and sleep began to overwhelm him. Suddenly, his skin began to crawl and his pulse raced as he sensed someone else moving in the tent. He slowly moved his head toward the back wall and let his eyes fully adjust to the darkness. A shadow seemed to transform before him and move slowly toward his cot. Prudenciano caught his breath and prepared to fight. The figure seemed to float above the ground in total silence. It stopped before him and remained motionless.

Prudenciano let his eyes search for the figure's face. The filtered moonlight barely illuminated the man who stood before him. Suddenly, his features jumped out at him. Prudenciano recognized him as the Indian he had glimpsed in the canyon. Prudenciano's fear rose to his throat.

John Smoke Rider stood next to the big man lying on a cot. Curiosity had driven him to sneak into the tent and study this man. Never before had a man outmaneuvered and escaped him. When Smoke Rider leaned over the cot and saw him, he was stunned to discover that his opponent was middle-aged. He watched him quietly with awe and respect because his grandfather Augustine had taught him to respect wisdom and bravery. This man that lay before him certainly had both.

Smoke Rider could easily kill this man with a quick thrust of his knife, but the thought never occurred to him. Instead, he slowly reached out and gently touched Prudenciano on the shoulder—the symbolic gesture of collecting coup from an adversary. This was an Apache belief that a brave could claim some of his opponent's medicine or spiritual powers. John wanted this man's spiritual gifts. Then with incredible swiftness, he whirled toward the tent wall and disappeared.

Prudenciano exhaled and felt beads of perspiration trickle down his face. He timidly reached over and felt his shoulder. It was still there with no perceivable injury, but Prudenciano was convinced that he had just been touched by the Angel of Death.

Morning came quickly at the lumber mill. By dawn, the cooking shack operated in high gear. The men woke, dressed and trudged over to the mess tent, their conversation low and friendly. So when Canuto ran to Frank and Edith's cabin with frantic news that John Smoke Rider had slipped away during the night, it caused a stir in

the camp. Edith immediately checked on her two strays and was relieved to see both men were well. The crew quickly looked around
and could not find anything missing.

"I guess he figured that he had to git," said Tom as he adjusted
his hat. "I reckon he'll tell the sheriff about those two Mexicans you
found down the road, Maw."

Edith replied, "Maybe he will and maybe he won't, but I think that
they are healthy enough to do a few chores around here. Please give
them something to do and see how they work out. If they don't, send
them on their way."

"Maw," pleaded Tom with a thread of exasperation, "they ain't
worth it. Let's turn them loose now."

Edith smiled at her son and said, "All I am asking is for you to give
them a chance. That is all. If they cause trouble, then kick them out,
Okay?" She struggled not to say "honey" or "dear" at the end of her
sentence. It embarrassed Tom immensely when she called him that
in front of the men. Tom shook his head, but reluctantly agreed.
"Good," exclaimed Edith as she sealed the decision, "have Canuto
supervise them. They do not speak English."

"Great," muttered Tom. Canuto was listening in the background. At
Tom's signal, he came forward. Tom spoke not a word, but wagged his
head toward the tent where the two vagabonds were staying. Canuto
smiled his understanding and started walking to the tent with a bounce
in his step. He had a feeling that the day was going to be amusing.

When Canuto reached the tent, he flipped the front flaps open and
let the early morning sun blast inside. Much to his surprise, he found
Prudenciano sitting on the edge of his cot and Silva already rousted
from his bed. Prudenciano sat bare-chested with his pants and boots
on. Canuto was impressed with his muscular build and flat stomach, especially since his gray hair, beard, and body hair indicated an advanced
age. Prudenciano's bandaged head was his only sign of injury.

"*¡Dios mío!*" exclaimed Silva as he struggled to get up while squint-
ing into the sun. "I could have slept for another day."

Canuto produced a wicked grin and greeted them, "*Buenos días,
Señores*. I hope you enjoyed our hospitality for the last two days."

"Two days!" blurted Prudenciano in an unbelieving tone. He must
have slept longer than he thought.

"*Sí*," answered Canuto with laughter in his voice. "Now, I am afraid
we must determine what we are going to do with you."

Silva asked, "Oh? And how are you going to do that?" Silva did not
like the sadistic tone in the man's voice.

Canuto seemed to relish this moment and delayed a few delicious
seconds before answering. "Well, I suppose the first thing to do is get

you two cleaned up and fed. Then we will ask you a few questions. If we think you are worth having around, then we will see how well you work. After that ..." Canuto shrugged and produced another smirk. Prudenciano and Silva had a feeling that the next few days were going to be extremely hard if they wanted to stay here.

After another uneasy few moments, Prudenciano spoke first. "Where are our shirts?"

As if on cue, a woman's voice called behind Canuto, "Are they decent?"

Prudenciano saw the deep respect in the man's eyes as he turned to address her. "*Sí, Señora.* They are covered, if that is what you mean, but I doubt that they are decent."

Edith ignored his remark and came forward. On each arm, she had a freshly washed and neatly pressed shirt with a towel and a bar of soap placed on top. "Here you go," she said as she handed her load to each man. "Canuto will take you to the washtubs. I suggest you two spend some time there. You will find some shaving supplies there too. Afterward, we will feed you and figure out what to do next." She appraised each one quickly with her confident stare. The men found her scrutiny uncomfortable and shifted nervously in front of her. Seemingly satisfied, Edith left without saying another word.

Canuto announced, "All right, *hombres. ¡Vámanos!*" He led the men through camp. Many of the workers stopped what they were doing and stared at them as they walked by. Prudenciano felt their suspicious and wary looks as he passed. They finally came to a large canvas shelter that had a smoking stovepipe in the middle of its roof. As they entered it, they found that the canvas was actually a wind shelter and screen for a series of large tubs that sat within stalls of rough-cut lumber. A spring provided water for a wood boiler and a cold water reservoir. By combining the flow of each, a bather could adjust the water temperature in each tub. Prudenciano thought it was an incredible luxury. Canuto led them to separate tubs and showed them how to operate the water controls. Then he pointed out the shaving mirrors and the supplies at the far end of the bathhouse and left them.

Prudenciano and Silva quickly stripped, filled their tubs, and slid gingerly into the steaming water. They could hear each other's moans of pain and pleasure through the cracked walls as they became accustomed to the temperature. Finally, silence prevailed as each soaked in paradise.

After about an half an hour of silent bliss, Silva broke the silence. "Nava, can you hear me?"

"*Sí*," answered Prudenciano gruffly. He was annoyed that Silva wrecked his tranquility, and sank deeper into the tub.

Silva continued, "I have been doing some thinking." He waited for a response and after getting none, he resumed. "These people are going to ask why we were running. If we tell them the truth that we killed a man, then they will turn us in to the law, ¿qué no?"

Prudenciano had to admit that Silva had a point, but he did not know where he was going with his discussion. So, he grunted back his agreement.

Mollified, Silva went on with his thoughts. "What if we tell them that this is all a case of mistaken identity? We can change our names just like Pancho Villa and live here. What do you think?" Prudenciano had to admit that Silva was making a lot of sense. He especially liked the correlation between them and Villa. It excited him to think that he was living a life like the notorious outlaw he had once pursued.

Prudenciano finally answered, "I think that is a very good idea. What name should I choose?"

Silva laughed and said, "I can't pick it for you, Nava. You have to do that, but this is what I suggest you do. You should select a first name of someone you like, you know, a past friend, then you will never forget it. Then you should chose a last name of your mother or grandfather so it is still part of your family."

Again, Prudenciano thought this was a very good idea. Before he could answer, Canuto's voice boomed over the partitions, "This is not a beauty salon! Get shaved and dressed now!" Both men moaned in response as they got up and dried themselves. They pulled the plugs in the tubs to drain the water and put their pants and fresh shirts on.

They shuffled out of their stalls and met Canuto pointing his finger toward the shaving basins. Metal mirrors lined the wall above the basins of steaming hot water. The mirrors gave a dull reflection, but they were still adequate for shaving. Canuto said, "I trust you two know how to use these? When you are done, meet us in the mess tent that is across the road. Hurry. We don't have all day." Canuto turned and left.

Silva and Prudenciano stared at themselves in the mirrors for a moment. Each contemplated two decisions—how much to shave and what to choose for a new name. Silva had a sparse beard so the choice was simple. He would shave his face smooth. As for his new name, he thought he should keep it simple and short. After a few seconds it came to him. "Santos Terra," he muttered. "Sí, Santos Terra it shall be." Santos smiled and briskly began preparing his face for shaving.

Prudenciano had a more difficult task. His beard was thick and full and he liked it. But he realized that a new identity often required a complete change of appearance. He looked at himself again in the mirror. He could not depart with all the facial hair. He would compromise and keep the mustache.

Next came the important decision of a new name. Prudenciano contemplated this for a moment and searched his memory for a suitable friend from his past whose name could assume. Suddenly, his brain seized on one man, Tereso Rodriguez. The memory brought a stab of remorse, but he knew the name would be a good choice. In a way, resurrecting the name would honor his friend of twenty years. Prudenciano blurted, "Tereso! I would never forget that name." His outburst startled Santos, who had already lathered his face up with the shaving brush. Prudenciano laughed at Santos's dark brown eyes peering through the white suds that puffed around his face.

Prudenciano returned to the mirror and thought about his last name. He recalled that his mother's last name was Minjares. "Tereso Minjares," murmured Prudenciano, "That is it! I shall be called Tereso Minjares." With the critical decisions made, Tereso confidently wetted the soap in the shaving jar and whisked it with a brush until a thick lather formed. Removing his thick beard was going to take some work.

When the two men stepped into the mess tent, the people inside scarcely recognized them. They looked scrubbed and polished in their clean shirts and wet combed hair. Their smooth brown faces had a raw appearance that resulted from fresh shaving. The taller of the two had a neatly trimmed mustache.

Edith waved them over to the plywood table where they were sitting. She greeted them in Spanish, *"Buenos días.* Sit here, *por favor.* We need to discuss your future." The men walked to the table and sat at the far end. They faced Edith, Frank, Tom, and Canuto, who were studying them closely. After a few awkward moments, Edith began. "What are your names?"

The two men stole a quick look at each other as if they each knew their names, but did not know their partner's. This was not lost on the others, who watched them with keen interest. Finally, the larger man spoke first, "My name is Tereso Minjares." Tereso stopped and turned to his friend to speak.

The younger and smaller man seemed to acknowledge his cue and continued, "My name is Santos Terra." Again, an unsettling silence fell over the table.

"Must be men of few words," muttered Frank to no one in particular.

Edith shot Frank a look of annoyance before asking her next question. "We heard one side of the story from Johnny. Now we want to hear from you two. What happened at the railroad and why were you chased?"

Tereso and Santos were deeply bothered by this question. They squirmed and traded uncomfortable glances at each other. Santos seemed to understand that he shouldered the responsibility of delivering the requested story. He took a deep breath to collect his thoughts and began weaving his tale. "Prud…, er, I mean, Tereso and I had to flag a train down south of Carrizozo to catch a ride to our camp. We missed the work train and it started raining." He stopped for a moment to see if his hosts were buying his story. They seemed intent on listening to every word that came out of his mouth and it bolstered him. He continued with renewed confidence, "We started a bonfire at the work site. The train stopped. The crew spoke no Spanish. A misunderstanding occurred. We fought. Then we ran." Santos lifted his hands in the air and shrugged to signify that there was nothing else to say.

Tom thundered, "That's it? Why did the law send Smoke Rider after you guys? They just wouldn't do that for fightin'. Something is not adding up!" Canuto and Frank nodded in agreement.

Santos felt his validity slipping and quickly came up with a response. "When Tereso and I were running, we heard that a man was killed close to the work site. The law thinks it was us. This explains why we are being chased." The story sounded good, but opened up many more questions.

Frank quickly pressed the question, "But, you guys did not do it?"

"No, *Señor*. We are innocent!" lied the new Santos with his arms spread out in a pleading manner. The story did not satisfy the men. For all they knew, they were sitting with two killers. A long silence prevailed over the meeting. Suddenly, the cook burst through a swinging door with a plate of steaming food in each hand. Edith nodded toward Santos and Tereso. The man slammed the plates on the table and expertly slid them in front of the starving men. They quickly wolfed down the ham, eggs, and potatoes and chased them with mugs of hot coffee. The others waited patiently until they were done before continuing the conversation.

Tom spoke first. "We're fixing on shutting down for the winter. In another month, we will have snow past your waist. You guys can either leave now or stay and help us with the shutdown. Your choice. If you stay and work, we will pay you, but you've got to work hard. If you screw up, I'll put your butts on the next wagon out of here, *comprende*?" The men nodded. "So, what's it going to be?"

Tereso and Santos glanced at each other before answering in unison, "We will stay."

Tom mumbled, "I was afraid of that." He looked at his mother as if to say, Are you satisfied, Maw? She just smiled back at him and sipped her coffee. "All right," sighed Tom, "Canuto, you have your work cut out for you. Take these men and see what you can do with them."

Canuto smiled and stood up from the table. "This way, *Señores*. Your day awaits you." He led them out into the camp. Tereso and Santos were wary and exchanged apprehensive glances. Canuto saw their expressions and chuckled as they walked toward the sawmill. As they came nearer, the screaming circular saw became louder until it was almost deafening. The mill rough-cut logs into planks and rail ties. The men stacked the cut wood in organized lots for wagons to haul the products to railroad warehouses or other markets. The mill also produced mountains of sawdust and scrap wood that required constant removal. Mill employees considered this to be the ugliest and most degrading work at the camp. Everyone started here and proved their worth before the Lesnetts promoted them into more desirable positions. Even Tom had cut his teeth here as a scrappy teenager before his father gave him additional responsibilities. The Lesnetts were about to initiate Tereso and Santos into mill life.

Canuto stopped in front of a large sawdust pile with an old freight wagon parked next to it. He put his hands on his hips and surveyed the situation. Then with a loud voice that was overwhelmed by the screeching saw, he explained their new tasks. "Do you see those two scoop shovels over there?" He pointed to the tools embedded in the enormous pile. "I want you *hombres* to load the sawdust into that wagon. When you are done, tell the mill foreman. He will hook the horses up and haul it away. *Comprende?*"

Tereso and Santos stood speechless as they sized up their job that Canuto so nonchalantly described. It would take them over two days to move this pile. Canuto read their minds and laughed loudly. "Oh, don't worry. See that conveyor belt over there?" The men turned to look where Canuto was pointing. A large conveyor belched fresh wet sawdust into a new pile that promised to be even bigger than the first. "That pile will be waiting for you when you are through with this one. We have plenty of work for you to enjoy. Have fun." He seemed to almost skip as he walked away. Although his back was toward them, they were sure that he had a smirk on his face.

Tereso and Santos glanced at each other as if to say, Ready? Then each grabbed a shovel and started chucking the sawdust into the wagon. They worked steadily without saying much, but after an hour, their backs and shoulders hurt in the thin air. The combination of hard labor and the warm autumn sun drew beads of sweat across their brows. The perspiration soaked Tereso's head bandage. Neither had a hat.

Tereso stopped to take a break. He wiped his forehead with the back of his hand and leaned on his shovel to watch Santos work.

Only a short time ago, Santos would have stopped too and sought a way to avoid further labor. However, the events of the past week had changed him. Never before had he faced death, hunger, exhaustion, and the unrelenting fear that someone deadly was chasing him. The experience rattled the very core of his existence and molded his spirit. He was more humble and he never wanted to repeat the past week. With the adoption of a new name, Santos vowed to change his life and that included developing a good work ethic. He continued to shovel.

Tereso, on the other hand, had learned little from their near-fatal adventure. His only thoughts were that his head ached from the high-pitched noise, his back and shoulders hurt, his hands felt raw, and the work seemed endless. In the deep recesses of his mind, he was vaguely aware that his recklessness had caused him to abandon his family and run. He believed that the past week resulted from bad luck and was not worthy of life-altering changes. He still wanted to get by with the least possible work while claiming the maximum amount of benefit.

Tereso watched Santos for a few minutes longer before counseling him on how to work better. He shouted over the saw, "Grab the handle closer to the shovel. Use your legs more." Santos bristled from Tereso's unsolicited advice. He gritted his teeth and continued to throw sawdust onto the growing pile in the wagon.

Tereso yelled louder, "Hey!" He hated to be ignored. "I said to grab the handle lower!"

Santos exploded. He hurtled his shovel over the wagon and turned on Tereso with clenched fists and screamed, "What the hell is wrong with you? Are you completely *loco*? These people are giving you a chance to start a new life and you are going to blow it!"

Santos's reaction caught Tereso flat-footed. He was clueless why Santos erupted. As for a new life, Tereso envisioned something much better than shoveling sawdust. He threw his shovel aside and prepared to retaliate when the mill foreman interrupted him.

The foreman walked up to the wagon and asked "Done?" He had seen Santos's flying shovel and came over to investigate. He found the wagon sufficiently filled and said, "*Bueno*." This was the extent of his Spanish. He held up one finger to indicate that he would be right back. The men nodded their understanding and sat down in the sawdust pile to rest. While they waited, their anger subsided. After a few minutes, the foreman returned with a team of four horses pulling an empty wagon. As he drew near, the high-pitched noise agitated the horses and made them unruly. A lead horse reared and bucked. Its harness yanked the other horses and they neighed and exhaled forcibly in response. The foreman tightly held the reins and fought for control.

Tereso stepped forward and laid his hands on the neck of the bucking horse. He gently stroked its neck and soothed its aching ears. The horse snorted in response and ceased thrashing. Its eyes rolled with pain. Tereso nuzzled the horse and led it by its bridle to pull the wagon alongside the sawdust pile. He signaled to the foreman to pull the pin that connected the team to the wagon. The man leaped off the buckboard and yanked the metal pin from the yoke. Tereso then calmly brought the team forward to the loaded wagon and skillfully backed them in place so that the yoke and wagon lined up and the foreman inserted the pin. When the foreman waved him forward, Tereso led the team and pulled the loaded wagon away from the noisy saw.

The foreman came running up to the team. Tereso stood holding the disturbed horse by the halter and stroking its nose. Tereso's horsemanship impressed the foreman and he signaled for Tereso to climb into the wagon with him. When Tereso got situated, the man gave him the reins and motioned for him to drive. Tereso gave the reins a firm snap and the horses moved forward down a forest road. Neither man looked back to see an exasperated Santos standing alone by a huge sawdust pile and an empty wagon that required filling.

The following weeks proved difficult for Santos and enjoyable for Tereso. Santos continued to work at the sawdust piles. His hands and back hardened from the torturous hours of shoveling. Much to his credit, Santos did not complain or shirk his duties. Tereso, on the other hand, became the camp's horse handler. He cared for the horses, harnessed them, and drove the teams. He seldom did any hard work and never lifted a finger to help Santos when he had free time. At least once a day, he shouted out some words of advice to Santos on how to work faster. Santos appeared to ignore his remarks, but the way he jammed his shovel into the pile, everyone except Tereso could see he was seething.

The nights grew colder and the trees filled with leaves of gold and yellow. Snow began to spurt from dark, heavy clouds. By the first week in November, the camp began shutting down. Tereso and Santos knew that their time was limited and soon they must look for another place to stay. So when Tom Lesnett called them to his office, they thought their time had ended. They both took off their hats as they entered the office and stood in front of Tom's desk. Tom was finishing his review of a ledger as he looked up.

"*Buenos días, Señores*. Thank you for coming." Tom motioned for them to take a seat. They sat down in the wooden chairs lining the wall directly across from the desk. Tom got directly to his point. "We are closing our doors for the winter. The big snows are coming very soon and we got to be out of here by then." Tom stopped for a second and studied the two men in front of him. He seemed to come to a decision before continuing. "Both of you proved to be good employees. I have to be honest and say that I am quite surprised. I thought you both would be long gone by now. So, I have a proposition for you two." The men were intrigued and leaned forward to hear what he had to say. "Every year, our sheds, cabins, and equipment shelters break under the heavy snowloads of winter. It takes time and money to get the camp in shape every spring. We want to try something new this winter. We want you two to stay here and keep the snow off the roofs. We can fix you guys up with firewood and food. I don't have to tell you that you men would be marooned up here for four months, but nobody is going to be coming up here looking for you either, catch my drift? So, what do you say?"

For Tereso and Santos, this was a dream come true. The camp would be a perfect hideaway. They both nodded yes.

Tom appeared pleased, but at the same time he looked at them quizzically as if there was more to these two men than what he knew. He finally concluded that it was probably best that he did not know.

The bitter cold clawed at Paz's back as she bent down to pick up a piece of dirty laundry that had fallen from her large basket. Her bare hand was so cold and numb that she could barely grasp the clothing. Her back ached as she straightened up and staggered toward her boxcar. The unceasing winter winds pushed and shoved her all the way.

When she got to the car, Paz used her last bit of strength to lift the basket into the sliding door. She was barely tall enough to accomplish this without the help of a stool. She reached up to grab the handrail when she heard someone call out to her, "¡Buenas tardes, Señora!" Paz looked over her shoulder and saw a young man from the bachelor car wave to her. He was one of several men in the *colonia* who had recently been trying to catch her attention.

Prudenciano and Silva had fled six months ago. Since then, rumors abounded that they had been caught and hung. Others said that the railroad posted a large reward for their capture and the Mescalero Apaches were hot on their trail. The *colonia* had moved several times and now were relocated south of Tularosa. She was beginning to give up hope that her husband would ever return. If he was still alive, how would he ever find them?

Paz kept her children fed by washing the clothes of the *colonia* families in a large metal tub within the drafty boxcar. The cold water and lye soap ate her hands raw. Her knees ached from kneeling all day. The *colonia* repaid her with food, some money, and by keeping her secret from the railroad section bosses that she had no husband.

Despite the hard work, Paz hated the nights the worst. After she tucked her children in bed, the loneliness pressed upon her like a giant weight. She longed to be held again, loved, and told that everything would work out. She would lie awake listening to the wind shaking the car and wondered if her husband was still alive. She sometimes cursed him for this fate and other times she just lay under her blankets and silently cried.

It would be so easy to invite a man over. After all, who would fault her? Her husband had killed a man. The law had probably caught him by now. She would never see him again. She was young and had three little children. She needed a reliable man, but she knew in her heart that she could never open herself to another without knowing if her husband was truly dead. She had made a vow to God and Prudenciano to see her marriage through. She would honor that vow. Paz smiled sadly back at the man and pulled herself up and into the car.

Alcaria and Joaquina pushed the heavy blanket aside when they heard their mother pull the laundry basket across the wooden floor and helped her into their living quarters. Paz strung ropes across the makeshift room to dry clothes. While she was gone, the girls had wrung the freshly washed clothes and hung them to dry. The damp clothing dripped on everything not covered. Paz had stacked their bedding in a corner in a feeble attempt to protect it, but the wet floor gradually seeped water into the mattress and rotted it.

Augustine crawled across the cold, wet wood to Paz and begged to be held. Ever since his father had left, he had refused to walk and frequently wet his pants. The trauma of seeing his father hurt and abandoning the family had deeply affected him. Every day he looked for his father and cried when he did not return by evening. Paz felt his agony twist in her heart and it added to her despair.

Paz stood up and let the curtain fall behind her. She put her hands into the small of her back and massaged her aching muscles. She closed her eyes and thought how wonderful it would be to have Prudenciano use his *sobador* talents on her back. Augustine interrupted her dream by tugging at her skirt. Paz looked down at the pitiful boy and forgot all about her pain. She brushed a hanging shirt to the side and lifted Augustine to her breast. "Oh!" she groaned, "You are a big boy."

Augustine did not feel like a big boy. He laid his head on his mother and kneaded her coat with his chubby hand. Paz held him tight and stroked his head. She ducked under more clothes and sat on a stool in front of the washtub. The girls came to her and sat on the folded bedding. Paz noticed dark circles under their eyes. Alcaria seemed to have lost weight over the past month.

Paz gathered up her courage and put on her best smile. The girls stared blankly back. Their father's absence had snuffed their little-girl spirits. They were cold and sad. The family sat in silence for a moment and listened to the wind blowing outside. Finally, Alcaria asked the question that was on all their minds, "Mama, will Papa ever come back?"

Paz stared back at her daughters as she tried to control her emotions. She wanted to give them some hope, something to cling to, but she had reached the end of her strength. She started to tremble as she raised her hand to her mouth to suppress a cry. Heavy tears flowed from her big brown eyes. Suddenly, she could not restrain herself and she let the waves of suppressed grief pour out. Her body convulsed with deep sobs. Augustine put his little arms around her neck to comfort her and let her tears fall on his face. The girls came forward and held their mother, too.

This little knot of a family continued to cry and hold each other as the wind seeped through the walls and fluttered the hanging clothes. A chill hung in the air as winter swirled around the *colonia*—scattered boxcars parked on a lonely sidetrack in the New Mexican desert.

Chapter 17
Sierra Blanca

March 1914 brought the end of the heavy snows on Sierra Blanca. The sun radiated warmth that melted the snow and glistened the surface. Santos beat on their cabin door until the frozen ice released its grip on the jamb and opened. He stepped out and squinted into the morning sun as it reflected brilliantly off the white landscape. Walls of snow mounded over twelve feet around the cabin. Deep trenches provided pathways to other areas of the camp. For the past two months, Santos and Tereso had lived like mice burrowing through snow. They shoveled relentlessly just to keep their cabin entry open. It made their labors on the sawdust pile seem trivial.

Santos stepped out and stretched his stiff back. He exhaled forcefully and watched his breath rise as steam into the crisp air. He turned and called back, "Hey, Tereso. Come out here. The day is warm." A few minutes later, Tereso emerged with his shoulders slouched forward and shuffled next to Santos. His hair was long and woolly and his beard was thick and ragged. Together, they looked like refugees from a hard-fought war.

Santos spread his arms wide and tilted his face to the sun. "Do you feel it, *amigo*? Spring is here."

Tereso straightened his back and let his eyes adjust to the surrounding glare. He took a long look around and sniffed the air. "It does feel like spring. About time. I have never seen so much snow. I thought it was going to smother us."

Santos laughed, "It almost did. Remember when the snow slid off the cabin roof? It took us two days to dig out."

Tereso shook his head at the memory. He had thought they were entombed forever. "Well, our shoveling days are over."

Santos countered, "Not really. Now we have to clear the mill house and the office to prevent water from seeping in. In a few weeks, the Lesnetts will reopen the camp."

Tereso grunted back. *More endless work*, he thought. This camp was starting to wear on him.

———•••••———

Spring came quickly in the mountains. By the last week in April, Frank and Tom Lesnett had moved most of the mill crew back to camp. After a four-month rest, the crew was eager to start work. Starting the camp was usually a slow and tedious process, but this year it went much more smoothly because the winter watchmen had removed the heavy snows from the buildings. The equipment was dry. The men had no crushed roofs and walls to repair or deep, wet snow to slog through to access buildings.

Tom was especially surprised and pleased at Tereso's and Santos's performance. He had expected them to wade out and disappear off the mountain. He reluctantly admitted that they had done an admirable job and his mother was a good judge of character. Tom was also amazed that no law official had paid them a visit to escort the two characters to jail. He thought, *I guess they earned their stay. We will probably never know what really happened, but nobody has come for them.*

Tom motioned for Canuto to come over. He finished giving instructions to some men retrofitting the sawmill and walked briskly to Tom. "*Sí, Jefe.*"

Tom smiled at the Mexican term for "boss" and said quietly to Canuto, "Move Tereso and Santos into the bunkhouse with the rest of the men. I think they will work out just fine here." Canuto smiled back and nodded. They impressed him, too. From now on, he would treat them with more respect.

———•••••———

Spring flew by and summer found the camp in full swing. Everyone worked hard every day to maximize the production. Even Tereso was not immune to the workload. He tried to extend his equestrian duties, but the foremen had grown wise to his tricks and dragged him off to help with other tasks.

When the stacks of ties and lumber began to overflow the warehouses, the Lesnetts sought faster ways to get their products to market. The obvious solution was to assign more men to drive the wagons to the buyers. When Tom asked Tereso if he was interested in driving a load to the railroad, Tereso reluctantly declined. He claimed that he did not know the area well enough, but Tom and Canuto could tell that Tereso probably did not want to be seen. Thus, Tom assigned Canuto to drive a wagon full of rail ties to the El Paso and Northeastern Railroad section house in Tularosa.

That evening, Tereso casually met Canuto outside the bunkhouse. The night was warm and clear. Canuto leaned against the wall and studied the incredible wealth of stars in the sky. He puffed white clouds of smoke through his pipe, that seemed to mix perfectly with the dull Milky Way that stretched across the horizon. Canuto spoke first without looking at Tereso, "A man can feel very small in this world when he gazes at the heavens, *¿qué no?*"

Tereso looked up and contemplated the stars for a moment. He self-consciously felt his old head wounds with his hand. Although his scalp had healed, the hammer blows had left permanent dents in his skull. The undulations in his bone bothered him. Finally he answered, "*Sí*. It makes a man think."

Canuto barely nodded and continued to look up. He had a feeling that Tereso had something interesting to say. Ever since he had turned down that freight job to Tularosa, he seemed perplexed. Canuto decided to lead him a little and asked, "What thoughts come to your mind, *amigo?*"

Tereso replied evasively, "Oh, like family. It has been a long time since I've seen them."

Ah, bah! thought Canuto. *So that's it.* Canuto remarked, "You never mentioned any family before, Tereso." He stopped his stargazing to study Tereso. "What family do you have and where are they?"

Tereso fell silent. Canuto thought that he looked like he was wrestling with a painful decision. Finally, Tereso nodded as he came to terms with his problem and slowly began to talk. "Canuto, I must ask you to do me an important favor."

Canuto nodded his head. "Go on."

Tereso gulped and looked nervously around him before continuing. "I have a wife and three children. I left them last fall, when Santos and I ran. They are probably still with the *colonia*, you know, a work train." Tereso stopped and kicked his toe at the ground. "I was wondering if you passed it on your trip, could you tell my wife that I am fine?"

Canuto pulled his pipe from his mouth and slowly exhaled the smoke in a long, quiet stream. He tapped the bowl against his palm before he replied. "Have you ever thought about bringing them up here? I am sure the Lesnetts would not mind, especially if you signed on for the winter again."

Tereso was stunned. The thought had never entered his mind. He stood dumbfounded for a moment as he mulled the idea around in his head. He missed his family terribly and the thought of having Paz share his bed again sent stabs of wanting through his groin. "*Sí*. I want my family here. Can you bring them back?"

Canuto smiled. Tereso could see his teeth in the dark. Canuto replied slyly, "I will discuss the matter tomorrow with *Señor* Tomas. By the way, what name shall I tell your wife that asks her to come back with me?"

Again, Tereso was surprised. "How do you know that Tereso is not my real name?"

Canuto laughed softly in the darkness and refilled his pipe. "This is wild country out here. Men are not always what they seem. So, what is your real name?"

Tereso leaned closer and whispered, "Prudenciano Nava. My wife's name is Paz."

Canuto nodded to signify that he heard. He stuff his pipe bowl with fresh tobacco and struck a match. It illuminated his face for a second with a yellow glow as he lit the packed bowl. After a few strong puffs, he developed an even burn and began a relaxed draw on the pipe. He resumed speaking in a soft voice. "I suppose Santos goes by another name, too? Well, no matter. You both worked out well and so far nobody has come looking for you. I will talk with you tomorrow on this. *Buenas noches.*" Canuto quietly turned and walked away.

Tereso felt he had shared some deep dark secret. He stood watching the darkness where Canuto had disappeared. As he turned to go back to the bunkhouse, an owl hooted nearby. The sound made his skin crawl. He was raised with the common Mexican mythology that owls foretold impending death. Tereso shook the feeling from his bones and walked briskly away.

After three days of riding, Canuto was bone tired. His team of six horses pulled the heavily laden wagon off Sierra Blanca, through the Mescalero reservation, and finally into Tularosa. Tereso and Santos had helped him tarp the stacked lumber and secure the straps. Between pulling the ropes tight and tying knots, Tereso had given Canuto an accurate description of his wife. Canuto was surprised how young Tereso said she was. *She probably ran off with someone by now*, he thought as he pulled up to El Paso and Northeastern Railroad office.

He jumped down from the buckboard and dusted himself off. It was still late morning. He had made good time, but the horses needed rest and good fodder. Canuto walked up to the lead mare and patted her neck affectionately. "Just a little farther, *niña*. Then we rest."

He pulled a purchase request from his breast pocket and walked up a small flight of stairs to the main door. The railroad office was meticulous, quiet, and well organized. Canuto felt that his mere presence disturbed the tranquility of the room. He tiptoed to the counter and peered respectfully at the clerk entering figures into a ledger. The young clerk dressed fastidiously in an immaculate white shirt that buttoned tightly around his neck. Black suspenders with brass snaps securely held his creased black slacks over highly polished black shoes. A black and gold visor and wire-rimmed glasses completed his attire.

Canuto fidgeted silently behind the counter until the clerk noticed him. "May I be of some assistance to you, sir?" asked the man as he stood and pushed his glasses to the bridge of his nose with a precise finger.

"*Sí*," replied Canuto with relief in his voice as he handed the clerk the manifest and billing. "I have a load of lumber that your company ordered from the Lesnett Mill." The man took the papers and committed his total attention to it. Canuto held his breath as the man analyzed every word and figure.

Finally, the clerk turned to his desk and retrieved a list of work orders. He ran a finger down the various descriptions until he stopped on mid page. He compared the orders with the inventory that Canuto had given him. The clerk looked up with a solemn face and said, "It appears, sir, that your company has fulfilled our order a week late." He let the revelation sink into Canuto and seemed to relish the discomfort it brought him. "Nonetheless," he continued, "you must deliver it to our work site that is a few miles north."

Canuto complained, "But I have traveled so far already."

The clerk's face remained neutral. "Think of it as compensation for your late delivery. When our company stipulates a delivery date, we mean it." The proclamation summarized the situation. The railroad wielded great power in this region and doing business meant jumping when they said jump.

Canuto swallowed hard to contain his anger and asked, "Where is the work site?"

The clerk searched his face for any animosity. Seeing none, he replied, "Follow the road north for five miles. You will see a work camp parked at a rail siding on the right. The section boss lives in the house next to the water tank. He will direct you where to deposit the lumber." The clerk picked up his clipboards to signify that their conversation was over and said, "Goodbye, sir."

Canuto was seething as he turned away from the obstinate clerk and marched back to the wagon. He stood next to the mare for a few minutes and let his anger subside. He subconsciously stroked the horse's head. She twisted her ear so that Canuto could scratch some hidden itch. Suddenly, it occurred to Canuto that maybe this was the work camp that Tereso had described. "Could it be?" he asked out loud to himself. "*Sí*, it makes sense. Well, old girl, I am afraid that we have a little further to go before we can unload." The mare flattened her ears to show that she understood and was mad. Canuto laughed and patted the neck for the last time. "We better go and see what we will find."

Canuto drove the wagon onto the lone road heading north along the foothills of Sierra Blanca. The sun glared hot in the dry, clear sky. He kept the horses to a slow trot to conserve their strength. Their methodical clopping steadily ate the miles. After an hour, he came across a side road that led to a group of boxcars and a rail siding. A large water tower loomed next to a railroad section house. The camp and house appeared quiet. "This must be it," Canuto said to himself. He steered the team onto the access road and proceeded to the house.

The wagon team crossed the tracks and skirted around the camp. To the untrained eye, it appeared abandoned. Only the flapping of freshly laundered clothes that clustered around one of the cars revealed recent human activity. Canuto knew that Mexican people often melted away into their homes and watched a stranger's every move through secret holes and parted curtains. Confirming his suspicions, he glimpsed an owl-eyed child peeking around a corner. Suddenly, a woman's arm reached out and snatched the child back. Canuto continued riding while he watched the camp from the corner of his eye.

He rode to the section house and parked the wagon in front. The house was a ranch-style home typical of the section houses built along the line. It had a large porch with a white railing. The gray water tank towered alongside with dark stains from water seeping between the weathered planks.

The section house seemed deserted. Canuto stepped down from the wagon and walked up to the front door. He knocked formally to announce his presence, took off his hat, and waited. Within a few moments, a woman came to the door with her hair wrapped in a scarf and wearing a cotton farm dress. She was pleasant looking with strong arms that told Canuto that she was not afraid of hard work. She pushed the screen door opened and asked, "Hello. May I help you?"

Canuto smiled and said, "*Buenas tardes, Señora.* I am from the Lesnett Mill and I have a load of lumber for the railroad. The Tularosa office told me to deliver it here."

"Oh, dear me," exclaimed the woman, "my husband is due back any minute from the work crews. He will show you where to unload."

Canto said, "I see. May I water my horses while I wait, *por favor.* The day is very hot."

"I don't see why not," replied the woman. She pointed to the spout that hung from the water tank. "Take the horses over there. There is a trough below the tank."

Canuto bowed and said, *"Gracias, Señora."* He put his hat back on and went back to the horses. He unhitched them from their harnesses and led them to the water trough. The horses shoved their noses deep in the water and drank noisily. Canuto added more water by pulling a chain that hung from the spout. Then he retrieved a large, stiff brush and stroked each horse's neck and back where the harness and bridles attached. Each horse bobbed its head with contentment during the rubdown.

Canuto had another reason for caring for the horses. It allowed him to casually observe the movements in the camp. As he brushed the horses, he noticed the camp residents gradually come out of their boxcars and resume their daily chores. Eventually, the women accepted his presence and walked through camp without looking in his direction. By the time he reached the last horse, Canuto had counted ten different families. None of them matched Tereso's description.

He was about to give up when he saw a small young woman climb down from a car. She reached up and took a baby from a little girl. Then the girl and her sister scaled down the metal rungs like monkeys. With one arm balancing the baby on her hip, the woman stood on her toes and pulled a large laundry basket down. Then the family walked over to the clothesline and began hanging the wet laundry.

Canuto watched them with keen interest. They fit the description perfectly. He put down his brush and prepared himself to walk over and ask their names. A soft chugging sound caught his attention. He turned and saw a white man driving a small rail tractor with four Mexican men holding on to the sides roll up to the section house. He sighed. His questions would have to wait.

Canuto assumed the driver was the section boss. He walked up to the man and tipped his hat to him as he said, *"Buenas tardes, Señor."*

The man jumped down from the tractor and sized Canuto up. He answered cautiously, "Just fine, partner. Do you speak any English?"

"Sí," replied Canuto out of habit. Then he awkwardly gestured toward the wagon and said, "Your Tularosa office told me to deliver your lumber here."

The boss swore and shook his head in disgust. "They did, huh? Damn bean counters." He stopped himself short and realized that this man had nothing to do with the asinine decisions from the area office. "Okay, partner. I didn't mean to vent on ya. I just get plumb upset about them office fellows planning my day for me. Let's get them horses rigged up and we will all pitch in and off-load this stuff."

By late afternoon, the men had unloaded the lumber and stacked it by the sidetrack. The boss signed off on the invoice and bid Canuto a good day. Canuto jumped up into the wagon and proceeded to drive down the access road toward the highway. When the wagon passed behind the boxcars, Canuto abruptly pulled up and jumped off. He walked directly to the car with the laundry streaming from numerous lines stretched from both ends.

As Canuto rounded the corner, he saw the woman lifting a basket of clothes into the sliding door. Each of her girls stood behind her with a basket overflowing with fresh laundry in their arms. The baby crawled around the woman's legs and begged to be held. Canuto steeled himself and walked timidly forward. He did not want to alarm her, so he announced his presence by speaking in a respectful voice. "*Buenas tardes, Señora.* Do not be afraid, *por favor.*"

The woman froze and the girls fled behind her. The baby grabbed the hem of her dress. Her maternal instincts flared and fortified her. She narrowed her eyes and studied him for a moment before speaking. "What do you want?"

Canuto offered his most disarming smile and replied, "My name is Canuto Reyes and your husband asked me to find you."

The statement momentarily stunned the woman. Canuto could see it in the way she took a step back. She quickly recovered, lifted her chin up and said, "Why would that be? My husband is working with the crew up north. He will be back in a few hours."

Canuto held his smile and continued with an understanding voice, "Your husband's name is Ter...er. I mean, Prudenciano Nava, *¿qué no?*" She nodded slowly. "*Bueno,*" said Canuto, relieved that he had found her. "Then your name is Paz and your children's names are Alcaria, Joaquina, and Augustine."

Paz was overwhelmed. *He could only know this if Prudenciano told him,* she thought. She looked quickly around her to make sure nobody was watching and then whispered, "What is it that he wants me to know?" The children were quiet as mice.

Canuto replied softly, "He wants me to take you and the children back to the lumber camp where he is staying. You will be safe there and he has a good job."

Paz again thoroughly studied his face for any signs of deception. She saw none. Finally, she said what was on her mind, "Why should I trust you?"

Canuto shrugged and said, "I believe family is important and Prudenciano is a good man. I promised him that I would try and bring you back. *Por favor, Señora.* Think about it. I will return tonight to bring you back. If you choose to stay, I will tell your husband that you are well." He tipped his hat and returned to his wagon.

Within a few minutes, Paz heard the wagon drive off. She stood motionless as she mulled the recent events over in her mind. Alcaria's small voice brought her back to reality. "Mama, are we going to see Papa?"

"Papa? Papa?" asked Augustine with a fragile desperation that squeezed Paz's heart.

Any doubts about *Señor* Reyes evaporated from Paz's mind. She took a deep breath and said, "*Sí*, little ones. We are going to see Papa, but first, we have a lot of work to do. We must deliver the laundry and pack. And, *Dios mío,* do not tell anyone that we are leaving. *Comprende?*" The children nodded and smiled broadly for the first time in months. Paz shook her head as she looked at them. She wished that she could be so joyous. She felt herself being pulled along a path that she had little choice but to follow. It gave her a very uneasy feeling.

The moon rose above the tall mountains in the northeast as Canuto entered the access road. He was grateful for the light and slowed the team to a walk to silence their approach. He parked the wagon next to the boxcar where the Nava family lived. Mindful of the clothes lines, he carefully walked around the car. Much to his surprise, he discovered that they had been removed. He continued to make his way to the doorway and found the giant sliding door halfway open. Canuto breathed a sigh of relief because opening it would have created enough noise to alert the other family that shared the car.

He grabbed the top rung to pull himself up when Paz magically appeared out of the darkness. She held a finger to her lips, then turned and motioned for the girls to come forward. They began to bring their belongings and stack them in front of the door. Canuto sized up the situation and suddenly had an idea. He lifted up one finger to signal that he would be right back and disappeared into the night. Minutes later, he drove the wagon back and stopped alongside the doorway. Now, he only had to stand in the wagon and lower the luggage a few feet into the bed. Within minutes, everything was silently loaded and Canuto reached up and gently lowered each child to the wagon. Finally, he lifted Paz to the buckboard. Augustine scrambled into her lap. Canuto wrapped the girls in wool blankets and gave one to their mother. Satisfied that all was secure, Canuto quietly shook the reins and the wagon started forward. The horses whisked them out of the camp with scarcely a sound.

Paz looked over her shoulder as the sleepy camp faded in the darkness. It had been home for many months, but she had no regrets. The boxcars represented loneliness and despair. She turned back to the front as the team headed south on the highway. She clutched her little boy tighter to her breast and contemplated how quickly she cast the dice of fate. She entrusted a stranger with the welfare of her family to seek a man she doubted that she still loved. "I did it for the children," Paz whispered to herself. To reassure herself, she peered under the blanket at Augustine. He looked up to her with big, trusting eyes and smiled. She smiled back and smoothed his hair. "*Sí*, I did it for my children."

⋅•⋅⋅•⋅

The subtle jarring of the wagon began to wear on the family's bones. After three days of travel, their bottoms hurt from absorbing the jolts of the iron-rimmed wheels rolling over the rutted road. Only Canuto seemed unaffected. His eyes sparkled with encouragement and he sang amusing songs to please the children. He stopped frequently to allow the children to play and stretch. Paz knew that he was doing his best to make the difficult trip enjoyable. She appreciated the effort and slowly let her guard down.

The road became steeper as they approached the big mountain that loomed in front of them. Sagebrush and grasses gradually gave way to towering pines. The air felt pleasantly cooler and lifted Paz's spirits. The country was a welcome change from the harsh deserts of the Tularosa valley.

Paz turned and watched Canuto for a moment. He hummed a tune as he gently cradled the reins in his strong hands. She looked behind her and saw her three children sleeping on blankets, their little heads rocking back and forth as the wagon lumbered forward. *This would be a good time to ask Señor Reyes some questions*, she thought. Paz softly cleared her throat and asked, "*Perdón, Señor* Reyes. Where is the lumber camp?"

Canuto smiled and pointed toward the towering mountain before them as he replied, "The camp is less than a day's drive from here. It is located on the backside of this mountain, Sierra Blanca."

"I see, and what exactly does my husband do at the camp?"

"Well," answered Canuto, "he handles and cares for the horses. He seems to have a way with them, *¿qué no?*" Paz nodded. Canuto turned his head forward and studied the road ahead for a moment. By the way he moved his jaw, Paz could tell that he was struggling with something. Finally, he turned to her with a serious look and said, "*Señora*, there is something that I must tell you." Paz's eyes told him to continue. "Your husband has changed his name. He is known in camp as Tereso Minjares."

Paz gave him a level stare and asked, "Why?"

Canuto replied, "Last year I found your husband and his friend near death. We brought them to the camp. A few hours later, an Apache bounty hunter arrived and demanded them. The camp owner's wife refused and told him to get a warrant. The man left and never returned, but no *gringo* lawman came either. Your husband thought it was best to change his name."

Paz thought about this for a few minutes before asking another question, "Do you know what he did?"

Canuto shrugged his shoulders and said, "He said something about being mistaken for someone else. There was a train holdup and someone got hurt. He and his friend, Santos, were in the area and the law blamed them."

Paz snorted at the story. "That is not what happened. My husband and his friend, 'Santos,' got drunk, stopped a freight train for a ride home, and killed a man."

Canuto whistled lowly and continued to study the road for a while in silence. Finally, he asked, "If they killed a man, why hasn't the law come and snatched them by now?" He shook his head, "I don't understand it. *Por favor, Señora*, use your husband's new name. It will help protect your family."

Paz nodded. Then she asked, "Why did the owner's wife protect them?"

Canuto laughed at the question and answered, "Because *Señora* Lesnett loves all people. She is a strong-willed woman, but she has a heart of gold. You will see. She manages a store and hotel a few miles ahead. We will be stopping to take supplies up to the camp. I know that she will demand to meet you and your children."

They rode the rest of the way in silence. Each reflected on what they had learned. Soon, they entered Ruidoso and continued to the edge of town. Canuto stopped in front of the two-story building that composed the Lesnett store and hotel. He jumped down and assisted Paz off the buckboard. Then he reached up and lifted each child to the ground. The children had warmed to his kindness over the three days and threw themselves into his arms without restraint.

Paz flattened her rumpled dress with her hands and pushed back some errant strands of hair behind her ears. "Come," said Canuto and he led them up the porch stairs and into the store. Edith Lesnett was behind the counter completing an invoice. She was not aware of their presence until Canuto's low voice filtered into her concentration. "*Buenas tardes, Señora*. I bring visitors."

Edith looked up and saw Canuto standing before her with his hat in his hand and grinning from ear to ear. "Oh," she said, "I didn't hear you come in. You said that you brought visitors. Where are they?"

"Right here, *Señora*," said Canuto as he motioned for Paz and the children to step forward. The tall aisles filled with goods had hidden them from Edith's view. Paz quietly emerged from the aisle holding Augustine, with the girls close behind. "This is Tereso Minjares's family. They will be staying at the camp for a while."

Edith and Paz studied each other closely. Both saw the firmness of character in each other's eyes and liked what they saw. Shifting to Spanish, Edith greeted her, "*Hola*. I am Edith Lesnett. You and your family are welcome."

"*Gracias, Señora* Lesnett," replied Paz as she curtsied. "My name is Paz and this is Augustine and these two are Alcaria and Joaquina."

Edith smiled and came around the counter to inspect the children more closely. "Gracious, what nice-looking children." She ruffled Augustine's thick hair and he giggled back. "Augustine is the name of a great Indian chief that ruled in these parts. Well, I bet you kids would like a piece of hard candy, wouldn't you?" Edith grabbed a large jar on the counter and took off the lid. She tilted the jar toward the girls and invited them to reach in and take a piece. The girls looked uncertainly at their mother. She nodded and the girls quickly snatched a candy and popped it in their mouths. Squeals of delight emitted from their faces as they smacked their lips. Augustine stretched his little body to get a piece of candy, too. Paz put him down and he quickly jumped up on his toes and jammed his chubby arm into the jar. His fingers wrapped around a candy and he stuffed it into his mouth. He danced on his toes with joy. Paz was amazed. This was the first time in months that he had stood by himself.

Edith laughed and said, "I think he would dance forever for candy." She looked up to Paz and said, "The camp is about a four-hour ride from here. Why don't you spend the night? We could get the children cleaned up and you would have a good night's sleep before seeing Tereso." For a brief moment, Paz flashed the expression of uncertainty across her face at the mention of her husband. Then she quickly masked it. Edith caught it and the expression puzzled her.

Paz replied, "*Gracias, Señora.*"

Edith quietly closed the jar and returned it to the counter. With a sympathetic smile, she looked at Paz again with renewed interest. She saw a young woman who had seen hardships, but remained steadfast. Although the children were dirty, they appeared well cared for and loved. Edith thought, *What was she doing with a man as old as Tereso? Why is she reluctant to see him? I bet there is more to Tereso than what he told us. I will have Frank keep an eye on him.*

Edith turned to Canuto, who was waiting patiently against the wall. "Plan on leaving tomorrow morning. I have a list of supplies for the camp. You can load the wagon after caring for the horses." Canuto nodded and proceeded to the door when Edith stopped him. "Canuto, thank you for finding Tereso's family."

He smiled broadly back and said, *"De nada, Señora."* He put on his hat and bounced out the door with renewed energy.

Edith returned her attention to Paz. "Come. I will show you your room. Canuto will bring your things up. Then we will get some bath water for everyone." Paz smiled her thanks and scooped up Augustine. She put her reservations about tomorrow's meeting with her husband out of her mind and followed *Señora* Lesnett upstairs.

———◦••◦———

The wagon pulled into the noisy lumber camp in the early afternoon. Paz and the children looked wide-eyed at the activity around them. Men were piling freshly cut lumber into stacks. Others hustled to and fro, hauling equipment and supplies while the sawmill screamed in the background. Paz tried to identify Prudenciano in the confusion. She spotted one man pitching sawdust that looked strangely familiar, but her husband was nowhere to be seen.

Canuto jumped down and held his finger up to signal that he would be right back. He trotted off behind an equipment building. Paz used the moment to appraise herself and the children. *Señora* Lesnett had helped her to scrub the children and wash and darn their clothes. She had given Paz a beautiful scarf to wear on her head. It brought new life to her frayed dress. The children shone in their clean clothes and *Señora* Lesnett had made sure the girls had pretty ribbons to put in their hair. The family had never looked better.

As Paz turned back in her seat, she saw Canuto returning with a tall gray-haired man. It was only when he came closer that she recognized him. His smile gave him away. It was Prudenciano. He was clean shaven with a trimmed mustache and short hair. He wore a cotton work shirt with suspenders to secure his trousers.

The children identified their father and squealed with delight as they scampered off the wagon. Even little Augustine squirmed onto the ground and ran straight to the waiting arms of his father. Prudenciano got down on one knee to hug and kiss his children. They swarmed over him and smothered him with kisses. Augustine clung to Prudenciano's neck like a tick and burrowed his face into him.

Paz watched her children with the loving heart of a caring mother. She could not deny her children their father. They loved him fiercely and his absence had killed them. Augustine especially needed him. Because of her children, she would try to forgive her husband and forge ahead with him. With this decision made, she stepped down from the wagon and slowly walked to him.

Prudenciano spotted her walking across the grounds. He stopped wrestling with the children and stood up with Augustine holding tight. He had forgotten how beautiful she was. She looked so young and small as she came forward. He opened his arms and gently brought her to him. Paz reached up and stroked his face and said, "I have never seen you shaved."

"It is the new me," he said with a smile.

Paz replied, "And a new name I hear, ¿qué no?"

"Sí, among other things," Prudenciano said, still wearing that mischievous smile. He kissed her and Paz had to admit that it was very pleasant. "Come, I will show you where we will live." With that said, the new Tereso led the new Minjares family to their new home.

———◆◆◆◆———

Paz busied herself with picking up their belongings from the dirt floor. The wall tent they lived in proved to be more comfortable than she had first thought. Lately, she'd had a growing anxiety that everything was not in its place. She shuffled sleeping places and restacked clothes, but none of her arrangement brought any satisfaction. Then today, Tereso announced that they would be moving into the foreman's cabin within the week. This brought her a rush of unexplained relief.

She stood to survey her work when a sudden wave of nausea washed over her. Paz quickly grabbed the side of a cot to steady herself as she rode the pulsing sickness. It passed in a few minutes and she resumed her work. The nausea had started a few weeks ago. At first, Paz thought that she had a touch of the flu, but the missing of her menstruation told her that she had conceived. The discovery frightened her because winter was fast approaching and Tereso and Santos told stories of very deep snows and freezing winds. Carrying a baby in such conditions would be very difficult.

Paz kept herself busy to keep from fretting. She had not told Tereso. She had just admitted to herself that she was pregnant. Paz was afraid that he might get angry because the Lesnetts might not let them stay if they discovered a baby was coming. "I will tell him after the camp shuts down for the winter," she decided. "Nobody will know until next spring."

Augustine bolted into the tent and disrupted her thoughts. He wrapped his arms around her leg and buried his face into her skirt. She was about to ask what was wrong when she heard the girls giggle outside. Slowly they pushed the flap aside and stepped inside. Mischief danced across their faces. Despite her urge to smile, she put on her sternest face and said, "Are you two torturing your brother?"

"No, Mama," replied Alcaria, "we were just trying to paint his face with this." She stretched out her hands and presented a mashed concoction of cranberries and blueberries. Paz bent down and pulled Augustine's head back. Smeared berry stains streaked his forehead and cheeks.

"Oh, my poor boy," she crooned. "What have they done to you? Come. I will take you to the wash shack and clean your face." Facing her daughters, she shook her finger and rebuked them. "No more of this nonsense, *comprende?*" The girls nodded their heads like little angels. Paz knew that they would forget everything she told them within the hour. She sighed and took Augustine by the hand and led him outside.

Paz marched Augustine across the camp to the wash shack with the girls in close tow. Every man they passed smiled and waved to the children. When they caught sight of Augustine's face, they guffawed and pointed at him. The entire camp enjoyed the Minjares children and laughed at the trouble they brewed. Augustine was the camp favorite.

When they arrived at the wash shack, Paz knocked on the door to make sure the washroom was empty. Hearing no response, she reached for the latch when the door suddenly swung open. Santos stood in the doorway toweling his face. His presence startled her. During the past three months, they had successfully avoided each other. Both felt uncomfortable in each other's presence. Paz felt that he was largely responsible for her family's trouble. Santos felt her pain and disgust and surprisingly understood her feelings.

Santos froze and Paz took a step back. They analyzed each other for a moment. Finally, Paz broke the silence, "*Perdón*, I thought the room was empty. We will come back." She turned to leave when Santos's words stopped her.

"No, that is not necessary," he replied in a gentle voice as he lowered his towel. "I am just leaving. I had to wash a piece of sawdust out of my eye. The place is yours." He stepped aside and held the door for her. Paz was not accustomed to his politeness, but Tereso had told her that Santos had changed since arriving at the lumber camp. With his new name came a new outlook on life. She found it hard to believe that a scoundrel like Rafael Silva could have become a decent man named Santos Terra. Paz eyed him warily as she led her children into the wash area.

Santos spotted Augustine's face and cracked a wide smile. One look at the girls' colored hands told him what had happened. "*Por favor*, let me help you," he said with sincerity. Before Paz could respond, Santos grabbed a bar of soap from a shelf and motioned for

Augustine to come to the washbasin. The boy walked over to him without hesitation. Santos ran some hot water over a cloth and applied it gently over Augustine's face. He let it sit for a moment. Then he pull it off and lathered the soap on the boy's painted skin. With patience and gentleness, he rubbed the berry stains away and left Augustine with a clean, shining face.

Santos patted his face dry with a towel and stepped back to inspect his work. Augustine stood smiling with his face still turned upward and his eyes closed. He liked the attention given to him from a man. "There now," said Santos as he balled up the towel and threw it into a hamper, "that is much better, ¿qué no?" Augustine opened his eyes and slowly nodded.

Paz was stunned. The old Silva she knew would never have treated a child like this. Maybe he had changed. For the first time in two years, Paz smiled and thanked him for his kindness. "*Gracias.* He looks good as new."

Santos grasped the significance of her compliment. He suddenly became shy in her presence and said, "I guess I better get back to work. That pile is not getting any smaller." He looked down at Augustine and put his finger on the boy's nose. "And you better learn to run from your sisters when they try to paint you like a girl, eh?" Santos chuckled and walked out the door. Paz watched him go and thought that maybe something good has come out of that disastrous night at Carrizozo. Silva had finally grown up.

———

Edith Lesnett paid Paz a special visit just before leaving for the winter. Although the morning produced a heavy frost, the afternoon sun was unusually warm and melted all signs of the impending winter. Its rays filtered through golden leaves that fell sporadically and littered the ground. As she walked to the foreman's log cabin where the Minjares family had relocated for the winter, she savored the pungent smells and crisp air. Normally, these signs brought her feelings of well-being and the satisfaction of knowing that another successful season was coming to a close, but her concern about Paz Minjares overrode autumn's pleasantries. Her woman's intuition told her that something was not right with Paz. A few days ago, Edith had caught the look of despair in her eyes as the family prepared to settle in the cabin. Their eyes had locked together for a fleeting moment and shared thoughts that only women could fathom. The encounter haunted Edith and so she made a point of seeing her alone, away from the delicate and all-hearing ears of children and the unsympathetic views of men.

Edith walked up the porch stairs and knocked on the cabin door. She heard a rustling inside and then a momentary pause. The door slowly opened with a cautious Paz peering behind. Edith smiled and greeted her. "*Buenas tardes*, Paz. May I come in?" Paz's eyes darted outside to see if anyone was watching. Satisfied that they were alone, she nodded and stepped aside. *My*, thought Edith as she came inside, *she is very discreet. I wonder why?*

Edith stopped in the middle of the one-room cabin and assessed the situation. Paz had neatly organized the sleeping and cooking areas into functional units. She had arranged the bunks into couches for the family to lounge during the day. At night, they quickly converted back into beds. The cooking area could easily change to an all-purpose room for family projects. However, most importantly, Edith noticed that they were alone. The children were outside playing and her husband was setting the harnesses for the horses that would pull the last of the lumber and men off the mountain.

Edith turned her attention to Paz. She studied her in an awkward silence for a moment and thought, *She doesn't look right. She looks weak, maybe sickly.* Edith resumed her smile and said, "I wanted to talk with you privately before I left. Would that be all right?"

Paz enjoyed Edith and had grown to share Canuto's deep respect for her. She smiled weakly back and replied, "*Sí*, that would be nice. I will fix us some tea. *Por favor, Señora* Lesnett, sit here." Paz motioned to a set of hard-backed chairs at the kitchen table.

Edith graciously accepted and sighed as she sat down, grateful for resting her stiff legs. "*Gracias* and, please, do not call me *Señora* Lesnett. Edith is just fine," she said in an attempt to establish a friendly atmosphere. Paz smiled back over her shoulder as she lifted the puffing teapot from the woodstove. She poured the hot water into two mugs and steeped tea bags that she had acquired from the camp kitchen before it closed. Within a minute, the tea was brewed and Paz served Edith a steaming mug with a dab of honey.

Edith held the cup with both hands and sipped the delicious tea. She smacked her lips and said, "There is nothing like a good cup of tea between friends on a quiet afternoon." Paz nodded in agreement and savored the tea and camaraderie. Edith decided that the moment was right to discuss her foreboding. "Paz," she began in the voice of a loving mother, "I came over today because I am worried about you. You seemed to have something heavy on your mind. Please tell me what it is."

Paz studied her dark tea for a minute. Edith thought she was struggling with a hard decision to reveal some dark secret. Then in a soft voice, she whispered, "I am pregnant." The announcement hit Edith like a sack of flour. She could feel Paz's heavy burden slide onto her back and it made her shudder. Pregnant and snowbound for the entire winter on Sierra Blanca would be a horrible and lonely fate for any woman.

"Oh, my God!" exclaimed Edith as she reached out to caress Paz's hand. "How far along are you?"

Paz continued to stare into her cup. "I don't know. Two months, I guess." Edith did the math in her head. Paz would be in her third trimester by April when everyone returned to reopen the camp. In the meantime, if anything went wrong, she would be on her own.

Edith said, "Don't stay. We can get someone else to help Santos watch the place. Come with us."

Paz shook her head and looked up from her mug with dark, pitiful eyes, "We can't. Tereso must stay and the children need their father. My place is here." Her plight tore at Edith's heart. Sometimes women bore hardships far greater than any man could imagine. Edith thought, *She's trapped! Trapped between duty to her husband and love for her children.* Edith suddenly remembered Tereso strutting around the camp like a peacock soon after his family had arrived. He brazenly made everyone aware that he was sleeping with a young wife. The memory made her seethe with hatred.

Edith addressed Paz sternly, "Tereso is not innocent, is he?" Paz looked down at her tea again. Without mumbling a word, she slowly shook her head. "I didn't think so," said Edith bitterly.

Edith stood and came over to Paz. She grabbed Paz by the shoulders with both hands and drew her to her breast. Paz was not accustomed to such an embrace and stiffly complied, but when Edith stroked her hair, Paz felt her love and concern flow into her body. Paz's resolve cracked and she began to sob deeply into Edith's body. Edith, too, cried and dripped tears on Paz's head.

The women embraced each other for several minutes. Finally, Edith pushed Paz back and commanded, "Look at me." Paz wiped her tears with the back of her hand and hesitantly obeyed. Edith stood before her with a firm resolve written across her face. "I am going to have a talk with Tereso. He must take care of you."

Paz shook her head. "It will only make things worse."

Edith was not swayed. "We shall see. Now let's get cleaned up. Then I need to see how the wagon loading is faring."

When Edith marched into the loading area, every man stopped and paid attention. They saw that she was on the prowl and wondered whom she was hunting. She locked her jaw tight and balled her hands into tight fists. With unwavering determination, Edith stomped past her bewildered husband and son and headed directly for Tereso

Minjares. Frank jumped off the wagon and ran to catch her, but he was too late. Edith found the man who would receive her wrath.

Tereso never saw her coming. He was just throwing a harness over a horse when Edith exploded behind him. "Tereso Minjares! Do you have any idea what you have done to your wife?" Tereso turned around and faced Edith with complete bewilderment across his face. Frank caught up with her and also looked baffled.

Frank asked exasperated, "Edith. What on earth are you doing?"

Edith ignored him and never took her burning eyes off Tereso. "Did you know that Paz is two months pregnant?" Tereso's jaw dropped. "I thought not," spat Edith. "You are too busy telling everyone how much fun you are having with her to even notice that something is wrong." Tereso stood speechless. Frank squirmed with embarrassment because he could not believe that Edith would get involved in something as personal as this. He put his hands on her shoulders to turn her away, but Edith abruptly shook him off and roared back at Tereso. Edith pointed a finger at him and said, "I want you to do the right thing. You should come off the mountain for the winter. This is no place for a woman carrying a baby."

Tereso replied quietly, "I must stay."

Frank begged, "Edith, please. We should talk about this later."

Edith's anger ebbed as she realized that Tereso's mind was made up. No matter what she said, nothing would change and firing him would bring hardship on his family. She walked up to Tereso and tilted her head back until she practically stood below him. In a low, threatening voice, she said, "I gave you life. You owe me. If something happens to Paz, I will see that you pay dearly. *Comprende?*" Tereso stood silently without moving a muscle. Edith slowly backed away and allowed Frank to usher her from the loading area.

Tereso watched her leave and wondered what prompted her to react so violently. He felt the men's eyes on him and his anger flared. He thought, *Who does she think she is telling me in front of the men that my wife is pregnant? Paz carried Joaquina when we walked from Torreón to Chihuahua. This winter will be no harder.* However, as Edith disappeared from sight, he felt the first stirring of doubt creep into his mind. Suddenly, an owl hooted from the nearby woods. Its ghostly cry caused a shiver of dread to slide down his back. There was nothing more ominous than the daytime call of an owl. Tereso knew it foretold death.

The ride home was usually enjoyable, but this time a black cloud of despair hung over the Lesnett wagon. Edith scarcely said a word during the whole trip. She could not get Paz's forlorn eyes out of mind and fretted all the way back to Ruidoso. She desperately needed to send one last shipment of supplies up to the camp before the snows sealed the road shut. Edith thought as she wrung her hands, *Maybe some more warm clothes that would fit her and some medical supplies.*

Frank sat on the buckboard next to her and watched her worry while he drove the team. He finally shook his head and said, "Edith, you are worrying yourself sick over something that is not your business. The Minjareses will work it out."

Edith shot him a venomous stare and hissed, "How can you turn your back on her! Her life and her baby are in danger. Tereso will not lift his lazy hands to help her, either. If something happens to her, it will be on your conscience."

Frank sighed and replied, "She has a nice place to stay with plenty of firewood and food. She will make out just fine. When spring rolls around, we will ship the family to somewhere closer to a doctor so she can have the baby." Edith kept quiet. She did not share Frank's confidence that Paz would be all right.

Yes, thought Edith, *I will send up one more supply wagon to make sure.* When they arrived at their home, Edith jumped down and immediately began assembling goods and supplies for another wagon trip. She called Canuto to make ready.

Canuto put his hat in his hands and replied in a respectful voice, "*Señora*, the horses must rest. I will go in the early morning."

Edith bit her lip, but gave no rebuke. She nodded and said shortly, "Okay. Tomorrow at first light it is."

Tomorrow came with the first blowing snows of winter. It came suddenly with the ferocity of a lion. Canuto tried to bust through the elements, but he could drive his team only a mile up the road before having to turn back. The long winter on Sierra Blanca had begun.

The hunched figure waded knee-deep in the snow to the back of the cabin. A heavy wool blanket was draped over the small person and provided some shelter against the ceaseless February wind and stinging snow. When she got to a big drifted snow pile, Paz held her blanket closed with one bare hand and probed the snow with the other. Her numb fingers found chunks of frozen wood which she tried to hold in the folds of her blanket. She could carry only enough to feed the unquenchable woodstove for a few hours.

After finding a few logs, she staggered to keep her footing and turned slowly around. She almost bumped into Alcaria and Joaquina who came unexpectedly behind her. "*¡Dios mío!*" exclaimed Paz. "You two scared me! What are you girls doing out here?"

"We came to help you, Mama," answered little Joaquina. The girls had thrown on their father's thick wool shirts over their long dresses. Their bare legs waded through the snow with simple leather shoes on their feet. Their little teeth chattered in the cold.

Paz's heart broke for them. "Oh *gracias*, my little ones. Here, you can help me carry these."

Alcaria said, "Wait Mama, I can carry more." She trudged over to the pile and stuck her hand into the snow and fished out several split logs. She knocked the wood together to remove the snow and cradled them in her upturned arms. She turned around with a full load. Joaquina helped by taking a couple of pieces from her mother and sister. Together, they plowed their way back to the cabin with the girls in front and Paz close behind.

As the girls climbed up the porch steps, Paz hesitated as a sudden cramp grasped her protruding abdomen. Her wood spilled from her arms as she doubled over in pain. The girls had just reached the door when they saw their mother reaching out to the lower step to steady herself. Alcaria called, "Mama, Mama! Are you all right?" They dropped their loads and scampered down the stairs to her. Paz tried to speak, but her diaphragm squeezed her lungs tight. She struggled for breath and consciousness. She began to pitch backward when strong and gentle arms caught her and lifted her off her feet. The familiar voice was filled with concern and help.

"Girls, open the door for me," requested Santos. He had been walking by with his snow shovel on his shoulder when he heard the girls' distress. He arrived just as Paz blacked out and scooped her off her feet as she fell into his arms. He carefully carried her up the stairs and into the warm cabin. He stood in the middle of the room holding Paz as he said, "Quickly, close the door and clean off this bed." Joaquina slammed the door shut while Alcaria threw the clothing off a nearby bed. Augustine scampered over to see what was happening.

Santos gently laid Paz on the bed and took off her blanket and wet shoes. Paz looked ashen and her face was contorted in pain. Santos put his hand over the woodstove and felt that it was cooling. He went outside, gathered the dropped wood, and brought it in. After stoking the stove, he returned to Paz to check on her condition. She was still unconscious. He turned around and noticed the children staring at him as if he had the cure for their mother's illness. He gave them a smile of encouragement and said, "You must take care of your mother. She is carrying your baby brother or sister. She must not go outside and carry firewood again, *comprende?*" Three little heads nodded solemnly back. *"Bueno.* Now, Alcaria, put some blankets on her and let her rest, *por favor.*"

Alcaria retrieved some dry wool blankets and started to put them on her mother when she dropped them and backpedaled in horror. She put her hands on her mouth and let out a piercing scream. Santos whirled back to the bed and looked where Alcaria stared. Dark red blood soaked Paz's lower dress. "*¡Dios mío!*" gasped Santos. "I must get Tereso. Keep your mother warm."

He bolted from the cabin and jumped off the porch in a dead run. The deep snow sucked at his boots, but Santos kept flailing forward. He rounded the warehouse where Tereso was shoveling the roof. To his dismay, Tereso was not there. Santos frantically searched for him and then spotted the door to the warehouse office open. He sprinted for the door and jumped inside. He found Tereso leaning back in a chair with his feet propped up on the desk, smoking a hand-rolled cigarette. His shovel leaned against the wall.

He shouted, "Tereso! Come quick! Paz is hurt!"

Tereso kicked his feet to the floor and stood upright. "What happened?" he demanded.

Santos wheezed as he tried to catch his breath, "She strained herself carrying wood. She is bleeding and in pain. Come. We must hurry!" Tereso bolted out the door with Santos close behind. They slogged through the snow till they reached the cabin. Tereso crashed the door open and saw his three terror-stricken children standing around a bed. He gruffly moved through them and found Paz lying with her face twisted with agony. She had regained consciousness, but was very weak. Tereso spotted the blood-soaked clothes and sucked in his breath. For a second, Tereso could feel all eyes and hopes rest upon him. He cursed his predicament because he felt utterly helpless and alone. The deep snows prevented him from transporting Paz to proper medical care and the distance kept him from bringing help to the camp. He would have to care for Paz himself.

Tereso took a deep breath to steel himself and started issuing commands. "Alcaria, fill that big pot with water and put it on the woodstove. Joaquina, remove your mother's dress and put a blanket over her. I am going to the wash shack and get some clean towels."

"I can do that," offered Santos.

Tereso exploded and unfairly blamed Santos for Paz's condition. "No. You have done enough. I can handle this from now on. *Adios.*"

A bewildered Santos replied, "You must be joking." But one look at Tereso's angry face convinced him otherwise. Santos put his hat snugly on his head and left. As he walked away, he grabbed his shovel out of a snowbank. Suddenly he stopped in the deep snow and stood motionless for a moment as he thought, "He will never help her. I do not care if he gets mad. I am going to lend a hand."

Santos turned around and marched back to the cabin. He shoveled a path from the porch to the woodpile in back. While he threw the snow to the side, he saw Tereso walk toward the wash shack and come back with an arm load of towels. Neither said a word to the other. After Santos shoveled a pathway, he cleared the woodpile. Then he brought back armloads of wood and stacked it on the porch and next to the door.

Every day till spring, Santos carried wood from the pile. He also filled water jugs from the spring and dragged them to the cabin. During all of this, Tereso never thanked or helped him. Tereso became reclusive, and neglected his winter watchman duties. Santos never saw Paz again during the last of the winter months. The children seldom ventured outside. A glum set over the camp that the spring winds could not thaw.

The wagon sloshed through the mud and puddles on the soft road. Frank Lesnett drove the team while Edith sat anxiously next to him. This was the first year that Edith accompanied him to open the mill. She usually came a few weeks into the new season, but this time she was concerned about Paz Minjares. The mid-April day of 1915 gave fits of cold wind intermingled with bursts of warm sunshine. Traces of winter's snow lined the road and some drifts still existed close to camp. Frank coaxed the horses to pull extra hard to trudge through the snow. A few miles farther, they rounded the final corner and entered the camp.

Frank stopped the wagon in the middle of the yard and critically evaluated the buildings. The roofs appeared solid with no signs of collapse. He also saw no traces of fire. Frank breathed easier. The mill had survived another winter without catastrophic loss.

Edith did not share her husband's relief. She looked nervously around for some sign of the Minjares family. She expected to hear the shrieks and laughter of the children, but only the sounds of the wind blowing through the naked trees prevailed. The place looked deserted. As Edith turned in the buckboard, she spotted a man walking around the corner to them. Her hopes were immediately dashed when she realized that he was Santos and he wore a grim face.

Frank jumped down and walked briskly to him. They exchanged hearty handshakes and since Frank's Spanish was limited, their talk was brief. Edith wasted no time interrogating him. "*Señor* Terra, where is the Minjares family? Is Paz healthy?"

Santos's brief smile disappeared and he resumed his serious look. He caught her eye for a moment and then looked away. Edith demanded, "What is it? What is wrong?"

Santos slowly turned his head back to her. She stood silent, holding her husband's arm for emotional support. She was ready to hear what he had to say and she was not leaving until she heard it all. Santos took a deep breath and spoke in a quiet voice, "Paz hurt herself collecting wood two months ago. She has been bleeding and in pain ever since."

Edith put her hand to her mouth and gasped, "Oh my God! The poor dear! Where is she?" Santos pointed toward the foreman's cabin. Edith grabbed the hem of her skirt and ran as fast as she could. She bounded up the porch stairs and swung the door open. The inside of the cabin was dark and her eyes took a few moments to adjust. The smell of stale air filled her nostrils.

She saw the children sitting on a bed looking up at her. Their faces were filled with despair. Their father sat on a chair next to the dining table. In the other bed across from the children lay a small figure under a wool blanket. Edith felt her fear rise in her throat as she quietly walked to the bed. She bent down and pulled the blanket away from the face. She scarcely recognized the gaunt creature before her. "Paz, my dear sweet girl", whispered Edith with sobs rising in her voice. "What has happened to you?"

Paz opened her eyes and managed a weak smile. She spoke in a tired voice, "*Señora* Lesnett, it is good to see you." Edith could tell that she had lost weight. Her dark eyes looked big for her sunken face. Her dirty hair clung to her sweaty forehead. Edith pulled the covers back to reveal her swollen abdomen. The baby appeared to be carried much too low for her seventh month. Edith also noticed a towel wrapped between her legs as a makeshift bandage. It looked clean and recently applied.

Edith replaced the blanket and stood up straight as she found her resolve. She spoke with absolute confidence, "I am taking you to Ruidoso where there is a doctor and I can take care of you."

Tereso chose this time to make himself known. Edith's meddling irked him and wrenched his male pride. He came to his feet and declared, "I am taking care of Paz. She will not be leaving with you."

Edith squared off with him and snarled back in his face, "You are killing her! I am taking Paz and the children with me and there is nothing you can do!"

Tereso spoke through his gritted his teeth, "Oh, yes there is!" He firmly grabbed her arm and escorted her out of the cabin and slammed the door behind her. Edith was outraged. She stomped back to her husband and demanded that he take charge and bring the family to her at once.

Frank's anger was slow to kindle, but once ignited, it burned hot.

He had witnessed her increasing involvement with the Minjares family's affairs and kept silent until now. He believed that Edith had gone too far this time and it was time to stop. Frank shouted, "Edith Lesnett! Stop interfering with their lives, right now. If Tereso doesn't want his wife to go Ruidoso, then you have no right to take her."

Edith countered, "But she is dying!" She was unaccustomed to Frank's wrath and it unnerved her. "You can't just let her die."

"That's right. I can't let her die and I will tell Tereso that he must leave, but he will decide what is best for his family. Not you." Edith knew that once Frank put his foot down, his back became steel. She reluctantly nodded. Frank let out a deep breath and looked toward the foreman's cabin. He was about to walk over and speak with Tereso when Canuto Reyes arrived with the covered wagon that carried perishables such as flour, rice, and beans. Frank breathed a sigh of relief. He could use Canuto as an interpreter when dealing with Tereso.

As Canuto brought the wagon up along the Lesnetts, he could tell that something was amiss. Edith looked near tears and Frank's eyes burned with a deep purpose, a look that Canuto had seldom seen. He had a feeling that he had just driven into a firestorm and he was integral in snuffing it. Canuto waited solemnly for some hint of the problem, but Frank said simply, "Come," and started walking to the cabin where the Minjareses were staying. Canuto gave Edith a glance, but she quickly turned and looked away. He threw down the reins, jumped off the wagon, and ran to catch up with Frank. He fell in behind his boss and asked no questions as they approached the cabin.

Frank climbed the stairs and motioned for Canuto to follow. Frank came to the door and hesitated for a second before knocking. Within a few moments, Tereso came to the door. His face showed signs of strain under his grizzly beard. Frank turned to Canuto and said, "Ask him to come out onto the porch so we can talk in private." Canuto nodded and repeated the request in Spanish. Much to Frank's relief, Tereso gave them an agreeable look, stepped outside, and closed the door behind him.

Frank began talking and Canuto spoke the interpretation. Once Tereso got used to the offset wording, he conversed freely. "I do not want to be separated from my family again. There must be somewhere I can take them."

Frank rubbed his chin as he contemplated the problem, "Well Ruidoso doesn't have much work there and I guess you can't go back to the railroad."

Canuto interjected, "*Perdón*, perhaps I can help. I heard that the State just finished that new dam across the Rio Grande north of Las Cruces. It irrigates lots of new land for farming. The farmers are crying for workers. It's a quiet place where people can live without suspicion."

Tereso did not savor the idea of working on a farm again. Monte Escobedo had given him enough for a lifetime. However, the place did sound like the perfect place to hide. He slowly nodded as he accepted the idea.

Frank let out a deep breath as Tereso made his decision. There was one more issue that had to be addressed. "Well, that about settles it then, but what are you going to do about your wife? She is in no condition to ride." Canuto and Tereso became perplexed over the problem and scuffed their feet at the porch.

Edith stood by the wagon and watched with the eyes of a hawk as they discussed the situation. They appeared uncertain and vacillating between decisions. She decided to defy Frank's dictums and find out what was going on. She marched back to the cabin and stopped at the foot of the porch. She asked in a straightforward voice, "What's wrong?"

Tereso instantly clammed up and studied her with loathing eyes. Frank shook his head at his wife's presence. He knew that she could not stay away and hold her tongue for long. Frank sighed and said, "Looks like Tereso decided to take the family to the valley north of Las Cruces, but we can't figure how to best move Mrs. Minjares."

Edith retorted, "That's because you men know that she should not travel beyond Ruidoso. A long trip like that will kill her."

Again, Canuto offered a solution. "I could drive them in the covered wagon. We could make a nice bed for her so that she wouldn't have to sit up." Edith became silent and shot hard glances at the men.

Tereso took her silence as a sign that he had won and wholeheartedly agreed with Canuto. "*Bueno*. That would work out fine. May we borrow your wagon, *Señor* Lesnett?"

Frank could sense his wife's burning eyes roasting his skull. He knew that someone would be unhappy with whatever decision he made. It was a no-win situation. He took a deep breath and decided to let Canuto drive them to Las Cruces. Frank steeled himself and said, "Yes. Canuto will drive you in the covered wagon. You will leave in two days."

Edith snarled, "You bastards!" She pointed at them from the porch steps and shouted, "You have just killed the baby and probably Paz! The blood is on your hands!" Tears flooded her eyes as she turned and ran for her cabin. The men watched her go. Each of them had a sick feeling twisting in their guts.

***

Canuto and Santos gently lifted Paz to her husband in the bed of the wagon. Tereso bent low to clear the canvas covering and received her in his arms. He carried her awkwardly to a makeshift bed just behind the buckboard. A canvas curtain hung between the buckboard and the bed from the wire frame to provide the occupant privacy and shelter from dust and sun. The bed was a simple mattress with old flour sacks filled with blankets for pillows. Several blankets were at hand, but the morning was already hot and Paz refused them.

The men said their fond goodbyes to the children and playfully tossed them into the wagon. Tereso jumped down to supervise the loading of the scant family possessions. He shook hands with Frank Lesnett and thanked him for his help. Then he turned and faced Santos. They both felt uncomfortable and shuffled their feet in the dirt. Despite their differences, they shared the tight bond of men who have braved a life-and-death ordeal together. Tereso offered awkwardly, "You know that you are welcome to join us."

"No, *gracias amigo*," replied Santos. "I belong here. I would just get into trouble again."

Tereso nodded and scuffed the earth again. "Silva," he said quietly so only Santos could hear. "I appreciated your help this winter. *Gracias*. I will never forget you."

Santos stepped closer and hugged Tereso, "And I will never forget you, Prudenciano Nava. Thank you for bringing me here, *amigo*." They slapped each other's backs before releasing their embrace. Santos waved at the children and said, "Mind your parents and stay out of trouble." The children smiled and waved back.

Paz struggled up on one arm and called out to Santos, "Thank you for your help. It made the winter much easier." Santos smiled and nodded. "Also," added Paz, "You should think about settling down someday. You would make some woman a very nice husband." Her compliment stunned and deeply touched him. Never in his wildest dreams had he ever expected Paz to say that to him. He vividly remembered how much she had hated him. Tears almost came to his eyes as he silently mouthed, "*Gracias.*"

"*Perdón*," a voice interrupted behind Santos. He turned and saw Edith Lesnett standing behind him with a neatly folded bundle draped across her arms. Santos stepped back and let Edith approach the wagon. She balanced the material on her left arm and grasped the wagon gate with her right. Without hesitation, she stuffed her left foot into a metal rung and began to hoist herself up. Santos quickly came to her aid and helped her inside. She landed on the wagon floor with an "Ohff!"

"*Señora* Lesnett! Are you all right?" asked Paz with concern.

"*Muy bien*," replied Edith. "My old legs don't bend like they used too." She scooted herself over to Paz and caressed her head like a loving mother. Their eyes locked together and communicated deep thoughts that words could not convey. Finally, Edith spoke, "I brought you a gift for your baby. It's not much, but I thought you could use it." She unfolded the material and lifted it up, so that Paz could see. It was a beautiful satin blanket that reflected soft blue hues in the shade of the canvas.

Paz reached up and softly stroked the smooth, cool material and exclaimed, "It's gorgeous! Oh, *gracias, Señora. Muchas gracias!*"

Edith smiled and said, "I know it's a pale blue, but I think a girl would look pretty snuggled in it too, don't you think?" Paz nodded her head. Edith reached down and gave her a good long hug. "I shall miss you," she whispered. "Take care of yourself."

Paz whispered back, "I will. Thank you for all your help." Edith nodded and fought back her tears. She slapped her thighs and scooted out to the rear of the wagon. Then she hefted herself over the gate. Santos was there to help her down.

Tereso shook Frank's hand and joined Canuto on the buckboard. He waved to rest of the crew and Canuto snapped the reins to start the team forward. He drove the team around the grounds and toward the haul road to Ruidoso. Edith stood next to Frank as the wagon disappeared behind the trees. Pleased with himself, Frank looked down to Edith and said, "See there? Things are going to work out just fine."

Edith shot him a hard stare and looked back to where the wagon had been. When she spoke, her voice dripped with bitterness, "You sound so confident, Frank, but the truth is that we will never know if you did the right thing."

Frank followed her stare down the empty road and lost his grin. Her words hung on his mind. He hated it when she was right.

Chapter 18
The Hard Trek

The first day out was uneventful. The road to Ruidoso was clear and downhill so they made good time. They passed through town without stopping and turned south into the Mescalero reservation. As they left the protection of the pines, the temperature began to climb and the road deteriorated. Canuto pulled back on the reins to slow the horses to a walk. He grimaced at every rut and bump they crossed because he knew Paz felt every one. The stiff wagon springs helped absorb the severity of the jolts, but the wagon still shook and hopped as the metal-rimmed wheels rolled over the rough terrain. Anything not tied down bounced on the hard wagon floor. This included Paz. The girls tried in vain to keep the mattress from throwing their mother. The bedding shifted erratically and tossed Paz around like a rag doll. She held on to her stomach and gritted her teeth to squelch the pain.

They continued along the dusty road for several hours until Alcaria stuck her head out the front curtain and said, "Papa, Mama is in a lot of pain. Can we stop for a while?" Tereso looked at Canuto who nodded toward a small adobe hut in the distance.

Tereso understood and replied, "*Sí.* Tell your mother that we will stop soon." As they neared the house, Tereso saw that it commanded a wide view of the land to the west. The terrain gradually sloped away and left the observer with a completely unimpeded vista. Nothing could move across this area without being seen miles away. Tereso had a gut feeling that he had once walked through this vast country before making his way up Sierra Blanca.

He turned and studied the hut as they pulled to a stop alongside. Two stools leaned against the front wall, which indicated that the occupants spent hours watching the countryside. A dog shot out of a hole next to the house and challenged them with deep, low growls and snarling teeth. Tereso readied himself to holler at it when a man bounded out the door and shouted a sharp command in a tongue Tereso did not understand. The dog responded immediately and slunk behind the house to continue its watch in secrecy.

Tereso turned his attention to the approaching man. He wore a buckskin vest over his bare, muscular chest. His lean, powerful shoulders and arms flexed fluidly as he moved toward them. His stride contained an athletic bounce. Then Tereso saw the deeply chiseled face with raven dark blue hair bound into a single braid and felt his blood run cold. This man was the phantom pursuer who had almost killed him two years ago.

John Smoke Rider recognized Tereso at the same time and stopped dead in his tracks. His dark eyes focused on Tereso's face with the intense concentration of a hawk. Canuto understood instantly what was happening and swore at their bad luck of stumbling onto each other. He spoke fast to defuse the situation. "*Buenos días, Señor* Smoke Rider. How are you today?"

John only nodded and continued to stare at Tereso. Canuto let out a deep breath and jumped to the ground. This was not going well. He walked up to John and offered his hand. John did not acknowledge it and never took his eyes off Tereso. Finally, John asked, "Why did you come?"

"We are traveling to Las Cruces," answered Canuto, "but we have a sick woman in the wagon. May we rest for a moment, *por favor*? She is in much pain."

Silence prevailed for a few moments before John spoke. "Yes, but he must stay on the wagon."

"That's fine," Canuto agreed eagerly. Since his conversation consisted of a combination of English, Spanish, and Apache, he turned to Tereso to translate. However, Tereso could tell by John's body language what had transpired. He nodded to indicate that he understood.

Satisfied for the moment, John cautiously moved to the back of the wagon and flipped the curtain up. He surprised three children who looked at him with fascination and fear. Behind them he saw a small figure lying on its side. The children saw where he was looking and shrank back to the sides of the bed. John saw nothing dangerous hidden among the sparse belongings and lowered the flap.

John walked back to the front of the wagon to check on Tereso and was relieved to find him still on the buckboard. He called out in a loud voice, "Maria!" Within few moments, a small woman dressed in a buckskin dress and bare feet appeared at the door. She wore her black hair in two braids that rested on her shoulders. Her delicate features gave her the look of a Madonna. Her obsidian eyes contained mistrust and wariness. "Maria," he repeated, "Come here. I need your help."

She glided to him on silent feet and stood slightly behind him. She was very careful not to look directly at the other men. "Maria, there is a woman in the wagon who may need help. Go to her."

Maria nodded and moved cautiously to the back. She quietly parted the flap and peered in. She saw three little children blink back. Then she saw an elfin figure lying on her side in the middle of a worn mattress. Her trepidation dropped and she boldly climbed into the wagon. The children moved to the side and allowed her to move gently to the bedding. Maria saw that the woman was about her age and when she moved the blanket back she discovered that she was very pregnant. She noted that the woman and children were Mexican, so she spoke in hesitant Spanish, "*Hola*. Are you fine?"

The soft female voice seeped into Paz's consciousness. At first, she thought it was a dream. Then slowly she became aware of another presence. She opened her eyes and saw a lovely face looking at her with dark eyes that radiated concern. "Thirsty," Paz muttered through cracked lips.

Maria nodded and scurried out of the wagon. She ran past John into the house. After a few moments, she came out with a pitcher and some towels. She gave her husband a worried look and returned to the wagon. She knelt down beside the bed and poured Paz a cool drink of fresh water. Maria lifted her head up and allowed her to slowly sip the soothing drink. When Paz was through, Maria wet the towels and carefully washed Paz's face. "*Gracias*," whispered Paz.

Maria smiled for the first time and answered, "*De nada*." Then she added, "It must be hard to travel when you are carrying a child."

Paz sucked in her breath and said, "*Sí*. I don't know how I am going to make it. The baby is resting so low and the wagon shakes so much that my insides hurt." Maria put her hand on Paz's womb and nodded her head as she confirmed Paz's assessment.

"How far along are you?" asked Maria as she placed a blanket over Paz.

"About eight months."

Maria clucked her tongue and she studied Paz's face. She thought, *The baby will never go full term. The wagon ride will shake it right out of her.* She sat down with her legs tucked under her and clasped her hands over her lap. With her back straight and her head held high, she addressed Paz in a serious tone, "Your husband should stop soon and wait for the baby to be born."

Paz shook her head and said, "We can't. People may be searching for him. We must go to a safe place."

A look of disdain and then understanding crept across Maria's face. Families usually suffered dearly from men's follies. This was just another example, but Maria understood. Her John had caused her many sleepless nights worrying about his safety while he was off fighting outlaws. If he was a wanted man, he would think nothing of dragging her through the wilderness, pregnant or not. Men were so thoughtless.

Meanwhile, John Smoke Rider and Tereso Minjares continued to stare at each other. Augustine squirmed through the front curtain and popped up behind the buckboard. He looked past the man standing next to the wagon and spotted three children watching the newcomers through the open door. Augustine waved to them and they timidly returned the gesture. John swung around and barked an order at them. The children instantly vanished from the doorway and Augustine shrank back inside the wagon. The action seemed to loosen John's tongue for he spoke when he turned back to the wagon, "I reported your whereabouts to the Carrizozo sheriff. I guess they just didn't want you too badly, eh?"

Tereso shrugged and said, "Who knows? Maybe they thought it was too far to go."

John smiled at the answer, then he continued, "You know, if *Señora* Lesnett had not picked your carcass off that road, I would have caught you."

This time Tereso smiled back, "Maybe."

John had to laugh in spite of himself. "Yeah. Maybe you are right. You are the luckiest son-of-a-bitch I ever met." Maria walked up to him carrying a jug and damp towels. She cast an angry glance at Tereso before whispering something to John. He lost his smile and nodded solemnly to her. He looked back at Tereso and said, "Maria says your wife is very ill and you are an idiot for making her travel. She has done everything she can to help her. You must find some place to rest soon or you will lose your baby and your wife."

Tereso felt his anger bristle under his hat and snarled, "I will do what I think is best. We are leaving now." Canuto took this as his cue to climb back on board. Tereso snapped the reins violently, which startled the horses forward with a jerk. The wagon rumbled down the road at a fast rate.

John and Maria stood in silence next to each other as they watched the wagon disappear in the distance. Maria finally spoke. "I do not know what he did, but he is about to pay dearly for his crime." John studied her for a moment before returning his gaze to the road. He contemplated his wife's words. Life had way of eventually handing out justice, if not by his hands, then by God's.

———•••••———

The road dropped down into the Tularosa Valley and through the little town of Tularosa before meeting the main north-south highway that connected Carrizozo and Alamogordo. Here, Canuto turned the wagon south and followed the smooth and well-maintained road for thirteen miles to Alamogordo. Paz savored the tranquil ride and thought they were riding on air. Within a few hours, they arrived at the big town. They did not stop and briskly took the fork in the middle of town that led them west. When they left the settlement, the road quickly deteriorated into a wagon trail.

The trail stretched for sixty-three miles and crossed the scorching White Sands Desert and the San Agustin Pass before descending into Las Cruces. At first, the trail consisted of deep ruts from heavy wagons cutting into the hard ground. Each wheel rotation produced a bone-jarring jolt. The men slowed their advance to prevent the wagon from shaking apart. The water barrels sloshed precious water through vent holes in the lids as the wagon tilted and jerked forward. The wire frame that suspended the canopy whipped back and forth, which added to the abrupt movements.

As they progressed, the hard ground gradually gave way to the shifting gypsum sand of the White Sands Desert. The horses struggled to yank the wagon through sand dunes that periodically drifted across the trail. Through particularly difficult sections, the men jumped down and assisted the horses by pushing from behind. Alcaria would snap the reins to urge the animals ahead while Tereso and Canuto rammed their shoulders into the back gate and shoved the wagon forward. They squinted against the brilliant reflection off the surrounding sand and clenched their teeth as they locked their back and leg muscles and strained ahead. They progressed forward in agonizing steps.

The moderate elevation and spring season caused freezing nights and searing days. Only a few hours after dawn and again between sunset and night offered pleasant temperatures. Paz thought she had died and arrived in hell. She constantly pulled her blanket on and off her in an attempt to find a comfortable temperature. Sometimes she thought she had a fever and drifted in and out of consciousness. She accepted the water the children offered to her, but she could not keep down any food. Her condition grew worse as the slow wrenching trip progressed.

On the sixth day, the trail began to rise and make its way up the rugged Organ Mountains. The already exhausted horses strained forward to pull the wagon up. Finally, they reached the 5,700-foot summit of San Agustin Pass where Wayne Brazel had gunned down Pat Garrett only seven years ago.

Canuto stopped and rested the horses while Tereso scanned the valley before them. The clear afternoon air and high elevation allowed him to see nearly a hundred miles. The Rio Grande Valley stretched out before him. The stark landscape sloping to the valley floor reflected soft, rose-colored hues in the afternoon sunlight. Smooth bare rocks with sparse grasses and tough shrubs littered the countryside. The land rolled unchanged until it met the Rio Grande. Although Tereso could not see the river from his perch, he knew its location by the mile-wide swath of lush vegetation and trees. The river painted a deep green band that flowed from the north to the south and seemed to extend to infinity. Tereso also saw communities, a road, and a railroad along the eastern bank.

After an hour and a rationed watering, the horses plodded down the road for the last fifteen miles to Las Cruces. The initial descent was steep and required Canuto to apply the brake to keep from overtaking the team. He was thankful that he had paid the two Mexicans camping on the summit to grease the axles to prevent the brakes from over heating. Mexican "greasers" were found on most road summits in the southwest and they eked out a meager living by providing this messy, but needed service. The road soon shallowed and settled into a gradual two percent grade to the valley floor.

They arrived at the northern outskirts of Las Cruces in the early evening. The town consisted of adobe houses and buildings packed closely together. The streets were narrow and crooked, almost as if the town was haphazardly thrown together. Almost every structure except the church was a single-story building. People walked freely in the streets and mingled at corners. Many noticed the ragged wagon that arrived in their town.

Canuto parked the wagon on a side street and had a look around while Tereso checked on his family. When Tereso parted the rear flap and saw the despairing look in his children's eyes, he thought his wife had died during the last hours of the trip. He studied the withered form on the worn bed and detected a slight breathing movement. Relieved, Tereso climbed into the wagon and checked Paz's condition. Her forehead was hot and dry. He pulled the cover back and was astonished how much weight she had lost. Her ribs protruded like barrel straps and her arms and legs were emaciated. For the first time since they started their hard trek, Tereso felt pity for his wife and questioned his wisdom in pursuing this trip.

He mixed a tea from the lukewarm water left in one of the wagon barrels and some dried herbs from his frayed medicine pouch. He gently lifted her head and let her sip the mixture from a clay mug. Alcaria and Joaquina washed their mother's face and smoothed her hair back. Paz blinked a vacant stare at the ceiling and slowly fell back to sleep.

Tereso attempted to calm his children by saying, "Do not worry. We are almost done traveling. Then we can nurse your mother back to good health." Only Augustine gathered encouragement from his father's words. The girls were too scared to believe it.

Canuto arrived back as Tereso climbed down from the wagon. Canuto started to ask about Paz's condition, but checked himself when he saw the strain on Tereso's face. Instead, he reported his findings, "Man, the people around here are tight! Everyone knows everything that goes on. Reports of our wagon already are circulating through town."

"*Sí*, I can feel their eyes on us right now," replied Tereso, looking around as he spoke. "What about work? How are the prospects?"

Canuto answered, "There appears to be a building boom going on. The government is constructing new dams and canals to open up the Rio Grande valley for farming. According to the men that I spoke with, there are many new farming jobs too, just north of here. A small town called Doña Ana."

"*Bueno*," replied Tereso, "We will go there now. Paz must rest very soon and I want to get away from these prying eyes."

Canuto nodded and looked over to his team of horses. They stood with their heads held low still connected to their harnesses. The past week had been very hard on them. Pulling the wagon across the rugged desert, the heat, and lack of water all had taken their toll. The horses were exhausted. Canuto knew he would have to rest them soon. He walked over to his favorite mare and scratched the back of her ear. She swayed her head slightly to acknowledge his affection. "Just a little further tonight, *niña*," he whispered, "then I will rest you for a few days." The mare flattened her ears. She wanted to stop now. Canuto chuckled and patted her neck. Then he climbed aboard and waited for Tereso to secure the wagon and join him on the buckboard before starting the team forward.

The blackness of the deep night fell as they left Las Cruces. The bright stars lit the sky, but the distant mountains still hid the moon so the road was dark. They rode in silence for a few miles until one of the horses stumbled. It shuddered and continued with a limp. "Whoa," commanded Canuto as he pulled back on the reins. He looked over to Tereso and said, "I am afraid that this is as far as we go tonight. It is too dark to take a good look at the horse. The rest of them are very tired. We will have to make camp here."

Tereso looked around in the dark to see where "here" was. He could barely make out a set of railroad tracks in the distance and that was all. He nodded and waited for Canuto to pull off the road and into a grassy field. The men climbed down and unhitched the horses. The animals smelled water in a nearby ditch and made their way to it. Tereso and Canuto followed them and let them drink their fill before hobbling them for the night.

As Tereso walked back to the wagon, he felt strangely at home. The smells and the land seemed to welcome him. *Maybe this is where I should settle down*, he thought as he prepared to climb into the back of the wagon. *I will see what tomorrow brings.*

——•••——

Tereso woke to a strange man's voice calling from outside. At first he thought he had dreamed it. Then the voice called again in English. Tereso opened his sleepy eyes and let the dim light shift the cobwebs from his brain. He looked across the wagon bed and saw his family heaped on the single mattress, completely oblivious to their surroundings. He would have to see what the man wanted.

He slid the wool blanket from his cramped and aching body and struggled to sit up. Tereso blinked twice to clear his vision and smoothed his rumpled hair before reaching for the back flap of the canopy. Just as he was lifting himself over the gate, he heard Canuto answering the man. *Bueno*, thought Tereso, *Canuto will find out what the man wants. I can go back to sleep.*

He was about to return to his hard spot on the floor when Canuto called out to him, "Hey, Tereso! Come on out. This man wants to hire you!" Tereso swore under his breath before he tore open the flap and climbed over the gate. His hand slipped from the rail, which caused him to fall in an awkward manner. He almost tumbled to the ground, but he grabbed the wagon with a flailing hand and steadied himself. He quickly recovered and tried to gather the rest of his dignity before greeting his prospective employer.

Bill Taylor was a hard-working, straight-talking man. He stood with his hands on his hips and raked his assessing eyes over Tereso. Mr. Taylor wore bib overalls over a flannel shirt and a big straw hat to protect his balding head. His clean-shaven face and clean clothes gave him an air of superiority despite being four inches shorter than Tereso.

Taylor's wife, Nellie, had seen the wagon parked in the field when she was making breakfast. Ever mindful of the valley's shortage of farm help and the long hard days her husband put in because of it, she seized the possibility that the wagon held migrants searching for work and raced to tell Bill. To her amazement, Bill was not receptive to inspecting the wagon. After much cajoling and a small tantrum, Mr. Taylor finally relented and left his usually calm house without a morsel of food to start his day. Now he wondered if the early morning fuss and discomfort were worth the older rumpled man who wavered in front of him.

The men stood staring at each other in silence for a few moments until Canuto broke the ice and introduced them. "Tereso, this is *Señor* Taylor. He needs a family man to help him with his farm." Switching to English, Canuto continued, "*Señor* Taylor, this Tereso Minjares. I can attest to his work ethic. He is a good worker."

Taylor asked gruffly, "Can he speak English?"

"No," answered Canuto, "but he is very smart. Just show him what you want done and he will do it."

Taylor rubbed his chin as he continued to study Tereso. Then he spoke his thoughts, "He's a bit older than I would like."

Canuto sensed that Tereso's opportunity was slipping through his fingers. Suddenly, he had an idea and turned to Taylor and said, "He is also very good with horses. Look, see that horse over there?" Taylor looked to where Canuto was pointing. He saw a tired-looking wagon horse calmly grazing. As it took a step forward, it limped and favored its right hoof. "Let's go over there and watch Tereso check it out. You will see what I mean."

Canuto switched to Spanish and told Tereso, "Go over to that lame horse and find out what is the matter. *Señor* Taylor will see how good you are with horses and hire you." Tereso nodded and walked into the field to the limping horse. The other two men followed behind. Tereso circled the horse until he approached it from the front right side. With smooth, sure moves, he reached down and picked up the horse's leg and folded it back to expose the hoof. The shoe was misaligned and had sheared one of the pins that stapled it to the hoof. Tereso used the shoe as a lever to remove the remaining pins, which left a piece of the sheared pin still embedded. Tereso signaled that he would be right back and briskly strode to the wagon. He returned momentarily with large pliers and an old knife from the wagon's tool box. He lifted the leg again and cleaned around the pin with the knife. Then Tereso grabbed the exposed pin with the pliers and yanked it out. He examined the hoof to make sure the cuticle was not cracked and gently let it down. He gave the horse a pat on the neck before turning to face the men.

Canuto exclaimed, "See? What did I tell you? He has a way with horses. Could you not use a man like that?"

Taylor had to admit that having cheap Mexican help on the farm that could handle horses would be a big benefit. He rubbed his chin as he thought the situation over. "Well," drawled Taylor, "how do I know he just won't up and run off to take a job on one of those federal dams or canal projects? I can't pay as much as they can."

Canuto shrugged and said, "I will ask him." Switching to Spanish, he asked Tereso, "He wants to know if you will eventually leave him for a job digging ditches."

Tereso smiled and shook his head in response. "Tell *Señor* Taylor that I worked on a railroad and I prefer horses."

Canuto again took the liberty of modifying the translation and said to Taylor, "He says he'd rather work on a farm."

"All right," replied Bill Taylor as he stuck his hand out to shake Tereso's hand on the deal, "I will take him. You say he has a family in that wagon?"

"*Sí*," answered Canuto as he watched the men finish their hand-shake. "He has three children and his wife is very pregnant with their fourth." Canuto saw Taylor grimace at the mention of the pregnant wife, but he also recognized the look of resignation in Taylor's eyes that said nothing in life is perfect.

Taylor pushed his straw hat back off his forehead as he accepted the situation and said, "Well, I guess we should go back to the farm and get this shoe bent back into shape and refit this horse. Then we will take the wagon over to the helper's quarters and move the family in." Canuto smiled and explained everything to Tereso. This was working out better than either could have hoped.

———•◦•———

The wagon pulled up to a shack in the late morning. Mr. Taylor sat on the buckboard with the men to guide them. "This is it," he declared as Canuto reined in the horses. "I and the Missus live over yonder." Taylor pointed to a freshly painted two-story house about a quarter of a mile down the narrow dirt road. "This place used to be a duplex for bachelors, but we decided that it was best to have a family here. Less trouble, if you know what I mean. So we knocked a door through the dividing wall and turned one side into a kitchen. This place should work out fine."

Canuto and Tereso gave the helper's quarters a long hard look. The dwelling was a small, rectangular adobe structure situated a few feet from the road's edge. Dust from infrequent traffic caked the front. The mud bricks lay unevenly along the walls. Some stuck out while the face of others crumpled to the ground. There were no windows, but the front had a distinctive look with two front doors, evidence that it had once been a duplex. Each door had a rough, thick branch embedded over the jamb that kept the bricks from falling through. Wooden planks on top of two-by-four rafters supported the nearly flat sod roof. A rusty short stovepipe protruded above the sod on one side. This side contained the kitchen, which had a full-sized screened door to cool the room while cooking on the old woodstove.

A lone, massive cottonwood stood next to the west side of the house and provided precious afternoon shade. Alongside the house and next to the tree, someone had haphazardly stacked firewood. Some of it was cut cottonwood logs and the rest was weathered old wood salvaged from dilapidated buildings and wagons.

Large plowed fields stretched south behind the house. Crude irrigation ditches channeled brown water to planted portions of the fields that shimmered green from young shoots poking out of the fertile dark soil. This water came from the newly constructed Leasburg Canal, which brought water from the Leasburg Diversion Dam on the Rio Grande about thirteen miles north. A busy railroad ran from north to south along the western border of the fields.

The house sat halfway between the small, quiet town of Doña Ana and the bustling and growing Las Cruces. The Organ Mountains rose in the distant east and the outskirts of Las Cruces were clearly visible to the south.

Canuto let out a low whistle as he surveyed the home. He was used to the more sanitary and comfortable accommodations at the Lesnett Mill, but he knew he was luckier than most Mexicans. He had seen the conditions where the majority of Mexican laborers lived and this was better than some. It was also an improvement over the *colonia* boxcars where the Minjareses had lived in the past. He jumped down and motioned for Tereso to follow him.

The men tried the door closest to the wagon first. It would not budge. Tereso rattled the handle, but to no avail. "Wrong door," called Taylor as he got down from the buckboard. "Had to bolt it shut to make a wall out of it. Just the kitchen door works."

Tereso shrugged and went to the other door. He pulled the rickety screen door open and turned the knob to the solid door behind. The lock unlatched and he swung the door open. Shafts of sunlight beamed through the dusty air and illuminated the kitchen. Tereso stepped in and took a look around. His eye caught the scurrying movement of something along the far wall. A large woodstove sat against the eastern wall. The southern wall had some cupboards and a counter made from rough-cut lumber. In the middle of the room was a table with four chairs.

Tereso saw another door to his right and opened it. The adjoining room was dark as a dungeon. "There is a lantern by the stove," Taylor pointed out as he entered the house. "You will need it when you go in there."

Tereso grunted and walked over to the stove. The lantern sat on the counter nearby. He picked up the lantern and shook it. Fuel sloshed inside. He searched and found some matches and lit the wick. After trimming the flame, he carried the lantern into the bedroom. The room contained three wooden beds with rotten mattresses. Another furry creature with red, menacing eyes shot across the dirt floor and disappeared into a hole in the wall. Cobwebs hung in every corner and dust cloaked every surface. The place looked like it had been unoccupied for several months.

Tereso and Canuto looked at each other before leaving. Taylor could sense their apprehension and did not understand it. He asked with an irritated tone, "Something the matter? No one else ever complained. Do you Mexicans think you are too good for these accommodations or something?"

Canuto immediately answered without bothering to seek Tereso's view, "Oh, no *Señor*! We were just thinking that we will have to clean the house a little before moving in. His wife cannot help because her baby is due soon. So we will park the wagon here for a few days while we work."

Taylor put his hands on his hips and grunted while he gave them another hard look. The last thing he needed was some troublesome Mexicans living in his quarters. He made a mental note to keep an eye on them "All right then," he responded as he tilted his head toward his home, "I am going up to the house. The Missus will probably come soon with some food and stuff to help ya get on your feet. Tell him that I want him to start work in three days."

Canuto answered, "*Sí*. I will tell him." He felt like he had just dodged a bullet. Satisfied, Taylor pulled his hat over his forehead and started walking down the road.

Tereso watched him go and asked Canuto, "What was all that about?"

Again, Canuto smoothed the translation. "Oh, he said that he will give us three days to get this house ready before you have to start work. He also said that his wife will bring over some food and other things to get you going."

Tereso watched Canuto's eyes when he spoke. They flicked away from his probing stare. Tereso knew he was not telling the whole truth. "What is it that you are not telling me, *amigo*?"

Canuto hesitated for a moment and considered lying, but one look at Tereso wiped that option from his mind. He sighed and said, "I believe he thinks Mexicans are nothing more than mules to work his land. He is also suspicious of us. *Por favor*, Tereso, try to be good here. Work for a while and move on after you saved some money. Okay?"

Tereso snorted and replied, "I will do what I want to, but I will give this a try."

Canuto sighed again and knew Tereso would find his own way. "*Bueno*, I guess. Well, let's start getting this place fixed up."

———————

The men and the children had just finished hauling all the dilapidated furniture out of the house when Nellie Taylor arrived in a small, two horse wagon. She wore a full-length, blue cotton dress, plain with no frills. With her hair secured in a tight bun and her leather work boots protruding under the hem of her skirt, she radiated a businesslike attitude. However, when she jumped down, she smiled and revealed a softer core. She reminded Canuto of Edith Lesnett and he liked her instantly. Canuto greeted her, "*Buenos días, Señora.*"

"Good morning to you," replied Nellie. "I understand that you speak English?"

"*Sí,*" responded Canuto with a huge smile, "and you must be *Señora* Taylor. My name is Canuto Reyes and this is Tereso Minjares, your new farm help. These are his children Alcaria, Joaquina, and Augustine."

Nellie studied Tereso for a moment and then offered her hand. Tereso stared at the outstretched hand for an awkward second and then carefully shook it. Her grip impressed him. Then she closely inspected the children. They shifted nervously under her scrutiny. Canuto noticed a look of concern drop across her face as she looked at their dirty faces and torn clothing. Then she saw their gaunt bodies and realized they'd probably had infrequent meals.

She swallowed hard and quickly recovered her smile. "My goodness, children! You all look like you have been working hard. I bet you are hungry. Please help me get the food out of the wagon and I will help your mother prepare dinner." The children stood motionless and stared at her. Nellie looked questionably at them for a moment, then glanced back at Canuto.

Canuto smiled, "*Lo siento, Señora.* They do not speak English."

"Oh," exclaimed Nellie, "I see. Could you please tell them to help me?"

"*Sí*", replied Canuto. He spoke softly to the children. Alcaria timidly stepped forward and the other two followed shyly behind. Nellie climbed into her wagon, grabbed the food bags, and handed them down to the children. Each child carried a bag into the kitchen and placed them on the counter. Soon, they off loaded the vegetables, meat, and bread.

"There now," responded Nellie as she climbed down from the wagon, "that did not take long. Where is their mother? I will show her how to use the stove." Nellie noticed an uneasy silence around her as Canuto translated. Nellie asked Canuto, "What is the matter?"

Canuto stammered, "Ah, *Señora*. *Señora* Minjares is very ill."

Nellie replied, "Really? Where is she?" Canuto looked toward the covered wagon. Nellie nodded and cautiously proceeded to the back of the canopy. She parted the flap and peered inside. At first, she did not see anyone, but as her eyes adjusted to the darkness, she noticed a small figure lying on a worn mattress. Nellie called to the form, "Hello. Are you all right?" The person did not answer. Nellie felt a trickle of fear slide down her neck. She gathered her courage and climbed in.

Nellie scooted next to the bed and called gently again, "Can I help you?" Again, she heard no response, only shallow, ragged breathing. She reached out and gently rolled the person toward her so that she could see the face. Nellie gasped when she saw it. The woman's face was twisted in agony. Sweat plastered her hair against her forehead and beads of moisture lined her upper lip. Her cheekbones protruded from her skin, which revealed that she had not eaten for some time.

Nellie wailed, "Oh, you poor dear! I will be right back." She scampered to the wagon gate and stuck her head out of the flap and yelled, "Canuto! Get me that water jug and bundle of towels in the wagon. And put the oldest girl in here too. I need help!" Canuto jumped at her command and gathered the items. As he carried them over to Nellie, he told Alcaria to get into the wagon and assist *Señora* Taylor.

Nellie wasted no time in stripping the soiled clothing off Paz. She winced again when she saw her emaciated body and swollen abdomen. Paz seemed oblivious to what was happening to her. Nellie gave her a sponge bath and, with Alcaria's help, she dressed her in a loose cotton dress.

Nellie addressed Alcaria, "I am going to get a doctor. Try to give your mother some water." Alcaria stared back at her with dull eyes. Nellie realized that she did not understand her, "You don't speak English, do you?" Alcaria continued to stare questioningly back. Nellie picked up the water jug and a glass and made a drinking motion and then pointed back at Paz. Alcaria understood and nodded.

Satisfied, Nellie crawled out of the wagon and went straight for Tereso. She stopped in front of him and screamed, "You monster! How could move your wife in her condition? She is almost dead!"

Tereso did not need an interpreter to translate what *Señora* Taylor was saying. He stood motionless and watched the woman rant at him. Nellie quickly tired of Tereso's blank look and leaped onto her wagon. She snapped the reins and mustered the horses into a quick trot back to her house. Within minutes, she arrived at her house and ran inside to find her husband. She found him in the backyard mending the fence.

Nellie was breathless by the time she reached him. "Bill! Oh, Bill! Thank God I found you. You have to get a doctor. Your helper's wife is sick. She may be dying!"

Bill scarcely looked up from his work. He seemed to concentrate harder as he pulled the barbed wire tighter. "Damn cows. They keep busting this fence to get at the vegetable garden. This barbed wire ought to slow them down a bit."

Nellie stood stunned at his lack of response. "Bill, didn't you hear a single word I said? A woman is dying! We must get help!"

"Oh, I heard ya," replied Bill as he pounded in another staple. "Couldn't help but hear."

Nellie watched him work for a moment, still disbelieving his detachment from this crisis. "So," she prodded, "what are you going to do?"

"Do?" responded Bill as he put his hammer down and reexamined his work. "I intend to do nothing. I am not going to spend my hard-earned money on a doctor for some Mexican woman that just showed up here."

Nellie spat, "I can't believe you are saying this. She needs help. I don't care who she is."

Bill turned from his work and faced his wife for the first time. She could see fire in his eyes and a firm set in his jaw. "Now see here, Nellie. These Mexican folk take care of their own. A doctor is just wasted on them."

Nellie was furious. Bill realized that he would have to concede something or dinner would be a scant affair. He grumbled and said, "I tell you what. Since you are all worked up into a frenzy and all, I will go over to the Rosales and see if a midwife could come over and pay them a visit."

Nellie knew that this was the best she could do. She calmed herself down and said, "All right, you just do that. I am going back to help get things straightened out and cook those poor children dinner. If you want to eat tonight, I suggest you come over at about six o'clock." Without another word, she spun around and marched back into the house.

Bill watched her go. He kicked at the ground and cursed his luck before picking up his tools and preparing to leave. "Damn Mexicans," he muttered to himself, "they're just a bunch of trouble."

——◆◆◆——

True to her word, Nellie Taylor threw herself into rehabilitating the old helper's quarters. She organized the men and children to coordinated their cleaning and repairing tasks. Within three days, the place became a functional home, suitable for raising children. Before

Tereso began his first day at work, Canuto and he carried Paz into the home for the first time and laid her on the rebuilt bed in the back room. Under Nellie's and a midwife's care, Paz began to regain her strength and a little weight.

Canuto sensed that his time was over here and he needed to get back to the Lesnett Mill. He shook Tereso's hand and bent down to hug each child goodbye. When he kissed Alcaria on the cheek, the child surprised him by looking up into his eyes and proclaiming, "I think I will see you again someday."

Canuto laughed and said, "How can you be so sure? The world is very big and we are but two people."

Alcaria answered with confidence, "I know we will."

Canuto thought, *Perhaps she has her father's gift.* He smiled at her and faced Tereso again. "I will tell *Señora* Lesnett that all goes well here." Tereso remained quiet so Canuto continued, "*Por favor*, Tereso. Try to stay out of trouble. You have a way of attracting attention."

Tereso grinned and said, "I will try. You take it easy crossing the desert again."

"*De nada*," he answered, "I am taking extra water and a lighter load. We should make it just fine. Well, *adios amigo*." With no more delay, Canuto climbed up on the wagon and ordered the horses forward. They pulled the wagon onto the road and quickly picked up speed. Tereso watched him go and felt a loss. He had enjoyed his company and would miss him deeply.

He turned to walk back into the house when he heard Paz groan. He ran into the bedroom and saw the midwife holding Paz's hand and stroking her forehead. The Mexican woman looked up to him and said in a matter-of-fact tone, "It is time."

———— ⚬ ————

After a difficult labor, Paz Minjares gave birth to a baby boy on May 28, 1915. She named him Bernardo after Saint Bernard of Menthan, the patron saint of the day. The baby weighed less than five pounds and appeared weak. The rigors of the hard trek and scant food had taken their toll on the baby's development. As the days went by, Bernardo gained only little weight. Paz tried to breast-feed him, but her body was too spent to develop adequate quantities of nutritious milk. The Rosales midwife attempted to bottle-feed the infant, but Bernardo could not keep the food down. The baby continued to weaken and Paz's spirit began to die with him.

By the second week, Nellie sneaked a doctor into the house to examine the child. His examination found a heart murmur that indicated a defective heart. He sadly shook his head and proclaimed that there was nothing he could do. During the last of June, Bernardo died quietly in Paz's arms while she desperately tried to feed him.

The loss devastated her. She crumpled and sobbed mournfully while holding the lifeless infant. Tereso let her hold it for a few hours before prying the body from her hands. Then he looked awkwardly for something to cover the baby. Paz finally got enough control of herself to say, "Here. Wrap him in this." She unfolded the soft blue blanket that Edith Lesnett had given her as a farewell gift. Tereso gently placed the baby in the blanket and tucked it around him.

Paz came over and neatly pushed in the loose edges and smoothed out the covering. As she stood lovingly stroking the tiny bundle, Paz rained big tears down on the blanket. After a few minutes, she said softly, "We must bury him properly in a cemetery."

Tereso quietly agreed and said, "I think I saw a small one in Doña Ana. It's not far away. I will take him there now."

"I will come with you." Before Tereso could protest, Paz threw her shawl over her head and shoulders and shuffled into the kitchen. The children sat solemnly at the table with big, sad eyes. "Come, children," said Paz in a monotone, "we must bury your brother." The children saw their father come into the room carrying the little blue bundle. They quietly stood and followed him out the door. Paz walked slowly behind with her head down and her back bent.

Nellie Taylor was washing dishes when she saw the miserable-looking parade trudge past the house and down the road toward town. She brought her hand to her mouth to stifle a cry. The tiny package that Tereso carried left little doubt what it contained. The children followed in single file with their mother lagging behind. Nellie moaned, "Oh, my God! That poor woman!"

Her husband came to her and asked "What is the manner, Nellie?" He looked out the window and saw the makeshift funeral procession. It struck a deep chord of guilt and regret within Bill Taylor. The death of a child represents the death of a family's hopes and dreams. He knew that firsthand from the drowning of their own son in an irrigation ditch many years ago. Now, the death of the Minjares baby dredged up the old feelings of despair and tragic loss. *But this isn't the same thing*, he thought as he watched the family disappear in the distance. *Mexican babies die all the time.*

Chapter 19
Doña Ana

For thousands of years, civilizations occupied the land along the Rio Grande within central and southern New Mexico. The high elevation tempered the searing sun and the life-giving water nourished, bathed, and transported the residents. The Indians that first flourished along the river irrigated their crops with crude ditches and makeshift dams. The annual floods usually destroyed these drainage systems, but the Rio Grande deposited fertile silt as its waters ebbed back to its banks. Thus, the rhythm of life here consisted of reconstruction, planting, and harvesting.

Like most histories of the world, dramatic changes occurred when the lure of massive riches attracted powerful men. In January 1598, Don Juan de Oñate marched an expedition north from Santa Bárbara, Chihuahua to the *Nuevo México* territory under the King's orders to establish a settlement along the Rio Grande and convert the Indians to Christianity. Oñate and a few collaborators funded the expedition and had more capitalistic reasons for venturing to Spain's most distant province. They were convinced that the mountains along the Rio Grande contained gold and silver riches similar to that in the Sierra Madre range in Zacatecas. Oñate planned to search for valuable deposits in *Nuevo México* and if he stumbled upon the fabled Seven Cities of Gold, so much the better. His entourage consisted of about six hundred diverse individuals including soldiers, priests, families, Indians, and Africans. They had eighty-three wagons and more than seven thousand animals among them. When they marched, the procession stretched four miles.

The natives of the Rio Grande were awed by the enormous size of the expedition when Oñate arrived about four months later. Oñate lingered in the area of present-day Las Cruces while he sought information about the Rio Grande valley. During this time, the priests introduced Christianity and the alphabet to the residents and the expedition families traded a few horses and cattle for fresh vegetables and grains. After a few months of fruitless interviews, Oñate became angered as he perceived the Indians' reluctance to cooperate and reveal locations of promising ore bodies that must exist in the lofty San Andres Mountains. He abruptly pulled up stakes and ordered his group to continue marching north.

Oñate's plan was to follow the Rio Grande north and send scouts east and west to look for gold as they progressed. Unfortunately, deep canyons and abrupt ridges forced the expedition to travel east of the river and eventually to abandon the idea of following it altogether. Oñate decided to take the gap between two hills north of Las Cruces and lead his group into the wide, flat valley beyond. Later, travelers would call these hills the "Points of Rocks."

As the expedition marched northeast along the parched valley floor, they searched for signs of water. They found none. The land was so totally devoid of water that it did not support any vegetation except for an infrequent cactus. The streambeds looked like sun-bleached bones that had not seen the flow of water for centuries. The scorched land stretch for ninety miles with no respite.

The heat pounded the party and soon the animals began dropping dead in their tracks. After three agonizing days, Oñate feared that he had made a fatal mistake when he saw a pet dog trot by with muddy paws. He halted the expedition and quickly found the dog's owner. The owner coaxed the dog to show him where it had found the water. The dog happily led a group of men to a string of pools that contained enough water to quench the thirst of the entire party and livestock. Oñate named the watering holes *Los Charcos del Perillo* (the pools of the little dog).

Juan de Oñate regrouped his expedition and struck a northern course till they intercepted the Rio Grande by the village of Teipana. The Pueblo Indians gave food to the weary travelers. Oñate renamed their village *Socorro*, which means "help."

The expedition continued following the river north until they discovered the Tewa Pueblo of San Juan. San Juan lay in a fertile valley where the Chama River and the Rio Grande converged. Tewa Indians were friendly and gave the bedraggled Spaniards food from their surplus stores. Oñate thought that this would be a satisfactory place to build the first capital of *Nuevo México*. Within two short months, Oñate erected the villa of San Gabriel.

After three heartbreaking years of famine, Indian reprisals, and no treasure, Oñate returned to Mexico defeated and bankrupt. In 1607, the Spanish crown performed the final humiliation by removing Juan de Oñate from office. His soldiers, however, filed favorable reports about the Rio Grande and its suitability for settlement. These reports generated stories about the Rio Grande's rich land and ample water that circulated for years within Mexico.

Meanwhile, the brief interaction of Oñate's people with the natives of *Nuevo México* forever changed their simple rhythms of life. The Indians adapted to breeding cattle and goats for food. They infused the Christian God and Son into their pagan religions. The Apache and Comanche mastered the art of fighting on horseback and waged war against each other and against helpless, peaceful tribes. The horse allowed them to spread their terror far and wide.

In 1680, Pueblo Indians revolted against Spanish rule and killed many residents of San Gabriel. The survivors, more than two thousand colonists and loyal natives, gathered at a campsite on the east side of the Rio Grande. They decided to flee to the protected boundaries of El Paso and take the direct route through Oñate's valley to the Points of Rocks. This proved to be a fatal mistake. Nearly six hundred refugees died of thirst. First the elderly and the weak fell. Then the malnourished and sick succumbed to the unforgiving land. Henceforth, the Spaniards named Oñate's detour along the Rio Grande the *Jornada del Muerto* (the Journey of the Dead).

The Spanish became interested again in the *Nuevo México* territory in the early 1700s. They sent many missionaries and soldiers to tame this wilderness. However, the Apache and Comanche refused to be bridled and fought the Spanish occupation fiercely. The Spanish endured and established the settlement of Doña Ana.

The Americans also desired these rich farmlands and made sure that the Treaty of Guadalupe Hidalgo that ended the Mexican War transferred the land east of the Rio Grande to the United States in 1848. To the dismay of the Doña Ana residents, they had become American citizens with a stroke of a pen. They stood dumbfounded when U.S. Army troops under the command of Lieutenant Delos Bennett Sackett rode into town to protect them from marauding Indians and establish an American toehold in their new lands. Within a few months, American settlers began arriving in droves. The citizens of Doña Ana felt that the American intruders were forcing them out of their town and they petitioned their mayor, Don Pablo Melendres, to help them. Melendres met with Sackett and asked him to develop a new town within the area so that the new settlers could have a place to build their homes. Sackett agreed because he had noticed the frayed nerves of the residents and felt their tensions building. He thought Melendres had an excellent idea that would defuse the situation and provide land for settlement.

In 1849, Sackett and his men rode about five miles south of Doña

Ana. Using rawhide ropes and stakes, they laid out eighty-four blocks and subdivided each block into four lots. When they were finished, Sackett invited interested settlers to meet at the imaginary town square to assign home sites. About one hundred and twenty people gathered in the center of the town grid and drew for lots from a hat. The lottery was a success and the people immediately began building their homes. Since wood was scarce, they made adobe bricks by digging holes in the streets. Within a short period, a traveler had to negotiate countless pits just to cross town. Finally, Judge Richard Campbell declared a public emergency and ordered the townspeople to stop excavating Main Street. When the madness stopped, the town consisted of closely packed adobe homes lining narrow crooked streets with gaping holes large enough to swallow a wagon.

With their homes built, the people set forth to determine a fitting name for their new town. After much debate, the settlers decided on *Las Cruces,* which meant "The Crosses." Nobody could come up with a good reason why Las Cruces was chosen. Some thought the town site was the place where many settlers had died during an Apache attack. Others said that Indians had murdered a group of missionary priests here. Regardless of the name's importance, people liked it and the name stuck.

The creation of Las Cruces to relieve the overcrowding in Doña Ana worked, but Señor Melendres and Lieutenant Sackett soon discovered that their efforts were for naught. Many of the Mexican residents were deeply upset that they were now considered Americans because they lived on the east side of the river. In 1850, more than sixty Doña Ana families packed up their belongings and moved a short distance to the south, on the west side of Las Cruces, just across the new border in Mexico. Here, they founded the town of *Mesilla,* which means Little Mesa. Many more families would have moved also, but they had invested too much effort and money into their profitable farms to leave them behind. Thus, many begrudgingly accepted their American citizenry, but deep in their hearts they remained loyal to Mexico.

On June 6, 1852, Doña Ana established the county of Doña Ana that incorporated the lands east of the river and extended south of Las Cruces. The purpose of the county was to establish a tax base that would fund needed irrigation projects in the valley. However, many Mexican families saw it as another tyranny of American life.

Although the new Mesilla residents preserved their Mexican status, the hands of governmental change soon swept over them again. In 1854, the United States bowed to intense lobbying by railroad companies to purchase a 30,000-square-mile strip of land along the

United States-Mexican border from Mexico. The companies thought the land was perfect for building a straight railroad from California to the eastern states. The United States and Mexico signed the Gadsden Purchase by which Mexico sold the land to the United States for ten million dollars. Mesilla was part of the land deal and the residents were once again American citizens. When the residents discovered their fate, they seethed deep in their souls at the injustice. They believed that the United States once again had deceived and cheated them by denying their Mexican citizenship. Now both Doña Ana and Mesilla harbored dissenters who swore allegiance to Mexico and taught their children to do the same.

Just after the Civil War, the Sante Fe railroad began surveying their new north-south line through the New Mexican territory. Their first survey line passed through Mesilla. The towns' people were elated and met frequently with railroad officials to make sure that their town would be a regular stop. The railroad assured the town that their position on the line was secure and all that remained was to negotiate rights of way with the private landowners. Believing that the railroad was committed to purchasing their land, the landowners banned together and decided to sell their land at inflated prices. When the Santa Fe landsmen arrived, they were greeted by hardened Mesilla residents who refused to budge a nickel on their selling price. Dismayed, the railroad officials left without securing any land.

A group of businessmen from Las Cruces heard about the dispute and petitioned the railroad to consider their town as a refueling stop. To sweeten the offer, Las Cruces offered free platted rights of way to the railroad in exchange for the right to develop the land along the line. The surveyors investigated the proposed deviation and found it acceptable. The Santa Fe railroad accepted the terms and altered their route away from Mesilla.

When the trains began running through Las Cruces, the town experienced the immediate benefits of having another economic base to sustain their community. The town boomed and quickly became many times larger than Mesilla and Doña Ana. These towns suffered the same fate as Lincoln when the railroad went through Carrizozo. The once bustling towns withered and became quiet backwaters of society where the rest of the world did not pay much attention to their views and wants.

By the 1890s, the population in Doña Ana County surpassed ten thousand. The populace's demand for water, the intense irrigation along the Rio Grande in central New Mexico, and the enormous agriculture development in Southern Colorado drained the river's finite resources and caused the Rio Grande to dry up above El Paso in the summer. Engineers proposed elaborate water storage projects to solve the problem, but water rights were a volatile subject among the residents and many accused each other of hoarding. To make matters worse, Mexico proclaimed water rights that were based on historical usage. The squabbling and protests halted the construction of all storage projects along the Rio Grande.

At the beginning of the new century, two events finally settled the controversy and opened the door for water management. Congress passed the Reclamation Act in 1902, which provided money to construct large-scale water-storage projects. In 1904, the United States and Mexico reached an agreement to construct a large reservoir at Elephant Butte, which was about seventy miles north of Doña Ana. The new dam, named the Engle Dam, would store enough water to meet the needs along the Rio Grande during the dry summer months. The proposed structure was a large concrete gravity dam, over 300 feet high and more than 1,600 feet long. Construction began in 1908, but land disputes slowed the building. After several stops and starts, the Engle Dam, later renamed the Elephant Butte Dam, finally began storing water in January 1915.

During this time period, the government built other water management projects. Just north of Doña Ana, the Leasburg Diversion Dam and six miles of canal were completed in 1908. This project brought water to thirsty fields within the heart of Doña Ana. Other projects in the immediate area were in various stages of construction. These were the Mesilla Diversion Dam, the East Side and West Side Canals, Percha Diversion Dam, and the Rincon Valley Canal.

The surge in construction around Doña Ana completely overwhelmed the area's supply of labor. In mid-1915, every able-bodied man who was willing to work could easily find a well-paying construction job. Contractors for the government competed vigorously for labor in a desperate effort to meet their construction schedules. Labor agents besieged migrant workers as soon as they entered town to sign work contracts. In return, the labor agents received commissions for every man they secured.

Aggravating the labor shortage, the United States was considering entering the escalating war in Europe. A German U-boat torpedoed and sank the British ocean liner Lusitania on May 7, 1915. Nearly 1,200 people, including 128 Americans died and caused the nation to rally in support of Britain and France. Young American men were anxious to fight, more out of the thrill of excitement and adventure than out of a sense of patriotism and defending "dear old England." Many were already traveling to conscription centers so that they could be the first to leave. This deepened the labor shortage.

Doña Ana farmers were not blind to the potential windfall their crops would bring if America joined the war. The demand for their cotton, alfalfa, vegetables, pecans, and grains would skyrocket once America entered the conflict. A farmer who worked hard, got his share of Rio Grande water, and had reliable cheap labor could make a small fortune within a few years. The key was securing low-cost labor and the farmers believed that migrant Mexicans fulfilled the requirement.

Newly arrived Mexican families usually had very few possessions and no skills. They were fleeing a war-torn economy in Mexico that worked them very hard and paid them very little. Ideas of land ownership, individual rights, and organized labor were foreign to them. Therefore, Mexicans were ripe for exploitation. They were extremely thankful for the small wages given to them by the farmers because it was usually ten times more than what they would get in Mexico. The substandard housing that farmers provided was equal or better than what the Mexican families had left and much safer.

Doña Ana's population consisted of transient Mexicans and descendants of original Spanish settlers. The prominent family names were Vanegas, Garcia, Madrid, Ledesma, Flores, and Echavaria. For the most part, everyone got along and everyone knew each other's business. A new family arriving in the area was properly inspected from afar, then thoroughly discussed among the residents. Afterward, an embassy of three self-appointed women usually paid the family an unannounced visit under the guise of welcoming them into the community. The visit usually gave the women more material to gossip around town. Within a few hours after leaving the new household, Doña Ana knew everything there was to know about the newcomers.

The Minjares family was not spared the normal rituals of entering community life. When an elderly and two middle-aged women appeared at the door, the visitors were appalled by the obvious age difference between Tereso and Paz. This discovery provided juicy tidbits for eager ears around town. However, they were touched by Paz's attempt to recover from the tragic loss of her baby and this tempered their report. The women were in agreement that the children were well behaved, Mrs. Minjares was a strong and good woman, and Tereso Minjares was a scoundrel. They disliked his bravado and attempts to impress them with his wit and acts of strength. After the residents tired of discussing the Minjares family, the farming community accepted them for what they were, a poor Mexican family looking for a safe nurturing place to call home.

As the Minjares family settled into daily life in Doña Ana, they struggled to put Bernardo's death behind them. The family slowly fixed their shelter into a home. Neighbors brought small welcome gifts and helped Paz get organized. At first, she numbly accepted their help, but as the weeks progressed she became more receptive and even offered her guests coffee. The children met others their age and began romping through the vast fields together. Of course, Tereso enjoyed meeting the men and entertaining them with stories of his past exploits.

Work even agreed with Tereso despite the language barrier between him and his employer, Bill Taylor. Taylor knew only fragments of Spanish and Tereso could understand about the same in English. To solve this problem, they created a sign language that seemed to bridge the gap. By accompanying a spoken verb in either Spanish or English with a short pantomime, they could exchange needed information to accomplish the tasks at hand. For example, if Taylor said "water" and pointed to a field, Tereso would know to place the siphons in the canal to pull water into the vegetable plots. And, if Tereso stated "*trabajo*" and pretended to hoe, Taylor would understand that Tereso was going to weed the field.

A typical day began at seven in the morning just when the sun dried the dew from the growing crops. Tereso walked over to the Taylor farm and rounded up the plow horses. He attached their harnesses to a plow and walked them out to the field. He usually worked alone until Bill Taylor found him and directed his efforts elsewhere. At noon, he put the horses back in their pasture and hung up the gear. Then he walked back home for a two-hour lunch and rest. Afterward, he returned to the fields and moved irrigation siphons or weeded the vegetable plots. He worked until six in the evening and returned home at sunset.

Although the work was monotonous, Tereso enjoyed the slow pace. For the first time in two years, he did not feel hunted. No one seemed to care where he came from or what he did in the past. Doña Ana accepted him as Tereso Minjares, a farm worker. Although he wished he could reclaim his old *colleador* fame, he sensed a tremendous relief from slipping the lawman's noose. He felt safe at last.

His happy mood motivated him to liven up the house. He would grab Augustine as soon as he walked into the door and toss him into the air. The boy always shrieked with delight and gave his father a tight hug around the neck. Tereso then sat down at the table and asked for the girls to come forward and tell him about their day. Joaquina was still young enough to want to crawl into his lap and chatter like a bird. Alcaria was more reserved and stood close to him and planted a kiss on his cheek before reciting her day.

Paz stayed in the background finishing the family dinner. She did not partake in the teasing and happy banter, and appeared aloof.

However, the light family discussions were infectious and greatly improved her spirits. She still did not allow Tereso into her bed. Paz harbored too many hard feelings against him for the loss of Bernardo, but as time marched on, the bitterness ebbed. His sincere interest in the children helped, too.

Tereso also directed some of his unspent energies toward improving the family's general welfare. He borrowed Mr. Taylor's horses one day and plowed a plot behind the house for a family garden. He planted squash, beans, carrots, and melons. Paz and the girls weeded and watered the garden during the day. Afterward, he built a chicken coop and received four hens and a rooster from Nellie Taylor. By the end of the hot summer, the Minjares family flourished with a bountiful diet.

During the evening of the first day of September, the family was sitting around the table after dinner discussing a very important topic. Alcaria was going to attend school for the first time. She was seven years old. Tereso and Paz were very proud. Paz sewed her a new school dress and packed her a special lunch. Joaquina was jealous and made faces at her big sister. Augustine could not quite understand what the fuss was all about, but he was caught up in the joyfulness of the occasion and bounced on his father's knee.

"There now," Paz said as she took in the waist of the dress with a final stitch as Alcaria stood on a stool in the kitchen. "Turn around so I can see how it fits." Alcaria turned slowly on her bare feet to face her mother. She thoroughly searched her mother's face for a look of acceptance, but she only saw her intensely study the seams in the feeble lantern light with a sewing needle protruding from her mouth. Paz mumbled through clenched teeth, "Well, it seems to fit good."

"*Gracias*, Mama," Alcaria said as she jumped down and twirled on the dirt floor. "It's *muy bonita!*" Augustine clapped with approval, but Joaquina stomped behind her father and sulked.

Tereso laughed and said, "Well, I think your mother did a wonderful job, *¿qué no?* Your sister's nose may be out of joint for a while though."

Paz watched her husband wrap a strong arm around Joaquina and comfort her. Alcaria pranced around the room and Augustine snuggled up in his father's lap with sleepy eyelids. *This is so peaceful,* she thought. *Why couldn't we always have been like this? I hope Tereso doesn't destroy our peace. I don't think I could live through it again.*

Paz continued to watch the lively discussions. Augustine fell sound asleep with his head propped on his father's chest. Suddenly, there was a knock at the door. The talk stopped as everyone turned and looked at the closed door. Tereso pushed away from the table and stood up while holding on to the boy. He opened the door and let out a booming greeting when he recognized the visitor, "Miguel Echavaria! Come in."

"*Hola*," Miguel said as he took off his hat and shook Tereso's hand. As he entered the room, Miguel stopped and bowed to Paz. She smiled and nodded back. She had seen him before with his wife, Rosemary. Miguel came from an established family that had settled in the area over a hundred years ago. His above-average height and long mustache revealed his Spanish heritage, but his wiry, bow-legged walk and black eyes bespoke his Indian roots too. Paz noticed that he had groomed himself and put on clean clothes before paying his visit. He wore a dull red cotton shirt tucked into blue jeans, with black cowboy boots polished to full luster.

Miguel fidgeted for a moment and worked his hat in his hands before addressing Tereso. Paz suspected that he was nervous about discussing what was on his mind in front of her and the children. She had learned long ago not to turn her back on secret discussions that concerned her husband. She decided to sit down and wait quietly for him to explain the nature of his call. Miguel fumbled for a few minutes before getting to the subject at hand. "I am sorry for coming so late in the evening, but I wanted to see you while I had the chance," he said in an awkward voice. Tereso smiled and nodded his head to go on. Seeing that Paz and the children were staying, Miguel gulped and continued, "Well, the men always get together for Mexican Independence Day and I wanted to personally invite you to join our celebration this year."

Paz thought, *I knew it! Why do men always find an excuse to drink?* She looked over to her husband and saw his huge grin. Tereso appeared to be overjoyed at the prospect of attending an all-male party.

Tereso asked, "Where will it be?"

Miguel answered, "It will be at Augustine Madrid's farm. In fact, he asked me personally to invite you." This news pleased Tereso greatly. He had heard people talk about him. Many thought of him as a *mayordomo*. If this man wanted to meet him, then surely this was a sign that Doña Ana finally recognized his talents. Tereso knew that he was destined for far greater things than working as a simple farmhand. For a moment, Tereso stood smiling in front of Miguel while he stared blankly at the wall and dreamed about the implications. Miguel misinterpreted Tereso's silence as reluctance to accept. So he added, "Since you are new to the area, you do not have to bring anything. It's all free."

Paz emitted a groan as she thought, *This just keeps getting worse!* Miguel's eyes shot toward Paz and registered her displeasure. Then he abruptly looked back at Tereso.

"Uh?" said Tereso as he came back to reality. "Did you say something?"

"Ah, *Sí*," answered Miguel. He felt Paz's stare upon him and he shifted under its weight. "I . . er … said that you would be our honored guest."

Tereso beamed, "*Gracias*, Miguel. I gladly accept. What time should I arrive?"

Miguel had planned to escort Tereso to the party, but the thought of confronting Paz again changed his mind. "About two o'clock."

"*Bien*," said Tereso, "I will be there."

"*Bueno*," sighed Miguel as if he had just completed a difficult and unpleasant assignment. Not wanting to linger any longer, he put his hat back on his head and quickly departed with a curt, "*Buenas noches*."

Tereso repeated the departing wish and closed the door. When he turned around, Paz saw that he had a smile that stretched from ear to ear. He jostled little Augustine in his arms as he paced the floor. He was too keyed up to sit back down. Paz watched him for a moment with a stern look before speaking, "The last time you celebrated Independence Day you killed a man." The comment stopped him dead in his tracks.

He asked, "What do you mean?"

Paz stood, pointed a knowing finger at him, and spat, "You know exactly what I mean. It was only two years ago when you and your friend decided to drink yourselves drunk on Independence Day. You killed a man and ran away. You left me and the children to fend for ourselves. Now you are going to do it again!"

Tereso felt his anger roar through his veins. He involuntarily squeezed Augustine as he struggled to contain himself. The boy gasped awake and started to cry. Tereso shouted, "It was an accident!" Augustine began to wail louder and the girls scampered to a corner of the room and cowered. "It could have happened to anyone. That time has nothing to with this. *Comprende?*"

Paz walked fearlessly over to her husband and wrestled her son away from him. She smoothed Augustine's hair and cooed softly to him to soothe his fears. When he quieted down, she continued, "It has everything to do with this year's party. We have a good life here and you are going to ruin it. You are going to get drunk and do something stupid. I know this will happen and if you looked into your soul, you would see it too." Without waiting for a response, Paz motioned for the girls to follow her as she grabbed a lantern and walked into the back room.

When the door closed, Tereso found himself alone in the front room to contemplate his wife's words. But the more he turned them around in his mind, the more he wanted to go to Madrid's party.

Bill Taylor understood what Mexican Independence Day was all about and that he was powerless to stop it. Although September 16 fell on a Thursday, he begrudgingly allowed Tereso to quit early and get ready for the evening's event. Taylor knew Tereso would be worthless the next day and did not plan on him returning to his duties until Saturday. In the past, every one of his Mexican helpers had participated in the holiday and celebrated heavily. Some men failed to return at all. His only consolation was that Tereso was married and hopefully that responsibility would temper his activities.

Taylor pushed his hat off his brow and wiped his forehead with the back of his hand as he watched Tereso quickly throw his tools into the shed and race home. Taylor shook his head as he thought, *Why is it that every citizen in Doña Ana and Mesilla must celebrate this fool day? Isn't July fourth Independence Day?* He just had to accept that this custom was one of the quirks of living in the valley. Tereso slammed the door to the tool shed closed and took off to his house on a dead run. Taylor continued to watch him disappear down the road in a cloud of dust.

Tereso busted into the house and slid across the dirt floor. Paz was sitting at the table patiently waiting for his arrival. As she lifted her head to speak, Tereso blew by her without a second's notice. He threw open the door to the back room and snatched his clean shirt and pants from a wooden peg on the wall. He shucked his work clothes into the corner and tugged on his pants and shirt. He frantically tucked in his shirt and raced over to the sink. Tereso quickly filled a pan with a pitcher on the counter and splashed the water on his face. He gruffly dried his face with his sleeves and ran his fingers back through his graying hair.

As he stood up and searched for his hat to leave, Paz made her presence known. She spoke sharply, "Tereso. You do not have to do this. You can stop now before it is too late."

Tereso looked at her with annoyance. "What do you mean 'before its too late'? Too late for what?"

Paz snapped back, "Before you do something stupid that will haunt this family! That's what!"

Tereso smirked at her as he put on his hat. "You worry too much. I am going to have a few drinks with the men and tell a few stories. Nothing wrong with that."

"But you won't stop with a few drinks," continued Paz. "Then you will do something that causes us to flee and hide. I can't live like that again. *Por favor*, Tereso, don't go!"

Tereso's smirk changed to a leer as he opened the door and turned to her saying, "Those times are past, *comprende?* I will see you tonight." He saw her pleading eyes and lips compressed tightly together, all signs that his words did not console her. Exasperated, he shook his head and left.

As he stepped onto the road, his mind's eye opened and flashed a vision. At first, the vision startled him because it had been a long time since he'd had one so vivid. When he calmed himself, he noticed that the road before him transformed into a railroad track pointing north. He had that hunted feeling again, a desperate premonition of dread that slid down a man's back when he was certain that some predator was going to snatch him. Suddenly, the road reappeared and all looked normal. His vision left as quickly as it came, but the uneasy feeling remained. He knew in his heart that his wife was right. He should stay home, but he also felt powerless to resist the night's celebration. Tereso knew something bad was going to happen.

<hr />

Augustine Madrid stood at the gate to his *hacienda* and greeted his guests as they arrived. He was a stocky, dignified-looking man in his early sixties who radiated authority wherever he went. This evening he wore a black vest made of finely tooled calf leather over a crisp white shirt. A dark blue-green turquoise stone held in a silver clasp adorned his bolo tie and matched a similar arrangement on his belt buckle. His hair was short and freshly oiled back along his head. The gray hair around his temples and the thin black mustache completed the image of an exceptional *mayordomo*.

Every man passing the gate felt obligated to shake Madrid's hand and bow simultaneously. Madrid responded to each man with a solemn smile and nod, but kept looking over their heads as if he was searching for someone. After halfheartedly acknowledging about fifty guests, his eyes glimpsed Miguel Echavaria loitering outside the gate. He quickly excused himself and gracefully moved through the line of men in front of him. When Miguel saw Madrid walking toward him, he took off his hat and held the brim with two hands as he nervously looked down the road. When Madrid noticed that Miguel was alone, his eyes betrayed the anger that his reserved face hid.

Madrid addressed him sternly, "*Buenas tardes*, Miguel. Where is our honored guest that I entrusted to your care?"

Miguel bowed his head submissively and continued to rotate the hat in his hands. "We agreed to meet here. He should be here any minute."

Madrid seethed at hearing Miguel's reply. He spat, "Did I not tell you to bring him here personally? Why could you not follow my simple instructions? Are you aware that this man may be perfect for our cause?"

"*Lo siento*," answered Miguel weakly, "but his wife does not want him to come to our celebration tonight. I thought it best to meet him here and avoid making trouble."

A look of contempt crept across Madrid's face. "You mean you let your fear of his wife prevent you from bringing him here? Unbelievable! What if she convinces him not to come, eh? The movement needs him and that should have been your only concern!"

Madrid was about to fire off a string of rebukes when they heard heavy boots running up the road. Turning, they saw Tereso jogging up the road with a big smile on his face. He shouted, "Miguel! Sorry that I am late. It took longer to run here than I thought." He stopped in front of them with only a hint of perspiration across his brow, and a mild shortness of breath.

Relief washed across Miguel's face. He turned to Madrid and said, "Permit me to introduce you two. *Señor* Madrid, this is Tereso Minjares. Tereso, this is *Señor* Augustine Madrid."

Madrid's anger evaporated within the moment and his face beamed a wide smile. "I am very pleased to finally meet you, *Señor* Minjares." Madrid heartily shook Tereso's hand. "I have heard so much about you." He could see Tereso swagger under the compliments.

This was the first time Madrid had seen Tereso and he took a moment to analyze him. He was exceptionally tall and muscular. Judging by his hair color and crow's feet at the corners of his eyes, Madrid guessed him to be in his late fifties. Madrid smiled to himself. This man appeared perfect for their upcoming mission. He was a seasoned, reasonably fit man who appeared to respond well to praise. He could be controlled and manipulated to do their bidding. Madrid only had to properly recruit him and Tereso would be theirs.

Madrid stepped forward, put his hand on Tereso's back, and guided him through the gate. "Come," he said as if he was talking to a long-lost son, "there are some people I want you to meet and there are refreshments to partake." Tereso smiled back at Madrid. He forgot the dread that had lain heavily on his mind only a short time ago. He now felt important and happy, ready to show everyone how smart he was.

The kerosene lanterns hung like ornaments within the courtyard and cast a yellow, slightly wavering light on the party below. Madrid had elaborately decorated the yard with brightly colored ribbons and banners that said "*¡Viva México!*" The grass was freshly mowed and smelled pungent. Copious amounts of food lay on platters on top of long tables that bordered the entire yard. Madrid had assembled a bar at one end with waiters to hand out a choice of beer, tequila, or wine. As in all matters, Madrid proved his attention to detail by erecting a row of outhouses within a discreet distance from the party.

The courtyard was packed and the noise was deafening. Men stood face to face holding and spilling their drinks, laughing like hyenas, and slapping backs. Tereso thrived within this chaos. With his belly full of burritos and tequila, he roared and fought for attention and eventually got it. Being a head taller than most and with Augustine Madrid by his side, he found the men beginning to take notice. They thought he was a braggart and paid him only amused interest until he began to elaborate on his escapades with Don Louis Terrazas and Pancho Villa. On this subject, the men, including Madrid, became quiet and let Tereso rant.

"I was a guard for Terrazas in Chihuahua when I first met Villa," said Tereso to Madrid in a voice much louder than necessary. "At first we fought against each other until I realized what Villa stood for. Then I switched sides."

Madrid asked incredulously, "You know Villa?" This seemed too unbelievable and the men agreed by nodding their heads in unison.

There were very few things that angered Tereso more than not being believed. "*Sí,*" he replied with an edge to his voice. The tequila lit a deep arc of fire inside him. "I know him well. Some of the men that fought next to him were close friends of mine. I even saved him once from a traitor within his company!" Tereso looked around him to see if anyone was smirking. If there was, he was going to punch him.

Madrid sensed Tereso's ugly black mood and moved quickly to defuse it. "Tereso, *por favor,*" he said in a soothing voice. "It is not that we do not believe you. We all support Villa's cause, but never had your good fortune to meet him. I guess you can say that we are envious of your past, *comprende?*" For added emphasis, Madrid turned to the surrounding men and asked, "*¿Qué no?*" Slowly, the men began to nod out of respect for Madrid.

Madrid's words and the men's actions mollified Tereso. He took another swig from his glass and wiped his mouth with the back of his hand. Madrid broke the awkward silence by asking Tereso a pointed question, "Why did you change sides?"

Tereso smiled and replied, "Because Villa fights for the working Mexican man like me."

This was the response Madrid sought. He put an arm around Tereso's shoulder and turned to the other men. With a raised hand, he proclaimed, "Did you men hear that? This man has just summarized our cause in one sentence! Villa is fighting for the common man, not for some land baron or tyrant. All of you are Mexican in your hearts. You feel Mexico's distress and it tugs at your soul. That is why we gather tonight to celebrate its independence and cheer its struggle to preserve it." Madrid turned back to Tereso and placed both hands on his shoulders and grasped him hard. He spoke into his eyes, "We all must support Villa's cause. Some of us with special talents must step forward and help in unusual ways. Do you agree, *Señor* Minjares?"

Tereso was taken aback by Madrid's speech and personal attention in front of the men. He quickly looked around him and saw everyone staring back at him waiting for a response. He gulped and answered weakly, "*Sí.*"

"*Bueno*," replied Madrid. Then he grabbed Tereso by the head and pulled his face close to his and kissed him on the cheek. Madrid whispered in his ear, "I know you won't let us down." He released him and held up his hands and yelled, "*¡Viva México!*"

The men shouted back in chorus, "*¡Viva México!*" Some threw their hats in the air and others took a hearty drink. Tereso stood silently next to Madrid realizing something important had just happened, but failed to grasp what it was.

Paz heard the commotion in front of the house long before the door opened. Judging by the dimming stars and brightening day, she thought the hour to be around five in the morning. She heard several men dragging something heavy through the kitchen door and depositing the load on the floor. When she heard the wagon drive off, she got up and opened the bedroom door. On the kitchen floor, she saw her husband sprawled out in a drunken stupor. Paz stood over him for a moment and checked for signs of blood, broken bones, or slashed clothing. Seeing none, she walked back to the bedroom and closed the door. They would live in peace for another year.

Chapter 20
Gunrunner

The last weeks of September through the middle of October were very busy for Tereso. The crops required harvesting and Bill Taylor pushed him hard to collect them on time. Tereso pulled vegetables from the field and hauled them to large wagons. Once he carted them off the field, he removed the excess dirt and foliage and bagged them. Then he lugged the bags to a freight wagon and piled them high. Taylor drove the loads to market for sale.

Tereso toiled hard and long in the beating sun for weeks without a break. Nellie Taylor helped by carrying water out to the field and providing hearty lunches. Tereso would wolf down the food and chase it with huge gulps of water. It sustained him to push forward and complete the harvest. By the end of each day, he was so exhausted that he stumbled home and collapsed on the cool bedroom floor. Before Paz could help him with his boots, he was fast asleep and snoring deeply.

Work filled every minute of Tereso's life. He had no spare time to get into trouble. So when the harvest abruptly concluded, Tereso suddenly had his evenings free and energy to pursue other interests. He worked on small jobs around the house and Paz began to think that he was quite pleasant to be around. He chopped cottonwood and the girls stacked it neatly along the house. He plowed their garden over to make ready for fall, but most importantly, he installed a window that Taylor gave him for the bedroom. The natural light did wonders for the gloomy interior.

It was during this slower pace of life and cooler weather that Augustine Madrid's men began to pay Tereso unannounced visits in the field. Miguel Echavaria with one or two associates would stroll out to where Tereso was plowing and interrupt him for a short time. Tereso enjoyed these visits because they halted his monotonous work, gave him opportunities to brag, and the men usually asked his advice on particular matters, which always puffed up his ego.

Bill Taylor watched these visits from across the fields. He made a mental note to lecture Tereso about his meetings. He did not want to set a precedent of socializing during work, but the lecture would have to wait until he could find someone who could translate reliably. Their hand signals would not cover the intricacies of this subject. Thus, when he saw two men walk out to Tereso for the third time this week, all Taylor could do was grit his teeth and swear that he would find a translator soon.

Miguel waved as he stumbled toward Tereso across the freshly turned soil. Tereso smiled when he saw them and pulled the reins of the two plow horses to stop. He wiped the sweat off his brow with the back of his hand and greeted them. *"Buenos días, Señores.* How goes it?"

Miguel stopped next to Tereso and shook his hand. "Oh, not bad," he replied as he nodded his head toward his partner, "Do you know Julio?"

"Sí," answered Tereso. He vaguely remembered him from the Independence party. Julio was the young man with a cocky smile and a glint of evil behind his eyes. Tereso had a feeling that he could not trust him.

"Bueno," continued Miguel, "I don't want to take much of your time, but *Señor* Madrid requests the pleasure of your company tonight."

Tereso squirmed in pleasure in front of the men. He thought, *Madrid must think that I am very important to seek me.* Tereso's thoughts showed plainly across his face and the men easily read them. Julio cracked a mischievous grin. Tereso finally answered, "I would be happy to attend."

Miguel smiled and said, *"Bueno.* We will see you tonight at eight." He tipped his hat and motioned for Julio to follow. Tereso leaned on his plow and watched them walk through the field and back toward the road. A horse snorted and brought him back to reality. Tereso felt his energy rejuvenate and readied the plow. He could hardly wait until tonight. At that moment, he felt a set of eyes burn upon him. He glanced toward the house and saw Bill Taylor watching him over the livestock fence. Tereso thought that he looked mad, but he had not a clue why. He shrugged and snapped the reins to signal the horses forward. Tereso was convinced that tonight was the start of his rise in affluence in the community and, within a short time, he would no longer have to plow another man's field.

When Tereso arrived at Madrid's *rancho*, he scarcely recognized the place. In stark contrast to the gala atmosphere of the Independence party, the grounds were dark and silent. Only a single lantern burned on the front porch and gave the home an almost secretive look. The scene triggered a memory of approaching Villa's dark house in Chihuahua. The image produced a shiver down Tereso's spine.

"*Buenas noches, Señor* Minjares," a servant announced unexpectedly from behind the gate. Tereso almost jumped in fright. "We have been expecting you." He unlatched the gate and swung it open.

"*Gracias*," mumbled Tereso as he strained to calm his voice and walk boldly forward. The servant motioned for him to follow and walked straight to a side door of the house. The entry was concealed, which allowed people to come and go completely undetected by any traveler on the road. The servant quietly opened the door and whispered something to an attendant standing inside. The man nodded and quickly went to another room. The servant stepped back and signaled for Tereso to go inside. Tereso nodded, took off his *sombrero*, which the servant deftly took from him, and entered the home.

The entryway was small, so he shuffled to one side and stood silently until someone came for him. He could hear muffled voices with serious tones coming from a room at the end of a hallway. The voices suddenly died and within a few moments, Augustine Madrid came bounding down the hall toward him. His face was solemn with only a hint of a smile. Tereso thought, *This must be a very important matter. They must really need my advice.*

Madrid greeted him in hushed tones, "You are right on time, *gracias*. It shows that you are very dependable and we need such a man now." Tereso soaked the praise up like a fine wine. "Come. There are many important people that I must introduce you to." Madrid took him by the arm and led him down the hall and into a large room. Decorative oil sconces along the natural wood paneled walls threw soft lighted tones across the hardwood floor. About a dozen well-dressed men were present; some were standing and others sat comfortably in leather chairs. All had tumblers of tequila, and a few smoked cigars that left a haze along the ceiling. Tereso felt their eyes upon him as Madrid brought him forward.

"Gentlemen," announced Madrid as he escorted Tereso to the middle of the room, "let me introduce *Señor* Tereso Minjares." The men stared back in silence. Only a few faintly nodded. Unfazed, Madrid continued, "Tereso, these men are from Mesilla. The others I am sure you recognize from around here, *Señores* Vanegas, Garcia, Ledesma, Flores, and Rosales." They all studied him behind guarded expressions. A few nodded curtly, but no one extended his hand.

Behind them, a smirking young man walked out into view. Madrid said, "Ah, and I believe you already know Julio, *¿qué no?*"

"*Sí*," replied Tereso. Julio irritated him, but he checked his anger.

He let Madrid lead him to the bar where Madrid poured him a drink. Tereso took a hard swig and felt the tequila burn down his throat and bolster his courage and spirit.

Madrid walked back into the middle of the room and resumed running the meeting. "Now that we are all here, I will recap the events that have led us to this meeting. First, my sources have confirmed the rumor that Victoriano Huerta is in an El Paso prison for conspiring to incite another revolution in Mexico. His tyranny is over. Second, the new provisional head of Mexico is now Venustiano Carranza. Many believe that he is actually a dictator in disguise. Francisco Villa saw through his facade and declared war against his regime. Third, and the reason we are here tonight, President Wilson has imposed an arms embargo against Villa's army. The *Estados Unidos* has turned its cowardly back on Mexico's revolutionary needs. Villa must have arms to fight for freedom and we must supply them."

Madrid looked around the room for agreement. At first, the men talked quietly among themselves. Several rubbed their chins and contemplated Madrid's words. Finally, an older, distinguished man who represented Mesilla stepped forward. "*Señor* Madrid, may I speak frankly?"

"Of course, *Señor* Olveria," answered Madrid. "You may speak your mind here."

"*Gracias*," replied Olveria as he walked to the middle of the room. He stopped and looked carefully into every eye. Then he spoke in a low and authoritative voice, "I speak only for the men from Mesilla, but I am sure many others feel the way we do. We support Mexico's struggle for democracy and deplore the *Estados Unidos* blockade of arms. This is just one of many past discriminations against Mexico's residents. Villa desperately needs reliable weapons to repel the Mexican *federales*. We have connections to obtain rifles, but they are not cheap and we cannot afford to fund Villa's revolutionaries ourselves. Where will the money come and, once the guns are paid for, how will we get them to Villa?"

Madrid replied, "Villa has received some funds from Mexican citizens. Our contributions, of course, are needed too. Between these sources, we can pay for the guns. As for how we get them to Villa …" Madrid paused and swirled his drink for a moment as he contemplated his response. Then he looked over to Tereso and smiled as he said, "This is why I invited *Señor* Minjares to our meeting tonight. Minjares possesses some unique talents that we may find useful. He is brave, good with guns, can handle horses, and knows some of Villa's men. He will be our wagon driver for our gun shipments."

Tereso almost choked on his drink. The surprised look on his face produced a chuckle from Julio. Madrid continued as if nothing was wrong. "I have made contact with the *Villistas* in El Paso. They will meet us south of Las Cruces once a week. We will exchange wagons along with payment for the rifles."

Olveria seemed impressed. He paused in silence for a few moments to contemplate Madrid's words and then asked, "With all due respect *Señor*, why Minjares? Why not one of my men whom we have known from birth?"

"Because of all the reasons I mentioned before, and because I believe we can trust this senior man to promptly deliver the goods and collect the money. However, I realize that he is a newcomer, so I am sending a man of good standing within our communities with him. That man is Julio." Tereso shot Julio a hard glance. He returned an infuriating smirk. Olveria appeared mollified and bowed his head respectfully to Madrid before returning to his chair.

Sensing some insurgence, Madrid moved quickly to counter any resistance to his plan. He walked directly to Tereso and looked him squarely in the face as he addressed him. "*Señor* Minjares. I must be frank with you. Delivering these weapons will be dangerous. There are many who would kill to prevent those guns from being transferred to the *Villistas*. Others will want to steal them for their own profit. Minjares, Mexico needs you to perform this duty." Madrid spread his arms wide to signify the whole room and added, "We need you. There is no one more brave and skilled than you. Do you accept the challenge?"

Tereso's mind flooded with a surge of conflicting emotions. He was outraged that Madrid had staged this entire meeting to trap him into doing his bidding. However, his ego and vanity soared under the thick compliments Madrid pronounced in front of so many important men. Also, the mention of the danger poked a sliver of excitement through his gut. It had been a while since he had last felt it and he savored it like a fine wine. Tereso stood ramrod straight as he faced Madrid and said, "I do."

"*Bueno*," replied Madrid with a relieved look upon his face. He had anticipated an argument and that was why he had showered the compliments so thickly. Madrid reached out with both hands and clasped Tereso on the shoulders and said, "I knew we could depend on you. Now, I want you to slip out the door that you came in and go home. We will contact you next Tuesday and tell you about the arrangements." Tereso nodded his understanding, but Madrid kept his grip on his shoulders. "I have one more demand. You must not tell a soul about this meeting or your special mission. *Comprende?* Not even your wife must know. There are too many eyes upon us. *Sí?*"

Tereso loved secrets, but he was at a loss on how to handle Paz. She was too sharp not to pick up on his Wednesday night excursions. He nodded and asked, "*Sí*, but what do I tell my wife?"

"Tell her that you are attending local government meetings at my *rancho*," replied Madrid. "It is partly true, *¿qué no?*" Tereso smiled and nodded again. Madrid patted him on the shoulder and released his hold. "*Bueno*. Now go home. I will see you next week." Tereso took one last look around the room. Every man's eyes were upon him and this made him feel both uneasy and important. Only Julio continued to wear a disrespectful leer across his face, which produced an almost uncontrollable urge to punch him in the nose. Tereso steadied himself and turned to the hallway. The servant was waiting for him with his sombrero in one hand and pointing down the hall with the other. Tereso took his hat and walked quickly toward the door.

When Augustine Madrid heard the door close, he turned back to the men. Olveria smiled from his chair and asked, "*Verdad*, why have you chosen him?"

Madrid went silently over to the bar and poured himself a stiff drink. He lifted up the glass and took a large swallow. Then he faced Olveria with an uneasy smile and answered him. "He does possess some traits that I believe will be useful. However, he is expendable if something should happen during a shipment."

Olveria asked, "What if he is captured by the law and talks? He can finger everyone here."

Madrid took another drink and walked over to Julio. He gave him a knowing look and answered Olveria while staring at Julio, "This is why Julio is going with him. Julio will make sure Minjares never utters a word to anyone." Julio only nodded back and smiled wider.

———

During the past week, Paz had noticed that Tereso was exceptionally well behaved and almost subdued. He went to work without complaint, spent every free moment with the children or in the family garden, and was very attentive to her needs. At first she thought he was trying to woo her into sharing her bed, but the way he jumped every time someone knocked at the door made her think something else was afoot. She watched him with a wary eye as he went about his daily duties.

On Tuesday evening, Tereso returned from work with an unusual bounce to his step. He announced that Augustine Madrid had asked him to attend a political meeting at his home on Wednesday night. Had Paz not known *Señor* Madrid, she would have thought that Tereso was going to some drunken brawl. Still, she was suspicious of this Wednesday meeting. She found it hard to believe that someone as wise as Madrid would seek out her husband for political advice.

As the sun set on Wednesday evening, Tereso abruptly bounded through the door from work. He pranced back and forth nervously as he collected his knapsack and water bag. His normally jovial mood was gone and replaced by a serious and almost scared look. Paz watched him with keen interest. None of his actions made sense to her. She thought, *Why would he pack his field gear if he was attending a political meeting?* Then she saw Tereso grab his knife and sheath and strap it to his waist. Paz now knew that he was going somewhere else than Madrid's *rancho*.

Paz quietly walked up to Tereso and asked him point-blank, "Tereso, where are you really going?"

He stopped dead in his tracks with his back to her and replied, "What do you mean?"

"You know that you are not going to Madrid's *rancho*. What are you up to? Are you going somewhere to drink?"

Tereso felt trapped and a little angry that she would question him on such an important night. He turned around and said with absolute conviction in his voice, "I am meeting Madrid on a very important issue. I want to make sure that I am prepared. I will not drink tonight. You will see when I return." With that proclamation, Tereso cinched up his knapsack and grabbed his coat and hat. He gave each child a hug and kiss and waved goodbye to Paz. Then he left as abruptly as he had arrived.

Paz continued to stare at the closed door for several minutes. She was baffled at his actions. His nervous behavior was different from his party moods. She thought, *No, he is not going to drink. He looked like he is going to do something unusual, almost dangerous.* Paz knew her husband had a flair for attracting danger. A cold shiver suddenly crept though her body. She turned back to the kitchen to complete the evening meal. She murmured bitterly as she picked up a pot, "I just hope he doesn't bring the whole world down upon us." It was going to be a long night waiting for him to return.

Tereso started off with a loping gait. He headed west along Taylor Road and soon crossed the railroad tracks and the Leasburg Canal. The sun buried itself behind the stark mountains and deep night fell. He broke into a run to ensure that he arrived at the meeting place on time. He kept the brisk pace until he saw the intersection ahead. The damp, fertile smells told him that he was close to the Rio Grande. Tereso slowed down to a cautious walk and stretched his senses to detect anyone near.

The intersection with the north-south road was vacant. Tereso suddenly feared that he was late and had missed his rendezvous. He looked nervously up and down the road for signs of the wagon that the messenger who had come to him in the field yesterday had told him to meet. If he missed the wagon, it would be an embarrassing blunder that would be hard to amend. Tereso gulped and strained his eyes into the dark and up the road. He noticed that his night vision was not as sharp as it used to be.

He heard the clomping of horse hooves coming from the north before he saw the team. The wagon appeared furtively out of the night. A lone figure rode on the buckboard with his sombrero pushed down over his eyes. The rider pulled the wagon to a quiet stop alongside Tereso. It was not until he spoke that Tereso realized it was Julio. "Get in, Minjares. We do not have all night." The lack of respect in his voice rankled Tereso, but the relief of knowing that he had met the wagon on time nullified the insult. Tereso climbed quickly aboard. Without saying another word, Julio shook the reins and the four horses started forward.

They headed south in silence for two miles until they arrived at the outskirts of Las Cruces. Julio turned the wagon onto a small road that hugged the heavily wooded Rio Grande and missed the populated areas. Only an occasional farmhouse could be seen. When the lights of the city lay northeast of their position, the road abruptly rose and met an approach to a bridge that crossed the river next to the little town of Mesilla. Julio halted the wagon at the intersection and waited without explanation to Tereso.

Tereso ignored the rebuff by looking carefully at his surroundings. The moon had risen and its soft light filtered through the thick foliage above. An occasional bat darted across the starlit night. Tereso felt that they were alone and nothing was unusual. He thought, *We must be waiting for someone.* The lack of information about their mission irritated him. He watched Julio casually hold the reins and glance occasionally across the bridge. *The little brat must know what's going on.* He had an overwhelming urge to grab Julio by the neck and beat the hell out of him. *I could make him talk*, stewed Tereso as he forced himself to remain calm.

The sound of the bridge creaking under a heavy load startled the two of them. A dark form slowly materialized on the far end of the bridge and rolled toward them. As it drew closer, Tereso saw that it was a stout wagon pulled by two horses. By the strain on the horses and the jerking movements of the wheels, Tereso knew that the cargo must be burdensome. He made out two men on the buckboard. Each had a rifle. Tereso suddenly felt naked with only his knife to protect him. He glanced back at Julio, who secretly moved his vest back with his left hand and exposed a small pistol in a shoulder holster. This surprised and angered Tereso. Madrid should have given him a gun, too. He wondered what other secrets were hidden from him.

The men came to a stop directly in front of them. All remained quiet for moment before Julio hailed them in a quiet voice. "The people of Mesilla are loyal to Mexico."

"And the people of Doña Ana are loyal too," was the reply. The exchange was correct and Julio and the others seemed to breathe a sigh of relief.

Julio whispered, "They checked out. Jump down and help them switch out their horses. We will swap wagons here." Tereso begrudgingly obeyed the younger man. He slipped off the buckboard and walked over to the other wagon. When he got closer, Tereso could barely make out the men's faces in the dark. He recognized them as young men from last week's meeting at Madrid's *rancho*. He noticed that the wagon was covered with a heavy tarp that was strapped to the sides.

Tereso looked down at the harness arrangement and found the pins that connected the team to the wagon. He motioned for the driver to set his brake before disconnecting the horses. Tereso pointed at the other man and said, "I need you." The man looked at the driver for approval before jumping down with his rifle in his left hand.

Tereso led the team away from the wagon and told the man to hold the horses still. Then he walked over to Julio's wagon and released the team. Within minutes, Tereso had swapped horses and adjusted the harnesses. Even Julio was impressed with the skill and efficiency with which Tereso accomplished the task. They climbed aboard the new wagons and signaled goodbye.

"Remember to collect the money," the driver said to Julio as he passed.

"*Sí*," replied Julio sharply. He snapped the reins and prodded the horses forward. They strained to move the heavy wagon down the road.

Tereso asked, "Money? What money?"

Julio kept his eyes forward and said, "You ask too many questions, Minjares." He offered no further explanation.

Julio's silence began to boil Tereso's blood. He thought, *Who does he think he is?* Finally, he could not contain himself any longer. He reached over and grabbed the reins from Julio and yanked the horses to a stop.

Julio snarled, "What are you doing!" Tereso's swift action caught him by surprise.

"Since you will not tell me," replied Tereso as he climbed onto the wagon cover, "I am going to find out what is going on."

Julio commanded, "Get back here! Or I will…"

"You will what?" asked Tereso as he unfastened some straps and pulled the tarp back. The dull moonlight reflected coldly off blue steel. Tereso whistled softly as he gazed at the neatly stacked carbine rifles, each carefully packed in a straw-lined box with the name "Western Cartridge Company" stamped along the sides. Then he spotted a small, deep box directly behind the buckboard. Tereso pulled the straw packing from the top and found two bundles wrapped in wax paper. He lifted one up and unwrapped it. Julio watched him with raging eyes. Tereso unfolded the last of the paper and gasped at what he revealed. He beheld the most beautiful revolver that he had ever seen. It was a beautiful Colt pistol. Tereso ran his eyes along the blued barrel to its finely machined cylinder. The workmanship was exquisite, but it was the handle that made the piece extraordinary. It consisted of carved ivory with the Mexican double-eagle stamp on the side. The pistol was obviously a gift to some unknown benefactor. He held it up and felt its balanced weight rest naturally in his grip.

Julio barked, "Put that back!" Tereso ignored him. There was no way that he would part with such a stunning weapon. He thrust the pistol under his waistband and grabbed the other bundle. It contained a matching gun. He put his hand back in the box, fished around for a moment, and pulled out a small box of bullets. He placed them on the seat and threw back the tarp. Then he casually sat down and began loading the guns. "What are you doing?" asked Julio with a thread of exasperation in his voice.

Tereso finished loading the last pistol and snapped the cylinder back in place. He took a final loving look at the gun before stuffing it into his belt, opposite the other pistol with the handles facing inward. "Just preparing myself, that is all," he replied with a large, satisfied smile.

Julio could see Tereso's smiling teeth in the moonlight. It infuriated him and made him feel helpless. He blurted, "I am going to tell *Señor* Madrid."

Tereso answered nonchalantly, "So, tell him. Now, *vámanos*." Julio glared at him in the darkness for a moment before collecting the reins and prodding the horses forward. They rode south in silence for several hours. The heavy load slowed their progress to a crawl. The lights of Las Cruces seemed to hang forever in the north until they finally disappeared below the horizon. By the rising and falling of constellations and the position of the moon, Tereso estimated the time to be around one in the morning. He started to feel tired and involuntarily yawned.

Without warning, Julio pulled on to a small side road and entered a spent gravel pit, which was hidden from the road by a high berm built from overburden. The soft ground bogged the horses down. Finally, Julio pulled the reins to stop.

Tereso looked around him and did not like what he saw. A twenty-foot-high berm bordered the entire perimeter. He felt like a *matador* trapped in an unfamiliar arena. Anyone could be watching him at this moment with a rifle trained on his belly. The horses could barely budge the wagon in the soft dirt, which would restrict their mobility if a fight broke out. Lastly, there was only one way in and out of the pit. If enemies positioned themselves at the entrance, they would trap them like slow-moving turtles in a box.

"This is stupid," spoke Tereso to no one particular.

Julio's temper broke at the comment and he screamed, "What do you mean 'stupid,' you dumb ox! What do you know about planning? If you don't shut your big mouth *pronto,* I am going to...." Tereso saw Julio make a move for his gun and instinctively reacted. He grabbed Julio's windpipe with his left hand and trapped his right arm across his chest. At the same time, Tereso slammed his body against him. They tumbled off the wagon with Julio landing flat on his back and Tereso falling squarely on his chest and maintaining his grip on his neck. The fall and blow smashed the air out of Julio's lungs. Julio felt his grip on his pistol weaken as his vision blurred.

Tereso jammed his knee into Julio's groin and punched him in the face with his right fist. After two more crushing blows, the fight went out of Julio. His body went limp in Tereso's hands. Suddenly, a chuckling voice filtered into Tereso's brain and broke through his madness. "These *hombres* fight more than we do. Maybe they should fight this war and we deliver guns, *¿qué no?*"

That voice, thought Tereso as he struggled to stand. *I have heard that voice before.* He strained to see where it had come from. It sounded like they were watching him from the top of the berm. Then he heard a deep, rumbling reply.

"No. They fight among themselves like crows. They would kill themselves before they had a chance to fight the *federales.*"

Tereso recognized the low, strong voice too, and it triggered a distant and pleasant memory. He smiled and said in a loud and mocking voice, "Anastacio Currandas and Victoriano Vallejo! Come down here right now and show me your rotting carcasses."

A shocked silence prevailed for a long second until Victoriano yelled, "*¡Dios mío!* Tacio, it's Nava!" The two men jumped up from their hiding place and ran down the loose embankment. Victoriano floated like a bird, but Tacio lumbered awkwardly down the slope. Tereso held his arms out wide and grabbed Victoriano in a bear hug.

For the moment, he became Prudenciano Nava again. Tacio smashed into them and wrapped them both into his big arms.

Victoriano struggled loose and playfully punched Prudenciano in the arm in an attempt to hide his tears and regain his masculinity. Finally he asked, "It is good to see you again, Prudenciano. How in the hell did you end up here?"

Prudenciano chuckled and said, "It is a long story. One that would take many bottles of tequila to tell."

Tacio said in a serious tone, "We heard a rumor that you were wanted by the law. Is that true?"

"Let's just say that I had an adventure," replied Prudenciano. He did not feel that this was the place to discuss what had happened. They needed to be alone where he could share his secret with them. Just then, a moan distracted them. They turned around and saw Julio sitting up and holding his head.

Tacio asked, "Who is that?"

Prudenciano pushed Julio back down with his foot and took the pistol from his holster. "Oh, just some kid with a toy that he shouldn't have. I had to beat some manners into him."

Victoriano threw this head back and let out huge laugh and said with tears in his eyes, "You always were a good teacher, Nava."

Prudenciano cringed at the mention of his real name. He grabbed Victoriano and Tacio by their arms and led them away from the wagon. "Look," he said in a hushed tone as they walked, "there is something very important that I must tell you without that brat listening." Victoriano maintained his amused expression, but Tacio sensed the seriousness of Prudenciano's tone. When they arrived at the far edge of the pit, Prudenciano stopped and looked back at the wagon. He could barely see it in the dark. He sighed and released his grip on the men. Then he spoke in a quiet tone. "The rumors you heard about me are true." Victoriano's smile left his face and Tacio stood quietly waiting for him to continue. "I killed a *gringo* a couple of years ago by Carrizozo. It was an accident and I have been running ever since."

Victoriano let out a low whistle, but otherwise they stayed quiet. Victoriano and Tacio were men accustomed to killing. The revolution had hardened them and revealed the savagery of unbridled war. If the lawmen ever caught them running guns out of the *Estados Unidos*, the *gringos* would shoot them without hesitation. They understood their friend's plight and sympathized with his situation.

Prudenciano continued, "To protect myself, I changed my name to Tereso Minjares."

Tacio nodded and said, "It is fitting to take the name of your *jaripeo* partner, Tereso Rodriguez. Wasn't your mother's name Minjares?"

"*Sí*," said Prudenciano, "and you must never use my real name again, *comprende?*"

"Okay, Tereso," replied Victoriano with added emphasis on the name. "We will try, but it will be difficult at first."

Mollified, Tereso changed the subject. He asked, "What happens to the guns now?"

Tacio answered, "We have a team of horses and a wagon on the south side of the berm. We will switch wagons and take the guns to a warehouse in El Paso. From there, we will slip them across the border to Villa."

Tereso commented, "You must be receiving weapons from other sources too."

Currandas replied, "*Sí*. We have many other supply routes. Sometimes we use the train and pack the guns in vegetable crates. Other times we pull guns in from the border towns. It sounds like a lot, but we can barely keep Villa's troops outfitted."

"So," Victoriano interjected, "who gets the money?"

The question startled Tereso for a moment until he remembered the Mesilla man at the bridge. He reminded Julio to collect the money. "Ah, I guess I do," answered Tereso.

"*Bueno*," replied Victoriano. "It's under the buckboard. Now, I guess we better get going. We need to get back to El Paso before dawn."

They walked back to the wagon and found Julio struggling to climb up to the bench. Tereso shoved Julio up and across the buckboard. Then he turned and said, "Victoriano, get up there and drive the horses. Tacio and I will have to push from behind to move this wagon out of here." Victoriano jumped up and grabbed the reins. Julio kept silent as Victoriano drove the horses forward and the two large men rammed their shoulders into the back and pushed. The wagon moved slowly at first and finally picked up enough speed to roll up the slight incline out of the pit and back onto the road. Victoriano halted the wagon, jumped down, and raced around the corner. He soon returned driving another wagon. Tacio and Tereso caught their breath and then worked quickly to switch the wagons.

Victoriano said, "Well, Tereso. I guess we will be working together again. Be careful and we will see each other soon." He offered his hand and Tereso shook it with a solid handshake.

Tacio did the same and leaned his head close to Tereso and whispered, "Be careful of that young man, Nava. He may kill you if he gets the chance."

Tereso playfully punched Tacio in the shoulder and said, "Don't worry. I will keep an eye on him. Travel safely, my *amigo*." Tacio nodded and shot Julio a wary glance before lumbering over to Victoriano and laboriously climbing aboard. Victoriano lifted his hat in the air as a parting farewell and signaled the horses forward. The wagon started with a jolt and turned south on the road to El Paso.

Tereso walked back to his wagon and climbed aboard. Julio momentarily glared at him through swollen eyes and then looked away. Tereso ignored him, snatched the reins, and snapped them. The horses moved cautiously first, then picked up speed when they realized the wagon was light. They made good time on the return trip to Doña Ana. Neither spoke during the ride home, but Tereso could feel the heat of Julio's anger burn holes in his skull. Tacio was right. Julio was mad enough to kill.

Augustine Madrid was waiting for them when they arrived at his gate. The early morning sky was turning deep indigo blue, which indicated that the sun was just below the eastern horizon. Madrid's face looked strained from a night of worry. For a moment, he beamed brightly at their arrival until he saw Julio's face. Then his brow pinched with concern. As Tereso jumped down, he asked, "What happened?"

Tereso wagged his head toward Julio and said, "I had to beat some manners into this young man. Other than that, everything went well."

Julio screamed, "He lies!" He awkwardly slipped off the wagon and ran to Madrid. "He almost spoiled everything! He attacked me for no reason, took my gun, and stole two pistols from the wagon." Julio's voice was laced with hysteria.

Madrid looked back to Tereso and asked, "Is this true?"

"Some of it," answered Tereso. He handed over Julio's pistol to Madrid, but kept his own safely hidden under his coat. He had a feeling that if Madrid saw the magnificent guns he would demand that he hand them over. "I took the pistols only to arm myself. I should not have been out there without one. I picked up the guns and delivered them to the *Villistas* as planned. Julio had an attitude problem that I solved. Nothing more."

Madrid believed that Minjares was understating the situation. He knew the question to ask to determine what he said was true. "Minjares, do you have the money?"

Julio let out a quick laugh and resumed his condescending smirk. *Madrid has got him now*, he thought with glee.

Tereso casually went over to the wagon, reached under the buckboard, and retrieved a wooden box. He walked back to Madrid and handed it to him. Madrid undid the metal clasp and opened the box. Inside were neatly stacked bills. Julio's jaw fell open when he saw the money. Madrid quickly estimated the value and found the correct amount was there. He looked up from his counting with a relieved smile and said to Tereso, "You did very well, tonight, Minjares. I can see that you are a valuable member to our cause."

The praise sang in Tereso's ears and made him swagger. Conversely, it inflamed Julio. Through clenched teeth he hissed, "*Señor* Madrid, this man is not worthy of such compliments."

Madrid silenced Julio with a quick wave of his hand and rebuked him by saying, "Enough! Were not the guns delivered and the money collected? You did not even know where the money was. Go home, Julio. You have done enough tonight." The words stung Julio like a slap across the face. He staggered backward for a few steps before recovering and left without saying another word.

Madrid watched him go, then resumed his smile. "You go home too, Minjares. It has been a full night and you have to work in a few hours. Try to get a little sleep. Thank you for your help."

"*De nada*," replied Tereso. His smile stretched from ear to ear as he placed his hat upon his head and headed down the road. His high spirits seemed to lift his feet above the ground and float them in the air. He was so distracted by his happy thoughts that he did not see Julio until he jammed his hands upon his chest. Julio stood in front of him with his face distorted in rage.

Julio shoved him again and growled, "You fooled Madrid, but I know what a screwup you are, Minjares." Tereso brushed Julio's hands away as he would remove dirt from his clothing and took a step forward. Julio did not budge an inch and stuck his swollen face in front of Tereso. "I heard those *Villistas* call you by another name. What was it? Nava? I bet you are running from something, *¿qué no?* Well, I am going to find out and then Madrid will know the truth about you!" Before Tereso could answer, Julio spun on his heels and took off down the road at a fast pace. Tereso watched him disappear before continuing on his way home. While the possibility that Julio might discover that he had killed a man in Carrizozo weighed heavily on his mind, Tereso was so elated from the night's adventure and Madrid's praises that he quickly forgot the confrontation and let his inflated ego return.

Dawn broke just as Tereso bounded through the kitchen door. He pulled the pistols from his pants and wrapped them lovingly in a piece of canvas. He stashed them on top of the kitchen cupboard, out of reach and sight of the family. Then he felt tremendously hungry and began to root around the kitchen for any remnants of last night's dinner. The banging pots and ransacking of goods woke Paz and she shuffled out of the bedroom in a large flannel shirt and with her hair disheveled. Tereso caught sight of her bare legs and felt a different kind of hunger boil in his loins. He dropped the pans and came to her. She asked sarcastically as she rubbed the sleep from her eyes, "How was the meeting?"

"It was *muy bueno*," he replied in a husky voice. He slipped his arms around her waist and pulled her to him. As she looked up at him in surprise, he kissed her hard and full. She tasted his warm mouth and found it devoid of alcohol and tobacco. He smelled like the fresh outdoors. Wherever he had been, it was certainly not a party which she had expected. He felt so strong and virile that she began to tremble as he tightened his hold on her. It had been a long time since she had been intimate with her husband and, in spite of the bitterness that she harbored toward him, she had missed his embrace. She knew his passions this time were not spawned by tequila but from the penned-up need generated from abstinence and it made her want him even more.

Tereso gently picked her up and laid her across the table. Then he slowly unbuttoned her shirt as he continued to give her lingering kisses. He parted her shirt and exposed her light brown skin and full breasts. His hands traced the round contours of her body as he gazed upon her beauty. Then he bent down and ran his lips and tongue along her skin. Her taste and smell inflamed him. Finally, he could not contain himself any longer. He stepped back, untied his pants, and let them fall to the ground. Paz sighed deeply when she saw his swollen manhood before her. Tereso carefully lifted her up by her buttocks and she wrapped her legs around his waist as they came together. They became husband and wife again.

———

The next months were pleasant for the Minjares family. Tereso's workload at the Taylor farm slowed to a mere couple of hours per day. Bill delegated the care of his horses and livestock to Tereso. He accomplished all his work by midmorning and was free to do as he liked. He still ran guns once a week, but the nights and routes varied. He would receive his instructions from Miguel and meet a wagon destined to some clandestine spot where the exchange took place. Madrid made sure that Tereso had full knowledge of every operation. Sometimes Julio came along and was icily silent during the entire trip. Tereso occasionally caught Julio glaring at him under the brim of his sombrero. Tereso would smile back and subconsciously touch one of his finely-tooled pistols tucked under his coat. Its weight felt reassuring against his waist.

Miguel alternated with Julio as Tereso's partner during the gun deliveries. Tereso liked Miguel and enjoyed telling him stories of Zacatecas and Chihuahua. Miguel sat quietly, listened intently, and asked questions at the right time. He also completely relied on Tereso to handle the wagon exchanges with the Mesilla men and the *Villistas*. Tereso thought these traits made Miguel the perfect traveling partner.

Over the next four months, Tereso made dozens of trips, each without a single problem. Madrid openly praised him for his exceptional service for the Revolution and told many of Tereso's heroic service. The lavish flatteries swelled his head so big that his neck threatened to collapse under the weight. He felt that people were finally realizing his intelligence and importance. He also revealed his *sobador* talents and many locals stopped by their home for a visit and a consultation.

Paz was mystified by the unaccustomed attention the locals gave her. Women stopped her in the streets of Doña Ana and commented how proud she must be of her husband. Paz would shrug her shoulders and state that she did not understand. The women always laughed and gave her a knowing smile before moving on. Paz could not make any sense out of their behavior. She believed that Tereso's weekly political meetings were the basis for their comments. It seemed that entire town knew what was afoot but her.

Not knowing what happening at Tereso's mysterious meetings frustrated Paz, but when she considered that he had been on his best behavior during the past few months, she was reluctant to get angry. Paz liked the way Tereso treated the family. Even with all the spare time he had during the winter season, he kept his drinking to a bare minimum. The minimum was the American Thanksgiving, Christmas, and New Year's. This holiday season was the first she had enjoyed in many years. Nellie Taylor brought her a turkey and a ham for the special dinners. Her family had their fill of good food and Tereso entertained them with exciting stories about lost treasures and the Seven Cities of Gold that were still hidden in the Mexican wilderness.

Then, in mid-January 1916, she discovered that she was pregnant. When she told her husband, he threw his arms around her and gently hugged and kissed her. He became even more attentive and helped around the home.

Paz reflected on his behavior and noticed that it had started after his first political meeting several months ago. The weekly, all-night meetings seemed to energize him. He always looked forward to the next one and not once did he come back with liquor on his breath, and seldom tobacco. He smelled fresh and clean like he had been outside all night. She knew that if she badgered him to tell her what he did those nights, he might get angry and clam up, but she had to know. Even with all the positive attributes the meetings generated, she knew that Tereso had a way of getting himself in serious trouble.

She would have to find a way of questioning him, so that he would reveal what happened at those meetings.

Paz chose a blustery February evening to discuss her husband's political endeavors. The family was snug inside their home and adsorbed in various activities. Alcaria sat at the kitchen table with a kerosene lamp and concentrated on her homework. Tereso had Augustine on his lap and related to his son the secrets of handling horses. Paz and Joaquina baked cookies. Joaquina was covered in flour as she mixed the ingredients in a large bowl. Her little tongue poked out the side of her mouth as she laboriously turned the mix.

Paz stopped her baking for a moment and brushed her hair from her face with the back of her dough-covered hand. She took in the serene atmosphere of the room and it filled her with contentment. Everyone was happy and Tereso looked like he was in especially good spirits. As if he read her mind, he stopped his instructions to Augustine in mid-sentence and looked up at Paz. A mischievous grin crept across his face and he winked at her before resuming his one-sided conversation.

Paz took this moment to walk over to him and nuzzled his thick gray hair. She whispered in his ear, "We need to talk after the kids are in bed." Tereso raised one eyebrow in response and then shrugged to signify that he would participate.

Later that evening after completing the bedroom rituals and the children were at last asleep, Paz met her husband in the kitchen. She put her arms around his waist and said, "Today, so many women told me that I should be proud of your accomplishments. Perhaps, I should be jealous, *¿qué no?*" She could feel his body puff up from the compliments, so she pressed, "What exactly does my husband do that makes women so appreciative?"

Tereso put his arms around her and said, "Oh, I just help things out around here. That is all."

"*Verdad?*" asked Paz. "How do you help around? *Por favor*, tell me so I can praise you too."

Tereso was never one to refuse praise. He mulled a few thoughts in his head for a few moments before answering. *After all*, he thought, *everyone in town knows what I am doing. So Madrid would not be mad if I told her.* He took a deep breath and finally spoke, "I am helping Villa win the Revolution."

Paz's eyes flew open in surprise as she tightened her grip around his waist. She had imagined a hundred things that he might be doing at his weekly meetings, but never had she considered this possibility. She prodded him to go on, "How do you help?"

"I shuttle guns to his men south of Las Cruces."

She asked, "Is that not dangerous?"

Tereso chuckled deeply and replied, "Some think so, but you would never guess who I deliver the guns to. Anastacio Currandas and Victoriano Vallejo. What a small world, ¿qué no?"

Paz pushed herself away from Tereso and looked up to him with serious eyes. With a slight edge to her voice, she asked, "This is illegal, ¿qué no?"

Tereso waved his hands in the air to brush the comment away and answered nonchalantly, "There is an arms embargo against Villa's army, but no one seems to care. Besides, what is the harm of shipping guns south of the border? No one in the *Estados Unidos* will care."

There was something incredibly ignorant in Tereso's reasoning that irked Paz. He was illegally delivering arms to a man known for unpredictable violence. As she stood there staring back at him, she knew that either his little adventures would eventually kill him or bring misfortune on the family. She just hoped that the gun shipments would stop before someone got hurt.

During the evening of March 1, 1916, Pancho Villa sat brooding in a small Ciudad Juarez *cantina*. A small cadre of trusted men silently watched him take another sip of his beer and stroke his mustache in thought. The *cantina* was spacious, but Villa and his men were the only patrons. Many men would enter and see the group of hardened revolutionaries glaring back at them and correctly interpret this as a signal to leave. A nervous bartender washing mugs behind the counter was the only non-*Villista* in the room. The dim yellow light from the overhead gas lamps reflected dully on the heavy atmosphere of cigar smoke from Rodolfo Fierro.

Villa took another gulp of beer and mulled his situation. Villa had tried every method he could conceive of to gain recognition from the United States. He had participated in public appearances with *Americano* officers like General Hugh Scott. He'd sent emissaries to Washington, Austin, and Santa Fe to ask for support in fighting for Mexico's democracy. They all paid him lip service with no deeds to back up their hollow words. Now President Wilson had stabbed him in the back by declaring an arms embargo against his regime and supporting Mexico's new dictatorial president, Venustiano Carranza. Villa grimaced when he remembered how Wilson had almost killed him when he allowed Carranza's troops to ride the El Paso & Southwestern train through Texas, New Mexico, and Arizona. Then, from Douglas, Arizona, Carranza had launched a surprise attack at the rear of Villa's defenses at Aqua Prieta on the evening of November

2, 1915. Mexican border guards had used spotlights to target the *Villistas* like jackrabbits on the open Mexican desert. Carranza's troops had a field day shooting Villa's men as they scampered for cover. Only a rapid retreat saved the *Villista* army from annihilation.

"I have done everything that a civilized man could do," muttered Villa as he picked up his mug. His words broke the heavy silence that hung in the room. The men looked puzzled and glanced at each other for clues to their meaning. Villa seemed dimly aware of their presence as he continued his ranting. "I sent them good men. Posed for pictures with their officers. Offered my support. For what? To be strangled by their embargo?" He took a large gulp and wiped his mouth with the back of his hand.

"Maybe it is time for action, my General," replied Fierro with his cigar clenched between his teeth. His fierce eyes burned angrily through dense smoke.

"Action?" replied Villa as he shook himself out his self pity, "What action?"

Fierro took his cigar out of his mouth and examined it for a moment as he contemplated his reply. When he finally spoke, his voice sounded strangely like a philosopher. "Nations only respect those they fear. And they fear men of definite action. Those who do not falter to use the sword to achieve their goals."

Villa sat back in his chair for a moment and studied the man before him. Fierro was never one to shy from battle. In fact, war seemed to release the beast in the man. His officers were appalled by his sheer brutality and wanted him shot, but Villa always protected Fierro because he knew the man was loyal and would generate the results he required. And Villa was right. One by one, his officers had abandoned or betrayed him, but Fierro had remained by his side. Villa trusted Fierro.

"All right, Rodolfo," asked Villa with his eyes focused on Fierro's serious face. "What action do you suggest?"

Fierro took out his cigar and blew a thick stream of cold blue smoke through the air. The men thought he looked like a dragoon. "I propose that we take the guns delivered to us from Doña Ana and Mesilla and strike at a small *Americano* army garrison. We will hit them hard and fast and retreat into Mexico. Then the *Estados Unidos* will know of our might and purpose and pay us the respect that we are due."

At first, Villa thought he was joking. The room became deathly quiet as Fierro produced an evil grin and resumed smoking. Villa thought, *He is serious!* Fierro calmly waited for his reply. Villa remained silent for a moment longer before finally responding. "They will think of us as butchers."

Fierro roared back as he slammed his fist on the table, "They will think of us as men!" Fire shot from his eyes.

Villa felt Fierro's words seep deep into his soul and create images of grandeur within him. Villa steadied himself and asked, "Do you have a place in mind?"

Fierro replied in a calmer tone, "*Sí*. Columbus, New Mexico."

Villa asked in a puzzled voice, "Columbus? Why Columbus?" He vaguely knew the town and passed by it once or twice in the past decade. It was a nondescript, adobe hovel of a town scarcely inside America's border, with a small army camp.

Fierro stood straighter with a confident poise and pulled his cigar from his mouth. With smoke swirling around his ruggedly handsome face and fierce eyes, he looked like a smiling Satan. "I will tell you why we should attack Columbus. Columbus is within a mile or two of the border. It sits at the bottom of low hills where we can stay hidden until we descend upon them. The small army base there is lightly defended, but my sources say that they have lots of supplies and horses. If we catch them by surprise, we will encounter little resistance and retrieve guns, ammunition, and food. Our attack will be a decisive blow against the *Estados Unidos*. If they want to protect their border citizens, they will have to deal with us."

Pancho Villa again sized up his trusted officer. Fierro obviously had thought about this move for a while. The idea was bold and ruthless, but Villa also recognized its brilliance. If anything would draw attention to his army, attacking Columbus would do it and God knew that he desperately needed supplies for his beleaguered army. During the raid, he might even pay the Ravel brothers a visit and settle an old debt that the brothers owed him for taking his money and failing to deliver arms and ammunition. The thought of Sam and Arthur Ravel groveling at his feet and begging for mercy brought a smile to Villa's lips.

Villa looked around the table to see if anyone agreed with Fierro's plan, but they all stared back and watched him for his reaction. None of them offered an opinion. The decision was on his shoulders.

Villa took a deep breath and let it out slowly. Then he reached out and grabbed his mug. As he brought it to his mouth, he announced in a low voice, "All right. We will do it within a few days." Some of the men stepped back in astonishment and muttered their disagreement to a close confidant. Others were giddy with excitement and began to talk rapidly. Only Rodolfo Fierro stood quietly, slowly rolling his cigar in his mouth and smiling.

———

On March 9, 1916, at four in the morning, Pancho Villa sat hunched on his horse and tried to shield his body from the cold. He had ridden hard throughout the night to arrive at the outskirts of Columbus and it had sapped his strength. The sky was filled with stars and dawn was more than an hour away. He sat alone and surveyed the dark lifeless town and army camp below. The time for optimum surprise, that period between two-thirty and four-thirty in the morning when humans are at their lowest ebb, was almost past. They would have to attack soon before the first ranchers stirred.

Villa knew that Fierro was now in position with his half of the men. Each of them would lead about three hundred rebels. Fierro would attack from the south and Villa from the east. Fierro would charge when he heard the first gunshot and try to overwhelm the camp before the soldiers could mount a defense. All the plan needed now was a signal from Villa to start the advance.

Villa took out his revolver and checked the load. Then he strained his eyes into the darkness to evaluate his men. Everyone seemed poised for action with weapons drawn and horses readied. Villa could feel the butterflies rise in his belly in anticipation of battle. He gave the town a quick final look before raising his arm and pointing his pistol to the sky. Pancho Villa tilted his head back and bellowed at the top of his lungs, *"¡Váyanse adelante, muchachos!"* He shot his pistol in the air and his column surged forward. Many shouted *"¡Viva Villa!"* as their peaked sombreros blew backward off their heads when they pitched down the slope, and swooped into the town. As they reached the first homes undetected, Villa knew that they had the enormous advantage of complete surprise.

Private David Smith lay on his cot in the dark early morning and dreaded the start of another boring day in Camp Furlong. A year ago, he had joined the army in an attempt to escape the monotony of his family's Missouri farm. David had grand illusions of seeing the world and partaking in glorious adventures, but army life had proved to be a bitter disappointment. His one and only assignment was with the Thirteenth Calvary and stationed at this godforsaken place called Camp Furlong next to Columbus, New Mexico. According to Smith, there was absolutely nothing for an ambitious nineteen-year-old to do in Columbus. The barren landscape offered no alluring scenes for exploration. The climate was always clear, hot, and monotonous. Only the Columbus residents seemed contented to trudge down their dirt streets and live their boring, predictable lives.

Smith was particularly caustic this morning because yesterday half the regiment had left for Deming to support fellow soldiers in a polo tournament. A senior officer had denied his one chance to escape Camp Furlong for a few days. The officer told him, "You are needed to secure the fort."

Fort? thought Smith as he stomped back to his conical canvas tent identical to the hundreds of other tents pitched in perfect formation. *What fort? Why is this place even here?* Even the serious and career-minded Lieutenant George Patton was going. David watched him ride away in formation with a scowl on his face. Clearly, the man wanted to do something else instead of going to a polo match. *It just isn't fair*, thought Smith as Patton passed by and disappeared into the scorched hills.

Lying on his back, David let his eyes drift through the darkness. He barely could make out the center pole that supported the tent above him. He thought, *"Today is going to be a lonely one."* With only half the men to perform the regular duties, he was either going to be stuck with tending the horses all day or posting guard duty for an eternity. He dreaded either prospect.

David rolled on his side to relieve the aches from the wooden cot frame. His face rubbed across the abrasive canvas cover as he fluffed his pillow and tried to get a few more minutes of sleep before the bugle blew reveille. Damn, how he hated that piercing tune every morning! He shoved the thought out of his troubled mind and sank into a light, uncomfortable rest.

David Smith's next conscious thought was struggling to rise amid wild screams and random gunfire. The cobwebs in his mind muffled his senses and added to his confusion. The dark tent erupted in chaos. Men jumped up and down on one leg while they frantically tried to put on their trousers until they were bowled over by other half-dressed comrades clutching their rifles and rolling their eyes in fear. The tent shook from soldiers tripping over the tent lines in the dark. David could hear a few officers outside shout commands and direct their scattering troops into some type of order.

A young man slammed into David as he rushed for the tent door. David grabbed him and screamed in his face, "What's happening?"

The private jerked his arm free from David's hold and yelled back in a desperate voice, "We are under attack! Run!" The man bolted out the door bare chested and without boots. His terror was infectious. David jumped into his pants and threw on his shirt. He shoved his feet into his boots and groped for his rifle in the feeble light. His trembling hands found it lying on a ground cloth under his cot where he had placed it the night before. He grabbed it and instinctively executed his army training. He jerked the bolt back and stuck his finger into the breach. His touch told him that it was clear and he could feel a bullet in the magazine ready to slide into the action. He shoved the bolt forward and down and heard the satisfying click that signified that the rifle was loaded and the pin drawn back. David reached under his cot again for his ammo pouch, but he could not find it. During the melee, someone must have taken it. The bullet in his chamber and the two in his magazine would have to do. Smith clutched his gun with both hands and plunged out the door.

The night engulfed him as he raced into the central compound. Sounds and sights exploded around him and threatened to shred his last bit of sanity. Nothing made sense to him. Men were running in every direction. Guns blazed randomly and bullets buzzed through the air. Inhuman screams echoed through the night. David ran like a man possessed through lines of parked trucks and horse wagons. When he reached the yard, he found the only assemblage of order. A tough, looking sergeant named Michael Fody was directing men and shouting orders. David barely heard him over the noise.

"We've got to form a defensive position," screamed the sergeant. "We don't have enough men to counterattack. Position yourselves around the barracks and dig in! Do it now! Move, move, move!" Fody began pushing the men to individual spots to set up.

David needed some purpose to direct his fury. He yelled back at the sergeant, "Sarge, who are we fighting?"

Fody looked back over his shoulder at David and cursed. He did not have time to explain everything, but on the other hand, this private was the only one who was not in a state of panic. He grabbed David by the shoulder and steered him toward the feeble defensive line. As he held him, the sergeant said, "I don't know, but I got a hunch they are making a move for the supply house. There's a lot of them, son, so keep your..."

Fody was stopped in mid-sentence when a young private slammed into him at a full run. The impact broke the sergeant's grip on David's shoulder and spun him around. The blow stunned the private for a second as he crashed to the ground.

Sergeant Fody bellowed, "What the hell do you think you are doing, private?"

The dazed man answered, "What?" He shook his head to clear his senses and bounced back up. "Sir! We have just detected another large assault force attacking the town just north of us. We have reports of civilian casualties, sir!"

Fody swore a blue streak at the news. Now, instead of concentrating on protecting the camp, he would have to pull men from his meager troops to defend the townspeople. He had a sinking feeling that he was greatly outnumbered. "I need something to swing the battle in our favor," he thought out loud. "But what?" Nearby, several guns from the soldiers fired simultaneously at a group of charging men on horseback. The volley cut down two and forced the retreat of the others. Fody cried, "That's it! The machine guns!" He grabbed the young men with each hand and said, "Come with me."

Fody practically dragged the men with him. Along the way, he grabbed two more men to help. When they reached the guard tent, they could hear the rebels storming the camp, but the soldiers repelled them with accurate fire. Fody led the men to the tent flap and they jumped inside. The room was darker than outside, but the sergeant knew where to go. He went straight for a set of stoutly built shelves. On the shelves were rectangular wooden crates with thick rope handles and heavy locks. Fody produced a key from his belt, unlocked one box, and swung the lid open.

In the dim light, David got his first glimpse of the French-made Benet-Mercier machine gun. Its compact firing mechanism and fat stubby barrel belied its lethal potential. David reached out and touched its cold smooth surface. The blue steel seemed to suck the life out of his fingers. He quickly snatched his hand back.

"All right, men," shouted Fody as he snapped the box shut. "Let's get these two boxes out of here. Two men to a gun. I will grab the ammo belts." The men grunted when they yanked the boxes from the shelves. The guns were much heavier than they looked. They lugged them out of the room and the sergeant followed close behind with several belts of bullets draped over his shoulders. "Drag them into town, boys," Fody directed. "We've got work to do."

The center of town was not far, but the weight of the crates caused the men to labor fiercely. As they approached the town square, sounds of the fighting intensified. Gulping ragged breaths through his open mouth, David looked up as he and his partner rounded the final corner and beheld a scene straight out of the annals of hell. Terrified people were running in several directions. Women dressed in nightgowns held their screaming babies to their breasts and desperately prodded their sleepy children forward. Men in nightshirts stopped and fell to one knee as they brought their rifles to aim. They fired and quickly resumed running. David saw rebels wearing tall sombreros ransacking stores and throwing their pillage on their horses. The whole scene was backlit by burning buildings.

Michael Fody halted their advance while he assessed the situation. Most people were seeking shelter in either the two-story Hoover Hotel or in the school. Both buildings had thick adobe walls that resisted gunfire. The sergeant realized that he had to concentrate his efforts to protect both places. Being an excellent judge of ground, Fody quickly surveyed the area to select the optimum sites for the machine guns. He decided to set one gun in front of the hotel and place the other gun farther south on East Boundary Street. If each team concentrated its fire on the Broadway/East Boundary intersection, the crossfire would shred anything in its path. Fody rallied his men with encouragement, "Quickly, men! To the hotel. We are almost there."

They bolted across the street and wove with their crates through the frantic people. Panting, they arrived at the front door. Fody wasted no time in ripping the cover off and removing the oiled packing from the gun. He straddled the crate and gritted his teeth as he lifted the heavy gun. The folding tripod dangled underneath the weapon like limp spider legs. Fody set the machine gun down beside the box and spread the tripod legs until they locked into position. He reached out along the barrel and flipped the folding sites up. Then he grabbed one of the soldiers and showed him how to feed the ammo belt into the action. Satisfied, he looked up at David and said, "Get behind this gun and protect the hotel. Be careful not to hit any civilians."

David asked incredulously, "Me? I've never fired one of these things."

"Well, no better time than the present," answered the sergeant. "Spray some bullets down Broadway so we can set up the other post." David gingerly grabbed the pistol grip and pointed the sight down the street. Several rebels were riding toward them at about seventy-five yards away. Not knowing what to expect, David squeezed the trigger. Within a fraction of a second, the Benet-Mercier emitted a quick roar as it smoothly fired a dense cluster of bullets. A stream of spent shells ejected sideways from the gun. The rebels and their horses disintegrated before them. David was shocked by the murderous rampage that he released by the simple pull of the trigger. It amazed and sickened him.

"Good man!" shouted Fody as he slapped David across the back. "That'll teach them! Now keep it up. We got to go while the way is clear. Good luck!" David vaguely nodded as he continued to survey the carnage he had unleashed.

His partner cried, "David! Quick! Over there!" David looked and saw ten more rebels storming the square. Without thinking, David swivelled the gun toward the invaders and sprayed a stream of bullets at them. The fusillade mowed them down within a blink of an eye. It was almost too simple. David had a gut feeling that the machine gun was going to change the face of warfare forever.

———•••———

Pancho Villa led his men straight for the Columbus business district.

The plan was to hit the stores as fast as they could before the Americans and residents could mount a defense. Their goal was to steal as much ammo, clothing, and food as they could carry. Pancho made it clear to his troops to leave the homes alone. However, the heat of battle fogs memories and several rebels found the homes of sleepy residents irresistible. Splinter groups of the main charge fell behind and began raiding houses. The *Villistas* chased terrified residents away at gunpoint and set off a chain reaction of hysteria through the town. Displaced families ran to a brother's or cousin's home to seek shelter. Warnings sprang throughout the community like ripples from a stone plunked into a quiet pond. Within minutes, the entire town was aware that armed forces were storming the village.

Villa pointed to various businesses that he wanted plundered as he galloped past. Men peeled off the main column and smashed down a door or window to gain entry. Villa made sure that his men ravaged the Commercial Hotel and raided the vault. Sam Ravel owned the hotel and as the *Villistas* carried out their loot and set the building on fire, Villa thought, *Your debt is paid in full, Señor Ravel. Now for your brother.*

As the plundering continued, Villa kept an eye out for a particular house on Broadway. When he finally spotted it, an evil grin crept across his face. He grabbed two of his men and said, "Follow me. We must pay a visit to another *Señor* Ravel."

Villa led the men to the home and jumped off his horse. He motioned for the men to follow and pulled his pistol from his holster. He waited for the men to position themselves around the door before kicking it open and rushing inside. Finding the living room empty, Villa ran straight to the back bedroom. They smashed the bedroom door off its hinges and found Ravel still in bed with his wife.

"*Buenos días, Señora* Ravel," Villa said in a mocking tone as he took off his hat and bowed to her. Terrified, she sat up in bed and pulled the blanket up to her chin. Arthur plunged under the covers. "*Perdón,* but we have some unfinished business with your husband. Is that not so, *Señor* Ravel?" Villa poked the covered lump with his pistol.

Ravel emitted a muffled scream under the blanket, "Yi-yi-yi-yi! Get away from me! I have nothing that you want!"

"Oh, but you do!" Villa answered with glee in his voice. "And we shall discuss it now." He motioned to his men and they stepped forward and dragged Ravel from his bed. The man was too scared to walk, so the *Villistas* carried him into the front room and threw him on the floor. Arthur squirmed on the floor at Villa's feet.

Ravel asked in a pitiful voice, "What is it that you want? I have nothing here that is of value."

"Now that is a shame," Villa pretended to brood as he fingered his pistol, "for you see, I thought you might have some rifles that I bought from you but never received, *¿qué no?*" Ravel's eyes reeked with fear. He had been caught cheating Pancho Villa and now death was his punishment.

Ravel blurted out, "I have some money! It's in a safe under my bed. I will show you."

Villa sneered and thought, *Weak men always break.* He said, "No. I will get it and bring it in here. Lift him to his feet and hold him. I will be right back." The men grabbed Arthur by each arm and hoisted him up. Villa took one last look at the defeated man in his nightshirt with his outstretched arms held securely by fierce rebels. He knew he was not going anywhere. Satisfied, Villa turned and went back into the bedroom. *Señora* Ravel had not moved an inch since he had yanked her husband from the room. She was still sitting up and trembling.

Villa again tipped his hat to her and knelt down at the foot of the bed. He threw the covers back and looked under the mattress. At that precise moment, a roar thundered into the house. Villa thought a dragon had stormed though the front door. The bedroom walls seemed to dissolve around him. *Señora* Ravel emitted a piecing screaming that made his skin crawl. Villa whirled around with his pistol drawn as bits of brick and dust pelted him. It took him a second to recognize the fresh bullet holes and scorings throughout the house. He jumped up and ran into the front room. He saw Arthur Ravel standing petrified with his head in hands. The two guards lay perforated at his feet. Miraculously, the gunfire had straddled Ravel and hit his abductors.

Stunned, Villa pushed past Ravel and stumbled out into the street. His horse and another lay slaughtered on the ground. The third horse had a flesh wound, but was still standing. Another blur of gunshots roared from down the street. Villa looked in the direction of the sound to see about thirty of his troops galloping madly toward him. In the wavering light of burning buildings, Villa could see the terror in their eyes. They looked like they were racing away from some horrible evil. Another roar erupted behind them. *That sound*, Villa thought, *could only be from a machine gun!*

Suddenly it occurred to him that the machine gun fire that hit the Ravel house could not have come from the current firing position on East Boundary. That gunfire must have come from somewhere closer. Villa turned and glanced across Broadway Street. He immediately saw the machine gun in front of the Hoover Hotel. Somehow, the Americans had slipped in and set up the deadly device within close proximity of their raid. Villa noticed that the two young soldiers had turned their weapon toward the intersection of Broadway and East

Boundary. His men were blindly riding into an ambush that would grind them into pulverized meat.

Villa yelled at the top of his lungs, "No...!" His warning was too late. The machine guns roared like lions and ripped the fabric of the night air as they tore into the fleeing *Villistas*. Villa threw himself to the ground and beheld the devastating effects of the crossfire. Men were literally ripped in half. The bullets spun the horses around like they were pirouetting in a ballet before the projectiles chewed them to bits. Within seconds, the bloodbath was over and an equally deafening silence prevailed. Nothing in the street moved. They were all dead.

Villa heard the distinctive "ker-chink" sound as the Americans re-loaded their machine gun and realized that this was his opportunity to escape. He jumped on the wounded horse and rode away from the Hoover Hotel. The encounter had unnerved him. He had just lost many trusted men and discovered that the Americans were retaliating with superior weapons. He gazed above him and noticed that the stars were starting to fade and a trace of dawn lay on the eastern horizon. Villa knew that the waning night and the solidifying American defenses signified the end of the *Villista* raid. He decided to order the retreat, but with his men spread throughout the town, it would not be an easy task. Villa rode quickly through the town and spoke to every rebel he saw to evacuate and carry as many stolen goods as possible. By six-thirty in the morning, he managed to get the word out to most of his men that the raid was over.

Villa rendezvoused with Rodolfo Fierro on the eastern outskirts of town. Fierro had succeeded in stealing wagon loads of rifles, ammunition, and some food. He had even acquired two boxed machine guns. Ahead of the wagons, his men herded about one hundred U.S. army horses and a few mules. His success, however, came at a steep price. Fierro lost twenty men when he stormed the supply tents and commandeered the wagons. In addition, Villa grasped that the valuable stolen goods would be an added incentive for the soldiers to retaliate and mount a pursuit. He saw the heavy wagons sink into the soft ground and burden the horses. The wagons would slow their escape. He would have to create a defense to deter any pursuers.

Villa quickly selected thirty brave men and rode ahead. He stationed them at the crest of a low hill directly east of Columbus. They fortified their positions with rocks and boulders. Villa issued a rifle, several pouches of ammunition, and a canteen of water to each man. Then he ordered them to keep the army at bay until the main column had a chance to escape. Afterward, they were to retreat and report on the size and status of the force pursuing them. Villa took his place with them to oversee the defense and directed Fierro to retreat with all haste.

By eight o'clock, the *Villistas* could see wisps of dust rising in the distance and a large column of equipment and horses moving toward them. As the army drew nearer, Villa realized that his riflemen were facing a superior and motivated force that they would have little effect in deterring. He could see a well-equipped calvary leading the advance. Several trucks followed closely behind, undoubtedly filled with supplies to sustain the pursuit for several days and, God forbid, artillery. Villa ran a calculating eye down the column and estimated that two hundred men pursued him.

Villa ordered a man to ready the horses for a quick retreat. Then he told his men to prepare themselves for a hard fast fight. They were to shoot quickly and accurately, but if the army overran them, they were to fall back and ride to the next defensive position. Although his men nodded and assumed their positions, their silence hid the fear they felt inside. Villa felt it, too. He crouched behind a low stone wall, took a swig of water from his canteen, and waited. The waiting was always the hardest part of battle.

Major Frank Tompkins set a brutal pace for his troops to follow. His soul burned with outrage that a group of ruffians would unjustifiably attack a helpless town and ruthlessly kill its citizens and burn its buildings. They had stolen valuable army equipment and killed eight of his men outright. "Those son-of-bitches are going to pay!" murmured Tompkins as he signaled viciously to his column to fall in tighter. The cavalry could move much faster than his mechanized division in these soft soils, but he did not want the trucks to linger too far behind in case he needed them in a pinch. He knew his impatience was driven by his need for revenge, but he was helpless to control it. The deep wagon ruts along the rebels' retreat told him that their plunder was slowing them down. With an hour's head start, they were only a few miles ahead. Tompkins also knew that the Mexican border was only two miles to the south. If Villa crossed it, Tompkins did not have the authority to pursue him and he was not going to let that happen.

The army quickly followed the rebels' well-marked trail like a bloodhound on a fresh cougar scent. Like the hound, Tompkins felt like baying as the trail became fresher. They were gaining rapidly on the rebels. The rising terrain, reasoned Tompkins, was probably the cause for the slower retreat.

As they started up the low hill, he noticed jumbles of rocks that appeared artificially placed. A flag of caution sprang up in his mind. He watched them warily as they drew closer. Suddenly, his eye caught a movement behind one. Tompkins barely screamed his warning when the *Villistas* popped up along the ridges and started firing.

Two soldiers were hit immediately. Tompkins ordered the cavalry to fall back until they were just out of accurate firing range.

"Bring the trucks forward," he ordered. The cavalry gave way to the five fortified Model-T trucks that lumbered through their ranks. In each truck bed were four infantry riflemen. One of them was David Smith, whose body still throbbed on adrenaline. He sat uncomfortably behind the cab holding onto the side of the bed with his left hand and clutching his rifle with his right. Tompkins wasted no time in directing them. "You men drive these things up this hill as fast as you can and run over the top of those bastards. The cavalry will be right behind you. You infantry, hang on and shoot like hell! Now, go!"

The trucks' tires spun in the loose soil as the drivers threw the transmissions into low gear and let out the clutches. David barely stopped himself from somersaulting backward as the truck accelerated and began climbing the slope. His unit was third in line. He crouched down behind the cab and peered over the top. The engine whined in his ear and the wind began to blow his cap off his head as the truck picked up speed. Close ahead was the low ridge. He could clearly see the peaked sombreros of the *Villistas* bobbing above rock piles that lined the hill.

The gunfire began in earnest as the trucks neared the top. The army soldiers desperately tried to shoot accurately by resting their guns on the roof of the truck cab, but the trucks wove and bucked violently, throwing off even the best marksman. Bullets whizzed through the air and a few of them struck glancing blows on the armored cab. David realized that the rebels could shoot much more accurately than he possibly could.

Suddenly, a geyser of steam erupted from the lead truck. A bullet had penetrated the fragile radiator and spewed hot water in the air. The truck pulled over and let the others go by. As his truck drew abreast of the disabled vehicle, David saw the riflemen use the stationary cab as a elevated perch to pick off rebels with deadly accuracy. He spotted bandits with their arms windmilling in the air as they were hit. David looked behind him and saw the cavalry riding close behind and using the trucks as a moving shield. The riders were firing their pistols at the rock revetments.

The rest of the trucks quickly closed the final distance to the top of the hill. As they breached the summit, they were surprised to find no one to fight. A few corpses lay twisted on the ground, but the rest of the rebels were nowhere to be seen. A private yelled out, "Look! Over there!" David squinted into the morning sun and saw about twenty men riding hard into the distance.

Tompkins crested the hill and yelled loudly when he saw the rebels fleeing, "We've got them now, men! Cavalry, ho!" He led the mounted troops in a full-gallop chase. David took his place in the truck bed and held on. He watched as the army horses quickly outdistanced the motorized division. He had a feeling that the cavalry would effectively deal with the rebels before he had a chance to arrive.

———————

Villa rode for his life. The Americans had smashed through his defenses with startling speed. He had not anticipated the trucks shielding the advance and he had barely ordered the retreat in time to escape. He raced for Fierro's retreating column for support. He needed a plan and he was quickly running out of options. Villa glanced over his shoulder and saw the cavalry in hot pursuit. He had only minutes to assemble a counter attack.

Fierro steered the wagons to the south for a quick dash to the border. He looked behind him to check on two lingering wagon teams and spotted the defenders in a full gallop coming toward him. Then he saw the reason for their speed. A huge dust cloud rose from behind as more than a hundred mounted soldiers rumbled after them. Fierro assessed the situation and knew that at his current pace he would not make it to Mexico. He would have to turn and fight. He quickly ordered the wagons to be driven at all haste and rode off to assemble his troops.

Fierro chose ground that offered some relief and stationed his troops accordingly. He believed that their only chance was to dig in and hold the soldiers at bay until the wagons had a chance to escape. Then they would flee as fast as they could across the border.

His men readied their weapons behind scattered rocks and scant brush that offered little protection. Fierro saw their fear and fatigue. Most of them had been awake for more than twenty-four hours with little to eat. They were functioning on raw nerves, the type that snaps without warning. In a cornered situation such as this, their performance was unpredictable.

The men held themselves steady as Pancho Villa and his surviving riflemen streaked across their line. Villa jumped his horse over several prostrated men and leaped to the ground in one fluid motion. He drew his pistol, threw himself behind some rocks next to Fierro, and said quietly, "Here they come." A hundred set of horse hooves rumbled like a speeding locomotive and kicked dust several hundred feet in the air. The dust obscured half the approaching force and produced an awesome display of might. A few men lost control of their fear and ran as the cavalry drew near.

When the first horsemen came within one hundred yards, Fierro yelled, "Fire!" The *Villistas* responded by releasing a volley of bullets.

The highly trained cavalry immediately took evasive action and skirted the rebel defenses. As the *Villistas* repositioned themselves for another shot, the soldiers dismounted and began shooting. A fierce gun battle erupted. Within minutes, the rebels were overwhelmed and lost more than a hundred men.

Villa looked back and saw the wagons crossing the Mexican border. They had done their job and now it was time to go. He screamed, "Fierro! *¡Vámanos!*" Fierro and Villa took off in a dead run for their horses. The rest of the men saw their leaders fleeing and bolted too. The cavalry continued to fire at the retreating rebels and killed many more.

When the Americans began mounting their horses to give chase, Major Tompkins stopped them with a raised hand. "We've killed them enough today, boys. The wagons are across the border now, so we can't chase 'em. I think they learned not to mess with us again." He continued to watch them ride off into the vast Mexican plains. Tompkins had a feeling that he would be hunting Pancho Villa soon.

America's newspapers heralded Villa's attack as a great victory for the rebels. They said that the *Villistas* routed the surprised army at Camp Furlong and captured huge amounts of valuable supplies, but in truth, the rebels paid a heavy price for their raid. Sixty-seven *Villistas* died during the raid. The machine guns slaughtered most of these. An additional thirteen died later from their wounds. The army captured another twelve rebels in town and jailed them. During Tompkins' twenty-mile pursuit of the rebels, the cavalry killed almost 150 more *Villistas*. Out of Villa's original 600-man army, only about 350 survived. In contrast, the American casualties included ten civilians and eight soldiers.

Sergeant Michael Fody fought hard to keep from vomiting from the stench. The hot sun baked the air and putrefied the corpses stacked along the deep long trench. The smoke from yesterday's smoldering fires coated his throat and nostrils with a greasy soot. The combination was sickening.

Fody adjusted the handkerchief tied to his face to blunt the smells and squinted at the task at hand. His men had just finished digging a gigantic mass grave and were now preparing to fill it with the dead rebels. He watched David Smith throw his shovel out of the pit and scramble up the steep side. He, too, had a sweat-soaked scarf across his face. Fody noticed how much older David looked after yesterday's raid. His eyes were haunted and aged.

Fody stepped forward, grabbed a dead rebel by the arm, and signaled for David to lift the legs. David complied with a tired nod and grabbed an ankle. Together, they swung the first body into the trench. It seemed to fall a long time before it struck the bottom with a lonely thud. The other soldiers joined them and soon the huge void was filled with dead men. David and the others retrieved their shovels and covered them up with mounded soil.

When the work was finished, Fody took his handkerchief off and wiped his brow with it. "Gentlemen," he said in an exhausted voice, "it is time to take a rest. Fall out and report back to the barracks." The men silently collected their shirts, hats, and tools and started walking away. David held back for a moment to gaze at the freshly mounded grave. Fody stood next to him and asked, "Still bothered by the killing?"

David let out a sigh and answered, "Yes, sir. I reckon that's still botherin' me." He fell silent for a moment longer and then asked, "Why? Why did they do it?"

Fody pushed his hat back and said, "Hell, kid, who knows? Probably for the guns and supplies. Who knows what gets in them Mexican heads?"

David faced the sergeant and asked, "Do you think we can catch Pancho Villa and his gang?"

Fody looked grimly back and replied, "I hear talk that old man Pershing is coming down with the entire United States Army. They'll sniff him out for sure, but I think we got some other people to hunt down, too."

David looked at Fody with a puzzled expression and asked, "What do you mean?"

"Why, I mean we have to find out who supplied those hellions with these rifles." Fody walked over to a nearby wagon where the army stored the confiscated weapons. He threw the tarp off and revealed a heap of guns taken from the rebels. He pulled a rifle out of the stack, threw it to David, and said, "Take a look at it." David inspected it and found the gun to be new and of satisfactory workmanship. "A nice piece for a Mexican *bandito*, isn't?" David had to agree. The rifle was of higher quality than the usual Mexican firearm. Fody continued, "Most of these guys were carrying them. Now, take a peek at the inscription on the barrel." David easily found the crisp stamped letters in the blued metal that spelled 'Western Cartridge Company.'

David asked, "What is the Western Cartridge Company?"

"It's a company in Saint Louis," answered Fody. "Rumor has it that they have been selling arms to Villa's crew. So, since there is an official arms embargo against Villa, we also need to track down the guys smuggling the rifles across the border. In my book, they are as much to blame as Villa himself."

David took a final look at the rifle and handed it back to Fody.

"Maybe so," he said," but if these guys are clever enough to sneak these guns to Villa, they are going to be hard to find."

Sergeant Fody carefully laid the rifle back on the stack and replaced the tarp. Then he spoke the words that David Smith would remember for the rest of his life. "A skunk always leaves a trail and his friends are unfaithful. Among these people, there is usually one that has a score to settle. And that one will talk. We will find them."

Miguel Echavaria shuffled nervously across the broken field in the early afternoon. Like a cat in the open, he would stop every so often and look around before continuing. He looked like a man who expected someone to pounce on him. Carefully, he picked his way to the irrigation ditch on the other side of the field. There he found the man he sought. He twisted his head back and forth to check the area as he half whispered, "Tereso!"

Tereso Minjares was hard at work clearing debris from the ditches. He was barefoot with his pants rolled up above his calves. His shirt and wide-brimmed hat were splattered with mud. He stood in the thick water while yanking on a branch submerged in the muck. The debris was part of a summer's accumulation of material that choked the flow. Tereso hated this miserable work. When he heard his name called, he was startled from his mundane task and whirled around with a start. "Huh? Miguel! What's wrong!"

Miguel put his finger to his lips and replied quietly, "I have come to tell you that something terrible has happened, but you have to be quiet, *amigo*. They might hear us!"

Tereso calmed down a bit, but Miguel's behavior baffled him. He waded out of the ditch and started climbing up the embankment. "What do you mean 'they will hear us'? Who is 'they'?"

"I don't know," answered Miguel in a scared voice, "but someone bad might see us together, too. Stay down there, *por favor*. I risked everything coming here."

Tereso stopped and put his hands on his hips. Miguel was starting to irritate him. "Either you tell me what is going on or I am going to kick your butt!"

Miguel took a final look around him before speaking. "Tereso, Pancho Villa attacked Columbus yesterday morning!"

Tereso stood in the ditch staring blankly back. "So?"

"So?" repeated Miguel in an exasperated voice. "So? I will tell you 'so'. Villa used the guns that we smuggled to him to kill *Americanos*! Now the *gringo* lawmen will track us down and hang us!" Tereso could hear the hysteria rise in his voice.

Tereso smacked his lips and shook his head in disgust. "Go home," he said in a calm, flat voice. "You have nothing to fear. Nobody will find us." Miguel looked uncertain and stood motionless. "Go home," Tereso repeated firmly. Miguel glanced around him again and then slowly turned and walked away. Tereso watched him leave until the embankment blocked his view.

Tereso walked back to the ditch, stood along the muddy bank, and watched the brown water slowly slide along. His mind filled with troubled thoughts. He stood for a moment and contemplated them. He had to admit that Miguel's visit had unnerved him. If anyone did come looking for him, he was sure that his secrets were safe in Doña Ana, but something in his subconscious bugged him, something that he had missed. He thought about it for a few minutes more as his feet sank deeper into the mud. Finally he snapped out of his brooding and began the slow shuffling movements to break himself free. As the mud reluctantly released him, he suddenly felt an old familiar emotion stir within him. It made him feel jumpy and on edge. Then he recognized for what it was, the feeling of being hunted.

Chapter 21
Lying Low

Tereso barely had returned home from the day's work when the terrifying news wafted through his door. Thousands of army troops were descending upon Columbus and preparing to mount a search for all persons responsible for the attack. Tereso ran to the railroad tracks with several local men to watch the troop cars roll south to Camp Furlong. They all stood speechless as the long train packed with men and equipment moved by. In the windows of the passing train, they saw the fresh, excited faces of young men thrilled to be on a wild adventure. Their enthusiasm diminished his hopes of not being pursued. Tereso returned home subdued and worried.

Paz met him at the door and greeted him with a troubled look. The news of the attack and of the troop movements scared her. It reminded her of Carrizozo and of the hopelessness and despair that had hung over her and her children when her husband fled the authorities. She did not know if she could live through it again. Paz instinctively put her hand over her womb. *The baby will be moving soon,* she thought to herself. *I will not travel like I did with Bernardo. I won't do it.* The pain of losing her baby boy came back to her and filled her with grief. With trembling lips and eyes brimming with tears she walked back to the kitchen and faced the wall, so she could grieve in private.

Tereso perceived her pain and felt powerless to comfort her. He hung his hat and coat on the hooks by the door and quietly sat down by the table. A few minutes later, Alcaria burst through the door. She was breathless like she had ran several miles, but her eyes danced with excitement. With ragged breath, she blurted, "Guess what my teacher told us today in school?"

Thankful for the diversion, Tereso smiled and said, "Tell us, *por favor*, what she said."

Alcaria took another deep breath before reciting her news. "A great army general is coming to chase down Pancho Villa, and, do you know what his name is?" She paused only to catch another breath before continuing, "His name is Black Jack Pershing! Doesn't that sound mean? My teacher said that he is the best general in America and nobody can hide from him! Isn't that something?"

Tereso shot her a fierce stare for a moment before bolting up and heading for the door. He grabbed this hat and coat and abruptly left. Alcaria was stunned and hurt by her father's reaction. She turned to her mother for support and an explanation, but she stopped when she saw her wiping tears from her face and mindlessly go through the motions of preparing the evening meal. Alcaria could tell that something much deeper was afoot, but remained quiet. Her developing female intuition told her that her father was responsible for her mother's behavior. She thought, *I wonder what he has done now.*

Evening fell thickly by the time Tereso reached Augustine Madrid's *rancho.* There were several fine horses tied to a post in front and two expensive wagons with their teams were parked in the large pull-through driveway. Even a Model T truck was present. Tereso assumed that Madrid must be having very important guests.

He made his way to the side entrance, which was dimly illuminated by a small lamp hanging from a metal hook beside the porch. As he stood at the doorway, he heard muffled voices within the home. He rapped softly on the thick wood door. The voices stopped and silence prevailed. A few minutes dragged by without a response. Tereso knocked again. This time the door creaked slightly open and a frightened servant peeked through the crack. He whispered, "What do you want?"

Tereso felt his fear rise too. He thought, *If Madrid is so cautious, then trouble must be near.* He gulped back his anxiety and addressed the man, "Tell *Señor* Madrid that Minjares is here to see him."

The servant nodded and said, "Stay there." He pulled the door shut. Tereso waited for a few minutes more and was about to knock again when the door slowly opened a few inches. The servant looked nervously around before speaking. "*Señor* Madrid will see you now. Come." Tereso had to squeeze through the narrow opening and muscle past the man. Once he made it to the hallway, the servant quickly shut the door and bolted it. He motioned for Tereso to follow him and led him down the long hallway to the receiving room.

At the doorway, the servant stepped aside and swung his arm toward the room as a gesture for Tereso to enter. Tereso took his hat off and walked into the room. He recognized the men from his first meeting here, but their demeanor was much more solemn, almost harsh. None of the younger men were present, only the patriarchs of Doña Ana and Mesilla. No one was drinking and only two men were smoking. They were all sitting in comfortable leather chairs that faced toward the middle of the room. Tereso stood before the men wearing his tattered coat and holding his worn *sombrero* before him. He was keenly aware of his disheveled appearance before these distinguished gentlemen. He sensed their criticizing eyes upon him as they labeled him among the lower caste of their society.

Augustine Madrid rose with a grim face and approached Tereso. "What is it that is so important to disturb us tonight?"

Tereso held his head high and responded with faked bravado, "Probably the same reason that you are meeting with these men. Villa's attack on Columbus."

Madrid did not mince words. "*Sí*, we are discussing that situation, but it does not concern you. Go home."

"It concerns me a greatly," growled Tereso. "I want to know what to do when the *Americanos* come calling."

Madrid replied, "What to do? Why, you will do nothing. *Comprende*? You will say or do nothing. Nobody will say anything. The *Americanos* will become frustrated and leave. Now, go home. I will send for you if we need you." Tereso search Madrid's eyes for some sign of deceit and found none. Then he evaluated the men in the room. They all looked blankly at him with no evidence of malice. Mollified, Tereso nodded, put his hat back on, and left the room without further comment.

Madrid remained standing and facing the hallway until he heard the door open and close. Then he slowly walked to the bar and poured himself a drink. No one spoke as he poured a shot glass full of tequila and threw it down his throat. He exhaled forcefully and licked his lips as he contemplated his discussion with Tereso. Mr. Olveria spoke what was on all their minds. "He appears agitated, Augustine. Are you sure we can trust him?"

Madrid turned and faced the men. "*Sí*, I believe we can trust him. He performed better than expected, don't you agree? What is more, we still need him to complete one last task, *¿qué no?*"

"True," replied Olveria, "but what if he becomes … unmanageable?"

Madrid walked over to his chair and slumped down upon the cushion. He sighed and clasped his hands together as he answered, "Then I will have him killed."

During the following weeks, residents of New Mexico witnessed an awesome buildup of military power within their state. The papers heralded the event as the "Great Punitive Expedition" led by Brigadier General John J. "Black Jack" Pershing. The force pushed deep into Mexico in hopes of capturing Pancho Villa. Waves of trucks and armored vehicles drove south to support the assault. Even the skies were not spared the intrusion, with Curtiss JN-3 biplanes sputtering overhead. The sights were enough to make even the bravest Mexican heart quail.

The population of Columbus soared with the military influx and the town quickly became the largest city in New Mexico, exceeding Albuquerque, Santa Fe, and Las Cruces. Military traffic came from all directions and modes—air, road, and railroad. It all converged on the once sleepy town. Mounds of freight and equipment were unloaded in Camp Furlong and the garrison expanded to receive and organize it. Hundreds of horses arrived by rail. Some were destined to carry cavalry and others were harnessed to drag small artillery and wheel-mounted machine guns.

Life was no longer boring for privates like David Smith. He and his fellow soldiers worked around the clock for days without end to assist with the buildup. Although the days were long, the excitement buoyed their spirits and drove them on. People from all walks of life descended upon Columbus. Military officers and enlisted men arrived in droves, but newspaper reporters, photographers, businessmen, and thrill seekers also besieged the town. David always had someone new and interesting for conversation.

"Well, do you reckon we will be joinin' old man Black Jack down south?" asked one young private as he and David heaved a box of ammunition onto a shelf in the supply tent.

David wiped his forehead with the back of his hand and smiled back at the young man. Judging by his accent, the private had to be from the Appalachian country and David liked him. The two had the same lust for adventure. "I hope so," answered David as he positioned himself behind another box. "I was here when them bandits attacked, you know, and I want another crack at them."

"Yep," replied the private with a groan as he grabbed the other end of the box and hefted it up. "I reckon I would too if I were in your shoes." They stopped for a moment to catch their breaths when a captain stepped into the tent. They quickly snapped to attention.

The captain waved casually at them and said "At ease, gentlemen." The privates relaxed a bit and watched the officer inspect the shelves. In his hand were two military green envelopes that were crisply sealed. "Well, it looks like you boys have been working hard. Good. For your rewards, I am bringing your orders." David and his friend looked at each other in excited anticipation. The captain saw the exchange and produced a sad smile. He knew what was in their hearts and what he had to tell them was not all good news.

The captain turned to the Appalachian and said "Here you go, Private Jones." He handed him one of the envelopes. "You are hereby assigned to the Thirteenth Cavalry to pursue the perpetrators of the attack on Columbus, New Mexico. You are to leave tomorrow morning and join the advancing column by next week."

"Hot damn!" the private yelled as he slapped his knee in joy. Then he realized his outburst was unmilitary and apologized, "I mean, thank you, sir!"

The captain smiled and said, "That is quite all right, private. Make us proud." The men stoically saluted each other. Then the captain turned to David and handed him his orders. "Private Smith, you are hereby assigned to assist special agents with investigating the movement of illegal arms through the state of New Mexico. The agents will be here within the next two weeks."

David almost stepped away from the envelope presented before him. Disappointment dripped from his face. "You mean I am not going south to join the rest?"

The captain knew what was going through David's heart. He, like all the rest of the privates, had never participated in a military action. They had been too young for any of the previous skirmishes that had flared up in the last twenty years, so many viewed this event as their one and only chance to fight, although many thought that it was just a matter of time before America jumped into the fray in Europe. The captain spoke in a consoling voice, "I know that you were hoping to chase after Villa and his clan, but we need you here, son. You were one of the few that got a good look at most of the attackers. There may be one or two holed up in this state. You will be a big help in spotting them for the agents."

David took the envelope and hung his head. The captain knew that he had done all that he could to soften the news. He snapped to attention and saluted. The privates did the same. The captain executed a precise turn and marched out of the tent.

Jones exclaimed, "Wow-ee! I get to take a shot at Villa's brown ass! Ain't that something?"

"Yeah, great," replied David as he looked at his unopened letter. He felt like he'd just got the short end of the stick again.

Tereso was now sixty years old with a young family, and another baby on the way, and he was scared. The rest of March dragged away with each passing day bringing impending doom. The spring planting began in April and filled his days with long hours of work. Tereso was thankful for the diversion because idleness would have crippled him with worry. Nonetheless, every so often he glanced over his shoulder to make sure that no one was stalking him. He decided that if some official unexpectedly arrived looking for him, he would throw down his tools and run. He would dash for the Rio Grande and hide forever within the thick foliage. He had left everything behind before. He would not hesitate to do it again.

Military traffic still streamed through town. Tereso saw Bill Taylor and his fellow farmers meet by the Taylor Road rail crossing and watch the flatbeds loaded with equipment and weapons roll south. The farmers dutifully watched this parade daily and it provided endless entertainment. Judging by Taylor's waves and smiles, Tereso knew that he supported the army's cause and, if Taylor knew of his involvement, he would report him within a heartbeat.

During the following weeks, Tereso was a model citizen and a tireless worker. He was never late to toil in the fields, his visitors ceased to come around, and he went straight home when evening came. Taylor noticed his diligence too and welcomed it. He always felt a little uneasy about Tereso Minjares. The man sometimes acted too smart for his britches for Taylor's liking, but now Tereso seemed subdued and even humbled. It was a personality change that Taylor hoped would continue.

Tereso quietly went about his business day after day when he heard whispered rumors run through Doña Ana that lawmen were making their way up the highway looking for gun smugglers. They had already stopped at Chamberino and San Miguel and interrogated several Mexican residents. Now they were in Mesilla questioning men and inspecting barns and other suspicious buildings. It was just a matter of time before they arrived in Doña Ana.

The news terrified Tereso. He was certain that they were coming for him. He had an overwhelming urge to rush over to Madrid's *rancho* and demand that Madrid do something, but his last uninvited meeting had left a bad taste in his mouth and he did not want to go through another uncomfortable confrontation. So he forced himself to go about his duties as before and tried not to jump when a truck drove by or when someone yelled a greeting to him from the road.

Paz and the children felt his fear when he returned home. Every night, Tereso found a chair and propped it against the wall. Then he plopped down and silently brooded as he pulled his mustache. He remained that way for the entire evening and returned questions with only a grunt. Paz heard the rumors too and knew that they were the source of Tereso's mood. The uncertainty of their future filled her with trepidation.

Five days later, Tereso was harnessing the horses at the Taylor farm when Miguel Echavaria bursted into the barn. He was completely out of breath, but his eyes reeked with fear. He blurted, "They're here!"

Tereso dropped what he was doing, grabbed Miguel by the shoulders, and asked, "Where?"

Miguel took another gulp of air and said, "In town. They just arrived. Three of them. One's an Indian!" Tereso took a step back to steady himself. Miguel shook himself free and continued, "I got to go. I must warn the others." Before Tereso could ask him anything else, Miguel was gone.

Tereso stood deathly still as he contemplated his next move. He was torn between many conflicting emotions. He wanted to bolt and hide along the Rio Grande, but another part of him wanted to see who was searching for him. While struggling with his decision, he never once thought about the repercussions to his family. This was definitely a time for self-preservation.

Slowly his fears quieted and he got ahold of his senses. The two plow horses turned their heads toward him with their ears stretched forward as if they expected him to tell them what he was going to do. He took a deep breath and wiped the cold sweat from his face. Then he made his decision. *I will stay here and work quietly at the farm*, he thought. *No one will suspect me if I lie low.* The horses seemed to nod their heads in agreement. Tereso scratched their necks and proceeded with the harnessing.

For the next two days, Tereso plowed the fields with his *sombrero* pushed low over his eyes. He showed up for work early and left late. Taylor was impressed and watched him work without complaint.

On the third day, Tereso was in the barn mending a broken plow when he heard voices outside. He set his tools down and carefully crept to the partially opened door. Peering through the crack, he saw three men on horseback talking down to Bill Taylor. They conversed in English, so Tereso could not follow it, but judging by the smile on Taylor's face, Tereso knew that these men were probably the investigators that Miguel had warned him about.

Tereso turned his attention back to the strangers. The youngest one looked like a boy dressed in an army uniform. He sat uncomfortably in his saddle with a bored expression on his face. The one doing most of the talking was a big man. He wore a large cowboy hat and slung a pistol around his waist in a natural manner. This man definitely knew how to handle a gun.

The cowboy shifted in his saddle and revealed the third man behind him. When Tereso saw him, his blood ran cold. It was the Indian who had chased him on Sierra Blanca. Tereso quickly retreated a few paces from the door. He watched Smoke Rider take in his surroundings with his obsidian-colored eyes. Suddenly, his gaze riveted on the barn door. Tereso's pulse raced as he thought, *He's seen me!*

He stood frozen in time, not wanting to move a whisker lest the Indian should see him. Then slowly Smoke Rider continued his searching. Tereso let out a slow, quiet breath.

"Where are you boys from?" asked Bill Taylor as he looked to up to the big cowboy in the saddle.

"Well, John and I are from Carrizozo and Dave, here, is from Columbus. My name is Roberts. I'm a Deputy and John is sworn to help me." Roberts stuck his hand out to Taylor.

Taylor grabbed it and gave him a solid handshake. Then he walked over to the Army private and asked, "What's your name, son?"

"Private David Smith, sir," answered David as he extended his hand. "Pleased to meet you."

Taylor shook his hand with respect in his eyes and asked, "Were you there during the attack?"

David let go of Taylor's hand and looked down at the ground. He spoke softly, "Yes, sir. I reckon I was." Taylor understood the short reply. Men who had experienced combat seldom talked about it.

Taylor slapped David on the thigh and said, "Good man." Then he approached the Indian, but stopped short. Bill Taylor did not trust Indians. Only a few years ago, the Apaches and Navajo had terrorized the farmers in these parts and tales of that time lived strong within Taylor's memory. He would avoid this John. *Too bad*, thought Taylor, *If it weren't for the Indian, I would invite the private and deputy in the house for some refreshment.* Johnny seemed to read his mind and sat motionless in his saddle. Taylor ignored the Indian and addressed the deputy. "How can I help you?"

"Well," answered Roberts, "we've been investigating a possible gun-smuggling operation in these parts and we're wondering if you have seen anything suspicious lately?" David flipped open a small book and prepared to jot down notes.

Taylor rubbed his chin for a moment, then shook his head. "No. I don't reckon I have seen anything out of the ordinary around these parts. Why in tarnation are a couple of fellas from Carrizozo way out here looking for gun smugglers?"

Roberts smiled and replied, "Well, our illustrious governor, William McDonald, was a rancher from Carrizozo and he seems to have taken a shine to our way of sniffing out outlaws. So he placed a call to the sheriff and a few army folks and here we are."

Taylor nodded and asked, "You guys finding anything?"

This time David spoke up. "Nothing! Every town we ride into it's the same thing. Nobody has seen anything. Especially the Mexicans. They act like they never spoke or heard English in their lives."

Taylor laughed, "Yep! Them Mexicans are a bit clannish. I have one that works for me. He can't speak a lick of English, but he sure in hell knows when quittin' time and payday is."

Roberts replied, "Really? Maybe we ought to talk with him."

"Well, you can if you want," answered Taylor. "He is just an older man, though. Doesn't cause any trouble. To tell you the truth, I really don't know where he is just now. Would you like me to look for him?"

Roberts contemplated this for a moment. "No. Don't bother yourself," replied Roberts as he shifted his reins in his hands in preparation to leave. "It was just a thought. Well, Mr. Taylor, thank you for your time. We best be getting on." Roberts tipped his hat.

Taylor waved and said, "Thanks for stopping by. I hope you catch'em."

Roberts smiled as he led his horse back onto the road. "We will," he said with a confident voice. "Outlaws eventually make mistakes."

Tereso watched the men ride down the road and out of sight before relaxing. He felt like he had just missed being captured for either the Carrizozo incident or for smuggling arms, or worse, for both transgressions. He swore an oath to himself that from now on he was going to be very careful.

<hr>

On September 1, 1916, Paz gave birth to a beautiful girl in the bedroom of her two-room adobe brick home. The baby's features were perfect, as if made from porcelain. Nellie Taylor and Paz breathed a sigh of relief when they saw that the baby was healthy. Nellie said that she looked like a little angel. Paz agreed and named her Angelita after Saint Anna, the patron saint of the day. Alcaria and Joaquina hovered around the bed like little hummingbirds, trying to catch a glimpse of the baby.

Nellie gave Paz a soft green blanket to wrap the baby. As Paz gently laid Angelita into the folds, she was suddenly struck by the poignant memory of bundling little Bernardo in the soft blue blanket that *Senora* Lesnett had given her two years ago. Paz struggled to hold back the tears as she lovingly lifted her daughter to her breast. She did not know how she could go on if something ever happened to another one of her babies. The pain was too great.

Nellie watched Paz nurse the baby for a few minutes before reluctantly standing to leave. She was tired from having assisted with the birth since early in the morning. A Mexican midwife had summoned her, not because she needed help, but because she felt she had a duty to inform the owners of the farm about the situation. Nellie liked the Minjares family and watched over their welfare a little more closely than her husband liked. She felt a responsibility for this family that shared her farm.

Nellie walked over to Paz and kissed her on the forehead. Paz looked up at her with exhausted eyes and managed a weak smile on her pain-racked face. Nellie whispered, "I will be back soon, honey." Paz did not understand the English, but got the gist of what she was saying. Nellie stood back up and gave the midwife a quick look of thanks. The woman nodded and came forward to check on Paz. There was nothing else for Nellie to do now except inform Tereso of the outcome.

She came into the kitchen to see Tereso sitting quietly by the table with Augustine on his lap. Nellie pushed back her graying hair and said in half English and half Spanish, "Congratulations, Tereso. *Tienes una niña. Se llama* Angelita." Tereso got the message. Paz had a girl and named it Angelita.

Tereso smiled back and said, "*Gracias.*" Nellie managed a smile and gave Tereso a long look. She still found it hard to believe that Paz would marry such an old man. She subconsciously sighed and shook her head in disbelief, then caught herself. Embarrassed, Nellie pointed to the bedroom door and indicated that it was all right for him to visit his wife. Tereso seemed undaunted. He nodded and lifted Augustine off his lap. Nellie chose this time to leave and waved as she walked out the door.

Holding Augustine's hand, Tereso walked quietly into the bedroom. He saw the girls dancing on their toes around the bed, completely entranced with the new addition to the family. Tereso awkwardly led Augustine to the bed and stopped short as if they were waiting for permission to continue. Tereso looked at the midwife for approval. She stood next to the head of the bed with her arms crossed. A simple nod told them to come forward, but stay only briefly. Augustine crept forward to his mother. Paz smiled at him and moved the baby closer to him so he could take a peek. His eyes went big when he saw the tiny face. Paz looked up at her husband. Tereso managed a gruff smile, then his face resumed its worried look—a look that Paz had seen him wear constantly these last months.

Paz cleared her throat and spoke in a weary voice, "She is beautiful, *¿que no?*" Tereso nodded. She continued, "She needs her father, Tereso. You cannot be chasing adventures. Promise me that you will stay close to home."

Tereso wanted to answer, but his voice lodged in his throat. He knew that he was part of something that was out of his control. He believed that eventually the men of Doña Ana and Mesilla would need him to perform another mission or the lawmen would come back seeking him. Either would require him to leave at a second's notice.

Paz had to settle for a simple nod. She watched him put his hand behind Augustine's back and gently steer him out of the room. Tereso closed the door quietly behind him.

——◆——

Life slowly returned to normal in the Minjares household. Within a few weeks, Paz completely healed from childbirth and resumed her domestic duties. The girls eagerly helped her care for the baby. Accustomed to being the youngest in the family, Augustine felt displaced and jealous of the attention that his mother and sisters lavished on his new sister. The five-year-old would hang on his mother's skirt and cry for attention. Paz understood Augustine's behavior and frequently stopped what she was doing and gave him a special hug and kiss. Gradually, he accepted the baby and assisted his sisters with Angelita's care.

Harvest time once again consumed Tereso's time. He worked from dawn to after dusk to bring in the vegetables, fruits, and grains. For the first time, Taylor hired two extra workers to help with the harvest. He had planted more this year than usual in anticipation of the army demands for more supplies. The gamble paid off in that the U.S. Government requisitioned all the crops grown along the Rio Grande Valley to feed the thousands of soldiers in Columbus. After years of hard work, Bill Taylor was finally going to make a fortune. All he needed to do was to harvest his crops and get them to market.

Crops in the ground meant loss of potential profit, so Taylor pushed his workers hard to harvest them. Tereso bristled at Taylor's sharp, barked orders and exasperated hand gestures. At another time, Tereso would have told Taylor just what he thought about his insults and might have even swung at him too, but today was different. Tereso wanted to stay inconspicuous and living in his house, so he gritted his teeth and kept his feelings to himself. He even remained aloof to the two temporary workers. Both men were Mexican migrants who followed the harvest season through the Southwest. Tereso did not know them and, therefore, did not trust them.

The hard work melted September and October away until finally the harvest was over. The temporary help moved on and Tereso settled into a quiet and slower pace. Home life was peaceful and serene. Tereso was beginning to relax at night and breathe easier now that so many months had gone by since the lawmen's visit. So when the knock came at the door in the cool evening of November, Tereso thought another family wanted to see their new baby or required his *sobador* talents. Paz sat quietly at the table rocking Angelita in her arms and barely looked up when Tereso went to the door. He opened it and found Augustine Madrid waiting for him. Tereso involuntarily stiffened and sucked in his breath.

Madrid stood holding his hat with both hands and wearing a sincere smile across his lips. He looked over at Paz and bowed respectively to her. Paz's eyes narrowed as she glared back. She instinctively cradled her baby closer to her breast as if to protect her from his presence. Madrid read her thoughts and returned his attention to Tereso and asked, "May I have a moment of your time outside, Tereso? There is something of importance that we must discuss."

No matter what the situation was, Tereso was not the sort of man to refuse to discuss something important. He nodded and proceeded to follow Madrid outside. He could feel Paz's eyes burn into the back of his skull and warn him not to get involved with anything foolish. Tereso closed the door and saw Madrid motioning for him to walk beside him. Tereso complied and fell into an uneasy cadence as they strolled into the evening darkness.

Madrid finally broke the silence. "Your family looks well," he casually mentioned as a means of starting conversation. Tereso barely nodded. Madrid seemed unabashed and continued, "I know that the past months have been difficult for you. The past events have been trying on all of us."

At this, Tereso snorted and said, "Why is that? I am the one who drove the shipments south. You and your *hacendados* have nothing to fear."

Madrid spun around and confronted Tereso, grabbing his arms with both hands. He snarled, "How can you be so stupid? My associates and I risked everything to ship arms to the revolutionaries. I am even taking a big risk meeting with you tonight. We are in this together!" Madrid slowly released his grip on Tereso and the tension faded from his face. Tereso was taken back by his outburst and remained silent.

"I am sorry for taking my anxiety out on you," sighed Madrid. "I have been on edge for a long time as, I am sure, you have been too." Madrid's words had a soothing effect on Tereso and he began to feel pity for him. Sensing Tereso's mood had changed, Madrid decided to reveal the true purpose of his visit. "Tereso, I need your help one last time. In fact, all of New Mexico needs your bravery and talents." Tereso swaggered under Madrid's salvos of compliments. "*Verdad*, Tereso. There is no one else who can do this one last task. Will you help us?"

Tereso felt very important now. His fears and trepidations fluttered away in the darkness like bats through the night. He looked down at Madrid through slitted eyes and asked, "What is it that you need done?"

Madrid produced a sly grin. He knew what motivated this man—pride, praise, and adventure. Even at his advanced age, Tereso was still a thrill seeker. Madrid massaged these traits to his advantage. He lowered his voice and said, "We have one last shipment that we must deliver. It is the last of the guns, and therefore, the last of the evidence against us. The weapons are hidden in a shed in Las Cruces. You must deliver them to *Villistas* in San Agustin Pass just east of town. It will be dangerous, Tereso, and will require all your skill and courage to pull it off. You are the only man that I believe could successfully accomplish the task. Will you do it?"

Tereso sucked in the cool night air and straightened his back while he collected his thoughts. He did not want to go and knew that he could refuse, but here was another chance to show people his bravery. The thought of taking the wagon up into the Organ Mountains appealed to him, too. He could make it to the pass and back in a single night. Simple. He would do it.

As he looked down to Madrid's waiting eyes, a thought suddenly struck him. *Why not ask for something in return?* Tereso answered, "I will do it." A wave of relief washed over Madrid's face. "But, I want something for the danger."

"Oh," replied Madrid lifting an eyebrow in response. "What would that be?"

"I want a holster belt for my pistols."

"I see," answered Madrid with a hint of irritation in his voice. "That can be arranged. It will be on the wagon when it comes for you in, say, two days at first dark?" Tereso nodded. "*Bueno*," Madrid said, "well, I better get going. It's getting late. Thank you for your help, Tereso. *Buenas noches.*"

Tereso watched him walk away from the house and disappear into the night. "Well, that is that," he said to himself as he turned and walked back to the door. He steeled himself for Paz's questions before entering. As he came in, he saw her rocking the baby. She looked up and shot him a piercing stare.

Paz picked up Angelita and placed her across her shoulder to burp her. As she patted the baby's back, she asked, "What did he want?"

Tereso shrugged his shoulders as he walked over to the kitchen and rummaged through some leftover tortillas from dinner. After a few moments, he nonchalantly said, "He wanted to discuss some things." He stuffed a cold tortilla in his mouth more in an attempt to stave off conversation than to still his hunger. Paz would have none of it.

"What kind of questions?"

Tereso motioned that his mouth was full and he could not answer right away. This irritated Paz because he had never exercised such restraint before, but she held her anger and let him continue eating. After much fanfare, he smacked his lips and started for the bedroom.

"I asked you what he said," repeated Paz with an edge to her voice.

Tereso threw his hands in the air and appeared to have forgotten. "Oh, that. Madrid needed help with something important and I said I would lend a hand. That is all."

Paz narrowed her eyes and spoke sharply, "You are going to run guns again, ¿qué no?"

Tereso had enough of this conversation. He clenched his teeth and yelled, "I will go and do as I please!" Then he stomped into the bedroom and slammed the door. Paz continued to stare at the closed door for several minutes. It seemed to represent the hardness of her husband's mind. She pulled Angelita from her shoulder and cradled her lovingly in her arms. As she looked upon her angelic face, she made a silent vow to be strong for her children, no matter what trouble her husband brought them.

———•◦•◦•———

The wagon came swiftly down the road in the feeble light of a waning sunset. Tereso was nervous about meeting it in the early evening, but the long trip ahead required a timely start. The wagon slowed and came to a stop close to Tereso. He jumped up onto the buckboard and prepared to take the reins, but an outstretched hand stopped him. "That wouldn't be necessary, Tereso," the voice said in a pleasant tone. "I will be happy to drive."

Tereso squinted in the darkness and recognized the smiling face of Julio sitting next to him. Tereso involuntarily lurched backward at the discovery. He expected to see Miguel, not this cocky man. Tereso suddenly had a gut feeling to jump off the wagon and abandon the mission. Julio seemed to read Tereso's mind. He reached behind the bench, retrieved a long flexible object, and tossed it to Tereso. "Here is something I believe you wanted."

Tereso looked down in his lap and saw a finely tooled double holster. The dark brown leather looked black in the darkness. It felt good in his hands. He quickly pulled the pistols from his waistband and slid them into the pouches. Then he buckled the belt around his hip. The guns rested comfortably along his sides and made him feel powerful and important. The holster also calmed him and banished any further thoughts of leaving. He relaxed a bit and casually asked Julio as he snapped the reins, "Where is Miguel?"

Julio let out a good-natured laugh and said, "Echavaria is still shaking in his boots. The man would have frightened himself to death if he had come along." Tereso thought the explanation was reasonable, but the levity in Julio's voice was out of character. It seemed fake and caused Tereso to suspect that Julio was up to something. He made a mental note not to let his guard down.

The short trip to Las Cruces was uneventful and smooth. The temperatures fell as the sky became darker and the stars became crisper. The men responded by squishing their hats over their heads and buttoning their coats tightly around their necks. The horses plodded along with an even and constant tempo that quickly carried them into the city.

The streets were mostly vacant with an occasional pedestrian crossing quickly before them or a solitary man standing by a doorway smoking a cigarette or pipe, obeying orders from his wife not to smoke in the home. Nobody paid them any heed and they slipped unnoticed to a small building toward the center of town. Julio stopped the wagon in front of two large doors that were built to accept freight. He looked over to Tereso and asked, "Tereso, *por favor,* back the team up so the wagon's gate is against the doors."

Tereso was unaccustomed to Julio's respectful tone and courtesies. His suspicions flared as he warily climbed down from the wagon and walked to the head of the team. He grabbed the bridles and backed the horses to the doors.

"*Bueno.* Now, knock on the doors and let them know we are here."

Tereso hissed, "No! You do it." His right hand fell on his pistol to let Julio know that he was ready for anything.

Julio threw his hands in the air and sighed. "All right. I will do it. Honestly, Tereso, you need to trust people more often." He jumped down and banged on the door. Within a few moments, the doors creaked open a bit and man asked who was there. Julio identified himself and the doors swung wide. Tereso suddenly felt vulnerable because he could not see inside, but he was sure they could see him standing in the street. If someone was going to shoot him, he would never see it coming. Julio came out and motioned for him to back the wagon inside. Tereso was thankful for the limited shielding the wagon provided as he guided the horses backward.

Once inside, Tereso saw a few oblong boxes stacked directly behind the wagon. If this was all they were going to carry up to the pass, their load was going to be very light. *Almost not worth the effort*, thought Tereso.

Again, Julio seemed to anticipate what Tereso was thinking. "This is all that's left of the arm shipments. Once we get rid of these rifles, there is nothing left to tie us to the gun smuggling, *¿qué no?* Let's get it loaded and get out of here." Tereso thought the explanation was plausible, but it stirred grave doubts in his mind. He nodded and helped Julio lift the boxes into the wagon. Then they secured the load with a tarp.

They rode out of town as quietly and unnoticed as they had arrived and headed east toward the Organ Mountains. A partial moon cast a feeble light along the countryside. Tereso could barely see the road as the wagon began the gradual ascent to the mountain pass. Dangers seemed to lurk behind every bush and rock, putting his nerves on edge. He glanced sideways at Julio and saw him grinning as he steered the team up the road. *Something is not right*, thought Tereso. His senses began to prickle with warnings.

As the wagon neared the summit, portions of the road gave away to steep embankments and cliffs along one side. Tereso remembered that some places had drops exceeding several hundred feet. He felt his stomach twist at the thought of the wheels riding so perilously close to the edge. He reached for the reins and said, "I will drive."

"Oh, that's right," replied Julio as he jerked the reins away from Tereso's outstretched hand. "You traveled this way before, *¿qué no?* Now, where did you say you came from?"

Tereso did not like where this conversation was going. "I didn't," he answered.

"Oh, you didn't? Well, let me guess then. How about Carrizozo?" Tereso remained silent and tried to watch his face. "Am I right or am I confusing you with someone else? Maybe someone named Prudenciano Nava?"

Tereso stiffened and said, "What do you want?"

Julio laughed, "What do I want? I will show you what I want." He steered the wagon into a pullout, put his fingers in his mouth, and blew a loud whistle. Three men emerged with rifles drawn and began approaching the wagon from both sides. "You see Nava," continued Julio, "I knew you were hiding something from the moment I met you. I asked around and found out that a man described like you got into some trouble in Carrizozo. Then I remember what those *Villistas* called you in that gravel pit where you sucker-punched me. Guess whose name matched up? Yours. So I worked a little deal with those lawmen who passed thorough town a few months ago. I told them I would deliver you to them with evidence that you were gun smuggling. Now you are going to do everyone in Doña Ana a favor and take the blame." Julio tilted back his head and let out a long wicked laugh.

Tereso glanced sideways and saw that the men had almost reached the wagon. Without thinking, he swung his left arm and struck Julio with a powerful backhand, silencing the laughter and knocking him unconscious. He snatched the reins and yelled "*¡Adelante!*" to the horses as he frantically whipped their flanks. The horses bolted in surprise.

A voice rang out in English, "Hey! Stop, you crazy fool! There's a cliff in front of you!" Tereso drove on and suddenly the world dropped out from underneath him. The wagon pitched downward as he felt that sickly feeling of free fall in his stomach. Tereso let go of the reins and pushed away from the buckboard with his arms flailing frantically in the pitch-black night, trying desperately to claw into something solid that would stop his fall. His fingertips dug into soft earth and Tereso fought to find more of it. He could feel his fingernails rip off as he drove his hands deeper into the soil. Slowly his speed diminished and he stopped on a rock pile. He could hear the wagon bounce on the steep incline and the horses scream in terror as it plummeted down into the black abyss. The noise gradually became fainter until it terminated in a thunderous crash.

Tereso froze, not wanting to move a muscle. He was unsure if he was hurt, the situation of his precarious position, or the whereabouts of the armed men. He could hear his heart pound with fear against his heaving chest. The disturbed slope rained dirt upon his body, partially burying his head. As he gathered his senses he became aware of voices yelling above him.

"Oh, Dear Mother of God! They went right over the edge! Why in the hell did they do that?" Private David Smith stood stunned looking over the cliff.

"Because that big guy thought he was trapped," answered Deputy Albert Roberts as he stared down into the inky blackness. "I reckon he thought he had no choice." Roberts looked over to his trusted companion John Smoke Rider for confirmation, but Smoke Rider seemed tense as his nocturnal eyes scanned the black ravine below. "What'cha looking for, John? They're as good as dead."

Smoke Rider continued looking for a moment longer before replying, "The big man has many lives."

Roberts shook his head in disbelief. "We'll find out how many lives he has tomorrow. Let's go back to Las Cruces and notify the authorities. Then return in the morning."

Smoke Rider straightened up and looked back at Roberts. Even in the darkness, Smoke Rider's obsidian eyes shone like black polished orbs. He said flatly, "I'm staying."

Roberts sighed and refrained from arguing. He knew that it was hopeless to persuade him to leave. "Suit yourself. Come on, David. Time to go. We'll see ya, John, at first light." David followed Roberts aimlessly back to the horses, still totally disbelieving what had happened. Roberts put his rifle in his scabbard and mounted his horse.

He turned in his saddle and watched Private Smith fumble with his reins and awkwardly climb onto his horse. The accident had badly shaken him. When David was ready, Roberts gave Smoke Rider a final look that said, *Be careful and don't kill anybody*, before setting off in a slow trot toward town.

Smoke Rider watched them leave and disappear in the darkness. He continued to stare in their direction for a moment and reflected on why he had chosen to stay. He had an unexplained feeling that the big man was still alive. The man possessed a warrior's spirit and a warrior would exploit any chance to survive, no matter how slim that chance was. If there was any possibility of surviving that crash, Smoke Rider was certain that he would find it and escape. Smoke Rider felt the hunter inside him unleash itself and tantalize his senses. The prospect of a challenging manhunt excited him.

Smoke Rider knew the best chance of capturing the man would be to anticipate where he would flee, get ahead of him, and wait for him to arrive. He remembered that the road followed the lip of a deep ravine to the valley floor. The man would most likely follow the bottom of the ravine until he met the north-south highway. Smoke Rider decided that he would move down the mountain a few miles and set up a sniper's post. If he guessed right, by dawn he would have him. Smoke Rider slid his rifle into his buckskin sheath on his back and led his horse down the dark road. He vowed to himself that the man would not slip from his grasp again.

When the voices finally receded, Tereso slowly mustered the courage to move. He carefully lifted his head up and let the dirt rain off his face as he searched the ridge above him for any signs of movement. He saw the stars and the Milky Way shine brightly above until they abruptly stopped at the inky black mountain above him. He watched the ridge for a few minutes more until he was satisfied that there was no movement. Then he relaxed for a moment and considered his options. He could make his way back up the mountain to the road, but there was a chance that the lawmen would still be there, ready to snatch him and take him to jail. His only other alternative was to make his way down the slope and find his way out the canyon.

With his decision made, Tereso began to inch his way down. His progress was slow, sometimes interrupted when his legs suddenly thrust out over a rock cliff. Then he blindly traversed the obstacle and continued sliding slowly down the steep slope. After an hour of painstaking effort, Tereso finally reached the canyon floor. He stood up and stretched his aching back and brushed the soil from his hair and clothes.

In the feeble starlight, he recognized pieces of the wagon scattered over the rocky floor. He stepped carefully among the debris and found the horses mangled and still harnessed to their yoke. Tereso took a step backward and tripped over a soft lump on the ground. He fell and landed roughly on his back. He sat up and saw his feet lying on top of something. He quickly got to his knees and felt the object before him. It was a body. He rolled it over and discovered it was Julio. His neck was grotesquely twisted. Tereso put his head on his chest and confirmed that he was indeed dead.

Suddenly, the horror of what had happened descended upon Tereso. He scampered backward away from Julio. He was sure that the law was going to blame him for this death, too. Now he was wanted for two murders. His mind screamed for him to run. He jumped up and fled into the dark canyon toward home.

Dawn of the next morning found Deputy Roberts and Private Smith back at the accident site with the Las Cruces sheriff and his two sworn deputies. While David sat exhausted in his saddle from the lack of sleep, Roberts scanned the area for John. The sheriff and his deputies dismounted first and looked over the edge. "Wow—ee!" exclaimed the sheriff as he pushed his hat back. "Yes sir. They're as dead as doornails for sure. I reckon we will be scraping them up come close to noon."

Roberts did not respond and kept looking for his partner. He thought, *Where in blue blazes is he? Even his horse is gone.*

The sheriff saw him scanning the mountains and said, "What's the matter? You lost yer Injin? I bet he hightailed it to some squaw he had squirreled up in some cave. You know how them people are." The sheriff's comments irritated Roberts. He was about to respond when he heard a faint gunshot echo from down the mountain. Without commenting, he kicked his horse into a gallop down the road toward the sound. He had a gut feeling that John was handing out his own special brand of justice that had made him infamous.

John Smoke Rider chose his perch in a boulder patch with the skill of a seasoned hunter. It faced south and overlooked the mouth of the canyon and a half mile of flat terrain before the main highway. Anyone venturing into his killing field would be an easy target. He was confident that he could hit any down-gradient shot offered. The only disadvantage of his hideout was that a large boulder on his left prevented him from looking up the ravine.

He sat cross-legged with his rifle across his lap and watched the panorama unfold before him. Dawn broke over the mountains and spilled its light over the land like water smoothly cresting a dam. Objects leaped into view where only minutes before they had lain hidden in darkness. He studied the landscape below and took in every detail. He saw the white tail of a deer spring up like a flag as it bounded quietly for cover. His eye caught the scurrying of a furry creature frantically searching for its burrow before a hawk found it. He saw everything.

Minutes slowly ticked by and still no man walked into his trap. Smoke Rider began to doubt his theory. *Maybe he died*, he mused, *or maybe he went over the pass*. More time crept by and his doubts increased. He was so preoccupied in thought that he barely noticed a sprinkle of dirt spill down the side of the boulder next to him. His eyes flicked up and saw a man falling on top of him. He instantly knew that his rifle was useless.

Tereso stumbled along in almost total darkness, tripping over rocks and brush. His fingers ached and his thirst was almost crippling. His progress was much slower than he wanted, but under the circumstances, it was the best he could do. The twinkling starlight revealed the inky black edge of the canyon walls. As the night wore on, the walls appeared to shrink in height. Tereso knew that this indicated that he was nearing the foothills and the Rio Grande valley beyond.

As dawn broke, Tereso found a rock to sit on and rest. He was exhausted and took a few minutes to assess his situation. For the first time since the accident, he closely examined his hands. Several nails were missing and his fingers were caked with blood and dirt. He grimaced as he assessed their condition. He would have to clean them soon or infection would set in. He checked his pistols and much to his relief found them intact but packed with dirt.

He looked around his position and felt a premonition that he had been here before. The narrow canyon was just like the one at the base of Sierra Blanca where he and Silva had stumbled into a deadly trap laid by that Indian bounty hunter. He turned to the west and saw the mouth of the canyon and the barely visible highway below. It was tempting just to walk out the canyon and into the valley, but he would be easily spotted by anyone desiring to kill him. Therefore, he had two choices. Either he could hide in this hot, arid canyon until nightfall or climb out before reaching the mouth and hide among the rocks while creeping to the road. Since he did not think that he could last the day without water, he chose to climb.

He spotted a jumble of rocks and boulders not far ahead that offered a reasonable route up the north wall. The rock pile lay close to the end of the gully. If he traveled much farther, his cover would be lost. He decided that the rocks would be his way out.

He hugged the wall and moved quietly to base of the boulder pile before climbing carefully up the rock screed. His fingers stung every time he grasped a hand hold. He gritted his teeth and pushed on. Sometimes a loose rock shifted when he put his weight on it and almost caused a small avalanche. He had trouble identifying the potentially hazardous rocks until he committed his weight to them and by then it was too late. He slowed his ascent and tried to pick his way up as quietly as possible.

He soon neared the top and chose to follow the lip of the canyon to stay out of sight. He rounded a corner and started up the side of a smooth boulder. His footing slipped and knocked a few pebbles loose. His eyes followed the path of the falling stones and suddenly froze with fear. Directly beneath him sat the Indian, motionless and nearly invisible to the unwary eye. Tereso's mind whirled at lightning speed and caused the most minute details to resonate with crystal clarity. He could see the dust particles and stones churning in slow motion as they delicately fell away. There was no sound, only the sight of the dirt landing next to the man with the rifle lying across his lap. Fear propelled Tereso off the boulder and into the thin air. He was not conscious of what he was doing, but reacting to the deeply inbred instinct to fight and survive, and he wanted to live. He had no sensation of falling, just the wonderment of why it was taking so long to travel the seemingly short distance. He saw the Indian's eyes turn toward him and noted his futile attempt to lift his rifle. Then he landed on him, feet first, and the sound of rifle fire cracked through his mind and returned him to reality.

Tereso's left foot smacked the rifle out of Smoke Rider's hands. It discharged harmlessly into space. His right foot drove into his shoulder, but Smoke Rider spun into the blow and deflected most of its power. The impact still threw John onto his back and momentarily drove the air out of his lungs. Tereso came down in a heap and rolled off the perch and onto a small ledge below. As he struggled to his feet, Smoke Rider grabbed the knife from his belt and lunged for Tereso's back, but his lungs were still fighting for breath and drained his strength. He collapsed on Tereso with the blade pointed out. Tereso reared up and sent Smoke Rider flying backward, slamming him against the rocks and driving the remaining air out of him. Tereso threw himself on the Indian and snatched the knife.

Suddenly, all time seemed to stop as Tereso held the knife with his arm outstretched above him and the blade pointed down toward Smoke Rider. Time and fate rested in a balance. Smoke Rider lay calmly looking into Tereso's wild eyes, ready to accept what life was about to serve him. Sweat dripped down Tereso's forehead as he struggled with his emotions. Then he plunged the knife into the ground next to Smoke Rider's left ear. Tereso let out a lung full of air and felt the weariness creep through his body as the adrenaline left his blood. He put his hand on Smoke Rider's shoulder to steady himself and slowly stood up.

Smoke Rider stayed where he was, still as stone and watched the man with reverence in his eyes. This big man just spared his life and took a coup, as he had in the tent on Sierra Blanca three years ago. Tereso had unknowingly earned honor in this warrior's eyes. Smoke Rider watched him look with uncertainly around before quickly disappearing into the rocks below.

John waited for a few minutes before trying to sit up. His chest and shoulder ached from the attack. As he came wobbling to his feet, he heard heavy footsteps come his way. He thought that the big man was returning until he saw Deputy Roberts crest the rise. "John!" Roberts yelled, "Are you all right? Is someone shot?"

Smoke Rider lowered his eyes and shook his head.

Roberts came closer. "Hell's fire, John! You ain't making any sense. Was that your rifle I heard or wasn't it?"

Smoke Rider vaguely remembered his rifle flying out of his hands. He could not recall if it fired. Battle sometimes robbed the mind of trivial details while ingraining others. He staggered over to the ledge and spotted its shattered remains on the rocks below. John looked back at Roberts and shrugged his shoulders.

Albert Roberts took a couple of steps closer and stopped short when he saw John's condition. "John, talk to me. You look like you tangled with a den of cougars or something. Did you see that big Mexican?"

Smoke Rider looked out toward the highway and the Rio Grande Valley. Traffic was beginning to move on the road. His eagle eyes could see the laborers walking slowly into the fields as the world prepared to start another day. Then for an instant, he saw a speck quickly cross the highway and disappear into an irrigation ditch like a fugitive fleeing from the law. Smoke Rider turned toward Roberts and straightened his aching back. He said quietly, "I fell. There was no one else."

Roberts did not believe a word of it, but when he looked into John Smoke Rider's eyes and saw them plead, *Please don't ask*, he dropped the matter. During the following days when only one body was found within the wagon wreckage and no trace of the big man was discovered, Roberts peppered Smoke Rider with questions and his answer was always the same. He had seen nothing. Roberts finally concluded the investigation out of frustration and sent Private David Smith back to Camp Furlong. John and he rode back to the Tularosa Valley and parted company. The mystery of the missing man would haunt Roberts for the rest of his life.

———•••••———

Paz stood silently crying in front of the rough-cut kitchen counter during the December afternoon. Alcaria, Joaquina, and Augustine were outside playing. The baby lay sleeping in a padded crate on the table. The tranquil serenity was rare within the Minjares household and Paz usually savored every moment, but times had suddenly changed ever since her husband had bounded through the door that late morning scared and hurt. He was terrified that someone was hunting him and wanted to run away forever. Only her constant pleading had kept him from fleeing and her prodding pushed him back to work at Taylor's farm.

She subconsciously put her hand over her womb and trembled with fright. She had just discovered that she was pregnant again. If her husband left her, Paz wondered how she could feed and clothe her children with a baby and carrying another. With Christmas near, she should be happy and looking forward to the holidays, but instead she felt deep loneliness and despair. Paz thought it was strange how history repeated itself. She doubted that she had the strength to run again. "I won't do it," she whispered to herself. The pain of losing her baby boy came back to her and filled her with grief. With trembling lips and eyes brimming with tears, she faced the wall again so she could grieve in private.

Chapter 22
Changes

Paz Minjares gave birth to a girl on July 26, 1917 and named her Anita after the patron Saint Anne, the mother of Mary. She was born amidst calamitous events rocking the Rio Grande valley and the world. Armies of the European nations swept across the face of Europe and collided in eastern France. Britain, France, and Italy begged the United States to join the fray and help them defeat the Kaiser, but President Wilson refused and doggedly pursued a peaceful solution. America narrowly reelected Woodrow Wilson for a second term in November 1916, mainly because of his isolationist views. His campaign slogan was "He kept us out of the war." However, when Germany broke the Sussex pledge to limit submarine warfare in February 1917, Wilson became outraged and recalled the U.S. ambassador from Germany.

At roughly the same time, British intelligence intercepted a coded telegram from the German Foreign Minister Arthur Zimmermann to Von Eckhardt, the German ambassador to Mexico. British cryptographers labored with the code and finally deciphered its message. Its content shocked the stalwart leaders of the world. Germany proposed an alliance with Mexico to jointly fight the United States. If Mexico agreed to wage war against its neighbor, Germany pledged financial support and formal recognition of its sovereignty. As an added bonus, Germany offered the lost territories of Texas, New Mexico, and Arizona as payment for Mexico's efforts.

The British waited until February 24 to present the telegram to President Wilson. The telegram arrived at the same time when Wilson recalled General "Black Jack" Pershing and his great Punitive Expedition from Mexico. Pershing had been unsuccessful in capturing Pancho Villa and his army. Villa had eluded the superior force and vanished into the rugged Sierra Madre mountains. The telegram infuriated Wilson and he immediately told his favorite general to prepare to lead the American forces in Europe.

The Punitive Expedition had provided one key benefit to the United States. It propelled the U.S. military and manufacturing industries into a high state of readiness. America's factories and military regime were in prime shape to enter the European conflict. Thousands of young men returning from Mexico were disappointed in the hide-and-seek games with the *Villistas* and hungered to see real action. When the press published the telegram on March 1, America clamored to take up arms against Germany. Wilson had little trouble convincing Congress to declare war.

The Zimmermann telegram had other repercussions than triggering war with Germany. Americans became suspicious of Mexican immigrants and citizens of Spanish and Mexican heritage and considered them a threat to national security. Border patrols increased and U.S. ports of entry curtailed their once liberal entry standards. Mexican laborers were suddenly shunned and ostracized when only a short while ago, American industries welcomed them with open arms. Some U.S. senators even suggested legislation banning the further admittance of Mexicans.

To defuse the building hatred and fears, the governor of New Mexico called upon his constituents to volunteer for military service. His hope was to show the nation that New Mexicans were deeply patriotic and posed no threat to the Union. The governor's plea worked as thousands of New Mexican residents, mostly from the Rio Grande Valley, enlisted. Although America took little notice of New Mexico's contribution to the war, this sparsely populated state supplied more recruits per capita than any other state in the nation.

During the summer of 1917, Tereso Minjares worked hard in the fields alongside Bill Taylor. Taylor's worst nightmare had unfolded this year. The war created a huge demand for agricultural products, but it sucked every able-bodied man out of the valley. The Texas Rangers and other border patrols ruthlessly harassed Mexicans to the point of deterring the flow of new laborers. Therefore, if Taylor wanted to reap the benefits of the market, he had to plant, weed, irrigate, and harvest his crops himself. He was deeply grateful for Tereso's help and asked Nellie to provide more food and supplies to the Minjares family.

Taylor stopped his hoeing for a moment and stood up to stretch his aching back. He reached for the canteen slung around his neck, twisted the cap off, and took a long swig. He held the water in his mouth for awhile and savored its wetness. Tereso continued to work with his *sombrero* pushed over his eyes. Taylor watched him and thought he looked preoccupied with some serious thoughts. Taylor could barely speak a word of Spanish so he could not ask him what was on his mind. Their relationship was purely business and their language and cultural barriers prevented anything different. Taylor slid the canteen onto his back and went back to the weeding.

Tereso was deep in thought as he chopped the weeds from around the beets and made a shallow trench parallel to the planting. He labored without thought, almost by reflex as he turned the soil around each vegetable. The long handle allowed him to stand with only a slight stoop and shuffle slowly down the row. Later, when he opened the irrigation ditch, water would flow down each hoed row next to the receiving crops.

He kept wondering why the law had never come for him. The Indian bounty hunter had gotten a good look at him, but he'd let him escape. Tereso knew he should have killed him when he had the chance, but contrary to everyone's opinion of him, he was not a killer. Doña Ana residents kept a respectful distance from him and seldom stopped by the fields to talk. He heard their whispers that he and Julio had fought the lawmen and only he had barely escaped. The area Mexicans were sure that Tereso Minjares was a wanted man with a price on his head. To add to the mystery, Augustine Madrid never asked him what happened on that fateful last trip. It was as if he had never known anything about the mission. None of this made sense to Tereso.

The sick feeling of not knowing when the other shoe was going to fall made Tereso nervous. Every passing day gave him more dread and the belief that surely someone was coming for him. He kept to himself and worked in silence.

Life in the Minjares household had changed too. The family had swelled to five children, two of them in diapers, which added to Paz's already heavy workload. Alcaria and Joaquina were ten and seven years old, respectively, and helped with the chores in little ways. Augustine was a big five-year-old and struggled to keep up with his big sisters. He would grab big loads of wood and lug them into the kitchen for his mother's stove. All three children helped feed the chickens, collect the eggs, and tend the family garden.

Paz noticed the subtle change in community behavior and guessed that it was the her husband's handiwork. When she went to the store, women would ask to see her new baby or inquire about the welfare of her family, then give her a knowing and concerned smile. The clerk would total her goods in a business-like manner and take her money with a sage nod. Often, he deftly slipped a free can of tobacco into her bag with a sleight of hand that rivaled the most skilled magician. Paz was certain that Doña Ana knew more about her husband's secrets than she did.

Doña Ana wrapped itself tightly its Mexican culture and hid from the world crises and border disputes. If a white man ventured into the town, he would mistake the brown faces that looked downward at his glances for backwardness and laziness. What he failed to see was a whole town watching his every move. The stories of Texas Rangers indiscriminately killing all Mexicans they encountered along the border left Doña Ana distrustful and wary of all strangers. Newcomers never stayed long.

In the late afternoon of autumn, Paz walked out of the front door with a load of laundered clothes to hang and dry. She was making the most of both babies napping at once. The older girls were in school and Augustine was drawing pictures on the kitchen table. Paz wanted to get the clothes hung and return before one of her three children decided they needed her. She hurried out along the house when she saw a team of four mules pulling a covered wagon. Driving the team was a man with night-black hair and a thick, matching mustache that was drawn to handlebar points. He wore a black hat and a white shirt with a black leather vest. Sitting next to him was a woman with long black braids that lay against her back and almost reached her waist. She wore a long dark dress and a red scarf on her head. Her arms jangled with lots of bracelets, and rings adorned every finger. As the wagon drew closer, Paz could see the heads of children pop out from under the canvas like crows peering out of a nest. She froze and watched them approach.

As the wagon came alongside Paz, the woman slapped the man on his arm and signaled for him to stop. He quickly pulled back on the reins and halted the wagon. The woman leaned over the man and said in heavily accented Castellano Spanish, "Good afternoon, *Señora*. We wish to have one of your chickens. Please give us one."

Paz was taken back by her forwardness and stood silently staring back at them while holding the basket of wet clothes. Suddenly, she recognized who they were and took a step back. They were gypsies and her mother had warned her to avoid them at all costs. Mexicans firmly believed that gypsies stole everything they could get their hands on, including children. They possessed black magic and would curse you at the slightest provocation. The best course of action was just to run back into the house and lock the door.

Paz wanted to run, but she knew the gypsies would go into the backyard and help themselves to her vegetables and chickens. Therefore, she decided to hold her ground and stand up to these thieves. Paz lifted her chin up and said, "I need those chickens to feed my family. I have nothing for you."

The woman responded in a shrill voice, "What did you say? Do you know who we are? Go get one of those chickens before you regret it."

"No."

The woman was outraged. She stood up and slowly raised her pointed finger at Paz. Through clenched teeth she hissed, "Then behold my wrath. I cast a hex on you, you selfish wench!" Paz dropped the basket in horror and stumbled backward into the house. She breathlessly slammed the door and locked it.

"What's going on, Mother?" asked Augustine as he looked up from his drawing.

"Nothing," replied Paz as she ran to the window and looked out. To her relief, the man signaled the mule team forward and continued to move down the road. She watched them until they were out of sight before turning around and letting out her breath. Then the thought struck her. *The hex! She threw a hex on me!* Paz checked her hands and feet for signs of affliction and then ran to the mirror over the kitchen sink. She intensely studied her face for injury and saw none. She looked nervously back at her son and said, "It's nothing. Go back to your drawing." Paz subconsciously scratched an itch on her arm and went back outside to retrieve her laundry. Augustine watched her leave, with a puzzled look on his face.

Paz did not tell Tereso about the gypsies when he returned that evening. He noticed that she was unusually quiet that night, but let her behavior go without comment. He thought it was odd that she frequently scratched her arm and seemed to fuss over a particular patch of skin. He made a note to ask her about it tomorrow. He was too tired from his day's work to care about anything else but sleep.

By midmorning of the next day, Paz had worked her nervous scratching into a full-blown rash. She was certain that the outbreak of redness on her arm was the manifestation of the dreaded hex. It never occurred to her that her skin was suffering from her chafing. She was scared and rubbed the rash harder, which increased its size and severity and bolstered her fear.

Finally, Paz could no longer keep silent. While on a trip to the store with Anita in her arms and Alcaria holding Angelita, *Señora* Rodriguez inquired about the family's well-being. Paz, who usually kept her family's affairs secret, blurted out, "A gypsy woman hexed me! See!" She freed her afflicted arm and showed *Señora* Rodriguez her bright red rash.

Señora Rodriguez recoiled in horror. "*¡Dios mío!* You poor child! Her black magic must be working on you." Now *Señora* Rodriguez had something important and fascinating to tell the other Doña Ana women and she wasted little time informing them of Paz's misfortune. By the afternoon of the same day, the town's women elected Miguel Echavaria to tell Tereso about his wife's condition and immediately shoved him in the direction of the Taylor farm.

Tereso was deep in thought as he hoed the weeds along the long row of vegetables. His back and head slumped forward and his sombrero slid low over his forehead and hid his face. His eyes were closed and he was virtually asleep on his feet as he methodically went through the motions of weeding. His progress had slowed to a mere crawl in the late summer heat.

Miguel walked carefully along a single furrow to prevent trampling the crops. He arrived alongside Tereso unnoticed and waited a few minutes for some sign of recognition. When he received none, he cleared his throat to announce his presence.

Tereso startled awake, "Huh? Miguel! What are you doing here?"

Miguel cowered and took a step backward in case Tereso swung his hoe at him. When he realized that Tereso was in control of his faculties, he slowly straightened up and spoke, "Tereso, some women in town want me to discuss something important with you."

Tereso snorted, "You came out here to see me because some women told you to? You must be joking? What is this about?"

"*Verdad*, Tereso," blurted Miguel. "You see, it seems a powerful gypsy woman cast a hex on Paz and now she has developed a rash on her arm. You must help her."

Tereso stood silently with his arm propped on the hoe handle and stared at Miguel. He found it hard to believe that the women of Doña Ana would get involved in such petty affairs and talk Miguel into coming out here to tell him the news, but such was life in a small town. He let out a long sigh of disgust and looked up at the sun. Its position told him that he still had a few more hours of work before he could go home. "All right," he finally said, "tell the *señoras* that I will tend to her when I come home tonight. They will see a marked improvement in her condition tomorrow."

"*Gracias*," replied Miguel. He looked relieved that his mission was successful and that he had something favorable to report back. "I better be going before *Señor* Taylor chases me off. *Adios*." He turned and left with considerably more spring to his step than before.

Tereso watched him leave before returning to his mind-numbing work. As he chopped at the weeds with his hoe, he wondered how his *sobador* talents would stack against a gypsy curse.

Immediately after dinner, Tereso directed Paz to sit in the chair next to him by the dinner table and examined her arm. The children stood silently around them and watched their father carefully inspect the rash. He emitted some low grunts and tugged at his mustache before reaching into his bag and pulling out his small ceramic jar of aloe vera leaves. He popped the wire that secured the lid and pulled out a thick, green, rubbery leaf. Tereso crushed the leaf between his thumb and forefinger and mashed it into a green, fibrous paste. He applied the pulp over the red spot on Paz's arm and massaged it in. Then he wrapped her arm with torn strips from a dish towel and bound it with a final strip of cloth.

"There," he said with a satisfied look as he gave his work a final inspection. "You should feel much better tomorrow."

"How can you be so sure?" Paz snapped as she took her arm back and rubbed the bandage. "A gypsy curse can last a long time."

Tereso smirked at her and answered, "I know how to heal a rash caused by a gypsy. My treatment has not failed yet." Paz gave him a hard look before returning to her chores. She had a feeling that he was making fun of her and that he had never before encountered a gypsy curse.

By the next day, Paz's arm ceased to itch. She was tempted to take the bandage off and inspect her wound, but Tereso was adamant that she leave it alone for three days. The bandage also satisfied the women around town that Tereso had finally administered proper care. After three days, Tereso unwound the bandage and revealed a healthy arm. Paz examined it intensely for a few minutes before believing that she was truly cured. She smiled her thanks to her husband and ran off to show the rest of the community her miraculous recovery. This testimony restored Doña Ana's confidence in Tereso's *sobador* talents and tore down the last of their reservations about him. Before long, residents once again stopped by the house for Tereso to examine and treat their ailments. In return, they brought food, liquor, and tobacco, but best of all, they listened to his stories of being a *colleador* and applauded his bravery, which pumped up Tereso's ego and made him feel very good.

———

War and all its horrors was often thought of as man's deadliest enemy, but other scourges rampaged the earth that ripped through humans like a scythe through a wheat field. These calamities would lie dormant for centuries with only a faint heartbeat until roaring into life with a lethal vengeance. The bubonic plague erupted across Europe in the sixth, fourteenth, and seventeenth centuries and claimed a total of 137 million victims. At its worst, the plague killed about two million people a year. However, in the spring 1918, a far deadlier epidemic pounced on the world and killed at least 30 million people within one year, more than three times as many people than died in World War I.

On March 11, 1918, an army cook named Albert Mitchell reported to the infirmary at Camp Funston, Kansas. He complained about a mild fever, a sore throat, and slight head and muscle aches. The doctor diagnosed him with the flu and assigned him to the barracks for bed rest. By noon, 107 soldiers had reported sick with the same symptoms. Within two days, 522 soldiers fell prey to the same sickness and Mitchell died from drowning in his own fluids.

Suddenly, reports came in from other military bases around the country. Thousands of sailors in supply ships docked on the East Coast were sick with the mysterious flu. Within seven days, the disease had spread to every state in the Union. As quickly as the disease would strike a city, it would disappear only to resurface in another town close by.

The influenza defied the normal patterns of attacking the very young, the old, and the sick. It preferred the young and robust, often infecting adults aged twenty-one to thirty-six years. America quickly lost many of its most productive citizens, which threatened to rip the country's social fabric.

Although the flu was clearly airborne, the supply efforts of the war provided the means to spread the influenza throughout the world. The crowded troop and supply ships contained infected men who appeared healthy and robust at the start, but quickly deteriorated once at sea. The close quarters functioned as an incubator, allowing the virus to spread like wildfire throughout the ships. By April, every ship had lost at least 10 percent of its passengers while crossing the Atlantic.

Within one month, the influenza raced across Europe. The disease ravaged the troops fighting trench warfare. As on the ships, the high concentrations of men tightly packed in the trenches proved to be fertile ground for the virus. By June, more men had died from the influenza than from enemy fire.

All countries fighting in the war concealed the news of the influenza epidemic. Leaders feared that the news would bolster their enemy's spirits if word ever leaked out how devastating the disease was to their troops and countrymen back home. Spain was neutral during the war and thus, had no censorship. Spanish newspapers broke the story and graphically told the world about the disease. This was the first time that citizens were informed about the global impact of the influenza and they quickly dubbed it the "Spanish Flu" after the articles that proclaimed it.

The disease spread to India, China, and Japan where it killed millions every month. As the virus continued to move across the face of the earth, it mutated into an even deadlier form. When it finally returned to America, the virus unleashed its fury again among the already stunned Americans. People were caught totally unprepared for its ferociousness. In Philadelphia, 16 percent of its population died. Baltimore lost 15 percent and, in Washington D.C., 10 percent perished. Civic leaders scurried to limit the disease in their communities by restricting public gatherings like dances, theaters, and church. The mayor of San Diego instituted a five-dollar fine if anyone was caught not wearing a mask. Men partially complied by cutting a hole over the mouth so they could smoke a cigar and women sewed decorative veils that hid their mouths in a Persian style.

The accelerated death rate completely overwhelmed the mortuaries. Churches, undertakers' homes, streets, and front yards were filled with pine boxes containing victims waiting for burial. Most of the boxes were made from rough lumber because finely made caskets were all taken. Children returned to school after surviving the flu to find only half their classmates alive. Funeral processions seemed never to end as they occurred every day around the clock.

Amidst of this death came a poem that children and adults recited daily:

I had a little bird,
Its name was Enza.
I opened the window,
And in-flu-enza.

The Spanish Flu was particularly devastating to Native Americans. This was partially due to the incomplete adaptation of their immune systems to European diseases, but their substandard living conditions also played a major role. The Sioux and Cherokee lost 65 percent of their members. In Alaska, 60 percent of the Nome Inupiat Eskimo population perished and, in Brevig Mission, 85 percent died within one week.

The Mexican population with its Mexican Indian heritage also suffered. The Spanish Flu struck like a knife through the Rio Grande settlements and killed hundreds every week. County officials with white masks covering their faces tacked quarantine signs on telephone poles outside small towns that warned travelers not to stop. Mexicans were forced to bury their dead immediately, sometimes without a priest to issue the last rites. The small-town cemeteries quickly filled to capacity and residents resorted to burying their relatives in their backyards and in the fields where they worked.

Despite the global impact of the virus, many Americans placed the blame of the flu on the Mexican laborers. *After all*, they reasoned, *the Spanish Flu came from the Spanish and they are clearly Spanish. See how they die from it?* The unfounded prejudice resounded in the Congressional halls again as senators and congressmen floated bills to "remove the Mexican vermin from our soils." Although no Mexican expulsion laws passed, the anti-Mexican sentiment among whites slowed medical assistance to regions of high Mexican concentrations. These poor laborers of America's agricultural sector were on their own to combat the influenza by whatever means they could.

By November 1918, the Mexicans of New Mexico were amidst an internal epidemic. Word had trickled down that the Great War was over, but few New Mexicans were coming home—most were dead from either a German bullet or the flu. Along the Rio Grande, cramped little adobe hovels held scores of dying family members. The virus flourished within the crude homes without adequate heating, clean water, and suitable toilet facilities. People were dying in their relatives' helpless arms.

Health officials quarantined Doña Ana and strictly ordered all residents to stay put. They could not even walk to Las Cruces for supplies or medical help. They were shut off from the rest of society and forced to face their fears alone. Residents sought anyone among them with any medical knowledge to help. Tereso Minjares was besieged by mothers and fathers begging him to visit their home and use his *sobador* skills to cure a loved one.

At first, Tereso tried to help, but he was soon overwhelmed by the sheer magnitude of the afflicted. Never in his life had he seen a sickness ravage a body so quickly. He would administer to an ailing man in the morning, only to see him die in the evening. He could do little to battle it and his fruitless efforts only succeeded in exhausting him before going home late at night.

Then the sickness struck the Minjares family. The eighteen-month-old baby, Anita, became seriously ill. Paz had just set her down after a feeding when suddenly she vomited her meal. She quickly felt her baby's forehead and found it hot. *¡Dios mío!*, Paz thought, *she was feeling fine before I fed her. I must find Tereso!* Paz turned to her daughters, who were diligently completing their schoolwork. She fought to keep her voice calm. "Alcaria, I want you to find your father and bring him home now, *comprende?*"

Alcaria seemed troubled by her mother's request and asked, "Why, Mother? Is everything all right?"

Paz snapped back, "Never mind! Just do as I tell you. Now go!" Alcaria staggered back from her mother's rebuke. She sensed something was terribly wrong. Then her eyes fell upon the fussy baby in Mother's arms. Beads of perspiration trickled down Anita's face. Alcaria recognized it for what it was and clasped both of her hands over her mouth to keep from screaming.

Alcaria wailed, "Anita has the flu! Doesn't she? Is she going to die? Oh God!" Joaquina jumped alongside her sister with eyes of fear staring back.

"*¡Silencio!*" shouted Paz. "Get your father, now!" Alcaria took a slow step backward with horror etched across her face. Then suddenly she snapped out of her trance and grabbed her coat from the wall peg and raced out the door. Joaquina was left standing alone with trembling lips as she looked at her mother for some ray of hope. Paz took a deep breath and said, "Come here, honey. I need your help. Being scared isn't going to make Anita well. Let's change her into some warm clothes." Joaquina nodded her head, her thick black braids bobbing back and forth and came forward to assist her mother.

Tereso could not believe it. Miguel Echavaria was dead. He had been by his friend's bedside since morning, trying to abate the consuming fever. Miguel's eyes had pleaded for his big older friend to save him but he had drowned in his own fluids by nightfall. The last hour of his life was hideous. Miguel's young wife, Rosemary, and her children watched as Tereso pulled the sweat-soaked bedsheet over his friend's head. She made the sign of the cross and began to cry. Tereso slumped down on a stool and buried his head in his hands. He had never felt so tired and hopeless in his life.

Alcaria burst through the door and saw the heartbreaking sight before her. Her father looked old and tired. The children and woman were devastated, holding each other for support. The scene tempered her fear as she quietly approached her father. "Father," said Alcaria softly, "Father. Anita is sick. Mother wants you home to help."

Alcaria's voice took a moment to seep past his misery and register in his mind. Tereso slowly lifted his head and turned toward her. Alcaria saw the rough stubble on his face and the deep circles of fatigue around his dull eyes. He looked dead on his feet. He asked, "What did you say?"

"Anita is sick. Mother needs you now." Tereso nodded as if he accepted his child's sickness as inevitable and slowly stood up. He walked over to Rosemary and put his hand on her grieving shoulder. She placed her hand on his and patted it in a silent way to thank him for trying to help her husband. The gesture tore Tereso's heart. He quietly grabbed his hat and walked his daughter out the door.

It was late in the evening when Tereso and Alcaria arrived home. Paz sat in the kitchen next to a makeshift bed she had hurriedly fashioned from a fruit crate and blankets. She looked up at her husband with worried eyes. Tereso momentarily forgot his grief and weariness and approached the bed. When he looked inside, he scarcely recognized the tiny, withered figure lying in the box as his baby Anita. Perspiration dripped from her face, and her breath was short and shallow. Tereso put his hand on her forehead and felt the heat of the fever. Anita moaned in response and fussed for him to remove his hand.

Tereso took a step back and looked back at Paz with a look of resignation. He said, "She has the flu. There is little that we can do for her."

Paz put her hand to her mouth to stifle a scream, then bit her hand. The pain seemed to steel her. She suddenly launched into Tereso, beating her fists into his chest and screamed, "No! You can't just let her die! Damn you! I want you to fight. *Comprende*? Fight for her!"

Her ferocity shocked him. He gently grabbed her wrists and looked into her wild eyes. He thought, *How can I tell her the horrors that I saw these past days? She would never understand.* Tereso took a deep breath and said, "All right. I will do what I can. The next twelve hours will be the most critical." His words calmed her and she stopped struggling.

When he released her, Paz smoothed her hair back with her hand and asked, "What do you want me to do?"

"Boil some water and make some mint tea. I put some dried leaves in the cupboard." Paz nodded and immediately set to work stoking the stove fire and setting the water to boil. She executed her tasks like a highly trained soldier readying for battle.

Tereso wedged the door ajar to allow cool air to circulate in the room and provide Anita with some relief from her fever. Then he rolled her on her side and propped her with extra blankets to allow her lungs to drain. Satisfied, he turned to his children sitting at the table, who watched his every move. "I want you kids to go to bed. Your mother and I will tend to Anita. Now go."

They all mumbled and slowly walked toward the back room except for Angelita. She lingered behind for moment and walked up to her father and asked, "Is Anita sick?"

"*Sí*, little one. She is sick."

Angelita considered this for a moment and asked another question, "Will she get better?"

Tereso sighed and scooped her up in his arms and looked down at her angelic little face. His heart squeezed when he gazed into her beautiful dark eyes that searched his face for an answer. Tereso swallowed hard and said, "You know something? You ask too many questions. Now go to bed. You must help your mother tomorrow." He put her back down and playfully swatted her bottom. Angelita padded off to the bedroom without a second thought.

———••••———

By midmorning of the second day, Anita was still dreadfully sick. Tereso could not see any improvement in her condition, but she had survived far longer than other afflicted people he had tried to help. This gave him hope and he told Paz that Anita had a chance.

During the next five days, Anita fell in and out of delirium. The fever drained the life out of her and the hacking cough seemed to tear her in half. Each family member took turns watching over her day and night. Finally, on the sixth day her fever broke and she began to sleep easier. Everyone but Tereso felt relieved. He knew that intense fevers sometimes damaged toddlers' hearts and the ultimate effects would not be seen until years later. He would have to keep a special eye on Anita as she got older.

In the following days, the children would sit with Anita and keep her company. Alcaria, Joaquina, and Augustine played games with her and drew her pictures. Angelita, however, did not possess these skills yet, but this did not deter her from entertaining her little sister. She would scoot a chair beside the wooden bed and pull herself up. Then Angelita spent a good five minutes straightening her dress, fixing her braids, and tying her bows before finally looking into the bed and addressing Anita.

"You know," she would begin as she swung her bare legs and feet back and forth over the edge of the chair, "everyone thinks that I am so pretty. That's why they call me Angelita, because I look like a little angel. Did you know that?" Anita was not quite old enough to understand that her sister was conceited and accepted everything she said as fact. She responded by slowly shaking her head.

"Well, they do," Angelita continued. She looked around her and rattled on about how she had noticed several girls eyeing her dress and what she thought about that and about a hundred other unrelated subjects. The one-sided discussion enthralled Anita and she listened to every word. Angelita acknowledged this by chatting nonstop for hours until Paz shooed her away.

"She needs to rest now," Paz scolded. "You probably talked her ear off." Angelita put her nose up in the air and stomped off to sulk for thirty seconds before forgetting her mother's rebuke and racing off with her sisters.

As January 1919 emerged, the Minjares household rejoiced over Anita's recovery; she could now leave the confines of her tiny kitchen bed. But their joy was short-lived as a second and final wave of influenza washed through Doña Ana and killed many more of its residents. One of the new victims was Angelita. Tereso and Paz were stunned by the suddenness of her death. In the morning, Angelita complained of a sore throat and by nightfall she was dead. Tereso had to pry his wife's fingers from their daughter's hands as Paz could not bear the thought of letting her precious child go.

Tereso knew he had to bury Angelita quickly to prevent spreading the disease. Since the town cemetery was full, he chose a plot behind the house. Normally, a Mexican laborer would ask his landlord's permission first, but time was essential and the sickness too vicious to worry about protocol. He placed her little body in the same fruit crate that Anita had used as a bed and started to carry her outside.

Paz cried, "Wait!" She ran into the back room and came out with the green blanket Nellie Taylor had given her three and a half years ago when Angelita was born. She lovingly wrapped the little figure in the soft cloth and said a silent goodbye as she tucked in the corners. Tears flowed down her face when Tereso lifted the crate and walked outside. She had just seen another of her babies die and carried off to be buried, wrapped in the child's baby gift. Her knees buckled and she slumped to the floor in a heap of misery.

Tereso walked around the house and placed the crate on the cold dark ground and reached for his lantern. He struck a match and lit the wick. Its wavering light glowed softly over the tiny crate. He hung it on a cottonwood tree and grabbed a shovel. He took one last look at the makeshift coffin before starting to dig. He could hear Paz's sobs through the adobe wall as he sank his spade into the lifeless dirt.

The year 1919 dragged by and went. The residents of Doña Ana picked up the pieces of their shattered lives and carried on. Many miseries went unsaid and were pushed into the recesses of their minds to only be pulled out during special ceremonies and quiet, brooding evenings with tequila. The Minjareses were no exception. With the loving support of her children and the persistent pestering of her husband, Paz managed to live with her loss and opened her heart again. She became pregnant and expected to give birth by the first of March of the next year.

The last days of January 1920 found Tereso tilling Taylor's fields for the spring planting. He ripped the earth with a heavy plow pulled by a team of two horses. He wrestled with the shoulder-high handles that jostled from side to side as the plow bounced along the uneven ground. As the plow turned the soil over, Tereso had to waddle over the furrow to prevent trampling it. It was hard and wrenching work for a healthy man, but it was especially rough on one who was sixty-four years old.

Tereso pulled the reins to halt the horses and took a short rest. He took the flask from his shoulder, uncorked the top, and took a long drink of the warm water. Water flowed down both sides of his mouth as he tilted his head back to drain the flask. When he had finished, he replaced the cork and wiped his mouth with the back of his sleeve. He looked across the field to the Taylor house and abruptly froze. He saw two men in business suits walk up to the door and knock. A few moments later, Nellie Taylor greeted them. The men appeared to introduce themselves and showed her some papers. Nellie quickly scanned them and then invited the men inside.

Tereso was certain that they were the law and had a warrant for his arrest. He panicked and looked for a place to hide, but there was none, only the vastness of the field. His restlessness caused both horses to bend their heads around and look at him in bewilderment. Tereso felt trapped and made a rash decision. He snapped the reins and quickly drove the horses back to the barn. Without wasting any time, he unhitched the team and dragged them into their stalls. When the horses were secure, he turned to flee for the safety of the lush vegetation along the Rio Grande. However, when he got to the door, Nellie stood there talking with the two strangers. Tereso tried to backpedal into the barn, but it was too late. Nellie spotted him and immediately addressed him.

"Tereso! There you are. *Un momento, por favor.*" Tereso froze dead in his tracks. "These men are from the government Census Bureau. Oh, how do you say it in Spanish?"

One of the men stepped forward. "Please, Ma'am. Allow me." He addressed Tereso directly in fluent Spanish, "*Por favor*, do not be alarmed. We are from the United States Census Bureau and we would like to pay your home a short visit."

Tereso did not trust this man and did not want him in his home, but he sensed Nellie wanted him to cooperate, so he asked, "Why?"

"We must count all people residing in this area for government purposes. That is all. We could come over now. It will not take long."

Tereso thought wildly, *They are going to find out that I am a wanted man. I must do something to throw them off my trail!* He looked nervously around and finally blurted out, "First, I must tell my wife that you are coming. She is very pregnant and I do not want you to scare her. After I explain the reason for your visit, you may come over."

"All right," replied the man in an easy manner. He had seen this unfounded suspicion and fear many times before when he interviewed Mexican laborers south of Las Cruces. "We will be along in a few minutes." Tereso nodded and immediately walked briskly around the barn. When he turned the corner and was out of sight of the others, he broke out in a run that he madly maintained for the entire distance. When he arrived home, he burst through the kitchen door breathless and drenched in sweat.

Paz was folding laundry on the table and looked up in alarm. She asked, "What's the matter?"

Tereso's voice was ragged and strained, "Two men. Coming here. Ask you questions about me. Tell them that my name is something else. You know, like ... Santos or something. You change your name too. I must go now and hide." Tereso ran into the bedroom and jumped out the back window.

Paz could not believe what had taken place. She stood silently for a few moments with her hands on her bulging abdomen and tried to think of what scared her husband so badly. Anita brought her back to reality by tugging on her skirt and saying as she pointed out the window, "Pappa gone."

Paz flattened the folds of her dress with the palms of her hands as she got a grip on herself. Then she took Anita by the hand and led her outside and to the garden in back of the home. She quickly grabbed a hoe and began to weed with alacrity. Normally, the added weight of the baby would have strained her back, but not today. She could have hoed an entire vegetable field just to look busy.

A few minutes later, Paz heard Nellie's voice calling for her in front of the home. Paz pretended not to hear as she chopped harder at the nonexistent weeds. She continued her show as Nellie appeared around the corner with the two strangers. The sight of the men dressed in suits and ties made her think that Tereso was right in fearing that they were the law.

Nellie hailed her. "Oh, there you are. Paz, I have two men that want to meet you." Paz stopped her hoeing and shot the men a piercing stare. Nellie tried to allay her distrust with a comforting smile, but as Nellie walked closer, she brushed against a crude cross planted in the ground. She looked at it and realized that it marked Angelita's little grave. Nellie quickly looked back to Paz and saw her watching her. Nellie suddenly felt ashamed and awkward, ashamed because she felt that she could have done something to save this child, awkward because these men were going to ask questions about her family, questions that would have had different answers only one year ago.

One of the men stepped forward and spoke to Paz in Spanish. "*Buenos días, Señora*. We are taking a census for the government. We would like to ask you some questions about your family. We trust that your husband informed you of our coming? By the way, where is he?"

Paz shrugged and remained silent. Nellie swallowed hard and said, "I really must be going back now. If you need anything, please come see me." She turned and briskly left.

The other man pulled out a ledger with specific questions arranged along the top. He readied his pencil to jot down the information. The first man continued the interview. "All right. We just need to ask you a few questions, then we will be going. First, what is your husband's name?"

Paz's mind reeled for a second and she fought to remember what he told her. Suddenly, she remembered the name "Santos". *Of course,* she thought, *Rafael Silva chose that name.* She lifted her head and said, "Santos Minjares."

The man replied, "Santos? I thought *Señora* Taylor said 'Tereso'?"

Paz stood firm. "His name is Santos."

The man nodded to his partner who wrote "Santos Minjares." "How old is he?"

Paz again shrugged her shoulders and said, "In his sixties."

The man was beginning to get annoyed, but her answers were no different than those from others that he had interviewed. His partner wrote "61" in the column and then proceeded to check "rented" under housing, entered "farm labor - working out" under occupation, and wrote "spoke no English and unable to read or write" in the remarks column. He did this without consulting Paz because he had recorded hundreds of Mexican families along the Rio Grande and their stories were always the same.

"Now," continued the man, "What is your name and age?"

Paz thought fast on her feet and said, "My name is Iza and I am thirty."

The man registered a puzzled look because he thought Ms. Taylor said her name was Paz, but he let it go. "Now we need to know your children's names and ages."

Paz was not going give the names of her children to two total strangers. So, she started making names up as fast as she could invent them. "Let's see, Manuela is 14, Antonia is 7, and ..."

Anita thumped her chest and said, "My name is Anita!" Paz wanted to stuff her in a gunny sack to silence her.

"I see little girl," replied the man with a smile. "And how old are you?"

Anita proudly held up three fingers. "I am three."

"My, my," remarked the man as he squatted down beside Anita. "Perhaps you can tell me about the rest of your family. Do you have any brothers?" Anita started to nod when her mother jerked her away and sternly told her to go inside the house. Anita looked bewildered and hurt for a moment, but complied without fussing.

When Anita was out of earshot, Paz answered the question, "We have one son. His name is Miguel and he is six."

"Is that everyone?"

"*Sí*."

The man sighed and knew that the information was, at best, incomplete. "I have one more question before we go. When did your family arrive in Doña Ana?"

Paz's mind whirled. She thought, *If I tell them the truth, they will find out that we were running from the law.* She swallowed hard and answered, "Oh, about four years ago." The census taker wrote "1916" in his final column. He accented the completion of the entry by stuffing his pen in his pocket and snapping the ledger book shut.

Both men bowed and one said, "*Gracias, Señora,* for taking time from your chores to talk with us. *Buenas tardes.*" Without any hesitation, they turned and promptly left. Paz watched them leave as she contemplated her answers. She worried that her replies might haunt her family later. Her baby seemed to move within her in response.

Tereso crept back into the house during the darkest hour of the night. He had laid in the lush grasses along the Rio Grande for hours and watched the roads for pursuers. He finally worked up the courage to go home and discover what revealing questions the government men had asked Paz. Tereso was convinced that this was the law's method of tracking him down. He walked in the door and found Paz sitting at the table waiting for him.

Tereso gulped back his fear and steeled himself for the worst. He sat down next to her and asked, "What did they say? Did they ask about me?"

Paz was relieved that Tereso returned home. She thought that he might try to bolt for freedom and never come back. She also knew that this was a real possibility if his fears were not abated. So, Paz quieted her own misgivings and smoothed her reply. "The men were only taking a head count of people living in the area. There is nothing to be afraid of."

"But did they ask about me?"

"*Sí*, but only your name and age. Nothing more."

Tereso leaned forward and asked, "What did you tell them?"

Paz smiled and said, "I told them that your name was Santos Minjares and you are in your sixties."

Tereso nodded. He believed that her answers were safe, but he still had a nagging feeling that someone was coming for him. He spoke his thoughts out loud, "I think we should think about moving away. Some people here know what I did in Carrizozo. It is only time till the law comes looking."

Paz put her hand on her womb and said, "The baby is due soon. We can't leave for several months. Besides, Tereso, where would we go? Farther north? Let's stay here and make the best of our situation, ¿qué no?" She purposely mentioned "we" to remind him of his family responsibilities.

Tereso tugged at his mustache as he contemplated her words. After a few minutes, he replied, "All right. We will stay a little longer, but I am going to keep my eye open for other opportunities. When something good comes along, we will move." Paz breathed easier. Her husband was not going to run or demand that the family move immediately. She would have her baby in peace and stay at home to nurture it. With any luck at all, Tereso's fear would ebb away and he would forget his desire to travel.

On February 25, 1920, Paz gave birth to a boy. Tereso took the privilege of naming him Benjamin and he was proud to have another son. Ben was healthy and plump and he gave Paz incredible joy when he actively sought her breast for milk.

The birth had a calming effect on Tereso. Ben reminded him that family matters were important and brought him joy. During the following weeks, he concentrated on working hard and helping out at home. He gradually lost his fear of being captured, but kept a watchful eye for any signs of lawmen.

In the spring, Tereso surprised everyone by presenting Augustine with a white colt for his eighth birthday. A deeply appreciative husband had given the little filly to Tereso for realigning his wife's shoulder. The woman had fallen while carrying their baby and dislocated her shoulder joint. The pain was excruciating and her husband could find no one with either the nerve or the skill to reset it. After she suffered two agonizing days without sleep, the man sent a desperate plea through the neighborhood for help. A relative remembered Tereso, but was hesitant because he acted like a ruffian. Finally, the woman's dire condition forced the family to seek all alternatives and summoned Tereso Minjares.

Tereso arrived promptly and knelt beside the woman's bed. With delicate fingers, he analyzed the positioning of the joint and ligaments. Then he surprised everyone present by asking for an unopened can of coffee. At first, the husband thought he was asking for payment in advance and the request shocked him, but Tereso explained that he needed it to reset the shoulder. When the man presented the can, he stood transfixed as he watched Tereso gently slide the can under her armpit. Then Tereso looked softly into her tearful eyes like a man gazing at his lover while his hand slid over her wrist. He leaned forward as if he was going to whisper something in her ear and suddenly yanked her arm down and over the can. The can acted as a fulcrum to lever the joint into the socket. The woman gasped once and it was over.

Tereso stepped back to appraise the situation and let the woman recover from his treatment. The appalled husband started to yell at Tereso for torturing his wife, but she lifted her good arm and silenced him with a wave of her hand. Then slowly she sat up and gingerly moved her injured arm. It was sore, but totally functional. She smiled and said, "I have no more pain. *Gracias, Señor.* I can live again."

After reconfirming her claims, the husband profusely apologized to Tereso and presented him with the colt. Tereso proudly brought the horse home and tied it to a tree in the back of the house. Then he walked inside and sternly told Augustine to march outside because he had a task for him. Augustine put his head down and followed his father to the backyard where he was sure that some mindless chore awaited him. As he turned the corner of the house, he spotted the colt staring back at him with expectation. Augustine stopped speechless and stared.

Tereso chuckled and said, "Well, just don't stand there with your mouth open. Go see if your horse needs water."

Augustine looked at his father with wide eyes and asked, "You mean she's mine?"

"*Sí*, but you must take care of her. If you don't, I will give her away, *comprende?*"

Augustine nodded and quietly walked up to the colt. He hesitantly put his hand on her neck and stroked her mane. The horse bobbed her head in response. Augustine laughed and turned his head to comment to his father when his sisters and mother came out. Joaquina put her hands to her face and let out a gasp. Paz and the other girls were too stunned to speak. Never before had such an extravagant gift been bestowed upon their family. Their reaction made Tereso and Augustine very proud—Tereso because he provided the colt and Augustine because he now owned such a splendid animal.

Tereso broke the silence by remarking, "The boy needed a horse. It's time he learned how to take care of one."

Paz recovered her wits and asked, "How much did it cost?"

Tereso stood a little straighter and replied, "*Nada.* I fixed a woman's shoulder. Her husband gave it to me."

Paz had to admit that she was impressed. She nodded and thought to herself, *Perhaps this will make him want to stay in Doña Ana.*

Chapter 23
El Renganche

During the midmorning of March 24, 1922, Paz delivered another son to the world. Nellie Taylor and a midwife helped her with the birth. Paz's labor lasted only a few hours and she had no complications. Nellie stood up and pressed her palms into her lower back as she stretched. She looked down on the tranquil sight as Paz sat up and cradled her baby. Her three daughters stood beside her like little angelic attendants and stroked the child's face. A stab of envy crossed her mind as she wished that she and Bill could have had more children. Their big house seemed empty while this small adobe shack bulged at the seams with kids. To Nellie, the situation did not seem right.

She shook the hurtful thoughts from her head and put on a soft smile. Nellie bent over Paz and smoothed her hair off her brow as she said, "Paz, *niño es bonito*. However, Paz, I think you should tell Tereso not to be so frisky. You can't be having babies all the time. It is too hard on you. Stop while you are ahead, Okay?" Paz frowned as she tried to understand Nellie's English. Nellie sighed and looked at the midwife. The midwife understood some English and nodded her head slightly to indicate that she would explain the comment to Paz at a later time.

Nellie smiled again at Paz, picked up her shawl, and walked quietly out of the bedroom. She saw Tereso holding little Ben on his lap and Augustine sitting next to him. She smiled and said, "Es *un niño*." Tereso smiled broadly and nodded that he understood. Nellie started to give him the same advice that she had told Paz, but held her tongue. She did not possess the language skills to convey her thoughts, nor did she believe that Tereso would curtail any of his activities if she had been able to speak fluent Spanish.

Instead, she looked around the kitchen to see if the family was in need of anything. The open cupboards appeared full and the cooking utensils looked in good condition. Then she noticed a sag in the thatched roof above the stove. A timber had rotted, bowed under the weight, and misaligned an adobe block in the wall. Nellie pointed to it and said, "Did you see this? This is dangerous. It could fall and pull part of the wall with it. Somebody could be seriously hurt. Tereso, *comprende?*"

Tereso only understood the "*comprende*" part, but he looked where she pointed and shrugged. His indifference infuriated her. "Tereso, fix it. Okay?" Tereso only smiled back at her. "Oh, forget it. I will tell Bill about it. Go see your new baby." Nellie took one last look at the failing roof and marched out the door.

Tereso watched her go and could not understand why she was in such a huff. The roof had been like that for some time. There was no reason to be upset. He dismissed her distress with a wave of his hand and wagged his head at the bedroom door. "Come on, Augustine. Let's see your new brother." Augustine's face glowed with anticipation. They walked into the room and saw Paz holding the baby with the girls standing around her. The midwife was cleaning up the sheets and disposing the evidence of the birth.

Paz looked up and said, "I want to name him José after Saint Joseph. Is that all right with you?" Her strong voice surprised Tereso. The past births had always drained her.

Her suggestion angered Tereso. He thought, *The father should name a boy. Not his mother.* He spoke gruffly, "Was not Saint Joseph's day on the nineteenth ? We should name him something else."

Paz held the baby protectively to her breast and challenged her husband. "Okay. What do you suggest?"

Tereso made a vague gesture and replied, "Well, how about Agapito? That is a fine name, *¿qué no?*"

Paz lifted her baby and looked at his face. "Hum … no, he looks like a José, *¿qué no?*" The girls nodded in unison. Paz smiled and said, "*Sí.* José is a good name." Tereso felt his anger brew. To cement her proclamation, she directed Tereso to walk into Las Cruces and register the birth. Tereso nodded that he would, but set his stubborn jaw tight.

Relieved that her son was properly named, Paz took a moment to look at her family as they stood around her. She marveled how quickly her family had grown. She now had three girls and three boys. She was thirty-one years old and had given birth eight times. Although she felt relaxed, Paz felt her age in her bones, but having her family home, safe, and healthy comforted her. *And*, Paz thought, *what more could I hope for?*

———————

The following morning, as the sun broke over the serrated San Andres Mountains, Tereso set out to visit the Las Cruces courthouse and report the birth of his son. This was the first time that he attempted the task by himself. For Angelita, Anita, and Ben, he had sought the assistance of men who could read and write. He felt nervous and set a brisk pace to complete the task and return to Taylor's fields before the morning passed.

Tereso wore his *sombrero* high on his head and his work clothes were freshly washed. He strode down the railroad tracks in his work boots with his eyes focused straight ahead at the emerging town. He ignored the cheerful bird songs and the fresh dew smells of the early morning and concentrated on the duty before him. Various thoughts ran through his head. *What if some lawman recognizes me? Will I have to write? Why did I not take someone with me?* And finally, *I should have the right to name my son. Not Paz.*

He was flustered and mentally occupied by the time he reached Las Cruces. He made his way through the awakening streets and soon found himself standing in front of the single-story courthouse. It was one of the few cement buildings in town. The thick, dull white walls held a small prison, courtroom, and several city offices. He tried the door and discovered it locked. He sighed and sat down on the small concrete steps to wait for the business day to start.

By the time the sun rose above the rooftops, a man appeared with a large ring of keys and opened the front door. He motioned for Tereso to stay put and disappeared inside. He reappeared shortly, carrying two neatly folded flags. With care and reverence, he un-folded the American flag first and ran it up the shiny metal pole. The red, white, and blue colors unfurled and added an air of authority to the courthouse. Then he carefully unfolded the yellow flag of New Mexico with its blazing orange sun and sent it up the pole to its des-ignated place beneath the American flag.

Tereso thought the man was going to salute as he stared for a mo-ment at the flags in silence, but instead, he turned and motioned for Tereso to come inside. Tereso followed the man into the courthouse and found it surprisingly cool. The man finally broke the silence and asked Tereso in Spanish, "What do you want?"

Tereso answered, "I need to report the birth of my son."

The man nodded and pointed toward an open door. "Please wait in this office. The clerk will be here in a few minutes." Tereso en-tered the sterile office and found a stiff wooden chair to sit in. He waited uncomfortably for nearly a half hour before a middle-aged man arrived. His surprised expression told Tereso that he was not accustomed to having citizens wait for him. The bureaucrat nodded a "good morning" as he quickly organized his desk and prepared for the day. Finally, he laid his pens and forms down in front of him and carefully addressed Tereso.

"How may I be of service, *Señor*?"

Tereso scooted his chair to the desk and said, "I want to report the birth of my son."

"Ah," replied the man, "I can register your son's birth. *Uno momento, por favor.*" He rustled through a leaf of papers and selected the correct form. "All right. When and where was your son born?"

"He was born yesterday in Doña Ana."

The clerk wrote this down and asked without looking up, "And, who is the mother?"

Tereso answered, "Paz Esparza Minjares."

The clerk continued, "And the father?"

This question rankled Tereso. He thought, *I just told him that it is my son. Does he think that I am too old to sire a child?* He answered angrily, "I am."

"Okay, just a routine question," the clerk said smoothly, "And what is your name?"

"Tereso Minjares."

The man wrote this down and asked, "What is your son's name?"

With his anger already piqued, Tereso suddenly remembered his resentment at Paz for naming his son José. Out of pure spite, he answered, "His name is Agapito Esparza Minjares." The clerk wrote this name down and signed the birth certificate to authenticate it. He punctuated his signature with a hard dot of the i.

"Done! Your son is a registered citizen of the *Estados Unidos.* Congratulations!" Baffled at the ease and brevity of the recording, Tereso looked around to see if there was any other paperwork he had to file. The clerk had seen this expression on many other immigrants and knew what was on his mind. He smiled and said, "You can go now. There is nothing more to do." Tereso nodded and slowly stood up to leave. He gave the clerk one more glance to ensure that all was in order and walked out of the room.

Later that night, Paz questioned him about José's registration. Tereso replied that he had handled the entire affair and correctly recorded their son's birth. Paz never pursued the topic further, but her intuition told her that her husband might have screwed up the paperwork. She would never know that her beautiful little José was really Agapito.

The late May evening was unusually hot. Tereso opened the door wide to let the night air circulate through the fragile screen door and into the house. The air was thick with the musky smells of the fertile, irrigated fields. The Minjares family clustered in the front room and participated in several unrelated activities. The baby slept on the floor along the wall in a vegetable crate padded with blankets. Paz knelt next to Anita and showed her how to grind a corn mash called *nixtamal* into a dough with a cylindrical stone on a *metate*. Alcaria, Joaquina, and Augustine worked diligently on their homework assignments and Ben worked equally hard on his doodling and art work.

Tereso sat apart from his family and carefully unwrapped the worn canvas from his most prized possessions. He reverently opened the package and revealed the two ivory-handled pistols securely tucked in black leather holsters. For a moment, he simply looked at them as they lay before him. As he studied the stunning workmanship of the Mexican double eagles on the handles, he subconsciously ran his fingers along the dents on his skull. He had developed a habit of tracing the indentations from that ill-fated night south of Carrizozo whenever he was in deep thought.

Then, with the caring of a loving mother handling her baby, Tereso gently pulled one of the pistols from its holster and gazed upon the blued steel. The gun seemed to come alive in his hand. The barrel balanced perfectly with the weight of the chamber and handle. He pulled the hammer back with his right thumb and half-cocked it. He spun the chamber with his left hand and listened to the purring of the finely machined action. He had never seen a finer weapon in his life.

After the plunge off the cliff by San Agustin Pass and Tereso's groveling through the dust and muck to get home, the guns were packed with dirt. Tereso had spent days dismantling the pistols and thoroughly cleaning every piece. With tender loving care, he restored them to their original beauty and treasured them.

Paz looked up from her teaching and frowned when she saw her husband fondling the guns. He told her that they were unloaded, but she never really knew if Tereso told her the truth. The sight of the pistols around her children bothered her. Suddenly, he looked up and saw her staring at him. He smiled and stroked the barrel one more time before putting it back in the holster and wrapping the canvas around the guns. He stood up and placed the package on top of the cupboards, high above the reach of little hands and out of sight of strangers.

Paz returned to her task of demonstrating the *metate* to Anita. The *metate* was a stone slab, slightly dished, that sloped down to a ridge along the bottom. Two days before, Paz had soaked corn kernels in a diluted lye solution overnight. The next morning, she had washed and rinsed the corn. The process removed the tough outer shells around the kernels and created the pasty *nixtamal*. She dried the nixtamal before grinding it into a dough called *masa*.

Paz took a handful of *nixtamal* and placed it on top on the slab. Then she put a small cylindrical stone in her right palm and set it over the grain. Kneeling in front of the *metate*, she placed her left hand over her right, locked her elbows straight, and pressed the rolling stone into the *nixtamal*. The stone crunched and pulverized the *nixtamal* into *masa* as she rolled it from the bottom to the top of the slab. The *masa* sifted down to the ridge along the bottom. Paz halted her grinding periodically to lift the *metate* and dump the accumulated *masa* into a bowl.

Women had used a *metate* for thousands of years. Hours of grinding flour for the family meal wore heavily on their bodies. Skeletal remains showed significant deterioration of their wrists, shoulders, and, especially their knees by the time they reached their early thirties.

Paz placed a small blanket under the *metate* to catch any *masa* that fell and to cushion her knees. After a few minutes of grinding, she stopped and straightened her aching back. She looked at Anita and said, "Oh, little one. I think Mama needs a rest. Do you want to try?" Anita nodded and knelt next to her mother. "*Bueno*. See, you hold the stone like this." She put it in Anita's little hand. "Now, hold your arms straight and push the rock into the corn." After several tries, Anita started to mimic her mother's rocking motion and pulverize the *nixtamal*.

Paz stood up to give her knees a rest and watched Anita work for several minutes. Her little daughter soon tired and struggled to press on. Paz thought, *Poor little girl. She tires much too quickly. Tereso said that the flu might have harmed her*. She stopped Anita and said, "*Bueno*. Now let's make *tortillas*." She emptied the *metate* into the bowl and brought the *masa* to the counter.

Paz added just enough water to moisten the mixture. She kneaded the *masa* into a smooth ball and pulled small, pliable globs from it. From these portions, Paz rotated the dough in the palm of her hand and patted a thin circular layer. She threw the thin patty on the hot iron skillet on the stove. The *tortilla* cooked rapidly on the bottom. Paz deftly flipped it over with a flick of her hand. The *tortilla* began to rise as the cooked top trapped the hot air within. When she was satisfied that it was done, she flipped the *tortilla* onto a dish towel and covered it to keep it warm.

Paz looked over to Anita and said, "Now you try." Anita nodded and walked over to the ball of raw *masa*. Without any hesitation, she plunged her hand into the ball and yanked out a hand full. Paz advised, "That is too much, honey. Put some back." Anita tried to peel some of the dough off, but it clung to her fingers and made a mess.

"Here." Paz produced a dish towel and cleaned the excess dough off her hands. With the remaining portion, Anita tried to make a neat little *tortilla*. Instead, she made an irregular shape that resembled a horse. Paz smiled as Anita carefully laid it on the skillet.

As Paz watched Anita try to flip the *tortilla* on her own, she felt dust trickle down her neck. She looked up and saw the bulge in the sod roof. It appeared more ominous than before. She pointed to the ceiling and asked, "Tereso, have you seen this? Will it fall?"

Tereso was busy telling Ben about where he had buried a rich treasure in the central mountains of Zacatecas. After Paz called to him again, he stopped his story and looked where she pointed. He simply shrugged and resumed his tale. Her temper flared, but when Anita yelped in pain from scorching her fingers, Paz quickly forgot the failing roof and tended to her daughter's needs.

By the late afternoon of the hot August day, Tereso smelled the rain coming before he saw the towering cumulus clouds in the west. The hazy blue sky was clear, but the wet ozone scent was unmistakable. They were due for rain soon. If he had been able to speak English, he would have mentioned his forecast to Bill Taylor, but he could not and more important matters were at hand.

They were working in the southernmost field that bordered the outskirts of Las Cruces. Their horse team struggled to open a buried sluice box that flumed water from a large irrigation ditch to a smaller channel that paralleled the field. Mud had accumulated along the bottom of the sliding gate and sealed it shut. The men attached ropes to the horses and tried to pull the gate open. The horses faltered as they dug their hooves into the soft tilled soil for purchase.

Taylor's patience wore thin. The unusually dry month had parched his crops. He needed the water to save his field. He thought, *By gawd, I'll dynamite this son-of-a-bitch open if I have to!* The horses snorted in response and strained in their harnesses.

Tereso jumped into the ditch with a shovel and shoved the point under the gate. With all his might, he tried to pry the gate up. The horses pulled, Tereso pushed, and Taylor cursed. Slowly the mud lost its grip and the gate moved. Water trickled underneath, then gushed out over Tereso's trousers. The gate moved easily as it opened wide.

Tereso struggled back to the bank and a happy Taylor helped him up. He slapped him on the back and said, "*Bueno*, Tereso, *bueno*." Tereso was out of breath from the effort and only nodded his response. Suddenly, a deafening clap of thunder boomed nearby. They looked to the west and saw huge anvil-shaped clouds high in the sky where only minutes ago it had been clear. The thunder seemed to stir the air and a cool wind began to blow.

Taylor yelled above the rising wind, "Man, that came up fast! We've got to get out of here before those clouds rip their seams and dump on us. *Vámonos!*" Tereso understood what Taylor said and quickly untied the ropes to the sluice gate. Taylor gathered their tools and slapped the horses on their flanks to move forward. They had to go around the field to prevent trampling the crops, which added to the distance they had to travel to the barn. The raindrops started pelting them before they were halfway around the field. By the time they reached the barn, they were drenched. The sky seemed to open up and dump buckets of water on top of them. Taylor fell down and fought the torrential rain to get up. Tereso threw open the front door. The wind caught it and slammed it against the wall. The noise startled the already frightened horses and caused them to buck.

Taylor rasped, "Get them inside! Go! Inside!" Lightning flashed again and a deafening clap of thunder immediately followed. Tereso grabbed the bridles and led the horses forward. Once inside, the horses quieted down and allowed Tereso to pull their harnesses off. "Ah, damn!" cursed Taylor as he threw his wet hat to the ground. "First no rain, now a gawd-forsaken flood! Those crops are getting the hell beat out of them. Just listen to that wind scream. It sounds almost human ..."

The men froze as the wailing and screaming became clearer. It was the sounds of terrified children. Tereso pushed past the horses and ran out the door. Alcaria slammed into him at a full run. The rain plastered her disheveled hair against her face and her eyes were wild with fear.

Tereso grabbed her with both hands and shook her as he yelled, "What is it? What's wrong?"

Alcaria cried out with a heart-tearing sob, "It's Mamma! The roof fell on top of her! She's screaming! Oh, God! She's screaming!"

Tereso's blood ran cold. He looked over to the house and saw Anita and Joaquina, holding Ben, racing toward him with terror in their eyes. He released Alcaria and bolted for the house. Taylor did not understand Alcaria's Spanish, but grasped that something terrible had happened at the Minjareses' home. He ran after Tereso and fought through the raging storm. The rain poured into his mouth and nostrils with each ragged breath he took and threatened to drown him.

Tereso smashed through the doorway and stopped to get his bearings and adjust his eyes to the dark room. The roof had fallen on top of the stove and pulled part of the south wall down with it. Lightning flashed above the gaping dark hole in the roof and revealed the slumping sod and broken timbers against the brilliantly white background. Rivulets of water poured through the hole and splattered on the pile. Thunder broke and shook the house.

Tereso's senses whirled at the scene before him. He heard the baby cry from the back room. Augustine clawed furiously at the pile of wet sod and adobe brick. Then he heard a bloodcurdling scream come from underneath. It was Paz. Tereso momentarily froze at the horror before diving into the debris. He knocked Augustine to the side and began throwing chunks of sod across the room.

Taylor arrived a moment later and gasped at what he saw. "Oh, Christ!" He jumped beside Tereso and grabbed pieces of broken timbers and wrestled them loose. Suddenly, a moving foot protruded from the pile. Taylor yelled, "Here she is!" Tereso grabbed it and tried to pull Paz out, but the heavy sod held her fast. Taylor removed more wood and brick and Tereso yanked Paz free.

He held her in his arms and wiped the mud from her eyes and nose. Her face was contorted in pain and she breathed in short spasms. She held her left hand slightly above her body as if the slightest touch would kill her. Tereso grimaced when he saw the third-degree burns along the back of her hand. The sod had pushed her into the hot stove while she was cooking.

Augustine crawled up to his father and asked, "Papa, is she going to die?" Tereso did know how to answer. Paz was critically injured and he had no way of knowing if she would survive. He looked into his son's desperate eyes and tried to reply, but the words stuck in his throat. Augustine steeled himself for his father's answer and waited. Tereso tried to speak again when the girls returned with Nellie Taylor.

Nellie wailed when she saw the small form shaking in Tereso's arms. She threw herself at Paz and checked her body for broken bones. Paz sucked in her breath when she touched her back. Nellie then saw her burnt hand and gasped. She looked up and saw the roof had collapsed at the very spot she had warned Tereso and her husband about many months before. Her anger raged as she screamed, "God damn you! God damn you both! You never lifted a finger to rebuild that roof—now look what happened!" Bill looked away as she glared at him. "Now, Bill Taylor, you are going ride out in this storm and get a doctor. And take Tereso with you. He can bring the wagon down and we will take her to our house."

Bill Taylor did not argue. His guilt was too great. He slowly walked over to Tereso and tapped him on the shoulder. Tereso looked bewildered at first, but when he saw Nellie seething at him and the look of resignation on Bill's face, he realized that he was supposed to follow. He gently laid Paz on the floor and quietly left.

Nellie wasted little time taking control of the situation. She told Alcaria to get the baby and comfort him. Then she directed Joaquina to pull the wool blankets from the beds. Nellie wrapped Paz in these and made a pillow for her head. When Paz was secure, Nellie grabbed a dish towel and carefully wrapped her hand.

Satisfied that she had done everything possible, Nellie motioned for the children to gather around her. They came close to her without hesitation and sat next to her. Nellie threw a blanket around them to comfort them and waited for their father to return.

The storm broke as suddenly as it had come. A light mist continued to fall, but the wind ceased and a quiet evening fell. Tereso pulled up with Taylor's wagon. Nellie helped him to carefully lift Paz into the wagon. Tereso quickly got several sacks of corn and used them to prop Paz's back as she laid on the floor boards. The children climbed in and Tereso slowly drove the horses to the Taylor home.

———————

The doctor discovered three crushed vertebrae and two broken ribs along Paz's back. He wrapped her torso to support them. Then he cleaned her burn and bandaged it with gauze. It was the best he could do. If she had been white or had come from a respectable Hispanic family, he would have prescribed an opium-based painkiller, but society frowned on Mexican laborers receiving such treatment so he left her a bottle of aspirin.

Bill Taylor and Tereso spent the next two weeks renovating the Minjares home. They rebuilt the south wall, tore the sod roof off, and replaced it with sheet metal. They shoveled the muck out of the front room and repaired the cooking stove. Nellie cleaned the house and made it liveable again.

By the third week, Paz was ready to move back. Tereso and Bill carried her on a stretcher from the Taylor house to her home. They laid her on her bed and made sure that she was comfortable. Nellie fussed about the home until Bill put his arm around her and led her away.

As soon as they closed the door, Tereso took matters in his own hands. For several weeks, he had yearned to treat Paz, but Nellie Taylor had prevented his intervention. Now he was free to use his *sobador* skills. He laid a blanket on the floor and placed sacks of flour on top. Then he lifted Paz and gently laid her down on her side on top of the blanket. Tereso placed the sacks strategically behind her, then slowly rolled her on top of them. The sacks of flour conformed to the curvature of her spine and provided comfortable support. Paz could now breathe easier.

Next, Tereso unwrapped the gauze from her left hand and inspected the wound. The charred skin was sloughing off and scar tissue forming underneath. The deformed skin was beginning to tighten and contort her hand. Tereso cleaned her hand with soap and water, then applied a healthy coating of aloe vera pulp over the burn. Then he carefully dressed and rewrapped the hand.

Tereso stepped back and evaluated Paz's condition. She appeared as comfortable as possible, warm, and her left hand protected, but there was something else that disturbed him. She was different, changed somehow. He knelt beside her for a closer look—then he saw it. Her eyes had changed. They no longer contained the spirit of a young and vivacious woman. They looked hard, cold, and years older. The roof had crushed more than her bones. It squeezed life out of her and left a bitter shell.

Nellie hired a midwife to nurse Paz a few hours a day and cook a meal. Under the direction of Tereso, the midwife slowly bent Paz backward over the sacks of flour to stretch and realign her back. Paz would numbly go through the exercise and winced when the stabbing pain became too great. Tereso wanted Paz to regularly squeeze a ball of cloth in her left hand to stretch the healing skin and muscles. Paz only halfheartedly complied. The midwife tried to force her to compress the ball, but Paz would let it drop out of her limp, withering hand.

Tereso entered another harvest season with a sad home life, guilt hanging over his head like a dark cloud, and the scrutinizing eyes of Doña Ana upon him. He worked with Bill Taylor to collect the year's meager yield. Daily, he caught people walking by the fields and watching him out of the corner of their eye. They looked at him, then over at the new shiny metal roof on his house, and back to him and shook their heads. Tereso felt their accusing stares and it rankled him. Taylor felt them too. They both worked in silence, each mired in deep, brooding thoughts.

The harvest gradually concluded in October and Tereso began his reduced workday schedule. This meant more time to spend at home, but this prospect was not a happy one. Nellie Taylor had dismissed the midwife because Paz could now direct her daughters to perform the basic housekeeping tasks. This suited Tereso just fine because he was tired of the midwife's scornful looks.

Paz was healing and could sit up by herself, but her back was bent and her burnt hand had atrophied. When Tereso tried to massage her back muscles and spine, she snapped at him to leave her alone. So he often went on long evening walks after dinner, anything to stay out of the house.

During his strolls through Doña Ana, he encountered people he knew who lived in the area. He would nod or greet them with a "*Buenas noches*," but they usually looked the other way or pulled their *sombreros* over their eyes and kept walking. For someone who loved to be the center of attention, this was hard to take.

On a cold February night in 1923, Tereso wandered through the lonely streets when a voice called out to him, "Bitter night for walking, *¿qué no?*" Tereso stopped and stared at the dark figure sitting in a chair under a store awning.

"Who are you?" he asked.

The man chuckled and struck a match to light a cigarette in his mouth. The soft flickering glow lit his face for a moment before he snuffed it out. Tereso recognized him and said, "*Señor* Madrid. A little cold for smoking outside."

Madrid slowly got up and walked up to him. The glow of his cigarette looked like a red eye. "Actually, I was waiting for you to come by." When Tereso remained silent, Madrid continued, "I have a business proposition for you."

Tereso answered flatly, "I am through with running guns."

Madrid managed a forced laugh and said, "That is all in the past. No, you have something that I want, and I am prepared to make you an attractive offer. Interested?"

Tereso was suspicious and felt reluctant to carry this conversation any further. He answered carefully, "What is it that you want?"

Madrid sensed his hesitation and decided he needed to soothe Tereso with two very powerful tools, praise and liquor. He put his hand on Tereso's shoulder and steered him toward his *rancho* as he said, "*Por favor*, Tereso. Let us get out of the cold. Come to my warm home and we will discuss the details over a fine tequila, *¿qué no?*" Tereso had not had a drink or been invited into someone's home for many months. Despite his trepidation, he decided to accept Madrid's offer and walked to his home.

When they were inside Augustine Madrid's rancho, Madrid wasted little time in seating Tereso in one of his comfortable leather chairs and pouring him a tall stiff drink. Tereso soaked in the attention and savored the mild burning of the tequila sliding down his throat. Gradually, his inhibitions loosened and he began to tell grand stories of his days on the *jaripeo* circuit. Madrid appeared to enjoy the yarns and laughed at the appropriate times. All of this made Tereso feel very good.

When the time seemed right, Madrid finally got to the point of their meeting. He leaned toward him with his drink in his hand and said, "Tereso, you have something that I am prepared to pay a lot of money to have."

Tereso's curiosity rose. He raised an eyebrow and asked, "What would that be?"

Madrid smiled and replied, "You possess a remarkable pair of pistols. They were destined as a gift to a very important person before you took them. I said nothing because you deserved them for the danger that you faced on every trip, but the gun deliveries are over and the danger is gone."

Tereso looked at his glass and swallowed hard. He loved those guns. Scarcely a night would go by without his taking them down from their hiding place and fondling them. They represented his only extravagant possession. Tereso slowly shook his head and said, "They are not for sale."

"Oh, come now!" retorted Madrid. "Anything is for sale for the right price. I bet you never even fired them, *¿qué no?*"

The comment rankled Tereso. He set his jaw firm and repeated, "They are not for sale."

Madrid got up and walked over to the bar. He shook his head as he poured another drink. "You don't know the significance of what you have. Surely you must have wondered who would have been worthy of wearing ivory-handled pistols with the double-eagle insignia?" Tereso remained silent and watched him over the rim of his glass as he sipped his drink. Madrid returned to his chair and continued, "Those pistols were destined for Pancho Villa to wear as he brought Mexico out of the tyranny of dictatorship. You have no right to keep them. I want to deliver them to their rightful owner."

Madrid's revelation momentarily stunned Tereso. Until now, he had never given the pistols' ownership a second thought. He possessed them and that was all that mattered. Now, the knowledge that the guns had been meant for Villa made them even more valuable. He was also amazed at how his life intertwined with the rebel leader. They were like brothers.

Tereso put down his glass, stood up, and said, "They are mine. I will not sell them." He grabbed his hat and coat and started for the door.

"Minjares!" Madrid's voice halted him. Augustine Madrid remained sitting and nursed his drink. After a moment's silence, he spoke in a low, authoritative voice, "You are not liked here in Doña Ana. People say that your laziness caused your wife's accident. If I were you, I would take the money and move away from here. *Comprende?*" Tereso answered by putting on his *sombrero* and resumed leaving. "All right," continued Madrid with resignation in his voice, "have it your way. At least see that new labor agent in Las Cruces. I understand that he has some new opportunities up north." Tereso pretended not to hear and closed the door behind him.

The obese man strolled down the Las Cruces street with a pained and laborious gait. His three-piece wool suit fit tightly around his girth and his tight shirt collar made his face slightly red. Life had been good to John Dillon, but he had lived it excessively. He ate and drank without restraint, smoked too many expensive cigars, and dabbled in frivolous luxuries. Once he even had supported a mistress in Missouri while lavishing expensive gifts on his wife in El Paso. Now, the money was spent, his wife had divorced him and taken more than half his net worth, the mistress had abandoned him, and his body was wrecked.

Dillon was not a man who mourned misfortune. Instead, he'd picked up his shingle and moved to the greener pastures of Las Cruces. He had absolute confidence that he could hit it big again. All he needed to do was find another brown wave of Mexican labor to ride and roll in the cash. His instincts told him that another wave was forming and it promised to be as big as the last. He had heard talk of the government finishing a large irrigation project in Montana that opened thousands of acres to farming. Adequate water combined with hot summers and fertile soil made this region suitable for America's newest cash crop, the sugar beet.

The only ingredient needed to turn the farmers and sugar companies into wealthy businessmen was cheap labor and this is where John Dillon entered the scene. He contacted Holly Sugar and Great Western Sugar and formed an arrangement that would be immensely profitable to all. For a fee, Dillon would recruit Mexicans willing to relocate to Montana to work the sugar beet fields. The sugar companies would charter old passenger train cars to haul the workers and their families north to the waiting fields.

Dillon smiled to himself as he thought about his arrangement. His body sweated profusely by the time he reached the small adobe building that he rented for his office. The building was a plain single-story structure with a front and back room. Once he installed the necessary window between the rooms, it was perfect for his business. Dillon hired local women to clean it and men to build a sturdy shelf to support his enormous coffeemaker. Tomorrow was Saturday, a day when men had a chance to escape their jobs and move freely around the community. Dillon craftily chose that day to open for business. He would hang his banners, make his coffee, and see whom his aromas attracted.

Dillon reviewed his arrangements and smacked his lips with satisfaction. He had one more factor weighing in his favor. Last week, he had contacted the civil leaders of Doña Ana, Las Cruces, Mesilla, and Chamberino and offered them a business deal. If they referred potential recruits to him, he would pay them a dollar for every man who signed up. The response was very positive and Dillon could almost smell the future profits.

• • • •

It was a beautiful May morning and Tereso decided to take the Saturday off. Bill Taylor seldom lectured him anymore and Tereso felt that he had earned the vacation. Since both home and Doña Ana held people who despised him, he chose to walk to Las Cruces and seek out men who would appreciate his company. The walk lifted his spirits and put him in a jovial mood as he entered the town and began to mingle. He struck up a conversation with a few men by a street corner and quickly became engrossed in trading stories. He drank up their attention like a fine wine. It had been a long time since he had people to entertain.

Suddenly, a booming voice distracted him. "I knew we would find him talking men's ears off."

"*Sí*, Tacio, except his tales are even more unbelievable than before."

Tereso whirled around and faced Anastacio Currandas and Victoriano Vallejo, both grinning from ear to ear. He spread his arms out wide and engulfed them in a massive bear hug. "Tacio. Victoriano. It is good to see you. What are you *hombres* doing here?"

Victoriano shrugged and said, "We are unemployed and looking for work. How goes it for you?"

Tereso brushed off the question with a wave of his hand and replied, "*Bueno.* There is plenty of work to be found in digging ditches for the *federales*, also some farm work, too."

Anastacio shook his head and said, "I am getting too old for digging ditches and we should stay far away from the *federales*, *¿qué no?*"

Tereso demeanor turned grim for a moment as he contemplated the last few years. While gunrunning was exciting, it had taken a heavy toll on them. They would always be looking over their shoulder.

A warm wind stirred the light morning air and carried the fresh aromas of the wakening town. Victoriano inhaled deeply and exclaimed, "*¡Dios mío!* Smell those fresh *tortillas* cooking and I can almost taste that coffee!"

Anastacio moaned as he sampled the air. "I haven't had a decent cup of coffee in years. It smells heavenly."

Tereso agreed. He closed his eyes as he took in the smells. The coffee triggered a vague memory of deceit and gave him an uneasy feeling. He searched his mind for an answer to his foreboding when

Victoriano interrupted his concentration with a shout. "Look! Those men are running to that building with the sign that says 'Work Now'! and some are leaving with coffee."

Anastacio set his jaw firm and proclaimed, "I am going see what jobs are available and have some of that coffee at the same time."

Victoriano nodded excitedly, "*Sí*, that sounds *muy bueno*! I am coming too. How about you, Prud...er—I mean Tereso."

Tereso felt that he had crossed this path before and his sixth sense prickled, but he was never a man to pass up a free cup of coffee with old friends. He smiled and said, "Let's go." With that affirmation, the river of fate once again carried him and his friends to their next destination and deposited them at the doorstep of John Dillon, Labor Agent.

When they arrived at the building, a line had already formed and stretched outside. The delicious coffee aroma wafted from the door and made the men's mouths water. Every so often, a man would muscle his way out with a steaming mug of coffee in his hands, but the majority of the men stayed and socialized. When Tereso finally got inside, he felt like he had been there before. The front room was large and crowded. A massive coffeemaker perked on a sturdy counter that also supported stacks of cups and generous amounts of cream and sugar. Men turned the tap on the reservoir and poured mugfuls of coffee. Then they shoveled in copious amounts of cream and sugar to make a lip-smacking mixture. Of course, all of this took time and none of the waiting men had any patience. Many pushed and shoved to prod the line to move faster.

Tereso looked around the room and inspected the pictures on the wall. His eyes riveted to one that displayed a proud man standing next to his adoring wife and a man who Tereso recognized as *Señor* Dillon. He remembered how that picture had affected him ten years before in El Paso. He looked to the back wall with a large window that exposed the back room and saw a large, worn man discussing something important with three men who seemed to hang on his every word. Tereso studied the hefty man and suddenly recognized him. It was Dillon. Tereso thought that his physical appearance had changed substantially, but his mannerisms were identical to the first time they met. He still put on a good and believable show for all his prospective victims.

Tereso leaned over to Tacio and said, "I know the proprietor. He is a snake. Let's drink his coffee and scoot." Tacio raised his eyebrow at the comment, then nodded. Victoriano, on the other hand, did not hear Tereso's warning and became enthralled with the charged atmosphere of the room. Men all around him talked about the golden opportunities north. They chugged down their steaming mugs of sweetened coffee and chatted about the pictures of men just like themselves who had found success. The excitement was infectious.

Suddenly, three men burst from the back room with official-looking documents in their hands. One man proclaimed, "I am going to be rich! I just got a high-paying job in Montana and I leave on a train in two days!" Jealous men crowded around him to catch a peek at his contract, although none of them could read English.

A smiling Dillon walked into the front room, rubbing his hands together like a cat cleaning his paws. As soon as the crowd spotted him, a riot ensued as men fought for their turn to join the train. Dillon raised his fleshy hands to calm them and yelled, "*Señores*, no need to fight, *por favor*. I have many lucrative contracts ready for your signature on the back table, see?" Dillon pointed toward a long table along the back wall with neatly stacked forms strategically placed along its length. "Take one, *por favor*, and read it. I am here to answer your questions. If you were sent by your town leader, please tell me, so I can personally thank him."

The crowd bolted for the table. Victoriano got swept up in the moment, but Tacio grabbed him by the collar and held him back. Victoriano yelped, "Let go of me, you big ox!"

Anastacio answered calmly, "There is plenty of time. Besides, you are next in line for coffee."

The gold fever left Victoriano's eyes as he turned toward the coffee canister. He looked briefly over his shoulder at the scattered forms and frenzied men as he poured himself a cup. Tacio and Tereso followed close behind and, in short order, they were all sipping their sweetened creamy mixtures and watched the scene before them. Men tried or pretended to read the English-written contracts. Others blindly signed and waved the completed forms at Dillon. Dillon appeared calm as he wrote down their personal information on a notepad. His eyes flicked at each written name like a cash register ringing up a sale.

After Dillon congratulated each recruit, the man would run out the door with his contract in hand and proclaimed to the world that he had just snatched a golden opportunity. His proclamation attracted more curious men to Dillon's door. If they had any reservations about entering, the delicious coffee aromas usually overwhelmed them and broke down their defenses. Potential laborers poured in and Dillon's fortune soared.

Victoriano, Anastacio, and Tereso watched the whole process in fascination and poured themselves another mug of coffee. "You know, *amigos*," said Victoriano as he stirred the cream into his coffee, "I need a job and if this *gringo* can get me a good one, what is the harm of talking to him, *¿qué no?*"

Tereso answered gruffly, "Because I swallowed his bull in El Paso and ended up in Carrizozo. That's why. I worked hard and made little money."

"You also got yourself in trouble, *¿qué no?*" Anastacio reminded him.

Tereso grumbled something unintelligible as he sipped his drink. As if signaled, Dillon lifted his eyes from his notepad and studied the three men by his coffeemaker. Dillon had a gift of reading men and heading off trouble. These men appeared unaffected by the frenzied activity and, therefore, represented a potential problem. The last thing Dillon needed was three independent thinkers wrecking his business. He had to silence them before they started convincing people to stay away from his establishment.

Dillon snapped his book shut and motioned to the men around him that he would be right back. Then he strode confidently to the three troublemakers who stood a part from the crowd. He put on his most charming smile as he greeted them, "Ah, *buenos días, Señores.* Do you have any questions that I might be able to help you with?"

At first the men glanced at each other to see who was responsible for calling Dillon over to them. After they exchanged baffled looks, the men turned to Dillon and shrugged in unison. Unperturbed, Dillon continued, "Well, enjoy your coffee. You are under no obligation to sign up for this exciting opportunity. It is not for everyone. I am sure you can find work digging ditches around here. I hear the government is hiring. *Adios.*" Dillon turned to leave.

Anastacio snapped first. "Wait! I am not a ditch digger. Tell us more about this opportunity, *por favor.*"

Dillon smiled as he slowly turned to face the stout man and thought, *I have a bite.* "Well, now," he said as he sized Anastacio Currandas up, "I would be honored to explain the details. Would you be so kind as to step into my office in the back room?"

"No!" commanded Tereso with an edge to his voice. "You will tell us together out here, *comprende?*"

John Dillon was unaccustomed to orders. He thought, *Who does he think he is?* Dillon stepped toward Tereso for a closer look. *The man looks familiar, but I can't place from where. He certainly is in good shape for a man of his age.* Dillon gave Tereso a disarming smile as he replied, "That is no problem. I thought you might be more comfortable sitting down."

Then Dillon addressed all three in a voice that easily carried throughout the room. "The opportunity that I speak of can be summed up in two words, Sugar Beets. Ever heard of them? I am not surprised if you have not. Sugar beets represent the newest cash crop to hit the markets. They grow like giant turnips. The leading sugar manufacturers of the *Estados Unidos* discovered a method for distilling sugar from this bulbous root. Imagine, making sugar without buying high-priced sugar cane from Puerto Rico or Cuba. At today's sugar prices, the farmers and manufacturers are capturing large profits from sugar beets. What does this mean to you, *mis amigos?* It means that the farmers and sugar companies can afford to pay you high wages for bringing in this crop and building a new sugar plant plus many side benefits such as transportation, housing, relocation assistance, and the list goes on and on. Do you see why I am so excited for you?"

Dillon dangled the same lure that silk traders, diamond buyers, and sellers of gold claims have used for centuries, the possibility of becoming rich. Men who worked and struggled every day to make ends meet kept their sanity by perpetuating dreams of striking it rich. They dreamt of the respect and adoration of their families and peers that their newfound wealth would bring them. When they finally perceived that an opportunity to achieve riches was near, an irrational fear exploded in their minds that their one and only chance would escape forever if they did not jump at it. This emotion caused men to abandon solid, dependable jobs and loving families and stampede to the California goldfields or claw their way to the Klondike where the gold seams were plentiful. After the dust settled and sanity once again prevailed, the men returned defeated, depressed, broke, and with a verified tale that someone else got rich.

The revelation of sugar beets captivated Victoriano Vallejo, Anastacio Currandas, and even Tereso Minjares. They could feel the chance-of-a-lifetime opportunity rise before them and beckon them to ride it. Then, fear set in that they might miss this opportunity and caused them to press forward. Anastacio momentarily broke the spell by asking, "Where are the sugar beet fields located?"

Dillon pretended to check a list in front of him, but this was just a show because he already knew the answer. "Well, let's see here. It says the next train will be leaving June 9 to Sydney, Montana to build the new Holly Sugar factory."

"Sydney, Montana?" replied Victoriano, "Where in the hell is that?"

Dillon casually waved in a northerly direction, "Oh, a little ways north. I hear that the summers are cooler than here. That sounds *muy bueno*, eh?"

"*Sí*," replied Tacio, "but how do we know that you are telling the truth?"

Dillon snapped out an important-looking paper from his tablet and said, "It is all written down here in this contract. See?"

Tacio took it and tried to read the English. After a few moments, he gave it back to Dillon and nodded. "You are right. It is all in writing."

Even though Tacio could not read a word of it, he was not about to admit his shortcomings in front of all these men.

Dillon smiled slyly as he took the vague contract back and thought, *Pride gets them every time. Now to set the hook.* He swung his arm toward the back table and said, "If you are still interested, you may take one of the contracts on the table. You can sign anytime you like, but please remember that the companies may fulfill their labor requirements soon and cancel any future offers. The risk is yours."

Victoriano and Anastacio looked at each other for a full second before bolting for the table. Tereso held back. He was not immune to Dillon's persuasion, but he had seen Dillon's empty promises dissolve the minute he and his family stepped off the train. The El Paso & Northeastern Railroad experience had left a bad taste in his mouth. Despite his reckless nature, Tereso Minjares did not want to repeat a mistake.

Dillon noted Tereso's reservation and approached him with caution. "Is there something that I can answer for you?" he asked. Tereso shook his head and remained quiet. "Come now," persisted Dillon, "why are you afraid of this glorious opportunity?"

Tereso jutted out his jaw and snapped, "I am not afraid."

"Well, what then? Why are you not joining your friends?"

Tereso looked Dillon straight in the eye and said, "You don't remember me, do you? The railroad job in El Paso? You made the same promises then as you do now and they turned out to be lies."

If Dillon was ruffled, he did not show it. He smiled back at Tereso and replied, "I am sorry, but I don't remember you. I meet a lot of men in my business. It is impossible to remember everyone, but I believe you. I can only offer what the companies agree to. It is not my fault if they fail to honor their contracts." Then he leaned toward Tereso and continued in a low voice, "All I can assure you is that sugar beets are making a lot of people rich. This means that there is much more money to pay you than what the railroad could. Besides, an experienced man like you would most likely be a foreman. I can tell that you are a natural leader."

Dillon's words mollified Tereso and fed his ego. "You really think so?" he asked.

Dillon knew he had him. He answered, "Most certainly. So, tell me, *Señor.* Are you satisfied with your current job? Do they treat you well and use your leadership capabilities to their fullest? I bet not. What do you have to lose, eh?"

Tereso had to admit that he had a point. In addition, nobody in Doña Ana, including his wife, liked him anymore. He thought, *"Maybe if I got a job as a boss, Paz would like me better."*

As if Dillon read Tereso's mind, he added, "Just think how proud your wife will be when she finds out how important her husband has become."

That cinched it. Tereso smiled and straightened his back to his full height and proclaimed, "I will do it!" He marched over to the table and grabbed a contract and a pen. With much concentration, he signed his name in bold, awkward letters and swallowed *El Gancho* again.

Dillon stuck out his fleshy hand and gave Tereso a friendly handshake. "Congratulations, *Señor*. You have made a wise decision. You must keep this contract with you. It will allow you and your family to board the train. Now, remember, you must bring only the essentials. The company cannot be expected to move all your household possessions. I am counting on you as a future leader to set an example, *comprende?*" Tereso pumped his chest out and nodded. "*Bueno.* Be at the train station in Las Cruces by eight o'clock in the morning on June 9 and we will load you in."

Dillon escorted Tereso, Victoriano, and Anastacio to the door and waved as they left. All three walked with buoyed spirits and discussed their future prospects with great anticipation. They passed an old man sitting against a wall about half a block away from John Dillon's office. He chuckled as they walked by and called out, "So, you *hombres* going take a ride on *El Renganche*, eh?" His comment stopped them dead in their tracks. Mexicans sometimes called a work train *El Renganche*, which roughly meant "surrendering to the hook", a term that referred to a worker's lack of choices and the real possibility that he would never return.

Tereso faced the man and quipped, "Why do you say *El Renganche?* We are doing this of our own free will."

At this, the old man really guffawed and slapped his knee. Wiping the tears from his eyes, he said, "Oh, that was a good one. *Señor* Dillon really knows how to put on a show, *¿qué no?* I bet the only choice you had was whether your 'free' coffee needed one sugar lump or two. You were hog-tied and slapped on the butt before you knew it."

The man's comments angered Tereso. If this irritating old man had been younger, Tereso would have slugged him. Tacio tugged at his sleeve and said, "Come on, Tereso. Leave him to his senseless cackling."

The old man quickly retorted, "Then ask yourself this question. Are you coming back? If so, how? That train won't take you. This is a one-way trip, *Señores.* You *hombres* bit the hook Dillon dangled in front of you and when you board that train, the *gringos* will have you trapped. You must do their bidding, work their fields, and accept their terms. You have no choice. Enjoy your ride on *El Renganche*."

Anastacio grabbed Tereso by both shoulders and steered him

away from the laughing man. They walked in silence for a few blocks farther, each deep in his own thoughts, bothered by the man's comments. Finally, Victoriano broke their thoughts by asking, "Did we do wrong?"

Anastacio shook his head and said, "We needed jobs and I am not going to dig ditches for the *federales*. So, who knows? Going to Montana is about as good of an idea as any." Victoriano took heart in this and continued in silence.

Tereso, on the other hand, was still troubled by his decision. He fretted that Dillon had suckered him again. He thought about the trip north and saw the similarities to his last train ride to Carrizozo; the incredible opportunity, the chance to make lots of money, promises of housing and food, the formal contract. He needed more time to think. "*Amigos*, I must go home and prepare for the trip. I will see you in less than two weeks, *¿qué no?*"

Tacio saw the turmoil in his eyes and understood that he needed to be alone. He said, "*Sí*. We will meet you at the train." He and Victoriano watched Tereso turn and slowly walk toward Doña Ana.

Tereso followed the railroad tracks home. He walked down the center of the ties and contemplated how fate pulled him along. He thought, *Why must I always move? But, I cannot stay here. Everyone despises me. What kind of life awaits me in Montana?* At that moment, he looked up and saw the tracks stretch north to infinity. It gave him an uneasy feeling as he remembered a vision he'd had many years ago. Then he understood its significance and said quietly to himself, "I am not coming back, am I?"

———•••———

Paz cursed him silently as she stuffed the last of her children's clothes in the old trunk. She was mad enough about moving, but his insistence that they take only one trunk for the whole family was ludicrous. Tereso declared that the terms of the contract that he waved in her face specifically stated that each family was allotted one piece of luggage. Paz could not read English, but she doubted that such a clause existed.

She stepped back from her packing and tried to straighten her aching back. Her ribs and vertebrae had healed, but her spine was slightly bent, causing her to slouch. She pressed her hands into the small of her back to support herself as she looked at the packed crate. Paz had packed one change of clothes for each of her six children, a few precious photos, a skillet and a pot, and two blankets. There was no more room for any more basic necessities. She would have to struggle to close the lid.

Anita walked up to her, holding a special dress. "Mama, I want to take this one, too."

Paz felt her heart tear as she looked at her daughter. "I am sorry, little one, but I can only put so much inside this trunk." Anita slowly lowered her arms and pursed her lips into a pout. Paz forgot about her backache and bent down to give Anita a hug. "I know what we can do," she cooed. "I will make you a little backpack to wear and we will fold your dress into it. Okay?" Anita nodded and wiped the tears from her eyes. Then she looked up to her mother and beamed. Paz smiled at her and told her to put the dress on the bed.

As Paz watched her leave, she felt her anger rise again. She had lived in Doña Ana for eight years and accumulated the most possessions she had ever had. Now she had to leave them all behind because of her husband's stupid directive. In addition, he packed his beloved pistols that occupied precious volume that Paz could have used for the family. She stared at the impossibly small trunk again and shook her head.

Tereso bounded in the door and announced, "*Señor* Taylor will take us to the train tomorrow. He will pick us up at seven."

Paz responded by narrowing her eyes and saying, "We need another trunk. I can't fit the children's clothes in just one."

Tereso shook his head, "No. The labor agent said to take only one trunk. My contract says so too."

Paz snapped, "I bet your contract doesn't say a word about luggage! Nobody can read it because it is written in that pig-English."

Tereso held a finger up and said, "Just one." Then he left as abruptly as he had come.

Paz stood fuming as she glared at the closing door. She had a hunch that he had invented this one-luggage requirement to enhance his own standing in someone's eyes. She gritted her teeth and prepared for tomorrow.

Bill Taylor helped Tereso slide the heavy trunk off the wagon and carry it to the train platform. Tens of families were already there and milled in small groups with their possessions stacked behind them. Taylor squinted into the low morning sun and looked at the multitude of people. *It looks like a mass migration*, he thought with dismay. He accepted the loss of Tereso Minjares and knew it was time for him to leave. He had stayed far longer than any of his previous help, but by the way everyone was leaving in droves, Taylor anticipated being hard pressed to find a replacement.

Taylor gave Tereso his final pay and wished him well. He turned to bid Paz farewell, but one look at her hard face and he stopped cold. He managed a weak wave, climbed onto his wagon, and left.

Paz watched Taylor drive off before looking around her. She saw familiar faces, but most appeared from other outlying towns. Then she saw the heaps of luggage that every family was taking and her eyes narrowed in anger. She pointed toward the piles of goods and said to her husband, "How come they can bring so much and we can take only one trunk? Don't they have the same contract?"

Tereso seemed undaunted. He shrugged his shoulders, "Well, we will see what kind of jobs they get in Montana." His flippant response only infuriated her more.

"Tereso! There you are!" shouted a man from the crowd.

Grateful for the chance to look away from his wife's piercing stare, Tereso turned to the voice and smiled when he recognized its source. "Anastacio! *¡Hola!*" Anastacio and Victoriano made their way across the train platform to the Minjares family. The men winked at the children and tipped their hats to Paz before engaging Tereso in friendly banter.

"Ready to ride *El Renganche, amigo?*" laughed Victoriano.

Tereso chuckled and replied, "*Sí*, it is time to leave this place, *¿qué no?*"

Anastacio answered, "I think so, but I think one of your beautiful daughters is having second thoughts." He pointed toward Alcaria.

Tereso was puzzled. "Huh? What do you mean?" He glanced at his fifteen-year-old daughter and saw her casting mournful looks toward a boy standing behind the platform. The boy also appeared distraught and beckoned Alcaria to come to him.

Tereso had absolutely no idea about what was taking place under his nose, but Paz wasted no time in disrupting the lovesick couple. She grabbed Alcaria by the arm and jerked her behind Tereso. Then she shot daggers of hatred at the poor brokenhearted boy. The young man quickly backpedaled out of sight.

Joaquina was holding José and squealed with delight at the spectacle. Alcaria spat back and Paz hushed them both. Tereso rolled his eyes at his family and shrugged his shoulders at his friends.

Suddenly, a man shouted and the crowd pressed forward to peer down the tracks. A train was backing up to the platform. A conductor waved the crowd back to prevent someone falling beneath the wheels. Soon, railroad employees took the men's contracts and checked rosters before letting each family load their luggage and board the train. When the conductor took Tereso's contract and matched the name to his roster, he asked Tereso where the rest of his luggage was. Tereso proudly said that the one trunk was it. The man just shook his head and waved them aboard.

Soon, the last families were loaded and the train began to chug forward. The children hung out the windows and chatted excitedly as the world moved past. Even Alcaria temporarily forgot her shattered love life and became engulfed in the excitement. Tereso, however, felt strangely reserved and took a moment to review his life. He was now sixty-seven years old. He had six young children and one trunk of possessions to show for his lifelong efforts. He was embarking on another venture in the northern state of Montana, which was very far away. He did not know what he was going to do when he got there, where they would live, or how they would exist. He suddenly felt fragile, like his life was out of his control. Then the thought hit him. *I really am on El Renganche.*

——•◆◆•——

During the early morning of July 20, 1923, Francisco Villa drove his new black Dodge down a small side street in Parral, Chihuahua. Although he had driven a full hour from his ranch, he still overcorrected when he steered and veered from side to side. His chauffeur, Rosalío Rosales, made his driving even more comical by hanging from the open window and balancing on the runner board as he shouted instructions to Villa. The five passengers inside the vehicle braced themselves for a crash. His impeccably dressed secretary, Miguel Trillo, sat in the back between two burly bodyguards, Rafael Medrano and Claro Hurtado. In the front seat sat Villa's assistant, Daniel Tamayo, and another bodyguard named Ramón Contreras.

Villa careened toward the intersection of Gabino Barreda and Calle de San Juan de Dios at about seven o'clock. Rosales screamed as he pointed at the floorboard, "The brake! *¡Dios mío!* The brake!" Villa cursed as he struggled to push the middle pedal with his left foot, then switched to his right without engaging the clutch. The car began to bog down and lurch forward as the engine struggled against the high gear.

Rosales banged the soft convertible top with his fist to get Villa's attention. "The clutch! Push the clutch in!" Villa uttered some derogatory remark as he depressed the clutch pedal and ground the gears as he shifted. Trillo crossed himself and rapidly muttered a prayer to the Virgin Mary. It had been his idea to meet at the bank at such an early hour to complete their business transactions. Rumors abounded about possible ambushes and attempts on Villa's life. Because of these threats, Trillo thought that the early morning would be safer than arriving when crowds choked the streets.

Villa looked up from battling with the stick shift and saw that he was entering the intersection. At the same time, he noticed a nut and candy vendor standing behind his cart. The man looked straight at Villa as he passed and saluted. Villa thought that this was odd because cart vendors usually started pushing their products around noon and the salute was oddly timed, like a signal. The groaning of the engine snapped Villa's attention back to his driving. The car almost died as Villa started his turn onto San Juan de Dios.

Suddenly, a door kicked open from the corner store. Four British-made 303 rifle barrels protruded and fired hollow-point "Dum-Dum" bullets into the Dodge. The bullets, designed to penetrate its target and explode, ripped into Rosales and reduced him to a pile of shredded flesh. The car died partway through the intersection as Villa pulled his revolver and fired through his open window. A gun barrel flipped up and disappeared into the doorway as one assailant fell dead. A second door blew open and four more rifles appeared. The next volley concentrated on Villa and eviscerated him and Tamayo. Francisco Villa, the infamous and revered leader of the Mexican Revolution, died at the age of forty-five.

The bodyguards, seasoned men from years of battle, instinctively rolled out of the restrictive car and into the street. Trillo drew his pistol and chose to stay within the vehicle. Within a heartbeat, eleven Dum-Dum bullets blew him apart. The remaining three men fought bravely and managed to escape toward the safety of the Guanajuato bridge. Horribly wounded, Contreras and Hurtado died a few hours later on the riverbank. Medrano suffered from an abdominal wound and died eight agonizing days later.

The Parral undertaker did his best to make Villa's corpse presentable. By holding the internal organs together with celluloid, he managed to keep the body intact and dressed him in a suit. A photographer snapped a picture of the body lying in a coffin in the foyer of the Hidalgo Hotel. The picture soon found its way into most Mexican homes in Mexico and the United States, a grave remembrance of a man who had fought for them.

Chapter 24
Sydney

When the small flotilla led by William Clark navigated the lower Yellowstone River in 1806, they noted the oceans of waving grass that stretched to infinity across the vast plains. Rumbling herds of buffalo, fat mule deer, and fleet-footed antelope dotted the landscape. The land seemed rich, capable of supporting livestock, and the Lewis and Clark expedition eventually submitted reports to President Thomas Jefferson stating such.

Within two decades, small groups of adventure-seeking cowboys drove stringy longhorns and other tough breeds from Texas to these plains to fatten and multiply, but the frequent blasts of arctic air produced devastating blizzards in the winter. During some years, the harsh winters almost wiped out entire herds, leaving only a few standing skeletons on frostbitten hoofs to recuperate in the spring. To add to the cattlemen's hardships, the long trek to the markets in Kansas City and Omaha depleted the herds and, ultimately, their profits. The completion of the Utah & Northern Railroad in 1880 solved this transportation problem and greatly assisted the cattlemen in establishing a foothold in eastern Montana.

After Montana achieved statehood in 1889, dry-land farmers trickled into the area to try their luck at growing wheat and oats. The settlers concentrated their farms along the banks of the Yellowstone River. The deep, sandy soil proved adequate to sustain intensive agriculture, but the fourteen inches of average yearly precipitation presented the farmers with a problematic choice. In years of below-average rainfall, the semi-arid land required irrigation. However, during above-average years, the fields sustained crops without assistance. Thus, the farmers wanted an irrigation system, but did not want to commit large amounts of money and capital to achieve it. Their irrigation attempts resulted in a disorganized system of small ditches, modest canals, and a few dams on local streams that severe weather often destroyed.

The farmers' feeble efforts finally attracted the attention of the Bureau of Reclamation in 1903. The Bureau commissioned several studies of the Lower Yellowstone and determined that a diversion dam and canal built eighteen miles downstream of Glendive, Montana would irrigate about 64,000 acres. Consulting engineers estimated the cost of construction to be a whopping $1.8 million, a huge sum for land marginally deficient in water. Nonetheless, Secretary of the Interior Ethan Hitchcock authorized the construction in 1904 and directed the Bureau to start construction by 1906 and complete it by 1908.

Construction went poorly during the course of the project. Inadequate geotechnical design of the dam caused several failures. Floods, severe winters, and expensive materials and labor forced many contractors to default on their contracts. When the dam and the canal were finally completed in 1909, the delay and construction problems had pushed the costs to $2.3 million.

Undaunted, the Bureau continued to expand the irrigation system and eventually extended it to North Dakota. Farming communities such as Intake, Burns, Savage, Crane, and Fairview sprung up by the system's dams, reservoirs, and pump stations. These settlements contained clusters of Germans, Danes, and Russians who worked on the canal system.

Sidney was the largest community along the canal. Farming, ranching, and the railroad had established this community before the Bureau started construction. Crane and Fairview straddled Sidney and a single two-lane road connected all the farming towns. When residents escaped their farms or homes for a night out, they usually came to Sidney. The town supported a movie theater, a few night clubs, and many bars.

At first, the stable source of water substantially increased wheat production along the lower Yellowstone Valley, but the farmers failed to properly rotate their crops and yields began to drop steadily after 1910. The Bureau responded by advocating the planting of alfalfa and sugar beets to replenish the soil. The plan worked as crop values rose from $130,000 in 1910 to $730,000 in 1918.

The land's suitability for raising sugar beets caught the attention of the Great Western Sugar Company. In 1917, Great Western cultivated three hundred acres to validate previous production claims. The experimental plot produced favorable results and the company began encouraging the planting of beets. By 1920, sugar beets were the second most prevalent crop grown in the Yellowstone Valley, producing an average of $130 per acre. To poor dirt farmers, this was real money and spurred the expansion for further cultivation.

To get their product to market, farmers carted their beets to distant railroad sidings and stacked them in long, high piles. Later, the railroads sent gondola railcars to haul the beets to Great Western's sugar reduction plant in Billings, Montana or to other factories farther south, and charged a substantial fee for the service. The Holly Sugar Company recognized this transportation problem and saw a tremendous opportunity to break into the Valley's sugar beet production. In 1923, Holly Sugar announced that they would start the construction of a new sugar reduction plant in Sidney. The result of building this plant so close to the beet fields was to save the farmers a staggering $100,000 in annual freight charges. The farmers quickly responded by turning more land into sugar beet production.

Since the cultivation of sugar beets was labor intensive, the increased production quickly outstripped the local labor force. Determined not to repeat the Bureau of Reclamation's experience with high-priced labor, Holly Sugar sought to import cheap manpower to help build the plant and work the fields. Mexican labor proved to satisfy both of these needs. The company eventually found agents in New Mexico and Texas to gather the Mexicans and bring them to Sidney, but like so many great plans, the devil was in the details. Disputes in landownership and late delivery of materials delayed the plant's construction. Instead of postponing the importation of workers and their families, the company decided to exercise their labor agreements and bring them anyway. When the trains brought the Mexican families to Sidney in early June 1923, they found no one waiting for them and no shelter and food. They were truly marooned in an alien world that spoke no Spanish, and far from anywhere that did.

The train slowed as it approached the outskirts of Billings. Anita poked her head out the open window and let the warm summer wind blow her dark braids back. She squinted into the mid- morning sun and took in the glorious sounds, smells, and sights around her. Above the rhythmic clacking of the rail wheels, she heard the sweet call of the meadowlark. Red cliffs rose to the north and seemed to form an impenetrable wall that stretched forever and hemmed in a bustling town. On the other side of the car, Anita saw thick stands of tall cottonwood trees that sometimes opened and gave her glimpses of a river. She smiled and returned to her seat.

Anita prodded Alcaria to look out the window, but she could only produce a sleepy moan from her sister to leave her alone. Anita looked at the other members of her family and found all except her father in various forms of sleep. He was gone and nowhere in sight. She wanted to tell him about the town ahead, so she slipped off her bench and walked down the swaying railcars to find him. As she neared the end of the last car, she saw her father gesturing to several men as he described something out the window. She stepped closer to hear.

"The conductor told me that is the Great Western sugar beet factory," explained Tereso. The men shuffled up to the windows to get a good look. Large smoke stacks protruded from the enormous three-story facility, and huge sheet metal silos towered beside the building and amplified its size. Tereso noticed that the ground and side railings were littered with dark brown turnip-like roots and they piqued his interest.

Victoriano exclaimed, "They must be *loco* if they expect us to build a factory like that! We will die as old men before we are done."

Anastacio agreed, "It will take many men to build this. Much more than we have in this train." Several men murmured concurrences as the train rolled by the factory.

Soon, the train cleared the clustered neighborhoods and picked up its speed. Tereso was lost in thought as he gazed upon the farmlands along the Yellowstone River. Anita shuffled up to him and peered out the window. Her father put his arm around her and gently held her to him. She buried her head into his side and reveled in her father's smell and strength. Tereso subconsciously stroked her hair and continued to stare at the changing landscape. *This land is so different than Doña Ana*, he thought. *It must be colder. There are no fruit trees.*

Anita sensed her father's brooding and asked, "Papa, when will we get to Sidney?"

Her soft voice melted into Tereso's thoughts and brought him back to reality. He looked down at her and said, "The conductor told me that we will arrive in the early evening. Not that much longer, *¿qué no?*"

Anita sighed and pushed her head back into his side as she replied, "I guess not. We have been traveling for so long." Tereso smiled and continued to look out the window. He remembered the ordeal of walking to El Paso. In comparison, a few days' riding a train was a luxury that his little daughter could not possibly comprehend.

The train continued at a steady pace for hours until stopping briefly at the switchyards of Miles City. When Tereso took a quick stroll to stretch, he noticed something vaguely familiar about the landscape. It wasn't until the train turned north after passing through Glendive that he could put his finger on it. The countryside looked strikingly similar to the terrain around Monte Escobedo, the same sweeping barren land with plateaus and rugged hills. Only the land bordering the river and the canal system was green. Tereso suddenly felt at peace and comfortable with his decision to come to Montana.

They rolled into Sidney as the sun split its last rays of light over the horizon. The soft glows illuminated the lonely station as the train squeaked to a gradual stop. The men and their families stood clutching their meager belongings, ready to end their long and uncomfortable journey. Paz stood next to her husband and held a small pouch of some food and possessions. Because her back was still weak, Alcaria held little José. The rest of the children clustered around their parents as they stretched their necks and stood on their toes to catch their first glimpse of their new home.

The conductor placed a portable step at the foot of each car's stairway and signaled for the passengers to disembark. Everyone stepped down with an orderly calmness and quietly reassembled on the station platform. At first everyone looked around and then at each other for some sign of what to do next. Finally, Paz broke the silence with a concise question to her husband that seemed to be on every mind, "Where are the company bosses that you promised?"

All eyes seemed to swivel to Tereso and rivet on his face. Tereso momentarily squirmed under the accusing stares until he regained control of his composure. With false bravado he quipped, "They will be here shortly. The train probably arrived sooner than expected. In the meantime, I suggest we all make ourselves comfortable." A groan rose from the crowd as people began to sit down under the awning and unload their burdens.

"I bet no one comes," spat Paz as she adjusted her dress and sat on the floor. Her comment generated a few grumbles of agreement around her and made Tereso mad.

"*¡Jesús!*" he yelled, "I told you that they would come. They will come and you will see! Who here doubts me?" Everyone except Paz looked at the wooden floor. She continued to glare at him until it became too dark to see and even then he felt her hot eyes bore into his skull.

Victoriano woke with an aching back and a kink in his neck from sleeping on the hard floor and using his knapsack as a pillow. He pushed his hat off his forehead and painfully sat up. The brilliant early-morning sun skipped its rays under the awning of the rail station and warmed him. He squinted through the glare as he massaged his neck and looked around him. Anastacio snored softly beside him, and a few people were stirring and making their way to the one and only outhouse. Victoriano licked his dry lips and rocked to his feet.

He pressed his hand into the small of his back and strained to stand up straight. He groaned, "*¡Dios mío!* I must be getting old."

He took a couple of awkward steps toward the edge of the train platform and suddenly stopped. Facing him were two farmers silently standing before him with deep curiosity. They each wore faded bib overalls with flannel cotton shirts and wide-brimmed straw hats. They stared at each other for a moment before Victoriano slowly raised his hand and waved. The men slowly nodded, but kept their silence. Without taking his eyes off the farmers, Victoriano cleared his throat and called out to Tereso, "Ah, Tereso. Wake up! We have visitors."

Tereso woke not knowing why and lay in a stupor for a moment as he tried to get his bearings. Then he heard someone call out his name again. This time he struggled into a sitting position and blinked his eyes into focus. His throat was dry and made his voice sound hoarse, "*Sí*, what is it?"

A voice answered, "Tereso, are these the men from the company?"

Tereso turned his head toward the voice and saw Victoriano facing two men. He quickly gathered his senses, stood up, and came alongside Victoriano. He raised his hand to the men and said, "*¡Hola! Buenos días, Señores.*"

One of the farmers leaned to the other one and whispered through the side of his mouth, "What the hell did he just say?"

The other replied, "I don't likely know, Leon. I think he is talkin' Spanish or something."

"Well, how in the hell are we going to get them to work in our fields if we can't talk with them? And just take a look at all them young'ins and womenfolk. There must be fifty or sixty of them. What are we goin' a do with all of them? I ain't got places for another two or three families. How about you, Josh?"

Josh shook his head and said, "I reckon that I am in the same boat ya're in, Leon, but Lord knows that I need help with my crops. My wheat is about ready to fall and my beets sure need thinning. I say we go a git that Mexican butcher down at the Sidney Provision Meat Market and bring him over here to interpret for us."

Josh shoved his hands deep into his pockets and nodded, "Yep. I think that's a plum good idea. I gotta git my wheat in too and my beet fields need some attention. Let's go grab him before someone else comes round." The men turned and walked backed to their wagon and left without another word or a wave.

With puzzled looks on their faces, Tereso and Victoriano watched them go. When the farmers drove off, Victoriano turned to Tereso and asked, "What was that all about? They did not even answer you."

Tereso shrugged and replied, "I don't know, but the company men should be here any time, now." He said this with a false confidence in his voice. Victoriano sensed his uncertainty and shook his head as he walked away. Tereso watched him go and knew that his leadership was going to be severely challenged if the company representatives did not arrive soon. His group had limited food and water, and judging by the hazy blue sky, the day was going to be a scorcher. Tempers were going to flare.

An hour later, Tereso's worries materialized. It started when Paz fired a barrage of insults at her husband. Then several other women joined the fray offering their opinions on the matter. When Tereso retaliated, several men rose to defend their wives. The whole scene might have degenerated into a lynching if Anastacio had not stepped in and pointed to the group of men standing in front of the platform. They had arrived during the heat of the battle and stood watching the drama unfold. The combatants stopped in mid-sentence and after a few awkward moments of silence, moved back into their family units.

Tereso moved slowly to the front and nodded to the men. Ten farmers stood mystified at what had caused such a ruckus. Tereso's gesture snapped Leon back into reality and he prodded a Mexican man who looked to be in his thirties to step forward. The man wore a white shirt and black pants that were speckled with blood. He took off his hat, revealing a balding head, and held it in front of him with both hands. By the way he fiddled the brim, Tereso could tell that he was very nervous. The man slowly walked up to the platform and tilted his head back to address Tereso. The platform's height caused Tereso to tower over him. He nervously cleared his throat and addressed Tereso in Spanish, "*Buenos días, Señor.* Are you and your people looking for work?"

Tereso smiled and thought, "*Finally, someone that I can talk to.*" He pulled back his shoulders, stuck out his chest, and answered, "*Sí.* Holly Sugar brought us to build the factory and work in the fields. Are you from the company?" The man appeared puzzled by the question and looked uncertainly back to the farmers.

Leon asked, "What did he just say, Antonio?"

Antonio replied, "He's looking for a Holly Sugar representative. He says he is here to build a factory and work in the fields."

Josh scratched the back of his neck as he contemplated the situation. "Well, I hear tell that Holly is gonna delay the plant construction for a year. So, the way I figure it, these people are free to work where they see fit."

"Yep," agreed Leon, "that's the way I see it too. Antonio, tell these people about the delay and we all here have work for them."

Antonio nodded and turned back to the huge man in front of him. "*Señor*, it appears that the factory construction will start next year. So, these men have farms that need your people. Will you go with them?"

The news temporarily caught Tereso off balance, but he forced his expression to remain calm. He quickly recovered and held his finger up to signal that he needed a moment. He turned to the crowd in back of him and boldly announced, "Holly Sugar has decided to delay construction for a year."

Paz cut in, "I knew it!" Several people renewed their argument.

Tereso silenced it with a chop of his hand, "Enough! These men own farms that need our help. They are willing to take us. I say that we go with them, *¿qué no?*"

Everyone looked at each other in silence for a moment. Finally Anastacio shrugged and said, "It makes no difference. They have work and we are here to work. I say that we go with them."

Tereso smiled, turned to Antonio and said, "We will go to their farms."

Antonio nodded and returned to the waiting farmers. "They will go."

"Great," said Leon, "now you need to help us divide them up. We will take them in our wagons."

Antonio hated his newly appointed position of interpreter. He wandered back to the crowd and explained that the farmers would take them to their new homes and that he would help introduce them to their employers. People looked at each other for a moment before slowly gathering their belongings and moving toward the wagons. The men walked ahead to meet the farmers and Antonio introduced each one. Anastacio went north with a farmer who owned sugar beet fields south of Fairview. Victoriano rode south with a man who owned a ranch and farm outside of Savage.

By pure chance, Leon was paired with Tereso. He was hesitant to hire an older man, but he looked strong and capable. As far as Leon was concerned, beggars couldn't be choosers. He needed help or he would lose his harvest. Leon asked Antonio to tell the family to load into the wagon. Antonio turned to face the Minjares family when his eyes fell upon Alcaria and he was thunderstruck with love. He stood speechless and stared at her. Alcaria felt embarrassed by his obvious attention and looked shyly at the ground. Antonio stepped around Tereso and walked up to her. After an awkward moment, he nervously asked her name. Alcaria brushed a strand of hair behind her ear and blushed, but before she could speak, Paz grabbed her by the hand and yanked her away. She stuck her face up to Antonio and hissed, "She is too young for you! Go away!" Then Paz dragged Alcaria to the wagon and shoved her in.

Antonio stood speechless as he saw this beauty prepare to ride away. There were so few Mexican women in Sidney and he always told himself that when he finally met a nice girl, then he would pursue her aggressively. Antonio also knew that this trainload of Mexicans was just the beginning of many more to come. Those trains would carry more women, but many more men. He had to find out who she was and talk with her before competition arrived.

Looking for another option than the mother, Antonio approached the father. He was lugging a heavy trunk to the wagon. Antonio put on his hat and ran to him and grabbed a handle. His action surprised Tereso, but he accepted the help with a grunt of thanks. Together they carried the trunk to the waiting wagon and swung it aboard. Tereso let out a deep breath and said, "*Gracias*. I appreciated the help."

"*De nada*," replied Antonio. "By the way, my name is Antonio Borrego." He stuck his hand out to Tereso.

Tereso took it and said, "My name is Tereso Minjares."

Antonio was on a roll and pressed forward. "Minjares, eh? And is this your lovely family, *¿qué no?*"

"*Sí*," replied Tereso as he pointed to members in the wagon, "this is my wife Paz and this is my oldest daughter ..." He stopped speaking when he saw Paz grit her teeth and shake her head at him to be quiet. *Has she gone loco?* thought Tereso. *What is she doing?* He shrugged and continued, "and this is my daughter Alcaria." Paz groaned and slapped her forehead. Her actions bewildered and annoyed Tereso.

Antonio reacted quiet differently. He pounced on the name and said it slowly, "Alcaria Minjares."

"*Sí*, that is what I said." Tereso was again bewildered by what he regarded as weird behavior. "Well, we best be getting off. *Adios*."

"*Sí, adios, Señor*," replied Antonio as he watched Tereso climb aboard and Leon snapped the reins. The wagon started with a jolt and began to pull away. He waved to Alcaria. She returned a weak wave and quickly looked away. *Well, it's a start*, thought Antonio, *until I come to visit*.

———————

The farmers of Sidney were not prepared to house their Mexican helpers, nor did many really care. The farmers had three temporary needs for the Mexicans and no desire to keep them for the entire year. The three needs were harvesting the wheat in early June, thinning and weeding the sugar beets during the summer, and harvesting the beets in the fall. The farmers could meet all other demands of their farms with local labor. Thus, the farmers looked for temporary solutions to fulfill the year-around housing problem and saw no need to build expensive permanent homes for their field workers. With little thought, they pushed their Mexican help into their chicken coops, cattle shelters, tool sheds, and run-down shacks. These structures stunk from animal waste, and had no water or sewer. Lucky occupants had a solid roof and an outhouse in the back. Others coped with drafty walls and makeshift latrines in discreet places.

The Minjares family was luckier than most. Leon asked his hired help, Mr. Hansen, if he could share his one-room house with the family. The elderly gentleman valued his privacy, but he also was a compassionate man and realized that this family had no place to go. So Mr. Hansen agreed on the condition that Tereso did not drink. "I won't live with a drunk under this small roof," Mr. Hansen said. Leon agreed and promised that the next time he found Antonio Borrego, he would make sure that Tereso knew the ultimatum.

Mr. Hansen hung some old blankets across half of the room and signaled to the Minjareses that one side was his and the other was theirs. Hansen also gestured that they would share the kitchen in the middle. Tereso and Paz got the idea and immediately began settling in. Although their meager possessions took up little room, their six children filled the cramped space. Paz was not looking forward to arranging sleeping quarters.

Leon came early the next morning to fetch Tereso for work. He simply pulled his wagon up in front of the house and pounded on the door. Hansen had rustled Tereso out of bed an hour earlier and fed him some cornbread, beans, and coffee. Tereso knew that it was time to start work, but it grated on his nerves just the same to be woken up and told to get going. He grudgingly agreed and trudged out the door to meet his employer. Leon pointed toward the wagon and Tereso climbed silently aboard with Hansen.

The wagon bumped and jarred down a narrow dirt road as Leon urged the horses to maintain a fast trot. Tereso sat in the back and surveyed his surroundings as they sped along the countryside. Tall, massive cottonwoods lined both sides of the road. He caught the fertile smells of freshly turned earth and heard birds singing sweetly in the clear morning air. The weather was already warm and it promised to be a hot day.

Since the rising sun was on his right, Tereso judged that they were heading north. Soon, they broke out of the cover of the cottonwoods and rode out into vast fields of wheat. The road narrowed and became rougher as they skirted field boundaries. Tereso looked over the top of Leon and Hansen and saw a congregation of men and equipment ahead. Leon drove straight toward them and reined in the horses next to the group.

Leon greeted the men as he jumped down and walked toward them, "Howdy, gents. I brought an extra man to help out." Leon jerked his thumb back toward the wagon. In unison, the farmers looked over at Tereso and raked their evaluating eyes over him.

"A Mexican!" exclaimed a man. "Kinda old, ain't he? Hell, can he even talk English?"

Leon anticipated this response. He pushed his hat back and said, "We need help and this is the best that I can do. I suggest we make the most of it." The men started to grumble. Tereso caught their drift and it angered him. He jumped off the wagon and walked toward them. The men went silent when they saw his size and fierce eyes.

Leon waited until Tereso was beside him to give him his orders, "Tereso." Tereso looked at Leon. Leon pointed toward the thrasher. Then he pointed toward the waiting team of horses. Tereso got the idea. Leon wanted him to hook the thrasher to the horse team. Tereso nodded and walked over to the equipment. He had never seen this odd contraption before, but he recognized the tongue and grabbed it. The thrasher was heavy and pulled stiffly. Tereso put his back into it and gradually it moved forward. He managed to drag it a few feet before stopping.

The men never offered a hand and watched him closely. Tereso thought that they were setting him up to fail and felt his anger rise again. He threw the tongue down and marched over to the six-horse team. He grabbed the lead horses by their bridles and coaxed them backward. The team moved awkwardly back until they were directly in front of the thrasher. Tereso released his grip on the bridles, walked to the back of the team, and connected the equipment to the yoke. The men were impressed. Seizing the moment, Tereso grabbed the reins and swung up to the driving seat. He was ready to drive. The farmers laughed and one cried, "By Jimmy, he's ready to go! Better get him down, Leon, before he thinks he owns the place."

"Nope," replied Leon. "I think he earned it and he seems to know his way around horses, too. Let's try him out." Leon climbed up on the thrasher and stood behind Tereso. He put his hands on Tereso's shoulders for support and signaled to drive on. Tereso snapped the reins and the team moved forward.

For the rest of the day, Leon explained how the harvesting process worked to Tereso through a series of hand signals and pantomimes. Tereso would line up with the furrows of wheat and guide the horses as straight as possible. As he started his run, he pulled a lever next to his seat that activated a wide paddle wheel that pushed the wheat across a cutting bar. The bar cut the stalks and dropped them to the ground in a neat row, ready to be raked later.

Several men fired up a steam-powered grain harvester in the corner of the field. The men strategically positioned the enormous harvester at the juncture of several fields. The farmers had collectively rented the equipment to harvest the grain from all their fields. They took turns processing their grain. Leon's field was first.

After the wheat was cut, Leon directed Tereso to hook the team to the rake and wagon. The rake had long metal tines on a large wheel that scooped the wheat stalks and dumped them in the wagon. Leon elected to drive the horses and commanded Tereso to spread the wheat evenly through the wagon as the rake heaped it on board. Tereso plunged his pitch fork into the billowing waves of wheat and tried to prevent any from spilling over the sides of the wagon. Within minutes, Tereso was covered with itchy chaff.

When the wagon became full, Leon drove the team to the puffing harvester. Using pitchforks, Tereso and the farmers threw the wheat into the receiving bin. The harvester separated the grain from the stalks and chaff. A large auger removed the grain and deposited it into large grain wagons pulled alongside the harvester. When the grain wagons filled to their limits, the farmers drove them to nearby grain elevators for storage until the train carried their crop to market.

Under the searing sun, harvesting became a grueling process. The heat soaked through Tereso's body like hot water and throbbed within him in cadence to the pulsating drone of the locusts that emanated from the trees around them. As the temperature rose, the insects became louder. Tereso chugged down a massive gulp of water before resuming the driver's post and moving the team forward.

The heat forced the men to rest their horses regularly. Usually, this entailed a break in the morning, an hour lunch, another break in the afternoon, and working till dark. Then the exhausted animals and men stumbled home for the night.

When Tereso finally staggered through the door haggard, sunburnt, and filthy, even Paz felt sympathy for him. The children pulled his boots off and Paz wiped his face with a wet cloth before feeding him a simple meal of tortillas and beans. Paz also served Mr. Hansen, who nodded his thanks before slowly eating his meal. This work was hard on elderly men. They were both asleep before their heads hit their pillows.

———•••———

Not everyone was excited about the prospect of Holly Sugar building their new sugar plant near Sidney. In particular, an elderly gentleman locals called Old Man Hardy wanted the plant built elsewhere. He lived alone in an old shack east of town, not far from the railroad tracks. An eccentric, he wore rags for clothes and an old, moth-eaten buffalo cape for a coat that he kept strapped to his back even during the heat of summer. Despite his appearance and living conditions, he was not poor. He owned vast wheat fields around his ramshackle home, which generated a sizeable income.

Hardy's problem stemmed from the fact that he did not believe in paying property taxes or repaying bank loans he had acquired for seed or equipment. In his altered way of thinking, he believed the community owed him because his family had settled these parts long ago and successfully accumulated wealth and power. In Sidney, residents associated the Hardy name with prominence and named a school, bank, and countless other institutions after the family. The majority of the Hardy family did not share their wayward relative's opinions and distanced themselves from him. They viewed him as an outcast and publicly disavowed any relationship.

The Hardy family wanted the Holly Sugar plant built next to Sidney. They feverishly believed that the facility would increase the value of their farm holdings and their profits in the sugar beet trade. The family lobbied the company and offered any assistance required to facilitate building the new plant. Company officials responded by stating three main parameters for their preferred building site. They wanted level property alongside the main rail line with adequate room for several side tracks, vast agricultural land surrounding the building site, and close proximity to the Yellowstone River canal system to provide adequate production water. If Sidney could provide a site with these attributes, Holly Sugar would invest in a plant.

The Hardys thought about the requirements and realized that their weird relative possessed the perfect site. Since he was in default on loan payments and taxes, the sensible thing to do would be to foreclose on his property. Once the city and the bank foreclosed, the Hardys would arrange it to be sold at a nominal price to Holly Sugar to cover outstanding debts and expenses. The city and the bank readily accepted the idea with the condition of the bank harvesting the wheat before the property was transferred to the company. There was only one unpleasant task before them and that was to break the news to Old Man Hardy.

An elder Hardy drove his shiny new black Ford pickup to his relative's shack to discuss the arrangements with him. Within minutes, the discussion degenerated into a shouting match and the buffalo-caped Hardy's discharging his Hawkins 50-caliber rifle into his cousin's truck. The elder Hardy drove off in haste and promptly filed assault charges against his wayward relative. The Sidney police responded with every able-bodied man they could muster. With sirens blaring, they roared down narrow dirt roads to the Hardy farm.

Paz was outside hanging freshly washed clothes to dry when she heard the sirens. She had never heard the sound before and was at a loss to comprehend its significance. Her children were playing in the front yard next to the street. As the noise grew louder, the children stopped what they were doing and stared in the direction of the oncoming sound. Suddenly, the police cars rounded a corner and came barreling down the street. The children shrieked and ran for the house. The cars blew by them at breakneck speed. Paz saw the officers inside holding rifles and scared her. The Minjares family watched the cars disappear in a cloud of dust.

The sirens did not completely fade, but seemed to halt a short distance away. Loud, amplified voices carried through the air that Paz did not understand.

"Okay, Mr. Hardy, we don't want any trouble now. Give yourself up and come out real peaceful like."

Hardy bellowed back, "I will give up all right! One lead ball at a time!" Then he shot his black powder rifle at the sheriff and blew the windshield out of the squad car. The men scattered and took cover. "I've got plenty more where that came from, you yellow-bellied land grabbers!"

The siege of Old Man Hardy had begun. The sheriff sent for reinforcements and by the afternoon he surrounded the Hardy shack with men. Hardy exchanged shots with his visitors throughout the day, inflicting no wounds, but keeping them at bay. The standoff continued into the evening until Hardy discharged another shot into the side of an already perforated squad car. By now, the sheriff had estimated that Hardy required about one minute to reload his Hawkins rifle. Sensing that the minute was his, the sheriff charged the shack and overpowered Hardy without firing a shot. The bank and the city now controlled the property.

The day's events terrified Paz. She kept her children hidden inside until Tereso came home. She told him about the racing cars, the lawmen, and gunshots. Paz was certain that this area was bad and they should make arrangements to leave immediately.

Tereso was too tired to care. He and Mr. Hansen had finished the wheat harvest and Leon dragged Antonio back to tell him to rest up because the sugar beet thinning began next week. Tereso did not know what that entailed, but it sounded like hard work. Antonio also told him that some of his children could also work the fields with him, especially Alcaria. Tereso thought Antonio strange to mention Alcaria when he should have emphasized Augustine, but shrugged it off as a mistake. He was going to take his three oldest children with him and make four times the money and that was all that mattered.

During 1923, prohibition of alcohol was a major topic of conversation in Sidney. Prohibition baffled the immigrants that came to work the canal and farms. To them, the restriction was illogical within the very country that trumpeted freedom. The law appeared reckless and implemented without forethought.

However, prohibition was not a spontaneous invention, but a concept that took almost a century to materialize. Throughout the 1800s, American reform groups had lobbied for the prohibition of the sale and shipment of alcohol. Their efforts usually won some initial support before withering in the echoing halls of Congress. Between 1900 and 1920, the reformists persisted in their cause and finally convinced politicians that alcohol was the root of America's problems. They claimed it caused poverty because people drank themselves into a stupor and caused health problems that American taxpayers eventually paid to cure. Alcohol also caused abusive husbands to beat their children and wives. The reformists proclaimed that immigrants would become more "American" if their drinking habits were curbed. Religious groups even preached that drinking was immoral.

Congress bent to their feverous constituency and passed the Webb-Kenyon Act in 1913, which forbade the mailing and shipping of liquor into any state that banned such shipments. The reformists, or "drys" as some called them, were not satisfied with the Act and called for a prohibition amendment to the Constitution. World War 1 provided the drys with the impetus to attain such an amendment. In 1917, Americans were prepared to give up luxuries so that their boys could be well equipped and nourished overseas. When the amendment for forfeiting their liquor came up for debate in Congress, the American public overwhelmingly supported it. Some thought the sacrifice would somehow help win the war. In December 1917, Congress approved the Eighteenth Amendment that prohibited the manufacture, sale, transportation, import, and export of "intoxicating liquors." The states ratified the amendment in January 1919. In October 1919, Congress passed the Volstead Act that enforced the amendment and defined intoxicating liquors as those containing at least a half of a percent of alcohol. The Eighteenth Amendment went into effect in 1920.

Although prohibition may have throttled the alcoholic consumption of many Americans, it did little to curb the deep-seated social habits of Sidney's immigrants. Liquor was an important element of customs and rituals performed by the Russians, Poles, Irish, and Italians who came to this region to build the canal. They viewed drinking as necessary to socialize with friends and relatives. The immigrants could not understand prohibition and refused to comply.

To meet Sidney's insatiable demand, bootleggers like Antonio Borrego rose to the challenge to quench their thirst. He came to Sidney in 1920 in search of stable work on the Yellowstone River canal and took a part-time job as a butcher at the Sidney Provision Meat Market while he waited for openings. He quickly proved to be the fastest and most skilled butcher in the valley by setting a new town record for fully butchering a complete steer. "The secret to fast and accurate butchering is razor-sharp knives," Antonio confided to a customer who watched him work one day. Twice a day he honed his steel blades to a precise sharpness that easily shaved the hair off the back of his hand. People would come to the store just to watch him cut perfect pieces of meat to fill custom orders. The store promoted him to head butcher and he put away his plans for canal work.

However, Antonio was actually an entrepreneur at heart for he was not satisfied with a steady paycheck. He desired the finer things in life and was willing to take daring risks to have them. Prohibition presented Antonio with a lucrative opportunity to make a lot of money by shuttling booze from Canada to the liquor-deprived people of northeastern Montana. Bootlegging meant taking risks and, if he avoided capture, reaping large rewards.

It all started innocently enough. A customer quietly asked Antonio if he wanted to make a little extra cash. It just required a night's work with some "deliveries." When Antonio lifted the packages that night, the sloshing contents told him exactly what was inside. Antonio knew what he was doing was wrong, but the money was good and the work light. A few nights later, he borrowed a pickup and drove the hundred miles north to Big Beaver, Canada and loaded the truck bed full of beer, whiskey, and vodka. Antonio thought the whole transaction was hilarious because Canada had a prohibition law too, but nobody paid much heed. The drive back was uneventful and by dawn he had sold his entire inventory at an incredible profit.

Within one month of bootlegging, Antonio bought a new Ford pickup truck. He paid cash for it at a dealership in Miles City and proudly drove it back to Sidney. While some citizens wondered how a Mexican butcher could afford such a vehicle, most overlooked the luxury and continued to buy their custom meats from him.

The new truck eliminated Antonio's rental expenses, which increased his overall profits. Twice a week he drove to the Canadian border, always taking a slightly different route, and loading up with booze for the run home. He tried not to sell the liquor out of the meat market, but an occasional Russian immigrant would come and ask for a lamb roast and give Antonio a sly wink for a fifth of vodka. Antonio would carve the roast and sell it to his customer. Then he took him around back of the store and sold him the vodka.

The arrangement was incredibly profitable for Antonio and he quickly began to amass a small fortune. Antonio knew if he just lay low and did not call attention to himself, he could become independently wealthy. He purchased new clothes, but not extravagantly. He bought a nice two-story home, but not gaudy. He seemed to live a prosperous life that was a little above what his butcher salary could support, but just below the level that would generate suspicion.

Life was good for Antonio until he violated the golden rule of bootleggers, "Never drink your merchandise." He did not intend to drink, it just happened. Feeling particularly lonely one night, he decided to crack the seal on a pint of whiskey. After downing its contents, things did not seem so bad, so he had another. The next morning he woke with a horrible hangover and dragged himself to work. Within two hours, his employer sent him home for poor work performance and sour mood. Antonio retaliated by drinking more whiskey. He went on a drunk for three days until he hit bottom and pushed himself away from the booze. Although he denied it, Antonio exhibited all the signs of an alcoholic.

Antonio was smart enough to know that he had to stay away from alcohol, but that was very hard to do. Friends would invite him over to have a drink, or a fellow bootlegger would want to solidify an agreement with a swig. Antonio loved to comply, but every time he felt the liquor's smooth fingers glide over his mind and pull him into the bottle, it took all his will power to resist guzzling the whole jug.

Now he had another reason to resist drinking, a new goal to help fortify his resolve. Antonio Borrego wanted to court Alcaria Minjares. He contemplated his approach and immediately dismissed trying to charm her mother. *The woman looked mean*, thought Antonio shaking his head. *No, I will have to befriend her father if I want to get close to Alcaria. I should visit soon before the beet thinning begins.* With his mind made up, he decided on a surprise visit that very evening. He chose a comfortable attire of a white cotton shirt with pair of dress slacks and snappy felt hat. Antonio held the clothing up and thought with satisfaction, *Not too fancy, but distinguished.* Next, he needed to bring an appropriate gift for the father. Antonio rubbed his chin as he gave this topic serious consideration. In the end, he simply defaulted to the universal gifts that most older gentlemen receive, tobacco and a bottle of booze. Little did Antonio know that these gifts would set in motion a series of decisions that would shape Tereso Minjares's destiny.

The hot evening was beginning to cool when Paz heard the knock at the door. She quickly grabbed a dish towel and wrapped it around her left hand. Although the burnt hand had regained most of its mobility, she was self-conscious about the scars and frequently hid it from view. Paz looked nervously at her husband, who was relaxing on a kitchen chair with his legs stretched out. Alcaria, Joaquina, and Anita had just cleared the remnants of their simple meal from the table and now the girls were helping their mother with the dishes. Mr. Hansen was puffing on a corncob pipe and enjoying the tranquil mood.

Paz waited for a moment for some sign that Tereso was going to rise and answer the knock, but saw none. Augustine sat on the bed reading a paperback book to Ben. He quickly realized that his father expected someone to see who it was, so he put his book down and carefully walked to the door and pushed the screen open. As his eyes adjusted to the dim evening light, Augustine saw a man who looked vaguely familiar standing on the front porch with a package in one hand and a dress hat held to his chest with the other. He was smartly dressed with his receding hair neatly combed and his mustache meticulously trimmed.

"*Hola*," the man addressed Augustine with a wide smile. "I would like to talk with your father, *por favor*. Is he available?"

The man's formality took Augustine by surprise and made him wary. Then he got a whiff of the man's hair tonic and cologne and his nose wrinkled. Augustine did not know what this man wanted, but he definitely did not come to talk about work. He turned his head and called to his father, "Papa, there is a man here to see you."

Tereso leaned forward in his chair and answered in a loud voice, "Well boy, tell him to come in." Augustine stepped back and held the screen door open for the man. The entire family and Mr. Hansen watched as the man appeared in the doorway. Suddenly they recognized him. Tereso smiled. Paz swore. Alcaria blushed. Joaquina giggled. Mr. Hansen shook his head.

An awkward moment of silence followed before Antonio finally spoke and addressed the men first, "*Buenas noches, Señores*." Then he bowed to Paz, "You look breathtaking tonight, *Señora*." Paz kept silent, but her eyes shot fire back. Lastly and purposely, he gazed at Alcaria and seemed to become transfixed. Alcaria squirmed under his gaze and looked shyly at the floor.

Paz opened her mouth to launch a salvo of heated words, but Tereso stepped in front of her and shook Antonio's hand. "Your name is Antonio, *¿qué no?* What brings you here tonight?"

Antonio returned the handshake with gusto and answered, "I brought you a small gift to welcome you to Sidney. I thought maybe we could visit and get to know each other some." He offered his small bundle to Tereso.

Tereso was touched by this simple act of hospitality. He gratefully accepted the package and noted that it quietly sloshed when moved. Tereso waved his hand to the table and said, "*Por favor*, sit with us and ..."

"No!" thundered Hansen. His outburst shocked Tereso and stunned the rest of the family. "This man is a bootlegger! A scoundrel, I tell you. If you let him ..." Hansen stopped as he realized that he was babbling in English and that Tereso and Paz could not understand him. They looked at him with confusion. The children knew English well enough from school to grasp Mr. Hansen's warning. Antonio appeared agitated and glanced nervously around him for the family's reaction. Hansen shifted to his limited Spanish, "*Malo hombre. Muy malo.*"

Tereso did not understand any of this tirade. He brushed Hansen's comments aside and was about to restate his offer to Antonio when Paz seized the moment and made her feelings known. She shook her finger at Antonio and said, "I don't know what *Señor* Hansen has against you, but I trust him much more than I trust you. You don't want to welcome us. You want my daughter and you can't have her. Now leave us."

Paz's comments deeply embarrassed and angered Tereso. He gritted his teeth and yelled, "*¡Silencio!* I say he stays and I am not going to allow the ranting of an old man or woman tell me differently."

Antonio nervously worked the brim of his hat through his fingers. He had thought that his visit might be controversial, but nothing like this. He cleared his throat and said, "Perhaps I should leave."

Tereso whipped around and faced him. His eyes burned with fury for a moment longer before mellowing. He sighed and said, "Let's go out onto the porch. We can talk there." Antonio nodded in agreement and carefully bowed to Paz, Alcaria, and Joaquina. Mr. Hansen stuffed his pipe back into his mouth and chomped down on the mouthpiece as he glared back. Antonio put his hat on and followed Tereso outside.

The darkness fully enveloped the warm evening. The men settled themselves on the wooden porch and listened to the chirping crickets for a moment. The soft glow of the kitchen lights filtered through the screen door and illuminated their faces. Antonio pointed at the small package that Tereso held as a reminder to open it. Tereso loved presents and quickly unwrapped the gift. When he unfolded the brown paper wrapping, he found a tin can of Prince Albert tobacco, a package of cigarette paper, and a pint of whiskey. Antonio watched Tereso's face as he examined the gifts and felt a rush of satisfaction and relief when Tereso beamed a wide smile.

"*Gracias*, Antonio," Tereso grinned, "These are very nice gifts."

"*De nada*," answered Antonio, "I was hoping you would like them."

Tereso wasted no time in popping the lid off the tobacco can and rolling a fresh cigarette. Antonio produced a match and Tereso allowed him to light it. Tereso took a couple of long, satisfying puffs before he nodded his gratitude to Antonio. Then Tereso focused his attention to the pint. He twisted the cap off and took a huge swig from the bottle. He seemed to savor the taste for a moment before he exhaled forcefully and wiped his mouth with the back of his hand. He then placed his cigarette back into his mouth to complete the luxury and handed the whiskey to Antonio.

Antonio took a sip and passed the bottle back as he asked, "How do you like Sidney?"

Tereso took a long drag on his cigarette that produced a dark red glow on the end. He blew out a stream of smoke before answering, "It's all right. Seems quiet." He took another swig of whiskey. It had been a long time since he had last tasted such good liquor and tobacco.

"You will get used to it," said Antonio as he received the bottle again and took another drink. "People here are good. There is lots of work around. More coming if Holly Sugar builds that refinery here. If a man met the right woman, he could settle down here and raise a family, *¿qué no?*"

The whiskey and cigarette put Tereso in a very good mood. He calmly replied, "*Sí*, a man could put roots down here." Antonio nodded enthusiastically and took a long swig to reaffirm Tereso's comment.

Their conversation then began to weave though a variety of topics as they proceeded to consume the entire bottle. Tereso smoked a few more cigarettes and, before either man knew it, they had finished the pint, completing their first male bonding experience. They shook hands and parted in good spirits. Tereso was pleased to meet a new friend who appeared to see the world as he did and had access to life's simple luxuries. Antonio was overjoyed at making a very positive impression on Alcaria's father. Both would serve each other's needs very well.

The late June heat pressed down on Alcaria's head like a hot iron. A wide-brimmed hat provided shade, but it sizzled like an oven around her brow and caused beads of sweat to trickle down her face. She wore a man's cotton shirt and dungarees that hung loosely on her slim body. The clothing was hot and stifling, but protected her skin from the searing sun and the rigors of working on her knees as she thinned and weeded the sprouting sugar beets.

Alcaria stopped for a moment to wipe her forehead with the back of her dirty cotton glove and stretch her aching back. She scanned the wide field for her family and found them scattered among the endless rows. They moved slowly along, oblivious to the world around them. Her father, Mr. Hansen, and Augustine waddled ahead with a short-handled hoe in each hand. They chopped the ground and removed the excess beets and intermingled weeds. Their efforts were rough and required Alcaria and Joaquina to follow behind and finish the job. Joaquina was roughly parallel to her, working several rows over. Her thick black braids dangled from under her hat and swung forward close to the dirt as she removed the remaining plants with her fingers. After the girls' efforts, solitary sugar beet sprouts stood about a foot apart, allowing the bulbous root to expand and mature.

It was midmorning and Alcaria was tired. Her day had started at 4:30 AM with her mother rustling in the kitchen preparing a breakfast of beans and tortillas. By five, she, her sister and brother, her father, and Mr. Hansen trudged off into the cool dark morning to the sugar beet fields with only a hint of dawn on the horizon over the thick cottonwood forest of the Yellowstone River to the east. They worked until about 11 AM when the sun became unbearable and broke for lunch and a short *siesta*. Then they resumed work at around 3 PM and continued until seven when darkness halted their labors. The work was hard and tedious. The repetitive schedule drained Alcaria's energy until she felt that she had become a zombie. As the days wore on, she grew to hate the work, the monotony, and the unrelenting heat.

As she continued to pluck the weeds and young beet plants, her mind wandered through many random thoughts. She thought about Diego, the boy she had left in Doña Ana. *Surely, we would have married*, she reflected wistfully. Alcaria languished on this pleasurable thought and smiled to herself as she conjured up a happy and perfect life with him.

Suddenly, her dreams were interrupted by thoughts of Antonio Borrego. Alcaria shook her head as she contemplated his recent advances. He came to the house almost nightly, always bringing her father a bottle and sometimes tobacco. Her mother was furious because her father was now drinking and smoking more than he ever did. It was only a matter of time before her father either got too drunk to work or got himself into trouble. She could tell that Mr. Hansen was seething at these visits too. Something bad was going to happen.

During each visit, Antonio would find some way to speak with her. Alcaria laughed softly to herself as she remembered how her mother always knew when he tried to get her attention and would cut his conversations short. But he kept coming, night after night.

Alcaria stopped her weeding for a moment and gave *Señor* Borrego some serious thought. *I bet that he is twice my age. That is less than the difference between Mamma and Papa, but it is still a lot.* She reached out and grabbed a handful of plants and yanked them out of the ground as she continued to contemplate Antonio. *He is not handsome, but he is not ugly either and he certainly appears to be well off. He drives a new truck and dresses very nice. People say that he is the best butcher in the valley! I certainly could do worse.* She scooted forward on her knees to the next clump of weeds. *Maybe I should try to talk to him. He seems nice.* As she gave this subject more thought, her work seemed less tedious and she began to look forward to the evening.

The dinner dishes were scarcely washed and put away when they heard the usual knock on the door. Tereso smiled broadly as he leaned back in his chair and patted his full belly. A drink and a good smoke would top off his meal quite nicely. He signaled for Augustine to greet the visitor. Augustine rolled his eyes and walked with a bored shuffle to the door as he had so many times before. Alcaria quickly glanced at her reflection in a pocket mirror that sat against the sink and made last-second refinements. Then she quickly removed her apron and threw it behind the cupboard.

Paz noticed her daughter's primping and scowled. She purposely turned her back to the door and refused to acknowledge the knock.

Augustine reached the door and went blindly through the motion of opening it, paying no attention to who stood on the steps. He was about to walk away when he noticed that the man was taller than usual and did not exude the normal aroma of aftershave. Augustine studied him for a moment as the man stepped into the light. "Uh, Papa," stammered Augustine, "I think you better come here."

Before Tereso could look up from the kitchen table, Alcaria gasped and put her hands to her face. "*¡Dios mío!* Diego! What are you doing here?" Tereso snapped to his feet as Paz spun on her toes. Joaquina squealed with delight. To her, this was the beginning of a perfect night.

Diego stood quietly in the doorway. His disheveled thick black hair and rumpled clothes revealed nights of sleeping on the ground. His boyish face was gaunt from starvation, but his deep brown eyes burned with passion and love. In front of the stunned family, he spoke as if Alcaria was the only person in the room and the universe, "Alcaria, my love and my soul, I could not eat or sleep when you left. My world came to an end. I had to find you and make you mine."

Alcaria's knees went weak with love and she felt herself drawn to his outstretched arms. Paz moved quickly to break Diego's enchanting spell. She spurred her husband to intervene by stabbing him repeatedly in the back with her finger. Tereso winced in pain as he stepped forward and twisted away from his wife. He looked back as if to say, *What do you want me to do about this?* Paz responded by jerking her head toward Diego. Tereso sighed and reluctantly faced the young man and asked, "Who are you and what do you want?"

Paz moaned at her husband's question and slapped her head. *How can the man be so dumb?* she thought. *A blind man could see what this kid wants!*

Diego bowed his head respectfully to Tereso and replied, "*Perdón,* I did not mean to call unannounced, but I have been traveling for so long. Sidney is a long way from Doña Ana. I arrived just this morning and finally found someone who knew where you live. I decided to come directly here." Tereso looked at him with a puzzled expression, so Diego continued. "I knew Alcaria in Doña Ana and fell in love with her. When she left, I thought my heart would rip out of my chest. *Por favor, Señor.* Let me talk with her for a while."

Tereso felt a little sorry for the love-struck fellow and was about to grant his request when he noticed Paz struggling to hold Alcaria at bay. Paz signaled for him to help her and when she saw that he was about to capitulate, loathing poured from her eyes. She started to launch a salvo of insults when another knock came from the door. The sound stopped everyone dead in their tracks.

Joaquina broke the silence with a high-pitched laugh and said gleefully, "Now, this should be interesting!"

Augustine gulped when he realized that he was the delegated greeter and awkwardly walked back to the door and opened it. Antonio stepped in, dressed smartly, neatly scrubbed and shaved, his receding hair impeccably trimmed and combed. In his left hand, he held a tin of tobacco and small flask, the sight of which made Tereso moan. In Antonio's right hand, he delicately held a tiny bouquet of daisies, which caused Alcaria to groan. He stood next to Diego and each looked at the other with puzzled expressions.

Anita sat on the bed and held the baby with Ben sitting close to her. The children were quiet as mice watching the drama unfold.

Suddenly, Paz realized that the events were teetering in her favor and all she needed to do was push them a little further. She let go of Alcaria and waltzed up to the two uncomfortable men and announced to Antonio, "This young fellow is Alcaria's boyfriend from Doña Ana and he has come to ask for her hand in marriage." She looked at Diego for confirmation and asked, "*¿Qué no?*" Diego managed a weak nod. "*Bueno*," Paz continued. "Now, *Señor* Borrego, go home. Do not bother us again."

At first Antonio stood expressionless, stunned by what he heard. His flowers seemed to wilt in his hand as he lowered his head, shoulders slumping forward with resignation. Paz smiled with satisfaction at the devastation her words produced. Then her smile ceased as she saw something manifest in his expression, something sinister that almost avoided detection except for her close inspection. Through slitted eyes, Antonio was glaring hatred at Diego. They burned like a viper, ready to strike, silent and deadly. Paz gulped and took a step back.

Slowly, Antonio turned toward Diego and faced him, almost nose to nose. Diego at first looked scared, but then squared his jaw and returned the stare. The silence thickened for a moment as Antonio bored his rage into Diego's skull. Then Antonio twisted away from Diego, kicked the screen door open, and stomped out. Moments later, they heard his pickup grind into gear and roar onto the road, throwing rocks and dirt high into the air.

As the sound of Antonio's pickup disappeared into the night, the Minjareses returned their attention to Diego. Paz spoke first, "Well, you can see that we have had a busy night. So, we bid you good night, *adios*."

"Mama," exclaimed Alcaria, "you just can't send him away after he traveled for so long! Please let him stay."

Paz snorted with disgust. She could just imagine what kind of sleep everyone would get if Diego stayed the night, but Alcaria was right. She could not cast Diego out like a bag of trash at night. She would do that in the morning.

"All right," replied Paz as she put her hands on her hips. "He can stay in the tool shed out back. Tereso, help him make a bed and, Alcaria, you are staying inside where I can keep an eye on you, *comprende?*"

———◆———

Antonio smashed his front door open with a kick from his polished boot. He could have turned the doorknob, but this was much more satisfying. He balled his hands into fists of rage and stomped around the living room, occasionally sending a coffee table or a stool flying across the room. Finally, as his anger abated, he collapsed on the sofa and buried his head in his hands.

"It's not fair," he muttered. "Not fair at all. I am better for Alcaria than that flea-bitten puppy. What could he give her? Nothing! I could give her a home, security, and a loving hand. That boy offers nothing! *¡Nada!*" He continued to blubber for a few minutes longer until a familiar craving gradually seeped into his despair. Without another thought, he got up and went to his bedroom closet and removed a bottle of Canadian whiskey from a hidden trunk.

He sat on his bed, dejected and lonely, and cracked the seal around the cap. He took a long hard swallow and felt the liquid burn, then comfort, as it slid down his throat. It dulled the pain. Antonio closed his eyes for a moment as he savored the taste and then took another swig. As he drained the bottle of its contents, the world began to once more come into focus. He sat up ramrod straight and clutched the bottle with his left hand as his world suddenly became clear and he knew what he had to do.

"I'm going to kill him." He said this as if he had a clear vision of the future. Antonio took another long drink and wiped his mouth with the back of his hand. "*Sí*, I will kill him. Tonight. I will show that kid a thing or two."

He struggled to get up and spilled whiskey on his dress pants. Antonio staggered to his dresser and wrestled the top drawer with his free hand. He finally jerked it open and reached under his folded shirts. His hand probed around until he felt the familiar leather sheath. He grabbed it and pulled it out. A smile broke across his face as he set his bottle on top of the dresser and examined the object. It was a long knife with a beautifully carved ebony handle. A highly polished black leather sheath snugly protected the blade. He carefully pulled the blade from the sheath and examined it in the moonlight. The polished metal gleamed flawlessly along the slim ten-inch blade. He carefully ran his finger along the sharp edge to reconfirm that he had honed it to perfection.

Knives gave him confidence and strength, a gratifying feeling when he butchered. They felt good in his hands. He took care of them, kept them clean and sharp, and the knives responded flawlessly. He used them like high-quality tools to precisely slice meat or as a deadly weapon to protect what he perceived was his. Knives had always served him well.

Antonio slowly slid the blade back into the black sheath. He found his bottle and took another swig. He exhaled forcefully as the liquid burned down his throat. "Tonight," he muttered in the darkness, "tonight I will show him."

———◆◆◆———

Diego slept fitfully in the early morning upon his makeshift straw bed with only a thin blanket to cover him. Temperatures in the predawn summer hours in Sidney were similar to those of the high mountain climates of New Mexico—the colder the morning, the hotter the day. Diego's teeth chattered and he swore he could see his breath. The coming day would be a scorcher.

As he lay in his delirium, he heard the faint creaking of the shed door. He smiled and thought, *Alcaria must have sneaked away. I knew that she would come!* Diego rolled over to receive his sweet love. As he slowly stretched out his arms, a pungent alcoholic stench suddenly wafted across his face. He threw his eyes open and saw a deranged man with murderous eyes plunging down upon him. Diego tried to twist away, but it was too late. The man had him by the throat and pinned him to the ground.

Terrified, Diego clawed at the man's wrist, but his grip was strong and he could not pry it open. He began to choke. Then with deliberate slowness, the man drew a knife and carefully slid it against Diego's neck. Diego felt his fear scream as the long cold blade pressed against his young skin. A hot steaming stream of urine flooded his pants. This man was going to kill him.

With his dying breath, Diego rasped, "What do you want?"

His voice seemed to jolt his assailant into reality. For a moment, the man appeared perplexed, unsure of his next move. Then menace resurfaced in his eyes as his put his face directly over Diego's. As he spoke, his spittle and foul breath rained down upon the boy and made his stomach wretch. "Want? Why, you little tick, I want you dead! *Comprende?* I am going to cut you up into little tiny pieces and feed your sorry ass to the hogs!" The man twisted the knife ever so slightly and nicked his neck.

Diego felt blood trickle down his collar and thought his throat had just been cut. He trembled at the thought of death and pleaded with his last breath, "*¡Por favor!* Don't kill me. What can I do to make you change your mind?"

Again, the man appeared uncertain how to proceed. For the first time, Diego thought he saw a flicker of sanity in the man's eyes and it gave him a little hope. The man hesitated for a moment longer before forming a decision. He stuck his face back over Diego and spoke through clenched teeth as if to accent his point. "I want you to get up and go straight to the train station. I will give you money to go back to wherever the hell you came from. If you decide not to get on that train or turn back, I will kill you where you stand. *Comprende?* I will be watching every move you make."

Diego nodded and felt the stranglehold relax and the knife lift off his skin. The man struggled to his feet and stood hunched over him with his hair rumpled around his balding head, still holding the long-bladed knife in his right hand. He fumbled in his pockets with his left hand and produced some crumpled bills. He eyed them quickly and then threw them onto Diego's chest. "Here. This should be enough. Now go and don't look back or I swear I will kill you."

Diego bolted to his feet and ran out the door. The cold night air felt like ice through his wet pants as he found his way onto the dirt road that led back to town. He never looked back as he could feel the man's presence behind him.

The man stood silently watching the boy disappear like a jackrabbit into the night. He felt his anger and adrenaline subside as exhaustion filled his body. With his shoulders slumped forward and the effects of the alcohol wearing off, he looked at the peaceful house for a moment. Then a soft light appeared in the window and signaled that the Minjares family was waking to start another day in the beet fields.

"Soon, Alcaria," spoke Antonio is a soft quiet voice, "soon I will make you mine." He turned and walked home.

———

By the first of August, the field workers had finished the second weeding of the sugar beets and enjoyed some relaxation before the harvest in late September. However, Leon had Mr. Hansen, Tereso, and Augustine manage the irrigation in the fields. Since August was usually the hottest month of the year, the fragile plants required constant watering. The men maintained a maze of sluice gates and ditches that channeled water from the canal. Where the grade allowed, they pulled water from the ditches with siphons made from large rubber hoses and let the water flow down the furrows they had hoed earlier. They shifted the hoses in the early morning and again in the evening, so that they avoided working in the searing midday sun.

Tereso preferred to work in bare feet with his pants rolled up to his knees and a wide-brimmed straw *sombrero* to shelter his head. Mr. Hansen wore old leather boots that looked like they were rotting off his feet and traditional bib overalls with a small straw hat. Augustine wore what his mother provided, which was usually men's clothing that other families had discarded. They hung loosely on his thin frame. He too worked barefooted, but with no hat to cover his thick black hair from absorbing the hot sunlight.

Tereso invariably tried to shuck his duties onto his son and Mr. Hansen. He proclaimed himself the foreman and started bossing them. Hansen, whose patience was already stretched because of Tereso's drinking, would have none of his nonsense. Although he was five years Tereso's senior, Hansen still possessed fire in his belly and could produce it at will. Standing in muck up to his ankles, Hansen squared off with Tereso with gritted teeth and balled fists. He glared at him for a moment and then yelled in English, "I have just about had it up to my eyeballs with your crap!" Tereso looked blankly back without a hint of comprehension. This infuriated Hansen even more because he knew very little Spanish to convey his message. "All right. You are not my boss. *No jefé, comprende?*" Hansen vigorously shook his head to accent this point. Tereso took a step back and sneered.

Hansen's anger exploded at the flippant response. "And another thing," he bellowed, "No more drinking at the house. You know. No drinking at *la casa.*" Hansen performed a quick pantomime of holding a bottle and tipping it back in his mouth.

For Tereso, this was too much to contain. He tilted his head back and roared with laughter. Hansen cocked his fist back to sock him square in the jaw when Augustine intervened. The boy grabbed Hansen's arm and pleaded in accented English, "*Señor Hansen,* please, let me talk to him." In the fury of the moment, Hansen had forgotten that the Minjares children were bilingual.

The boy's voice dampened Hansen's wrath and he slowly dropped his arm. Augustine walked to his father and said, "Pappa, Mr. Hansen doesn't like you bossing him around."

Tereso looked down at his son and answered, "So what?"

Augustine quietly tried to reason with his father, "Pappa, I think it is best not to get him mad. He is a good man and he is letting us stay in his home." Tereso thought about this for a moment and nodded his head. Augustine let out a sigh of relief at his father's agreement and continued with the hardest part of his interpretation. "Mr. Hansen also wants you to quit drinking at home."

Tereso bristled at the comment and replied, "You can tell *Señor* Hansen that if he were more of a man, he would drink too. Tell him that!"

Hansen could tell that he was the target of Tereso's terse reply, but he did not catch the meaning. He asked Augustine, "What did he say?"

Augustine looked at the mud oozing through his toes and answered, "He said that he will try." Hansen emitted a grunt of disbelief and shuffled off to open another sluice gate. Tereso watched him go and then, without further comment, returned to moving siphon tubes to drier parts of the field. Augustine observed both men go through the motions of their tasks without confronting the central issue of Tereso's drinking. He knew in his heart that this unresolved issue would resurface very soon.

The sugar beet was a member of the goosefoot family of plants that includes red beets and spinach. It originated in the Mediterranean area and the Germans perfected its cultivation and processing in the late 1800s. By 1900, immigrants imported the seed to America and planted experimental plots from Arizona to Canada. It grew well at various altitudes, but required voluminous amounts of water, which ultimately was its demise in areas whose residents were constantly waging "water wars" against competing needs. These regions were New Mexico, Arizona, southern California, and southern Colorado.

The sugar beet grew a fat bulbous root in mellow soils and possessed an unique trait among the goosefoot family in that it concentrated sucrose instead of starches during its final weeks of maturity. It was the root's high sucrose content that allowed processors to capture the sugar and refine it.

Two parameters established the price paid for sugar beets—the sugar content measured in percent of the sugar beet tonnage and the net selling price for sugar on the world market. Whereas the farmers could do little to control the world's fluctuating sugar prices, they strived to harvest their beets when the sugar content was at its highest.

The sucrose content increased until subfreezing temperatures stopped the beet's photosynthesis. At this critical moment, the beet's sucrose content was at its highest. If it was not harvested before the frost killed the plant tops, the sucrose quality and quantity dropped sharply with its value plummeting proportionally. Therefore, the farmers held off harvesting the beets until the weather forecasts or the Farmer's Almanac predicted a hard frost in the near future and then furiously gathered the beets with every man, animal, and piece of equipment they could get their hands on. Every season was littered with reports of farmers who waited one day too long and their crops froze into the ground, requiring expensive and hard labor to harvest the devalued beets.

In northeast Montana, the second week of September usually marked the beginning of the sugar beet harvest. By this time, each beet had grown a massive bulbous root that filled the gap created by weeding and thinning two months earlier. The mornings were very cold and the workers could see their breath as they trudged out into the field. Sometimes they woke to a light dusting of snow that quickly melted by midmorning.

Since every hand was needed to harvest the beets, field hands usually pulled their children out of school for three weeks. Most children of immigrant field workers went to one of the two schools in town. The schools were next to each other and were located within four blocks of the town center, next to the Catholic and Methodist churches. One school was a smaller, wood-framed, two-story structure that housed the first grade on the ground floor and the second grade on the top floor. The third through twelfth grades were taught in the larger, brick-built, two-story building. Although the classrooms were small and stark, the teachers were dedicated to giving each student a good basic education and understood that their pupils' families lived an almost hand-to-mouth existence. Thus, they adapted their curriculum around the cycle of sugar beet farming by excusing the children for part of September and October so they could help their parents in the fields. The children made up this time during the summer of the following year.

When a farmer judged that the sucrose level of his crops was peaking, he enlisted all the help he could muster to pull his beets. Farmers realized that if they cooperated, they could more effectively use the limited labor force. So, they met daily for early-morning coffee a small restaurant at the eastern edge of town to discuss the progression of harvesting. Their planning was not perfect in that the earliest and latest harvested plots were not optimum, but it was better than waging all-out war between men who were normally close friends.

As Sidney swung into full harvesting, word got around formally and informally as to where labor was needed. The workers would walk on the crunchy frozen soil in the early, dark morning and began pulling the beets by the foliated tops. If the beet was frozen in the ground, a field hand would chop it out with a short-handled hoe. Men would follow behind the beet pickers with a wicked-looking, sickle-shaped tool called a topping knife. With a fluid dipping motion, they sank the tip of the knife into the beet and picked it off the ground. As the beet rose into the air, they snapped their wrist and freed it from the knife, caught it in midair with their left hand, deftly chopped the top off, dropped the beet, and proceeded to the next one. Sometimes, a procession of twenty to thirty beet pickers and toppers worked along separate rows and advanced across a field together.

Men with pitchforks followed the pickers and toppers and threw the beets into horse-drawn carts. When the carts were full, men drove them to nearest storage yard along the railroad for shipment to a sugar reduction factory. After the beets were removed, the farmers usually herded their sheep and cattle onto the fields to graze on the beet tops and fertilize the fields. If weather permitted, the farmer plowed the field to turn the soil before winter set in, thus completing the sugar beet farming cycle.

Alcaria's hands and back were stiff with cold as she plucked the beets from the ground. She waddled over a furrow, bent forward with her arms dangling in front. She wore a man's denim coat and large cotton gloves with a scarf on her head to shield her from the bitter north wind, but the cold cut through her clothing and stole her body heat. She shivered and bit her lower lip to keep it from trembling.

The hardships of the harvest were starting to extract a heavy toll from her body. The long days of yanking beets out of the frozen ground, hour after hour, was mind numbing and crippling. She felt like a walking zombie by the afternoon, which blunted her embarrassment when she squatted in front of everyone in the middle of the field to relieve herself because there were no bathroom facilities. Alcaria hated this work.

As she plodded forward, pulling beets as she went, her mind began to wander. She thought of Diego and wondered why he had disappeared after traveling so far to find her and confessing his love for her. She shook her head in disappointment. *He must have changed his mind*, Alcaria thought and reached for another beet.

Then she thought about Antonio. Her developing woman's intuition told her that he might have had something to do with Diego's quick departure, but she was at a loss to guess how. He still came around at night and always spoke to her in a charming way. Her mother had given up preventing the conversation and ceased to harass them.

Alcaria spoke softly to herself, "If I married him, he would take me away from this drudgery. I would live with him in his big house and have many nice clothes." Suddenly, she stopped in her tracks and stood up. Her back screamed with relief as she stretched and gave her statement serious consideration. "All I have to do is say yes and I am gone. That's all." She smiled and realized that being married to a rich man had some definite benefits. She then resumed her work with a renewed spirit that came from knowing that the end of her troubles was near.

———————

Alcaria Minjares and Antonio Borrego were married in December 1923, shortly after her sixteenth birthday, at St. Philomena Catholic church. Antonio spared no expense and made sure that his bride had a beautiful white dress and matching wedding decorations that were rare in Sidney. He bought his attendants and his future father-in-law each a new white shirt, an extravagance that none of them could afford on their own. He also financed the dresses for the bridesmaids. Finally, he bought his loving and supportive future mother-in-law a lovely cotton flower-printed dress. Paz accepted it at first with solemn disdain, but her stubborn heart warmed when she put it on, and Alcaria and Joaquina fussed with the final alterations.

The wedding radiated success and happiness. Victoriano and Anastacio came from their outlying towns and reunited with their old friend. The men congratulated Tereso for acquiring such a prosperous son-in-law and toasted his good fortune. The wedding celebration engulfed Tereso and he made the most of it. He gulped gargantuan amounts of liquor from his son-in-law's inexhaustible stash. He ate plate-loads of delicious foods from the well-stocked tables and he told marvelous stories to all who would listen. Tereso could not remember a better time.

In the wee hours of the next morning, many hours after the bride and groom had slipped from the crowd, Tereso dragged Victoriano and Anastacio back to his house to continue the celebration. The two friends felt awkward when Tereso banged the door open and stormed inside. Sleepy-eyed children squinted at them as Tereso belched some profanity and lit an oil lamp. Paz lifted her head and glared back at them before rolling over and smashing her pillow over her head.

"Huh, Tereso," stammered Victoriano, "I don't think we should be here, *comprende? Buenas noches, amigo.*"

Tereso thundered back, "Stay! Nobody cares that we are here."

"All the same," replied Anastacio with a soft and reasonable voice, "it's late and we should be going. Great wedding, old friend."

"No!" bellowed Tereso. "I want you to stay and help me finish this bottle. How about one more bottle between friends, *¿qué no?*"

Anastacio was about to refuse when he saw Mr. Hansen part the curtain around his bed and stand up. He wore his one-piece long john underwear. His disheveled, thin gray hair, and the white stubble on his chin seemed to accent the anger in his eyes. Hansen stomped toward them, shaking his finger as he approached. He scolded them in English, "I told you no more drinking, Tereso. Now get your drunken friends out of here, now! I mean it. I won't warn you again!"

Tereso flashed Hansen an obnoxious grin and asked his friends, "Does anyone know what this old man is ranting about?"

Victoriano slapped Tereso on the shoulder and answered, "I think that he wants us to leave and I can't blame him. It's late, *amigo*, and time to call it a night. *Adios.*"

According to Tereso's simple view of the world, only Hansen stood in his way of sharing a good bottle of tequila with his two best friends. Therefore, he had to silence Hansen. Without another thought, Tereso caught Hansen's face with his right hand, clenched it, and shoved him backward and through the curtain. The elderly man slammed against the wall and slid down in a heap upon his bed. Tereso's brutality shocked the men. They stood silent and watched Hansen struggle to regain his breath.

Anastacio broke the silence. "Enough! He doesn't deserve to be hurt. We are in the wrong!" He turned to Victoriano and said, "Come on. *¡Vámanos!*" They put their hats on and left without another word. Tereso watched them go, still clutching his bottle with his left hand. Then he heard Hansen put on his clothes behind the curtain. A moment later, Hansen emerged fully dressed, carrying his boots.

He pulled out a chair from the kitchen table, sat down, and put the boots on. Without speaking to Tereso, Hansen marched to the door, grabbed his coat and hat, and disappeared into the early dawn. Tereso watched the door slam shut behind him. He had a feeling that the slamming door also meant the end of their arrangement.

It took Leon a couple of days to find Antonio Borrego. He and Alcaria had disappeared to some discreet location for a relaxing honeymoon. When they returned home, Leon was waiting for them and he explained that Antonio's new father-in-law had gotten drunk and assaulted Mr. Hansen. "I hate to do this to ya. I mean, ya being just married and all, but I need ya to come with me and explain to Tereso that he and his family got to move on now. I can't be havin' that kind of behavior on my farm, ya know."

Antonio knew that marriage had its drawbacks, but he had never figured this scenario into his plans. He suddenly felt Alcaria's family land heavily upon his shoulders. Alcaria interjected and spoke Antonio's thoughts, "Where will they go?"

Leon looked directly at Alcaria and said, "That's not my problem, Ma'am."

Antonio felt the crushing weight of responsibility attach firmly to his back. With downcast eyes, he slowly turned his head toward Alcaria. He saw her staring at him and he knew what she would say before she spoke. "Then they can stay with us until they can find another home. We have plenty of room. They can live on the ground floor and we will live above them, *¿qué no?*" Antonio had just tasted his beautiful wife's sweet love and knew if he ever hoped to have it again that he had better not refuse. He gulped and nodded. "*Bueno*," said Alcaria sweetly, "you are such a good husband."

Leon pushed his hat off his forehead and said dryly, "Well, how ever ya want to handle it is your business, but I think ya're bitin' off way more than ya can chew with Tereso. It's your call though. So, I reckon that we better git my wagon and mosey on over there and fetch them. Mr. Hansen needs his place back."

Alcaria squealed with delight and picked up the hem of her dress and scurried into the house to ready it for her family. Antonio watched helplessly as she skipped through the door. He felt a sickening feeling as uncontrollable events hurtled his life forward. He thought, *I only wanted her father to like me. Now he will drink my liquor like a pig and smoke my tobacco like a steam engine in my own house. And what about her mother? ¡Dios mío!, we will kill each other within a month!*

"Coming, Antonio?" Leon's voice broke into Antonio's thoughts.

"*Sí*," answered Antonio. He walked with leaden feet toward his shiny new pickup—the feet of a condemned man when he shuffles toward the gallows.

Chapter 25
Holly Sugar

The cold arctic winds of January 1924 screamed across Sidney's stark farmlands and raked the homes with a chill factor of sixty degrees below zero. Only a few hardy souls ventured outside to feed sheltered livestock. The intense cold froze machinery and vehicles into metallic statues awaiting the winter thaw or human intervention to free them. Dark cottonwoods spread their barren branches upward to the bluish white sky and broke the monotonous skyline.

However, the occupants of the Borrego home were oblivious to the raging wind buffeting against the windowpanes. The owner in particular was howling louder than the storm's worst blow. "She's pregnant!" screamed Antonio, "What do you mean your mother is pregnant? How could that have happened?" Antonio stood shaking with shocked disbelief in his own kitchen, staring at his wife and sisters-in-laws. Alcaria, Joaquina, and Anita clustered around their mother who sat at the table with her face buried in her hands. Alcaria replied with a weak shrug and a trembling smile.

Paz spoke in a low voice through her fingers, "I felt sorry for him during the beet harvest. So I let him have me. It must have happened then."

"¡Jesús!" swore Antonio as he shot his father-in-law a hot glare. Tereso sat in Antonio's favorite chair smoking his dwindling stash of high-quality tobacco. He seemed detached from the commotion bellowing from the room next door. Antonio's anger seethed as he watched him casually blow smoke at the ceiling. Antonio turned back to his wife and proclaimed, "You should be pregnant, not her!"

Alcaria shrugged again and replied calmly, "These things happen, Antonio. Mother is only thirty-three years old. Older women have babies all the time." Her explanation did little to douse her husband's anger. He abruptly left them and stomped into the living room. Augustine, Ben, and little José played with their toys scattered around them. Antonio kicked a small truck and sent it flying across the room. The boys stopped playing and watched him.

Ashamed at his outburst, he turned away from them and stared out the frosted window. *This house is a prison*, he thought. *I feel like a trapped animal.* Tobacco smoke wafted across his face and refocused his attention on his father-in-law, the cause of all his problems. Tereso sat totally relaxed, pulling his white mustache with his left hand and lovingly holding his rolled cigarette with his right. The sight was too much for Antonio. He marched to the coat rack, grabbed this coat, hat, scarf, and gloves and aggressively stuffed them on.

"*¡Dios mío!*" exclaimed Alcaria, "Where are you going on such a cold day?"

Antonio growled back, "Out!" He yanked the door open and felt the winter air slap his face and rob his breath as it sent pins of ice into his body. He hesitated for moment as he reconsidered his actions. Then he heard his father-in-law's irritating voice, "Close the damn door!" That was all the incentive Antonio needed to keep marching forward. He slammed the door behind him and strode briskly down the street. He needed friends and good conversation now and he knew just where to find it—a place where he had relocated his liquor stash to keep it safe from Tereso's searching hands, a place away from useless fathers-in-law and pregnant mothers-in-law.

During the first week in March, Anastacio Currandas paid the Borrego household a rare visit. Tereso had not seen his friend since the ill-fated night after Alcaria's wedding and suspected that he harbored bad feelings, but when he saw his solemn expression, Tereso knew this was not a social call. Tacio carried a paper scroll bounded neatly with a string and, after the usual greetings and small talk, he handed it to him. Tereso examined it briefly before asking, "What is this?"

Tacio nodded toward the scroll and replied, "Open it. You will see."

Tereso raised his eyebrow at the response and slowly undid the knot. The heavy paper spun open and revealed a black and white photograph. Tereso took it out and carefully straightened it. He studied it for a moment before slowly sinking back into his chair. Augustine looked over his father's shoulder and gawked at the photograph of a man dressed in a three-piece suit and hat, lying in a coffin. Several men stood proudly behind the display. "Papa," the boy asked, "who was he?"

Tereso continued to stare quietly at the photograph for several minutes before answering in a sad low voice, "His name was Francisco Villa."

"Villa," repeated Augustine, "Is that the same Villa that you told me about from Chihuahua?"

Tereso nodded, "*Sí*, the same." The room remained quiet for a few minutes longer until Tereso asked Tacio, "How did it happen?"

Anastacio let out a long breath and answered, "A man arrived the other day from Chihuahua selling these photographs. I bought this one for twenty-five cents and asked him if he knew anything. He said that a bunch of *banditos* ambushed him outside Chihuahua. They shot him up bad."

"When?"

Tacio shrugged his shoulders and replied, "The man said sometime last July."

Tereso continued to stare at the picture. It conjured up deep memories and feelings of a time past, a time when he wanted to kill Villa. Now he felt that a piece of himself had died, something irretrievable was lost. Tereso suddenly felt old and lonely, like a survivor of some past grueling struggle.

They continued with small talk for about an hour until Anastacio sensed that it was time to leave. He grabbed his hat and bid his friend farewell. Tereso caught Anastacio by the arm as he opened the door and said, "*Gracias*, Tacio. I appreciate you coming down from Fairview to bring me this picture. It means a lot to me."

"I know it does, *amigo mío*," answered Anastacio with softness in his eyes. "Villa's movement affected us all. *Adios*." The men shook hands before parting.

Tereso sat back down in his chair and studied the photograph for a few minutes more. Then, without saying another word, he rose and searched for the family trunk. He found it where Paz had stored it, neatly tucked under a table next to the wall. He slid it out, opened the latch, and lifted the lid. The trunk bulged with neatly folded clothes carefully arranged by Paz. Tereso slid his hand between the clothes and fished for his prize along the bottom. He quickly found it and pulled the pistols free.

Tereso lovingly cradled the guns and brought them back to his chair. As he resettled himself, he pulled the guns from the black, polished holsters and held them up to the light. The sight of the pistols brought Augustine and Ben scurrying to their father for a closer look. The double-eagle insignia shone brightly from each pearl handle. The pistols were as immaculate as the night Tereso snatched them from the back of the gun-running wagon in New Mexico. The boys uttered appreciative "oohs" and "aahs" as their father rotated the guns in the lantern light.

"Papa," Ben asked, "are those yours?"

Tereso smiled at his little son and said, "*Sí*." Then he picked up the photograph and used a pistol barrel to point. " Do you see the man lying down in this picture?" Ben nodded. His thick black hair bounced with each nod. "These pistols were supposed to be his, but I got to them first."

Ben contemplated this information for moment as he studied the picture. Then he looked up at his father with innocent dark eyes and said, "Looks like he could have used them, *¿qué no?*"

The boy's revelation stunned Tereso. He sat back in his chair speechless as he looked at the picture again in a new light. He thought, *Could it be that I caused Villa's death?* He looked back at Ben who stood patiently by his side waiting for an answer. "You know, boy," Tereso finally replied, "I think you are right, but we will never know."

———•••———

During the first week in May, Antonio aggressively hacked the meat off a leg bone as he contemplated his plight. Each chop with his cleaver represented a blow against his worthless father-in-law. "The man just eats and sleeps," he muttered as he worked. "I can't wait until beet thinning starts. I will make sure that he gets his lazy butt up and gets it to work. Oh, I can't wait." He slammed the scraped bone into the waste barrel and reached for another leg. Antonio was in a trance, oblivious to the world around him. All he wanted to do was to take out his frustrations on the cold meat in front of him. Suddenly, a shout destroyed his concentration.

"Antonio! Antonio, what the hell is the matter with you? Are you going deaf?"

"Huh?" answered Antonio. He looked up and saw Leon pounding on the counter. "Oh, *¡hola!* What can I do for you, *Señor?*"

"Do for me? Hell, Antonio, I damn near had to club you over the head to get yer attention. Now, pull off that butchering apron and git yourself cleaned up. Holly Sugar is in town and they're going to need someone to translate to the Mexicans. They's meeting right now. So, let's git."

Antonio looked over at his employer, who waved him on. Without further delay, Antonio ripped off his smock and went to the sink to wash his hands and arms and comb the sides of his head. After he had removed most of the blood and dried himself on a soiled towel, Antonio grabbed his hat and coat and bounded out the door with Leon.

Leon motioned to his old truck. Antonio went straight to the cab to open the passenger door. He grabbed the handle and suddenly recoiled when he saw who was inside waiting for him. Antonio yelled out in a high voice, "What's he doing here?"

"Now, don't git yer shorts in a bunch," Leon replied over the top of the truck cab. "Yer father-in-law is considered a leader of the Mexican folk in these parts and I thought it best to have him along, Okay? Now git in. We don't have much time."

Antonio gulped back his anger and said, "No. I will drive my own truck and follow you."

Leon sighed and said, "Suit yourself. Git a move on it." Tereso remained silent and smiled irritatingly at his only son-in-law through the side window. Antonio shoved himself away from the cab and strode briskly to his truck. A few minutes later, they arrived at the Sidney City Hall. The streets were filled with cars and trucks, forcing them to park several blocks away.

They raced inside and found the meeting room packed with men. Leon searched the crowd for a familiar face. A shout rang out, "Leon! Over here!" Leon looked to the front of the room and saw his friend Josh waving to him. He grabbed Tereso and Antonio by the collars and steered them through the multitudes until they reached a long table. Josh signaled toward some empty chairs and they quickly settled themselves.

An official-looking man dressed in an expensive suit glanced at Josh for an indication to begin. Josh sat back in his chair, folded his arms across his chest, and nodded to the man to proceed. The man stood up and spread his arms wide to silence the crowd. The gesture seemed to have a magical effect on the men and quickly silenced even the most persistent talker. He cleared his throat and began, "Welcome, gentlemen. Thank you for coming at such short notice. My name is Paul Johnson and I am vice president of operations for Holly Sugar. I am here to announce that our company will start construction this year on a sugar reduction plant in Sidney."

A voice rang out, "About gawd-damn time!"

"Um, yes," stammered Johnson. He quickly gathered his composure and continued, "The new site will be a few miles east of town by the railroad."

Another voice shouted, "You mean the old Hardy place? The city plum stole it from that old coot. He went out fightin' worse than a wildcat." A burst of laughter rippled through the crowd.

Johnson began to feel uncomfortably warm. "Right. Well, like I was saying. We plan to start preparing the site this summer and erecting the building and equipment next year. We should be operational by next harvest time. I called this meeting to tell you this and gather your support to make this a successful venture. First, my company would like your opinions on any special needs that must be met before the construction can begin."

The men looked at each other, and a few murmured suggestions.

Finally, a farmer stood up with his hat in his hand and said, "A few of us here would like you to provide some housing for all these Mexicans showing up. I mean, none of us folk can afford to put these people up. Especially since we can only use them a couple of months out of the year. The way we look at it, they are here because of you, and you need them to build the plant. So, you should take care of them and not the hard-working farmers of this town." A rumble of agreement went through the crowd.

Johnson had not anticipated this request and his face showed it. He countered, "I understand your problem, but lumber is expensive and I cannot commit the company to build a huge housing project. We have never done that before and I can see no reason to start now."

The men's voices began to rise and a feeling of agitation swept over the crowd. Tereso could sense it, but he was at a loss to understand its basis. He leaned over to his son-in-law and asked, "What is happening?"

Antonio put aside his contempt for his father-in-law for the moment and answered, "The farmers want Holly Sugar to provide housing for the Mexicans coming to build the new plant, but *Señor* Johnson refuses. He says that lumber is too expensive."

Tereso replied, "Lumber? Tell him that we can make adobe brick homes. It's cheaper and warmer, too."

Antonio reluctantly admitted that Tereso had a good idea. He stood up and timidly raised his hand for a moment's quiet. The sporadic conversations gradually tapered off and left Antonio at the center of attention, a position he hated. He gulped and addressed Paul Johnson. "*Señor,* my father-in-law suggests that we use adobe to construct the homes or, as we say, a *colonia,* group homes."

Johnson looked incredulously at Antonio. "Adobe? You mean mud?"

"Oh, no *Señor,*" replied Antonio, "I mean adobe bricks. We can make them out of local materials. When made right, they are extremely strong and cheap, too."

Johnson rubbed his chin and said, "Adobe, huh? Do you know someone around here that knows how to make it?"

Antonio suddenly realized that this was his opportunity to get his in-laws out of his house. He pointed to Tereso and said, "*Sí, Señor.* This man is my father-in-law and he makes fine adobe bricks. He can supervise the brick making."

Johnson looked back at the crowd. The men were quietly staring back at him. They knew Antonio's concept was economical and feasible. All that was needed was for Johnson to approve it. Johnson swore under his breath and turned toward the big elderly man sitting next to Antonio. He appeared to be cocky and enjoying the attention. Johnson thought, *What the hell? If it doesn't work, I'll tell the farmers that I tried.* He addressed Antonio, "Please tell your father-in-law that I wish to employ his services to supervise the brick-building."

Antonio almost shouted with joy. The men emitted a huge roar of agreement and the noise level skyrocketed. Tereso again leaned over to Antonio and asked, "What did he say?"

Antonio put his mouth up to Tereso's left ear and shouted, "He wants you to supervise the adobe brick making for the new *colonia.* Congratulations! You got yourself a job."

Tereso smiled broadly and boldly stood up and shook Johnson's hand. Johnson was surprised by the strength of the elderly man's grip. He slapped Tereso on the shoulder and waved back to the crowd. He was very pleased to make a positive impression in the community. Tereso, on the other hand, could hardly wait to supervise. It was like a dream come true.

The hot summer afternoon of June 14 settled heavily on the workers and snuffed their energy. There was no shade and the only respite from the heat was the muddy water that flowed along the narrow irrigation ditch beside their wooden bins. Ten men slaved beneath the blazing sun under the direction of their impossible boss, Tereso Minjares. Tereso paired the men in five groups. Each group mixed the clay, straw, and water into the proportions dictated by Tereso. When he was satisfied with the mixture, the men scooped the concoction into wooden brick forms. After the men filled each set of forms, they scraped off the excess and allowed the mud to harden into adobe bricks. The bricks took about two days to cure before the men knocked them out of the forms for other crews to haul to the building site.

Tereso usually allowed the men to break from 11 AM to 2 PM to miss the heat of the day. They would all go home and enjoy a relaxing lunch and *siesta* before returning to work. However, Paz was extremely irritable during the last stages of her pregnancy and Tereso wanted to avoid her at all costs. So, he stayed away and ordered his men to stay at their posts. If he was going to suffer, then they would too.

The men were too tired to grumble. They silently went about their tasks like zombies until Tereso vented his irrational anger at them for some minor infraction. It was during such an outburst when Antonio drove up undetected in his truck. Tereso bellowed, "I told you to put more straw in this clay. Now these bricks are useless!"

The young man pushed his *sombrero* off his forehead and glared back. He seethed through clenched teeth, "I mixed it like you told me, old man. You can't remember what you told me, can you? Go home. We don't need you here."

Tereso balled his hands into huge fists and came after the insolent man. The young rebel threw down his shovel and prepared to meet him. Antonio watched the drama unfold with keen interest. He wanted to watch strength and experience pitted against youth and speed, but Alcaria had sent him to fetch his rogue father-in-law and he knew that she wanted him in one piece. Reluctantly, Antonio called out, "Tereso!"

Tereso stopped in his tracks with his fists cocked for action. He turned his head to Antonio and barked, "What!"

Antonio waved him toward the truck, "Come on. Your wife is in labor. You must come now!" Tereso seemed to teeter between jumping into Antonio's truck and knocking the young buck's block off. Antonio sensed his indecision and coaxed him back, "*Vámanos*, Tereso. Paz needs you now. You can always come back and settle this disagreement, *¿qué no?*"

"*Sí*," grunted Tereso. He abruptly lowered his arms and swiftly strode to the truck. He jumped into the cab and slammed the door. Antonio sighed and slid behind the wheel. He put the truck into gear and glanced at this father-in-law. Tereso was staring straight ahead with his jaw set. Antonio shook his head and drove forward.

As they opened the screen door to Antonio's house, they were greeted by a newborn's squall. The sound emanated from the master bedroom, a room that Antonio had not yet shared with his wife. The boys were sitting in the living room with looks of concern on their faces. Tereso stepped forward and slowly opened the bedroom door. He saw a midwife bundling the baby in blankets. Alcaria, Joaquina, and Anita were helping their mother clean up and get comfortable.

The midwife cooed and gently rocked the baby. The infant responded to the loving voice and gradually stopped crying. When the baby quit fussing, the woman looked up and saw Tereso standing before her. She smiled and presented the tiny bundle to him. Tereso solemnly took his child and carefully held it his chest. He swallowed hard when he saw its angelic face and asked gruffly, "What is it?"

The woman laughed softly and said, "Can't you tell? It's a girl, of course." Tereso nodded, not sure how a baby girl looked any different from a baby boy. The woman tilted her head toward the bed and continued, "You should see your wife now." He smiled his gratitude and carried the baby to Paz. The girls parted to let him through and he knelt down by her. She smiled at him. He did not realize how much he had missed seeing her smile until now. It took years off her face.

Tereso awkwardly handed her the baby. Paz deftly took the child like a seasoned professional and offered a breast to its tiny mouth. The baby instinctively found the nipple and began to suck. The act of nourishing her baby comforted Paz and relaxed her. After a few gratifying minutes, she spoke softly to her husband, "Tereso, I think that we should name her Antonia after my mother. The name also pays respect to Antonio who has let us live in his house, ¿qué no?"

Alcaria squealed with delight.

Tereso emitted a deep chuckle and said, "All right. Let's name her Antonia. That's a good name." Alcaria spun on her toes and rushed out the room to tell her husband. She wanted to give Antonio the good news for she knew that their first six months of marriage had been difficult. Naming the first baby born in the house after him would help, even if it belonged to his mother-in-law.

By the last week in August, the *colonia* was nearing completion. It resembled an ice cube tray with fifteen units on each side of its length. The building paralleled the railroad tracks and was close to where Holly Sugar would build the sugar reduction plant. The thick and sturdy adobe bricks supported long timbers that bolstered the massive flat sod roof. The company had supplied windows, cheap wooden doors, kitchen cabinets, and woodstoves.

Each unit consisted of a large open space that functioned as a kitchen-dining-living room and two bedrooms. The floors were brick and slightly uneven. Bathrooms consisted of several outhouses in back of the *colonia*. Although rough and drab, the apartments were snug, warm, and dry.

Mexican families moved into the units and got settled before the sugar beet harvest began. Much to the relief of Antonio, this included the Minjares family. Tereso, Paz, Joaquina, Augustine, Anita, Ben, José, and baby Antonia sandwiched into the apartment. Tereso and Paz took one bedroom and brought the baby to their bed. In the other room, Joaquina and Anita shared a bed and the three boys slept together on a mattress on the floor. Despite the closeness, Paz turned their small apartment into a cozy home and the children enjoyed being a family again without Antonio's scrutiny.

Tereso had little time to rest from building when the beet harvest moved into full swing. He took Augustine and Joaquina out of school and ordered them to work the harvest with him. Together, they made enough money to buy food and clothing for the family until Holly Sugar began the plant construction the following year.

Tereso was overwhelmed by the flurry of activity that the plant construction brought to Sidney in the spring of 1925. He sat on the buckboard, cradling the leather reins in his big, sore hands. His wagon creaked and groaned from the weight of five cubic yards of gravel the steam-powered clam shovel excavator had dumped into the bed. His team of four horses strained under the weight and plodded mindlessly along the one-and-a-half mile route from the gravel pit to the construction site. The team completed the round trip ten times a day, seven days a week, and could now walk the route in their sleep: an easy stroll down to the pit next to the Yellowstone River, the hard pull up the pit ramp with Tereso snapping the reins and urging them to pull harder, and finally the long strain of the load back.

Tereso sat hunched from fatigue and boredom as he drove his team forward. He met tens of empty wagon teams driving back out to the pit for another load. At the beginning of the season, he used to wave to every driver. As the season progressed, Tereso lapsed into nodding as the drivers passed. Now, he blindly looked forward, scarcely acknowledging their existence.

There were two exceptions to his indifference, Anastacio Currandas and Victoriano Vallejo. When either passed, they would shout out, "*Buenos días, amigo!*" or "*¡Hola!* This beats pulling weeds, *¿qué no?*" Their words of encouragement bolstered Tereso and made the day go better.

As Tereso approached the construction site, he gently pulled on the reins, but his actions were unnecessary because the horses instinctively slowed to a walk. Ahead were several teams off-loading the gravel where crews mixed concrete for the massive foundations and walls. A man with a red flag signaled Tereso to park behind another team pulling away. Tereso obeyed with a simple nod and steered his team into the slot. When he stopped, he set the brake and took a deep breath. This was the part he hated. The company expected him to help the four laborers who jumped into the back of his wagon to off-load the gravel. This was done with scoop shovels and Tereso's sixty-nine-year-old back ached from the strain. He looked wistfully at the boys who carried water and some oats to replenish the horses while the gravel was removed. *The company treats the horses better than us*, he thought.

Tereso took a deep breath, stored the reins, and grabbed the shovel he stashed under the buckboard. He slowly climbed in the wagon and joined the other men. Tereso was the only Mexican of the group. The group consisted of two Russians, a Pole, and an Italian. The two Russians spoke to each other in their native tongue. The Pole and Italian kept quiet. Tereso hated them all.

Together, the five men shoveled the gravel out within thirty minutes. Tereso's shoulders and back throbbed with pain. He took a swig from his water pouch and sloshed some water on his face to wash off some sweat. With a laborious effort, Tereso pulled his aching body into the wagon and untied the reins. With a flick of the wrist, he restarted the gravel-hauling cycle for the ten-thousandth time.

The plant construction sucked all the available labor from the lower Yellowstone River valley. The farmers knew that the plant would increase their profits, so they complained quietly and used children and women to meet their needs. Trains provided a steady flow of Mexican labor from Las Cruces. Some worked in the fields while others filled temporary jobs at the plant. Housing became a problem again and most took over the shacks the first wave of Mexicans had used.

Sidney bulged at its seams from the sudden population influx. Town merchants could not keep food, clothing, and supplies stocked on their shelves. As fast as they could replace their merchandise, someone bought it. The Sidney economy soared and many made small fortunes during the summer of 1925.

Antonio's fortunes also skyrocketed. Demand for his butchering services was at an all-time high, but the real profits were in his bootlegging business. The surge of immigrants produced an insatiable thirst for his products. He raised his prices to ridiculous levels and scarcely saw a drop in sales. He had no trouble selling an entire pickup-load of liquor in one night.

Antonio was making a ton of money and he could barely fathom it. He stashed money in shoe boxes and hid them in the crawl space under his house. He fretted about the money constantly while he worked at the meat market. Alcaria had only an inkling of how much money her husband was hiding. Finally, Antonio opted to find a safer place to put his money. He grabbed a shoe box and took it to the local bank. He walked up to the cashier and said, "Good morning. I would like to open an account."

The cashier was an elderly woman who liked her world to function in an orderly fashion. She did not acknowledge Antonio immediately and continued to complete her paperwork with her reading glasses slid to the end of her nose. Antonio shifted uneasily for several minutes. *She must be deaf*, he thought and was about to repeat his request when she suddenly looked up at him and said, "I will be with you in a moment, young man."

Antonio gulped and waited. Five more uncomfortable minutes passed before she finished her task and was ready for her customer. "Now," she said as she slid her papers into an out box and folded her hands in front of her, "how can I help you?"

Antonio stepped forward and presented his box to her. "I would like to open a savings account and deposit this money."

"That seems simple enough," she replied with a dignified air. "Please fill out this card. How much will be your initial deposit?"

Antonio took the card the clerk slid toward him and began to write his name and address in the blanks. "Oh, I really don't know how much is in this box. Perhaps you could count it?"

The clerk smiled as if she was dealing with a two-year-old, carefully slid the box on the polished counter to her and took off the lid. She let out a startled gasp. "There must be close to ten thousand dollars in here!"

Antonio lifted his head momentarily and replied, "Yes, there probably is."

She shook her head and mumbled as she quickly counted the bills, "This is irregular. Highly irregular."

Antonio completed the card and handed it back to the troubled clerk as she finished counting the money. "Here you go. I hope I answered each question correctly. How much was in the box?"

The woman looked over her glasses at him with astonishment and said, "Ten thousand, five hundred and sixty dollars!"

"Good! I would like to deposit all of it please."

The clerk glanced at the card and then gave Antonio a hard look and said, "All right, Mr. Borrego. I will give you a receipt in a moment." She bound the money and placed it back into the shoe box. Then she rang up the deposit and generated a bank receipt. "Here you go. Thank you, Mr. Borrego, for your business."

Antonio smiled as he took the receipt and reviewed the information on it. Then he neatly folded it and placed it in his breast pocket, tipped his hat, and happily strode out the door. He left with the buoyant feeling that comes from knowing that you just completed a secure and wise financial transaction.

The clerk watched him leave with the evaluating eyes of an old schoolteacher. As soon as the door closed behind him, she quickly picked up the money and closed her window. Then she stomped upstairs to the administrative office tightly clutching the box to her breast and marched into the bank president's office without a knock. She shook the box at the startled secretary and announced, "I must bring this to the president's attention. I think Mr. Borrego is up to no good."

As the foundation and massive walls formed, the Holly Sugar Company was busy acquiring the equipment to fill the plant. To keep costs low, the company searched for used machinery they could pick up at bargain prices. Their search paid off when they learned that the Anaheim Sugar Company in Anaheim, California had gone bankrupt and the bank was selling the assets for pennies on the dollar to recoup their losses. The components were large enough to give the new Sidney plant a processing capacity of 1,800 tons of sliced beets per day.

Holly Sugar sent laborers to Anaheim to dismantle the plant and ship the equipment by train to Sidney. One month later, a train of flatbed cars with mounds of equipment stopped in front of the *colonia* for off-loading. Tereso and his son Augustine, Anastacio, and Victoriano stared in amazement at the immensity of the materials.

Victoriano wore leather gloves and pushed his frayed *sombrero* off his forehead as he assessed the job before him. "*¡Dios mío!* How is all this junk going to fit inside this building?"

Anastacio answered, "Never mind that. How does it go together, *¿qué no?*"

"*Sí,*" agreed Tereso, "It will take a special man to make the pieces fit and work."

Augustine stood silently behind them entranced by the machinery. He spoke quietly, "I could do it." His father gave him a side glance and a smirk. Augustine stiffened his jaw and repeated louder, "I could do it."

This time Tereso faced his son and studied him for a moment. Suddenly, Tereso's premonition flashed and revealed an image of Augustine dressed in blue coveralls holding a huge wrench in his hand. In his vision, Augustine was a man, solidly built with a thin mustache and thick black hair combed back along the sides. Behind him turned a gigantic drum with wheels and gears grinding along its base. Then the scene dissolved and left Tereso staring at a young boy glaring back with determination and confidence. Tereso took a deep breath to clear his mind and said, "I believe you will."

———

Holly Sugar finished the plant shortly after the sugar beet harvest in the early winter of 1925. A road that led directly to Sidney bordered the huge facility's north side, and the railroad formed its west boundary. To the south and east, the company owned large, unplowed fields that provided a buffer between the surrounding residents and the plant.

The processing plant required enormous amounts of water to clean and refine the beets. Holly Sugar enhanced the water storage of a nearby lake by building a small dam at its outlet. The lake stored unused irrigation water over the summer and reached its crest in fall when the sugar beet harvest began. A pipeline carried the water to the plant.

The sugar beet processing started with the local farmers loading their beets directly into gondola railcars. When these were filled, the farmers continued to stack beets in huge, long piles close to the plant. Plant workers washed the dirt off the beets outside and let them freeze to prevent rotting.

The plant processed the beets twenty-four hours per day, seven days per week to minimize sugar loss because the beet quality deteriorated in storage. The washed beets entered mechanical slicers and emerged as long, thin strips called cossettes. Tall silo-like diffusers boiled the cossettes into a thick molasses-like fluid known as raw juice. The diffusers discharged the sugar-depleted cossettes—now called pulp—into a gigantic pulp pit behind the plant to ferment and stabilize. During the following summer, a large pulp dryer designed and built in Lyons, New York removed the excess moisture. The plant sold the final product as cattle silage.

The raw juice contained 10 to 15 percent sugar by weight and required purification and concentration. The plant accomplished this by adding lime to the raw juice, causing a precipitate to form and settle colloidal materials such as bits of pulp and dirt. A massive filter press removed the sludge and created a refined product called thin juice. Tall evaporators heated the thin juice and condensed it to a thick juice, which contained 50 to 60 percent sugar.

Large low-pressure vessels gently boiled the thick juice at low temperatures and created a supersaturated solution. Highly trained workers then saturated the juice by adding a small amount of powdered sugar to form crystals. The workers controlled the crystal size by maintaining a delicate balance between vacuum pressure, temperature, and powered sugar additions.

After the crystallization process, the plant gave the raw sugar two brief washes with clean hot water. This produced a wet, white sugar that required drying, cooling, and screening before the company could store it. Holly Sugar used three very tall bulk bins to store and package the sugar. They painted these white with the company emblem, a tilted three-leafed holly sprig, and the words HOLLY SUGAR printed underneath. The company positioned the bulk bins next to the sidetrack, which allowed the plant to discharge directly into metal container railcars for transportation to markets.

The plant also produced noxious odors that required the nearby residents, especially the workers living in the *colonia*, to tolerate or move. During normal plant operations, the cooking of the cossettes, evaporation of the thin juice, and crystallization of sugar emitted thick, pungent smells that wafted over the *colonia* and sometimes over the entire community. At times the odor was so repugnant that it brought tears to the eyes and made sleep nearly impossible.

During the summer months when the plant was dormant, the large pulp pit that contained a season's worth of fermenting pulp burped methane gas and other odious fumes. The pulp dryer emitted more odors as it churned and dehydrated the pulp into animal feed. Seldom were the *colonia* residents not subjected to some sort of annoying smell.

Plant operations also discharged massive amounts of wastewater. From the initial beet washing through the final sugar rinse, the plant consumed millions of gallons of water per day from the lake. In addition, periodic plant shutdowns for cleaning also required gargantuan amounts of water. The plant discharged the resulting wastewater into a ditch that flowed into a series of smaller ditches that functioned like a manifold and evenly spread the water across the company fields. The wastewater contained a high concentration of lime from the precipitation process required to remove dirt and plant matter from the sugar water. The lime stabilized the pH of the waste stream, which turned the wastewater into a liquid fertilizer. The wastes flowed over the rough fields and settled into the voids. Over the years, the field began to level with the annual deposits of organic matter. The company eventually cultivated the land and it produced high yields of sugar beets.

Despite the odors, the citizens of Sidney overwhelmingly approved the plant and welcomed the prosperity it brought to their small town. The plant provided many residents with stable employment. The increase in sugar beet production created hundreds of seasonal jobs. Field workers could now make enough money to make it through the lean winter and spring months until beet thinning. So, while the populace gagged and wheezed as they went about their lives, they smiled at their good fortune to have a Holly Sugar plant in their community.

The winter of 1925-1926 was brutally cold. The thermometer plummeted to sixty-below-zero Fahrenheit. The howling north wind drove the chill factor to minus ninety-five. The residents of Sidney huddled in their homes and waited for the chill to break. The Minjares family was no exception. The thick adobe walls kept the family snug, but the small apartment seemed to close around them like a cage. Tereso would sit all day in a wooden kitchen chair and rock back and forth on the back two legs as he smoked a rolled cigarette and gazed out the frosted window.

The three older children had the luxury and hardship of trudging off to school each day. School provided Joaquina, Augustine, and Anita an escape from the boredom of home life, but forced them to endure the bitter winds. Dressed in frayed coats and shawls wrapped over their heads and faces, the children struggled against the wind and darkness as they walked the two miles to the school. By the time they arrived, ice glazed their eyelashes together and nearly blinded them.

The darkness and cold brought out the worst in people. Everyone knew this and seldom talked about it, but when violence flared up, it still shocked area citizens.

Late one cold winter night, Tereso sat sullenly in his chair leaning back on two legs and staring out the dark window. He had run out of tobacco that morning without any hope of procuring more. His nicotine withdrawal soured his already foul mood. Paz worked quietly in the kitchen, afraid to disturb him. The children were tucked in their beds in the back room.

A bang at the door broke the uneasy stillness. At first, no one moved. Paz slowly set down a dish and deliberately dried her hands on her apron as she looked over at her husband. Tereso snapped his chair forward and abruptly stood up. He suddenly had a bad feeling about his visitor. His body ached with stiffness from sitting too long. He shuffled to the door and slowly opened the latch. The door blew out of his hand and a small, frozen figure slumped into his arms. Tereso barely had time to catch the body to prevent it from falling. He quickly dragged the person in and shut the door.

He gently laid the small bundle on the floor and took a step back. Paz walked quietly toward the unmoving figure with her hand on her mouth. Her voice quivered as she whispered, "*¡Dios mío!* Don't let it be her, *por favor*. Not her."

Tereso felt her fear, but was puzzled by her words. "Do you know this person?" he asked.

Paz answered by falling to her knees and unwrapping the shawl around the head. Tereso recognized her the moment Paz gasped as she revealed the swollen and bloodied face. It was Alcaria.

Tereso swooped down, picked his daughter up, and set her on the table. Paz and Tereso quickly opened her coat and took off her mittens. Her hands were like ice, but not frozen. Her ragged breath seemed to slow as her body warmed. Tereso examined her and found bruises, but no broken bones. Paz brought a bowl of warm water to the table and carefully washed the blood from her face.

Alcaria slowly opened her swollen eyes and looked up at her parents. Her voice croaked through her split lips, "Mama. Papa. I ..." Suddenly, her body shook as she emitted a loud sob. Tears poured from her eyes.

Paz wrapped her arms around her and held her to her breast. "Its all right now," she cooed.

Tereso felt his anger rage through his body. He thundered, "What happened? Did Antonio do this to you? Tell me!"

Alcaria cried out, "He didn't mean to. He's drinking too much. He can't help it. He ..." Another wave of sobbing overtook her.

Paz gently rocked her in her arms and said, "Hush, now. You can stay with us. Tomorrow is another day."

Tereso felt torn with emotion. Part of him wanted to stomp into the cold night and beat the hell out of his son-in-law. The other half respected a man's right to discipline his wife and he always turned a blind eye to an occasional heavy hand, but this was different. This young woman was his daughter. Tereso finally threw himself in his chair and wished silently for a drink. Paz was right. Tomorrow was another day.

Antonio woke in a silent, dark room, confused and sick. He lay still and let his blurry eyes grow accustomed to the dim light provided by the lone streetlight shining through a frosted windowpane. Gradually, he became aware that he was sitting in the kitchen with his torso sprawled across the table, a sea of empty bottles around him. His head pounded like a steam locomotive when he tried to lift it. As he pushed himself up, his hands knocked over some bottles and sent them crashing to the floor.

"*Dios mío*," he croaked. "What happened to me?" Antonio looked around for an explanation or someone to blame, but he was alone. He decided to postpone the inquiries and focused on his current situation. He staggered toward the window and peered outside. The winter darkness gave him no hint of the time. It could be the early morning, evening, or night. He needed to know the time.

Antonio tilted his head back and bellowed, "Alcaria! Come here!" Silence greeted him. The night's coldness seemed to seep through the walls and grab him. Suddenly, he remembered why Alcaria was not home. Her arguing, screaming, and crying rang hauntingly in his ears. His eyes flashed scenes of his fists hammering down upon her as his rage boiled over. Then his memory clouded over and stopped, drowned by the smuggled liquor he should have sold long ago, but had chosen to hoard.

Antonio slumped back into his chair. He grabbed a half-drunk bottle that had survived his last binge and poured a glass full of the amber-colored liquid. As he brought the glass to his lips, Antonio hesitated for a moment before letting the alcohol tumble down his throat and smash against his stomach. The liquor immediately carried him back to a hazy world where he was king.

He began to rant. "A woman should not leave her husband." Hearing no rebuttal, he took another drink and continued. "Alcaria was wrong to leave me. Where did she go? To her family at the *colonia*? Ha! They live like rats there." He poured another drink, slammed the bottle down on the table, and fumed about the injustice of his life. "I bet her mother is filling her with lies about me. She hates me. *Jesús*, she's probably convincing her worthless husband to keep me away, too." Antonio took a long drink and let it completely rip him from reality. "Well I won't stand for it! I am going to the *colonia* and drag her back and I will kill anyone who stands in my way!"

He pushed away from the table and stumbled down the hallway to his bedroom. He went straight to the top drawer of his dresser and quickly found his prized possession—the long, incredibly sharp butcher knife sheathed in black leather. Antonio slowly pulled the knife out and examined the blade. It was flawless and honed to perfection. He smiled as he slid it back into the sheath and snickered, "It's time to pay the Minjares family a visit."

———

It was late and Tereso was about to finish another boring day when a fist began pounding on the door. He jumped up from his chair and stood still, unsure if he was going to answer the door or run. The pounding became louder as the visitor started kicking the door in irregular intervals. The thick wooden door shook at its hinges with each blow. Then, as abruptly as the pounding began, it stopped.

Suddenly, a drunken voice bellowed, "I know you're in there, Alcaria! I have come to bring you home."

Tereso recognized Antonio's voice and tried to peer through the front window to see if he was armed. Between the frost and glare from the lantern, he could not see a thing. Tereso heard sounds from behind. He carefully backed away from the window, turned, and saw his entire family peering from the back room. The older kids occupied the top sections of the bedroom doorway while the littler ones poked their heads through the bottom. Their eyes were big with fear. Alcaria and Paz stood in the kitchen quietly holding each other.

The pounding and kicking suddenly resumed. It jolted Tereso into action. He unlatched the door and jerked it open, catching Antonio by surprise. He stumbled forward and sprawled across the floor at Tereso's feet. A blast of arctic cold swept through the room. Tereso reached over his son-in-law's body and slammed the door shut. Then he stepped back and positioned himself between Antonio and his family. No one spoke a word.

At first, Antonio lay still, breathing ragged like a dull saw caught in a dry board. He was dressed in a heavy winter coat that hid his upper body. Slowly, he picked himself up and resumed an unsteady stance. His foul breath wafted across the room and caused Tereso to wince. "I have come for Alcaria," he announced.

Tereso answered, "No. You are drunk. Go home."

Antonio reacted to his refusal like a slap across his face. He gritted his teeth and hissed, "Who are you to tell me what to do?" He reached into his coat and pulled out the butcher knife. The blade flashed wickedly in the flickering lantern light.

Alcaria gasped, "Oh, no, Antonio! *Por favor*, put that away before it's too late!"

Her words made her husband feel invincible. He sneered and waved the knife menacingly in front of Tereso's face. "See? I could cut you to shreds if I wanted to, so give me Alcaria and I will not hurt you, *comprende?*" Tereso stood as still as a statue with his muscles tensed. Antonio made a few mock stabbing motions at Tereso and turned his attention to his wife. "Alcaria ! Time to...." In mid-sentence, Tereso exploded forward and grasped his knife hand by the wrist. With a savage twist, he yanked Antonio's arm behind his back and forced him to drop the knife. Antonio screeched in pain as Tereso lifted him off his feet and opened the door. Then with a running start, Tereso threw him outside and into the snow. Antonio landed headfirst and skidded across the ice on his face. Tereso stayed only long enough to ensure that Antonio was not coming back and then went back inside, shutting the door behind him.

Alcaria put her hands to her face and cried, "*¡Dios mío!* I must make sure that he is all right."

Paz restrained her and held her back. "No. Let him sober up first before deciding what to do. Let him go."

Tereso stooped down and picked up the butcher knife. He examined it in front of Alcaria. She stopped struggling with her mother and watched her father. He suddenly stabbed it into the table and walked past her to bed. Her eyes were glued to the quivering knife and grasped its meaning. If she went back to her husband tonight, Antonio would kill her. Alcaria surrendered to her mother's arms and began to weep.

———

By the time Antonio stumbled back to his house, he was numb with cold and slightly sober. He struggled weakly to remove his coat, but his wounded arm refused to cooperate. He finally gave up and collapsed on the sofa with his coat half off. His arm hurt like hell and he gingerly placed it on his lap. Then he felt along his face and head and found bloody scrapes and hard knots from smacking the ground. He took a deep breath to ease the pain and clear his mind.

What the hell happened? Antonio thought as he closed his eyes. *Did I just let an old man throw me out of his home? ¡Jesús! I must be drunk!* He gulped as another wave of pain radiated from his arm. He announced out loud, "I need a drink." Antonio struggled to his feet and stumbled to his closet. With his good arm, he reached inside and slid the coats to the side to reveal his secret hiding place behind a false panel. However, when Antonio looked at the wall, the panel was already removed and shoved haphazardly aside.

"No!" he roared, "I've been robbed!" Forgetting his injuries, he fought inside the nook and found it empty. He slumped against the closet door and lamented his loss. Then, like a thunderbolt from the night sky, he remembered that he had dug out his stash of liquor last night. This was not the work of a robber. He took some solace in this revelation, but he still faced the undesirable situation of not having any booze.

Suddenly, he hit upon an incredible idea. *Why not drive up to Canada and buy a truckload? I could sell most of it by tomorrow morning and keep a few bottles for myself.* Antonio laughed for the first time that night as he formulated his plan. He struggled to his feet and fumbled with his coat and hat. Within minutes, he was grinding the reluctant engine in his truck to start and drove the stiff-steering vehicle north.

———

The bright headlights almost blinded Antonio as he neared the intersection of Highway 16 and Route 201, a deserted crossroads only twelve miles north of Sidney. He was weary and hung over from his all-night ride to Canada and back. The liquor purchase had been smooth and routine. The entire transaction and loading took only a matter of minutes within a nondescript barn on a southern Saskatchewan farm. Antonio cursed as he squinted into the lights that seemed to hang motionless in his windshield. He down-shifted to slow his heavily laden truck as he fought to hug the narrow shoulder.

Antonio thought it strange that the vehicle sat motionless in the intersection and pointed its lights straight at him. He applied his brakes and slowed the truck to a crawl as he came up to the car. The bright headlights prevented him from determining the vehicle's type or its occupants. He rolled down his window to get a better look as he drove by.

Suddenly, red and blue rotating lights exploded from the roof of the parked car. Before Antonio could react, a second car jumped in front of him and blocked his way. The same colored lights magically appeared on its roof, too. Antonio slammed on his brakes to avoid a collision. Two spotlights immediately bore down on him. The searing lights rendered him blind and forced him to look away. He felt confused and scared.

A tall, uniformed man walked slowly to his truck. He held a large flashlight in his hand while his free hand hovered over a holstered pistol on his hip. He silently checked the interior of the cab and then gave Antonio a good look. "Show me your license," he barked.

Antonio jumped in his seat at the command and quickly found his wallet in his coat pocket. He took out his driver's license and handed it to the police officer. The officer took his time examining it while the second officer walked to the back of the truck bed. He pried the lid off one of the boxes and reached inside. "Oh, boy!" the officer exclaimed as he pulled out a bottle of whiskey, "Look what we have here! Yes sir, we have us here a bona fide bootlegger. Yep, we sure do."

The policeman holding Antonio's license smiled and opened the truck door. "Better come out of there and let me check you for weapons." Numbly, Antonio obeyed. As the officer checked Antonio's pockets, he continued to talk. "You know, we got a report about you some time ago. Seems that old lady Applebee at the bank had you pegged right as a bootlegger. We've been looking for you for a long time. Now, stand up and put your hands behind your back, so I can cuff ya." Antonio complied and winced as the handcuffs clamped down on his wrists.

"Okay, pal, now you get a ride to town."

As the officer pushed Antonio into the back of the squad car, Antonio asked, "What about my truck?"

The officer laughed and said, "What truck? You don't own a truck anymore. In fact, a whole lot of things are going to change for a long time, just you wait and see." He slammed the door in Antonio's face.

Chapter 26
La Colonia

The spring of 1927 brought a feeling of rebirth and happiness to the *colonia*. Fresh green grass and daffodils sprouted around the apartments, which gave the adobe bricks an earth-friendly ambiance. The long harsh winter was finally over and people were working and playing outdoors. The warm sun and blue skies seemed to wash winter's glum from minds. Now was the time for fun and newfound love before the beet-thinning season began.

Joaquina and José were skipping back with a basketful of young fiddleheads to help stretch the family meal, when they spotted a 1920 Ford parked in front of the *colonia*. A tall young man dressed in a fancy suit with a red satin scarf wrapped around his neck was peering inside the open hood at the engine. A faint wisp of steam rose from the radiator and he paused to inspect it more closely.

Joaquina vaguely recognized him as one of the new residents who had moved into the bachelor apartment. Until now, she had not had an opportunity to get a good look at him. She stopped skipping and slowed to a walk. José was irritated at her refusal to skip and tugged at her sleeve to walk faster. Joaquina shook her head, but continued to stare at the stranger as they drew closer. José finally gave up and took up his sister's interest in the man by the black car.

When they were almost alongside the car, the man stepped back from the hood and turned toward them. Joaquina stopped dead in her tracks and let out a quiet, deep moan from the back of her throat. Standing before her was the most handsome young man she had ever seen. He was tall and lean with broad shoulders, but it was his perfectly formed nose and full lips that stole her heart.

José thought she was sick and began to worry about her until he saw the man do an incredible trick that made him forget all about his groaning sister. The man produced a raw egg from his coat pocket and cracked it against the car frame. Then he opened the radiator cap and dumped it into the radiator. Within a few minutes, the steam ceased rising from the grill and the man happily replaced the cap. José was impressed.

"Joe," whispered Joaquina, "take these plants and go home." Several of the white plant workers called José "Joe" and the name stuck. Joe made a face and shook his head. "I mean it, you little brat. Go home to Mother, now!" Joe suddenly realized that his sister was no longer a fun playmate, but had changed into a boring adult. In retaliation, he knocked the basket out of her hands, spilling the fiddleheads on the ground, and ran off.

Joaquina momentarily forgot her love sickness and took a swipe at her fleeing little brother. A low, soft chuckle stopped her from chasing him. She looked up to see the handsome man leaning against his car and laughing at her. He had seen the entire spat and seemed to enjoy it immensely. Joaquina froze in horror.

He smiled and said, "That little *niño* must give his pretty Mama lots of trouble, *¿qué no?*"

"Oh, I am not his mother," exclaimed Joaquina breathlessly. "He is my little brother. And, yes, he is a handful."

"I see," responded the young man. He seemed to look at her with renewed interest. Then, with fluid style and grace, he rose from his car and strode toward her. Joaquina stood paralyzed as he approached. He stopped a few feet in front of her and slowly offered his manicured hand. "Please allow me the honor to introduce myself. My name is José Cabello. May I have the pleasure of knowing yours?"

Joaquina felt her tongue tie into knots as she tried to speak. All she could do was take his warm hand and look into his soft brown eyes and marvel at his thick black wavy hair. José waited patiently for a reply. Finally, she got hold of herself and answered, "My name is Joaquina Minjares."

"Well, *Senorita* Minjares, I am very pleased to meet you. I take it that you live in *colonia*, too?"

"*Sí*, with my family."

"*Bueno*," replied José with a brilliant smile, "then you must come to the dance this Saturday at our apartment, *¿qué no?*"

In a rare exhibition of forethought, Tereso and others had decided to remove the center wall dividing the last two apartments with the intention of creating a large room for meetings and dances. The bachelors used the outlying bedrooms and cots in the common room for sleeping. When the residents scheduled a special event, the men quickly cleaned up their messes and crammed it into one of the bedrooms. This Saturday would be the first dance of the summer to be held at the *colonia*. Joaquina collected her thoughts and answered, "I will attend with my older brother and my younger sister."

José beamed and said, "Excellent! I shall look forward to seeing you there. However, I am afraid that I cannot dance with you."

Joaquina dropped her jaw in disappointment and stammered, "But why not?"

José smoothly replied, "Because I will be playing some of the instruments, but I can assure you that I will be watching you every minute that you are there. Until then, *adios*." He carefully dropped her hand and walked back to his car.

Joaquina could not believe what had just happened to her. She had met and talked to the most incredible young man she had ever seen and he was going to look for her at the upcoming dance. He was also a musician with a nice car and fancy clothes. She could hardly contain herself. Joaquina knew that she must try to keep this meeting a secret or Augustine might try to intervene. Worse yet, her mother might forbid her to go to the dance. *Well, this will be my own little secret*, she thought as she floated home in her dream world.

Suddenly, a horrible thought stopped her dead in her tracks. "*¡Dios mío!*" she wailed, "Joe! Joe knows. That little brat will tell everyone! I must get my hands around his neck and make sure that he keeps quiet." Joaquina bolted for home with the remaining fiddleheads streaming from the basket behind her.

When Joaquina reached her family's apartment, she slowed to a walk and entered. Everything seemed tranquil. Her mother was stirring a pot of beans on the stove. Anita and Ben were playing with Antonia on the floor. Nothing seemed out of the ordinary. Relieved, Joaquina let out a heavy sigh. Then she saw Joe standing in the back of the kitchen staring at her with a wicked smile and gleaming eyes. *The brat knows something*, she thought. She put on her best fake smile and said, "Mother, Joe was such a good boy when we were outside. I think we should make something nice for him." Joaquina continued to smile sweetly as she slowly walked toward him.

Paz scarcely looked up from her cooking. "I am glad Joe behaved himself. What did you have in mind?"

Joaquina replied sincerely, "Oh, I don't know, Mama. Maybe something sweet." She was getting closer to him. Just a little more and she could nab him. Joe's smile got even bigger as he watched her approach. He seemed to be thoroughly enjoying this cat-and-mouse game. Joaquina edged a little closer, then lunged for her brother. Joe dodged his big sister and darted to his mother.

"Mama! Mama!" squealed Joe as he tugged on her apron, "Joaquina likes a man! Joaquina likes a man!"

"I see," said Paz as she tapped her spoon clean on the rim of the pot. Now she understood her daughter's unusual words of praise. She stood between the warring siblings and wiped her hands clean on her apron. Then she ruffled Joe's thick hair as he stuck his tongue out at his sister. Paz suppressed a smile as she confronted Joaquina. "What is Joe talking about? Are you seeing someone?"

Joaquina hissed at her brother to quiet him and then composed herself before speaking to her mother. "Joe is talking nonsense, Mama. You know how he makes up stories all the time." There was something about her demeanor that convinced Paz that Joe had been speaking the truth. She started to open her mouth to speak when Alcaria came into the room tying a ribbon in her hair. She wore a long summer dress with ankle-high shoes.

"Mama," Alcaria said, "I am going down to the jail to visit Antonio. I should be back in an hour, Okay?"

Joe jumped out and grabbed her hand. "I want to go, too!"

Alcaria answered, "Oh, no, Joe. You are too little to go with me. Stay here, *comprende?*"

Joe took one look at Joaquina and tightened his grip on Alcaria. "No, I want to come!" Alcaria sighed and proceeded to peel him off her hand and shove him back to their mother. Joe would have none of it and began to throw a fit. Paz wrapped her arms around him and tried to soothe his temper. Alcaria chose this moment to briskly walk out the door.

A block away from the *colonia*, Alcaria slowed to a walk and looked over her shoulder to see if Joe was following her, like he had done in the past. All was clear, so she continued down the road that she had walked so many times these past months.

Four months before, the court had convicted Antonio of bootlegging. Since this was his first arrest, the judge gave him a light sentence of six months. So, he still had two months to sit idly in the Sidney jail. Alcaria saw the boredom slowly gnawing at her husband's mind and drive him mad, but the positive side to his incarceration was that it forced him to quit drinking. The first two weeks were rough on him, but afterward, he had slowly stopped begging her to smuggle something into his cell. She had firmly denied his requests and let him dry out.

Alcaria was lost in her thoughts and failed to notice a little boy trailing her. It was not until she neared the jail when a passerby laughed and pointed behind her. Alcaria turned and saw Joe racing behind a parked car to hide. She shouted at him with exasperation, "*¡Dios mío!* Have you been following me all this time? Well, it's too late to take you back so you might as well come along. Come here and take my hand. I don't want you to get into trouble." Joe came out from behind the car with a triumphant smile and skipped over to his sister. "Now, stay with me and don't wander off, *comprende?*" Joe never answered her. He was excited to see the prisoners in their cells.

The Sidney jail was a simple, nondescript building that stood out from the rest because of its drab features. The one-story brick structure had a barred window in front that provided light for the sheriff's office. A narrow hallway led to six small jail cells in the back of the building. Four small cells lined the back wall and each adjoining wall had a larger cell that held groups of detainees for short periods of time.

When Alcaria walked up the steps of the jailhouse holding Joe by the hand, the sheriff held the door open for her. He was a big man with an infectious smile. One hand held the door while the other rested comfortably on his holstered pistol. He greeted her with a deep, low voice. "Good afternoon, ma'am. Right on time as usual. I see you got yer tag-a-long again. Couldn't shake him, huh?"

Alcaria gave him a smile as she entered and said, "*Hola*. No, Joe broke away from Mother again. I will keep him by my side."

The sheriff chuckled as he bent over to look at Joe. Joe squirmed behind his sister and peered around her dress. "That's right, little man. You stay real close to yer sister. Last time you darn near got pulled through the bars by that crazy migrant!"

Alcaria shuddered at the memory. She and Antonio had been deep in conversation and failed to notice Joe wandering off to gawk at the strange men behind the bars. One particularly deranged individual had enticed Joe over to his cell with the promise of candy. The sheriff had miraculously appeared and yanked Joe back just as the prisoner lunged for him. Had the sheriff been one second slower …

The sheriff produced the sign-in ledger and Alcaria signed and wrote in the time of the visit. The sheriff then led them down the hallway to the jail cells in back. Alcaria's arrival always produced cat-calls and derogatory comments from the surrounding inmates, which was followed by Antonio telling them to shut up or he would kill them when he got the chance. After a few minutes, the comments died down to a couple of snickers. After the sheriff was satisfied that all was well, he walked Alcaria to Antonio's small cell along the back wall and left her alone.

They were quiet at first, getting used to each other's company again. Alcaria noticed that he seemed more agitated than usual, so she asked him, "Antonio, what is wrong? Did something happen today?"

Antonio grabbed the bars with both hands and rested his head in the middle gap. He closed his eyes for a second as if he was steeling himself for what he had to say. "This morning," he whispered, "I got a letter from the bank. The federal government seized my account. They took everything."

Alcaria let his announcement sink in for a few moments before responding. When she did speak, Antonio was surprised how strong she sounded. "Antonio, I have lived through times when I did not have anything to eat and nowhere to live. We might not have any money, but we have a house and when you get out, you can go back to work at the Provision Meat Market. We will be all right."

Antonio snorted, "Nobody would hire me as a butcher in this town."

"Oh, yes they would," countered Alcaria. "You are the fastest butcher in the valley. They will hire you as soon as you are out. Just you see."

Antonio took a deep breath and produced a tired grin. "You are too good for me."

Alcaria tilted her head and answered, "*Sí.* You have a lot of making up to do." Antonio nodded and began to speak to her in the relaxed tone in which a loving husband speaks to his wife. They were soon engrossed in conversation and forgot that little Joe was at their feet.

Joe, on the other hand, could not care less. He walked to the middle of the room and gaped at the men staring back at him. Their hardened faces and jackal sneers fascinated him. One man with a scar running down his mustached face and a skull tattooed on his arm motioned for Joe to come closer. Joe balled his chubby hands tight and held his ground, but he felt drawn to him as if he was connected to him.

"Time's up, Mrs. Borrego." The sheriff's voice broke the spell the ruffian was trying to weave over Joe. The man turned away and walked to the back of his cell. "You will have to conclude your visit." Alcaria and Antonio said their goodbyes and gave each other an awkward kiss through the bars. Then she dragged Joe out of the room and headed for home.

———•••••———

Within their back bedroom, Anita and Joaquina fussed with last-minute preparations for the dance. They shared a handheld mirror they propped up on a crate next to the wall. Sixteen-year-old Joaquina wanted that special sophisticated look and her ten-year-old sister strove for a mature appearance. Joaquina introduced Anita to the marvels of lipstick and eye shadow. When the two finally emerged from the bedroom, they found Augustine patiently waiting at the kitchen table, neatly scrubbed, brushed, and dressed fashionably in a simple suit. Their mother, however, stood with her hands on her hips and a scowl on her face.

"Anita!" scolded Paz, "You are much too young to be wearing heavy makeup. Come to the sink and wash it off, *pronto!*"

"But, Mama," protested Anita, "All the other girls are wearing it."

"I don't care. Wash it off or stay home. Your choice."

Sobbing, Anita shuffled over to the wash basin. She dribbled some water on a washcloth and dabbed her face with it. Paz stood silently watching her daughter painstakingly remove some of the makeup. Finally, Paz could not wait any longer and took matters into her own hands. She grabbed the washcloth away from Anita, doused it with water, and scrubbed Anita's face. Anita howled as her mother removed the last of the false coloring.

"There," said Paz as she stepped back and admired her work, "Augustine, you may take your sisters to the dance." Anita stood reeling from her mother's assault as Augustine rose and walked to the door. Joaquina put her arm around her sister and ushered her out the door.

When they heard the door close behind them, Joaquina whispered in Anita's ear, "Don't worry. I will put some lipstick on you when we get to the dance."

The three of them walked toward the corner apartment where the bachelors stayed. In the deepening evening, they could see the other residents entering the door. Laughter and warm lights spilled out through windows of the apartment. The Minjares children felt their excitement and anticipation rise as they came to the doorway. Joaquina grabbed Anita by the arm and pulled her to the side. "Here," she said as she produced her special tube of lipstick. "Let me put a little on." Anita pucker up her lips and let her sister touch her up. "You look great! Let's go in."

As they stepped through the doorway, they were engulfed in a milling crowd of familiar faces and neighbors. A three-piece band was setting up in the far corner. Joaquina swept her eyes across the floor until they fell upon José tuning his guitar. She felt her stomach tighten when she saw how impossibly handsome he looked in his fancy musician's suit. Joaquina turned to her sister and whispered, "There he is, Anita! Look!"

Anita peered over the moving heads and spotted the tall, lean man. "*¡Dios mío!*" she gasped. "He is so handsome. You actually talked to him?"

"*Sí*, and he said that he would look for me at the dance. Can you believe it?" The girls mooned over José for a few minutes as he began to strap his instruments to his body. His right foot operated a bass drum while he strummed a guitar and played a harmonica. He played a few practice bars and then nodded to the men next to him that he was ready. A man with a fiddle returned the gesture. The third man with another guitar began to sound out a cadence. Suddenly, they launched into a Mexican two-step dance tune. Men began to hoot and laugh and sweep women onto the dance floor. Anita jumped at the first offer to dance, but Joaquina held back. She was transfixed on José and watched how skillfully he played his instruments without error. He tapped out a lively beat on the bass drum as he strummed the strings and played the harmonica.

The trio played song after song without stopping until the crowd begged them to stop and yelled for mercy. Men took off their hats and wiped their brows with their handkerchiefs. The women fanned their faces with their hands. Several couples chose to step outside to cool off. As the crowd thinned, the musicians carefully set down their instruments and sought a drink to soothe their throats. José took longer than his partners to disconnect from his equipment and was by himself by the time he set his guitar down. When he stood up to join them, he found his way blocked by Joaquina Minjares.

"*Hola*, José," she greeted him shyly.

José stood momentarily at a loss for where he had met her. Then his memory rekindled his chance meeting a few days ago. "Ah, *hola*. And you look ravishing tonight … um …"

"Joaquina," she injected with hurt in her voice.

"*Sí*, Joaquina," he replied smoothly, "How could I forget such a lovely name?" José flashed a sexy smile that caused Joaquina to forgive him a hundred times over. "Are you enjoying the dance?"

Joaquina beamed back, "*Sí*. You play very well. You sing well, too."

"*Gracias, señorita*. Your pleasure is my only concern." José deftly swooped up her hand and kissed it. Then he held it gently and softly looked into her eyes. Joaquina felt her knees buckle and her body melt in front of him. His magic spell wrapped around her and penetrated her heart.

Suddenly, a voice cracked into Joaquina's fantasy land and let the shafts of reality shine through. "*Perdón*, but I don't believe that I have had the honor of meeting you." Augustine stood beside them with his jaw set tight. At only thirteen-years-old, Augustine assumed his role as the oldest brother very seriously. José slowly dropped Joaquina's hand and faced Augustine with a sneer on his face. Although José towered over him, Augustine stood solid and unflinchingly met his stare.

Joaquina said quickly, "Augustine, we were just talking." Augustine ignored her and remained transfixed on José.

Finally, José realized that intimidation would not work. He slowly offered his hand to Augustine and said, "Let me introduce myself, *por favor*. I am José Cabello. I live here in this apartment."

Augustine carefully grasped José's hand and shook it. He replied in a serious tone, "I am Augustine Minjares and my parents tasked me with chaperoning my sisters tonight."

José choked back a laugh and dropped Augustine's hand. "I understand and I assure you that my intentions are honorable. Besides, as the lead musician, I cannot even have the pleasure of dancing with Joaquina, *¿qué no?*"

Augustine admitted to himself that José had a point, but he still did not trust him. He replied, "I can see that you are a busy man tonight, so we will not delay you any longer. Come, Joaquina. Let's get a drink."

Joaquina was about to protest when one of the band members yelled, "José! Time to start again. Come on." José winked at Joaquina and strode back to the makeshift stage. Augustine left his love-struck sister to gawk at the insolent man and made his way to the punch bowl. The band started with a musical coyote howl from the band before belting out another Mexican two-step tune. The room erupted with laughter and foot-stomping. Augustine made it to the punch bowl and fought to ladle some punch amidst the jarring throes of the crowd. After pouring his drink, he retreated to a doorway for protection and so he could enjoy his drink in peace.

Augustine scanned the room as he tasted his punch. He spotted Anita whirling across the floor, laughing and enjoying herself immensely. He saw Joaquina disgustingly swaying in front of the stage, trying to catch the pompous José's attention. Then much to his surprise, he noticed his father and mother entering the door. Tereso wore a plain white shirt, buttoned to the collar. Paz wore a simple, full-length dress. Augustine also detected that each had a different expression. His father's eyes revealed that he was planning on finding friends and telling stories. His mother carried a reserved air about her that announced that she was only here because of her husband. She looked like she was only tolerating the situation and had no intention of enjoying herself.

Within minutes of entering, Tereso proved Augustine right. He spotted his new friend Juan Gonzalez and made a beeline for him, leaving Paz to fend for herself. Augustine felt sorry for her and wormed his way through the crowd to her. When he finally got to his mother, Paz gave him a grateful look and then resumed her stately pose.

The Mexican polkas came in groups of threes. When couples started to dance the first one, they were usually committed to dance the whole set. This suited Anita well, but toward the end of the second set, her heart began to pound and she became lightheaded from lack of breath. She reluctantly refused the next offer to dance and groped her way to the outside door. Unfortunately, her path led her directly in front of her mother.

Paz spotted her ailing daughter and motioned for Augustine to help her. Augustine grabbed Anita's arm just as she began to faint. He gracefully caught her as she fell backward and let her slump gently to the floor. Paz roughly pushed a few gawking people away before kneeling before Anita and examining her. During this close inspection, Paz noticed the same bright lipstick that she had washed off earlier had miraculously reappeared.

Paz suddenly felt a flood of emotions. She was concerned about her unconscious daughter sprawled on the floor, but she was angry at her defiance. Then Paz felt the prodding of many eyes and looked up to see most of the crowd staring at her. She desperately wanted to leave, but she needed her husband's help. Suddenly, she heard his bellowing laughter reverberate through the room, followed by a backslap. Paz spotted him across the floor engrossed in telling a wild tale. He and Juan were the only ones oblivious to Anita's plight. Then Paz saw Joaquina swooning in front of a fancy-dressed young man and realized that she had two family members who had not a clue to what was happening.

Paz decided to take control of the situation. She stood up, put her hands on hips, and yelled, "That does it! Augustine, tell your father to come here and help me. Then grab your sister over there and take her home, now! The rest of you, leave us alone. *Comprende?*" With much fanfare, Augustine finally pried Tereso away from Juan and steered his father back to his mother. Then Augustine dragged Joaquina, kicking and screaming, away from her newfound love. Under his wife's firm direction, Tereso reluctantly scooped up Anita and carried her out the door. Augustine consoled his sobbing sister as they followed their father home. Trailing behind her estranged family, Paz walked with her arms tightly crossed and a stern look that a passerby could clearly see in the dark.

———

After the beet thinning in June, life for Tereso slowed to a comfortable pace. Augustine found work helping at the pulp dryer and draining the pulp pits in preparation for the upcoming sugar beet processing. The little money Augustine made plus the family's earnings from beet thinning allowed the Minjareses to live comfortably until the beet harvest in the fall. Tereso could have found work irrigating fields, but without hunger as a motive, he was not inclined to seek employment. Instead, he spent his idle time exaggerating his old *colleador* days in Zacatecas to Juan Gonzalez

Juan was ten years younger than Tereso and a scoundrel at heart. If there was a way to cut a corner and profit by it, Juan would think of it. Tereso and Juan were kindred spirits. Each sought wealth by exploitation and discovery. Neither considered hard work and saving the way to riches. So when their talk eventually wandered to money, they schemed up elaborate ways to gather it.

"*Amigo*," said Juan as he sat leaning against a tall cottonwood contemplating life in the cool shade, "we need to think of something to sell. You know, something that everyone wants. Then we can buy it cheap and sell it *mucho* high. We would be rich in no time, *¿qué no?*"

Tereso was lying on the ground with his sombrero pulled over his face half-listening to the hypnotic buzz of the locusts. They were especially loud during the heat of the day. He eventually replied, "My numbskull son-in-law tried that and ended up in jail."

"*Sí*, but he made lots of money until then, *¿qué no?*"

Tereso grunted in return.

"Well then," continued Juan, "all we have to do is think of something that everyone wants, but doesn't have. You know, like liquor. Something that we could make. That would keep costs down and profits high. You see, *amigo*, Antonio had the right idea. He just got dumb. We are a lot smarter. We would not make the same mistakes, *¿qué no?*"

Tereso slid his hat off his face and gave Juan a hard look. "*Sí*, we are smarter than that idiot. He couldn't keep his hands off the stuff and got caught. Are you thinking that we should make our own liquor?"

Juan opened his eyes and rubbed the stubble on his chin as he thought it out. "That is a possibility, but someone might find our still and then our business would be over. No, maybe something else that would not be as much work …"

Tereso looked up into the tree and studied the fluttering leaves. When he finally spoke, he sounded like he was acting out a dream, "We could grow marijuana."

Juan's eyes flew open. "What did you say?"

"I said we could grow marijuana. The workers never seem to have enough of it. They bring it up from Mexico and run out within a few weeks. Anyone that has any extra always seems to sell it for *mucho dinero*."

Juan jumped to his feet and said, "*¡Dios mío!* That's it! You are a genius." Then he looked around him to make sure that no one was listening and continued in a low voice, "Where do we grow it? How can we get the seed?"

Lying on his back, Tereso saw Juan towering over him, his eyes bugging out with excitement. He thought that he looked ridiculous and started to laugh. "Why, *amigo*, we can just ask for the seed from any field hand who has an empty pouch. They don't want them." Then Tereso struggled to sit up. *Damn, my joints hurt!* he thought. *I am start-*

ing to feel old. When he regained his composure, Tereso continued, "As for where to grow the plants, we find some place fertile with lots of water. Someplace that is out of the way and can hide our crop."

"You mean like the river?"

Tereso had to admit that sometimes Juan had good ideas. "*Sí,* the river would be a good place."

"*Bueno,*" exclaimed Juan as he slapped Tereso across his back. "Let's start collecting seeds now and plant a crop before it gets too late in the season, *¿qué no?*"

Tereso let out a huff and shook his head. He really wanted a nap now, but he knew Juan would pester him without mercy. Tereso struggled to his feet and adjusted his sombrero. "Okay. *Vámanos,*" he said with resignation. The partnership of Juan Gonzalez and Tereso Minjares had begun.

———————

On a hot August day, a man in his thirties, dressed sharply in a brown three-pieced suit, stepped off the train at the Sidney depot. He wore a matching brown derby that rested on his head with a slight cant. In contrast to his clothing, his boots were old and scuffed and looked like they belonged with a different outfit. Probably the man's most remarkable feature was his face. It bore a perpetual smile and his eyes shone with a cockiness that screamed, "I feel lucky!"

With a small, ragged suitcase in his hand, he left the station and marched up to the first Mexican he saw and asked, "*Perdón,* could you tell me where Prudenciano and Paz Nava live?"

The man screwed up his face in concentration for a moment and then replied, "There is no family in these parts with that name." The stranger was undaunted. He thanked the man and bounded off to find another. Over and over, he asked for the whereabouts of the Nava family and the answer was always the same, "Never heard of them." "No, not here." "Are you sure they live in these parts?"

Toward late afternoon, the man began to show signs of despair. His smile had deteriorated to a slight grin, his posture stooped forward, and his suitcase hung low at his side. Standing on Main Street, he saw two older men talking by a store and decided to ask them if they knew of the Nava family. As he approached them, he noticed that these two must be longtime friends. They appeared to be completely at ease with each other and enjoying the conversation. One man was enormous, with big shoulders and a powerful chest. Unfortunately, his girth matched his muscled top and hung over his belt, but he still looked ominous. The other man was smaller and wiry with a laughing face. The stranger chose to address the smaller man first.

The man walked up to the men and took off his derby and held it to his chest with his left hand. He waited for a moment for the men to acknowledge him, but they were engrossed in their conversation and paid him no heed. Then he cleared his throat. The noise interrupted the men. They turned and stared at the strangely dressed man standing next to them with a suitcase in his hand.

The stranger put on his best smile and asked, "*Perdón*, I was wondering if any of you could tell me where Prudenciano and Paz Nava live?" The man saw their eyes snap wide open and their heads reel back at the mention of the names.

"Who are you? Why do you ask for them?" demanded the smaller man. His smile was gone.

The stranger was troubled by the response. He quickly answered, "Prudenciano is my uncle and Paz is my half-sister."

"*¡Dios mío!*" gasped the big man. "Are you José Nava!"

Stunned, the stranger looked up to the large man and said, "*Sí*, how did you ..." He stopped in mid-sentence as he recognized the huge presence in front of him. "Anastacio Currandas?" The big man solemnly nodded. José turned to the smaller man and said, "And you must be Victoriano Vallejo!" Victoriano grinned broadly in response.

José was confused about what he should do next. Part of him wanted to run away from these dangerous men of his past. The other half wanted to embrace them for saving him from a certain death by the *Villistas* rebels. He settled for standing awkwardly motionless and silent.

Anastacio broke the ice by offering his big, meaty hand. José gingerly shook it. "Welcome to Sidney," Anastacio said in a low deep voice. "*Sí*, we know where your family is, but you must never mention their real names again, *comprende?*"

José shook his head and said, "No, I don't understand. What has happened?"

Victoriano answered with a question, "How did you track them to Sidney? Your uncle has never used his real name in fifteen years?"

José shrugged and replied, "I overheard some *hombre* in a *cantina* in Fresno, California talk about an old *colleador* that he met in Sidney, Montana. When I questioned him further, he said that this man was from Monte Escobedo, Zacatecas. I figured that he probably met my uncle, so I came north to find him."

José's answer impressed Anastacio. He did not think José was capable of such logic. "*Sí*, your uncle can sure talk. Victoriano, do you think that we can pay the Minjares family a visit and drop off this ruffian?"

Victoriano almost danced with excitement. "That's a great idea,

Tacio! My wagon is just around the corner. *Vámanos!*" Anastacio put his big hand on José's shoulder and steered him down the street.

After a half-hour wagon ride, Victoriano pulled up to the *colonia*. The sun was setting and delicious dinner smells wafted from the apartments. The wagon bobbed as Anastacio lumbered out. In contrast, Victoriano leaped from the buckboard and landed like a cat. José followed with his suitcase in tow. Anastacio walked up to the Minjares door and pounded on it with his fist. The family noises inside ceased and the door slowly opened, revealing a tall elderly man.

When Tereso recognized his two dear friends, he smiled and boomed, "Tacio and Victoriano! Come in, my *amigos*. Please have something to eat with us."

Anastacio grinned and said, "We would love to, but first, we brought you something." Victoriano flashed a mischievous smile as they slowly parted and revealed a strange man standing behind them. Tereso's expression changed to puzzlement as the man came forward and the kitchen light spilled across his face. *There is something familiar about him*, thought Tereso.

The man set down his suitcase, took off his derby, and said softly, "*Tío*, it is good to see you again. It has been a long time."

Tereso said quietly, "*Tío*? I haven't been called *Tío* since ..." Suddenly, Tereso recognized him. He stepped forward and engulfed José in a bear hug and kissed him on the cheek. Then Tereso turned toward the kitchen and yelled, "Paz! Come quick! See who is here!"

Paz emerged from the kitchen, wiping her hands on her apron. She was mad that her husband's carousing friends had interrupted her dinner preparation and showed it. "*Sí*," she said with annoyance, "what is it now?" Tereso ushered the man into the kitchen and Anastacio and Victoriano followed. Paz frowned as she studied the strange man standing in front of her. *Whoever this is*, she thought, *he looks as if he is going to stay a while.*

Then he spoke, "Paz, don't you recognize me? It's me. José."

The name took a second to register before causing a miraculous transformation. Paz's stern expression melted and tears rolled down her face. "José! My dear José!" She grabbed him and buried her face into his chest. Between great heaves and sobs, she whispered, "I thought you were dead."

José was overcome with emotion, too. He murmured into her hair as he held her, "You were hard to find."

The two cried and embraced each other for a few minutes while the children watched quietly with puzzled looks upon their faces. Finally, curiosity got the better of Ben. He walked over to his mother, tugged on her skirt and asked, "Mamma, who is this?"

Paz reluctantly released José and wiped the tears from her face. She smiled as she looked down at her little son and said, "This man is my brother." Then she faced the rest of her brood and gave a formal introduction, "Children, this is your Uncle José. I have not seen him for many years. José, this is Joaquina, Augustine, Anita, Ben, Joe, and the baby is Antonia. Our oldest, Alcaria, is married and lives here in Sidney. She is expecting her first child later this year."

The large family impressed José as he scanned the children's inquisitive faces. "So many beautiful children," he said softly. "Has that much time gone by?"

"*Sí*," answered Paz, "I'm afraid it has."

José shook his head in disbelief and sadness as he whispered, "So much time lost."

Tereso put his arm around José's shoulders and steered him to the table. "We have much to talk about," he said.

José flashed him a smile and said, "*Sí*, like what's with the new name? Tereso Minjares? Where did that come from?"

Victoriano let out a long whistle and laughed as he said, "Your uncle will love retelling that story! I wonder how much will change from the last time I heard it?"

Tereso shot his friend a hard look to silence him and took a seat next to José. "I will tell you all about it, but first, tell us about the family, *por favor*. Have you seen any of them?" Paz moved closer to her brother to hear better.

"Well," started José, "I bumped into our sister Estranda in Los Angeles. She is married now and has a family. She said Father brought her and our youngest sister to California to find work. He died a few years ago." Tereso and Paz nodded. They had last seen Abundio twenty years ago in Torreón as he led the two little girls on horseback to Durango. José continued, "When I was in the army, I traveled through Monte Escobedo. Only Father and the girls got out in time. Mother and the rest of the family were killed by the typhus epidemic in 1906. Father saved me by taking me to the army hospital in Zacatecas. Of course when I got out, I had to join the army for eight years to pay for the treatment. Then that tyrant Díaz stole our land. Father willed Paz and me a small parcel in town. That is all that is left of our property."

Paz put her hand on José's chair to steady herself as she contemplated her past. *I would have died with them had I not left the year before*, she thought. She shook her head and sighed, "I must finish dinner." Paz patted her brother on his shoulder before walking thoughtfully back to the stove. She motioned for Joaquina and Anita to help her. They dutifully rose and assisted with the meal preparations.

———•••••———

Just before the beet harvest and the first killing frost, Tereso and Juan met on a remote mud bar along the Yellowstone River. For the past two months, they had slipped secretly into the lush floodplain forest and visited their maturing marijuana crop. During this time, they weeded the neatly seeded rows, carefully thinned excess plants, and lovingly pruned the stalks so that the plants would grow thick and strong. They had chosen their site well. The thick canopy of the cottonwood trees trapped the heat and moisture along the ground, causing a greenhouse effect. The plants grew fast within this environment as their roots sank deep into the fertile, wet soil. The men now stood among their chest-high plants and admired their crop.

Juan pushed his *sombrero* back and wiped his brow with the back of his hand as he said, "We have done well, eh *amigo?*"

Tereso grunted, "*Sí*, I would like to see them grow some more before we harvest them, but if we wait any longer, the frost will kill them."

Juan produced a sickle and waved it in the air. "Well, let's cut them down and drag them home. Our money is just around the corner. *Vámanos.*"

The men worked hard all day cutting the fibrous stalks and gently carrying the bundles to a wagon parked above the riverbank. Tereso had borrowed it for this occasion. They were careful not to damage a single leaf. When the sun slid beneath the western horizon, they finished loading the last marijuana bundle and covered their crop with a tarp. With tired, happy faces, the scoundrels climbed aboard and encouraged their ragged horse to plod home.

———•••••———

One evening after dinner, Paz and her daughters were washing the dishes and clearing the table. The room was unusually quiet because Tereso had slipped outside to handle some "business arrangements" with Juan Gonzalez. Antonia was fast asleep in the corner and the boys were playing just outside the door.

José Nava came bounding inside dressed in his brown suit and derby. His face seemed to bubble over with excitement as he announced, "Tonight's the night, girls, tonight's the night! I can feel it in my bones." He grabbed Paz and twirled her around the kitchen.

"*¡Dios mío!*" she gasped, "What's gotten into you?"

"I feel lucky, that's all."

Paz smiled at her younger brother and asked, "And what are you going to do with such luck?"

José gave her a mischievous smile and replied, "I am going to make a lot of money tonight. *Verdad.* All I need is a little something to get things going, you know, a little money to make *mucho dinero.*"

Paz gave him a dubious look. "How much do you need?"

José waved his hand in the air and said, "Oh, I don't know, maybe ten dollars."

"Ten dollars!" shouted Anita. She had been silently watching José as she dried the dishes. For the past week, she had suspected that he had been borrowing money from her mother. Now, her suspicions were upheld and she could no longer hold her tongue. "Ten dollars is a lot of money. Don't do it, Mamma, *por favor.* He will just gamble it away."

"Shush," scolded Paz, "this doesn't concern you!"

Anita felt that the situation did concern her. She marched up to José and put her finger into his chest and said, "Stop taking money from my mother, *comprende?* Go out and find a job!"

Paz screamed at her daughter, "*¡Silencio!* Go outside and leave us alone!" Anita glared hotly at José before storming outside.

A moment of awkward silence prevailed before José cleared his throat and said, "I guess I better be going."

Paz wiped her hands on her apron and said, "Just a moment." She dashed into the bedroom and quickly emerged with a few dollars in her hand.

"Mamma!" exclaimed Joaquina.

Paz cut her off with a chop of her hand. Then she turned to her brother and said, "Here you go. Have fun tonight."

José stuffed the money into his breast pocket and regenerated his cocky smile. "*Gracias.* I will make it big tonight. Just you see." He tipped his hat to Joaquina and gave Paz a kiss on her cheek before skipping out the door.

During each beet harvest season, Holly Sugar sought to perfect harvest techniques and increase efficiency. Reducing production costs was the underlying reason to constantly improve the harvest process. As the fields increased in size, more workers were needed to bring the sugar beets to the factory within a reasonable amount of time. Although the Mexicans and other migrants worked cheaply, the overall payroll cut sharply into profits. Expanding the harvest season was not an option because the beets lost the peak sugar content if picked too soon or late. Also, late season harvests promoted rot and increased spoilage within the storage piles. Thus, the only solution was to increase harvest efficiency.

Every year, the company floated innovative ideas past farmers and tried new machinery in the fields. During a frosty morning in September 1927, Tereso, a sleepy and shivering José Nava, and an impeccably dressed José Cabello stood at the edge of a beet field with a large group of field workers and watched a tractor belch thick smoke into the cold air as it dragged a large plow and a level behind it. The plow fit perfectly between rows of beets. It turned the earth and rolled the beets out of the ground. The level broadened the plowed cut into a flat, shallow trough.

A man standing next to Tereso muttered, "What now? Looks like some *gringo* found a way to dig up beets, *¿qué no?*"

Tereso grunted back, "*Sí*, no more pulling, but we still have to clean them and top them."

After a couple of passes, the tractor stopped and the farmer jumped off the metal seat. He walked over to the waiting men and women and addressed them in English. "I hope ya all can understand me. If not, you that can will just have to explain to the others." The farmer waited for some indication of acknowledgment, but all he saw was a sea of unresponsive faces. He sighed and continued, "Okay, then. I want the women and children to walk into the troughs and grab the beets, shake the dirt off them and lay them down with the tops facing the trough. Understand? *Comprende?*"

No one moved. Exasperated, the farmer jumped into the trough and vigorously yanked the beets up and shook them. Then he threw them on the ground with the tops facing in. "See? Like this. *Comprende?*"

José Cabello leaned over to Tereso and asked, "How long are we going to play dumb? Until he pulls up every beet in the field?"

Tereso grunted, "*Sí*, that would be good to watch, but we would lose our pay." Reluctantly, he turned to the crowd and said, "All women and children. Pull the beets and lay them down like this man has shown us. Go on now." Slowly, the people moved into place and began pulling the beets as the farmer had demonstrated. Joaquina, Anita, and Augustine assumed their positions inside the trench and began working. Periodically, Joaquina stole a quick glance at the handsome José Cabello and usually she found him smiling at her, which caused her heart to skip a beat.

The farmer stood with his hands on his hips for a few minutes and watched them work. When he was satisfied with their progress, he turned his attention back to the men behind him. "All right, now, gentlemen. I want half of you to grab these topping knives and lop off the tops." The men stared silently back. The farmer's patience was wearing thin. He grabbed the sickle-shaped knife and said angrily, "Like this." He picked up a beet with his left hand and cut off the top with the knife. The top dropped into the trench and he plopped the beet down. Then he stooped over and grabbed another one and repeated the process. "See? Like this. *Comprende?*" Again, no response.

The farmer exploded, "Damn it! I know you varmints understand me! By gawd, if ya don't start coming around, I will get another crew! How does that make yer keister pucker, eh?"

José Cabello whispered to Tereso through the side of his mouth, "He says that if we don't start working soon, he will fire us. I think he means it." Tereso nodded and signaled for the men to step forward and grab a knife.

"Wait," shouted the farmer, "only half of ya." He arbitrarily pushed half of the men back, including José Nava.

Nava smiled as he wiped his brow with the back of his hand and said, "Well, it looks like there is no work for me here today. I think I will go home."

"Not so fast, *amigo*," said Juan Gonzalez. "This *hombre* has something else planned for us. See?" Sure enough, the farmer was pointing to a wagon and motioning the rest of the men to throw the beets inside. "I think he wants us to load the wagon. Better start working."

Nava swore under his breath. He was counting on slipping back to the warm confines of the *colonia*. There was no hope for escape. Too many people were watching. José Nava muttered, "I hate this place," and began throwing the topped beets into the wagon.

Although the new process went faster than the old way of yanking beets through frozen ground, it still required many hours of back-breaking work. The shifts started at dawn and stopped at dusk. Some enterprising farmers extended the shift by illuminating the fields with lanterns. The workers toiled on with the knowledge that the harvest would last only three weeks. They had to make their money now to sustain them over the idle winter as they rested for next year's beet-thinning season.

As the harvest season progressed, workers began to slow down as the long hours wore on. The hardships forced a person's character to emerge and reveal the true mettle inside. Big, strong men buckled from maintaining a stooped position while relentlessly topping the beets with the wicked topping knife. To save time, some men mastered the art of stabbing the beet with the sickle, flinging the beet into the air, catching it with their free hand, and lopping off the top. Unfortunately, this technique also produced nasty gashes and missing fingers.

Other men and women who appeared fragile at the beginning of the season proved to be stalwarts of the workforce. Despite his fancy clothes, José Cabello demonstrated that he was a hard worker. No matter the task, he worked steadily until it was completed. Joaquina, Anita, and Augustine crawled over acres of frozen fields shaking sugar beets clean. They did not complain once.

In contrast, Tereso found every excuse to stop and watch everyone work. He would offer some unwanted advice to a worker whose only thought was to mind his own business and get the job done. He also made a big show of connecting the horse's harness to the haul wagon and wasted hours in the process. Most irritatingly, he would stand in the middle of the field, slowly roll a cigarette, and smoke it down to a nub. Sometimes a farmer interrupted Tereso during these frequent smoke breaks and forced him back to work, but mostly he stood leaning on a hoe or shovel appearing completely oblivious to the hard labor around him.

José Nava took advantage of his uncle's work breaks and visited him regularly. He felt that if his uncle could get away with not working, then so could he. One afternoon, José found Tereso standing in the middle of the field enjoying a long smoke break. José greeted him, "*Hola, Tío.* How goes it?"

Tereso nodded as he let out a long stream of smoke through his nostrils as he leaned against a hoe. He appeared to watch a set of laborers top beets at a far corner of the field. Tereso pulled his cigarette from his mouth and pointed it at them. "They are doing that all wrong. They need to be farther apart, see?" José looked at the men and failed to notice their subtle shortcomings. Tereso continued, "I should tell them."

José ignored his uncle's comment and spoke what was on his mind, "Uh, *Tío*, I was thinking about returning to Fresno."

Tereso turned his attention to his nephew. "Why? You have family here, *¿qué no?*"

"*Sí*," stammered José, "but it's too cold here and I like a bigger city. You understand, don't you?"

Tereso contemplated his nephew's latest revelation and exhaled another stream of smoke. He remembered what it was like to be young and seek excitement. Sidney was a remote backwater of the United States. Young men seemed to suffocate here. He understood how José felt. At last he spoke, "Okay. You must do what you feel is best. Paz will be upset."

José thought, *But Anita won't.* He had been avoiding her since their last confrontation two weeks ago.

"Hey! Get to work, you two!" The farmer who owned the field came stomping toward them. "I have just about had enough of your lazy ways. Either get to work or leave."

Tereso and José gave each other a "What's wrong with him?" look before slowly returning to their tasks. The beet fields were not getting any smaller.

The whisper came like a bat out of the night, quiet and with purpose. Tereso was leaning against a stark cottonwood tree smoking a cigarette in the chilly evening in front of the *colonia* when he heard it. He was used to these type of meetings now, so the hushed voice did not startle him.

"*Señor* Minjares? I would like to buy some of your weed. You have some, *¿qué no?*"

Tereso took another long drag on his cigarette and pretended not to hear his customer while his eyes scanned the night for clues of other men hiding in the darkness. After a few moments of silence, he said quietly, "*Sí*, I have some. Do you have a can?"

"*Sí*, here it is. Just like *Señor* Juan Gonzalez told me."

A hand holding a Prince Albert tobacco can emerged from the dark. Tereso put his cigarette in his mouth and casually took it with both hands. He opened it and felt the dollar bills inside. Satisfied, he nodded and said, "Stay here. I will be right back." Tereso walked into his family's apartment.

Paz was soaking beans for tomorrow's meal when her husband entered the home, walked over to the kitchen cupboards, and placed a tobacco can on the high shelf before retrieving another. She noticed that he been shuttling many tobacco cans in the last two weeks. At first, she thought he was assembling some bizarre collection of Prince Albert cans, but now she knew something was up. He was being too careful.

Paz addressed her husband, "What is in those cans?"

Tereso shrugged and answered, "Stuff," as he walked back out the door.

Paz waited for the door to close before dragging a chair over to the cupboard to investigate. She pried the first can open and gasped when she saw the money stuffed inside. Her eyes flicked through the bills and estimated that she was holding at least fifty dollars. She quickly resealed the lid and replaced the can on the shelf. Then she grabbed another can and opened it. This one held dried plant material that took Paz a few seconds to recognize.

"What are you doing! Get down from there!"

Paz whirled around and saw Tereso standing in the doorway with fierce eyes. Paz jumped down with the can and confronted her husband. "Are you selling this stuff?" she said as she shook the can at him.

Tereso snatched the can from her grip, "It's none of your business, *comprende?*"

"None of my business?" replied Paz. "What do you mean this is none of my business? You are going to bring more trouble to this family. Didn't Antonio's misfortune teach you anything?"

Tereso snarled back, "Antonio was an idiot!"

"No he wasn't," Paz yelled, "he was greedy like you!"

Tereso gritted his teeth and pointed his finger at his wife, "Antonio was stupid! He did not know how to conduct business and he got caught. That's not going to happen to me."

Paz shot back, "You are fooling yourself! Something bad is going to happen. I can feel it."

Tereso snorted in contempt. He marched over to the cupboard and replace the tin on the top shelf. "I don't want you or the children touching these cans, *comprende?* I mean it." He gave Paz a hard look to emphasize his point before stomping back outside. Paz watched the door slam shut and felt the old familiar feeling of worry creep up her bones.

———

During the second week in October 1927, the Minjares family stood on the train platform at the Sidney depot saying their good-byes to their long-lost relative, José Nava. He wore his fancy brown suit with the matching derby. His face seemed to beam with relief at the prospect of leaving this town. The emotions on the faces of the Minjares family ranged from Paz showing regret and sorrow to Anita displaying a look of "good riddance!"

Paz sobbed, "Oh, but do you have to go? I like having you here."

Her pleading caused José to reconsider until he glanced at Anita and found her glaring at him. He managed to smile warmly at his sister before gently shaking his head. "I must go, Paz. It is too cold here and no work during the winter. I must go back to Fresno. They are crying down there for construction and farm workers."

Paz nodded her head and gave him a long hard hug. José gently pushed her back and shook Tereso's hand. "I like your new beard. It reminds me of the old days back home. I shall miss you, Tío."

Tereso smiled broadly and tugged on his new facial hair. He replied, "*Sí*, it has been a long time since I grew a beard. It feels good. Thank you for looking us up. I will miss you, too." José then gave each child except Anita a warm smile and goodbye before grabbing his suitcase and climbing aboard the train. He made his way back to the caboose and waved to the family as the train pulled away.

Tereso was suddenly struck by the familiar scene before him. Like his vision so many years ago in the little *cantina* in Monte Escobedo, José was dressed in a brown suit, waving a derby from the back of a train. The train rolled by a sidetrack containing gondola cars overflowing with sugar beets. The beets looked like giant brown turnips. Every detail was exactly as he had foreseen. It made him feel old, a major chapter of his life was over. He stroked his gray beard and turned away.

———

By the last week of October, life in the *colonia* slowed to a comfortable, dull pace, which was perfect for pursuing love interests. Joaquina was determined to make the most of it. She primped and preened in the little wall mirror before running outside and strategically positioning herself in front of a large cottonwood tree that stood directly across the bachelor apartment. Then she waited for José Cabello to appear. Around ten in the morning, he would emerge finely dressed and looking breathtaking. Every time she saw him, Joaquina felt her heart race and struggled to control herself. She tried to look disinterested and gaze to some far-off spot. José always seemed amused and glided over to her on his long legs. Today was no exception.

"*Señorita*," he began as he gently took her hand and kissed it, "you look absolutely stunning this morning."

Joaquina beamed back, "*Gracias, Señor*. What a pleasant surprise to see you."

José flashed her a devastating smile and said, "No, *señorita*, the pleasure is all mine, I can assure you. Say, would you be interested in a ride to town in my car? It is a splendid day for a drive, *¿qué no?*"

"*Sí*," Joaquina blurted a little too quickly. Embarrassed, she caught herself and continued with more control, "I mean, I would love to ride to town."

"*Bueno*," replied José with a smile, "I will wait for you to get your shawl."

Joaquina grabbed him by the hand and said, "Oh, that won't be necessary. *Vámanos!*" She practically dragged him toward his car. José laughed at her exuberance and barely had a chance to open the car door for her. By the time he climbed behind the steering wheel, Joaquina was nicely settled and anxious to get going.

They drove off into the crisp autumn morning as their laughter carried off into the remarkably blue sky. Joaquina soaked up all his lavish attention like it was a fine wine. His charm and good looks made her drunk with love. She felt special and beautiful around him. The trip to town was glorious and soon they were parking in front of the Ben Franklin department store.

José gallantly bounced outside, rolled over the car hood, and solemnly opened her door. She beamed a smile of gratitude as she delicately stepped out on to the sidewalk. José closed the door and took her hand. She gladly gave it and started to walk next to him when a young white woman stepped in front of them and blocked their path. She wore a pretty blue dress with matching ribbons in her hair. She subtly swayed her hips as she gave José a teasing smile. Joaquina knew in an instant that this girl meant trouble, and possessively squeezed José's hand.

The girl spoke to José as if they were the only two people on earth. "Hello, José. Fancy meeting you here today."

José flushed a little before flashing a smile and responding in perfect English, "Helen. What a pleasant surprise. I thought you would be in school today."

His reaction was exactly what Helen expected. He was off balance and she had the advantage. She waltzed up to him and ran her finger down his chest as she purred, "What Daddy doesn't know can't hurt him, now, can it?"

Joaquina seethed at the girl's insolence and thought, *Who does she think she is? She acts as if I don't exist.* Then she felt José tremble at Helen's touch. Joaquina finally exploded, "Leave us alone you little wench!"

Helen stepped back amused. "Why, how cute! She speaks English. Where on earth did you find her? I thought she was a transient farmhand." Joaquina lunged at Helen to claw her eyes out, but José threw his arms around her waist and held her back. Helen pursed her lips in a rebuke and exclaimed, "My! What a temper! Well, José, if you ever want a more refined companion, you know how to find me." She gave him a sly wink and calmly strolled into the department store.

Joaquina positively wanted to kill her. She made one last effort to break free from José before relaxing in his arms. When she spoke, her voice sounded ragged with hatred, "How do you know this girl?"

José slowly turned her around so that he could look into her eyes. "I met her when I was playing at her father's summer dinner party."

Joaquina looked up at his handsome face and asked, "Do you see her often?"

José's expression turned serious and he answered, "No. I only want to see you." Joaquina searched his eyes for betrayal, but found only truth and passion. His look drained the rage out of her heart and filled it again with love. "Come, let's enjoy the rest of the day." He offered his arm to her and she took it without hesitation. She had a feeling that there would always be women vying for his attention and, if she wanted to be with him, she would have to learn how deal with them.

But for now, they were together and the morning was warm and pleasant. She refused to let a rude girl spoil her special time.

————

Her screams came in short spasms, signaling that the time was near. Paz and Joaquina stood by each side of Alcaria's bed and gripped her hands for moral support. Paz bent over and wiped her brow while cooing soothing words. "Now, hush, my daughter. It is almost over. Soon you will be holding your little one." The change of events was not lost on Paz. Only three years ago in the very same house, Alcaria had helped Paz give birth to Antonia. Now, she was rightfully assisting her oldest daughter.

The house was cool from the frosty autumn night. Antonio sat motionless in his chair, crippled by worry, and made no effort to stoke the coal furnace. For the first time in his married life, Antonio appreciated having in-laws nearby. He felt alone and helpless and considered Paz and Joaquina angels from heaven. He completely placed his wife's and unborn child's welfare into their hands. Now, he could do nothing else but wait and wince each time Alcaria cried out.

Alcaria's screams of agony suddenly increased and reached a screeching climax. Then silence prevailed. A few moments later, the new sound of a squalling baby filled the home. Antonio sat frozen in place. He could hear Paz murmuring soft gentle words and the crying gradually subsided. Then, after what seemed an eternity, Paz came into the living room holding a tiny bundle.

She proudly announced, "It's a girl. Strong and healthy. Would you like to hold her?" Antonio slowly nodded and got up from his chair. He dangled his arms along his side and stared down at the little face. Paz sighed and said, "Lift up your arms and hold your baby. Go ahead. She won't break."

Antonio awkwardly stretched out his arms and Paz plunked the baby into them. Antonio slowly brought the baby to his chest and held it like a basket of eggs. After he realized that he could handle the child, Antonio relaxed a little and spoke for the first time. "How is Alcaria? She seemed to have a tough time of it, ¿qué no?"

Paz smiled and answered, "She is fine and resting. Some women have a hard time with their firstborn. The next one should be easier. Would you care to see her?"

Antonio seemed stunned. "You mean it's permissible?" he asked. Paz shook her head at Antonio's comment and pushed him toward the bedroom. Antonio gingerly walked into the room carrying the baby. Joaquina was just finishing cleaning the room when she saw Antonio. She quickly grabbed the soiled towels and left.

Once alone, Antonio walked quietly to the bed and looked down on Alcaria. She seemed to be sleeping, but after a minute, she sensed his presence and slightly opened her eyes. Alcaria smiled and asked, "What should we name her?" Antonio gulped and shook his head. Alcaria knew that he would not have any girl names, so she offered one. "How about Frances?"

Antonio immediately nodded and said, "*Sí*, Frances is a good name."

Alcaria murmured, "Frances it is, then." Her voice trailed off as she closed her eyes and fell into a deep sleep. She was content knowing that her mother and sister would take care of Frances and her baby had a name. Paz and Tereso had their first grandchild and all was right with the world.

Nothing stimulates an unwed woman to find a man more than holding her sister's newborn baby. As Joaquina looked upon little Frances's angelic face as she rocked her in her arms, she felt her maternal instincts fire up. With these arousals came the conviction that José Cabello would be that man. *He just needs a little coaxing, that's all*, she thought and she began scheming how to convince him that marriage was in his near plans.

Finding time alone with José was a problem. With the holiday season upon them, his musical talents were in constant demand. He and his two band members would play for parties and dances in faraway places such as Wolf Point and Glendive. He juggled these engagements with his steady commitment to play four nights a week at the Star Bar in Savage. José was either playing, driving to his next performance, or catching a catnap wherever he fell. His clothes looked rumpled and dark circles were forming under his eyes.

Joaquina gave this problem some thought as she gently laid Frances in her bed. Suddenly, an idea popped into her head and she froze as it solidified into a plan. *I could arrange it to be alone with him*, she thought, *and I know just how to do it.*

The following Sunday morning, Joaquina crept over to the bachelor apartment and stopped at the doorway. She had told her mother that she was going to the early-morning service. Except for Anita, whom she sharply told not to accompany her, no one in her family suspected that Joaquina had other plans. She spotted José's car parked in front and gave a sigh of relief. She feared that he might not have driven back from Savage last night.

Joaquina took a few moments to smooth her white dress and push some errant strands of hair in place. Then, after a quick glance to ensure no one was watching, she slowly opened the door and stepped inside. While her eyes adjusted to the dim light, her nose wrinkled with disgust. The place was a pigsty with dirt, garbage, and clothes scattered throughout the floor. She noticed a few men sleeping on floor mats among the filth. José had told her that he shared one of the bedrooms, so she ignored them and walked carefully to the door on her right.

Joaquina had no idea which of the two bedrooms he used. She quietly opened the first door and peeked inside. The room was darker than the center room, but after a few moments, she could tell that four men slept here. Two were on beds and the others on sleeping mats. Clothing was strewn everywhere. Neither the men nor the clothes looked familiar.

She softly shut the door and tiptoed to the other bedroom. She silently turned the doorknob and tried to push the door open, but something heavy seemed to hold it closed. Joaquina put her shoulder to the door and shoved it forward with all her might. As the door slowly yielded, she heard a groan come from inside. A man had fallen asleep across the doorway and she had shoved him along the floor.

The man groggily lifted his head and asked, "Who are you?"

Joaquina ignored him and searched the room. The place was somewhat cleaner than the last, but clothes were still thrown around like trash. Her eyes told her that three men shared this room. On the wall were three dress coats that Joaquina recognized as band uniforms. She had found José and his band. She stepped over the man and walked up to the beds. In the feeble light, she saw José softly snoring, totally oblivious to her presence.

So far so good, she thought, *now the hard part*. Joaquina turned and rousted the man in the other bed awake.

The man squinted his eyes and sputtered, "Uh? What's the matter? Who are you?"

"Never mind that," Joaquina answered as she helped him up, "You must go into the center room, now!"

The man on the floor was now sitting up and rubbing his eyes. "Is there something wrong?"

Joaquina grabbed him by the arm and said, "You too. Now, the both of you, out the door. Hurry." Numbed by the lack of sleep, both men allowed Joaquina to lead them like sheep out the door with their blankets and pillows. "*Bueno*, now go back to sleep." She shut the bedroom door in their faces.

Joaquina took a deep breath and waited, but within a few moments, she heard some grumbles and the sound of collapsing bodies. The men were too tired to protest their fate. Joaquina let out her breath. She had done it. She was now alone with José.

She came quietly back to the bed and sat down next to José. He looked so tired that Joaquina's heart ached for him. She began to softly stroke his head and the sides of his handsome face. José stirred slowly. He moved his face toward her hand and smiled. Suddenly, he woke up and bolted upright. Joaquina almost screamed with fright.

"Who are you?" he demanded.

Joaquina answered, "José, it is me, Joaquina."

"Joaquina?" José squinted to get a closer look. "*¡Dios mío!,* it is you! What are you doing here?"

"I came to see you. I missed you."

José shook his head in disbelief and said, "You shouldn't be here. People will talk."

Joaquina flung herself at him and wrapped her arms around his neck. "Oh, don't you see, José? We were meant to be together. I don't care what others think."

José slipped his arms around her waist and held her to him. "Joaquina, I care what people say."

Joaquina buried her face into his thick hair and asked, "Why?"

"Because I love you."

Joaquina held him tighter. "I love you, too."

José pulled her down to him and brought her face level to his. He stared at her for a moment before kissing her fully on her lips. When they parted, Joaquina was breathless. He looked at her again and asked softly, "Joaquina, will you marry me?"

Joaquina began to cry. "Oh, José. You have no idea how much I want to marry you. *Sí,* I will marry you, but we must do this soon or I swear I will do something rash!"

José chuckled and looked around the room. "I'd say that you already did something rash. Hey, where is everyone?"

Joaquina laughed and said, "I threw them outside so that we could be alone."

José gave her a hard look and shook his head. "I can see that you are capable of doing anything."

"*Sí,*" answered Joaquina as she leaned toward him. "That's why you must marry me soon or I will make sure that people will really have something to say about us, *¿qué no?*" She kissed him hard to emphasize her point. Before he could think about it, José Cabello became the second son-in-law of Tereso and Paz Minjares.

--- * ---

The summers of 1928 and '29 went well for Tereso Minjares and Juan Gonzalez. Between beet thinning and harvesting, their cash crops grew tall and strong along the hidden mud bars of the Yellowstone River. They built a drying shack in back of the *colonia* to properly dry and store their product. They took turns guarding it from potential customers who sought free samples.

By October 1929, their business boomed. Tired harvest workers flush with money visited Tereso and Juan at all hours of the day and night. Everyone brought an empty Prince Albert can and a few dollars. Then they left with another tobacco can filled to the brim with leaves, and Tereso and Juan counting their money.

But easy money attracts evil like a light draws moths. Juan liked to frequent bars around Sidney and buy drinks for anyone willing to listen to his loud boasting. He flashed money and swaggered like a successful businessman. Unfortunately for Juan, his fanfare attracted a sinister man named Pedro Casares.

Pedro was in his thirties but carried the bitter, cold heart of an eighty-year old. He had crossed the Rio Grande in March in search of employment and a higher quality of life, but all he found were broken promises and piecemeal work. He wandered to Sidney, performing farming labor on a temporary basis. The pay was low and sporadic, which caused him to live like a tramp, the lowest level of life possible. Now he was stuck in Sidney facing a long winter with only a few dollars in his pockets.

"I should have stayed in Mexico," he groused to no one particular as he nursed a stale beer on a bar stool. A loud braggart at the end of the bar caught his attention.

"Take my word for it. The stock market crash is only temporary. It won't affect us here. Hey, do you want another drink?" The man produced a large roll of bills and peeled off some onto the counter. "Here, bartender, buy these *amigos* some tequila." Pedro began to watch this man with keen interest.

"Hey, Juan," yelled a man from a distant table, "how about drinks over here for old friends, eh?"

Pedro noticed Juan strain to recognize the "old friends" and then shrug his shoulders and direct the bartender to serve them. Pedro decided to move closer to this popular and rich man.

"Now then," continued Juan, "as I was saying, there are plenty of opportunities in *los Estados Unidos*. You just have to look for them, *¿qué no?*"

Pedro snorted in disagreement, causing Juan to notice him for the first time. Juan turned to him and asked, "*Amigo*, you think that I don't know what I am talking about? Just take a look at me. Do I not look prosperous, *¿qué no?*"

Pedro now had Juan's full attention, which was exactly what Pedro intended. Pedro casually sipped his awful beer and said, "You look like you have done all right. I could probably learn a thing or two from a highly successful businessman like yourself."

The effect of Pedro's words was devastating. Juan moved closer to Pedro and motioned to the bartender to buy him another drink. "*Sí*, I could teach you a thing or two. Let me introduce myself, *por favor*. My name is Juan Gonzalez."

Pedro shook his hand and said, "Pedro Casares."

Juan puzzled over his name and asked, "Casares, I don't remember hearing that name before or seeing you around. Are you new to the area?"

"*Sí*, I arrived in Sidney just before harvest. I remember you, though. We worked in the same field by the plant."

Juan nodded and accepted his statement as the truth. There were so many transient workers during the beet harvest that he could have worked next to Pedro and never recognized him. But if they did work together, they shared a bond. Juan put his arm around Pedro's shoulders and lied, "Of course, now I remember. We worked long and hard together. Here, accept this drink with my compliments."

Pedro slid his used beer mug away and accepted the fresh tumbler of tequila. He picked up the glass and toasted Juan, "To old friends."

Juan clicked the glass and replied, "To old friends," and belted down the drink.

———•••••———

"Shhh ... Be quiet!" Juan loudly warned Pedro as he stumbled toward the drying shack. Then he doubled over in a fit of laughter.

Pedro followed close behind. "What's the matter?" he asked.

Juan wiped the tears from his eyes and answered, "My partner, Tereso Minjares, said that people would try and steal our crop. He never thought that it would be me."

He is very drunk, thought Pedro. He let Juan lead him to a flimsy shack hidden in the cottonwoods behind the *colonia*. Juan put his finger to his lips to indicate silence before throwing open the door. The door almost broke from the hinges when it slammed against the wall. The bang echoed into the night.

They stood still for a moment and waited for someone to respond, but the night seemed tranquil. Hearing nothing, they peered inside. They did not have a lantern, but in the feeble starlight, Pedro could see remnants of dried plant material on the floor of the empty shed. Juan was stunned and yelled, "I've been robbed! It's gone. All gone!"

Pedro asked, "What's gone?"

"My crop!" Then Juan slapped his forehead and said, "Oops! Wait a minute. We sold it all. That's right! We sold it all."

Pedro's anger flared. "You idiot! You dragged me out here to look at an empty shed?"

"Idiot?" retorted Juan, "What do you mean, 'idiot'? We sold our crop and split the profits. See?" Juan pulled out a huge roll of dollar bills and shook it at Pedro. "Do you have money like this? I bet you only have a few pesos to your name, ¿qué no? Now, who's the 'idiot', idiot?"

Pedro exploded, partly because Juan was right and partly because he could not accept that someone as foolish as Juan would have lots of money. He pulled a hidden stiletto from his sleeve and plunged it deep into Juan's chest. Juan gasped and looked at Pedro with a shocked face. Pedro twisted the knife and blood gushed over his hand. Juan fell to his knees and pitched forward on his face. Pedro yanked the knife out and grabbed the money from Juan's outstretched hand before vanishing into the night.

The early morning commotion behind the *colonia* caught Tereso's attention as he stood outside smoking a hand-rolled cigarette. A screaming boy brought him and several men running to the woods in back. When Tereso arrived, he found a body lying in a pool of dried blood in front of the wide open door of the drying shed. He rolled the man over and looked at his face. The blood-plastered leaves and dirt on his face made identification difficult. Suddenly, he recognized him. "*¡Dios mío!*" gasped Tereso, "It's Juan Gonzalez!"

The men gathered around and stared in silence. Finally, one asked, "What do you think happened?"

Tereso got up and wanted to wipe the blood off his hands. They felt filthy, but he found nothing suitable to clean them so he hung them awkwardly at his sides. He looked at the shed for a moment and said, "I bet he brought someone to show off our drying shed. He probably had some money and was killed for it." There were murmurs of agreement among the men. They had all seen how Juan flaunted his money.

Tereso took a deep breath to clear his mind before speaking. "Someone near us killed Juan. Did anyone see who he was with last night?"

The men shuffled their feet and looked at each other with expectation. Finally, the youngest raised his hand and said, "I saw him in the *cantina* last night. He was buying everyone drinks."

Tereso nodded. "*Bueno.* Now, who was with him? Did he leave with anyone?"

The man wrinkled his forehead in thought for a moment. Suddenly, he looked up at Tereso and exclaimed, "*Sí*, I remember now. Juan was talking to a man that worked the beet harvest. The *hombre* is new around here. I know his name. We worked in the same fields."

Tereso snapped, "What's his name!"

The man twisted his hands as he desperately racked his brains. "*Un momento, por favor.* I know it. Wait! I remember! His name is Pedro. Pedro Casares. *Sí*, that's it."

Tereso rolled the name around in his mind. He had a good suspect. Tereso addressed the young man again, "Pedro Casares. Where can I find Pedro Casares?"

The young man shrugged and replied, "I have seen him around town. I don't know where he lives."

An older man stepped forward and said, "Tereso. Leave this for the sheriff to handle, *¿qué no?* You can't take the law into your own hands."

Tereso turned on the man and hissed, "I'm taking the law into my hands! You think some gringo sheriff is going to find Casares? We are nothing in their eyes! Dirt! No, I must avenge Juan's death. He was my friend. I won't have his murder swept under a carpet and forgotten." The man opened his mouth to respond, but held his words when he saw the fire in Tereso's eyes. Tereso clenched his fists and stomped back to the *colonia*. The men watched him go before notifying the authorities.

For three days, Paz watched her husband brood by the kitchen table. She felt an inkling of sympathy for him, but her anger at his foolishness squashed it. Paz held him accountable for his friend's death. He had scoffed at her warnings and blundered into tragedy. So, she ignored him and went about her household tasks as if he was invisible.

The day was entering the early afternoon when a young man bolted through the door, breathless with excitement. His brashness irked Paz. *He should have knocked*, she thought.

The man was oblivious to Paz's cold stare. He blurted, "*Señor* Minjares! I saw him. I saw Casares!"

Tereso pushed away from the table and bolted upright, sending his chair crashing against the wall. "Where? Tell me now!" he demanded.

The man swallowed hard to catch his breath and replied, "At the hardware store, downtown. He was buying some camping gear."

Tereso stared at him for a moment as he considered this information. Then he said, "*Bueno*. Wait outside for a moment while I get a few things. Then you will take me to him." The man nodded and left. Tereso waited for the door to close before walking over to the kitchen cupboard and retrieving a box from the top shelf. Paz watched him closely. He carried the box to the table and carefully set it down. Tereso removed the lid and reverently unwound the cloth packing, revealing the twin pistols in the black leather holsters.

Paz gasped, "*¡Dios mío!* You are going to shoot that man, *¿qué no?* You can not do this! The law will hang you!"

Tereso rolled the cylinders and listened to the pistols purr. Then slowly and deliberately, he loaded the bullets. Paz went hysterical. "Are you listening to me? Kill this man and you will hang!"

Tereso snapped the breach shut and answered, "Juan was my friend."

"Your friend? He was a scoundrel! He would have cheated you blind had you not watched him like a hawk."

Tereso put the gun belt around his waist and fastened the clasp. "Casares murdered my friend. He must pay."

Paz grabbed his shirt with both hands and screamed, "You don't care about Juan! You want everyone to think you are a big man. *¡Machismo!* That's it, isn't? You are an idiot and your babies will suffer from your foolishness!"

Tereso firmly pried her hands from his shirt. She collapsed into a chair and buried her face into her folded arms on the table. Between sobs she asked quietly, "Don't go. Please don't go." Tereso took his hat from the wall hook and strode out the door.

The sheriff sat in his squad car and watched the sidewalks of east Main Street. He had taken this post since yesterday after receiving a tip that someone was planning revenge for the murder of the Mexican that occurred three days ago. He had no idea what the avenger would look like, but he had no murder suspects either. So, his instincts told him to watch the streets and see what unfolded. *Mexicans have a way of handling their own affairs*, he thought as he studied the people walking by.

Suddenly, he spotted an unusual sight. A tall, elderly Mexican strode toward him with a younger man leading him forward and pointing down the street. The man wore farm clothes and a wide-brimmed hat. His gray hair spilled to his shoulders and complemented his full gray beard. Besides his impressive size, the double-pistol holster caught the sheriff's attention. The sheriff smiled at his luck. He spoke out loud, "Here's one of them."

The sheriff vaguely knew Tereso from quieting past disputes at the *colonia*. The Mexicans seemed to hold him in some unofficial position of authority. He also suspected him as the ringleader for the illegal marijuana trafficking in the area, but he had never had enough evidence to arrest him, so the sheriff let him slide. Now, discovering that Tereso looked bent on revenge, he wondered if the murder and marijuana were related. The sheriff shifted in his seat for a better view.

Tereso walked with purpose as he neared the hardware store. His young assistant danced with excitement. "*Señor* Minjares, there is the store. What do you want me to do?"

Without breaking stride, Tereso responded, "I want you to go inside and see if he is still there."

The man nodded and ran ahead to the hardware store. He stopped in front of the door and caught his breath before entering. Tereso waited outside for his scout to return. As he stood waiting, Tereso felt eyes staring at him. He slowly looked around when the young man burst from the store and said, "He is gone! The storekeeper thinks that he is still around."

Tereso grunted and said, "I will hang around for a while. I want you to walk through town and see if you can find him, *comprende?*"

The young man nodded and said, "*Sí*. Where will you be?"

Tereso looked around and saw the barbershop across the street. He subconsciously stroked his beard and realized that he could use a trim and a haircut. "I will be in there," he said as he pointed toward the barbershop. "Come get me if you see Casares." The man nodded again and left with a brisk walk.

One block down and across the street, Pedro Casares spotted the big man with pistols strapped to his waist talking to a man in front of the hardware store where he had been only minutes ago. He knew that they were looking for him. He threw the burlap sackful of goods he had purchased over his shoulder and hid behind a building. Pedro felt his breath become ragged with fear. *I must get out of here!* he thought. *I got to make it to the river.*

Tereso walked casually across the street and entered the barbershop. The sheriff sensed that this was an opportunity to defuse the situation. He waited for fifteen minutes before leaving his car and walking toward the store. Business was slow and only the barber and Tereso were in the shop. As the sheriff entered, he saw Tereso in the reclined barber chair with a hot towel wrapped around his face. The barber was shaving his neck with a straight razor. Without saying a word, the sheriff put his finger to his lips to tell the barber to remain quiet. The barber froze with his razor against Tereso's neck.

Tereso sensed something wrong, but the towel blinded him and the razor prevented him from moving. He sputtered in English, "What?"

The sheriff shook his head at the barber to remain quiet and knelt behind the chair. With both hands, he pulled the pistols from the holsters. "No!" screamed Tereso. He felt the razor nick his skin, and stopped struggling.

The sheriff stood up and spoke for the first time. "It's for your own good. I can't have you take the law into your own hands." Tereso understood little of what he was saying. The sheriff turned to leave when he noticed the exquisite workmanship of the guns. The white pearl handles and double-eagle insignia indicated that these were treasures. He shook his head in amazement and asked, "Where on earth did you get these guns?"

Tereso quivered in silence under the razor's edge. The sheriff shrugged and carried the pistols out the door. "Damn Mexicans," mumbled the sheriff as he left, "They're always dragging the darndest things across the border."

When the sheriff left, the barber lifted his razor from Tereso's neck. Tereso jumped up from the reclined chair and ripped the hot towel from his face. "Where are my guns?" he demanded. The barber pointed his razor toward the door. Tereso ran outside with a bib still tied around his neck. He halted when he spotted the sheriff placing the guns into the squad car. The sheriff smiled at him as he got in and slammed his door shut. Then Tereso watched the sheriff drive off with his beloved pistols and a special part of his life.

Tereso was still seething when he returned to the *colonia*. He kicked the door open and marched inside. Anita shrieked as the door crashed into the wall. Paz and the rest of the family remained quiet, but fear radiated from their faces. Tereso stood in the middle of the room with his fists clenched and his eyes glowing hot. For a moment, the only sound was his ragged breath sawing through the silence. He gave each member a hard look before exploding.

"I lost my pistols! All because of that coward Casares. I am going to kill him!" No one answered. Tereso gave everyone another hard look. Then his eyes locked onto a machete hanging on the wall. He had used the knife to top beets. The blade was soft, but thick and sharp. He grabbed the wooden handle and pulled it off the hook. It felt heavy and unyielding in his hand, but it looked wicked and powerful. He made a quick show of slicing the air to show his family that he meant what he had said.

"I heard that Casares crawled off to the river. I am going to hunt him down and chop his head off!" Tereso spun around and blasted out the door.

Augustine watched his father go before turning to his mother and saying, "Mother, I think he means it." Paz did not answer. She shook her head in disgust and went back to her duties.

Pedro Casares was tired, hungry, and cold. He had slept fitfully for the past two nights on the damp sandbars of the Yellowstone. Although he had adequate canned goods and pots to cook his meals, Casares was afraid to build a fire because it might reveal his hiding place to the menace that he surely knew was lurking in the thick forest, looking for him. Thus, he was forced to shiver miserably within his thin coat and spoon cold beans from a can.

The sound of a twig snapping from a heavy footfall snatched his attention. He froze in terror. For the next moment, silence prevailed. He strained his ears to hear the slightest movement. After a hundred heartbeats, Casares heard another footstep. The sound was unmistakable and confirmed his greatest fear. The person was stalking him.

Casares slowly lay down on the damp earth and looked through the thick underbrush. Amid the horsetails and ferns, he searched for the source of the sound. A boot was planted into the sand only a few feet from his face. Casares stopped breathing. Out of the dense vegetation emerged a large man with a full white beard moving carefully forward. He crept like a lion, constantly searching for prey, with a machete in his hand. Casares's blood ran cold as he watched the man jab it into the brush around him.

Tereso felt his blood boiling for revenge. For the past two days, he had hunted for Juan's killer. He knew that Casares was hiding somewhere within the lush river bottom and it was only a matter of time before he found him. He walked slowly and carefully, a few steps at a time, then rested and listened before continuing on. He assumed the hunter's stare, searching for anything that resembled his prey. In this case, the silhouette of a man.

Suddenly, the brush erupted behind him. Tereso spun on his heels and spotted a man sprinting across the forest toward the riverbank. Tereso realized that he had almost stepped on the man only moments before. He gathered his wits and yelled, "Casares!" The man never looked back as he vaulted over a log and hit the ground at full speed. Tereso screamed again, "I am going to kill you, Casares!" and ran after him.

Pedro Casares broke out of the brush in a full panic and scrambled up a low hill that formed the transition from the river floodplain to the dry prairie. His lungs seared in pain and his heart felt like it was going to beat out of his chest, but fear drove him on. He was convinced that Minjares was right on his heels wielding that menacing knife. Casares never looked back. He ran all the way back to Sidney and turned himself in to the sheriff. The thought of facing trial was much less frightening than facing a wild man with a machete.

———

When Tereso stumbled into the colonia late that night, he was tired and hungry. Paz and the children watched quietly as he collapsed at the dinner table and held his head in his hands. Without saying a word, Paz got up and fetched him some dinner. She set a plate of beans and chilies in front of him. Tereso tore a tortilla in half, shoveled some beans into his mouth and ate it slowly and silently. He felt so tired, not just physically tired, but spiritually, too. For the first time in his life, he felt old, so very old ....

Chapter 27
The Final Hook

"Father. Wake up, Dad!"

Tereso shook himself awake. The rolled cigarette he was smoking dropped a huge ash onto his pants. Tereso brushed it off before it could burn through the fabric. He felt disorientated, unsure of the time and his surroundings. He muttered, "Huh, what's wrong?"

"Nothing is wrong, Father," Augustine replied, "except that you are not working. Why don't you stay home and tend the garden, *¿qué no?*"

Tereso had heard stories that a man could see his entire life replay within a heartbeat, but until now he had never believed them. Had he been sitting here contemplating his life for only a few minutes? His burning cigarette told him so, but his senses said the duration was a lifetime. Time was like the ground he broke his back hoeing. He worked hard against it every year and never got rid of it. He realized that the summer of 1930 was no different. There was always another field to plant, weed, and harvest. He was tired of field work and worn out from living.

He finally flicked his burning stub into the field and answered his son, "I am going home."

"*Bueno,*" replied Augustine, "*Señor* Currandas is in the next field. He can give you a ride."

Tereso nodded and used the thick cottonwood tree to help himself up to his feet. He pulled his sombrero over his eyes and began to walk to the end of the field. Damn, his joints hurt! He eventually stopped when he came to an irrigation ditch and stared across the channel to the field beyond. Several workers were spread throughout the field weeding the rows. Tereso watched them for a few moments before spotting his friend among the group. Tereso took off his hat and waved and shouted, "Tacio! It's me! Come here!"

A large man slowly straightened and pushed his wide-brimmed hat off his forehead with a dirty gloved hand. He stared in Tereso's direction for a moment before waving an acknowledgment and slowly started making his way across the field. Tereso noticed that Anastacio had a limp to his walk. Tereso shook his head and thought, *We are getting old.*

When Anastacio came within earshot of Tereso, he said, "*Hola, amigo.* What do you need?"

Tereso smiled at his old friend and replied, "I need to go home. I am through with field work. Can you drive me?"

Anastacio looked back at the workers. They appeared to be making good progress—he could leave them for a while. "*Sí.* I can drive you, but I must come right back, *¿qué no?*" Tereso snorted in response and started walking toward the road. The brilliant sun beat its heat into his head and made him faint. He took his hat off and slid his fingers through his thinning hair. He felt the indentations along the side of his skull and momentarily remembered how he got them. The distant memory made him smile as he put his hat back on and waited for Anastacio.

Within a few minutes, Anastacio fired up the old 1923 pickup and drove to where Tereso was standing. Tereso opened the creaking, heavy metal door and climbed into the hard seat. The truck backfired and slowly chugged forward as Anastacio double-clutched the gear and pressed the accelerator down. Tereso watched the fields pass by through the side window without comment. Anastacio noticed his unusual silence and finally asked, "Are you sick? Why aren't you working?"

Tereso did not answer immediately, but continued to stare out the window and let the hot wind blow through his hair. When he finally spoke, he seemed to speak to himself. "Life is short. Time has slipped away from my grasp."

Anastacio chuckled and asked, "I think you have been out in the sun too long, *¿qué no?*"

Tereso ignored him and continued, "It seems like yesterday when I pulled your big carcass away from that bull. Remember that day? Damn, did we drink that night!"

"*Sí, amigo*, but that was many years ago."

Tereso turned to his friend and replied, "It feels like yesterday to me. *Verdad.* Just like yesterday!" He looked back to the never ending sugar beet fields. "How did we get so old?"

Anastacio shook his head and said, "You are suffering from the heat. When did you become such a philosopher? If you know what's good for you, you will start thinking about what to say to Paz when I get you home. She doesn't take kindly to you skipping work."

Within a few minutes, Anastacio drove to the *colonia*. Even during the heat of the day, women were quietly completing their daily chores. As they pulled up to the aging apartment complex, the men spotted Paz hanging freshly washed sheets on the clothesline in front of building to dry. When she caught sight of them, she hesitated for a moment before resuming her work. Tereso shook his head and cursed as he struggled with the truck door. He knew by just looking at her that she was brewing for a fight. It was going to be a long, hot afternoon. Anastacio grabbed Tereso by the arm and held him in his rock-solid grip. "*Amigo*, don't let the heat of the day or wife's anger get the best of you. You still have many years in front of you, *¿qué no?* Take it easy these next few days. I will come and have a drink with you on Saturday night. We will get drunk and reminisce about the glory days, *¿qué no?* What do you say, *amigo?*"

Tereso smiled for the first time. "*Sí, gracias.* I will look forward to it." Anastacio released him and waved him on. Tereso slid out of the truck and let Anastacio drive forward. When the truck passed and the dust settled, Tereso had an unobstructed view of his wife glaring at him as she finished hanging the last sheet. Tereso sighed and decided to bypass her by walking directly to the house. Paz anticipated his move and intercepted him at the porch.

"So," she said with a tinge of bitterness, "skipping work again, *¿qué no?*"

Tereso paused at the door as he looked down at her before answering. "The heat was bothering me. Augustine told me to go home."

Paz snorted and replied, "I bet he did. You were probably dozing under a tree somewhere." Tereso had enough. He opened the screen door and marched inside. Paz watched him go with disdain. She had a feeling that he was never setting foot in the beet fields again.

———

On August 30, 1939, Anita's two year-old daughter Carmen held the medicine spoon and the unopened bottle up to her bedridden grandfather and said again in a clear little voice, "Take your medicine!"

Tereso grunted and waved her off. "Go away."

Carmen held her ground. "Take your medicine," she repeated. Tereso groaned and rolled his eyes. He knew that his life would be far easier if he swallowed that godforsaken stuff than trying refuse her. Carmen would stand next to his bed like a parrot repeating her command over and over again. And forget trying to fake it. Carmen had a knack for seeing through trickery.

"*¡Jesús!*" swore Tereso, "You are worse than your mother and grandmother combined!" He painfully turned over and took the spoon and bottle from her. His stomach burned like fire and his strength was nearly gone. The cancer the doctor had found earlier that year consumed him. Carmen stood on the tips of her toes to closely watch her grandfather feebly twist the cap off and gulp a mouthful of medicine. Carmen winced at her grandfather's crude way of taking the medicine. She would rather see him use the spoon, but the medicine got inside of him anyway and that was more important. She watched him screw his face up as he swallowed and wipe his lips with the back of his hand. Satisfied, Carmen reached out for the bottle and spoon. Tereso handed them to her and rolled over on his side. "*Gracias,*" Carmen said as she marched triumphantly out of the bedroom and into the kitchen.

Anita was washing the morning dishes when she saw her daughter. By the smug look on her face, Anita knew that she had been successful. "Did Grandfather take his medicine?" Carmen vigorously nodded her little head. Anita smiled because she knew her father had a soft spot for Carmen and found it hard to refuse her. "*Bueno,* little one. Now let Grandfather rest. We will clean him up in a little while, *¿qué no?*" Carmen handed her mother the spoon and bottle and skipped out the door to play outside.

Anita finished her chores and checked her father. He appeared to be sleeping, but his breathing was ragged and loud. Anita walked up to him and asked softly, "Father, how are you feeling?" Tereso did not immediately respond, so she put her hand on his shoulder and slowly rolled him on his back. Blood oozed from the corners of his lips. His eyes fluttered open and stared blankly back. Anita put her hand to her mouth and stepped back.

His voice was low and rough. "Bring everyone here."

Anita did not understand. "What did you say."

Tereso spoke louder. "Go, now. Bring everyone here. Get Vallejo and Currandas, too. Go!"

Anita looked at him blankly for a moment before she grasped his meaning. Tears welled up in her eyes as she said, "I will go and get everyone as fast as I can. I will get Mama to watch over you." She stayed only long enough to see if he understood. After a few precious moments with no response, Anita left the room to fetch Carmen and gather the family.

Anita drove the 1926 black Ford pickup truck that she, Joe, and Ben bought after beet thinning season. Little Carmen bounced on the seat with joy as her mother negotiated the narrow highway nineteen miles south to Savage. There she found Victoriano Vallejo supervising the branding of cattle at his newly purchased ranch.

Victoriano pushed back his cowboy hat and watched Anita get out of the truck and carry Carmen toward him. As soon as he saw her eyes, he knew why she had come.

Anita came to the point, "Father asked for you."

Victoriano nodded and replied, "I know. I will be there soon. Have you told *Señor* Currandas yet?"

Anita shook her head and said, "No. I am going there next." Victoriano turned his head and stared out over the rolling prairie. He seemed to turn very old in front of her. Finally, he tipped his hat in thanks and walked toward his house without saying a word.

Anita drove back to Sidney and then headed north on Highway 200 for 11 miles to Fairview. Anastacio Currandas was supervising several crews in the sugar beet fields located in the outskirts of town. Anita easily identified his massive bulk among the workers and drove along a makeshift dirt road to get as close as possible to him. She stopped the truck and waved her handkerchief to get his attention. Several workers spotted her first and called out to Tacio. He leaned on his hoe and squinted at her for a moment. Upon recognizing her, Tacio threw his hoe toward the edge of the field and began a very laborious walk toward her. He was out of breath by the time he reached the truck.

"I am very sorry, *Señor* Currandas," Anita began, "but my father believes that his time has come and he asked to see you."

Tacio wiped his sweating jowls with his handkerchief and nodded. "I understand. I have to finish this field before I can leave. I will be there in the early evening." Like Victoriano, Tacio tipped his *sombrero* and wandered off in silence. He looked like an old man struggling to walk in the soft tilled earth.

———

The family gathered around Tereso's bed in the early muggy evening before the moon rose. The dark room was lit by candles that gave everyone a soft yellow glow to their faces. Tereso looked gaunt but peaceful as he looked around him with weak eyes. The family stood quietly around the bed while Victoriano and Anastacio said goodbye to their old friend.

Tacio laboriously and painfully knelt down beside the bed before speaking softly to Tereso. "My dear *amigo*, do you remember when men called you *El Gancho*? We threw thousands of bulls in our time, *¿qué no?*"

"Well, I remember when Prudenciano and I worked the mines in Torreón. Then we fought on opposite sides of the revolution in Chihuahua. Damn, that seems so long ago!" piped Victoriano.

"Prudenciano," mused Tacio as he pulled on his long drooping mustache, "now there is a name that I haven't heard in a long time, *¿qué no?*"

Tereso managed a weak smile and slowly lifted his finger to signal that he wanted his friends to come closer. Tacio and Victoriano leaned forward and Tereso gently grabbed their arms and mouthed, "*Gracias*". The men were overcome with emotion and tried to choke back their tears. Tacio smoothed Tereso's long white hair back and ran his fingers over the familiar bumps along his head. Tereso took a shallow breath and murmured, "It's time." Tacio and Victoriano came to their feet with the help of Augustine, Ben, and Joe and stepped back behind the family.

Surrounding Tereso were his wife, his daughters and his sons. Only Alcaria was missing. Carmen held on to her mother and watched with big eyes as her grandfather held his hand up, made the sign of the cross before the family, and gave them his final blessing. His hand slowly came down and he died.

———•»«•———

Tereso felt himself rising from his body and lifting slowly above his grieving family. Then he seemed to gain speed as he shot through the ceiling and vaulted toward the sky. He looked south and could see beyond the curvature of the earth, past Carrizozo, Doña Ana, El Paso, Chihuahua, Torreón, and finally Monte Escobedo. In his previous life, the distance had seemed immense—now it was nothing.

Tereso smiled as he felt himself drawn to a light. He was being pulled by the ultimate *El Gancho*, but this time it felt good.

www.ingramcontent.com/pod-product-compliance
Lightning Source LLC
Chambersburg PA
CBHW070536030726
47505CB00001B/59